2.

not a cloud —
was a clear —
there seemed
tangible pall over the
of things, made the
that and that
dark and that
due to the absen
sun. I lie fast did
not worry the man.
was used to the h
sun. It had bee
days since he h
seen the sun, a few
he knew that a few
more days that
pass ere d
south, would just
above the sky-line
dip immediately from sight

The man
flung
along the war

SHORT STORIES OF
JACK LONDON

SS

SHORT STORIES OF
JACK
LONDON

35.00

AUTHORIZED ONE-VOLUME
EDITION

Edited by

EARLE LABOR, ROBERT C. LEITZ III,
I. MILO SHEPARD

MACMILLAN PUBLISHING COMPANY
New York

COLLIER MACMILLAN CANADA
Toronto

MAXWELL MACMILLAN INTERNATIONAL
New York   Oxford   Singapore   Sidney

Macmillan Publishing Company
866 Third Avenue, New York, NY 10022

Collier Macmillan Canada, Inc
1200 Eglinton Avenue East, Suite 200
Dan Mills, Ontario M3C 3N1

Library of Congress Cataloging-in-Publication Data
London, Jack, 1876–1916.
  [Short stories]
  Short stories of Jack London: authorized one-volume edition /
edited by Earle Labor, Robert C. Leitz III,
I. Milo Shepard.
     p.   cm.
  Includes bibliographical references (p.   ).
  ISBN 0-02-567180-4
  I. Labor, Earle, 1928–   . II. Leitz, Robert C., 1944–   .
III. Shepard, I. Milo (Irving Milo)   IV. Title.
PS3523.046A6   1990b
813'.52—dc20   90-6175   CIP

The endpapers of this edition are facsimile reproductions of the autograph manuscript of "To Build a Fire" (1908), by permission of the Henry E. Huntington Library, San Marino, California.

Design by Janet Tingey

10 9 8 7 6 5 4 3 2 1

Printed in the United States of America

CONTENTS

ABOUT THIS EDITION

It is particularly fitting that Jack London's own major publisher should bring out this special one-volume edition of his stories, most of which were first issued in book form by the Macmillan Publishing Company. Our only difficulty has been the problem of *exclusion:* not so much the question of which stories do we include as that of which of London's two hundred stories do we leave out? Of necessity, we have been forced to leave out at least a hundred very good stories—and to all London buffs who may miss one or more of their favorites we extend our sincerest apologies.

On the other hand, the process of *inclusion* has been a delight. At least a score of these stories must surely be included in any collection of London's "best"—for example, "To Build a Fire," "The Law of Life," "Love of Life," "All Gold Canyon," "The Apostate," "Koolau the Leper," "Samuel," "War," "A Piece of Steak," "The Mexican," "Told in the Drooling Ward," "The Red One," and "The Water Baby," to mention a baker's dozen that must be rated exceptional by any artistic measure.

Beyond simply selecting London's best, however, what we have attempted is to include works that represent the astonishing scope both of his subject matter and of his creative genius. We believe, for instance, that Jack's readers will be interested in seeing his first ("Story of a Typhoon Off the Coast of Japan") as well as his last story ("The Water Baby"), even though his first is neither his best nor, in the strictest sense, a short story. Certainly the 1902 *Youth's Companion* version of "To Build a Fire" cannot be ranked among his masterpieces (though it is an effective *exemplum* or moral fable); we have included it for purposes of comparison and contrast with the 1908 version, which is a universally acknowledged classic of short fiction, probably translated into more languages than any other work of short fiction in world literature. Such comparison eloquently answers the question, what is the difference between a good story and a great one? Furthermore, neither "A Relic of the Pliocene" nor "Moon-Face" can accurately be called a masterwork; yet the first is interesting as a sample of Jack's tall tales, and the second because of the apparent influence of Poe and because of the charges of plagiarism when London and Frank Norris almost simultaneously published stories with the same motif. On the other hand, London's fine gift for philosophic satire has been completely overlooked by the critics in a little nugget like "Nam-Bok the Unveracious" (his humorous northland version of Plato's "The Cave"). Even more neglected has been his story inspired by a quotation from Thoreau: "The Night-Born," a masterpiece virtually unknown because—except for a limited edition recently issued by the Jack London Research Center—it has been out of print for more than a half-century.

All of these, and more, we have been happy to include in this edition of London's stories. It is our hope that they will provide a wealth of pleasure as well as a new appreciation of this too-often-underrated literary artist's extraordinary achievement.

We wish to acknowledge the gracious cooperation of the Trust of Irving Shepard and the Henry E. Huntington Library in the preparation of this edition.

E.L.
R.C.L. III
I.M.S.

INTRODUCTION

"This is the twentieth century, and we stink of gasoline," mutters the Oxford-educated gentleman whose sole legacy of an age rich in myth and belief is the dry shin bone of a great earth princess three centuries dead. The theme might have been borrowed from T. S. Eliot, except that the author, Jack London, was dead before Eliot's first book was published.

"Kipling of the Klondike," "Poet of Darwinism," "Wonderboy of the Naturalist Carnival"—these are the usual stereotypes with which Jack London has been labeled and dismissed by our literary critics. And even the common reader may only dimly recollect London as the flamboyant adventurer who wrote a handful of splendid stories about the supermen and superdogs of the northland—stuff we properly laid aside on coming of age. It may therefore come as a surprise to learn that several years before Eliot had so brilliantly delineated the spiritual malaise of the twentieth century in *The Waste Land,* London had found the skeleton key to modern humanity's "lost-ness" in the primitive folklore of Hawaii and in the writings of Carl Gustav Jung. "I tell you I am standing on the edge of a world so new, so terrible, so wonderful, that I am almost afraid to look over into it," he exclaimed to his wife, Charmian, when he discovered Jung early in the summer of 1916. And during the next few months before his death, London worked to incorporate Jung's radical new psychology of the collective unconscious and racial memory into a half-dozen remarkable stories, the best of which are included in this edition.

These are only a handful of what we hope will be the many pleasant surprises in this volume. But perhaps we should first rehearse some salient facts about their author and his extraordinary career. There is considerable merit in Alfred Kazin's remark that "the greatest story Jack

London ever wrote was the story he lived." That fantastic story became legend even during London's brief lifetime.

Jack London was born in San Francisco on January 12, 1876, the son of Flora Wellman Chaney, wayward daughter of a respectable Ohio family and common-law wife of Professor William Henry Chaney, author, astrologer, and itinerant lecturer, who had denied his paternity and deserted her when Flora revealed her pregnancy. (Twenty-one years later, in reply to Jack's inquiries, Chaney still insisted that he was not his father; and while the majority of London's biographers suggest that Chaney's denials are outweighed by contrary factors, the evidence remains largely circumstantial.) On September 7, 1876, Flora married John London, a Civil War veteran and widower who had been forced to place his two younger daughters, Eliza and Ida, in an orphanage while he worked as a carpenter. It was evidently a marriage of convenience rather than of love, providing a father for the infant boy and a home for the two girls. Nevertheless, John London, a gentle, loving man, gave his name to the boy and treated him as his own son.

The circumstances of Jack's early years shaped the essential attitudes of his adulthood, and throughout his mature years he compensated—sometimes overcompensated—for what he considered to have been a deprived childhood. "My body and soul were starved when I was a child," he said. Indeed, he never fully outgrew his deep-seated resentment of his boyhood poverty and his mother's detachment. Flora was an unhappy, restless woman whose body had been dwarfed by a girlhood attack of typhoid fever and whose dreams of the genteel life had been aborted by the birth of an unwanted child. Too frail to nurse the infant herself, she had been forced to find a wetnurse: Mrs. Virginia Prentiss, a black woman who had lost her own baby in childbirth (and whose husband was one of John London's fellow carpenters). The only maternal affection Jack received as a youngster was what he got from "Aunt Jennie" and from his older stepsister Eliza—not from his mother, who was more interested in her seances than in her son. One of the most significant factors in London's development both as person and writer was his conscious rejection of the occult, the supernatural, and the mystical—all of which he associated with his mother's cold spiritualism—and it was not until his discovery of Jung that he could at last admit to himself that science, logic, and his avowed "materialistic monism" might not adequately account for all the mysteries of God's creation and humanity's place in the grand scheme of things.

London's youth was as insecure financially as it was emotionally. The family moved often from one rented house to another in the Bay Area as John London tried to make a living: carpentering, contracting, selling sewing machines from door-to-door, storekeeping, and farming. On Jack's seventh birthday they moved from Alameda to a farm down the coast. "We had horses and a farm wagon," he recalled, "and onto that we piled all our household belongings, all hands climbing up on the top of the load, and with the cow tied behind, we moved 'bag and baggage' to the coast in San Mateo County, six miles beyond Colma." The next year, encouraged by his ambitious wife, John London bought an eighty-seven-acre ranch in Livermore, and they moved once again.

His loneliness led London at a very early age to seek the companionship of books. "I always could read and write," he claimed in an early letter to Houghton Mifflin, his first book publisher, "and have no recollection antedating such a condition. Folks say I simply insisted upon being taught." Washington Irving's exotic sketches in *The Alhambra* and Ouida's *Signa,* the story of a peasant girl's illegitimate son who rose to fame as a great Italian composer, were among his early favorites—as were Captain James Cook's *Voyages* and Horatio Alger's success stories —all of which were clearly instrumental in molding the shape of London's own life and career. In 1885, when the Londons moved back to the city after an epidemic had destroyed their chicken flocks and forced John to give up the Livermore ranch, Jack found that he could freely check out books from the Oakland Public Library as fast as he could read them. "It was this world of books, now accessible, that practically gave me the basis of my education," he later wrote.

Other, less gentle and less genteel worlds also influenced his education: worlds of the gutter, the factory, the saloon, and the sea. Though John London was a conscientious provider, his vitality had been sapped by Civil War injuries and poor health. Furthermore, his efforts to succeed in various enterprises were repeatedly thwarted by bad luck and Flora's insatiable ambition and instability. Consequently, even as a grade schooler "Johnny" (as he was called until old enough to insist on "Jack") had been forced to help support the family, later attesting that "from my ninth year, with the exception of hours spent at school (and I earned them by hard labor), my life has been one of toil."

At first the work was part time: delivering newspapers, setting pins at a bowling alley, sweeping saloon floors, and doing whatever odd jobs would bring a few extra pennies into the family budget. When he finished grade school in 1889, he went to work full time in a West Oakland cannery, spending as many as eighteen hours a day at ten cents an hour stuffing pickles into jars. It was a traumatic ordeal, impressing upon him a lifetime loathing of physical labor. Years later that trauma was translated into art in one of London's most poignant stories, "The Apostate." Describing the plight of his protagonist (a teenaged factory worker named "Johnny"), London wrote: "There was no joyousness in life for him. The procession of days he never saw. The nights he slept away in twitching unconsciousness. . . . He had no mental life whatever; yet deep down in the crypts of his mind, unknown to him, were being weighed and sifted every hour of his toil, every moment of his hands, every twitch of his muscles, and preparations were making for a future course of action that would amaze him and all his little world." That "course of action" was escape: in the mode of his real-life model, the hero of "The Apostate" suddenly deserts the tattered army of "work beasts," abandoning the factory in favor of the adventure trail.

The pattern of London's own life, reflected in much of his fiction, might be rightly viewed as a series of escapes—first from the drudgery of poverty, later from the monotony of labor: a constant alternation between commitment and escape, routine and recreation, work and adventure. At the age of fifteen, with three hundred dollars borrowed from "Aunt Jennie," Jack bought a sloop from one of the hoodlums who made their living by raiding the commercial oyster beds and achieved notoriety on the Oakland waterfront as "Prince of the Oyster Pirates." He followed this dangerous career for a year before, fearing that he might wind up dead or in prison like many of his comrades, he then took up more legitimate work as a member of the California Fish Patrol. Many of his escapades during these two years were later fictionalized in *The Cruise of the Dazzler* and *Tales of the Fish Patrol*.

Jack's maritime adventures took on a wider scope the next year when, a few days after his seventeenth birthday, he shipped as an able-bodied seaman aboard the *Sophia Sutherland,* a sealing schooner bound for hunting grounds in the Northwest Pacific. This seven-month voyage provided the raw materials not only for his immensely popular novel *The Sea-Wolf* but also for his first successful literary effort. Two months after his ship had docked back home, the San Francisco *Morning Call* sponsored a contest for young writers, the first prize being twenty-five dollars (nearly a month's pay at the jute mill where he was working). Encouraged by his mother, London wrote a brief narrative sketch describing the typhoon he had experienced during his recent voyage. Simply titled "Story of a Typhoon Off the Coast of Japan," the piece was a remarkable accomplishment for a seventeen-year-old youth with only a grade-school education. Fresh, vivid, and unpretentious, it still reads well. Moreover, the sketch contains not only good descriptive detail but also narrative suspense and human interest. It so impressed the *Call* that London's story received the first-place prize and was published in that newspaper on November 12, 1893.

Subsequent experiences that winter working in the jute mill and, later, at the power plant of the Oakland and San Leandro Electric Railway intensified his wanderlust: "The thought of work was repulsive," London recollected in his semiautobiographical novel *John Barleycorn*. "It was a whole lot better to royster and frolic over the world in the way I had previously done. So I headed out on the adventure-path again, starting to tramp east by beating my way on the railroads." At first he rode with the West Coast contingent of Coxey's Industrial Army, a group of unemployed men who went to Washington to petition Congress for relief following the Panic of 1893. But this army moved too slowly to suit Jack's adventurous spirit, and he deserted at Hannibal, Missouri, on May 25, 1894, making his own way northeast via the World's Fairgrounds in Chicago. Arrested for vagrancy in Niagara in late June, he served thirty days in the Erie County Penitentiary, then headed back home to Oakland, determined to raise himself up from what he perceived as "the submerged tenth" of American society. London's tramping experiences, later recounted in *The Road,* were crucially important in the shaping of his career as a fictionist: "I have often thought that to this training of my tramp days is due much of my success as a story-writer," he said. "In order to get the food whereby I lived, I was compelled to tell tales that rang true. At the back door, out of inexorable necessity, is developed the convincingness and sincerity laid down by all authorities on the art of the short-story." Beyond this, his ramblings —and especially his prison experiences—drove home the realization that to raise himself from "the shambles at the bottom of the Social Pit," he must resume his formal education. Consequently, he wrote, "I ran back to California and opened the books."

Within the year he was reading Darwin's *On the Origin of Species,* Spencer's *First Principles,* and Marx's *Communist Manifesto.* In January of 1895 he enrolled in Oakland High School and began regularly contributing essays and sketches to the student literary journal, the *High School Aegis*. That spring he joined the Socialist Labor Party, and his activism won him notoriety as Oakland's "Boy Socialist." Then, in the late summer of 1896, after feverish cramming for the entrance exams, he was admitted to the University of California at Berkeley. Forced by lack of funds to withdraw after one semester, he plunged into his newfound career as a writer: "Heavens, how I wrote!" he recalled; "I wrote everything—ponderous essays, scientific and sociological, short stories, humorous verse, verse of all kinds from triolets and sonnets to blank verse tragedy and elephantine epics in Spenserian stanzas. On occasion I composed steadily, day after day, for fifteen hours a day. At times I forgot to eat, or refused to tear myself away from my passionate outpouring in order to eat." This Herculean expenditure of energy earned him nothing, however, but rejection slips, and he was forced to return to manual labor, this time in a backbreaking and soul-wrenching job in the laundry at the Belmont Academy, a private boys' school, later dramatized in *Martin Eden*.

He found escape once more that summer, when Eliza's husband, Captain J. H. Shepard, mortgaged his house for their stake and invited Jack to join him in the great Klondike gold rush. On July 25, 1897, they boarded the *Umatilla* en route to the Yukon via the Dyea Beach in southern Alaska, the four-hundred-mile trek over the rugged Chilkoot Pass, through the treacherous White Horse Rapids, and downriver to the mouth of the Stewart River, where Jack (without Shepard, whom age and frail health had forced to turn back home) spent most of the long Arctic winter listening to the tales that passed between the veteran "sourdoughs" and newly arrived "chechaquos."

Any illusions London may have entertained about the northland as paradise were thoroughly dissipated during that rigorous winter. In sharp contrast to the kind of nature that had been depicted by the Romantic poets and by the academic primitivists, this vast, still wilderness—portrayed in archetypal images of the White Silence throughout London's Northland Saga—was cold, impassive, awesome, inimical to puny and insignificant man. While nature's wellsprings might be pure in this region, they were also frozen, providing neither warmth nor security. London's early stories are filled with terror and dread of this deadly landscape. Describing the psychological disintegration of one of the main characters in the story "In a Far Country," he writes: "Everything in the Northland had that crushing effect—the absence of life and motion; the darkness; the infinite peace of the brooding land; the ghastly silence, which made the echo of each heartbeat a sacrilege; the solemn forest which seemed to guard an awful, inexpressible something, which neither word nor thought could compass." The only serenity available to man in this frozen-hearted Eden was the serenity of death.

This savage, pitiless wilderness was an ideal setting for the sensational new kind of fiction that was rapidly gaining currency at the turn of the century in the works of such young writers as Stephen Crane, Frank Norris, and Theodore Dreiser: literary naturalism. Denigrated by critics like Irving Babbitt as "romanticism on all fours," the new mode was not only a rebellious reaction against the prevailing "feminized" fiction of the Gilded Age and the Mauve Decade—that is, the popular sentimental romance and William Dean Howells's mild brand of "teacup realism"—but also a literary by-product of Charles Darwin's evolutionary theories and Herbert Spencer's "survival of the fittest" doctrine, compounded by the Progressive Era's obsession with rugged masculinity and outdoors adventure. Viewed through the philosophic lens of naturalism, man was not some divinely sponsored being descended from the angels but, instead, merely another among myriad creatures ascended from the primordial slime called "life." This human being was subject to the same inexorable laws that determined the fate of all other creatures in nature's mighty and ruthless scheme. "Nature was not kindly to the flesh. She had no concern for that concrete thing called the individual. Her interest lay in the species, the race," muses old Koskoosh, a once-powerful Indian chief, now blind and feeble, abandoned by his tribe to die in the snow in "The Law of Life": "Nature did not care. To life she set one task, gave one law. To perpetuate was the task of life, its law was death."

London managed to escape from this heartless wilderness, suffering from a severe case of scurvy, during the summer of 1898. Although he returned home with less than five dollars' worth of gold, he brought back an inexhaustible wealth of experiences—not only his own but also those of the argonauts with whom he had spent the richest winter in his life, experiences which his artistic genius would now transmute into marketable stories. "It was in the Klondike I found myself," he later testified. "There you get your perspective. I got mine."

He could scarcely have chosen a more propitious perspective for the American era in which he now found himself. Like Henry David Thoreau, he had been "born in the nick of time." The turn of the century was the golden age of the magazine—an age in which new technologies in printing and distribution created a lucrative mass market aimed at the affluent middle-class readers, an age in which the magazine profitably met those multifarious cultural needs subsequently filled by the more recent media of radio, films, and television. It was also the golden age of the short story, a genre ideally suited to the needs of the magazine. Finally, it was the golden age of America's he-manhood—the strenuous age of Teddy Roosevelt and other roughriders. Sated from a cloying diet of piety, propriety, and sentimental pap, the reading public was hungering for meatier, red-blooded fare; and an aggressive new breed of magazine editors like Frank Munsey (*Munsey's*), S. S. McClure (*McClure's*), Robert Collier (*Collier's Weekly*), George Horace Lorimer (*The Saturday Evening Post*), and John Brisben Walker (*Cosmopolitan*) were eager to satisfy this demand by providing "fiction in which there is a story, a force," as Munsey put it, "not washed out studies of effete human nature, not weak tales of sickly sentimentality, not 'pretty' writing. . . ." They were ready to pay good money for the right stuff, and Jack London was now ready to produce exactly the kind of forceful stories they wanted.

The fall of 1898 was for London a time of intense writing, more sensibly focused than his amateurish outpourings of the spring of 1897. The Klondike had truly given him his proper perspective—his métier, as Henry James might put it. No longer did he squander his energies on second-rate verse and third-rate imitations of the sentimental trash that had dominated the popular magazines. He began, instead, weaving first-rate fictions out of the raw materials he had stored in his memory during that marvelous year in the northland. By January 1899 he had broken into print with "To the Man on Trail" in the famous *Overland Monthly;* within a year his work was appearing in the most prestigious magazines in the country, including the *Atlantic Monthly,* which published "An Odyssey of the North" in its January 1900 issue. And that spring his first book was released by a highly respected Boston publishing house. Years later, answering those critics who complained about the incredibly swift rise to fame of his character Martin Eden, London wrote, "In three years, from a sailor with a common school education, I made a successful writer of him. The critics say this is impossible. Yet I was Martin Eden. At the end of three working years, two of which were spent in high school and the university and one spent in writing, and all three in studying immensely and intensely, I was publishing stories in magazines such as the *Atlantic Monthly,* was correcting proofs of my first book (issued by Houghton Mifflin), was selling sociological articles to *Cosmopolitan* and *McClure's,* had declined an associate editorship proffered me by telegraph from New York City, and was getting ready to marry."

The person London was "getting ready to marry" was Bessie Maddern, an athletically attractive, quietly intelligent young woman who had graduated from business school and who made her living as a tutor. She had been engaged to Jack's friend Fred Jacobs, who had recently died of food poisoning aboard a troopship en route to the Philippines. London had known Maddern for several years—in fact, she had tutored him in advanced mathematics during his intensive preparations for his university examinations—but evidently there was no stronger attachment than friendship between them when, having decided that marriage and family life should be a part of his new-won success, he abruptly proposed to her. They were married on April 7, 1900, the same day his first collection of stories, *The Son of the Wolf,* was published by Houghton Mifflin.

London's first book was an immediate hit. "The Klondike has waited three years for its storyteller and interpreter to set it in an imperishable literary mold," acclaimed the *New York Saturday Review of Books and Art.* "London catches the life and conflicts of the Far North with a sure touch, strong dramatic power, a keen eye for character drawing and a natural gift for storytelling." George Hamilton Fitch, in the *San Francisco Chronicle,* awarded London "a foremost place among American short story writers," calling him "the Bret Harte of the Frozen North, with a touch of Kipling's savage realism. . . ."

While Jack had found the key to literary success in his Northland Saga, he was frustrated in his quest for domestic happiness. He had impulsively proposed to Maddern because he believed he needed someone to tame his wildness, to give him a sense of roots and respectability, and to bear him "seven sturdy Saxon sons and seven beautiful daughters." Maddern, still trying to recover from the death of her fiancé, wanted someone to make a home for. The marriage seemed to make a good deal of sense at the time—except for one fatal flaw: neither partner was in love with the other. Love apparently came to Bessie after the wedding—but not to Jack—and it became evident early in their marriage that their personalities and interests were hardly compatible. He was gregarious and fun-loving; she disliked company, especially the kind of free-spirited crowd that gathered regularly around this coming young celebrity. Jack had counted on a son as their firstborn; instead, she gave him a daughter, Joan, on January 15, 1901, and another daughter, Bess (Becky), on October 20, 1902. Though he came to love both girls, his disappointment in not having a son was nonetheless acute.

A year or so after his wedding to Bessie, Jack fell in love with Anna Strunsky, a brilliant Stanford student whom he had first met in San Francisco at a lecture by Socialist Austin Lewis in early December 1899. London thought her a "beautiful genius" and quickly set up a correspondence. "Take me this way: a stray guest, a bird of passage, splashing with salt-rimed wings through a brief moment of your life—a rude and blundering bird, used to large airs and great spaces, unaccustomed to the amenities of confined existence," he wrote to her on December 21, 1899. "And further, should you know me, understand this: I, too, was a dreamer, on a farm, nay, a California ranch. But early, at only nine, the hard hand of the world was laid upon me. It was never relaxed. It has left me practical, so that I am known as harsh, stern, uncompromising. It has taught me that reason is mightier than imagination; that the scientific man is superior to the emotional man."

Some of the ideas of this early letter—most notably the dichotomy between the rational man and the emotional man—are central to much of London's work and constitute, particularly, the genesis of *The Kempton-Wace Letters,* an epistolary dialogue on love written in collaboration with Strunsky in 1901 and 1902, and published anonymously by Macmillan in 1903. As Dane Kempton, Strunsky argues for the ideal conception of love; behind the persona of Herbert Wace, London contends that romantic love is nothing but "prenuptial madness," an emotional trap set by nature and idealized by man as simply "a means for the perpetuation and development of the human type." A sensible union, he insists, "is based upon reason and service and healthy sacrifice." But these fine qualities, without love, were not enough to sustain a marriage, London subsequently realized. Because of his cold rationality, Herbert Wace's engagement to Hester Stebbins is broken; and by the time Jack and Anna had completed their collaboration on the *Letters,* London's marriage was clearly disintegrating. Writing to his friend Cloudesley Johns soon after his separation from Bessie in the late summer of 1903, London remarked, "It's all right for a man sometimes to marry philosophically, but remember, it's damned hard on the woman."

Although Strunsky was implicated when Bessie filed suit for divorce in 1904, there is no substantial evidence that her affair with Jack was ever consummated. She had apparently decided to end the romance while he was in England during the summer of 1902.

There Jack was researching and writing *The People of the Abyss,* his courageous, heartbreaking account of living conditions among the inhabitants of London's East End. Ignoring the warnings that he would never be seen alive again, he spent ten shillings at a secondhand clothing shop in Petticoat Lane for a change of wardrobe, and, disguised as a stranded and broke American sailor, disappeared into the black heart of the world's worst slums. On August 16, he wrote to Strunsky, "Am settled down and hard at work. The whole thing, all the conditions of life, the immensity of it, everything is overwhelming. I never conceived such a mass of misery in the world before." The next week he wrote to her again, saying that his book was one-fifth done: "Am rushing, for I am made sick by this human hellhole called London Town. I find it almost impossible to believe that some of the horrible things I have seen are really so." When he emerged a month later, he had the entire vivid record—manuscript with photographs—ready for Macmillan. He also had a new perspective on his relationship with Strunsky, for she had finally written to break off their affair. "And now it is all over and done with. So be it," he wrote to her on September 28. "Henceforth I shall dream romances for other people and transmute them into bread and butter."

London's "bread and butter" had already been assured by his long-term contract with Macmillan. In December of the previous year, Macmillan's president, George P. Brett, had written to him soliciting his longer manuscripts, with the comment that London's stories seemed to him "to represent very much the best work of the kind that has been done on this side of the water" (i.e., in America). Brett's letter was the start of a professional relationship that would not only last to the end of London's life but also bring out the best in him creatively. In response to Brett's inquiry, London agreed that Macmillan should publish all his books, starting with his collection *Children of the Frost* (including two of his very finest stories: "The Law of Life" and "The League of the Old Men"); Brett, in turn, agreed to send London a monthly check for one hundred and fifty dollars (which Jack had suggested as the amount needed to free him from the hackwork he had been forced to produce in order to meet his household expenses). Though often contemptuous of editors in general, London was seldom less than cordially respectful in his dealings with Brett. Moreover, he was uninhibited, often enthusiastic, in discussing his personal plans with Brett (e.g., his boat-building and ranching projects), partly because he was usually asking for advances on royalties, but also because he trusted Brett as a kind of benevolent father figure. Even more remarkably, Brett seldom lost patience with Jack's ambitious schemes and persistent requests for money to offset his habitual overspending.

London returned home from Europe in November 1902 shortly after the birth of his second daughter, hoping to make his marriage work. He settled down at once to produce what would become his most famous work. "By the way, you remember you found me at work on a story when you visited me," he wrote to George Brett on February 12, 1903. "It is an animal story, utterly different in subject & treatment from the rest of the animal stories which have been so successful; and yet it seems popular enough for the Saturday Evening Post, for they snapped it up right away." Macmillan also "snapped it up right away," and *The Call of the Wild,* published in July, was an instant best-seller. London's "utterly different" animal story has remained a best-seller ever since, having appeared in hundreds of editions in more than eighty different languages.

In May 1903, believing that a move from the city might lessen the tensions of his marriage, London took his family to Glen Ellen, California, a picturesque hamlet nestled in the heart of the Sonoma Valley (the Valley of the Moon), fifty-five miles north of Oakland. There he rented a cottage from Ninetta and Roscoe Eames, managing editor of the *Overland Monthly,* and began work on his next best-seller, *The Sea-Wolf.* But despite his efforts to hold his marriage together, it was increasingly evident that Jack and Bessie were personally incompatible. That summer he fell in love with Mrs. Eames's niece, Clara Charmian Kittredge. Though four years his elder and scarcely beautiful, Kittredge was a comely, vivacious woman with an excellent figure who not only knew how to make the most of her physical charms but also possessed an independent spirit that set her apart from the other young intellectuals, artists, and dilettantes who constituted "The Crowd" of Jack's acquaintances. The better he came to know her, the more she seemed endowed with all the qualities he associated with the ideal comrade and "mate-woman" he had dreamed about. In late July, without revealing that he was in love with another woman, he announced to his wife that he was leaving her. So discreet were he and Kittredge in their affair that it was more than a year before Bessie discovered the true identity of her husband's lover (whom she had mistakenly identified as Anna Strunsky).

In the meantime, Jack was finishing his novel *The Sea-Wolf*, using Charmian as his model for its heroine, Maud Brewster, and putting his own romantic sentiments into the mouth of his narrator-protagonist, Humphrey Van Weyden. In early 1903, Jack had written to George Brett that he had an unusual novel in mind: "My idea is to take a cultured, refined, super-civilized man and woman (whom the subtleties of artificial, civilized life have blinded to the real facts of life), and throw them into a primitive sea-environment where all is stress & struggle and life expresses itself, simply, in terms of food & shelter; and make this man & woman rise to the situation and come out of it with flying colors." By this time fully aware of his market, he shrewdly added: "Of course, this underlying motif, will be *underlying*; it will be subordinated to the love motif. The superficial reader will get the love story & the adventure; while the deeper reader will get all this, plus the bigger thing lying underneath." His plan worked. By combining the ingredients of the two major genres of the turn-of-the-century novel—the ever-popular sentimental romance and the new literary naturalism—London managed to produce one of his most successful novels, one which rivaled even *The Call of the Wild* in reprints and total sales (even exceeding that classic with seven film versions).

In January 1904, leaving the manuscript of *The Sea-Wolf* with Kittredge and his poet-pal George Sterling to edit and proofread, London sailed for Yokohama to report the Russo-Japanese War for the Hearst syndicate. He managed by considerable derring-do (including an eight-day voyage up the stormy Yellow Sea in a sampan he had privately chartered) to get closer to the front than any other reporter but was continually frustrated by Japanese officials who had imposed strict censorship on all reports of military activities. "Personally, I entered upon this campaign with the most gorgeous conceptions of what a war correspondent's work in the world must be," he wrote. "I had read 'The Light That Failed.' I remembered Stephen Crane's descriptions of being

under fire in Cuba. I had heard . . . of all sorts and conditions of correspondents in all sorts of battles and skirmishes, right in the thick of it,
where life was keen and immortal moments were being lived. In brief,
I came to war expecting to get thrills. My only thrills have been those
of indignation and irritation." After six months of thwarted attempts to
get into the action, London returned home with a high opinion of the
Japanese soldiers' toughness and discipline, but only disgust for the Japanese military bureaucrats' intransigence. Even so, this frustrating experience may have provided the germs for two of his most interesting
later stories: "War" and "The Unparalleled Invasion" as well as his
essay on "The Yellow Peril."

The year following his return from the Orient was one of the most
crucial in his life. He was served with divorce papers by Bessie's attor-
ney when he arrived in San Francisco. His finances were in a shambles,
but he was rescued by a three-thousand-dollar royalty check from Macmillan. That winter was probably the most depressing of his entire life;
in addition to his emotional worries, he was concerned about his physical health. He was defeated as Socialist candidate for mayor of Oakland,
and the bad publicity from that campaign detracted from his reputation
and his book sales. It is significant that he wrote no short stories during
this period. But his fortunes turned in the spring. An operation on
March 25 revealed that the tumor which had so worried him was non-
malignant, and in early April he took up permanent residence in the
Valley of the Moon and began writing again; on April 22 he mailed off
"The Sun-Dog Trail," one of his best Northland tales, to *Harper's*, who
immediately accepted it and paid the handsome fee of five hundred dollars. The first week of June he bought the 129-acre Hill Ranch (with
the help of a sixty-five-hundred-dollar advance from Macmillan) and
completed "All Gold Canyon," a fine story distinguished by lyrical passages of description obviously inspired by his new ranch. Later that
month he commenced his "companion-book" to *The Call of the Wild*
(which he fondly called "The Call of the Tame"): *White Fang*. With a
first printing of nearly fifty thousand copies, it was one of his most
commercially successful works.

It was during the summer of 1905 that Jack and Charmian (who
would be married as soon as his divorce was granted in November)
conceived the most highly publicized of all their adventures together:
the cruise of the *Snark*. "It was all due to Captain Joshua Slocum and
his *Spray*," recalled Charmian:

We read him aloud to the 1905 camp children at Wake Robin
Lodge, in the Valley of the Moon, as we sat in the hot sun resting

between water fights and games of tag in the deep swimming pool. *Sailing Alone Around the World* was the name of the book, and when Jack closed the cover on the last chapter, there was a new idea looking out of his eyes. Joshua Slocum did it all alone, in a thirty-seven-foot sloop. Why could not we do it, in a somewhat larger boat, with a little more sociable crew? Jack and I loved the water, and a long voyage was our dream.

What began as a dream became something of a nightmare. London had calculated that their boat would cost about seven thousand dollars —but the great San Francisco earthquake of April 1906 increased the prices of labor and materials fivefold and delayed the building of their craft for more than six months. Planned as a seven-year around-the-world cruise, their voyage lasted less than two years and got them only as far as Australia before having to call off the venture because of multiple tropical diseases Jack, Charmian, and their crew had contracted in the Solomon Islands. "If I were a king, the worst punishment I could inflict on my enemies would be to banish them to the Solomons," London remarked in *The Cruise of the Snark*. "On second thought," he added, "king or no king, I don't think I'd have the heart to do it."

But if the *Snark* voyage had been disastrous from the standpoint of London's health, it nevertheless enriched his fiction tremendously by providing a wealth of new subject matter and by adding significant new dimensions to his creative vision. The South Seas, particularly Hawaii and Polynesia, held forth the promise of warmth, good health, and life abundant—a paradise of flower-swept valleys peopled by bronzed youths and golden maidens. But what London discovered was that, thanks to "the inevitable white man," this was a modern-day paradise lost: a lovely land whose economy had been commercialized, whose political power had been usurped, and whose inhabitants had been contaminated and displaced by the "civilized" *haoles*. "They came like lambs, speaking softly," remarks the hero of "Koolau the Leper." "They were of two kinds. The one asked our permission, our gracious permission, to preach to us the word of God. The other asked our permission, our gracious permission, to trade with us. That was the beginning. To-day all the islands are theirs, all the land, all the cattle—everything is theirs." Also theirs, insidiously shared, is the "rotting sickness" of civilization, the leprosy that has metamorphosed a beautiful people into hideous monsters with stumps for arms and gaping holes for faces. "The sickness is not ours," says Koolau. "We have not sinned. The men who preached the word of God and the word of Rum brought sickness with the coolie slaves who work the stolen land." The situation was the same wherever London traveled in Polynesia. Expecting to find the natives of Typee as splendidly vigorous as Herman Melville had described them two generations before, he found, instead, nothing but a handful of wretched creatures, afflicted with leprosy, elephantiasis, and tuberculosis. Bitterly disillusioned, he wrote, "Life has rotted away in this wonderful garden spot, where the climate is as delightful and healthful as any to be found in the world. Not alone were the Typeans physically magnificent; they were pure. . . . When one considers the situation, one is almost driven to the conclusion that the white race flourishes on impurity and corruption." The purity symbolized in the Polynesians was spiritual as well as physical—and this symbolism is central to the theme of "The Heathen," London's South Seas version of Kipling's "Gunga Din," in which, with tragic irony, a Society Islander—rather than a white man—epitomizes the Christian virtues of agape and self-sacrifice.

By contrast, the natives of Melanesia are myrmidons of the Prince of Darkness—"a wild lot, with a hearty appetite for human flesh and a fad for collecting human heads," wrote London in "The Terrible Solomons." Their "highest instinct of sportsmanship is to catch a man with his back turned and to smite him a cunning blow with a tomahawk that severs the spinal column at the base of the brain. It is equally true that on some islands, such as Malaita, the profit and loss account of social intercourse is calculated in homicides." It was Melanesia, not the Klondike, that inspired London's bitterest naturalistic fiction. Unlike the northland, whose code inspired the best in those who survived, Melanesia tended to bring out the worst in the white man: "I've been in the tropics too long," confesses one character. "I'm a sick man, a damn sick man. And the whiskey, and the sun, and the fever made me sick in morals, too. Nothing's too mean or low for me now. . . ." This notion is central to "Mauki," which must be ranked alongside "The Red One" as the best of London's Melanesian tales, and in which the brutal German Max Bunster is hoisted upon his own sadistic petard by the very unheroic-seeming little black native he has so mercilessly abused.

The most salutary effect Melanesia had on London was to convince him that the paradise he had sought halfway around the globe was, in fact, back at home in the Valley of the Moon. Calling this his panacea, he added, "I defy any man to get a Solomon Island sore in the Valley of the Moon." Almost two years to the day after setting sail from San Francisco aboard the *Snark,* the Londons left Sydney, Australia, bound for home via Ecuador, Panama, New Orleans, and the Grand Canyon.

For the next seven years he would devote his major time and energy to fulfilling his agrarian dream in the building of "Beauty Ranch." "I believe the soil is our one indestructible asset," he avowed. "I am rebuilding worn-out hillside lands that were worked out and destroyed by our wasteful California farmers.... Everything I build is for years to come." Between 1909 and 1916 he increased the size of the ranch to fifteen hundred acres, and during those seven years he came to be regarded by agricultural experts as "one of California's leading farmers" whose ranch was "one of the best in the country." By combining modern agronomy with the wisdom of Oriental agriculture—using such techniques as terracing, drainage, and tillage—he succeeded in growing bumper crops of prunes, grapes, and alfalfa on land that had been abandoned as worthless by previous owners. He built the first concrete-block silo in California and constructed a "pig-palace" which was a model of sanitation and efficiency. He was a friend and neighbor to the famous "plant wizard" Luther Burbank, who paid him this tribute in his memoirs: "Jack London was a big healthy boy with a taste for serious things, but never cynical, never bitter, always good-humored and humorous, as I saw him, and with fingers and heart equally sensitive when he was in my gardens."

The period from the end of the *Snark* cruise until his death (1909–1916) has been generally dismissed by critics as London's "artistic decline," with the notion that as more and more of his vital time and energy were consumed by ranch activities, less was devoted to producing serious literature. Nothing could be farther from the truth. The fact is, even though he spent proportionately more time on longer works such as *Burning Daylight, John Barleycorn, The Valley of the Moon, The Star Rover,* and *The Little Lady of the Big House,* Jack produced some of his best—and certainly his most original—stories during these seven years.

For example, two outstanding socialist parables, "The Strength of the Strong" and "South of the Slot," were written during his stay in Australia in early 1909. "Samuel" and "A Piece of Steak" were composed in May and June, on his trip home. The first of these—the mythic drama of a magnificently courageous earth mother, who tells her story in authentic Scotch-Irish dialect—was so unusual that none of the major magazine editors would touch it. The second, overtly based on professional boxing, is at heart the timeless allegory of youth's inevitable triumph over age. "The Madness of John Harned," an ironic paradigm of Latin versus North American temperaments, was written immediately after the Londons' return to the Valley of the Moon in late July, with the drama of the bullfight they had seen in Quito, Ecuador, still vivid in Jack's memory.

In May of the following year, perhaps the happiest time in the Londons' marriage, when Charmian was pregnant with their first child, London wrote "The Night-Born" after witnessing the death of a young prizefighter during a bout in San Francisco. One of the thematically richest yet least known of his stories, this intricately framed narrative is not only a parable of romance and youth versus greed and decadence, but also a dramatization of the archetypal process of spiritual fulfillment that Jung calls "individuation" (double individuation in this story: one a success, the other a failure), and, furthermore, a tale of female liberation. "War," another little-known gem, reminiscent of Stephen Crane in its imagistic precision and of Ambrose Bierce in its sharp irony, was composed in September 1910.

In October, Jack wrote "Told in the Drooling Ward," a gently humorous view of the world through the eyes of one of the inmates of the Sonoma State Home for the Feeble-Minded. This pioneering study has been rightly praised a worthy forerunner of such later masterpieces as Faulkner's *The Sound and the Fury,* Steinbeck's *Of Mice and Men,* and Kesey's *One Flew Over the Cuckoo's Nest.*

All of these stories belie the critical notion that during these later years of his career London was producing little more than hackwork to satisfy the popular standards of the literary marketplace. The truth is, he was a professional who admittedly wrote for money (who, but a blockhead, ever wrote for anything else? inquired Dr. Johnson); and he contracted with both *The Saturday Evening Post* and *Cosmopolitan* to serialize his tales in 1911 and 1912 for seven hundred and fifty dollars apiece (subsequently collected in *A Son of the Sun* and *Smoke Bellew*). At the same time he was a craftsman with considerable integrity. He interrupted his South Seas tales for the *Post* to write his finest allegory of the revolutionary spirit, "The Mexican." Even his so-called potboilers of the period are distinguished by exceptional stories such as "The Pearls of Parlay" and "Wonder of Woman."

It is true, however, that London produced almost no short fiction from 1912 to 1916, concentrating instead on longer serialized works for the magazines. The year 1913 was perhaps the most notable of this period in terms of his personal fortunes—and misfortunes—for it witnessed a plethora of disasters: an appendicitis attack and operation which revealed that his kidneys were badly diseased; the loss of his fruit crop by a false spring and late frost; the accidental killing of one of his prize mares by a hunter; the threatened loss of his motion-picture copyrights by a lawsuit of the Balboa Amusement Company; and, on August 22, the burning of his nearly completed dream home, the splendid Wolf House, which had been designed to withstand earthquakes and other natural disasters for a thousand years.

Though London remained active, continuing his daily writing stint of one thousand words, his work on the ranch, and his traveling (including regular shorter trips aboard his yacht, the *Roamer*), his health steadily deteriorated over the next three years. Because of his bad kidneys, his physician prescribed a regimen of strict diet, adequate rest, and no alcohol; but, characteristically, except for limiting his alcoholic intake, Jack refused to follow his advice. Moreover, he also refused to cut down on his smoking; and his three-pack-a-day habit probably did more to undermine his already failing health than any other factor.

In the summer of 1914, he was sent home from Vera Cruz, Mexico (where *Collier's Weekly* had sent him to report the Mexican Revolution), with a near-fatal attack of dysentery. By the next year he was suffering chronically from edema, calculi, rheumatism, and the other symptoms of nephritis. Jack and Charmian spent most of 1915 and 1916 in Hawaii, where he hoped he might recapture his good health.

He did not find renewed health, but he did undergo a transformation of creative imagination. His finally awakened mythic awareness—so long repressed because of his deep aversion to the supernatural—began to respond to the folklore of Hawaii and to the theories of Jung, which he encountered in Dr. Beatrice M. Hinkle's 1916 edition of Jung's *Psychology of the Unconscious*.

In the late spring of 1916, for the first time in nearly four years, London began writing short stories again, stories unlike any he had written earlier. On May 20, he finished "The Message," which was retitled "The Red One" when published in *Cosmopolitan* two and a half years later. Something of an anachronism, it is at once both naturalistic and supernatural. Whether London had yet read his copy of Jung before writing the tale is problematical; regardless, the story is as archetypally rich as any London ever wrote. It clearly shows the influence of Conrad, particularly *Heart of Darkness,* in its atmosphere and theme. The title of one of Jung's major essays, "Modern Man in Search of a Soul," might even serve as a subtitle for London's story. Here the protagonist Bassett begins as a sterile, destructive man of science, the hyperconscious twentieth-century monster of rationality hell-bent on reducing all the great mysteries to formula. He has come to the Solomons (aptly named after the king who symbolized wisdom) to shoot down and dissect for science a great jungle butterfly, the mandalic image of soul, psychic wholeness, and spiritual regeneration. But his quest leads him instead into the heart of the jungle where he encounters an even greater cosmic mystery: the awesome sphere apparently sent to the planet earth by "those far distant and superior ones who had bridged the sky with their gigantic, red-iridescent, heaven-singing message." The implication of the story's haunting ending is that such ultimate reality as represented by the Red One is, in the final analysis, ineffable.

This idea—that the most profound knowledge transcends man's rational capacities and scientific processes—is also the theme of London's last story, "The Water Baby," which he completed just six weeks before his death. The setting for the narrative is a two-man fishing excursion, but there is remarkably little physical action—only one incident, in fact, when an intrepid Hawaiian native, past seventy years in age, nonchalantly dives to a depth of forty feet to overcome a nine-foot devilfish with his bare hands and teeth. Essentially, the action is cast in the form of a dialogue between the narrator and "central intelligence," John Lakana (the Hawaiian name for Jack London), and old Kohokumu, the fisherman, who persists in baiting his world-weary and skeptical companion with his "interminable chanting of the deeds and adventures of Maui, the Promethean god of Polynesia." Then, claiming the sea as his mother, Kohokumu articulates his primitive religious beliefs with those images which, according to Jung, emanate from mankind's collective unconscious. "But listen, O Young Wise One, to my elderly wisdom," admonishes Kohokumu in response to Lakana's comment that his is "a queer religion,"

> "This I know: as I grow old I seek less for the truth from without me, and find more of the truth from within me. Why have I thought this thought of my return to my mother and of my rebirth from my mother into the sun? You do not know. I do not know, save that, without whisper of man's voice or printed word, without prompting from otherwhere, this thought has arisen from within me, from the deeps of me that are as deep as the sea. . . . Is this thought that I have thought a dream?"
> "Perhaps it is you that are the dream," I laughed. . . .
> "There is much more in dreams than we know," he assured me with great solemnity. "Dreams go deep, all the way down, maybe to before the beginning. . . ."

Charmian London reports in *The Book of Jack London* that her husband finished writing "The Water Baby" on October 2, 1916, and that in his copy of Jung's *Psychology of the Unconscious* he underscored the quotation of Jesus's words to Nicodemus: "Think not carnally or thou art carnal, but think symbolically, and then thou art spirit." This suggests a notable change of attitude—one might call it "a sea-change"—in a writer who throughout his career had prided himself on being a "materialistic monist." Tragically, Jack London died on November 22, 1916 (from stroke and heart failure, according to the most recent evidence), before his new weltanschauung was fully developed. Even so, the sacred old world he had found in Hawaiian mythology and the brave new world he had discovered in the theories of Jung left an indelible imprint upon his last stories.

It has now been more than two generations since the death of Jack London, yet despite academic attempts to bury him, more of his books are currently in print than at any time in history, both in America and abroad. Beyond the United States, for example, London still holds his rank as the most popular foreign author in the Soviet Union. Moreover, his stock is high not only throughout Europe but also in the Orient—in India, China, and Japan (most recently Hon-No-Tomosha Publishers of Tokyo have issued a handsome twenty-five-volume edition of his works).

How may we account for this enduring, widespread appeal? First, because London is a master storyteller who knows how to hold his audience spellbound for a magical half-hour or two through his creation of narrative tension and what he called "atmosphere." Furthermore, among our great literary artists, he is one of the most eminently and consistently *readable* because of his unpretentious style. By writing plainly and clearly enough, he communicates with readers at all levels of literacy and education; it was therefore as easy for London to write a marketable story for *The Youth's Companion* as it was to write one for the *Atlantic Monthly*. Moreover, this classic simplicity—"purity of line," to use Hemingway's famous phrase—has facilitated the translation of London's writings, and therefore made them accessible to readers of all nationalities. As he attested in praising Herbert Spencer's *Philosophy of Style:*

> [Spencer's essay] taught me the subtle and manifold operations necessary to transmute thought, beauty, sensation and emotion into black symbols on white paper; which symbols, through the reader's eye, were taken into his brain, and by his brain transmuted into thoughts, beauty, sensations and emotions that fairly corresponded with mine. Among other things, this taught me to *know* the brain of my reader, in order to select the symbols that would compel his brain to realize my thought, or vision, or emotion. Also, I learned that the right symbols were the ones that would require the expenditure of the minimum of my reader's brain energy, leaving the maximum of his brain energy to realize and enjoy the content of my mind, as conveyed to his mind.

Along with Rudyard Kipling and Stephen Crane, London was a pioneer in popularizing this new kind of prose—uncluttered, straightfor-
ward, imagistic—a style of writing ideally suited both to the rapidly
developing genre of the short story and to the burgeoning magazine
market which demanded stories of narrative force and physical action.
In meeting this demand, London was able to reach an audience that
numerically overshadowed the devotees of the cool and distant fictions
of Henry James and Edith Wharton. And in producing fiction that was
thematically substantial enough to satisfy the editors of the most dis-
criminating magazines of the era—the *Atlantic, Century, Collier's, Cosmopolitan, Ladies' Home Journal,* and *Saturday Evening Post*—he was also
instrumental in establishing for this new kind of short story a respectable middle ground between the saloon and the salon. His thoughtful,
skillful treatment of physical violence (in his prizefighting stories, for
example) helped pave the way for the newer generations of Ernest
Hemingway, Ring Lardner, and Norman Mailer. And his extraordinary
leap from Darwin to Jung, from naturalism to supernaturalism, from
realistic stereotype to mythical archetype, signified the greater cultural
transition from the nineteenth century to the even more problematical
—and more challenging—twentieth.

But beneath London's mastery of narrative technique and clarity of
style lies another key to his perennial appeal: the essential vitality—the
spirit of humanistic affirmation—which transcends the deterministic,
negative aspects of literary naturalism. "Jack London's deep belief in
man's abilities in the face of overwhelming odds lends an optimistic
tone, a life-asserting force to his writings," notes his leading Soviet
critic, Vil Bykov. "Healthy people better understand a healthy person.
They believe in man and they tend toward that which is full of life. Jack
London brought to the Russian reader a world full of romanticism and
vigor, and the reader came to love him."

A "world full of romanticism and vigor" is an apt description of the
world we discover in London's stories, though perhaps "worlds" is the
more accurate word for describing his fictions. For his stories range
geographically from the frozen wilderness of the Klondike to the putrid
jungles of Melanesia, from Hawaii to Australia, from city to country,
from South America to the Valley of the Moon. In tone they vary from
the harsh naturalistic doom of the White Silence to the poignant gloom
of the child laborer's world, to the gentle humor of the Drooling Ward.
And they move in theme from the foolishness of pride, the ruthlessness
of greed, and the senselessness of war, to the indomitability of the human spirit, the unfailing salvation of comradeship and love, the incontrovertible wisdom of the Great Mother and the Water Baby.

But when all of the factors contributing to Jack London's greatness as a storyteller have been considered, there is one which remains paramount. Even while he was disavowing all mystical and mythical pretensions, it may have been London's own dreams from the deeps within him, "as deep as the sea," that from early on gave his best stories their universal and lasting appeal. Dreams such as these do, in truth, "go deep," as old Kohokumu tells us, "all the way down, maybe to before the beginning. . . ."

A NOTE ON THE TEXTS

Prior to submitting his manuscripts for a collection of stories to a book publisher, Jack London took advantage of the lucrative periodical market by having his short stories published in magazines both in the United States and, sometimes, in England. Often the magazine editors tampered with London's texts to contour them to their readership, to the physical format of the periodical, and to "house style." London had no control over these alterations, which usually took the form of deletions and changes in wording, punctuation, and paragraphing. He did, however, have the opportunity to restore the texts to their original form when the stories were collected in a book. And since London did not revise the first editions of his various collections of stories, we consider these texts authoritative; they are the ones we have chosen for this edition of stories. We have further opted to maintain the authenticity of these texts by retaining the original—and sometimes inconsistent—spelling, punctuation, and capitalization. There are, however, two exceptions to our procedure: We have made consistent the erratic spacing of contractions in the texts of the stories; also, because the 1902 version of "To Build a Fire" was never included in a collection of London's stories, we have used the text of the story which appeared in *The Youth's Companion*.

CHRONOLOGY

1876 Jack London born on January 12 in San Francisco, California. Named John Griffith Chaney by his mother, Flora Wellman, who had been deserted by her common-law husband, William Henry Chaney, when she informed him of her pregnancy. On September 7, Flora Wellman Chaney marries John London; the child is renamed John Griffith London and called "Johnny" until he insists on being called "Jack."

1878 To escape the diphtheria epidemic, which nearly killed Jack and his stepsister Eliza, John London moves his family across San Francisco Bay to Oakland, where he manages a grocery store and sells the produce he grows to local markets.

1881 The Londons move to a twenty-acre farm in Alameda.

1882 Jack begins grade school in Alameda.

1886 After living on farms in San Mateo County and in the Livermore Valley, the Londons buy a house in Oakland. Jack introduced to the world of books in the Oakland Public Library.

1891 Graduates from Cole Grammar School and begins working in Hickmott's Cannery. With three hundred dollars borrowed from his former wetnurse, "Aunt Jennie" Prentiss, buys the sloop *Razzle-Dazzle* and becomes an oyster pirate on San Francisco Bay.

1892 Joins the California Fish Patrol in Benecia as a deputy patrolman.

1893 From January through August serves as an able-bodied seaman aboard the sealing schooner *Sophia Sutherland* on its voyage to the Bering Sea via Hawaii, the Bonin Islands, and Japan. Upon his return to California, works in a jute mill for ten cents an hour for ten-hour workdays. "Story of a Typhoon Off the Coast of Japan" wins a writing contest sponsored by the San Francisco *Morning Call* and is published in that newspaper.

1894 Works as a coal heaver in a local electric railway power plant. In early April, joins Kelly's Army, the western contingent of Coxey's army of the unemployed, in its protest march to Washington. In late May leaves the group in Hannibal, Missouri, to tramp on his own. After visiting the World's Fair in Chicago, heads east. Is arrested in Niagra Falls, New York, and serves a thirty-day sentence for vagrancy. After release from the Erie County Penitentiary, returns to California.

1895 Attends Oakland High School and publishes short stories and articles in the school magazine, *The High School Aegis*. Falls in love with Mabel Applegarth, the Ruth Morse of his autobiographical novel, *Martin Eden*.

1896 Joins the Socialist Labor Party and becomes known as the "Boy Socialist" of Oakland. Leaves high school. Prepares to enter the University of California at Berkeley by attending the University Academy in Alameda, where he meets Bessie Maddern, his future wife.

1897 Attends Berkeley for one semester. Begins writing in order to support himself, but is unsuccessful. Takes a job at the Belmont Academy laundry. In July, with his brother-in-law, Captain James H. Shepard, journeys to Alaska to join the Klondike gold rush. Spends the winter in a cabin on Split-Up Island in the Yukon Territory.

1898 Suffering from scurvy, leaves the Klondike in early June. Works his way home as a coal stoker, arriving in Oakland in July. Begins an intense regimen to develop his skills as a writer.

1899 Sells his first story, "To the Man on Trail," to the *Overland Monthly* for five dollars. In August, the prestigious *Atlantic Monthly* accepts "An Odyssey of the North." In December, Jack meets Anna Strunsky, with whom he will collaborate on *The Kempton-Wace Letters*.

1900 On April 7, marries Bessie Maddern.
The Son of the Wolf (Klondike stories) published.

1901 Joan London, his first child, born on January 15. Jack commissioned by the Hearst newspaper syndicate to cover the Third National Bundes Shooting Championship, his first journalism assignment. Runs unsuccessfully for mayor of Oakland on the Socialist ticket.
The God of His Fathers (Klondike stories) published.

1902 Moves to Piedmont Hills and begins friendship with George Sterling, a poet who becomes the model for Russ Brissenden in *Martin Eden*. Spends six weeks in August and September in the East End of London to research and write *The People of the Abyss*. Second daughter, Becky, born on October 20.

Books published: *A Daughter of the Snows* (Klondike novel); *Children of the Frost* (Northland Indian stories); *The Cruise of the Dazzler* (juvenile stories featuring the 'Frisco Kid, based on London's adventures as an oyster pirate).

1903 Falls in love with Charmian Kittredge; is separated from Bessie London.

Books published: *The Kempton-Wace Letters,* with Anna Strunsky (epistolary dialogue on love); *The Call of the Wild* (Klondike novella); *The People of the Abyss* (sociological study of living conditions in the East End of London).

1904 Covers the Russo-Japanese War in Korea and Manchuria for the Hearst syndicate from January through June. Bessie London files suit for divorce on June 28; names Anna Strunsky as cause of the separation.

Books published: *The Faith of Men* (Klondike stories); *The Sea-Wolf* (novel based on London's experiences aboard the sealing schooner *Sophia Sutherland* in 1893).

1905 In March, runs unsuccessfully again as the Socialist candidate for mayor of Oakland. Moves to the Sonoma Valley town of Glen Ellen, purchases the 129-acre Hill Ranch, the beginning of what will become the fifteen-hundred-acre "Beauty Ranch." In October, starts socialist lecture tour throughout the Midwest and East, including lectures at Harvard and Yale. Divorce granted on November 18; marries Charmian Kittredge the following day in Chicago.

Books published: *War of the Classes* (essays); *The Game* (prizefighting novella); *Tales of the Fish Patrol* (stories based on London's adventures as a member of the California Fish Patrol in 1892).

1906 Resumes lecture tour in January after honeymoon in Jamaica. Becomes ill and cancels lecture tour. Returns to Glen Ellen in mid-February. Starts building the schooner *Snark* for his projected seven-year voyage around the world. Reports the San Francisco earthquake for *Collier's*.

Books published: *Moon-Face and Other Stories; White Fang* (companion novel to *The Call of the Wild); Scorn of Women* (three-act play based on his story of the same name).

1907 *Snark* sets sail from Oakland to Hawaiian Islands on April 23. Arrives at Pearl Harbor a month later. Departs Hawaii in October. Sails to the Marquesas Islands and then to Tahiti.

Books published: *Before Adam* (prehistoric adventure novel); *Love of Life and Other Stories* (Klondike stories); *The Road* (tramping reminiscences).

1908 In mid-January returns to Oakland from Tahiti for a month to attend to financial affairs. Resumes *Snark* voyage in April. Sails to Fiji Islands, New Hebrides, Solomon Islands, and Australia. Is hospitalized in Sydney, Australia, and forced to abandon the cruise. Buys more land for his ranch in Glen Ellen.

The Iron Heel (novel about socialist apocalypse) published.

1909 After recovering from illnesses in Sydney, returns to Glen Ellen, via Ecuador, Panama, and New Orleans, arriving home on July 24.

Martin Eden (autobiographical novel based on London's early writing career) published.

1910 Expands "Beauty Ranch" to nearly a thousand acres and hires stepsister Eliza Shepard as ranch superintendent and business manager. Visits friends at the artists' colony in Carmel. Daughter Joy born on June 19 and dies on June 21. Reports Johnson–Jeffries fight in Reno, Nevada, on July 4. Discusses plans to build "Wolf House" with architect Albert Farr.

Books published: *Lost Face* (Klondike stories); *Revolution and Other Essays; Burning Daylight* (the first of London's Sonoma novels); *Theft: A Play in Four Acts* (written for Olga Nethersole but never produced in the United States).

1911 Visits Los Angeles in January and February. With Charmian and his valet Nakata, drives four-horse wagon to Oregon and back in the summer. Departs on two-month trip to New York on December 24.

Books published: *When God Laughs and Other Stories; Adventure* (Melanesian novel); *The Cruise of the Snark* (travel sketches); *South Sea Tales* (Melanesian stories).

1912 In March, sails from Baltimore with Charmian aboard the barque *Dirigo* for a five-month voyage to Seattle around Cape Horn. Returns to Glen Ellen on August 4. Charmian miscarries second child on August 12.

Books published: *The House of Pride and Other Tales of Hawaii; A Son of the Sun* (South Sea stories); *Smoke Bellew* (Klondike stories).

1913 Discusses movie contract with producers in Los Angeles. Operated on for appendicitis in July. On August 22, "Wolf House" destroyed by fire. Cruises Sacramento and San Joaquin River deltas aboard the *Roamer* in the fall.

Books published: *The Night-Born* (miscellaneous stories); *The Abysmal Brute* (fictional exposé of professional boxing); *John Barleycorn* (autobiographical treatise on alcohol).

1914 Travels to New York to discuss business affairs. With Charmian, leaves for Vera Cruz in April to report on the Mexican Revolution for *Collier's*. Suffers from acute dysentery and returns to Glen Ellen in June.

Books published: *The Strength of the Strong* (miscellaneous stories); *The Mutiny of the Elsinore* (novel based in part on London's 1912 voyage around Cape Horn on the *Dirigo*).

1915 Suffers an attack of rheumatism in February. Sails to Hawaii and recuperates there for five months. Returns to Glen Ellen in July and sails back to Hawaii in December.

Books published: *The Scarlet Plague* (novella); *The Star Rover* (fantasy novel based, in part, on prison experiences of Ed Morrell).

1916 Remains in Hawaii until late July, when he returns to San Francisco. Visits California State Fair in Sacramento, where stricken again with rheumatism. Returns to Glen Ellen on September 16. Suffers a slight attack of ptomaine poisoning on November 10. Continues to have stomach problems and insomnia. On November 22, dies of "uraemia following renal colic" (more probably stroke and heart failure).

Books published: *The Acorn-Planter* (a Grove Play written for the Bohemian Club but never staged); *The Little Lady of the Big House* (farming novel); *The Turtles of Tasman* (miscellaneous stories).

Posthumously published books: *The Human Drift* (1917, miscellany), *Jerry of the Islands* (1917, dog novel), *Michael, Brother of Jerry* (1917, sequel novel to *Jerry*), *The Red One* (1918, stories), *On the Makaloa Mat* (1919, Hawaiian stories), *Hearts of Three* (1920, serialized cliff-hanger written in tandem with scenarist Charles Goddard), *Dutch Courage and Other Stories* (1922, early juvenile stories), *The Assassination Bureau*, completed by Robert L. Fish (1963, mystery thriller), *Letters from Jack London*, edited by King Hendricks and Irving Shepard (1965, one volume of selected letters), *Jack London Reports: War Correspondence, Sports Articles, and Miscellaneous Writings*, edited by King Hendricks and Irving Shepard (1970), *No Mentor But Myself: A Collection of Articles, Essays, Reviews and Letters by Jack London on Writing and Writers*, edited by Dale L. Walker (1979), *Jack London on the Road: The Tramp Diary and Other Hobo Writings*, edited by Richard W. Etulain (1979), *The Letters of Jack London*, edited by Earle Labor, Robert C. Leitz, III, and I. Milo Shepard (1988, three volumes of selected letters).

SHORT STORIES OF
JACK LONDON

STORY OF A
TYPHOON OFF THE
COAST OF JAPAN

It was four bells in the morning watch. We had just finished breakfast when the order came forward for the watch on deck to stand by to heave her to and all hands stand by the boats.

"Port! hard a port!" cried our sailing-master. "Clew up the topsails! Let the flying jib run down! Back the jib over to windward and run down the foresail!" And so was our schooner *Sophie Sutherland* hove to off the Japan coast, near Cape Jerimo, on April 10, 1893.

Then came moments of bustle and confusion. There were eighteen men to man the six boats. Some were hooking on the falls, others casting off the lashings; boat-steerers appeared with boat-compasses and water-breakers, and boat-pullers with the lunch boxes. Hunters were staggering under two or three shotguns, a rifle and heavy ammunition box, all of which were soon stowed away with their oilskins and mittens in the boats.

The sailing-master gave his last orders, and away we went, pulling three pairs of oars to gain our positions. We were in the weather boat, and so had a longer pull than the others. The first, second, and third lee boats soon had all sail set and were running off to the southward and westward with the wind beam, while the schooner was running off to leeward of them, so that in case of accident the boats would have fair wind home.

It was a glorious morning, but our boat-steerer shook his head ominously as he glanced at the rising sun and prophetically muttered: "Red sun in the morning, sailor take warning." The sun had an angry look, and a few light, fleecy "nigger-heads" in that quarter seemed abashed and frightened and soon disappeared.

Away off to the northward Cape Jerimo reared its black, forbidding

3

head like some huge monster rising from the deep. The winter's snow, not yet entirely dissipated by the sun, covered it in patches of glistening white, over which the light wind swept on its way out to sea. Huge gulls rose slowly, fluttering their wings in the light breeze and striking their webbed feet on the surface of the water for over half a mile before they could leave it. Hardly had the patter, patter died away when a flock of sea quail rose, and with whistling wings flew away to windward, where members of a large band of whales were disporting themselves, their blowings sounding like the exhaust of steam engines. The harsh, discordant cries of a sea-parrot grated unpleasantly on the ear, and set half a dozen alert in a small band of seals that were ahead of us. Away they went, breaching and jumping entirely out of water. A sea-gull with slow, deliberate flight and long, majestic curves circled round us, and as a reminder of home a little English sparrow perched impudently on the fo'castle head, and, cocking his head on one side, chirped merrily. The boats were soon among the seals, and the bang! bang! of the guns could be heard from down to leeward.

The wind was slowly rising, and by three o'clock as, with a dozen seals in our boat, we were deliberating whether to go on or turn back, the recall flag was run up at the schooner's mizzen—a sure sign that with the rising wind the barometer was falling and that our sailing-master was getting anxious for the welfare of the boats.

Away we went before the wind with a single reef in our sail. With clenched teeth sat the boat-steerer, grasping the steering oar firmly with both hands, his restless eyes on the alert—a glance at the schooner ahead, as we rose on a sea, another at the mainsheet, and then one astern where the dark ripple of the wind on the water told him of a coming puff or a large white-cap that threatened to overwhelm us. The waves were holding high carnival, performing the strangest antics, as with wild glee they danced along in fierce pursuit—now up, now down, here, there, and everywhere, until some great sea of liquid green with its milk-white crest of foam rose from the ocean's throbbing bosom and drove the others from view. But only for a moment, for again under new forms they reappeared. In the sun's path they wandered, where every ripple, great or small, every little spit or spray looked like molten silver, where the water lost its dark green color and became a dazzling, silvery flood, only to vanish and become a wild waste of sullen turbulence, each dark foreboding sea rising and breaking, then rolling on again. The dash, the sparkle, the silvery light soon vanished with the sun, which became obscured by black clouds that were rolling swiftly in from the west, northwest; apt heralds of the coming storm.

We soon reached the schooner and found ourselves the last aboard.

In a few minutes the seals were skinned, boats and decks washed, and we were down below by the roaring fo'castle fire, with a wash, change of clothes, and a hot, substantial supper before us. Sail had been put on the schooner, as we had a run of seventy-five miles to make to the southward before morning, so as to get in the midst of the seals, out of which we had strayed during the last two days' hunting.

We had the first watch from eight to midnight. The wind was soon blowing half a gale, and our sailing-master expected little sleep that night as he paced up and down the poop. The topsails were soon clewed up and made fast, then the flying jib run down and furled. Quite a sea was rolling by this time, occasionally breaking over the decks, flooding them and threatening to smash the boats. At six bells we were ordered to turn them over and put on storm lashings. This occupied us till eight bells, when we were relieved by the mid-watch. I was the last to go below, doing so just as the watch on deck was furling the spanker. Below all were asleep except our green hand, the "bricklayer," who was dying of consumption. The wildly dancing movements of the sea lamp cast a pale, flickering light through the fo'castle and turned to golden honey the drops of water on the yellow oilskins. In all the corners dark shadows seemed to come and go, while up in the eyes of her, beyond the pall bits, descending from deck to deck, where they seemed to lurk like some dragon at the cavern's mouth, it was dark as Erebus. Now and again, the light seemed to penetrate for a moment as the schooner rolled heavier than usual, only to recede, leaving it darker and blacker than before. The roar of the wind through the rigging came to the ear muffled like the distant rumble of a train crossing a trestle or the surf on the beach, while the loud crash of the seas on her weather bow seemed almost to rend the beams and planking asunder as it resounded through the fo'castle. The creaking and groaning of the timbers, stanchions, and bulkheads, as the strain the vessel was undergoing was felt, served to drown the groans of the dying man as he tossed uneasily in his bunk. The working of the foremast against the deck beams caused a shower of flaky powder to fall, and sent another sound mingling with the tumultuous storm. Small cascades of water streamed from the pall bits from the fo'castle head above, and, joining issue with the streams from the wet oilskins, ran along the floor and disappeared aft into the main hold.

At two bells in the middle watch—that is, in land parlance one o'clock in the morning—the order was roared out on the fo'castle: "All hands on deck and shorten sail!"

Then the sleepy sailors tumbled out of their bunk and into their clothes, oil-skins, and sea-boots and up on deck. 'Tis when that order comes on cold, blustering nights that "Jack" grimly mutters: "Who would not sell a farm and go to sea?"

It was on deck that the force of the wind could be fully appreciated, especially after leaving the stifling fo'castle. It seemed to stand up against you like a wall, making it almost impossible to move on the heaving decks or to breathe as the fierce gusts came dashing by. The schooner was hove to under jib, foresail, and mainsail. We proceeded to lower the foresail and make it fast. The night was dark, greatly impeding our labor. Still, though not a star or the moon could pierce the black masses of storm clouds that obscured the sky as they swept along before the gale, nature aided us in a measure. A soft light emanated from the movement of the ocean. Each mighty sea, all phosphorescent and glowing with the tiny lights of myriads of animalculæ, threatened to overwhelm us with a deluge of fire. Higher and higher, thinner and thinner, the crest grew as it began to curve and overtop preparatory to breaking, until with a roar it fell over the bulwarks, a mass of soft glowing light and tons of water which sent the sailors sprawling in all directions and left in each nook and cranny little specks of light that glowed and trembled till the next sea washed them away, depositing new ones in their places. Sometimes several seas following each other with great rapidity and thundering down on our decks filled them full to the bulwarks, but soon they were discharged through the lee scuppers.

To reef the mainsail we were forced to run off before the gale under the single reefed jib. By the time we had finished the wind had forced up such a tremendous sea that it was impossible to heave her to. Away we flew on the wings of the storm through the muck and flying spray. A wind sheer to starboard, then another to port as the enormous seas struck the schooner astern and nearly broached her to. As day broke we took in the jib, leaving not a sail unfurled. Since we had begun scudding she had ceased to take the seas over her bow, but amidships they broke fast and furious. It was a dry storm in the matter of rain, but the force of the wind filled the air with fine spray, which flew as high as the crosstrees and cut the face like a knife, making it impossible to see over a hundred yards ahead. The sea was a dark lead color as with long, slow, majestic roll it was heaped up by the wind into liquid mountains of foam. The wild antics of the schooner were sickening as she forged along. She would almost stop, as though climbing a mountain, then rapidly rolling to right and left as she gained the summit of a huge sea, she steadied herself and paused for a moment as though affrighted at the yawning precipice before her. Like an avalanche, she shot forward and down as the sea astern struck her with the force of a thousand battering rams, burying her bow to the catheads in the milky foam at the bottom that came on deck in all directions—forward, astern, to right and left, through the hawse-pipes and over the rail.

The wind began to drop, and by ten o'clock we were talking of heaving her to. We passed a ship, two schooners, and a four-masted barkentine under the smallest of canvas, and at eleven o'clock, running up the spanker and jib, we hove her to, and in another hour we were beating back again against the aftersea under full sail to regain the sealing ground away to the westward.

Below, a couple of men were sewing the "bricklayer's" body in canvas preparatory to the sea burial. And so with the storm passed away the "bricklayer's" soul.

THE WHITE SILENCE

"Carmen won't last more than a couple of days." Mason spat out a chunk of ice and surveyed the poor animal ruefully, then put her foot in his mouth and proceeded to bite out the ice which clustered cruelly between the toes.

"I never saw a dog with a highfalutin' name that ever was worth a rap," he said, as he concluded his task and shoved her aside. "They just fade away and die under the responsibility. Did ye ever see one go wrong with a sensible name like Cassiar, Siwash, or Husky? No, sir! Take a look at Shookum here, he's"—

Snap! The lean brute flashed up, the white teeth just missing Mason's throat.

"Ye will, will ye?" A shrewd clout behind the ear with the butt of the dogwhip stretched the animal in the snow, quivering softly, a yellow slaver dripping from its fangs.

"As I was saying, just look at Shookum, here—he's got the spirit. Bet ye he eats Carmen before the week's out."

"I'll bank another proposition against that," replied Malemute Kid, reversing the frozen bread placed before the fire to thaw. "We'll eat Shookum before the trip is over. What d' ye say, Ruth?"

The Indian woman settled the coffee with a piece of ice, glanced from Malemute Kid to her husband, then at the dogs, but vouchsafed no reply. It was such a palpable truism that none was necessary. Two hundred miles of unbroken trail in prospect, with a scant six days' grub for themselves and none for the dogs, could admit no other alternative. The two men and the woman grouped about the fire and began their meagre meal. The dogs lay in their harnesses, for it was a midday halt, and watched each mouthful enviously.

"No more lunches after to-day," said Malemute Kid. "And we've got to keep a close eye on the dogs,—they're getting vicious. They'd just as soon pull a fellow down as not, if they get a chance."

"And I was president of an Epworth once, and taught in the Sunday school." Having irrelevantly delivered himself of this, Mason fell into a dreamy contemplation of his steaming moccasins, but was aroused by Ruth filling his cup. "Thank God, we've got slathers of tea! I've seen it growing, down in Tennessee. What wouldn't I give for a hot corn pone just now! Never mind, Ruth; you won't starve much longer, nor wear moccasins either."

The woman threw off her gloom at this, and in her eyes welled up a great love for her white lord,—the first white man she had ever seen, —the first man whom she had known to treat a woman as something better than a mere animal or beast of burden.

"Yes, Ruth," continued her husband, having recourse to the macaronic jargon in which it was alone possible for them to understand each other; "wait till we clean up and pull for the Outside. We'll take the White Man's canoe and go to the Salt Water. Yes, bad water, rough water,—great mountains dance up and down all the time. And so big, so far, so far away,—you travel ten sleep, twenty sleep, forty sleep" (he graphically enumerated the days on his fingers), "all the time water, bad water. Then you come to great village, plenty people, just the same mosquitoes next summer. Wigwams oh, so high,—ten, twenty pines. Hi-yu skookum!"

He paused impotently, cast an appealing glance at Malemute Kid, then laboriously placed the twenty pines, end on end, by sign language. Malemute Kid smiled with cheery cynicism; but Ruth's eyes were wide with wonder, and with pleasure; for she half believed he was joking, and such condescension pleased her poor woman's heart.

"And then you step into a—a box, and pouf! up you go." He tossed his empty cup in the air by way of illustration, and as he deftly caught it, cried: "And biff! down you come. Oh, great medicine-men! You go Fort Yukon, I go Arctic City,—twenty-five sleep,—big string, all the time,—I catch him string,—I say, 'Hello, Ruth! How are ye?'—and you say, 'Is that my good husband?'—and I say 'Yes,'—and you say, 'No can bake good bread, no more soda,'—then I say, 'Look in cache, under flour; good-by.' You look and catch plenty soda. All the time you Fort Yukon, me Arctic City. Hi-yu medicine-man!"

Ruth smiled so ingenuously at the fairy story, that both men burst into laughter. A row among the dogs cut short the wonders of the Outside, and by the time the snarling combatants were separated, she had lashed the sleds and all was ready for the trail.

* * *

"Mush! Baldy! Hi! Mush on!" Mason worked his whip smartly, and as the dogs whined low in the traces, broke out the sled with the gee-pole. Ruth followed with the second team, leaving Malemute Kid, who had helped her start, to bring up the rear. Strong man, brute that he was, capable of felling an ox at a blow, he could not bear to beat the poor animals, but humored them as a dog-driver rarely does,—nay, almost wept with them in their misery.

"Come, mush on there, you poor sore-footed brutes!" he murmured, after several ineffectual attempts to start the load. But his patience was at last rewarded, and though whimpering with pain, they hastened to join their fellows.

No more conversation; the toil of the trail will not permit such extravagance. And of all deadening labors, that of the Northland trail is the worst. Happy is the man who can weather a day's travel at the price of silence, and that on a beaten track.

And of all heart-breaking labors, that of breaking trail is the worst. At every step the great webbed shoe sinks till the snow is level with the knee. Then up, straight up, the deviation of a fraction of an inch being a certain precursor of disaster, the snowshoe must be lifted till the surface is cleared; then forward, down, and the other foot is raised perpendicularly for the matter of half a yard. He who tries this for the first time, if haply he avoids bringing his shoes in dangerous propinquity and measures not his length on the treacherous footing, will give up exhausted at the end of a hundred yards; he who can keep out of the way of the dogs for a whole day may well crawl into his sleeping-bag with a clear conscience and a pride which passeth all understanding; and he who travels twenty sleeps on the Long Trail is a man whom the gods may envy.

The afternoon wore on, and with the awe, born of the White Silence, the voiceless travelers bent to their work. Nature has many tricks wherewith she convinces man of his finity,—the ceaseless flow of the tides, the fury of the storm, the shock of the earthquake, the long roll of heaven's artillery,—but the most tremendous, the most stupefying of all, is the passive phase of the White Silence. All movement ceases, the sky clears, the heavens are as brass; the slightest whisper seems sacrilege, and man becomes timid, affrighted at the sound of his own voice. Sole speck of life journeying across the ghostly wastes of a dead world, he trembles at his audacity, realizes that his is a maggot's life, nothing more. Strange thoughts arise unsummoned, and the mystery of all things strives for utterance. And the fear of death, of God, of the universe, comes over him,—the hope of the Resurrection and the Life, the yearning for immortality, the vain striving of the imprisoned essence,— it is then, if ever, man walks alone with God.

So wore the day away. The river took a great bend, and Mason headed his team for the cut-off across the narrow neck of land. But the dogs balked at the high bank. Again and again, though Ruth and Malemute Kid were shoving on the sled, they slipped back. Then came the concerted effort. The miserable creatures, weak from hunger, exerted their last strength. Up—up—the sled poised on the top of the bank; but the leader swung the string of dogs behind him to the right, fouling Mason's snowshoes. The result was grievous. Mason was whipped off his feet; one of the dogs fell in the traces; and the sled toppled back, dragging everything to the bottom again.

Slash! the whip fell among the dogs savagely, especially upon the one which had fallen.

"Don't, Mason," entreated Malemute Kid; "the poor devil's on its last legs. Wait and we'll put my team on."

Mason deliberately withheld the whip till the last word had fallen, then out flashed the long lash, completely curling about the offending creature's body. Carmen—for it was Carmen—cowered in the snow, cried piteously, then rolled over on her side.

It was a tragic moment, a pitiful incident of the trail,—a dying dog, two comrades in anger. Ruth glanced solicitously from man to man. But Malemute Kid restrained himself, though there was a world of reproach in his eyes, and bending over the dog, cut the traces. No word was spoken. The teams were double-spanned and the difficulty overcome; the sleds were under way again, the dying dog dragging herself along in the rear. As long as an animal can travel, it is not shot, and this last chance is accorded it,—the crawling into camp, if it can, in the hope of a moose being killed.

Already penitent for his angry action, but too stubborn to make amends, Mason toiled on at the head of the cavalcade, little dreaming that danger hovered in the air. The timber clustered thick in the sheltered bottom, and through this they threaded their way. Fifty feet or more from the trail towered a lofty pine. For generations it had stood there, and for generations destiny had had this one end in view,— perhaps the same had been decreed of Mason.

He stooped to fasten the loosened thong of his moccasin. The sleds came to a halt and the dogs lay down in the snow without a whimper. The stillness was weird; not a breath rustled the frost-encrusted forest;

the cold and silence of outer space had chilled the heart and smote the trembling lips of nature. A sigh pulsed through the air,—they did not seem to actually hear it, but rather felt it, like the premonition of movement in a motionless void. Then the great tree, burdened with its weight of years and snow, played its last part in the tragedy of life. He heard the warning crash and attempted to spring up, but almost erect, caught the blow squarely on the shoulder.

The sudden danger, the quick death,—how often had Malemute Kid faced it! The pine needles were still quivering as he gave his commands and sprang into action. Nor did the Indian girl faint or raise her voice in idle wailing, as might many of her white sisters. At his order, she threw her weight on the end of a quickly extemporized handspike, easing the pressure and listening to her husband's groans, while Malemute Kid attacked the tree with his axe. The steel rang merrily as it bit into the frozen trunk, each stroke being accompanied by a forced, audible respiration, the "Huh!" "Huh!" of the woodsman.

At last the Kid laid the pitiable thing that was once a man in the snow. But worse than his comrade's pain was the dumb anguish in the woman's face, the blended look of hopeful, hopeless query. Little was said; those of the Northland are early taught the futility of words and the inestimable value of deeds. With the temperature at sixty-five below zero, a man cannot lie many minutes in the snow and live. So the sled-lashings were cut, and the sufferer, rolled in furs, laid on a couch of boughs. Before him roared a fire, built of the very wood which wrought the mishap. Behind and partially over him was stretched the primitive fly,—a piece of canvas, which caught the radiating heat and threw it back and down upon him,—a trick which men may know who study physics at the fount.

And men who have shared their bed with death know when the call is sounded. Mason was terribly crushed. The most cursory examination revealed it. His right arm, leg, and back, were broken; his limbs were paralyzed from the hips; and the likelihood of internal injuries was large. An occasional moan was his only sign of life.

No hope; nothing to be done. The pitiless night crept slowly by,— Ruth's portion, the despairing stoicism of her race, and Malemute Kid adding new lines to his face of bronze. In fact, Mason suffered least of all, for he spent his time in Eastern Tennessee, in the Great Smoky Mountains, living over the scenes of his childhood. And most pathetic was the melody of his long-forgotten Southern vernacular, as he raved of swimming-holes and coon-hunts and watermelon raids. It was as Greek to Ruth, but the Kid understood and felt,—felt as only one can feel who has been shut out for years from all that civilization means.

Morning brought consciousness to the stricken man, and Malemute Kid bent closer to catch his whispers.

"You remember when we foregathered on the Tanana, four years come next ice-run? I didn't care so much for her then. It was more like she was pretty, and there was a smack of excitement about it, I think. But d' ye know, I've come to think a heap of her. She's been a good wife to me, always at my shoulder in the pinch. And when it comes to trading, you know there isn't her equal. D' ye recollect the time she shot the Moosehorn Rapids to pull you and me off that rock, the bullets whipping the water like hailstones?—and the time of the famine at Nuklukyeto?—or when she raced the ice-run to bring the news? Yes, she's been a good wife to me, better 'n that other one. Didn't know I'd been there? Never told you, eh? Well, I tried it once, down in the States. That's why I'm here. Been raised together, too. I came away to give her a chance for divorce. She got it.

"But that's got nothing to do with Ruth. I had thought of cleaning up and pulling for the Outside next year,—her and I,—but it's too late. Don't send her back to her people, Kid. It's beastly hard for a woman to go back. Think of it!—nearly four years on our bacon and beans and flour and dried fruit, and then to go back to her fish and cariboo. It's not good for her to have tried our ways, to come to know they're better 'n her people's, and then return to them. Take care of her, Kid,—why don't you,—but no, you always fought shy of them,—and you never told me why you came to this country. Be kind to her, and send her back to the States as soon as you can. But fix it so as she can come back,—liable to get homesick, you know.

"And the youngster—it's drawn us closer, Kid. I only hope it is a boy. Think of it!—flesh of my flesh, Kid. He mustn't stop in this country. And if it's a girl, why she can't. Sell my furs; they'll fetch at least five thousand, and I've got as much more with the company. And handle my interests with yours. I think that bench claim will show up. See that he gets a good schooling; and Kid, above all, don't let him come back. This country was not made for white men.

"I'm a gone man, Kid. Three or four sleeps at the best. You've got to go on. You must go on! Remember, it's my wife, it's my boy,—O God! I hope it's a boy! You can't stay by me,—and I charge you, a dying man, to pull on."

"Give me three days," pleaded Malemute Kid. "You may change for the better; something may turn up."

"No."

"Just three days."

"You must pull on."

"Two days."

"It's my wife and my boy, Kid. You would not ask it."

"One day."

"No, no! I charge"—

"Only one day. We can shave it through on the grub, and I might knock over a moose."

"No,—all right; one day, but not a minute more. And Kid, don't—don't leave me to face it alone. Just a shot, one pull on the trigger. You understand. Think of it! Think of it! Flesh of my flesh, and I'll never live to see him!

"Send Ruth here. I want to say good-by and tell her that she must think of the boy and not wait till I'm dead. She might refuse to go with you if I didn't. Good-by, old man; good-by.

"Kid! I say—a—sink a hole above the pup, next to the slide. I panned out forty cents on my shovel there.

"And Kid!" he stooped lower to catch the last faint words, the dying man's surrender of his pride. "I'm sorry—for—you know—Carmen."

Leaving the girl crying softly over her man, Malemute Kid slipped into his *parka* and snowshoes, tucked his rifle under his arm, and crept away into the forest. He was no tyro in the stern sorrows of the North-land, but never had he faced so stiff a problem as this. In the abstract, it was a plain, mathematical proposition,—three possible lives as against one doomed one. But now he hesitated. For five years, shoulder to shoulder, on the rivers and trails, in the camps and mines, facing death by field and flood and famine, had they knitted the bonds of their comradeship. So close was the tie, that he had often been conscious of a vague jealousy of Ruth, from the first time she had come between. And now it must be severed by his own hand.

Though he prayed for a moose, just one moose, all game seemed to have deserted the land, and nightfall found the exhausted man crawling into camp, light-handed, heavy-hearted. An uproar from the dogs and shrill cries from Ruth hastened him.

Bursting into the camp, he saw the girl in the midst of the snarling pack, laying about her with an axe. The dogs had broken the iron rule of their masters and were rushing the grub. He joined the issue with his rifle reversed, and the hoary game of natural selection was played out with all the ruthlessness of its primeval environment. Rifle and axe went up and down, hit or missed with monotonous regularity; lithe bodies flashed, with wild eyes and dripping fangs; and man and beast fought for supremacy to the bitterest conclusion. Then the beaten brutes crept to the edge of the firelight, licking their wounds, voicing their misery to the stars.

The whole stock of dried salmon had been devoured, and perhaps five pounds of flour remained to tide them over two hundred miles of wilderness. Ruth returned to her husband, while Malemute Kid cut up the warm body of one of the dogs, the skull of which had been crushed by the axe. Every portion was carefully put away, save the hide and offal, which were cast to his fellows of the moment before.

Morning brought fresh trouble. The animals were turning on each other. Carmen, who still clung to her slender thread of life, was downed by the pack. The lash fell among them unheeded. They cringed and cried under the blows, but refused to scatter till the last wretched bit had disappeared,—bones, hide, hair, everything.

Malemute Kid went about his work, listening to Mason, who was back in Tennessee, delivering tangled discourses and wild exhortations to his brethren of other days.

Taking advantage of neighboring pines, he worked rapidly, and Ruth watched him make a cache similar to those sometimes used by hunters to preserve their meat from the wolverines and dogs. One after the other, he bent the tops of two small pines toward each other and nearly to the ground, making them fast with thongs of moosehide. Then he beat the dogs into submission and harnessed them to two of the sleds, loading the same with everything but the furs which enveloped Mason. These he wrapped and lashed tightly about him, fastening either end of the robes to the bent pines. A single stroke of his hunting-knife would release them and send the body high in the air.

Ruth had received her husband's last wishes and made no struggle. Poor girl, she had learned the lesson of obedience well. From a child, she had bowed, and seen all women bow, to the lords of creation, and it did not seem in the nature of things for woman to resist. The Kid permitted her one outburst of grief, as she kissed her husband,—her own people had no such custom,—then led her to the foremost sled and helped her into her snowshoes. Blindly, instinctively, she took the gee-pole and whip, and "mushed" the dogs out on the trail. Then he returned to Mason, who had fallen into a coma; and long after she was out of sight, crouched by the fire, waiting, hoping, praying for his comrade to die.

It is not pleasant to be alone with painful thoughts in the White Silence. The silence of gloom is merciful, shrouding one as with protection and breathing a thousand intangible sympathies; but the bright White Silence, clear and cold, under steely skies, is pitiless.

An hour passed,—two hours,—but the man would not die. At high noon, the sun, without raising its rim above the southern horizon, threw a suggestion of fire athwart the heavens, then quickly drew it back. Malemute Kid roused and dragged himself to his comrade's side. He cast one glance about him. The White Silence seemed to sneer, and a great fear came upon him. There was a sharp report; Mason swung into his aerial sepulchre; and Malemute Kid lashed the dogs into a wild gallop as he fled across the snow.

TO THE MAN ON TRAIL

"Dump it in."

"But I say, Kid, is n't that going it a little too strong? Whiskey and alcohol's bad enough; but when it comes to brandy and pepper-sauce and"—

"Dump it in. Who's making this punch, anyway?" And Malemute Kid smiled benignantly through the clouds of steam. "By the time you've been in this country as long as I have, my son, and lived on rabbit-tracks and salmon-belly, you'll learn that Christmas comes only once per annum. And a Christmas without punch is sinking a hole to bedrock with nary a pay-streak."

"Stack up on that fer a high cyard," approved Big Jim Belden, who had come down from his claim on Mazy May to spend Christmas, and who, as every one knew, had been living the two months past on straight moose-meat. "Hain't fergot the *hooch* we-uns made on the Tanana, hev yeh?"

"Well, I guess yes. Boys, it would have done your hearts good to see that whole tribe fighting drunk—and all because of a glorious ferment of sugar and sour dough. That was before your time," Malemute Kid said as he turned to Stanley Prince, a young mining expert who had been in two years. "No white women in the country then, and Mason wanted to get married. Ruth's father was chief of the Tananas, and objected, like the rest of the tribe. Stiff? Why, I used my last pound of sugar; finest work in that line I ever did in my life. You should have seen the chase, down the river and across the portage."

"But the squaw?" asked Louis Savoy, the tall French-Canadian, becoming interested; for he had heard of this wild deed, when at Forty Mile the preceding winter.

Then Malemute Kid, who was a born raconteur, told the unvarnished tale of the Northland Lochinvar. More than one rough adventurer of the

North felt his heartstrings draw closer, and experienced vague yearnings for the sunnier pastures of the Southland, where life promised something more than a barren struggle with cold and death.

"We struck the Yukon just behind the first ice-run," he concluded, "and the tribe only a quarter of an hour behind. But that saved us; for the second run broke the jam above and shut them out. When they finally got into Nuklukyeto, the whole Post was ready for them. And as to the foregathering, ask Father Roubeau here: he performed the ceremony."

The Jesuit took the pipe from his lips, but could only express his gratification with patriarchal smiles, while Protestant and Catholic vigorously applauded.

"By gar!" ejaculated Louis Savoy, who seemed overcome by the romance of it. "La petite squaw; mon Mason brav. By gar!"

Then, as the first tin cups of punch went round, Bettles the Unquenchable sprang to his feet and struck up his favorite drinking song:—

> *"There's Henry Ward Beecher*
> *And Sunday-school teachers,*
> *   All drink of the sassafras root;*
> *But you bet all the same,*
> *If it had its right name,*
> *   It's the juice of the forbidden fruit."*

> *"Oh the juice of the forbidden fruit,"*

roared out the Bacchanalian chorus,—

> *"Oh the juice of the forbidden fruit;*
> *   But you bet all the same,*
> *   If it had its right name,*
> *It's the juice of the forbidden fruit."*

Malemute Kid's frightful concoction did its work; the men of the camps and trails unbent in its genial glow, and jest and song and tales of past adventure went round the board. Aliens from a dozen lands, they toasted each and all. It was the Englishman, Prince, who pledged "Uncle Sam, the precocious infant of the New World;" the Yankee, Bettles, who drank to "The Queen, God bless her;" and together, Savoy and Meyers, the German trader, clanged their cups to Alsace and Lorraine.

Then Malemute Kid arose, cup in hand, and glanced at the greased-paper window, where the frost stood full three inches thick. "A health to the man on trail this night; may his grub hold out; may his dogs keep their legs; may his matches never miss fire."

Crack! Crack!—they heard the familiar music of the dogwhip, the whining howl of the Malemutes, and the crunch of a sled as it drew up to the cabin. Conversation languished while they waited the issue.

"An old-timer; cares for his dogs and then himself," whispered Malemute Kid to Prince, as they listened to the snapping jaws and the wolfish snarls and yelps of pain which proclaimed to their practiced ears that the stranger was beating back their dogs while he fed his own.

Then came the expected knock, sharp and confident, and the stranger entered. Dazzled by the light, he hesitated a moment at the door, giving to all a chance for scrutiny. He was a striking personage, and a most picturesque one, in his Arctic dress of wool and fur. Standing six foot two or three, with proportionate breadth of shoulders and depth of chest, his smooth-shaven face nipped by the cold to a gleaming pink, his long lashes and eyebrows white with ice, and the ear and neck flaps of his great wolfskin cap loosely raised, he seemed, of a verity, the Frost King, just stepped in out of the night. Clasped outside his mackinaw jacket, a beaded belt held two large Colt's revolvers and a hunting-knife, while he carried, in addition to the inevitable dogwhip, a smokeless rifle of the largest bore and latest pattern. As he came forward, for all his step was firm and elastic, they could see that fatigue bore heavily upon him.

An awkward silence had fallen, but his hearty "What cheer, my lads?" put them quickly at ease, and the next instant Malemute Kid and he had gripped hands. Though they had never met, each had heard of the other, and the recognition was mutual. A sweeping introduction and a mug of punch were forced upon him before he could explain his errand.

"How long since that basket-sled, with three men and eight dogs, passed?" he asked.

"An even two days ahead. Are you after them?"

"Yes; my team. Run them off under my very nose, the cusses. I've gained two days on them already,—pick them up on the next run."

"Reckon they'll show spunk?" asked Belden, in order to keep up the conversation, for Malemute Kid already had the coffee-pot on and was busily frying bacon and moose-meat.

The stranger significantly tapped his revolvers.

"When 'd yeh leave Dawson?"

"Twelve o'clock."

"Last night?"—as a matter of course.

"To-day."

A murmur of surprise passed round the circle. And well it might; for it was just midnight, and seventy-five miles of rough river trail was not to be sneered at for a twelve hours' run.

The talk soon became impersonal, however, harking back to the trails of childhood. As the young stranger ate of the rude fare, Malemute Kid attentively studied his face. Nor was he long in deciding that it was fair, honest, and open, and that he liked it. Still youthful, the lines had been firmly traced by toil and hardship. Though genial in conversation, and mild when at rest, the blue eyes gave promise of the hard steel-glitter which comes when called into action, especially against odds. The heavy jaw and square-cut chin demonstrated rugged pertinacity and indomitability. Nor, though the attributes of the lion were there, was there wanting the certain softness, the hint of womanliness, which bespoke the emotional nature.

"So thet's how me an' the ol' woman got spliced," said Belden, concluding the exciting tale of his courtship. " 'Here we be, dad,' sez she. 'An' may yeh be damned,' sez he to her, an' then to me, 'Jim, yeh—yeh git outen them good duds o' yourn; I want a right peart slice o' thet forty acre ploughed 'fore dinner.' An' then he turns on her an' sez, 'An' yeh, Sal; yeh sail inter them dishes.' An' then he sort o' sniffled an' kissed her. An' I was thet happy,—but he seen me an' roars out, 'Yeh, Jim!' An' yeh bet I dusted fer the barn."

"Any kids waiting for you back in the States?" asked the stranger.

"Nope; Sal died 'fore any come. Thet's why I'm here." Belden abstractedly began to light his pipe, which had failed to go out, and then brightened up with, "How 'bout yerself, stranger,—married man?"

For reply, he opened his watch, slipped it from the thong which served for a chain, and passed it over. Belden pricked up the slush-lamp, surveyed the inside of the case critically, and swearing admiringly to himself, handed it over to Louis Savoy. With numerous "By gars!" he finally surrendered it to Prince, and they noticed that his hands trembled and his eyes took on a peculiar softness. And so it passed from horny hand to horny hand—the pasted photograph of a woman, the clinging kind that such men fancy, with a babe at the breast. Those who had not yet seen the wonder were keen with curiosity; those who had, became silent and retrospective. They could face the pinch of famine, the grip of scurvy, or the quick death by field or flood; but the pictured semblance of a stranger woman and child made women and children of them all.

"Never have seen the youngster yet,—he's a boy, she says, and two years old," said the stranger as he received the treasure back. A lingering moment he gazed upon it, then snapped the case and turned away, but not quick enough to hide the restrained rush of tears.

Malemute Kid led him to a bunk and bade him turn in.

"Call me at four, sharp. Don't fail me," were his last words, and a moment later he was breathing in the heaviness of exhausted sleep.

"By Jove! he's a plucky chap," commented Prince. "Three hours' sleep after seventy-five miles with the dogs, and then the trail again. Who is he, Kid?"

"Jack Westondale. Been in going on three years, with nothing but the name of working like a horse, and any amount of bad luck to his credit. I never knew him, but Sitka Charley told me about him."

"It seems hard that a man with a sweet young wife like his should be putting in his years in this God-forsaken hole, where every year counts two on the outside."

"The trouble with him is clean grit and stubbornness. He's cleaned up twice with a stake, but lost it both times."

Here the conversation was broken off by an uproar from Bettles, for the effect had begun to wear away. And soon the bleak years of monotonous grub and deadening toil were being forgotten in rough merriment. Malemute Kid alone seemed unable to lose himself, and cast many an anxious look at his watch. Once he put on his mittens and beaver-skin cap, and leaving the cabin, fell to rummaging about in the cache.

Nor could he wait the hour designated; for he was fifteen minutes ahead of time in rousing his guest. The young giant had stiffened badly, and brisk rubbing was necessary to bring him to his feet. He tottered painfully out of the cabin, to find his dogs harnessed and everything ready for the start. The company wished him good luck and a short chase, while Father Roubeau, hurriedly blessing him, led the stampede for the cabin; and small wonder, for it is not good to face seventy-four degrees below zero with naked ears and hands.

Malemute Kid saw him to the main trail, and there, gripping his hand heartily, gave him advice.

"You'll find a hundred pounds of salmon-eggs on the sled," he said. "The dogs will go as far on that as with one hundred and fifty of fish, and you can't get dog-food at Pelly, as you probably expected." The stranger started, and his eyes flashed, but he did not interrupt. "You can't get an ounce of food for dog or man till you reach Five Fingers, and that's a stiff two hundred miles. Watch out for open water on the Thirty Mile River, and be sure you take the big cut-off above Le Barge."

"How did you know it? Surely the news can't be ahead of me already?"

"I don't know it; and what's more, I don't want to know it. But you never owned that team you're chasing. Sitka Charley sold it to them last spring. But he sized you up to me as square once, and I believe him. I've seen your face; I like it. And I've seen—why, damn you, hit the high places for salt water and that wife of yours, and"— Here the Kid unmittened and jerked out his sack.

"No; I don't need it," and the tears froze on his cheeks as he convulsively gripped Malemute Kid's hand.

"Then don't spare the dogs; cut them out of the traces as fast as they drop; buy them, and think they're cheap at ten dollars a pound. You can get them at Five Fingers, Little Salmon, and the Hootalinqua. And watch out for wet feet," was his parting advice. "Keep a-traveling up to twenty-five, but if it gets below that, build a fire and change your socks."

Fifteen minutes had barely elapsed when the jingle of bells announced new arrivals. The door opened, and a mounted policeman of the Northwest Territory entered, followed by two half-breed dog-drivers. Like Westondale, they were heavily armed and showed signs of fatigue. The half-breeds had been born to the trail, and bore it easily; but the young policeman was badly exhausted. Still, the dogged obstinacy of his race held him to the pace he had set, and would hold him till he dropped in his tracks.

"When did Westondale pull out?" he asked. "He stopped here, didn't he?" This was supererogatory, for the tracks told their own tale too well.

Malemute Kid had caught Belden's eye, and he, scenting the wind, replied evasively, "A right peart while back."

"Come, my man; speak up," the policeman admonished.

"Yeh seem to want him right smart. Hez he ben gittin' cantankerous down Dawson way?"

"Held up Harry McFarland's for forty thousand; exchanged it at the P. C. store for a check on Seattle; and who's to stop the cashing of it if we don't overtake him? When did he pull out?"

Every eye suppressed its excitement, for Malemute Kid had given the cue, and the young officer encountered wooden faces on every hand.

Striding over to Prince, he put the question to him. Though it hurt him, gazing into the frank, earnest face of his fellow countryman, he replied inconsequentially on the state of the trail.

Then he espied Father Roubeau, who could not lie. "A quarter of an hour ago," the priest answered; "but he had four hours' rest for himself and dogs."

"Fifteen minutes' start, and he's fresh! My God!" The poor fellow staggered back, half fainting from exhaustion and disappointment, murmuring something about the run from Dawson in ten hours and the dogs being played out.

Malemute Kid forced a mug of punch upon him; then he turned for the door, ordering the dog-drivers to follow. But the warmth and promise of rest were too tempting, and they objected strenuously. The Kid was conversant with their French patois, and followed it anxiously.

They swore that the dogs were gone up; that Siwash and Babette would have to be shot before the first mile was covered; that the rest were almost as bad; and that it would be better for all hands to rest up.

"Lend me five dogs?" he asked, turning to Malemute Kid.

But the Kid shook his head.

"I'll sign a check on Captain Constantine for five thousand,—here's my papers,—I'm authorized to draw at my own discretion."

Again the silent refusal.

"Then I'll requisition them in the name of the Queen."

Smiling incredulously, the Kid glanced at his well-stocked arsenal, and the Englishman, realizing his impotency, turned for the door. But the dog-drivers still objecting, he whirled upon them fiercely, calling them women and curs. The swart face of the older half-breed flushed angrily, as he drew himself up and promised in good, round terms that he would travel his leader off his legs, and would then be delighted to plant him in the snow.

The young officer—and it required his whole will—walked steadily to the door, exhibiting a freshness he did not possess. But they all knew and appreciated his proud effort; nor could he veil the twinges of agony that shot across his face. Covered with frost, the dogs were curled up in the snow, and it was almost impossible to get them to their feet. The poor brutes whined under the stinging lash, for the dog-drivers were angry and cruel; nor till Babette, the leader, was cut from the traces, could they break out the sled and get under way.

"A dirty scoundrel and a liar!" "By gar! him no good!" "A thief!" "Worse than an Indian!" It was evident that they were angry—first, at the way they had been deceived; and second, at the outraged ethics of the Northland, where honesty, above all, was man's prime jewel. "An' we gave the cuss a hand, after knowin' what he'd did." All eyes were turned accusingly upon Malemute Kid, who rose from the corner where he had been making Babette comfortable, and silently emptied the bowl for a final round of punch.

"It's a cold night, boys,—a bitter cold night," was the irrelevant commencement of his defense. "You've all traveled trail, and know what that stands for. Don't jump a dog when he's down. You've only heard one side. A whiter man than Jack Westondale never ate from the same pot nor stretched blanket with you or me. Last fall he gave his whole clean-up, forty thousand, to Joe Castrell, to buy in on Dominion. To-day he'd be a millionaire. But while he stayed behind at Circle City, taking care of his partner with the scurvy, what does Castrell do? Goes into McFarland's, jumps the limit, and drops the whole sack. Found him dead in the snow the next day. And poor Jack laying his plans to go out this winter to his wife and the boy he's never seen. You'll notice he took exactly what his partner lost,—forty thousand. Well, he's gone out; and what are you going to do about it?"

The Kid glanced round the circle of his judges, noted the softening of their faces, then raised his mug aloft. "So a health to the man on trail this night; may his grub hold out; may his dogs keep their legs; may his matches never miss fire. God prosper him; good luck go with him; and"—

"Confusion to the Mounted Police!" cried Bettles, to the crash of the empty cups.

IN A FAR COUNTRY

When a man journeys into a far country, he must be prepared to forget many of the things he has learned, and to acquire such customs as are inherent with existence in the new land; he must abandon the old ideals and the old gods, and oftentimes he must reverse the very codes by which his conduct has hitherto been shaped. To those who have the protean faculty of adaptability, the novelty of such change may even be a source of pleasure; but to those who happen to be hardened to the ruts in which they were created, the pressure of the altered environment is unbearable, and they chafe in body and in spirit under the new restrictions which they do not understand. This chafing is bound to act and react, producing divers evils and leading to various misfortunes. It were better for the man who cannot fit himself to the new groove to return to his own country; if he delay too long, he will surely die.

The man who turns his back upon the comforts of an elder civilization, to face the savage youth, the primordial simplicity of the North, may estimate success at an inverse ratio to the quantity and quality of his hopelessly fixed habits. He will soon discover, if he be a fit candidate, that the material habits are the less important. The exchange of such things as a dainty menu for rough fare, of the stiff leather shoe for the soft, shapeless moccasin, of the feather bed for a couch in the snow, is after all a very easy matter. But his pinch will come in learning properly to shape his mind's attitude toward all things, and especially toward his fellow man. For the courtesies of ordinary life, he must substitute unselfishness, forbearance, and tolerance. Thus, and thus only, can he gain that pearl of great price,—true comradeship. He must not say "Thank you;" he must mean it without opening his mouth, and prove it by responding in kind. In short, he must substitute the deed for the word, the spirit for the letter.

When the world rang with the tale of Arctic gold, and the lure of the

North gripped the heartstrings of men, Carter Weatherbee threw up his snug clerkship, turned the half of his savings over to his wife, and with the remainder bought an outfit. There was no romance in his nature,— the bondage of commerce had crushed all that; he was simply tired of the ceaseless grind, and wished to risk great hazards in view of corresponding returns. Like many another fool, disdaining the old trails used by the Northland pioneers for a score of years, he hurried to Edmonton in the spring of the year; and there, unluckily for his soul's welfare, he allied himself with a party of men.

There was nothing unusual about this party, except its plans. Even its goal, like that of all other parties, was the Klondike. But the route it had mapped out to attain that goal took away the breath of the hardiest native, born and bred to the vicissitudes of the Northwest. Even Jacques Baptiste, born of a Chippewa woman and a renegade *voyageur* (having raised his first whimpers in a deerskin lodge north of the sixty-fifth parallel, and had the same hushed by blissful sucks of raw tallow), was surprised. Though he sold his services to them and agreed to travel even to the never-opening ice, he shook his head ominously whenever his advice was asked.

Percy Cuthfert's evil star must have been in the ascendant, for he, too, joined this company of argonauts. He was an ordinary man, with a bank account as deep as his culture, which is saying a good deal. He had no reason to embark on such a venture,—no reason in the world, save that he suffered from an abnormal development of sentimentality. He mistook this for the true spirit of romance and adventure. Many another man has done the like, and made as fatal a mistake.

The first break-up of spring found the party following the ice-run of Elk River. It was an imposing fleet, for the outfit was large, and they were accompanied by a disreputable contingent of half-breed *voyageurs* with their women and children. Day in and day out, they labored with the bateaux and canoes, fought mosquitoes and other kindred pests, or sweated and swore at the portages. Severe toil like this lays a man naked to the very roots of his soul, and ere Lake Athabasca was lost in the south, each member of the party had hoisted his true colors.

The two shirks and chronic grumblers were Carter Weatherbee and Percy Cuthfert. The whole party complained less of its aches and pains than did either of them. Not once did they volunteer for the thousand and one petty duties of the camp. A bucket of water to be brought, an extra armful of wood to be chopped, the dishes to be washed and wiped, a search to be made through the outfit for some suddenly indispensable article,—and these two effete scions of civilization discovered sprains or blisters requiring instant attention. They were the first to turn in at night, with a score of tasks yet undone; the last to turn out in the morning, when the start should be in readiness before the breakfast was begun. They were the first to fall to at meal-time, the last to have a hand in the cooking; the first to dive for a slim delicacy, the last to discover they had added to their own another man's share. If they toiled at the oars, they slyly cut the water at each stroke and allowed the boat's momentum to float up the blade. They thought nobody noticed; but their comrades swore under their breaths and grew to hate them, while Jacques Baptiste sneered openly and damned them from morning till night. But Jacques Baptiste was no gentleman.

At the Great Slave, Hudson Bay dogs were purchased, and the fleet sank to the guards with its added burden of dried fish and pemmican. Then canoe and bateau answered to the swift current of the Mackenzie, and they plunged into the Great Barren Ground. Every likely-looking "feeder" was prospected, but the elusive "pay-dirt" danced ever to the north. At the Great Bear, overcome by the common dread of the Unknown Lands, their *voyageurs* began to desert, and Fort of Good Hope saw the last and bravest bending to the tow-lines as they bucked the current down which they had so treacherously glided. Jacques Baptiste alone remained. Had he not sworn to travel even to the never-opening ice?

The lying charts, compiled in main from hearsay, were now constantly consulted. And they felt the need of hurry, for the sun had already passed its northern solstice and was leading the winter south again. Skirting the shores of the bay, where the Mackenzie disembogues into the Arctic Ocean, they entered the mouth of the Little Peel River. Then began the arduous up-stream toil, and the two Incapables fared worse than ever. Tow-line and pole, paddle and tump-line, rapids and portages,—such tortures served to give the one a deep disgust for great hazards, and printed for the other a fiery text on the true romance of adventure. One day they waxed mutinous, and being vilely cursed by Jacques Baptiste, turned, as worms sometimes will. But the half-breed thrashed the twain, and sent them, bruised and bleeding, about their work. It was the first time either had been man-handled.

Abandoning their river craft at the headwaters of the Little Peel, they consumed the rest of the summer in the great portage over the Mackenzie watershed to the West Rat. This little stream fed the Porcupine, which in turn joined the Yukon where that mighty highway of the North countermarches on the Arctic Circle. But they had lost in the race with winter, and one day they tied their rafts to the thick eddy-ice and hurried their goods ashore. That night the river jammed and broke several times; the following morning it had fallen asleep for good.

*   *   *

"We can't be more 'n four hundred miles from the Yukon," concluded
Sloper, multiplying his thumb nails by the scale of the map. The council,
in which the two Incapables had whined to excellent disadvantage, was
drawing to a close.

"Hudson Bay Post, long time ago. No use um now." Jacques Baptiste's father had made the trip for the Fur Company in the old days,
incidentally marking the trail with a couple of frozen toes.

"Sufferin' cracky!" cried another of the party. "No whites?"

"Nary white," Sloper sententiously affirmed; "but it's only five
hundred more up the Yukon to Dawson. Call it a rough thousand from
here."

Weatherbee and Cuthfert groaned in chorus.

"How long'll that take, Baptiste?"

The half-breed figured for a moment. "Workum like hell, no man
play out, ten—twenty—forty—fifty days. Um babies come" (designat-
ing the Incapables), "no can tell. Mebbe when hell freeze over; mebbe
not then."

The manufacture of snowshoes and moccasins ceased. Somebody
called the name of an absent member, who came out of an ancient cabin
at the edge of the camp-fire and joined them. The cabin was one of the
many mysteries which lurk in the vast recesses of the North. Built when
and by whom, no man could tell. Two graves in the open, piled high
with stones, perhaps contained the secret of those early wanderers. But
whose hand had piled the stones?

The moment had come. Jacques Baptiste paused in the fitting of a
harness and pinned the struggling dog in the snow. The cook made
mute protest for delay, threw a handful of bacon into a noisy pot of
beans, then came to attention. Sloper rose to his feet. His body was a
ludicrous contrast to the healthy physiques of the Incapables. Yellow
and weak, fleeing from a South American fever-hole, he had not broken
his flight across the zones, and was still able to toil with men. His
weight was probably ninety pounds, with the heavy hunting-knife
thrown in, and his grizzled hair told of a prime which had ceased to be.
The fresh young muscles of either Weatherbee or Cuthfert were equal
to ten times the endeavor of his; yet he could walk them into the earth
in a day's journey. And all this day he had whipped his stronger comrades into venturing a thousand miles of the stiffest hardship man can
conceive. He was the incarnation of the unrest of his race, and the old
Teutonic stubbornness, dashed with the quick grasp and action of the
Yankee, held the flesh in the bondage of the spirit.

"All those in favor of going on with the dogs as soon as the ice sets, say ay."

"Ay!" rang out eight voices,—voices destined to string a trail of oaths along many a hundred miles of pain.

"Contrary minded?"

"No!" For the first time the Incapables were united without some compromise of personal interests.

"And what are you going to do about it?" Weatherbee added belligerently.

"Majority rule! Majority rule!" clamored the rest of the party.

"I know the expedition is liable to fall through if you don't come," Sloper replied sweetly; "but I guess, if we try real hard, we can manage to do without you. What do you say, boys?"

The sentiment was cheered to the echo.

"But I say, you know," Cuthfert ventured apprehensively; "what's a chap like me to do?"

"Ain't you coming with us?"

"No-o."

"Then do as you damn well please. We won't have nothing to say."

"Kind o' calkilate yuh might settle it with that canoodlin' pardner of yourn," suggested a heavy-going Westerner from the Dakotas, at the same time pointing out Weatherbee. "He'll be shore to ask yuh what yur a-goin' to do when it comes to cookin' an' gatherin' the wood."

"Then we'll consider it all arranged," concluded Sloper. "We'll pull out to-morrow, if we camp within five miles,—just to get everything in running order and remember if we've forgotten anything."

The sleds groaned by on their steel-shod runners, and the dogs strained low in the harnesses in which they were born to die. Jacques Baptiste paused by the side of Sloper to get a last glimpse of the cabin. The smoke curled up pathetically from the Yukon stove-pipe. The two Incapables were watching them from the doorway.

Sloper laid his hand on the other's shoulder.

"Jacques Baptiste, did you ever hear of the Kilkenny cats?"

The half-breed shook his head.

"Well, my friend and good comrade, the Kilkenny cats fought till neither hide, not hair, nor yowl, was left. You understand?—till nothing was left. Very good. Now, these two men don't like work. They won't work. We know that. They'll be all alone in that cabin all winter,—a mighty long, dark winter. Kilkenny cats,—well?"

The Frenchman in Baptiste shrugged his shoulders, but the Indian in him was silent. Nevertheless, it was an eloquent shrug, pregnant with prophecy.

Things prospered in the little cabin at first. The rough badinage of their comrades had made Weatherbee and Cuthfert conscious of the mutual responsibility which had devolved upon them; besides, there was not so much work after all for two healthy men. And the removal of the cruel whip-hand, or in other words the bulldozing half-breed, had brought with it a joyous reaction. At first, each strove to outdo the other, and they performed petty tasks with an unction which would have opened the eyes of their comrades who were now wearing out bodies and souls on the Long Trail.

All care was banished. The forest, which shouldered in upon them from three sides, was an inexhaustible woodyard. A few yards from their door slept the Porcupine, and a hole through its winter robe formed a bubbling spring of water, crystal clear and painfully cold. But they soon grew to find fault with even that. The hole would persist in freezing up, and thus gave them many a miserable hour of ice-chopping. The unknown builders of the cabin had extended the side-logs so as to support a cache at the rear. In this was stored the bulk of the party's provisions. Food there was, without stint, for three times the men who were fated to live upon it. But the most of it was of the kind which built up brawn and sinew, but did not tickle the palate. True, there was sugar in plenty for two ordinary men; but these two were little else than children. They early discovered the virtues of hot water judiciously saturated with sugar, and they prodigally swam their flapjacks and soaked their crusts in the rich, white syrup. Then coffee and tea, and especially the dried fruits, made disastrous inroads upon it. The first words they had were over the sugar question. And it is a really serious thing when two men, wholly dependent upon each other for company, begin to quarrel.

Weatherbee loved to discourse blatantly on politics, while Cuthfert, who had been prone to clip his coupons and let the commonwealth jog on as best it might, either ignored the subject or delivered himself of startling epigrams. But the clerk was too obtuse to appreciate the clever shaping of thought, and this waste of ammunition irritated Cuthfert. He had been used to blinding people by his brilliancy, and it worked him quite a hardship, this loss of an audience. He felt personally aggrieved and unconsciously held his mutton-head companion responsible for it.

Save existence, they had nothing in common,—came in touch on no single point. Weatherbee was a clerk who had known naught but clerking all his life; Cuthfert was a master of arts, a dabbler in oils, and had written not a little. The one was a lower-class man who considered himself a gentleman, and the other was a gentleman who knew himself to be such. From this it may be remarked that a man can be a gentleman without possessing the first instinct of true comradeship. The clerk was as sensuous as the other was æsthetic, and his love adventures, told at great length and chiefly coined from his imagination, affected the supersensitive master of arts in the same way as so many whiffs of sewer gas. He deemed the clerk a filthy, uncultured brute, whose place was in the muck with the swine, and told him so; and he was reciprocally informed that he was a milk-and-water sissy and a cad. Weatherbee could not have defined "cad" for his life; but it satisfied its purpose, which after all seems the main point in life.

Weatherbee flatted every third note and sang such songs as "The Boston Burglar" and "The Handsome Cabin Boy," for hours at a time, while Cuthfert wept with rage, till he could stand it no longer and fled into the outer cold. But there was no escape. The intense frost could not be endured for long at a time, and the little cabin crowded them—beds, stove, table, and all—into a space of ten by twelve. The very presence of either became a personal affront to the other, and they lapsed into sullen silences which increased in length and strength as the days went by. Occasionally, the flash of an eye or the curl of a lip got the better of them, though they strove to wholly ignore each other during these mute periods. And a great wonder sprang up in the breast of each, as to how God had ever come to create the other.

With little to do, time became an intolerable burden to them. This naturally made them still lazier. They sank into a physical lethargy which there was no escaping, and which made them rebel at the performance of the smallest chore. One morning when it was his turn to cook the common breakfast, Weatherbee rolled out of his blankets, and to the snoring of his companion, lighted first the slush-lamp and then the fire. The kettles were frozen hard, and there was no water in the cabin with which to wash. But he did not mind that. Waiting for it to thaw, he sliced the bacon and plunged into the hateful task of bread-making. Cuthfert had been slyly watching through his half-closed lids. Consequently there was a scene, in which they fervently blessed each other, and agreed, thenceforth, that each do his own cooking. A week later, Cuthfert neglected his morning ablutions, but none the less complacently ate the meal which he had cooked. Weatherbee grinned. After that the foolish custom of washing passed out of their lives.

As the sugar-pile and other little luxuries dwindled, they began to be afraid they were not getting their proper shares, and in order that they might not be robbed, they fell to gorging themselves. The luxuries suffered in this gluttonous contest, as did also the men. In the absence of fresh vegetables and exercise, their blood became impoverished, and a loathsome, purplish rash crept over their bodies. Yet they refused to heed the warning. Next, their muscles and joints began to swell, the flesh turning black, while their mouths, gums, and lips took on the color of rich cream. Instead of being drawn together by their misery, each gloated over the other's symptoms as the scurvy took its course.

They lost all regard for personal appearance, and for that matter, common decency. The cabin became a pigpen, and never once were the beds made or fresh pine boughs laid underneath. Yet they could not keep to their blankets, as they would have wished; for the frost was inexorable, and the fire box consumed much fuel. The hair of their heads and faces grew long and shaggy, while their garments would have disgusted a ragpicker. But they did not care. They were sick, and there was no one to see; besides, it was very painful to move about.

To all this was added a new trouble,—the Fear of the North. This Fear was the joint child of the Great Cold and the Great Silence, and was born in the darkness of December, when the sun dipped below the southern horizon for good. It affected them according to their natures. Weatherbee fell prey to the grosser superstitions, and did his best to resurrect the spirits which slept in the forgotten graves. It was a fascinating thing, and in his dreams they came to him from out of the cold, and snuggled into his blankets, and told him of their toils and troubles ere they died. He shrank away from the clammy contact as they drew closer and twined their frozen limbs about him, and when they whispered in his ear of things to come, the cabin rang with his frightened shrieks. Cuthfert did not understand,—for they no longer spoke,—and when thus awakened he invariably grabbed for his revolver. Then he would sit up in bed, shivering nervously, with the weapon trained on the unconscious dreamer. Cuthfert deemed the man going mad, and so came to fear for his life.

His own malady assumed a less concrete form. The mysterious artisan who had laid the cabin, log by log, had pegged a wind-vane to the ridge-pole. Cuthfert noticed it always pointed south, and one day, irritated by its steadfastness of purpose, he turned it toward the east. He watched eagerly, but never a breath came by to disturb it. Then he turned the vane to the north, swearing never again to touch it till the wind did blow. But the air frightened him with its unearthly calm, and he often rose in the middle of the night to see if the vane had veered, —ten degrees would have satisfied him. But no, it poised above him as unchangeable as fate. His imagination ran riot, till it became to him a fetich. Sometimes he followed the path it pointed across the dismal do-

minions, and allowed his soul to become saturated with the Fear. He
dwelt upon the unseen and the unknown till the burden of eternity
appeared to be crushing him. Everything in the Northland had that
crushing effect,—the absence of life and motion; the darkness; the infinite peace of the brooding land; the ghastly silence, which made the
echo of each heart-beat a sacrilege; the solemn forest which seemed to
guard an awful, inexpressible something, which neither word nor
thought could compass.

The world he had so recently left, with its busy nations and great
enterprises, seemed very far away. Recollections occasionally obtruded,
—recollections of marts and galleries and crowded thoroughfares, of
evening dress and social functions, of good men and dear women he
had known,—but they were dim memories of a life he had lived long
centuries agone, on some other planet. This phantasm was the Reality.
Standing beneath the wind-vane, his eyes fixed on the polar skies, he
could not bring himself to realize that the Southland really existed, that
at that very moment it was a-roar with life and action. There was no
Southland, no men being born of women, no giving and taking in marriage. Beyond his bleak sky-line there stretched vast solitudes, and beyond these still vaster solitudes. There were no lands of sunshine, heavy
with the perfume of flowers. Such things were only old dreams of paradise. The sunlands of the West and the spicelands of the East, the
smiling Arcadias and blissful Island of the Blest,—ha! ha! His laughter
split the void and shocked him with its unwonted sound. There was no
sun. This was the Universe, dead and cold and dark, and he its only
citizen. Weatherbee? At such moments Weatherbee did not count. He
was a Caliban, a monstrous phantom, fettered to him for untold ages,
the penalty of some forgotten crime.

He lived with Death among the dead, emasculated by the sense of
his own insignificance, crushed by the passive mastery of the slumbering
ages. The magnitude of all things appalled him. Everything partook of
the superlative save himself,—the perfect cessation of wind and motion,
the immensity of the snow-covered wilderness, the height of the sky
and the depth of the silence. That wind-vane,—if it would only move.
If a thunderbolt would fall, or the forest flare up in flame. The rolling
up of the heavens as a scroll, the crash of Doom—anything, anything!
But no, nothing moved; the Silence crowded in, and the Fear of the
North laid icy fingers on his heart.

Once, like another Crusoe, by the edge of the river he came upon a
track,—the faint tracery of a snowshoe rabbit on the delicate snow-
crust. It was a revelation. There was life in the Northland. He would
follow it, look upon it, gloat over it. He forgot his swollen muscles,

plunging through the deep snow in an ecstasy of anticipation. The forest swallowed him up, and the brief midday twilight vanished; but he pursued his quest till exhausted nature asserted itself and laid him helpless in the snow. There he groaned and cursed his folly, and knew the track to be the fancy of his brain; and late that night he dragged himself into the cabin on hands and knees, his cheeks frozen and a strange numbness about his feet. Weatherbee grinned malevolently, but made no offer to help him. He thrust needles into his toes and thawed them out by the stove. A week later mortification set in.

But the clerk had his own troubles. The dead men came out of their graves more frequently now, and rarely left him, waking or sleeping. He grew to wait and dread their coming, never passing the twin cairns without a shudder. One night they came to him in his sleep and led him forth to an appointed task. Frightened into inarticulate horror, he awoke between the heaps of stones and fled wildly to the cabin. But he had lain there for some time, for his feet and cheeks were also frozen.

Sometimes he became frantic at their insistent presence, and danced about the cabin, cutting the empty air with an axe, and smashing everything within reach. During these ghostly encounters, Cuthfert huddled into his blankets and followed the madman about with a cocked revolver, ready to shoot him if he came too near. But, recovering from one of these spells, the clerk noticed the weapon trained upon him. His suspicions were aroused, and thenceforth he, too, lived in fear of his life. They watched each other closely after that, and faced about in startled fright whenever either passed behind the other's back. This apprehensiveness became a mania which controlled them even in their sleep. Through mutual fear they tacitly let the slush-lamp burn all night, and saw to a plentiful supply of bacon-grease before retiring. The slightest movement on the part of one was sufficient to arouse the other, and many a still watch their gazes countered as they shook beneath their blankets with fingers on the trigger-guards.

What with the Fear of the North, the mental strain, and the ravages of the disease, they lost all semblance of humanity, taking on the appearance of wild beasts, hunted and desperate. Their cheeks and noses, as an aftermath of the freezing, had turned black. Their frozen toes had begun to drop away at the first and second joints. Every movement brought pain, but the fire box was insatiable, wringing a ransom of torture from their miserable bodies. Day in, day out, it demanded its food,—a veritable pound of flesh,—and they dragged themselves into the forest to chop wood on their knees. Once, crawling thus in search of dry sticks, unknown to each other they entered a thicket from opposite sides. Suddenly, without warning, two peering death's-heads confronted each other. Suffering had so transformed them that recognition was impossible. They sprang to their feet, shrieking with terror, and dashed away on their mangled stumps; and falling at the cabin door, they clawed and scratched like demons till they discovered their mistake.

Occasionally they lapsed normal, and during one of these sane intervals, the chief bone of contention, the sugar, had been divided equally between them. They guarded their separate sacks, stored up in the cache, with jealous eyes; for there were but a few cupfuls left, and they were totally devoid of faith in each other. But one day Cuthfert made a mistake. Hardly able to move, sick with pain, with his head swimming and eyes blinded, he crept into the cache, sugar canister in hand, and mistook Weatherbee's sack for his own.

January had been born but a few days when this occurred. The sun had some time since passed its lowest southern declination, and at meridian now threw flaunting streaks of yellow light upon the northern sky. On the day following his mistake with the sugar-bag, Cuthfert found himself feeling better, both in body and in spirit. As noontime drew near and the day brightened, he dragged himself outside to feast on the evanescent glow, which was to him an earnest of the sun's future intentions. Weatherbee was also feeling somewhat better, and crawled out beside him. They propped themselves in the snow beneath the moveless wind-vane, and waited.

The stillness of death was about them. In other climes, when nature falls into such moods, there is a subdued air of expectancy, a waiting for some small voice to take up the broken strain. Not so in the North. The two men had lived seeming æons in this ghostly peace. They could remember no song of the past; they could conjure no song of the future. This unearthly calm had always been,—the tranquil silence of eternity.

Their eyes were fixed upon the north. Unseen, behind their backs, behind the towering mountains to the south, the sun swept toward the zenith of another sky than theirs. Sole spectators of the mighty canvas, they watched the false dawn slowly grow. A faint flame began to glow and smoulder. It deepened in intensity, ringing the changes of reddish-yellow, purple, and saffron. So bright did it become that Cuthfert thought the sun must surely be behind it,—a miracle, the sun rising in the north! Suddenly, without warning and without fading, the canvas was swept clean. There was no color in the sky. The light had gone out of the day. They caught their breaths in half-sobs. But lo! the air was a-glint with particles of scintillating frost, and there, to the north, the wind-vane lay in vague outline on the snow. A shadow! A shadow! It was exactly midday. They jerked their heads hurriedly to the south. A golden rim peeped over the mountain's snowy shoulder, smiled upon them an instant, then dipped from sight again.

There were tears in their eyes as they sought each other. A strange softening came over them. They felt irresistibly drawn toward each other. The sun was coming back again. It would be with them to-morrow, and the next day, and the next. And it would stay longer every visit, and a time would come when it would ride their heaven day and night, never once dropping below the sky-line. There would be no night. The ice-locked winter would be broken; the winds would blow and the forests answer; the land would bathe in the blessed sunshine, and life renew. Hand in hand, they would quit this horrid dream and journey back to the Southland. They lurched blindly forward, and their hands met,—their poor maimed hands, swollen and distorted beneath their mittens.

But the promise was destined to remain unfulfilled. The Northland is the Northland, and men work out their souls by strange rules, which other men, who have not journeyed into far countries, cannot come to understand.

An hour later, Cuthfert put a pan of bread into the oven, and fell to speculating on what the surgeons could do with his feet when he got back. Home did not seem so very far away now. Weatherbee was rummaging in the cache. Of a sudden, he raised a whirlwind of blasphemy, which in turn ceased with startling abruptness. The other man had robbed his sugar-sack. Still, things might have happened differently, had not the two dead men come out from under the stones and hushed the hot words in his throat. They led him quite gently from the cache, which he forgot to close. That consummation was reached; that something they had whispered to him in his dreams was about to happen. They guided him gently, very gently, to the woodpile, where they put the axe in his hands. Then they helped him shove open the cabin door, and he felt sure they shut it after him,—at least he heard it slam and the latch fall sharply into place. And he knew they were waiting just without, waiting for him to do his task.

"Carter! I say, Carter!"

Percy Cuthfert was frightened at the look on the clerk's face, and he made haste to put the table between them.

Carter Weatherbee followed, without haste and without enthusiasm. There was neither pity nor passion in his face, but rather the patient, stolid look of one who has certain work to do and goes about it methodically.

"I say, what's the matter?"

The clerk dodged back, cutting off his retreat to the door, but never opening his mouth.

"I say, Carter, I say; let's talk. There's a good chap."

The master of arts was thinking rapidly, now, shaping a skillful flank movement on the bed where his Smith & Wesson lay. Keeping his eyes on the madman, he rolled backward on the bunk, at the same time clutching the pistol.

"Carter!"

The powder flashed full in Weatherbee's face, but he swung his weapon and leaped forward. The axe bit deeply at the base of the spine, and Percy Cuthfert felt all consciousness of his lower limbs leave him. Then the clerk fell heavily upon him, clutching him by the throat with feeble fingers. The sharp bite of the axe had caused Cuthfert to drop the pistol, and as his lungs panted for release, he fumbled aimlessly for it among the blankets. Then he remembered. He slid a hand up the clerk's belt to the sheath-knife; and they drew very close to each other in that last clinch.

Percy Cuthfert felt his strength leave him. The lower portion of his body was useless. The inert weight of Weatherbee crushed him,— crushed him and pinned him there like a bear under a trap. The cabin became filled with a familiar odor, and he knew the bread to be burning. Yet what did it matter? He would never need it. And there were all of six cupfuls of sugar in the cache,—if he had foreseen this he would not have been so saving the last several days. Would the wind-vane ever move? It might even be veering now. Why not? Had he not seen the sun to-day? He would go and see. No; it was impossible to move. He had not thought the clerk so heavy a man.

How quickly the cabin cooled! The fire must be out. The cold was forcing in. It must be below zero already, and the ice creeping up the inside of the door. He could not see it, but his past experience enabled him to gauge its progress by the cabin's temperature. The lower hinge must be white ere now. Would the tale of this ever reach the world? How would his friends take it? They would read it over their coffee, most likely, and talk it over at the clubs. He could see them very clearly. "Poor Old Cuthfert," they murmured; "not such a bad sort of a chap, after all." He smiled at their eulogies, and passed on in search of a Turkish bath. It was the same old crowd upon the streets. Strange, they did not notice his moosehide moccasins and tattered German socks! He would take a cab. And after the bath a shave would not be bad. No; he would eat first. Steak, and potatoes, and green things,—how fresh it all was! And what was that? Squares of honey, streaming liquid amber! But why did they bring so much? Ha! ha! he could never eat it all. Shine! Why certainly. He put his foot on the box. The bootblack looked curiously up at him, and he remembered his moosehide moccasins and went away hastily.

Hark! The wind-vane must be surely spinning. No; a mere singing in his ears. That was all,—a mere singing. The ice must have passed the latch by now. More likely the upper hinge was covered. Between the moss-chinked roof-poles, little points of frost began to appear. How slowly they grew! No; not so slowly. There was a new one, and there another. Two—three—four; they were coming too fast to count. There were two growing together. And there, a third had joined them. Why, there were no more spots. They had run together and formed a sheet.

Well, he would have company. If Gabriel ever broke the silence of the North, they would stand together, hand in hand, before the great White Throne. And God would judge them, God would judge them!

Then Percy Cuthfert closed his eyes and dropped off to sleep.

AN ODYSSEY OF THE NORTH

The sleds were singing their eternal lament to the creaking of the harnesses and the tinkling bells of the leaders; but the men and dogs were tired and made no sound. The trail was heavy with new-fallen snow, and they had come far, and the runners, burdened with flint-like quarters of frozen moose, clung tenaciously to the unpacked surface and held back with a stubbornness almost human. Darkness was coming on, but there was no camp to pitch that night. The snow fell gently through the pulseless air, not in flakes, but in tiny frost crystals of delicate design. It was very warm,—barely ten below zero,—and the men did not mind. Meyers and Bettles had raised their earflaps, while Malemute Kid had even taken off his mittens.

The dogs had been fagged out early in the afternoon, but they now began to show new vigor. Among the more astute there was a certain restlessness,—an impatience at the restraint of the traces, an indecisive quickness of movement, a sniffing of snouts and pricking of ears. These became incensed at their more phlegmatic brothers, urging them on with numerous sly nips on their hinder-quarters. Those, thus chidden, also contracted and helped spread the contagion. At last, the leader of the foremost sled uttered a sharp whine of satisfaction, crouching lower in the snow and throwing himself against the collar. The rest followed suit. There was an ingathering of back-bands, a tightening of traces; the sleds leaped forward, and the men clung to the gee-poles, violently accelerating the uplift of their feet that they might escape going under the runners. The weariness of the day fell from them, and they whooped encouragement to the dogs. The animals responded with joyous yelps. They were swinging through the gathering darkness at a rattling gallop.

"Gee! Gee!" the men cried, each in turn, as their sleds abruptly left the main-trail, heeling over on single runners like luggers on the wind.

Then came a hundred yards' dash to the lighted parchment window, which told its own story of the home cabin, the roaring Yukon stove, and the steaming pots of tea. But the home cabin had been invaded. Three-score huskies chorused defiance, and as many furry forms precipitated themselves upon the dogs which drew the first sled. The door was flung open, and a man, clad in the scarlet tunic of the Northwest Police, waded knee-deep among the furious brutes, calmly and impartially dispensing soothing justice with the butt end of a dog-whip. After that, the men shook hands; and in this wise was Malemute Kid welcomed to his own cabin by a stranger.

Stanley Prince, who should have welcomed him, and who was responsible for the Yukon stove and hot tea aforementioned, was busy with his guests. There were a dozen or so of them, as nondescript a crowd as ever served the Queen in the enforcement of her laws or the delivery of her mails. They were of many breeds, but their common life had formed of them a certain type,—a lean and wiry type, with trail-hardened muscles, and sun-browned faces, and untroubled souls which gazed frankly forth, clear-eyed and steady. They drove the dogs of the Queen, wrought fear in the hearts of her enemies, ate of her meagre fare, and were happy. They had seen life, and done deeds, and lived romances; but they did not know it.

And they were very much at home. Two of them were sprawled upon Malemute Kid's bunk, singing chansons which their French forbears sang in the days when first they entered the Northwest-land and mated with its Indian women. Bettles' bunk had suffered a similar invasion, and three or four lusty *voyageurs* worked their toes among its blankets as they listened to the tale of one who had served on the boat brigade with Wolseley when he fought his way to Khartoum. And when he tired, a cowboy told of courts and kings and lords and ladies he had seen when Buffalo Bill toured the capitals of Europe. In a corner, two half-breeds, ancient comrades in a lost campaign, mended harnesses and talked of the days when the Northwest flamed with insurrection and Louis Reil was king.

Rough jests and rougher jokes went up and down, and great hazards by trail and river were spoken of in the light of commonplaces, only to be recalled by virtue of some grain of humor or ludicrous happening. Prince was led away by these uncrowned heroes who had seen history made, who regarded the great and the romantic as but the ordinary and the incidental in the routine of life. He passed his precious tobacco among them with lavish disregard, and rusty chains of reminiscence were loosened, and forgotten odysseys resurrected for his especial benefit.

When conversation dropped and the travelers filled the last pipes and unlashed their tight-rolled sleeping-furs, Prince fell back upon his comrade for further information.

"Well, you know what the cowboy is," Malemute Kid answered, beginning to unlace his moccasins; "and it's not hard to guess the British blood in his bed-partner. As for the rest, they're all children of the *coureurs du bois,* mingled with God knows how many other bloods. The two turning in by the door are the regulation 'breeds' or *bois brules.* That lad with the worsted breech scarf—notice his eyebrows and the turn of his jaw—shows a Scotchman wept in his mother's smoky tepee. And that handsome-looking fellow putting the capote under his head is a French half-breed,—you heard him talking; he doesn't like the two Indians turning in next to him. You see, when the 'breeds' rose under Reil the full-bloods kept the peace, and they've not lost much love for one another since."

"But I say, what's that glum-looking fellow by the stove? I'll swear he can't talk English. He hasn't opened his mouth all night."

"You're wrong. He knows English well enough. Did you follow his eyes when he listened? I did. But he's neither kith nor kin to the others. When they talked their own patois you could see he didn't understand. I've been wondering myself what he is. Let's find out."

"Fire a couple of sticks into the stove!" Malemute Kid commanded, raising his voice and looking squarely at the man in question.

He obeyed at once.

"Had discipline knocked into him somewhere," Prince commented in a low tone.

Malemute Kid nodded, took off his socks, and picked his way among the recumbent men to the stove. There he hung his damp footgear among a score or so of mates.

"When do you expect to get to Dawson?" he asked tentatively.

The man studied him a moment before replying. "They say seventy-five mile. So? Maybe two days."

The very slightest accent was perceptible, while there was no awkward hesitancy or groping for words.

"Been in the country before?"

"No."

"Northwest Territory?"

"Yes."

"Born there?"

"No."

"Well, where the devil were you born? You're none of these." Malemute Kid swept his hand over the dog-drivers, even including the two policemen who had turned into Prince's bunk. "Where did you come from? I've seen faces like yours before, though I can't remember just where."

"I know you," he irrelevantly replied, at once turning the drift of Malemute Kid's questions.

"Where? Ever see me?"

"No; your partner, him priest, Pastilik, long time ago. Him ask me if I see you, Malemute Kid. Him give me grub. I no stop long. You hear him speak 'bout me?"

"Oh! you're the fellow that traded the otter skins for the dogs?"

The man nodded, knocked out his pipe, and signified his disinclination for conversation by rolling up in his furs. Malemute Kid blew out the slush-lamp and crawled under the blankets with Prince.

"Well, what is he?"

"Don't know—turned me off, somehow, and then shut up like a clam. But he's a fellow to whet your curiosity. I've heard of him. All the Coast wondered about him eight years ago. Sort of mysterious, you know. He came down out of the North, in the dead of winter, many a thousand miles from here, skirting Bering Sea and traveling as though the devil were after him. No one ever learned where he came from, but he must have come far. He was badly travel-worn when he got food from the Swedish missionary on Golovin Bay and asked the way south. We heard of this afterward. Then he abandoned the shore-line, heading right across Norton Sound. Terrible weather, snowstorms and high winds, but he pulled through where a thousand other men would have died, missing St. Michael's and making the land at Pastilik. He'd lost all but two dogs, and was nearly gone with starvation.

"He was so anxious to go on that Father Roubeau fitted him out with grub; but he couldn't let him have any dogs, for he was only waiting my arrival to go on a trip himself. Mr. Ulysses knew too much to start on without animals, and fretted around for several days. He had on his sled a bunch of beautifully cured otter skins, sea-otters, you know, worth their weight in gold. There was also at Pastilik an old Shylock of a Russian trader, who had dogs to kill. Well, they didn't dicker very long, but when the Strange One headed south again, it was in the rear of a spanking dog-team. Mr. Shylock, by the way, had the otter skins. I saw them, and they were magnificent. We figured it up and found the dogs brought him at least five hundred apiece. And it wasn't as if the Strange One didn't know the value of sea-otter; he was an Indian of some sort, and what little he talked showed he'd been among white men.

"After the ice passed out of the Sea, word came up from Nunivak

Island that he'd gone in there for grub. Then he dropped from sight, and this is the first heard of him in eight years. Now where did he come from? and what was he doing there? and why did he come from there? He's Indian, he's been nobody knows where, and he's had discipline, which is unusual for an Indian. Another mystery of the North for you to solve, Prince."

"Thanks, awfully; but I've got too many on hand as it is," he replied.

Malemute Kid was already breathing heavily; but the young mining engineer gazed straight up through the thick darkness, waiting for the strange orgasm which stirred his blood to die away. And when he did sleep, his brain worked on, and for the nonce he, too, wandered through the white unknown, struggled with the dogs on endless trails, and saw men live, and toil, and die like men.

The next morning, hours before daylight, the dog-drivers and policemen pulled out for Dawson. But the powers that saw to her Majesty's interests, and ruled the destinies of her lesser creatures, gave the mailmen little rest; for a week later they appeared at Stuart River, heavily burdened with letters for Salt Water. However, their dogs had been replaced by fresh ones; but then, they were dogs.

The men had expected some sort of a lay-over in which to rest up; besides, this Klondike was a new section of the Northland, and they had wished to see a little something of the Golden City where dust flowed like water, and dance halls rang with never ending revelry. But they dried their socks and smoked their evening pipes with much the same gusto as on their former visit, though one or two bold spirits speculated on desertion and the possibility of crossing the unexplored Rockies to the east, and thence, by the Mackenzie Valley, of gaining their old stamping-grounds in the Chippewyan Country. Two or three even decided to return to their homes by that route when their terms of service had expired, and they began to lay plans forthwith, looking forward to the hazardous undertaking in much the same way a city-bred man would to a day's holiday in the woods.

He of the Otter Skins seemed very restless, though he took little interest in the discussion, and at last he drew Malemute Kid to one side and talked for some time in low tones. Prince cast curious eyes in their direction, and the mystery deepened when they put on caps and mittens, and went outside. When they returned, Malemute Kid placed his gold-scales on the table, weighed out the matter of sixty ounces, and transferred them to the Strange One's sack. Then the chief of the dog-drivers joined the conclave, and certain business was transacted with him. The next day the gang went on up river, but He of the Otter Skins took several pounds of grub and turned his steps back toward Dawson.

"Didn't know what to make of it," said Malemute Kid in response to Prince's queries; "but the poor beggar wanted to be quit of the service for some reason or other—at least it seemed a most important one to him, though he wouldn't let on what. You see, it's just like the army; he signed for two years, and the only way to get free was to buy himself out. He couldn't desert and then stay here, and he was just wild to remain in the country. Made up his mind when he got to Dawson, he said; but no one knew him, hadn't a cent, and I was the only one he'd spoken two words with. So he talked it over with the Lieutenant-Governor, and made arrangements in case he could get the money from me—loan, you know. Said he'd pay back in the year, and if I wanted, would put me onto something rich. Never'd seen it, but knew it was rich.

"And talk! why, when he got me outside he was ready to weep. Begged and pleaded; got down in the snow to me till I hauled him out of it. Palavered around like a crazy man. Swore he's worked to this very end for years and years, and couldn't bear to be disappointed now. Asked him what end, but he wouldn't say. Said they might keep him on the other half of the trail and he wouldn't get to Dawson in two years, and then it would be too late. Never saw a man take on so in my life. And when I said I'd let him have it, had to yank him out of the snow again. Told him to consider it in the light of a grub-stake. Think he'd have it? No, sir! Swore he'd give me all he found, make me rich beyond the dreams of avarice, and all such stuff. Now a man who puts his life and time against a grub-stake ordinarily finds it hard enough to turn over half of what he finds. Something behind all this, Prince; just you make a note of it. We'll hear of him if he stays in the country"—

"And if he doesn't?"

"Then my good nature gets a shock, and I'm sixty some odd ounces out."

The cold weather had come on with the long nights, and the sun had begun to play his ancient game of peekaboo along the southern snow-line ere aught was heard of Malemute Kid's grub-stake. And then, one bleak morning in early January, a heavily laden dog-train pulled into his cabin below Stuart River. He of the Otter Skins was there, and with him walked a man such as the gods have almost forgotten how to fashion. Men never talked of luck and pluck and five-hundred-dollar dirt without bringing in the name of Axel Gunderson; nor could tales of nerve or strength or daring pass up and down the camp-fire without the summoning of his presence. And when the conversation flagged, it blazed anew at mention of the woman who shared his fortunes.

As has been noted, in the making of Axel Gunderson the gods had remembered their old-time cunning, and cast him after the manner of men who were born when the world was young. Full seven feet he towered in his picturesque costume which marked a king of Eldorado. His chest, neck, and limbs were those of a giant. To bear his three hundred pounds of bone and muscle, his snowshoes were greater by a generous yard than those of other men. Rough-hewn, with rugged brow and massive jaw and unflinching eyes of palest blue, his face told the tale of one who knew but the law of might. Of the yellow of ripe corn silk, his frost-incrusted hair swept like day across the night, and fell far down his coat of bear-skin. A vague tradition of the sea seemed to cling about him, as he swung down the narrow trail in advance of the dogs; and he brought the butt of his dog-whip against Malemute Kid's door as a Norse sea rover, on southern foray, might thunder for admittance at the castle gate.

Prince bared his womanly arms and kneaded sour-dough bread, casting, as he did so, many a glance at the three guests,—three guests the like of which might never come under a man's roof in a lifetime. The Strange One, whom Malemute Kid had surnamed Ulysses, still fascinated him; but his interest chiefly gravitated between Axel Gunderson and Axel Gunderson's wife. She felt the day's journey, for she had softened in comfortable cabins during the many days since her husband mastered the wealth of frozen pay-streaks, and she was tired. She rested against his great breast like a slender flower against a wall, replying lazily to Malemute Kid's good-natured banter, and stirring Prince's blood strangely with an occasional sweep of her deep, dark eyes. For Prince was a man, and healthy, and had seen few women in many months. And she was older than he, and an Indian besides. But she was different from all native wives he had met: she had traveled,—had been in his country among others, he gathered from the conversation; and she knew most of the things the women of his own race knew, and much more that it was not in the nature of things for them to know. She could make a meal of sun-dried fish or a bed in the snow; yet she teased them with tantalizing details of many-course dinners, and caused strange internal dissensions to arise at the mention of various quondam dishes which they had well-nigh forgotten. She knew the ways of the moose, the bear, and the little blue fox, and of the wild amphibians of the Northern seas; she was skilled in the lore of the woods and the streams, and the tale writ by man and bird and beast upon the delicate snow crust was to her an open book; yet Prince caught the appreciative twinkle in her eye as she read the Rules of the Camp. These rules had been fathered by the Unquenchable Bettles at a time when his blood ran high, and were remarkable for the terse simplicity of their humor. Prince always turned them to the wall before the arrival of ladies; but who could suspect that this native wife— Well, it was too late now.

This, then, was the wife of Axel Gunderson, a woman whose name and fame had traveled with her husband's, hand in hand, through all the Northland. At table, Malemute Kid baited her with the assurance of an old friend, and Prince shook off the shyness of first acquaintance and joined in. But she held her own in the unequal contest, while her husband, slower in wit, ventured naught but applause. And he was very proud of her; his every look and action revealed the magnitude of the place she occupied in his life. He of the Otter Skins ate in silence, forgotten in the merry battle; and long ere the others were done he pushed back from the table and went out among the dogs. Yet all too soon his fellow travelers drew on their mittens and *parkas,* and followed him.

There had been no snow for many days, and the sleds slipped along the hard-packed Yukon trail as easily as if it had been glare ice. Ulysses led the first sled; with the second came Prince and Axel Gunderson's wife; while Malemute Kid and the yellow-haired giant brought up the third.

"It's only a 'hunch,' Kid," he said; "but I think it's straight. He's never been there, but he tells a good story, and shows a map I heard of when I was in the Kootenay country, years ago. I'd like to have you go along; but he's a strange one, and swore point-blank to throw it up if any one was brought in. But when I come back you'll get first tip, and I'll stake you next to me, and give you a half share in the town site besides.

"No! no!" he cried, as the other strove to interrupt. "I'm running this, and before I'm done it'll need two heads. If it's all right, why it'll be a second Cripple Creek, man; do you hear?—a second Cripple Creek! It's quartz, you know, not placer; and if we work it right we'll corral the whole thing,—millions upon millions. I've heard of the place before, and so have you. We'll build a town—thousands of workmen—good waterways—steamship lines—big carrying trade—light-draught steamers for head-reaches—survey a railroad, perhaps—sawmills—electric-light plant—do our own banking—commercial company—syndicate— Say! just you hold your hush till I get back!"

The sleds came to a halt where the trail crossed the mouth of Stuart River. An unbroken sea of frost, its wide expanse stretched away into the unknown east. The snowshoes were withdrawn from the lashings of the sleds. Axel Gunderson shook hands and stepped to the fore, his great webbed shoes sinking a fair half yard into the feathery surface and packing the snow so the dogs should not wallow. His wife fell in behind the last sled, betraying long practice in the art of handling the awkward footgear. The stillness was broken with cheery farewells; the dogs whined; and He of the Otter Skins talked with his whip to a recalcitrant wheeler.

An hour later, the train had taken on the likeness of a black pencil crawling in a long, straight line across a mighty sheet of foolscap.

· II ·

One night, many weeks later, Malemute Kid and Prince fell to solving chess problems from the torn page of an ancient magazine. The Kid had just returned from his Bonanza properties, and was resting up preparatory to a long moose hunt. Prince too had been on creek and trail nearly all winter, and had grown hungry for a blissful week of cabin life.

"Interpose the black knight, and force the king. No, that won't do. See, the next move"—

"Why advance the pawn two squares? Bound to take it in transit, and with the bishop out of the way"—

"But hold on! That leaves a hole, and"—

"No; it's protected. Go ahead! You'll see it works."

It was very interesting. Somebody knocked at the door a second time before Malemute Kid said, "Come in." The door swung open. Something staggered in. Prince caught one square look, and sprang to his feet. The horror in his eyes caused Malemute Kid to whirl about; and he too was startled, though he had seen bad things before. The thing tottered blindly toward them. Prince edged away till he reached the nail from which hung his Smith & Wesson.

"My God! what is it?" he whispered to Malemute Kid.

"Don't know. Looks like a case of freezing and no grub," replied the Kid, sliding away in the opposite direction. "Watch out! It may be mad," he warned, coming back from closing the door.

The thing advanced to the table. The bright flame of the slush-lamp caught its eye. It was amused, and gave voice to eldritch cackles which betokened mirth. Then, suddenly, he—for it was a man—swayed back, with a hitch to his skin trousers, and began to sing a chanty, such as men lift when they swing around the capstan circle and the sea snorts in their ears:—

> *"Yan-kee ship come down de ri-ib-er,*
>   *Pull! my bully boys! Pull!*
> *D'yeh want—to know de captain ru-uns her?*
>   *Pull! my bully boys! Pull!*
> *Jon-a-than Jones ob South Caho-li-in-a,*
>   *Pull! my bully"*—

He broke off abruptly, tottered with a wolfish snarl to the meat-shelf, and before they could intercept was tearing with his teeth at a chunk of raw bacon. The struggle was fierce between him and Malemute Kid; but his mad strength left him as suddenly as it had come, and he weakly surrendered the spoil. Between them they got him upon a stool, where he sprawled with half his body across the table. A small dose of whiskey strengthened him, so that he could dip a spoon into the sugar caddy which Malemute Kid placed before him. After his appetite had been somewhat cloyed, Prince, shuddering as he did so, passed him a mug of weak beef tea.

The creature's eyes were alight with a sombre frenzy, which blazed and waned with every mouthful. There was very little skin to the face. The face, for that matter, sunken and emaciated, bore very little likeness to human countenance. Frost after frost had bitten deeply, each depositing its stratum of scab upon the half-healed scar that went before. This dry, hard surface was of a bloody-black color, serrated by grievous cracks wherein the raw red flesh peeped forth. His skin garments were dirty and in tatters, and the fur of one side was singed and burned away, showing where he had lain upon his fire.

Malemute Kid pointed to where the sun-tanned hide had been cut away, strip by strip,—the grim signature of famine.

"Who—are—you?" slowly and distinctly enunciated the Kid.

The man paid no heed.

"Where do you come from?"

"Yan-kee ship come down de ri-ib-er," was the quavering response.

"Don't doubt the beggar came down the river," the Kid said, shaking him in an endeavor to start a more lucid flow of talk.

But the man shrieked at the contact, clapping a hand to his side in evident pain. He rose slowly to his feet, half leaning on the table.

"She laughed at me—so—with the hate in her eye; and she—would—not—come."

His voice died away, and he was sinking back when Malemute Kid gripped him by the wrist, and shouted, "Who? Who would not come?"

"She, Unga. She laughed, and struck at me, so, and so. And then"—

"Yes?"

"And then"—

"And then what?"

"And then he lay very still, in the snow, a long time. He is—still in —the—snow."

The two men looked at each other helplessly.

"Who is in the snow?"

"She, Unga. She looked at me with the hate in her eye, and then"—

"Yes, yes."

"And then she took the knife, so; and once, twice—she was weak. I traveled very slow. And there is much gold in that place, very much gold."

"Where is Unga?" For all Malemute Kid knew, she might be dying a mile away. He shook the man savagely, repeating again and again, "Where is Unga? Who is Unga?"

"She—is—in—the—snow."

"Go on!" The Kid was pressing his wrist cruelly.

"So—I—would—be—in—the snow—but—I—had—a—debt—to —pay. It—was—heavy—I—had—a—debt—to—pay—a—debt—to —pay—I—had"— The faltering monosyllables ceased, as he fumbled in his pouch and drew forth a buckskin sack. "A—debt—to—pay— five—pounds—of—gold—grub—stake—Mal—e—mute—Kid—I"— The exhausted head dropped upon the table; nor could Malemute Kid rouse it again.

"It's Ulysses," he said quietly, tossing the bag of dust on the table. "Guess it's all day with Axel Gunderson and the woman. Come on, let's get him between the blankets. He's Indian; he'll pull through, and tell a tale besides."

As they cut his garments from him, near his right breast could be seen two unhealed, hard-lipped knife thrusts.

·III·

"I will talk of the things which were, in my own way; but you will understand. I will begin at the beginning, and tell of myself and the woman, and, after that, of the man."

He of the Otter Skins drew over to the stove as do men who have been deprived of fire and are afraid the Promethean gift may vanish at any moment. Malemute Kid pricked up the slush-lamp, and placed it so its light might fall upon the face of the narrator. Prince slid his body over the edge of the bunk and joined them.

"I am Naass, a chief, and the son of a chief, born between a sunset and a rising, on the dark seas, in my father's oomiak. All of a night the men toiled at the paddles, and the women cast out the waves which threw in upon us, and we fought with the storm. The salt spray froze upon my mother's breast till her breath passed with the passing of the tide. But I,—I raised my voice with the wind and the storm, and lived.

"We dwelt in Akatan"—

"Where?" asked Malemute Kid.

"Akatan, which is in the Aleutians; Akatan, beyond Chignik, beyond Kardalak, beyond Unimak. As I say, we dwelt in Akatan, which lies in the midst of the sea on the edge of the world. We farmed the salt seas for the fish, the seal, and the otter; and our homes shouldered about one another on the rocky strip between the rim of the forest and the yellow beach where our kayaks lay. We were not many, and the world was very small. There were strange lands to the east,—islands like Akatan; so we thought all the world was islands, and did not mind.

"I was different from my people. In the sands of the beach were the crooked timbers and wave-warped planks of a boat such as my people never built; and I remember on the point of the island which overlooked the ocean three ways there stood a pine tree which never grew there, smooth and straight and tall. It is said the two men came to that spot, turn about, through many days, and watched with the passing of the light. These two men came from out of the sea in the boat which lay in pieces on the beach. And they were white like you, and weak as the little children when the seal have gone away and the hunters come home empty. I know of these things from the old men and the old women, who got them from their fathers and mothers before them. These strange white men did not take kindly to our ways at first, but they grew strong, what of the fish and the oil, and fierce. And they built them each his own house, and took the pick of our women, and in time children came. Thus he was born who was to become the father of my father's father.

"As I said, I was different from my people, for I carried the strong, strange blood of this white man who came out of the sea. It is said we had other laws in the days before these men; but they were fierce and quarrelsome, and fought with our men till there were no more left who dared to fight. Then they made themselves chiefs, and took away our old laws and gave us new ones, insomuch that the man was the son of his father, and not his mother, as our way had been. They also ruled that the son, firstborn, should have all things which were his father's before him, and that the brothers and sisters should shift for themselves. And they gave us other laws. They showed us new ways in the catching of fish and the killing of bear which were thick in the woods; and they taught us to lay by bigger stores for the time of famine. And these things were good.

"But when they had become chiefs, and there were no more men to face their anger, they fought, these strange white men, each with the other. And the one whose blood I carry drove his seal spear the length of an arm through the other's body. Their children took up the fight, and their children's children; and there was great hatred between them, and black doings, even to my time, so that in each family but one lived to pass down the blood of them that went before. Of my blood I was alone; of the other man's there was but a girl, Unga, who lived with her mother. Her father and my father did not come back from the fishing one night; but afterward they washed up to the beach on the big tides, and they held very close to each other.

"The people wondered, because of the hatred between the houses, and the old men shook their heads and said the fight would go on when children were born to her and children to me. They told me this as a boy, till I came to believe, and to look upon Unga as a foe, who was to be the mother of children which were to fight with mine. I thought of these things day by day, and when I grew to a stripling I came to ask why this should be so. And they answered, 'We do not know, but that in such way your fathers did.' And I marveled that those which were to come should fight the battles of those that were gone, and in it I could see no right. But the people said it must be, and I was only a stripling.

"And they said I must hurry, that my blood might be the older and grow strong before hers. This was easy, for I was head man, and the people looked up to me because of the deeds and the laws of my fathers, and the wealth which was mine. Any maiden would come to me, but I found none to my liking. And the old men and the mothers of maidens told me to hurry, for even then were the hunters bidding high to the mother of Unga; and should her children grow strong before mine, mine would surely die.

"Nor did I find a maiden till one night coming back from the fishing. The sunlight was lying, so, low and full in the eyes, the wind free, and the kayaks racing with the white seas. Of a sudden the kayak of Unga came driving past me, and she looked upon me, so, with her black hair flying like a cloud of night and the spray wet on her cheek. As I say, the sunlight was full in the eyes, and I was a stripling; but somehow it was all clear, and I knew it to be the call of kind to kind. As she whipped ahead she looked back within the space of two strokes,—looked as only the woman Unga could look,—and again I knew it as the call of kind. The people shouted as we ripped past the lazy oomiaks and left them far behind. But she was quick at the paddle, and my heart was like the belly of a sail, and I did not gain. The wind freshened, the sea whitened, and, leaping like the seals on the windward breech, we roared down the golden pathway of the sun."

Naass was crouched half out of his stool, in the attitude of one driving a paddle, as he ran the race anew. Somewhere across the stove he beheld the tossing kayak and the flying hair of Unga. The voice of the wind was in his ears, and its salt beat fresh upon his nostrils.

"But she made the shore, and ran up the sand, laughing, to the house of her mother. And a great thought came to me that night,—a thought worthy of him that was chief over all the people of Akatan. So, when the moon was up, I went down to the house of her mother, and looked upon the goods of Yash-Noosh, which were piled by the door,—the goods of Yash-Noosh, a strong hunter who had it in mind to be the father of the children of Unga. Other young men had piled their goods there, and taken them away again; and each young man had made a pile greater than the one before.

"And I laughed to the moon and the stars, and went to my own house where my wealth was stored. And many trips I made, till my pile was greater by the fingers of one hand than the pile of Yash-Noosh. There were fish, dried in the sun and smoked; and forty hides of the hair seal, and half as many of the fur, and each hide was tied at the mouth and big-bellied with oil; and ten skins of bear which I killed in the woods when they came out in the spring. And there were beads and blankets and scarlet cloths, such as I got in trade from the people who lived to the east, and who got them in trade from the people who lived still beyond in the east. And I looked upon the pile of Yash-Noosh and laughed; for I was head man in Akatan, and my wealth was greater than the wealth of all my young men, and my fathers had done deeds, and given laws, and put their names for all time in the mouths of the people.

"So, when the morning came, I went down to the beach, casting out of the corner of my eye at the house of the mother of Unga. My offer yet stood untouched. And the women smiled, and said sly things one to the other. I wondered, for never had such a price been offered; and that night I added more to the pile, and put beside it a kayak of well-tanned skins which never yet had swam in the sea. But in the day it was yet there, open to the laughter of all men. The mother of Unga was crafty, and I grew angry at the shame in which I stood before my people. So that night I added till it became a great pile, and I hauled up my oomiak, which was of the value of twenty kayaks. And in the morning there was no pile.

"Then made I preparation for the wedding, and the people that lived even to the east came for the food of the feast and the *potlach* token. Unga was older than I by the age of four suns in the way we reckoned the years. I was only a stripling; but then I was a chief, and the son of a chief, and it did not matter.

"But a ship shoved her sails above the floor of the ocean, and grew larger with the breath of the wind. From her scuppers she ran clear water, and the men were in haste and worked hard at the pumps. On the bow stood a mighty man, watching the depth of the water and giving commands with a voice of thunder. His eyes were of the pale blue of the deep waters, and his head was maned like that of a sea lion. And his hair was yellow, like the straw of a southern harvest or the manila rope-yarns which sailormen plait.

"Of late years we had seen ships from afar, but this was the first to come to the beach of Akatan. The feast was broken, and the women and children fled to the houses, while we men strung our bows and waited with spears in hand. But when the ship's forefoot smelt the beach the strange men took no notice of us, being busy with their own work. With the falling of the tide they careened the schooner and patched a great hole in her bottom. So the women crept back, and the feast went on.

"When the tide rose, the sea wanderers kedged the schooner to deep water, and then came among us. They bore presents and were friendly; so I made room for them, and out of the largeness of my heart gave them tokens such as I gave all the guests; for it was my wedding day, and I was head man in Akatan. And he with the mane of the sea lion was there, so tall and strong that one looked to see the earth shake with the fall of his feet. He looked much and straight at Unga, with his arms folded, so, and stayed till the sun went away and the stars came out. Then he went down to his ship. After that I took Unga by the hand and led her to my own house. And there was singing and great laughter, and the women said sly things, after the manner of women at such times. But we did not care. Then the people left us alone and went home.

"The last noise had not died away, when the chief of the sea wanderers came in by the door. And he had with him black bottles, from which we drank and made merry. You see, I was only a stripling, and had lived all my days on the edge of the world. So my blood became as fire, and my heart as light as the froth that flies from the surf to the cliff. Unga sat silent among the skins in the corner, her eyes wide, for she seemed to fear. And he with the mane of the sea lion looked upon her straight and long. Then his men came in with bundles of goods, and he piled before me wealth such as was not in all Akatan. There were guns, both large and small, and powder and shot and shell, and bright axes and knives of steel, and cunning tools, and strange things the like of which I had never seen. When he showed me by sign that it was all mine, I thought him a great man to be so free; but he showed me also that Unga was to go away with him in his ship. Do you understand?—that Unga was to go away with him in his ship. The blood of my fathers flamed hot on the sudden, and I made to drive him through with my spear. But the spirit of the bottles had stolen the life from my arm, and he took me by the neck, so, and knocked my head against the wall of the house. And I was made weak like a newborn child, and my legs would no more stand under me. Unga screamed, and she laid hold of the things of the house with her hands, till they fell all about us as he dragged her to the door. Then he took her in his great arms, and when she tore at his yellow hair laughed with a sound like that of the big bull seal in the rut.

"I crawled to the beach and called upon my people; but they were afraid. Only Yash-Noosh was a man, and they struck him on the head with an oar, till he lay with his face in the sand and did not move. And they raised the sails to the sound of their songs, and the ship went away on the wind.

"The people said it was good, for there would be no more war of the bloods in Akatan; but I said never a word, waiting till the time of the full moon, when I put fish and oil in my kayak, and went away to the east. I saw many islands and many people, and I, who had lived on the edge, saw that the world was very large. I talked by signs; but they had not seen a schooner nor a man with the mane of a sea lion, and they pointed always to the east. And I slept in queer places, and ate odd things, and met strange faces. Many laughed, for they thought me light of head; but sometimes old men turned my face to the light and blessed me, and the eyes of the young women grew soft as they asked me of the strange ship, and Unga, and the men of the sea.

"And in this manner, through rough seas and great storms, I came to Unalaska. There were two schooners there, but neither was the one I sought. So I passed on to the east, with the world growing ever larger, and in the Island of Unamok there was no word of the ship, nor in Kadiak, nor in Atognak. And so I came one day to a rocky land, where men dug great holes in the mountain. And there was a schooner, but not my schooner, and men loaded upon it the rocks which they dug. This I thought childish, for all the world was made of rocks; but they gave me food and set me to work. When the schooner was deep in the water, the captain gave me money and told me to go; but I asked which way he went, and he pointed south. I made signs that I would go with him; and he laughed at first, but then, being short of men, took me to help work the ship. So I came to talk after their manner, and to heave on ropes, and to reef the stiff sails in sudden squalls, and to take my turn at the wheel. But it was not strange, for the blood of my fathers was the blood of the men of the sea.

"I had thought it an easy task to find him I sought, once I got among his own people; and when we raised the land one day, and passed between a gateway of the sea to a port, I looked for perhaps as many schooners as there were fingers to my hands. But the ships lay against the wharves for miles, packed like so many little fish; and when I went among them to ask for a man with the mane of a sea lion, they laughed, and answered me in the tongues of many peoples. And I found that they hailed from the uttermost parts of the earth.

"And I went into the city to look upon the face of every man. But they were like the cod when they run thick on the banks, and I could not count them. And the noise smote upon me till I could not hear, and my head was dizzy with much movement. So I went on and on, through the lands which sang in the warm sunshine; where the harvests lay rich on the plains; and where great cities were fat with men that lived like women, with false words in their mouths and their hearts black with the lust of gold. And all the while my people of Akatan hunted and fished, and were happy in the thought that the world was small.

"But the look in the eyes of Unga coming home from the fishing was with me always, and I knew I would find her when the time was met. She walked down quiet lanes in the dusk of the evening, or led me chases across the thick fields wet with the morning dew, and there was a promise in her eyes such as only the woman Unga could give.

"So I wandered through a thousand cities. Some were gentle and gave me food, and others laughed, and still others cursed; but I kept my tongue between my teeth, and went strange ways and saw strange sights. Sometimes, I, who was a chief and the son of a chief, toiled for men,—men rough of speech and hard as iron, who wrung gold from the sweat and sorrow of their fellow men. Yet no word did I get of my quest, till I came back to the sea like a homing seal to the rookeries. But this was at another port, in another country which lay to the north. And there I heard dim tales of the yellow-haired sea wanderer, and I learned that he was a hunter of seals, and that even then he was abroad on the ocean.

"So I shipped on a seal schooner with the lazy Siwashes, and followed his trackless trail to the north where the hunt was then warm. And we were away weary months, and spoke many of the fleet, and heard much of the wild doings of him I sought; but never once did we raise him above the sea. We went north, even to the Pribyloffs, and killed the seals in herds on the beach, and brought their warm bodies aboard till our scuppers ran grease and blood and no man could stand upon the deck. Then were we chased by a ship of slow steam, which fired upon us with great guns. But we put on sail till the sea was over our decks and washed them clean, and lost ourselves in a fog.

"It is said, at this time, while we fled with fear at our hearts, that the yellow-haired sea wanderer put into the Pribyloffs, right to the factory, and while the part of his men held the servants of the company, the rest loaded ten thousand green skins from the salt-houses. I say it is said, but I believe; for in the voyages I made on the coast with never a meeting, the northern seas rang with his wildness and daring, till the three nations which have lands there sought him with their ships. And I heard of Unga, for the captains sang loud in her praise, and she was always with him. She had learned the ways of his people, they said, and was happy. But I knew better,—knew that her heart harked back to her own people by the yellow beach of Akatan.

"So, after a long time, I went back to the port which is by a gateway of the sea, and there I learned that he had gone across the girth of the great ocean to hunt for the seal to the east of the warm land which runs south from the Russian Seas. And I, who was become a sailorman, shipped with men of his own race, and went after him in the hunt of the seal. And there were few ships off that new land; but we hung on the flank of the seal pack and harried it north through all the spring of the year. And when the cows were heavy with pup and crossed the Russian line, our men grumbled and were afraid. For there was much fog, and every day men were lost in the boats. They would not work, so the captain turned the ship back toward the way it came. But I knew the yellow-haired sea wanderer was unafraid, and would hang by the pack, even to the Russian Isles, where few men go. So I took a boat, in the black of night, when the lookout dozed on the fok'slehead, and went alone to the warm, long land. And I journeyed south to meet the men by Yeddo Bay, who are wild and unafraid. And the Yoshiwara girls were small, and bright like steel, and good to look upon; but I could not stop, for I knew that Unga rolled on the tossing floor by the rook-eries of the north.

"The men by Yeddo Bay had met from the ends of the earth, and had neither gods nor homes, sailing under the flag of the Japanese. And with them I went to the rich beaches of Copper Island, where our salt-piles became high with skins. And in that silent sea we saw no man till we were ready to come away. Then, one day, the fog lifted on the edge of a heavy wind, and there jammed down upon us a schooner, with close in her wake the cloudy funnels of a Russian man-of-war. We fled away on the beam of the wind, with the schooner jamming still closer and plunging ahead three feet to our two. And upon her poop was the man with the mane of the sea lion, pressing the rails under with the canvas and laughing in his strength of life. And Unga was there,—I knew her on the moment,—but he sent her below when the cannons began to talk across the sea. As I say, with three feet to our two, till we saw the rudder lift green at every jump,—and I swinging on to the wheel and cursing, with my back to the Russian shot. For we knew he had it in mind to run before us, that he might get away while we were caught. And they knocked our masts out of us till we dragged into the wind like a wounded gull; but he went on over the edge of the sky-line,—he and Unga.

"What could we? The fresh hides spoke for themselves. So they took us to a Russian port, and after that to a lone country, where they set us to work in the mines to dig salt. And some died, and—and some did not die."

Naass swept the blanket from his shoulders, disclosing the gnarled and twisted flesh, marked with the unmistakable striations of the knout. Prince hastily covered him, for it was not nice to look upon.

"We were there a weary time; and sometimes men got away to the south, but they always came back. So, when we who hailed from Yeddo Bay rose in the night and took the guns from the guards, we went to the north. And the land was very large, with plains, soggy with water, and great forests. And the cold came, with much snow on the ground, and no man knew the way. Weary months we journeyed through the endless forest,—I do not remember, now, for there was little food and often we lay down to die. But at last we came to the cold sea, and but three were left to look upon it. One had shipped from Yeddo as captain, and he knew in his head the lay of the great lands, and of the place where men may cross from one to the other on the ice. And he led us, —I do not know, it was so long,—till there were but two. When we came to that place we found five of the strange people which live in that country, and they had dogs and skins, and we were very poor. We fought in the snow till they died, and the captain died, and the dogs and skins were mine. Then I crossed on the ice, which was broken, and once I drifted till a gale from the west put me upon the shore. And after that, Golovin Bay, Pastilik, and the priest. Then south, south, to the warm sunlands where first I wandered.

"But the sea was no longer fruitful, and those who went upon it after the seal went to little profit and great risk. The fleets scattered, and the captains and the men had no word of those I sought. So I turned away from the ocean which never rests, and went among the lands, where the trees, the houses, and the mountains sit always in one place and do not move. I journeyed far, and came to learn many things, even to the way of reading and writing from books. It was well I should do this, for it came upon me that Unga must know these things, and that some day, when the time was met—we—you understand, when the time was met.

"So I drifted, like those little fish which raise a sail to the wind, but cannot steer. But my eyes and my ears were open always, and I went among men who traveled much, for I knew they had but to see those I sought, to remember. At last there came a man, fresh from the mountains, with pieces of rock in which the free gold stood to the size of peas, and he had heard, he had met, he knew them. They were rich, he said, and lived in the place where they drew the gold from the ground.

"It was in a wild country, and very far away; but in time I came to the camp, hidden between the mountains, where men worked night and day, out of the sight of the sun. Yet the time was not come. I listened to the talk of the people. He had gone away,—they had gone away,—to England, it was said, in the matter of bringing men with much money together to form companies. I saw the house they had lived in; more like a palace, such as one sees in the old countries. In the nighttime I crept in through a window that I might see in what manner he treated her. I went from room to room, and in such way thought kings and queens must live, it was all so very good. And they all said he treated her like a queen, and many marveled as to what breed of woman she was; for there was other blood in her veins, and she was different from the women of Akatan, and no one knew her for what she was. Ay, she was a queen; but I was a chief, and the son of a chief, and I had paid for her an untold price of skin and boat and bead.

"But why so many words? I was a sailorman, and knew the way of the ships on the seas. I followed to England, and then to other countries. Sometimes I heard of them by word of mouth, sometimes I read of them in the papers; yet never once could I come by them, for they had much money, and traveled fast, while I was a poor man. Then came trouble upon them, and their wealth slipped away, one day, like a curl of smoke. The papers were full of it at the time; but after that nothing was said, and I knew they had gone back where more gold could be got from the ground.

"They had dropped out of the world, being now poor; and so I wandered from camp to camp, even north to the Kootenay Country, where

I picked up the cold scent. They had come and gone, some said this way, and some that, and still others that they had gone to the Country of the Yukon. And I went this way, and I went that, ever journeying from place to place, till it seemed I must grow weary of the world which was so large. But in the Kootenay I traveled a bad trail, and a long trail, with a 'breed' of the Northwest, who saw fit to die when the famine pinched. He had been to the Yukon by an unknown way over the mountains, and when he knew his time was near gave me the map and the secret of a place where he swore by his gods there was much gold.

"After that all the world began to flock into the north. I was a poor man; I sold myself to be a driver of dogs. The rest you know. I met him and her in Dawson. She did not know me, for I was only a stripling, and her life had been large, so she had no time to remember the one who had paid for her an untold price.

"So? You bought me from my term of service. I went back to bring things about in my own way; for I had waited long, and now that I had my hand upon him was in no hurry. As I say, I had it in mind to do my own way; for I read back in my life, through all I had seen and suffered, and remembered the cold and hunger of the endless forest by the Russian Seas. As you know, I led him into the east,—him and Unga,—into the east where many have gone and few returned. I led them to the spot where the bones and the curses of men lie with the gold which they may not have.

"The way was long and the trail unpacked. Our dogs were many and ate much; nor could our sleds carry till the break of spring. We must come back before the river ran free. So here and there we cached grub, that our sleds might be lightened and there be no chance of famine on the back trip. At the McQuestion there were three men, and near them we built a cache, as also did we at the Mayo, where was a hunting-camp of a dozen Pellys which had crossed the divide from the south. After that, as we went on into the east, we saw no men; only the sleeping river, the moveless forest, and the White Silence of the North. As I say, the way was long and the trail unpacked. Sometimes, in a day's toil, we made no more than eight miles, or ten, and at night we slept like dead men. And never once did they dream that I was Naass, head man of Akatan, the righter of wrongs.

"We now made smaller caches, and in the nighttime it was a small matter to go back on the trail we had broken, and change them in such way that one might deem the wolverines the thieves. Again, there be places where there is a fall to the river, and the water is unruly, and the ice makes above and is eaten away beneath. In such a spot the sled I drove broke through, and the dogs; and to him and Unga it was ill luck, but no more. And there was much grub on that sled, and the dogs the strongest. But he laughed, for he was strong of life, and gave the dogs that were left little grub till we cut them from the harnesses, one by one, and fed them to their mates. We would go home light, he said, traveling and eating from cache to cache, with neither dogs nor sleds; which was true, for our grub was very short, and the last dog died in the traces the night we came to the gold and the bones and the curses of men.

"To reach that place,—and the map spoke true,—in the heart of the great mountains, we cut ice steps against the wall of a divide. One looked for a valley beyond, but there was no valley; the snow spread away, level as the great harvest plains, and here and there about us mighty mountains shoved their white heads among the stars. And midway on that strange plain which should have been a valley, the earth and the snow fell away, straight down toward the heart of the world. Had we not been sailormen our heads would have swung round with the sight; but we stood on the dizzy edge that we might see a way to get down. And on one side, and one side only, the wall had fallen away till it was like the slope of the decks in a topsail breeze. I do not know why this thing should be so, but it was so. 'It is the mouth of hell,' he said; 'let us go down.' And we went down.

"And on the bottom there was a cabin, built by some man, of logs which he had cast down from above. It was a very old cabin; for men had died there alone at different times, and on pieces of birch bark which were there we read their last words and their curses. One had died of scurvy; another's partner had robbed him of his last grub and powder and stolen away; a third had been mauled by a bald-face grizzly; a fourth had hunted for game and starved,—and so it went, and they had been loath to leave the gold, and had died by the side of it in one way or another. And the worthless gold they had gathered yellowed the floor of the cabin like in a dream.

"But his soul was steady, and his head clear, this man I had led thus far. 'We have nothing to eat,' he said, 'and we will only look upon this gold, and see whence it comes and how much there be. Then we will go away quick, before it gets into our eyes and steals away our judgment. And in this way we may return in the end, with more grub, and possess it all.' So we looked upon the great vein, which cut the wall of the pit as a true vein should; and we measured it, and traced it from above and below, and drove the stakes of the claims and blazed the trees in token of our rights. Then, our knees shaking with lack of food, and a sickness in our bellies, and our hearts chugging close to our mouths, we climbed the mighty wall for the last time and turned our faces to the back trip.

"The last stretch we dragged Unga between us, and we fell often, but in the end we made the cache. And lo, there was no grub. It was well done, for he thought it the wolverines, and damned them and his gods in the one breath. But Unga was brave, and smiled, and put her hand in his, till I turned away that I might hold myself. 'We will rest by the fire,' she said, 'till morning, and we will gather strength from our moccasins.' So we cut the tops of our moccasins in strips, and boiled them half of the night, that we might chew them and swallow them. And in the morning we talked of our chance. The next cache was five days' journey; we could not make it. We must find game.

" 'We will go forth and hunt,' he said.

" 'Yes,' said I, 'we will go forth and hunt.'

"And he ruled that Unga stay by the fire and save her strength. And we went forth, he in quest of the moose, and I to the cache I had changed. But I ate little, so they might not see in me much strength. And in the night he fell many times as he drew into camp. And I too made to suffer great weakness, stumbling over my snowshoes as though each step might be my last. And we gathered strength from our moccasins.

"He was a great man. His soul lifted his body to the last; nor did he cry aloud, save for the sake of Unga. On the second day I followed him, that I might not miss the end. And he lay down to rest often. That night he was near gone; but in the morning he swore weakly and went forth again. He was like a drunken man, and I looked many times for him to give up; but his was the strength of the strong, and his soul the soul of a giant, for he lifted his body through all the weary day. And he shot two ptarmigan, but would not eat them. He needed no fire; they meant life; but his thought was for Unga, and he turned toward camp. He no longer walked, but crawled on hand and knee through the snow. I came to him, and read death in his eyes. Even then it was not too late to eat of the ptarmigan. He cast away his rifle, and carried the birds in his mouth like a dog. I walked by his side, upright. And he looked at me during the moments he rested, and wondered that I was so strong. I could see it, though he no longer spoke; and when his lips moved, they moved without sound. As I say, he was a great man, and my heart spoke for softness; but I read back in my life, and remembered the cold and hunger of the endless forest by the Russian Seas. Besides, Unga was mine, and I had paid for her an untold price of skin and boat and bead.

"And in this manner we came through the white forest, with the silence heavy upon us like a damp sea mist. And the ghosts of the past were in the air and all about us; and I saw the yellow beach of Akatan, and the kayaks racing home from the fishing, and the houses on the rim of the forest. And the men who had made themselves chiefs were there, the lawgivers whose blood I bore, and whose blood I had wedded in Unga. Ay, and Yash-Noosh walked with me, the wet sand in his hair, and his war spear, broken as he fell upon it, still in his hand. And I knew the time was met, and saw in the eyes of Unga the promise.

"As I say, we came thus through the forest, till the smell of the camp smoke was in our nostrils. And I bent above him, and tore the ptarmigan from his teeth. He turned on his side and rested, the wonder mounting in his eyes, and the hand which was under slipping slow toward the knife at his hip. But I took it from him, smiling close in his face. Even then he did not understand. So I made to drink from black bottles, and to build high upon the snow a pile of goods, and to live again the things which happened on the night of my marriage. I spoke no word, but he understood. Yet was he unafraid. There was a sneer to his lips, and cold anger, and he gathered new strength with the knowledge. It was not far, but the snow was deep, and he dragged himself very slow. Once, he lay so long, I turned him over and gazed into his eyes. And sometimes he looked forth, and sometimes death. And when I loosed him he struggled on again. In this way we came to the fire. Unga was at his side on the instant. His lips moved, without sound; then he pointed at me, that Unga might understand. And after that he lay in the snow, very still, for a long while. Even now is he there in the snow.

"I said no word till I had cooked the ptarmigan. Then I spoke to her, in her own tongue, which she had not heard in many years. She straightened herself, so, and her eyes were wonder-wide, and she asked who I was, and where I had learned that speech.

" 'I am Naass,' I said.

" 'You?' she said. 'You?' And she crept close that she might look upon me.

" 'Yes,' I answered; 'I am Naass, head man of Akatan, the last of the blood, as you are the last of the blood.'

"And she laughed. By all the things I have seen and the deeds I have done, may I never hear such a laugh again. It put the chill to my soul, sitting there in the White Silence, alone with death and this woman who laughed.

" 'Come!' I said, for I thought she wandered. 'Eat of the food and let us be gone. It is a far fetch from here to Akatan.'

"But she shoved her face in his yellow mane, and laughed till it seemed the heavens must fall about our ears. I had thought she would be overjoyed at the sight of me, and eager to go back to the memory of old times; but this seemed a strange form to take.

" 'Come!' I cried, taking her strong by the hand. 'The way is long and dark. Let us hurry!'

" 'Where?' she asked, sitting up, and ceasing from her strange mirth.

" 'To Akatan,' I answered, intent on the light to grow on her face at the thought. But it became like his, with a sneer to the lips, and cold anger.

" 'Yes,' she said; 'we will go, hand in hand, to Akatan, you and I. And we will live in the dirty huts, and eat of the fish and oil, and bring forth a spawn,—a spawn to be proud of all the days of our life. We will forget the world and be happy, very happy. It is good, most good. Come! Let us hurry. Let us go back to Akatan.'

"And she ran her hand through his yellow hair, and smiled in a way which was not good. And there was no promise in her eyes.

"I sat silent, and marveled at the strangeness of woman. I went back to the night when he dragged her from me, and she screamed and tore at his hair,—at his hair which now she played with and would not leave. Then I remembered the price and the long years of waiting; and I gripped her close, and dragged her away as he had done. And she held back, even as on that night, and fought like a she-cat for its whelp. And when the fire was between us and the man, I loosed her, and she sat and listened. And I told her of all that lay between, of all that had happened me on strange seas, of all that I had done in strange lands; of my weary quest, and the hungry years, and the promise which had been mine from the first. Ay, I told all, even to what had passed that day between the man and me, and in the days yet young. And as I spoke I saw the promise grow in her eyes, full and large like the break of dawn. And I read pity there, the tenderness of woman, the love, the heart and the soul of Unga. And I was a stripling again, for the look was the look of Unga as she ran up the beach, laughing, to the home of her mother. The stern unrest was gone, and the hunger, and the weary waiting. The time was met. I felt the call of her breast, and it seemed there I must pillow my head and forget. She opened her arms to me, and I came against her. Then, sudden, the hate flamed in her eye, her hand was at my hip. And once, twice, she passed the knife.

" 'Dog!' she sneered, as she flung me into the snow. 'Swine!' And then she laughed till the silence cracked, and went back to her dead.

"As I say, once she passed the knife, and twice; but she was weak with hunger, and it was not meant that I should die. Yet was I minded to stay in that place, and to close my eyes in the last long sleep with those whose lives had crossed with mine and led my feet on unknown trails. But there lay a debt upon me which would not let me rest.

"And the way was long, the cold bitter, and there was little grub. The Pellys had found no moose, and had robbed my cache. And so had the three white men; but they lay thin and dead in their cabin as I passed. After that I do not remember, till I came here, and found food and fire,—much fire."

As he finished, he crouched closely, even jealously, over the stove. For a long while the slush-lamp shadows played tragedies upon the wall.

"But Unga!" cried Prince, the vision still strong upon him.

"Unga? She would not eat of the ptarmigan. She lay with her arms about his neck, her face deep in his yellow hair. I drew the fire close, that she might not feel the frost; but she crept to the other side. And I built a fire there; yet it was little good, for she would not eat. And in this manner they still lie up there in the snow."

"And you?" asked Malemute Kid.

"I do not know; but Akatan is small, and I have little wish to go back and live on the edge of the world. Yet is there small use in life. I can go to Constantine, and he will put irons upon me, and one day they will tie a piece of rope, so, and I will sleep good. Yet—no; I do not know."

"But, Kid," protested Prince, "this is murder!"

"Hush!" commanded Malemute Kid. "There be things greater than our wisdom, beyond our justice. The right and the wrong of this we cannot say, and it is not for us to judge."

Naass drew yet closer to the fire. There was a great silence, and in each man's eyes many pictures came and went.

SEMPER IDEM

Doctor Bicknell was in a remarkably gracious mood. Through a minor accident, a slight bit of carelessness, that was all, a man who might have pulled through had died the preceding night. Though it had been only a sailorman, one of the innumerable unwashed, the steward of the receiving hospital had been on the anxious seat all the morning. It was not that the man had died that gave him discomfort, he knew the Doctor too well for that, but his distress lay in the fact that the operation had been done so well. One of the most delicate in surgery, it had been as successful as it was clever and audacious. All had then depended upon the treatment, the nurses, the steward. And the man had died. Nothing much, a bit of carelessness, yet enough to bring the professional wrath of Doctor Bicknell about his ears and to perturb the working of the staff and nurses for twenty-four hours to come.

But, as already stated, the Doctor was in a remarkably gracious mood. When informed by the steward, in fear and trembling, of the man's unexpected take-off, his lips did not so much as form one syllable of censure; nay, they were so pursed that snatches of rag-time floated softly from them, to be broken only by a pleasant query after the health of the other's eldest-born. The steward, deeming it impossible that he could have caught the gist of the case, repeated it.

"Yes, yes," Doctor Bicknell said impatiently; "I understand. But how about Semper Idem? Is he ready to leave?"

"Yes. They're helping him dress now," the steward answered, passing on to the round of his duties, content that peace still reigned within the iodine-saturated walls.

It was Semper Idem's recovery which had so fully compensated Doctor Bicknell for the loss of the sailorman. Lives were to him as nothing, the unpleasant but inevitable incidents of the profession, but cases, ah, cases were everything. People who knew him were prone to brand him a butcher, but his colleagues were at one in the belief that a bolder and yet a more capable man never stood over the table. He was not an imaginative man. He did not possess, and hence had no tolerance for, emotion. His nature was accurate, precise, scientific. Men were to him no more than pawns, without individuality or personal value. But as cases it was different. The more broken a man was, the more precarious his grip on life, the greater his significance in the eyes of Doctor Bicknell. He would as readily forsake a poet laureate suffering from a common accident for a nameless, mangled vagrant who defied every law of life by refusing to die, as would a child forsake a Punch and Judy for a circus.

So it had been in the case of Semper Idem. The mystery of the man had not appealed to him, nor had his silence and the veiled romance which the yellow reporters had so sensationally and so fruitlessly exploited in divers Sunday editions. But Semper Idem's throat had been cut. That was the point. That was where his interest had centred. Cut from ear to ear, and not one surgeon in a thousand to give a snap of the fingers for his chance of recovery. But, thanks to the swift municipal ambulance service and to Doctor Bicknell, he had been dragged back into the world he had sought to leave. The Doctor's co-workers had shaken their heads when the case was brought in. Impossible, they said. Throat, windpipe, jugular, all but actually severed, and the loss of blood frightful. As it was such a foregone conclusion, Doctor Bicknell had employed methods and done things which made them, even in their professional capacities, to shudder. And lo! the man had recovered.

So, on this morning that Semper Idem was to leave the hospital, hale and hearty, Doctor Bicknell's geniality was in nowise disturbed by the steward's report, and he proceeded cheerfully to bring order out of the chaos of a child's body which had been ground and crunched beneath the wheels of an electric car.

As many will remember, the case of Semper Idem aroused a vast deal of unseemly yet highly natural curiosity. He had been found in a slum lodging, with throat cut as aforementioned, and blood dripping down upon the inmates of the room below and disturbing their festivities. He had evidently done the deed standing, with head bowed forward that he might gaze his last upon a photograph which stood on the table propped against a candlestick. It was this attitude which had made it possible for Doctor Bicknell to save him. So terrific had been the sweep of the razor that had he had his head thrown back, as he should have done to have accomplished the act properly, with his neck stretched and the elastic vascular walls distended, he would have of a certainty well nigh decapitated himself.

At the hospital, during all the time he travelled the repugnant road back to life, not a word had left his lips. Nor could anything be learned of him by the sleuths detailed by the chief of police. Nobody knew him, nor had ever seen or heard of him before. He was strictly, uniquely, of the present. His clothes and surroundings were those of the lowest laborer, his hands the hands of a gentleman. But not a shred of writing was discovered, nothing, save in one particular, which would serve to indicate his past or his position in life.

And that one particular was the photograph. If it were at all a likeness, the woman who gazed frankly out upon the onlooker from the card-mount must have been a striking creature indeed. It was an amateur production, for the detectives were baffled in that no professional photographer's signature or studio was appended. Across a corner of the mount, in delicate feminine tracery, was written: "*Semper idem; semper fidelis.*" And she looked it. As many recollect, it was a face one could never forget. Clever half-tones, remarkably like, were published in all the leading papers at the time; but such procedure gave rise to nothing but the uncontrollable public curiosity and interminable copy to the space-writers.

For want of a better name, the rescued suicide was known to the hospital attendants, and to the world, as Semper Idem. And Semper Idem he remained. Reporters, detectives, and nurses gave him up in despair. Not one word could he be persuaded to utter; yet the flitting conscious light of his eyes showed that his ears heard and his brain grasped every question put to him.

But this mystery and romance played no part in Doctor Bicknell's interest when he paused in the office to have a parting word with his patient. He, the Doctor, had performed a prodigy in the matter of this man, done what was virtually unprecedented in the annals of surgery. He did not care who or what the man was, and it was highly improbable that he should ever see him again; but, like the artist gazing upon a finished creation, he wished to look for the last time upon the work of his hand and brain.

Semper Idem still remained mute. He seemed anxious to be gone. Not a word could the Doctor extract from him, and little the Doctor cared. He examined the throat of the convalescent carefully, idling over the hideous scar with the lingering, half-caressing fondness of a parent. It was not a particularly pleasing sight. An angry line circled the throat,—for all the world as though the man had just escaped the hangman's noose, and,—disappearing below the ear on either side, had the appearance of completing the fiery periphery at the nape of the neck.

Maintaining his dogged silence, yielding to the other's examination in much the manner of a leashed lion, Semper Idem betrayed only his desire to drop from out of the public eye.

"Well, I'll not keep you," Doctor Bicknell finally said, laying a hand on the man's shoulder and stealing a last glance at his own handiwork. "But let me give you a bit of advice. Next time you try it on, hold your chin up, so. Don't snuggle it down and butcher yourself like a cow. Neatness and despatch, you know. Neatness and despatch."

Semper Idem's eyes flashed in token that he heard, and a moment later the hospital door swung to on his heel.

It was a busy day for Doctor Bicknell, and the afternoon was well along when he lighted a cigar preparatory to leaving the table upon which it seemed the sufferers almost clamored to be laid. But the last one, an old rag-picker with a broken shoulder-blade, had been disposed of, and the first fragrant smoke wreaths had begun to curl about his head, when the gong of a hurrying ambulance came through the open window from the street, followed by the inevitable entry of the stretcher with its ghastly freight.

"Lay it on the table," the Doctor directed, turning for a moment to place his cigar in safety. "What is it?"

"Suicide—throat cut," responded one of the stretcher bearers. "Down on Morgan Alley. Little hope, I think, sir. He's 'most gone."

"Eh? Well, I'll give him a look, anyway." He leaned over the man at the moment when the quick made its last faint flutter and succumbed.

"It's Semper Idem come back again," the steward said.

"Ay," replied Doctor Bicknell, "and gone again. No bungling this time. Properly done, upon my life, sir, properly done. Took my advice to the letter. I'm not required here. Take it along to the morgue."

Doctor Bicknell secured his cigar and relighted it. "That," he said between the puffs, looking at the steward, "that evens up for the one you lost last night. We're quits now."

THE LAW OF LIFE

Old Koskoosh listened greedily. Though his sight had long since faded, his hearing was still acute, and the slightest sound penetrated to the glimmering intelligence which yet abode behind the withered forehead, but which no longer gazed forth upon the things of the world. Ah! that was Sit-cum-to-ha, shrilly anathematizing the dogs as she cuffed and beat them into the harnesses. Sit-cum-to-ha was his daughter's daughter, but she was too busy to waste a thought upon her broken grandfather, sitting alone there in the snow, forlorn and helpless. Camp must be broken. The long trail waited while the short day refused to linger. Life called her, and the duties of life, not death. And he was very close to death now.

The thought made the old man panicky for the moment, and he stretched forth a palsied hand which wandered tremblingly over the small heap of dry wood beside him. Reassured that it was indeed there, his hand returned to the shelter of his mangy furs, and he again fell to listening. The sulky crackling of half-frozen hides told him that the chief's moose-skin lodge had been struck, and even then was being rammed and jammed into portable compass. The chief was his son, stalwart and strong, head man of the tribesmen, and a mighty hunter. As the women toiled with the camp luggage, his voice rose, chiding them for their slowness. Old Koskoosh strained his ears. It was the last time he would hear that voice. There went Geehow's lodge! And Tusken's! Seven, eight, nine; only the shaman's could be still standing. There! They were at work upon it now. He could hear the shaman grunt as he piled it on the sled. A child whimpered, and a woman soothed it with soft, crooning gutturals. Little Koo-tee, the old man thought, a fretful child, and not overstrong. It would die soon, perhaps, and they would burn a hole through the frozen tundra and pile rocks above to keep the wolverines away. Well, what did it matter? A few years at best, and as many an empty belly as a full one. And in the end, Death waited, ever-hungry and hungriest of them all.

What was that? Oh, the men lashing the sleds and drawing tight the thongs. He listened, who would listen no more. The whip-lashes snarled and bit among the dogs. Hear them whine! How they hated the work and the trail! They were off! Sled after sled churned slowly away into the silence. They were gone. They had passed out of his life, and he faced the last bitter hour alone. No. The snow crunched beneath a moccasin; a man stood beside him; upon his head a hand rested gently. His son was good to do this thing. He remembered other old men whose sons had not waited after the tribe. But his son had. He wandered away into the past, till the young man's voice brought him back.

"Is it well with you?" he asked.

And the old man answered, "It is well."

"There be wood beside you," the younger man continued, "and the fire burns bright. The morning is gray, and the cold has broken. It will snow presently. Even now is it snowing."

"Ay, even now is it snowing."

"The tribesmen hurry. Their bales are heavy, and their bellies flat with lack of feasting. The trail is long and they travel fast. I go now. It is well?"

"It is well. I am as a last year's leaf, clinging lightly to the stem. The first breath that blows, and I fall. My voice is become like an old woman's. My eyes no longer show me the way of my feet, and my feet are heavy, and I am tired. It is well."

He bowed his head in content till the last noise of the complaining snow had died away, and he knew his son was beyond recall. Then his hand crept out in haste to the wood. It alone stood between him and the eternity that yawned in upon him. At last the measure of his life was a handful of fagots. One by one they would go to feed the fire, and just so, step by step, death would creep upon him. When the last stick had surrendered up its heat, the frost would begin to gather strength. First his feet would yield, then his hands; and the numbness would travel, slowly, from the extremities to the body. His head would fall forward upon his knees, and he would rest. It was easy. All men must die.

He did not complain. It was the way of life, and it was just. He had been born close to the earth, close to the earth had he lived, and the law thereof was not new to him. It was the law of all flesh. Nature was not kindly to the flesh. She had no concern for that concrete thing called the individual. Her interest lay in the species, the race. This was the deepest abstraction old Koskoosh's barbaric mind was capable of, but he grasped it firmly. He saw it exemplified in all life. The rise of the sap, the bursting greenness of the willow bud, the fall of the yellow leaf—in this alone was told the whole history. But one task did Nature set the individual. Did he not perform it, he died. Did he perform it, it was all the same, he died. Nature did not care; there were plenty who were obedient, and it was only the obedience in this matter, not the obedient, which lived and lived always. The tribe of Koskoosh was very old. The old men he had known when a boy, had known old men before them. Therefore it was true that the tribe lived, that it stood for the obedience of all its members, way down into the forgotten past, whose very resting-places were unremembered. They did not count; they were episodes. They had passed away like clouds from a summer sky. He also was an episode, and would pass away. Nature did not care. To life she set one task, gave one law. To perpetuate was the task of life, its law was death. A maiden was a good creature to look upon, full-breasted and strong, with spring to her step and light in her eyes. But her task was yet before her. The light in her eyes brightened, her step quickened, she was now bold with the young men, now timid, and she gave them of her own unrest. And ever she grew fairer and yet fairer to look upon, till some hunter, able no longer to withhold himself, took her to his lodge to cook and toil for him and to become the mother of his children. And with the coming of her offspring her looks left her. Her limbs dragged and shuffled, her eyes dimmed and bleared, and only the little children found joy against the withered cheek of the old squaw by the fire. Her task was done. But a little while, on the first pinch of famine or the first long trail, and she would be left, even as he had been left, in the snow, with a little pile of wood. Such was the law.

He placed a stick carefully upon the fire and resumed his meditations. It was the same everywhere, with all things. The mosquitoes vanished with the first frost. The little tree-squirrel crawled away to die. When age settled upon the rabbit it became slow and heavy, and could no longer outfoot its enemies. Even the big bald-face grew clumsy and blind and quarrelsome, in the end to be dragged down by a handful of yelping huskies. He remembered how he had abandoned his own father on an upper reach of the Klondike one winter, the winter before the missionary came with his talk-books and his box of medicines. Many a time had Koskoosh smacked his lips over the recollection of that box, though now his mouth refused to moisten. The "painkiller" had been especially good. But the missionary was a bother after all, for he brought no meat into the camp, and he ate heartily, and the hunters grumbled. But he chilled his lungs on the divide by the Mayo, and the dogs afterwards nosed the stones away and fought over his bones.

Koskoosh placed another stick on the fire and harked back deeper into the past. There was the time of the Great Famine, when the old men crouched empty-bellied to the fire, and let fall from their lips dim traditions of the ancient day when the Yukon ran wide open for three winters, and then lay frozen for three summers. He had lost his mother in that famine. In the summer the salmon run had failed, and the tribe looked forward to the winter and the coming of the caribou. Then the winter came, but with it there were no caribou. Never had the like been known, not even in the lives of the old men. But the caribou did not come, and it was the seventh year, and the rabbits had not replenished, and the dogs were naught but bundles of bones. And through the long darkness the children wailed and died, and the women, and the old men; and not one in ten of the tribe lived to meet the sun when it came back in the spring. That *was* a famine!

But he had seen times of plenty, too, when the meat spoiled on their hands, and the dogs were fat and worthless with overeating—times when they let the game go unkilled, and the women were fertile, and the lodges were cluttered with sprawling men-children and women-children. Then it was the men became high-stomached, and revived ancient quarrels, and crossed the divides to the south to kill the Pellys, and to the west that they might sit by the dead fires of the Tananas. He remembered, when a boy, during a time of plenty, when he saw a moose pulled down by the wolves. Zing-ha lay with him in the snow and watched—Zing-ha, who later became the craftiest of hunters, and who, in the end, fell through an air-hole on the Yukon. They found him, a month afterward, just as he had crawled halfway out and frozen stiff to the ice.

But the moose. Zing-ha and he had gone out that day to play at hunting after the manner of their fathers. On the bed of the creek they struck the fresh track of a moose, and with it the tracks of many wolves. "An old one," Zing-ha, who was quicker at reading the sign, said—"an old one who cannot keep up with the herd. The wolves have cut him out from his brothers, and they will never leave him." And it was so. It was their way. By day and by night, never resting, snarling on his heels, snapping at his nose, they would stay by him to the end. How Zing-ha and he felt the blood-lust quicken! The finish would be a sight to see!

Eager-footed, they took the trail, and even he, Koskoosh, slow of sight and an unversed tracker, could have followed it blind, it was so wide. Hot were they on the heels of the chase, reading the grim tragedy, fresh-written, at every step. Now they came to where the moose had made a stand. Thrice the length of a grown man's body, in every direction, had the snow been stamped about and uptossed. In the midst were

the deep impressions of the splay-hoofed game, and all about, everywhere, were the lighter footmarks of the wolves. Some, while their
brothers harried the kill, had lain to one side and rested. The full-
stretched impress of their bodies in the snow was as perfect as though
made the moment before. One wolf had been caught in a wild lunge of
the maddened victim and trampled to death. A few bones, well picked,
bore witness.

Again, they ceased the uplift of their snowshoes at a second stand.
Here the great animal had fought desperately. Twice had he been
dragged down, as the snow attested, and twice had he shaken his assailants clear and gained footing once more. He had done his task long
since, but none the less was life dear to him. Zing-ha said it was a
strange thing, a moose once down to get free again; but this one certainly had. The shaman would see signs and wonders in this when they
told him.

And yet again, they come to where the moose had made to mount
the bank and gain the timber. But his foes had laid on from behind, till
he reared and fell back upon them, crushing two deep into the snow. It
was plain the kill was at hand, for their brothers had left them untouched. Two more stands were hurried past, brief in time-length and
very close together. The trail was red now, and the clean stride of the
great beast had grown short and slovenly. Then they heard the first
sounds of the battle—not the full-throated chorus of the chase, but the
short, snappy bark which spoke of close quarters and teeth to flesh.
Crawling up the wind, Zing-ha bellied it through the snow, and with
him crept he, Koskoosh, who was to be chief of the tribesmen in the
years to come. Together they shoved aside the under branches of a
young spruce and peered forth. It was the end they saw.

The picture, like all of youth's impressions, was still strong with him,
and his dim eyes watched the end played out as vividly as in that far-
off time. Koskoosh marvelled at this, for in the days which followed,
when he was a leader of men and a head of councillors, he had done
great deeds and made his name a curse in the mouths of the Pellys, to
say naught of the strange white man he had killed, knife to knife, in
open fight.

For long he pondered on the days of his youth, till the fire died down
and the frost bit deeper. He replenished it with two sticks this time, and
gauged his grip on life by what remained. If Sit-cum-to-ha had only
remembered her grandfather, and gathered a larger armful, his hours
would have been longer. It would have been easy. But she was ever a
careless child, and honored not her ancestors from the time the Beaver,
son of the son of Zing-ha, first cast eyes upon her. Well, what mattered

it? Had he not done likewise in his own quick youth? For a while he listened to the silence. Perhaps the heart of his son might soften, and he would come back with the dogs to take his old father on with the tribe to where the caribou ran thick and the fat hung heavy upon them.

He strained his ears, his restless brain for the moment stilled. Not a stir, nothing. He alone took breath in the midst of the great silence. It was very lonely. Hark! What was that? A chill passed over his body. The familiar, long-drawn howl broke the void, and it was close at hand. Then on his darkened eyes was projected the vision of the moose—the old bull moose—the torn flanks and bloody sides, the riddled mane, and the great branching horns, down low and tossing to the last. He saw the flashing forms of gray, the gleaming eyes, the lolling tongues, the slavered fangs. And he saw the inexorable circle close in till it became a dark point in the midst of the stamped snow.

A cold muzzle thrust against his cheek, and at its touch his soul leaped back to the present. His hand shot into the fire and dragged out a burning faggot. Overcome for the nonce by his hereditary fear of man, the brute retreated, raising a prolonged call to his brothers; and greedily they answered, till a ring of crouching, jaw-slobbered gray was stretched round about. The old man listened to the drawing in of this circle. He waved his brand wildly, and sniffs turned to snarls; but the panting brutes refused to scatter. Now one wormed his chest forward, dragging his haunches after, now a second, now a third; but never a one drew back. Why should he cling to life? he asked, and dropped the blazing stick into the snow. It sizzled and went out. The circle grunted uneasily, but held its own. Again he saw the last stand of the old bull moose, and Koskoosh dropped his head wearily upon his knees. What did it matter after all? Was it not the law of life?

A RELIC OF THE PLIOCENE

I wash my hands of him at the start. I cannot father his tales, nor will I be responsible for them. I make these preliminary reservations, observe, as a guard upon my own integrity. I possess a certain definite position in a small way, also a wife; and for the good name of the community that honors my existence with its approval, and for the sake of her posterity and mine, I cannot take the chances I once did, nor foster probabilities with the careless improvidence of youth. So, I repeat, I wash my hands of him, this Nimrod, this mighty hunter, this homely, blue-eyed, freckle-faced Thomas Stevens.

Having been honest to myself, and to whatever prospective olive branches my wife may be pleased to tender me, I can now afford to be generous. I shall not criticise the tales told me by Thomas Stevens, and, further, I shall withhold my judgment. If it be asked why, I can only add that judgment I have none. Long have I pondered, weighed, and balanced, but never have my conclusions been twice the same—forsooth! because Thomas Stevens is a greater man than I. If he have told truths, well and good; if untruths, still well and good. For who can prove? or who disprove? I eliminate myself from the proposition, while those of little faith may do as I have done—go find the said Thomas Stevens, and discuss to his face the various matters which, if fortune serve, I shall relate. As to where he may be found? The directions are simple: anywhere between 53 north latitude and the Pole, on the one hand; and, on the other, the likeliest hunting grounds that lie between the east coast of Siberia and farthermost Labrador. That he is there, somewhere, within that clearly defined territory, I pledge the word of an honorable man whose expectations entail straight speaking and right living.

Thomas Stevens may have toyed prodigiously with truth, but when we first met (it were well to mark this point), he wandered into my camp when I thought myself a thousand miles beyond the outermost post of civilization. At the sight of his human face, the first in weary months, I could have sprung forward and folded him in my arms (and I am not by any means a demonstrative man); but to him his visit seemed the most casual thing under the sun. He just strolled into the light of my camp, passed the time of day after the custom of men on beaten trails, threw my snowshoes the one way and a couple of dogs the other, and so made room for himself by the fire. Said he'd just dropped in to borrow a pinch of soda and to see if I had any decent tobacco. He plucked forth an ancient pipe, loaded it with painstaking care, and, without as much as by your leave, whacked half the tobacco of my pouch into his. Yes, the stuff was fairly good. He sighed with the contentment of the just, and literally absorbed the smoke from the crisping yellow flakes, and it did my smoker's heart good to behold him.

Hunter? Trapper? Prospector? He shrugged his shoulders No; just sort of knocking round a bit. Had come up from the Great Slave some time since, and was thinking of trapsing over into the Yukon country. The Factor of Koshim had spoken about the discoveries on the Klondike, and he was of a mind to run over for a peep. I noticed that he spoke of the Klondike in the archaic vernacular, calling it the Reindeer River—a conceited custom that the Old Timers employ against the *che-cha-quas* and all tenderfeet in general. But he did it so naïvely and as such a matter of course, that there was no sting, and I forgave him. He also had it in view, he said, before he crossed the divide into the Yukon, to make a little run up Fort o' Good Hope way.

Now Fort o' Good Hope is a far journey to the north, over and beyond the Circle, in a place where the feet of few men have trod; and when a nondescript ragamuffin comes in out of the night, from nowhere in particular, to sit by one's fire and discourse on such in terms of "trapsing" and "a little run," it is fair time to rouse up and shake off the dream. Wherefore I looked about me; saw the fly, and, underneath, the pine boughs spread for the sleeping furs; saw the grub sacks, the camera, the frosty breaths of the dogs circling on the edge of the light; and, above, a great streamer of the aurora bridging the zenith from southeast to northwest. I shivered. There is a magic in the Northland night, that steals in on one like fevers from malarial marshes. You are clutched and downed before you are aware. Then I looked to the snowshoes, lying prone and crossed where he had flung them. Also I had an eye to my tobacco pouch. Half, at least, of its goodly store had vamosed. That settled it. Fancy had not tricked me after all.

Crazed with suffering, I thought, looking steadfastly at the man—one of those wild stampeders, strayed far from his bearings and wandering like a lost soul through great vastnesses and unknown deeps. Oh, well, let his moods slip on, until, mayhap, he gathers his tangled wits together. Who knows?—the mere sound of a fellow-creature's voice may bring all straight again.

So I led him on in talk, and soon I marvelled, for he talked of game and the ways thereof. He had killed the Siberian wolf of westernmost Alaska, and the chamois in the secret Rockies. He averred he knew the haunts where the last buffalo still roamed; that he had hung on the flanks of the caribou when they ran by the hundred thousand, and slept in the Great Barrens on the musk-ox's winter trail.

And I shifted my judgment accordingly (the first revision, but by no account the last), and deemed him a monumental effigy of truth. Why it was I know not, but the spirit moved me to repeat a tale told to me by a man who had dwelt in the land too long to know better. It was of the great bear that hugs the steep slopes of St. Elias, never descending to the levels of the gentler inclines. Now God so constituted this creature for its hillside habitat that the legs of one side are all of a foot longer than those of the other. This is mighty convenient, as will be readily admitted. So I hunted this rare beast in my own name, told it in the first person, present tense, painted the requisite locale, gave it the necessary garnishings and touches of verisimilitude, and looked to see the man stunned by the recital.

Not he. Had he doubted, I could have forgiven him. Had he objected, denying the dangers of such a hunt by virtue of the animal's inability to turn about and go the other way—had he done this, I say, I could have taken him by the hand for the true sportsman that he was. Not he. He sniffed, looked on me, and sniffed again; then gave my tobacco due praise, thrust one foot into my lap, and bade me examine the gear. It was a *mucluc* of the Innuit pattern, sewed together with sinew threads, and devoid of beads or furbelows. But it was the skin itself that was remarkable. In that it was all of half an inch thick, it reminded me of walrus-hide; but there the resemblance ceased, for no walrus ever bore so marvellous a growth of hair. On the side and ankles this hair was well-nigh worn away, what of friction with underbrush and snow; but around the top and down the more sheltered back it was coarse, dirty black, and very thick. I parted it with difficulty and looked beneath for the fine fur that is common with northern animals, but found it in this case to be absent. This, however, was compensated for by the length. Indeed, the tufts that had survived wear and tear measured all of seven or eight inches.

I looked up into the man's face, and he pulled his foot down and asked, "Find hide like that on your St. Elias bear?"

I shook my head. "Nor on any other creature of land or sea," I answered candidly. The thickness of it, and the length of the hair, puzzled me.

"That," he said, and said without the slightest hint of impressiveness, "that came from a mammoth."

"Nonsense!" I exclaimed, for I could not forbear the protest of my unbelief. "The mammoth, my dear sir, long ago vanished from the earth. We know it once existed by the fossil remains that we have unearthed, and by a frozen carcass that the Siberian sun saw fit to melt from out the bosom of a glacier; but we also know that no living specimen exists. Our explorers—"

At this word he broke in impatiently. "Your explorers? Pish! A weakly breed. Let us hear no more of them. But tell me, O man, what you may know of the mammoth and his ways."

Beyond contradiction, this was leading to a yarn; so I baited my hook by ransacking my memory for whatever data I possessed on the subject in hand. To begin with, I emphasized that the animal was prehistoric, and marshalled all my facts in support of this. I mentioned the Siberian sand bars that abounded with ancient mammoth bones; spoke of the large quantities of fossil ivory purchased from the Innuits by the Alaska Commercial Company; and acknowledged having myself mined six- and eight-foot tusks from the pay gravel of the Klondike creeks. "All fossils," I concluded, "found in the midst of débris deposited through countless ages."

"I remember when I was a kid," Thomas Stevens sniffed (he had a most confounded way of sniffing), "that I saw a petrified watermelon. Hence, though mistaken persons sometimes delude themselves into thinking that they are really raising or eating them, there are no such things as extant watermelons."

"But the question of food," I objected, ignoring his point, which was puerile and without bearing. "The soil must bring forth vegetable life in lavish abundance to support so monstrous creations. Nowhere in the North is the soil so prolific. Ergo, the mammoth cannot exist."

"I pardon your ignorance concerning many matters of this Northland, for you are a young man and have travelled little; but, at the same time, I am inclined to agree with you on one thing. The mammoth no longer exists. How do I know? I killed the last one with my own right arm."

Thus spake Nimrod, the Mighty Hunter. I threw a stick of firewood at the dogs and bade them quit their unholy howling, and waited. Undoubtedly this liar of singular felicity would open his mouth and requite me for my St. Elias bear.

"It was this way," he at last began, after the appropriate silence had intervened. "I was in camp one day—"

"Where?" I interrupted.

He waved his hand vaguely in the direction of the northeast, where stretched a terra incognita into which vastness few men have strayed and fewer emerged. "I was in camp one day with Klooch. Klooch was as handsome a little *kamooks* as ever whined betwixt the traces or shoved nose into a camp kettle. Her father was a full-blood Malemute from Russian Pastilik on Bering Sea, and I bred her, and with understanding, out of a clean-legged bitch of the Hudson Bay stock. I tell you, O man, she was a corker combination. And now, on this day I have in mind, she was brought to pup through a pure wild wolf of the woods—gray, and long of limb, with big lungs and no end of staying powers. Say! Was there ever the like? It was a new breed of dog I had started, and I could look forward to big things.

"As I have said, she was brought neatly to pup, and safely delivered. I was squatting on my hams over the litter—seven sturdy, blind little beggars—when from behind came a bray of trumpets and crash of brass. There was a rush, like the wind-squall that kicks the heels of the rain, and I was midway to my feet when knocked flat on my face. At the same instant I heard Klooch sigh, very much as a man does when you've planted your fist in his belly. You can stake your sack I lay quiet, but I twisted my head around and saw a huge bulk swaying above me. Then the blue sky flashed into view and I got to my feet. A hairy mountain of flesh was just disappearing in the underbrush on the edge of the open. I caught a rear-end glimpse, with a stiff tail, as big in girth as my body, standing out straight behind. The next second only a tremendous hole remained in the thicket, though I could still hear the sounds as of a tornado dying quickly away, underbrush ripping and tearing, and trees snapping and crashing.

"I cast about for my rifle. It had been lying on the ground with the muzzle against a log; but now the stock was smashed, the barrel out of line, and the working-gear in a thousand bits. Then I looked for the slut, and—and what do you suppose?"

I shook my head.

"May my soul burn in a thousand hells if there was anything left of her! Klooch, the seven sturdy, blind little beggars—gone, all gone. Where she had stretched was a slimy, bloody depression in the soft earth, all of a yard in diameter, and around the edges a few scattered hairs."

I measured three feet on the snow, threw about it a circle, and glanced at Nimrod.

"The beast was thirty long and twenty high," he answered, "and its tusks scaled over six times three feet. I couldn't believe, myself, at the time, for all that it had just happened. But if my senses had played me, there was the broken gun and the hole in the brush. And there was— or, rather, there was not—Klooch and the pups. O man, it makes me hot all over now when I think of it. Klooch! Another Eve! The mother of a new race! And a rampaging, ranting, old bull mammoth, like a second flood, wiping them, root and branch, off the face of the earth! Do you wonder that the blood-soaked earth cried out to high God? Or that I grabbed the hand-axe and took the trail?"

"The hand-axe?" I exclaimed, startled out of myself by the picture. "The hand-axe, and a big bull mammoth, thirty feet long, twenty feet—"

Nimrod joined me in my merriment, chuckling gleefully. "Wouldn't it kill you?" he cried. "Wasn't it a beaver's dream? Many's the time I've laughed about it since, but at the time it was no laughing matter, I was that danged mad, what of the gun and Klooch. Think of it, O man! A brand-new, unclassified, uncopyrighted breed, and wiped out before ever it opened its eyes or took out its intention papers! Well, so be it. Life's full of disappointments, and rightly so. Meat is best after a famine, and a bed soft after a hard trail.

"As I was saying, I took out after the beast with the hand-axe, and hung to its heels down the valley; but when he circled back toward the head, I was left winded at the lower end. Speaking of grub, I might as well stop long enough to explain a couple of points. Up thereabouts, in the midst of the mountains, is an almighty curious formation. There is no end of little valleys, each like the other much as peas in a pod, and all neatly tucked away with straight, rocky walls rising on all sides. And at the lower ends are always small openings where the drainage or glaciers must have broken out. The only way in is through these mouths, and they are all small, and some smaller than others. As to grub—you've slushed around on the rain-soaked islands of the Alaskan coast down Sitka way, most likely, seeing as you're a traveller. And you know how stuff grows there—big, and juicy, and jungly. Well, that's the way it was with those valleys. Thick, rich soil, with ferns and grasses and such things in patches higher than your head. Rain three days out of four during the summer months; and food in them for a thousand mammoths, to say nothing of small game for man.

"But to get back. Down at the lower end of the valley I got winded and gave over. I began to speculate, for when my wind left me my dander got hotter and hotter, and I knew I'd never know peace of mind till I dined on roasted mammoth-foot. And I knew, also, that that stood for *skookum mamook pukapuk*—excuse Chinook, I mean there was a big fight coming. Now the mouth of my valley was very narrow, and the walls steep. High up on one side was one of those big pivot rocks, or balancing rocks, as some call them, weighing all of a couple of hundred tons. Just the thing. I hit back for camp, keeping an eye open so the bull couldn't slip past, and got my ammunition. It wasn't worth anything with the rifle smashed; so I opened the shells, planted the powder under the rock, and touched it off with slow fuse. Wasn't much of a charge, but the old boulder tilted up lazily and dropped down into place, with just space enough to let the creek drain nicely. Now I had him."

"But how did you have him?" I queried. "Who ever heard of a man killing a mammoth with a hand-axe? And, for that matter, with anything else?"

"O man, have I not told you I was mad?" Nimrod replied, with a slight manifestation of sensitiveness. "Mad clean through, what of Klooch and the gun? Also, was I not a hunter? And was this not new and most unusual game? A hand-axe? Pish! I did not need it. Listen, and you shall hear of a hunt, such as might have happened in the youth of the world when caveman rounded up the kill with hand-axe of stone. Such would have served me as well. Now is it not a fact that man can outwalk the dog or horse? That he can wear them out with the intelligence of his endurance?"

I nodded.

"Well?"

The light broke in on me, and I bade him continue.

"My valley was perhaps five miles around. The mouth was closed. There was no way to get out. A timid beast was that bull mammoth, and I had him at my mercy. I got on his heels again, hollered like a fiend, pelted him with cobbles, and raced him around the valley three times before I knocked off for supper. Don't you see? A race-course! A man and a mammoth! A hippodrome, with sun, moon, and stars to referee!

"It took me two months to do it, but I did it. And that's no beaver dream. Round and round I ran him, me travelling on the inner circle, eating jerked meat and salmon berries on the run, and snatching winks of sleep between. Of course, he'd get desperate at times and turn. Then I'd head for soft ground where the creek spread out, and lay anathema upon him and his ancestry, and dare him to come on. But he was too wise to bog in a mud puddle. Once he pinned me in against the walls, and I crawled back into a deep crevice and waited. Whenever he felt for me with his trunk, I'd belt him with the hand-axe till he pulled out, shrieking fit to split my ear drums, he was that mad. He knew he had me and didn't have me, and it near drove him wild. But he was no man's fool. He knew he was safe as long as I stayed in the crevice, and he made up his mind to keep me there. And he was dead right, only he hadn't figured on the commissary. There was neither grub nor water around that spot, so on the face of it he couldn't keep up the siege. He'd stand before the opening for hours, keeping an eye on me and flapping mosquitoes away with his big blanket ears. Then the thirst would come on him and he'd ramp round and roar till the earth shook, calling me every name he could lay tongue to. This was to frighten me, of course; and when he thought I was sufficiently impressed, he'd back away softly and try to make a sneak for the creek. Sometimes I'd let him get almost there—only a couple of hundred yards away it was— when out I'd pop and back he'd come, lumbering along like the old landslide he was. After I'd done this a few times, and he'd figured it out, he changed his tactics. Grasped the time element, you see. Without a word of warning, away he'd go, tearing for the water like mad, scheming to get there and back before I ran away. Finally, after cursing me most horribly, he raised the seige and deliberately stalked off to the water hole.

"That was the only time he penned me,—three days of it,—but after that the hippodrome never stopped. Round, and round, and round, like a six days' go-as-I-please, for he never pleased. My clothes went to rags and tatters, but I never stopped to mend, till at last I ran naked as a son of earth, with nothing but the old hand-axe in one hand and a cobble in the other. In fact, I never stopped, save for peeps of sleep in the crannies and ledges of the cliffs. As for the bull, he got perceptibly thinner and thinner—must have lost several tons at least—and as nervous as a schoolmarm on the wrong side of matrimony. When I'd come up with him and yell, or lam him with a rock at long range, he'd jump like a skittish colt and tremble all over. Then he'd pull out on the run, tail and trunk waving stiff, head over one shoulder and wicked eyes blazing, and the way he'd swear at me was something dreadful. A most immoral beast he was, a murderer, and a blasphemer.

"But toward the end he quit all this, and fell to whimpering and crying like a baby. His spirit broke and he became a quivering jelly-mountain of misery. He'd get attacks of palpitation of the heart, and stagger around like a drunken man, and fall down and bark his shins. And then he'd cry, but always on the run. O man, the gods themselves would have wept with him, and you yourself or any other man. It was pitiful, and there was so much of it, but I only hardened my heart and hit up the pace. At last I wore him clean out, and he lay down, broken-winded, broken-hearted, hungry, and thirsty. When I found he wouldn't budge, I hamstrung him, and spent the better part of the day wading into him with the hand-axe, he a sniffing and sobbing till I worked in far enough to shut him off. Thirty feet long he was, and twenty high, and a man could sling a hammock between his tusks and sleep comfortably. Barring the fact that I had run most of the juices out of him, he was fair eating, and his four feet, alone, roasted whole, would have lasted a man a twelvemonth. I spent the winter there myself."

"And where is this valley?" I asked.

He waved his hand in the direction of the northeast, and said: "Your tobacco is very good. I carry a fair share of it in my pouch, but I shall carry the recollection of it until I die. In token of my appreciation, and in return for the moccasins on your own feet, I will present to you these *muclucs*. They commemorate Klooch and the seven blind little beggars. They are also souvenirs of an unparalleled event in history, namely, the destruction of the oldest breed of animal on earth, and the youngest. And their chief virtue lies in that they will never wear out."

Having effected the exchange, he knocked the ashes from his pipe, gripped my hand good night, and wandered off through the snow. Concerning this tale, for which I have already disclaimed responsibility, I would recommend those of little faith to make a visit to the Smithsonian Institute. If they bring the requisite credentials and do not come in vacation time, they will undoubtedly gain an audience with Professor Dolvidson. The *muclucs* are in his possession, and he will verify, not the manner in which they were obtained, but the material of which they are composed. When he states that they are made from the skin of the mammoth, the scientific world accepts his verdict. What more would you have?

NAM-BOK
THE UNVERACIOUS

"A Bidarka, is it not so? Look! a bidarka, and one man who drives clumsily with a paddle!"

Old Bask-Wah-Wan rose to her knees, trembling with weakness and eagerness, and gazed out over the sea.

"Nam-Bok was ever clumsy at the paddle," she maundered reminiscently, shading the sun from her eyes and staring across the silver-spilled water. "Nam-Bok was ever clumsy. I remember . . ."

But the women and children laughed loudly, and there was a gentle mockery in their laughter, and her voice dwindled till her lips moved without sound.

Koogah lifted his grizzled head from his bone-carving and followed the path of her eyes. Except when wide yaws took it off its course, a bidarka was heading in for the beach. Its occupant was paddling with more strength than dexterity, and made his approach along the zigzag line of most resistance. Koogah's head dropped to his work again, and on the ivory tusk between his knees he scratched the dorsal fin of a fish the like of which never swam in the sea.

"It is doubtless the man from the next village," he said finally, "come to consult with me about the marking of things on bone. And the man is a clumsy man. He will never know how."

"It is Nam-Bok," old Bask-Wah-Wan repeated. "Should I not know my son?" she demanded shrilly. "I say, and I say again, it is Nam-Bok."

"And so thou hast said these many summers," one of the women chided softly. "Ever when the ice passed out of the sea hast thou sat and watched through the long day, saying at each chance canoe, 'This is Nam-Bok.' Nam-Bok is dead, O Bask-Wah-Wan, and the dead do not come back. It cannot be that the dead come back."

"Nam-Bok!" the old woman cried, so loud and clear that the whole village was startled and looked at her.

She struggled to her feet and tottered down the sand. She stumbled over a baby lying in the sun, and the mother hushed its crying and hurled harsh words after the old woman, who took no notice. The children ran down the beach in advance of her, and as the man in the bidarka drew closer, nearly capsizing with one of his ill-directed strokes, the women followed. Koogah dropped his walrus tusk and went also, leaning heavily upon his staff, and after him loitered the men in twos and threes.

The bidarka turned broadside and the ripple of surf threatened to swamp it, only a naked boy ran into the water and pulled the bow high up on the sand. The man stood up and sent a questing glance along the line of villagers. A rainbow sweater, dirty and the worse for wear, clung loosely to his broad shoulders, and a red cotton handkerchief was knotted in sailor fashion about his throat. A fisherman's tam-o'-shanter on his close-clipped head, and dungaree trousers and heavy brogans, completed his outfit.

But he was none the less a striking personage to these simple fisherfolk of the great Yukon Delta, who, all their lives, had stared out on Bering Sea and in that time seen but two white men,—the census enumerator and a lost Jesuit priest. They were a poor people, with neither gold in the ground nor valuable furs in hand, so the whites had passed them afar. Also, the Yukon, through the thousands of years, had shoaled that portion of the sea with the detritus of Alaska till vessels grounded out of sight of land. So the sodden coast, with its long inside reaches and huge mud-land archipelagoes, was avoided by the ships of men, and the fisherfolk knew not that such things were.

Koogah, the Bone-Scratcher, retreated backward in sudden haste, tripping over his staff and falling to the ground. "Nam-Bok!" he cried, as he scrambled wildly for footing. "Nam-Bok, who was blown off to sea, come back!"

The men and women shrank away, and the children scuttled off between their legs. Only Opee-Kwan was brave, as befitted the head man of the village. He strode forward and gazed long and earnestly at the new-comer.

"It *is* Nam-Bok," he said at last, and at the conviction in his voice the women wailed apprehensively and drew farther away.

The lips of the stranger moved indecisively, and his brown throat writhed and wrestled with unspoken words.

"La la, it is Nam-Bok," Bask-Wah-Wan croaked, peering up into his face. "Ever did I say Nam-Bok would come back."

"Ay, it is Nam-Bok come back." This time it was Nam-Bok himself who spoke, putting a leg over the side of the bidarka and standing with one foot afloat and one ashore. Again his throat writhed and wrestled as he grappled after forgotten words. And when the words came forth they were strange of sound and a spluttering of the lips accompanied the gutturals. "Greeting, O brothers," he said, "brothers of old time before I went away with the off-shore wind."

He stepped out with both feet on the sand, and Opee-Kwan waved him back.

"Thou art dead, Nam-Bok," he said.

Nam-Bok laughed. "I am fat."

"Dead men are not fat," Opee-Kwan confessed. "Thou hast fared well, but it is strange. No man may mate with the off-shore wind and come back on the heels of the years."

"I have come back," Nam-Bok answered simply.

"Mayhap thou art a shadow, then, a passing shadow of the Nam-Bok that was. Shadows come back."

"I am hungry. Shadows do not eat."

But Opee-Kwan doubted, and brushed his hand across his brow in sore puzzlement. Nam-Bok was likewise puzzled, and as he looked up and down the line found no welcome in the eyes of the fisherfolk. The men and women whispered together. The children stole timidly back among their elders, and bristling dogs fawned up to him and sniffed suspiciously.

"I bore thee, Nam-Bok, and I gave thee suck when thou wast little," Bask-Wah-Wan whimpered, drawing closer; "and shadow though thou be, or no shadow, I will give thee to eat now."

Nam-Bok made to come to her, but a growl of fear and menace warned him back. He said something in a strange tongue which sounded like "Goddam," and added, "No shadow am I, but a man."

"Who may know concerning the things of mystery?" Opee-Kwan demanded, half of himself and half of his tribespeople. "We are, and in a breath we are not. If the man may become shadow, may not the shadow become man? Nam-Bok was, but is not. This we know, but we do not know if this be Nam-Bok or the shadow of Nam-Bok."

Nam-Bok cleared his throat and made answer. "In the old time long ago, thy father's father, Opee-Kwan, went away and came back on the heels of the years. Nor was a place by the fire denied him. It is said ..." He paused significantly, and they hung on his utterance. "It is said," he repeated, driving his point home with deliberation, "that Sip-sip, his *klooch*, bore him two sons after he came back."

"But he had no doings with the off-shore wind," Opee-Kwan retorted. "He went away into the heart of the land, and it is in the nature of things that a man may go on and on into the land."

"And likewise the sea. But that is neither here nor there. It is said . . . that thy father's father told strange tales of the things he saw."

"Ay, strange tales he told."

"I, too, have strange tales to tell," Nam-Bok stated insidiously. And, as they wavered, "And presents likewise."

He pulled from the bidarka a shawl, marvellous of texture and color, and flung it about his mother's shoulders. The women voiced a collective sigh of admiration, and old Bask-Wah-Wan ruffled the gay material and patted it and crooned in childish joy.

"He has tales to tell," Koogah muttered. "And presents," a woman seconded.

And Opee-Kwan knew that his people were eager, and further, he was aware himself of an itching curiosity concerning those untold tales. "The fishing has been good," he said judiciously, "and we have oil in plenty. So come, Nam-Bok, let us feast."

Two of the men hoisted the bidarka on their shoulders and carried it up to the fire. Nam-Bok walked by the side of Opee-Kwan, and the villagers followed after, save those of the women who lingered a moment to lay caressing fingers on the shawl.

There was little talk while the feast went on, though many and curious were the glances stolen at the son of Bask-Wah-Wan. This embarrassed him—not because he was modest of spirit, however, but for the fact that the stench of the seal-oil had robbed him of his appetite, and that he keenly desired to conceal his feelings on the subject.

"Eat; thou art hungry," Opee-Kwan commanded, and Nam-Bok shut both his eyes and shoved his fist into the big pot of putrid fish.

"La la, be not ashamed. The seal were many this year, and strong men are ever hungry." And Bask-Wah-Wan sopped a particularly offensive chunk of salmon into the oil and passed it fondly and dripping to her son.

In despair, when premonitory symptoms warned him that his stomach was not so strong as of old, he filled his pipe and struck up a smoke. The people fed on noisily and watched. Few of them could boast of intimate acquaintance with the precious weed, though now and again small quantities and abominable qualities were obtained in trade from the Eskimos to the northward. Koogah, sitting next to him, indicated that he was not averse to taking a draw, and between two mouthfuls, with the oil thick on his lips, sucked away at the amber stem. And thereupon Nam-Bok held his stomach with a shaky hand and declined the proffered return. Koogah could keep the pipe, he said, for he had intended so to honor him from the first. And the people licked their fingers and approved of his liberality.

Opee-Kwan rose to his feet. "And now, O Nam-Bok, the feast is ended, and we would listen concerning the strange things you have seen."

The fisherfolk applauded with their hands, and gathering about them their work, prepared to listen. The men were busy fashioning spears and carving on ivory, while the women scraped the fat from the hides of the hair seal and made them pliable or sewed muclucs with threads of sinew. Nam-Bok's eyes roved over the scene, but there was not the charm about it that his recollection had warranted him to expect. During the years of his wandering he had looked forward to just this scene, and now that it had come he was disappointed. It was a bare and meagre life, he deemed, and not to be compared to the one to which he had become used. Still, he would open their eyes a bit, and his own eyes sparkled at the thought.

"Brothers," he began, with the smug complacency of a man about to relate the big things he has done, "it was late summer of many summers back, with much such weather as this promises to be, when I went away. You all remember the day, when the gulls flew low, and the wind blew strong from the land, and I could not hold my bidarka against it. I tied the covering of the bidarka about me so that no water could get in, and all of the night I fought with the storm. And in the morning there was no land,—only the sea,—and the off-shore wind held me close in its arms and bore me along. Three such nights whitened into dawn and showed me no land, and the off-shore wind would not let me go.

"And when the fourth day came, I was as a madman. I could not dip my paddle for want of food; and my head went round and round, what of the thirst that was upon me. But the sea was no longer angry, and the soft south wind was blowing, and as I looked about me I saw a sight that made me think I was indeed mad."

Nam-Bok paused to pick away a sliver of salmon lodged between his teeth, and the men and women, with idle hands and heads craned forward, waited.

"It was a canoe, a big canoe. If all the canoes I have ever seen were made into one canoe, it would not be so large."

There were exclamations of doubt, and Koogah, whose years were many, shook his head.

"If each bidarka were as a grain of sand," Nam-Bok defiantly continued, "and if there were as many bidarkas as there be grains of sand in this beach, still would they not make so big a canoe as this I saw on the morning of the fourth day. It was a very big canoe, and it was called a *schooner*. I saw this thing of wonder, this great schooner, coming after me, and on it I saw men—"

"Hold, O Nam-Bok!" Opee-Kwan broke in. "What manner of men were they?—big men?"

"Nay, mere men like you and me."

"Did the big canoe come fast?"

"Ay."

"The sides were tall, the men short." Opee-Kwan stated the premises with conviction. "And did these men dip with long paddles?"

Nam-Bok grinned. "There were no paddles," he said.

Mouths remained open, and a long silence dropped down. Opee-Kwan borrowed Koogah's pipe for a couple of contemplative sucks. One of the younger women giggled nervously and drew upon herself angry eyes.

"There were no paddles?" Opee-Kwan asked softly, returning the pipe.

"The south wind was behind," Nam-Bok explained.

"But the wind-drift is slow."

"The schooner had wings—thus." He sketched a diagram of masts and sails in the sand, and the men crowded around and studied it. The wind was blowing briskly, and for more graphic elucidation he seized the corners of his mother's shawl and spread them out till it bellied like a sail. Bask-Wah-Wan scolded and struggled, but was blown down the beach for a score of feet and left breathless and stranded in a heap of driftwood. The men uttered sage grunts of comprehension, but Koogah suddenly tossed back his hoary head.

"Ho! Ho!" he laughed. "A foolish thing, this big canoe! A most foolish thing! The plaything of the wind! Wheresoever the wind goes, it goes too. No man who journeys therein may name the landing beach, for always he goes with the wind, and the wind goes everywhere, but no man knows where."

"It is so," Opee-Kwan supplemented gravely. "With the wind the going is easy, but against the wind a man striveth hard; and for that they had no paddles these men on the big canoe did not strive at all."

"Small need to strive," Nam-Bok cried angrily. "The schooner went likewise against the wind."

"And what said you made the sch—sch—schooner go?" Koogah asked, tripping craftily over the strange word.

"The wind," was the impatient response.

"Then the wind made the sch—sch—schooner go against the wind." Old Koogah dropped an open leer to Opee-Kwan, and, the laughter growing around him, continued: "The wind blows from the south and blows the schooner south. The wind blows against the wind. The wind blows one way and the other at the same time. It is very simple. We understand, Nam-Bok. We clearly understand."

"Thou art a fool!"

"Truth falls from thy lips," Koogah answered meekly. "I was over-long in understanding, and the thing was simple."

But Nam-Bok's face was dark, and he said rapid words which they had never heard before. Bone-scratching and skin-scraping were resumed, but he shut his lips tightly on the tongue that could not be believed.

"This sch—sch—schooner," Koogah imperturbably asked; "it was made of a big tree?"

"It was made of many trees," Nam-Bok snapped shortly. "It was very big."

He lapsed into sullen silence again, and Opee-Kwan nudged Koogah, who shook his head with slow amazement and murmured, "It is very strange."

Nam-Bok took the bait. "That is nothing," he said airily; "you should see the *steamer*. As the grain of sand is to the bidarka, as the bidarka is to the schooner, so the schooner is to the steamer. Further, the steamer is made of iron. It is all iron."

"Nay, nay, Nam-Bok," cried the head man; "how can that be? Always iron goes to the bottom. For behold, I received an iron knife in trade from the head man of the next village, and yesterday the iron knife slipped from my fingers and went down, down, into the sea. To all things there be law. Never was there one thing outside the law. This we know. And, moreover, we know that things of a kind have the one law, and that all iron has the one law. So unsay thy words, Nam-Bok, that we may yet honor thee."

"It is so," Nam-Bok persisted. "The steamer is all iron and does not sink."

"Nay, nay; this cannot be."

"With my own eyes I saw it."

"It is not in the nature of things."

"But tell me, Nam-Bok," Koogah interrupted, for fear the tale would go no farther, "tell me the manner of these men in finding their way across the sea when there is no land by which to steer."

"The sun points out the path."

"But how?"

"At midday the head man of the schooner takes a thing through which his eye looks at the sun, and then he makes the sun climb down out of the sky to the edge of the earth."

"Now this be evil medicine!" cried Opee-Kwan, aghast at the sacrilege. The men held up their hands in horror, and the women moaned. "This be evil medicine. It is not good to misdirect the great sun which drives away the night and gives us the seal, the salmon, and warm weather."

"What if it be evil medicine?" Nam-Bok demanded truculently. "I, too, have looked through the thing at the sun and made the sun climb down out of the sky."

Those who were nearest drew away from him hurriedly, and a woman covered the face of a child at her breast so that his eye might not fall upon it.

"But on the morning of the fourth day, O Nam-Bok," Koogah suggested; "on the morning of the fourth day when the sch—sch—schooner came after thee?"

"I had little strength left in me and could not run away. So I was taken on board and water was poured down my throat and good food given me. Twice, my brothers, you have seen a white man. These men were all white and as many as have I fingers and toes. And when I saw they were full of kindness, I took heart, and I resolved to bring away with me report of all that I saw. And they taught me the work they did, and gave me good food and a place to sleep.

"And day after day we went over the sea, and each day the head man drew the sun down out of the sky and made it tell where we were. And when the waves were kind, we hunted the fur seal and I marvelled much, for always did they fling the meat and the fat away and save only the skin."

Opee-Kwan's mouth was twitching violently, and he was about to make denunciation of such waste when Koogah kicked him to be still.

"After a weary time, when the sun was gone and the bite of the frost come into the air, the head man pointed the nose of the schooner south. South and east we travelled for days upon days, with never the land in sight, and we were near to the village from which hailed the men—"

"How did they know they were near?" Opee-Kwan, unable to contain himself longer, demanded. "There was no land to see."

Nam-Bok glowered on him wrathfully. "Did I not say the head man brought the sun down out of the sky?"

Koogah interposed, and Nam-Bok went on.

"As I say, when we were near to that village a great storm blew up, and in the night we were helpless and knew not where we were—"

"Thou hast just said the head man knew—"

"Oh, peace, Opee-Kwan! Thou art a fool and cannot understand. As I say, we were helpless in the night, when I heard, above the roar of the storm, the sound of the sea on the beach. And next we struck with a mighty crash and I was in the water, swimming. It was a rock-bound coast, with one patch of beach in many miles, and the law was that I should dig my hands into the sand and draw myself clear of the surf. The other men must have pounded against the rocks, for none of them came ashore but the head man, and him I knew only by the ring on his finger.

"When day came, there being nothing of the schooner, I turned my face to the land and journeyed into it that I might get food and look upon the faces of the people. And when I came to a house I was taken in and given to eat, for I had learned their speech, and the white men are ever kindly. And it was a house bigger than all the houses built by us and our fathers before us."

"It was a mighty house," Koogah said, masking his unbelief with wonder.

"And many trees went into the making of such a house," Opee-Kwan added, taking the cue.

"That is nothing." Nam-Bok shrugged his shoulders in belittling fashion. "As our houses are to that house, so that house was to the houses I was yet to see."

"And they are not big men?"

"Nay; mere men like you and me," Nam-Bok answered. "I had cut a stick that I might walk in comfort, and remembering that I was to bring report to you, my brothers, I cut a notch in the stick for each person who lived in that house. And I stayed there many days, and worked, for which they gave me *money*—a thing of which you know nothing, but which is very good.

"And one day I departed from that place to go farther into the land. And as I walked I met many people, and I cut smaller notches in the stick, that there might be room for all. Then I came upon a strange thing. On the ground before me was a bar of iron, as big in thickness as my arm, and a long step away was another bar of iron—"

"Then wert thou a rich man," Opee-Kwan asserted; "for iron be worth more than anything else in the world. It would have made many knives."

"Nay, it was not mine."

"It was a find, and a find be lawful."

"Not so; the white men had placed it there. And further, these bars were so long that no man could carry them away—so long that as far as I could see there was no end to them."

"Nam-Bok, that is very much iron," Opee-Kwan cautioned.

"Ay, it was hard to believe with my own eyes upon it; but I could not gainsay my eyes. And as I looked I heard . . ." He turned abruptly upon the head man. "Opee-Kwan, thou hast heard the sea-lion bellow in his anger. Make it plain in thy mind of as many sea-lions as there be waves to the sea, and make it plain that all these sea-lions be made into one sea-lion, and as that one sea-lion would bellow so bellowed the thing I heard."

The fisherfolk cried aloud in astonishment, and Opee-Kwan's jaw lowered and remained lowered.

"And in the distance I saw a monster like unto a thousand whales. It was one-eyed, and vomited smoke, and it snorted with exceeding loudness. I was afraid and ran with shaking legs along the path between the bars. But it came with the speed of the wind, this monster, and I leaped the iron bars with its breath hot on my face . . ."

Opee-Kwan gained control of his jaw again. "And—and then, O Nam-Bok?"

"Then it came by on the bars, and harmed me not; and when my legs could hold me up again it was gone from sight. And it is a very common thing in that country. Even the women and children are not afraid. Men make them to do work, these monsters."

"As we make our dogs do work?" Koogah asked, with sceptic twinkle in his eye.

"Ay, as we make our dogs do work."

"And how do they breed these—these things?" Opee-Kwan questioned.

"They breed not at all. Men fashion them cunningly of iron, and feed them with stone, and give them water to drink. The stone becomes fire, and the water becomes steam, and the steam of the water is the breath of their nostrils, and—"

"There, there, O Nam-Bok," Opee-Kwan interrupted. "Tell us of other wonders. We grow tired of this which we may not understand."

"You do not understand?" Nam-Bok asked despairingly.

"Nay, we do not understand," the men and women wailed back. "We cannot understand."

Nam-Bok thought of a combined harvester, and of the machines wherein visions of living men were to be seen, and of the machines from which came the voices of men, and he knew his people could never understand.

"Dare I say I rode this iron monster through the land?" he asked bitterly.

Opee-Kwan threw up his hands, palms outward, in open incredulity. "Say on; say anything. We listen."

"Then did I ride the iron monster, for which I gave money—"

"Thou saidst it was fed with stone."

"And likewise, thou fool, I said money was a thing of which you know nothing. As I say, I rode the monster through the land, and through many villages, until I came to a big village on a salt arm of the sea. And the houses shoved their roofs among the stars in the sky, and the clouds drifted by them, and everywhere was much smoke. And the roar of that village was like the roar of the sea in storm, and the people were so many that I flung away my stick and no longer remembered the notches upon it."

"Hadst thou made small notches," Koogah reproved, "thou mightst have brought report."

Nam-Bok whirled upon him in anger. "Had I made small notches! Listen, Koogah, thou scratcher of bone! If I had made small notches, neither the stick, nor twenty sticks, could have borne them—nay, not all the driftwood of all the beaches between this village and the next. And if all of you, the women and children as well, were twenty times as many, and if you had twenty hands each, and in each hand a stick and a knife, still the notches could not be cut for the people I saw, so many were they and so fast did they come and go."

"There cannot be so many people in all the world," Opee-Kwan objected, for he was stunned and his mind could not grasp such magnitude of numbers.

"What dost thou know of all the world and how large it is?" Nam-Bok demanded.

"But there cannot be so many people in one place."

"Who art thou to say what can be and what cannot be?"

"It stands to reason there cannot be so many people in one place. Their canoes would clutter the sea till there was no room. And they could empty the sea each day of its fish, and they would not all be fed."

"So it would seem," Nam-Bok made final answer; "yet it was so. With my own eyes I saw, and flung my stick away." He yawned heavily and rose to his feet. "I have paddled far. The day has been long, and I am tired. Now I will sleep, and to-morrow we will have further talk upon the things I have seen."

Bask-Wah-Wan, hobbling fearfully in advance, proud indeed, yet awed by her wonderful son, led him to her igloo and stowed him away among the greasy, ill-smelling furs. But the men lingered by the fire, and a council was held wherein was there much whispering and low-voiced discussion.

An hour passed, and a second, and Nam-Bok slept, and the talk went on. The evening sun dipped toward the northwest, and at eleven at night was nearly due north. Then it was that the head man and the bone-scratcher separated themselves from the council and aroused Nam-Bok. He blinked up into their faces and turned on his side to sleep again. Opee-Kwan gripped him by the arm and kindly but firmly shook his senses back into him.

"Come, Nam-Bok, arise!" he commanded. "It be time."

"Another feast?" Nam-Bok cried. "Nay, I am not hungry. Go on with the eating and let me sleep."

"Time to be gone!" Koogah thundered.

But Opee-Kwan spoke more softly. "Thou wast bidarka-mate with me when we were boys," he said. "Together we first chased the seal and drew the salmon from the traps. And thou didst drag me back to life, Nam-Bok, when the sea closed over me and I was sucked down to the black rocks. Together we hungered and bore the chill of the frost, and together we crawled beneath the one fur and lay close to each other. And because of these things, and the kindness in which I stood to thee, it grieves me sore that thou shouldst return such a remarkable liar. We cannot understand, and our heads be dizzy with the things thou hast spoken. It is not good, and there has been much talk in the council. Wherefore we send thee away, that our heads may remain clear and strong and be not troubled by the unaccountable things."

"These things thou speakest of be shadows," Koogah took up the strain. "From the shadow-world thou hast brought them, and to the shadow-world thou must return them. Thy bidarka be ready, and the tribespeople wait. They may not sleep until thou art gone."

Nam-Bok was perplexed, but hearkened to the voice of the head man.

"If thou art Nam-Bok," Opee-Kwan was saying, "thou art a fearful and most wonderful liar; if thou art the shadow of Nam-Bok, then thou speakest of shadows, concerning which it is not good that living men have knowledge. This great village thou hast spoken of we deem the village of shadows. Therein flutter the souls of the dead; for the dead be many and the living few. The dead do not come back. Never have the dead come back—save thou with thy wonder-tales. It is not meet that the dead come back, and should we permit it, great trouble may be our portion."

Nam-Bok knew his people well and was aware that the voice of the council was supreme. So he allowed himself to be led down to the water's edge, where he was put aboard his bidarka and a paddle thrust into his hand. A stray wild-fowl honked somewhere to seaward, and the surf broke limply and hollowly on the sand. A dim twilight brooded over land and water, and in the north the sun smouldered, vague and troubled, and draped about with blood-red mists. The gulls were flying low. The off-shore wind blew keen and chill, and the black-massed clouds behind it gave promise of bitter weather.

"Out of the sea thou camest," Opee-Kwan chanted oracularly, "and back into the sea thou goest. Thus is balance achieved and all things brought to law."

Bask-Wah-Wan limped to the froth-mark and cried, "I bless thee, Nam-Bok, for that thou remembered me."

But Koogah, shoving Nam-Bok clear of the beach, tore the shawl from her shoulders and flung it into the bidarka.

"It is cold in the long nights," she wailed; "and the frost is prone to nip old bones."

"The thing is a shadow," the bone-scratcher answered, "and shadows cannot keep thee warm."

Nam-Bok stood up that his voice might carry. "O Bask-Wah-Wan, mother that bore me!" he called. "Listen to the words of Nam-Bok, thy son. There be room in his bidarka for two, and he would that thou camest with him. For his journey is to where there are fish and oil in plenty. There the frost comes not, and life is easy, and the things of iron do the work of men. Wilt thou come, O Bask-Wah-Wan?"

She debated a moment, while the bidarka drifted swiftly from her, then raised her voice to a quavering treble. "I am old, Nam-Bok, and soon I shall pass down among the shadows. But I have no wish to go before my time. I am old, Nam-Bok, and I am afraid."

A shaft of light shot across the dim-lit sea and wrapped boat and man in a splendor of red and gold. Then a hush fell upon the fisherfolk, and only was heard the moan of the off-shore wind and the cries of the gulls flying low in the air.

THE ONE THOUSAND DOZEN

David Rasmunsen was a hustler, and, like many a greater man, a man of the one idea. Wherefore, when the clarion call of the North rang on his ear, he conceived an adventure in eggs and bent all his energy to its achievement. He figured briefly and to the point, and the adventure became iridescent-hued, splendid. That eggs would sell at Dawson for five dollars a dozen was a safe working premise. Whence it was incontrovertible that one thousand dozen would bring, in the Golden Metropolis, five thousand dollars.

On the other hand, expense was to be considered, and he considered it well, for he was a careful man, keenly practical, with a hard head and a heart that imagination never warmed. At fifteen cents a dozen, the initial cost of his thousand dozen would be one hundred and fifty dollars, a mere bagatelle in face of the enormous profit. And suppose, just suppose, to be wildly extravagant for once, that transportation for himself and eggs should run up eight hundred and fifty more; he would still have four thousand clear cash and clean when the last egg was disposed of and the last dust had rippled into his sack.

"You see, Alma,"—he figured it over with his wife, the cosy dining room submerged in a sea of maps, government surveys, guidebooks, and Alaskan itineraries,—"you see, expenses don't really begin till you make Dyea—fifty dollars'll cover it with a first-class passage thrown in. Now from Dyea to Lake Linderman, Indian packers take your goods over for twelve cents a pound, twelve dollars a hundred, or one hundred and twenty dollars a thousand. Say I have fifteen hundred pounds, it'll cost one hundred and eighty dollars—call it two hundred and be safe. I am creditably informed by a Klondiker just come out that I can buy a boat for three hundred. But the same man says I'm sure to get a couple of passengers for one hundred and fifty each, which will give me the boat for nothing, and, further, they can help me manage it. And . . .

that's all; I put my eggs ashore from the boat at Dawson. Now let me see how much is that?"

"Fifty dollars from San Francisco to Dyea, two hundred from Dyea to Linderman, passengers pay for the boat—two hundred and fifty all told," she summed up swiftly.

"And a hundred for my clothes and personal outfit," he went on happily; "that leaves a margin of five hundred for emergencies. And what possible emergencies can arise?"

Alma shrugged her shoulders and elevated her brows. If that vast Northland was capable of swallowing up a man and a thousand dozen eggs, surely there was room and to spare for whatever else he might happen to possess. So she thought, but she said nothing. She knew David Rasmunsen too well to say anything.

"Doubling the time because of chance delays, I should make the trip in two months. Think of it, Alma! Four thousand in two months! Beats the paltry hundred a month I'm getting now. Why, we'll build further out where we'll have more space, gas in every room, and a view, and the rent of the cottage'll pay taxes, insurance, and water, and leave something over. And then there's always the chance of my striking it and coming out a millionaire. Now tell me, Alma, don't you think I'm very moderate?"

And Alma could hardly think otherwise. Besides, had not her own cousin,—though a remote and distant one to be sure, the black sheep, the harum-scarum, the ne'er-do-well,—had not he come down out of that weird North country with a hundred thousand in yellow dust, to say nothing of a half-ownership in the hole from which it came?

David Rasmunsen's grocer was surprised when he found him weighing eggs in the scales at the end of the counter, and Rasmunsen himself was more surprised when he found that a dozen eggs weighed a pound and a half—fifteen hundred pounds for his thousand dozen! There would be no weight left for his clothes, blankets, and cooking utensils, to say nothing of the grub he must necessarily consume by the way. His calculations were all thrown out, and he was just proceeding to recast them when he hit upon the idea of weighing small eggs. "For whether they be large or small, a dozen eggs is a dozen eggs," he observed sagely to himself; and a dozen small ones he found to weigh but a pound and a quarter. Thereat the city of San Francisco was over-run by anxious-eyed emissaries, and commission houses and dairy as-sociations were startled by a sudden demand for eggs running not more than twenty ounces to the dozen.

Rasmunsen mortgaged the little cottage for a thousand dollars, arranged for his wife to make a prolonged stay among her own people, threw up his job, and started North. To keep within his schedule he compromised on a second-class passage, which, because of the rush, was worse than steerage; and in the late summer, a pale and wabbly man, he disembarked with his eggs on the Dyea beach. But it did not take him long to recover his land legs and appetite. His first interview with the Chilkoot packers straightened him up and stiffened his backbone. Forty cents a pound they demanded for the twenty-eight-mile portage, and while he caught his breath and swallowed, the price went up to forty-three. Fifteen husky Indians put the straps on his packs at forty-five, but took them off at an offer of forty-seven from a Skaguay Crœsus in dirty shirt and ragged overalls who had lost his horses on the White Pass Trail and was now making a last desperate drive at the country by way of Chilkoot.

But Rasmunsen was clean grit, and at fifty cents found takers, who, two days later, set his eggs down intact at Linderman. But fifty cents a pound is a thousand dollars a ton, and his fifteen hundred pounds had exhausted his emergency fund and left him stranded at the Tantalus point where each day he saw the fresh-whipsawed boats departing for Dawson. Further, a great anxiety brooded over the camp where the boats were built. Men worked frantically, early and late, at the height of their endurance, calking, nailing, and pitching in a frenzy of haste for which adequate explanation was not far to seek. Each day the snow-line crept farther down the bleak, rock-shouldered peaks, and gale followed gale, with sleet and slush and snow, and in the eddies and quiet places young ice formed and thickened through the fleeting hours. And each morn, toil-stiffened men turned wan faces across the lake to see if the freeze-up had come. For the freeze-up heralded the death of their hope—the hope that they would be floating down the swift river ere navigation closed on the chain of lakes.

To harrow Rasmunsen's soul further, he discovered three competitors in the egg business. It was true that one, a little German, had gone broke and was himself forlornly back-tripping the last pack of the portage; but the other two had boats nearly completed and were daily supplicating the god of merchants and traders to stay the iron hand of winter for just another day. But the iron hand closed down over the land. Men were being frozen in the blizzard, which swept Chilkoot, and Rasmunsen frosted his toes ere he was aware. He found a chance to go passenger with his freight in a boat just shoving off through the rubble, but two hundred, hard cash, was required, and he had no money.

"Ay tank you yust wait one leedle w'ile," said the Swedish boatbuilder, who had struck his Klondike right there and was wise enough to know it—"one leedle w'ile und I make you a tam fine skiff boat, sure Pete."

With this unpledged word to go on, Rasmunsen hit the back trail to Crater Lake, where he fell in with two press correspondents whose tangled baggage was strewn from Stone House, over across the Pass, and as far as Happy Camp.

"Yes," he said with consequence. "I've a thousand dozen eggs at Linderman, and my boat's just about got the last seam calked. Consider myself in luck to get it. Boats are at a premium, you know, and none to be had."

Whereupon and almost with bodily violence the correspondents clamored to go with him, fluttered greenbacks before his eyes, and spilled yellow twenties from hand to hand. He could not hear of it, but they overpersuaded him, and he reluctantly consented to take them at three hundred apiece. Also they pressed upon him the passage money in advance. And while they wrote to their respective journals concerning the good Samaritan with the thousand dozen eggs, the good Samaritan was hurrying back to the Swede at Linderman.

"Here, you! Gimme that boat!" was his salutation, his hand jingling the correspondents' gold pieces and his eyes hungrily bent upon the finished craft.

The Swede regarded him stolidly and shook his head.

"How much is the other fellow paying? Three hundred? Well, here's four. Take it."

He tried to press it upon him, but the man backed away.

"Ay tank not. Ay say him get der skiff boat. You yust wait—"

"Here's six hundred. Last call. Take it or leave it. Tell'm it's a mistake."

The Swede wavered. "Ay tank yes," he finally said, and the last Rasmunsen saw of him his vocabulary was going to wreck in a vain effort to explain the mistake to the other fellows.

The German slipped and broke his ankle on the steep hogback above Deep Lake, sold out his stock for a dollar a dozen, and with the proceeds hired Indian packers to carry him back to Dyea. But on the morning Rasmunsen shoved off with his correspondents, his two rivals followed suit.

"How many you got?" one of them, a lean little New Englander, called out.

"One thousand dozen," Rasmunsen answered proudly.

"Huh! I'll go you even stakes I beat you in with my eight hundred."

The correspondents offered to lend him the money; but Rasmunsen declined, and the Yankee closed with the remaining rival, a brawny son of the sea and sailor of ships and things, who promised to show them all a wrinkle or two when it came to cracking on. And crack on he did, with a large tarpaulin squaresail which pressed the bow half under at every jump. He was the first to run out of Linderman, but, disdaining the portage, piled his loaded boat on the rocks in the boiling rapids. Rasmunsen and the Yankee, who likewise had two passengers, portaged across on their backs and then lined their empty boats down through the bad water to Bennett.

Bennett was a twenty-five-mile lake, narrow and deep, a funnel between the mountains through which storms ever romped. Rasmunsen camped on the sand-pit at its head, where were many men and boats bound north in the teeth of the Arctic winter. He awoke in the morning to find a piping gale from the south, which caught the chill from the whited peaks and glacial valleys and blew as cold as north wind ever blew. But it was fair, and he also found the Yankee staggering past the first bold headland with all sail set. Boat after boat was getting under way, and the correspondents fell to with enthusiasm.

"We'll catch him before Cariboo Crossing," they assured Rasmunsen, as they ran up the sail and the *Alma* took the first icy spray over her bow.

Now Rasmunsen all his life had been prone to cowardice on water, but he clung to the kicking steering-oar with set face and determined jaw. His thousand dozen were there in the boat before his eyes, safely secured beneath the correspondents' baggage, and somehow, before his eyes, were the little cottage and the mortgage for a thousand dollars.

It was bitter cold. Now and again he hauled in the steering-sweep and put out a fresh one while his passengers chopped the ice from the blade. Wherever the spray struck, it turned instantly to frost, and the dipping boom of the spritsail was quickly fringed with icicles. The *Alma* strained and hammered through the big seas till the seams and butts began to spread, but in lieu of bailing the correspondents chopped ice and flung it overboard. There was no let-up. The mad race with winter was on, and the boats tore along in a desperate string.

"W-w-we can't stop to save our souls!" one of the correspondents chattered, from cold, not fright.

"That's right! Keep her down the middle, old man!" the other encouraged.

Rasmunsen replied with an idiotic grin. The iron-bound shores were in a lather of foam, and even down the middle the only hope was to keep running away from the big seas. To lower sail was to be overtaken and swamped. Time and again they passed boats pounding among the rocks, and once they saw one on the edge of the breakers about to strike. A little craft behind them, with two men, jibed over and turned bottom up.

"W-w-watch out, old man!" cried he of the chattering teeth.

Rasmunsen grinned and tightened his aching grip on the sweep. Scores of times had the send of the sea caught the big square stern of the *Alma* and thrown her off from dead before it till the after leach of the spritsail fluttered hollowly, and each time, and only with all his strength, had he forced her back. His grin by then had become fixed, and it disturbed the correspondents to look at him.

They roared down past an isolated rock a hundred yards from shore. From its wave-drenched top a man shrieked wildly, for the instant cutting the storm with his voice. But the next instant the *Alma* was by, and the rock growing a black speck in the troubled froth.

"That settles the Yankee! Where's the sailor?" shouted one of his passengers.

Rasmunsen shot a glance over his shoulder at a black squaresail. He had seen it leap up out of the gray to windward, and for an hour, off and on, had been watching it grow. The sailor had evidently repaired damages and was making up for lost time.

"Look at him come!"

Both passengers stopped chopping ice to watch. Twenty miles of Bennett were behind them—room and to spare for the sea to toss up its mountains toward the sky. Sinking and soaring like a storm god, the sailor drove by them. The huge sail seemed to grip the boat from the crests of the waves, to tear it bodily out of the water, and fling it crashing and smothering down into the yawning troughs.

"The sea'll never catch him!"

"But he'll r-r-run her nose under!"

Even as they spoke, the black tarpaulin swooped from sight behind a big comber. The next wave rolled over the spot, and the next, but the boat did not reappear. The *Alma* rushed by the place. A little riffraff of oars and boxes was seen. An arm thrust up and a shaggy head broke surface a score of yards away.

For a time there was silence. As the end of the lake came in sight, the waves began to leap aboard with such steady recurrence that the correspondents no longer chopped ice but flung the water out with buckets. Even this would not do, and, after a shouted conference with Rasmunsen, they attacked the baggage. Flour, bacon, beans, blankets, cooking stove, ropes, odds and ends, everything they could get hands on, flew overboard. The boat acknowledged it at once, taking less water and rising more buoyantly.

"That'll do!" Rasmunsen called sternly, as they applied themselves to the top layer of eggs.

"The h-hell it will!" answered the shivering one, savagely. With the exception of their notes, films, and cameras, they had sacrificed their outfit. He bent over, laid hold of an egg-box, and began to worry it out from under the lashing.

"Drop it! Drop it, I say!"

Rasmunsen had managed to draw his revolver, and with the crook of his arm over the sweep head was taking aim. The correspondent stood up on the thwart, balancing back and forth, his face twisted with menace and speechless anger.

"My God!"

So cried his brother correspondent, hurling himself, face downward, into the bottom of the boat. The *Alma*, under the divided attention of Rasmunsen, had been caught by a great mass of water and whirled around. The after leach hollowed, the sail emptied and jibed, and the boom, sweeping with terrific force across the boat, carried the angry correspondent overboard with a broken back. Mast and sail had gone over the side as well. A drenching sea followed, as the boat lost head-way, and Rasmunsen sprang to the bailing bucket.

Several boats hurtled past them in the next half-hour,—small boats, boats of their own size, boats afraid, unable to do aught but run madly on. Then a ten-ton barge, at imminent risk of destruction, lowered sail to windward and lumbered down upon them.

"Keep off! Keep off!" Rasmunsen screamed.

But his low gunwale ground against the heavy craft, and the remaining correspondent clambered aboard. Rasmunsen was over the eggs like a cat and in the bow of the *Alma,* striving with numb fingers to bend the hauling-lines together.

"Come on!" a red-whiskered man yelled at him.

"I've a thousand dozen eggs here," he shouted back. "Gimme a tow! I'll pay you!"

"Come on!" they howled in chorus.

A big whitecap broke just beyond, washing over the barge and leaving the *Alma* half swamped. The men cast off, cursing him as they ran up their sail. Rasmunsen cursed back and fell to bailing. The mast and sail, like a sea anchor, still fast by the halyards, held the boat head on to wind and sea and gave him a chance to fight the water out.

Three hours later, numbed, exhausted, blathering like a lunatic, but still bailing, he went ashore on an ice-strewn beach near Cariboo Crossing. Two men, a government courier and a half-breed voyageur, dragged him out of the surf, saved his cargo, and beached the *Alma.*

They were paddling out of the country in a Peterborough, and gave him shelter for the night in their storm-bound camp. Next morning they departed, but he elected to stay by his eggs. And thereafter the name and fame of the man with the thousand dozen eggs began to spread through the land. Gold-seekers who made in before the freeze-up carried the news of his coming. Grizzled old-timers of Forty Mile and Circle City, sour doughs with leathern jaws and bean-calloused stomachs, called up dream memories of chickens and green things at mention of his name. Dyea and Skaguay took an interest in his being, and questioned his progress from every man who came over the passes, while Dawson—golden, omeletless Dawson—fretted and worried, and waylaid every chance arrival for word of him.

But of this, Rasmunsen knew nothing. The day after the wreck he patched up the *Alma* and pulled out. A cruel east wind blew in his teeth from Tagish, but he got the oars over the side and bucked manfully into it, though half the time he was drifting backward and chopping ice from the blades. According to the custom of the country, he was driven ashore at Windy Arm; three times on Tagish saw him swamped and beached; and Lake Marsh held him at the freeze-up. The *Alma* was crushed in the jamming of the floes, but the eggs were intact. These he back-tripped two miles across the ice to the shore, where he built a caché, which stood for years after and was pointed out by men who knew.

Half a thousand frozen miles stretched between him and Dawson, and the waterway was closed. But Rasmunsen, with a peculiar tense look in his face, struck back up the lakes on foot. What he suffered on that lone trip, with naught but a single blanket, an axe, and a handful of beans, is not given to ordinary mortals to know. Only the Arctic adventurer may understand. Suffice that he was caught in a blizzard on Chilkoot and left two of his toes with the surgeon at Sheep Camp. Yet he stood on his feet and washed dishes in the scullery of the *Pawona* to the Puget Sound, and from there passed coal on a P. S. boat to San Francisco.

It was a haggard, unkempt man who limped across the shining office floor to raise a second mortgage from the bank people. His hollow cheeks betrayed themselves through the scraggly beard, and his eyes seemed to have retired into deep caverns where they burned with cold fires. His hands were grained from exposure and hard work, and the nails were rimmed with tight-packed dirt and coal dust. He spoke vaguely of eggs and ice-packs, winds and tides; but when they declined to let him have more than a second thousand, his talk became incoherent, concerning itself chiefly with the price of dogs and dog-food, and such things as snowshoes and moccasins and winter trails. They let him have fifteen hundred, which was more than the cottage warranted, and breathed easier when he scrawled his signature and passed out the door.

Two weeks later he went over Chilkoot with three dog sleds of five dogs each. One team he drove, the two Indians with him driving the others. At Lake Marsh they broke out the caché and loaded up. But there was no trail. He was the first in over the ice, and to him fell the task of packing the snow and hammering away through the rough river jams. Behind him he often observed a camp-fire smoke trickling thinly up through the quiet air, and he wondered why the people did not overtake him. For he was a stranger to the land and did not understand. Nor could he understand his Indians when they tried to explain. This they conceived to be a hardship, but when they balked and refused to break camp of mornings, he drove them to their work at pistol point.

When he slipped through an ice bridge near the White Horse and froze his foot, tender yet and oversensitive from the previous freezing, the Indians looked for him to lie up. But he sacrificed a blanket, and, with his foot incased in an enormous moccasin, big as a water-bucket, continued to take his regular turn with the front sled. Here was the cruelest work, and they respected him, though on the side they rapped their foreheads with their knuckles and significantly shook their heads. One night they tried to run away, but the zip-zip of his bullets in the snow brought them back, snarling but convinced. Whereupon, being only savage Chilkat men, they put their heads together to kill him; but he slept like a cat, and, waking or sleeping, the chance never came. Often they tried to tell him the import of the smoke wreath in the rear, but he could not comprehend and grew suspicious of them. And when they sulked or shirked, he was quick to let drive at them between the eyes, and quick to cool their heated souls with sight of his ready revolver.

And so it went—with mutinous men, wild dogs, and a trail that broke the heart. He fought the men to stay with him, fought the dogs to keep them away from the eggs, fought the ice, the cold, and the pain of his foot, which would not heal. As fast as the young tissue renewed, it was bitten and seared by the frost, so that a running sore developed, into which he could almost shove his fist. In the mornings, when he first put his weight upon it, his head went dizzy, and he was near to fainting from the pain; but later on in the day it usually grew numb, to recommence when he crawled into his blankets and tried to sleep. Yet he, who had been a clerk and sat at a desk all his days, toiled till the Indians were exhausted, and even outworked the dogs. How hard he worked, how much he suffered, he did not know. Being a man of the one idea, now that the idea had come, it mastered him. In the foreground of his consciousness was Dawson, in the background his thousand dozen eggs, and midway between the two his ego fluttered, striving alway to draw them together to a glittering golden point. This golden point was the five thousand dollars, the consummation of the idea and the point of departure for whatever new idea might present itself. For the rest, he was a mere automaton. He was unaware of other things, seeing them as through a glass darkly, and giving them no thought. The work of his hands he did with machine-like wisdom; likewise the work of his head. So the look on his face grew very tense, till even the Indians were afraid of it, and marvelled at the strange white man who had made them slaves and forced them to toil with such foolishness.

Then came a snap on Lake Le Barge, when the cold of outer space smote the tip of the planet, and the frost ranged sixty and odd degrees below zero. Here, laboring with open mouth that he might breathe more freely, he chilled his lungs, and for the rest of the trip he was troubled with a dry, hacking cough, especially irritable in smoke of camp or under stress of undue exertion. On the Thirty Mile river he found much open water, spanned by precarious ice bridges and fringed with narrow rim ice, tricky and uncertain. The rim ice was impossible to reckon on, and he dared it without reckoning, falling back on his revolver when his drivers demurred. But on the ice bridges, covered with snow though they were, precautions could be taken. These they crossed on their snowshoes, with long poles, held crosswise in their hands, to which to cling in case of accident. Once over, the dogs were called to follow. And on such a bridge, where the absence of the centre ice was masked by the snow, one of the Indians met his end. He went through as quickly and neatly as a knife through thin cream, and the current swept him from view down under the stream ice.

That night his mate fled away through the pale moonlight, Rasmunsen futilely puncturing the silence with his revolver—a thing that he handled with more celerity than cleverness. Thirty-six hours later the Indian made a police camp on the Big Salmon.

"Um—um—um funny mans—what you call?—top um head all loose," the interpreter explained to the puzzled captain. "Eh? Yep, clazy, much clazy mans. Eggs, eggs, all a time eggs—savvy? Come bime-by."

It was several days before Rasmunsen arrived, the three sleds lashed together, and all the dogs in a single team. It was awkward, and where the going was bad he was compelled to back-trip it sled by sled, though he managed most of the time, through herculean efforts, to bring all along on the one haul. He did not seem moved when the captain of police told him his man was hitting the high places for Dawson, and was by that time, probably, halfway between Selkirk and Stewart. Nor did he appear interested when informed that the police had broken the trail as far as Pelly; for he had attained to a fatalistic acceptance of all natural dispensations, good or ill. But when they told him that Dawson was in the bitter clutch of famine, he smiled, threw the harness on his dogs, and pulled out.

But it was at his next halt that the mystery of the smoke was explained. With the word at Big Salmon that the trail was broken to Pelly, there was no longer any need for the smoke wreath to linger in his wake; and Rasmunsen, crouching over his lonely fire, saw a motley string of sleds go by. First came the courier and the half-breed who had hauled him out from Bennett; then mail-carriers for Circle City, two sleds of them, and a mixed following of ingoing Klondikers. Dogs and men were fresh and fat, while Rasmunsen and his brutes were jaded and worn down to the skin and bone. They of the smoke wreath had travelled one day in three, resting and reserving their strength for the dash to come when broken trail was met with; while each day he had plunged and floundered forward, breaking the spirit of his dogs and robbing them of their mettle.

As for himself, he was unbreakable. They thanked him kindly for his efforts in their behalf, those fat, fresh men,—thanked him kindly, with broad grins and ribald laughter; and now, when he understood, he made no answer. Nor did he cherish silent bitterness. It was immaterial. The idea—the fact behind the idea—was not changed. Here he was and his thousand dozen; there was Dawson; the problem was unaltered.

At the Little Salmon, being short of dog food, the dogs got into his grub, and from there to Selkirk he lived on beans—coarse, brown beans, big beans, grossly nutritive, which griped his stomach and doubled him up at two-hour intervals. But the Factor at Selkirk had a notice on the door of the Post to the effect that no steamer had been up the Yukon for two years, and in consequence grub was beyond price. He offered to swap flour, however, at the rate of a cupful for each egg, but Rasmunsen shook his head and hit the trail. Below the Post he managed to buy frozen horse hide for the dogs, the horses having been slain by the Chilkat cattle men, and the scraps and offal preserved by the Indians. He tackled the hide himself, but the hair worked into the bean sores of his mouth, and was beyond endurance.

Here at Selkirk, he met the forerunners of the hungry exodus of Dawson, and from there on they crept over the trail, a dismal throng. "No grub!" was the song they sang. "No grub, and had to go." "Everybody holding candles for a rise in the spring." "Flour dollar'n a half a pound, and no sellers."

"Eggs?" one of them answered. "Dollar apiece, but they ain't none."

Rasmunsen made a rapid calculation. "Twelve thousand dollars," he said aloud.

"Hey?" the man asked.

"Nothing," he answered, and *mushed* the dogs along.

When he arrived at Stewart River, seventy miles from Dawson, five of his dogs were gone, and the remainder were falling in the traces. He, also, was in the traces, hauling with what little strength was left in him. Even then he was barely crawling along ten miles a day. His cheek-bones and nose, frost-bitten again and again, were turned bloody-black and hideous. The thumb, which was separated from the fingers by the gee-pole, had likewise been nipped and gave him great pain. The monstrous moccasin still incased his foot, and strange pains were beginning to rack the leg. At Sixty Mile, the last beans, which he had been rationing for some time, were finished; yet he steadfastly refused to touch the eggs. He could not reconcile his mind to the legitimacy of it, and staggered and fell along the way to Indian River. Here a fresh-killed moose and an open-handed old-timer gave him and his dogs new strength, and at Ainslie's he felt repaid for it all when a stampede, ripe from Dawson in five hours, was sure he could get a dollar and a quarter for every egg he possessed.

He came up the steep bank by the Dawson barracks with fluttering heart and shaking knees. The dogs were so weak that he was forced to rest them, and, waiting, he leaned limply against the gee-pole. A man, an eminently decorous-looking man, came sauntering by in a great bear-skin coat. He glanced at Rasmunsen curiously, then stopped and ran a speculative eye over the dogs and the three lashed sleds.

"What you got?" he asked.

"Eggs," Rasmunsen answered huskily, hardly able to pitch his voice above a whisper.

"Eggs! Whoopee! Whoopee!" He sprang up into the air, gyrated madly, and finished with half a dozen war steps. "You don't say—all of 'em?"

"All of 'em?"

"Say, you must be the Egg Man." He walked around and viewed Rasmunsen from the other side. "Come, now, ain't you the Egg Man?"

Rasmunsen didn't know, but supposed he was, and the man sobered down a bit.

"What d'ye expect to get for 'em?" he asked cautiously.

Rasmunsen became audacious. "Dollar'n a half," he said.

"Done!" the man came back promptly. "Gimme a dozen."

"I—I mean a dollar'n a half apiece," Rasmunsen hesitatingly explained.

"Sure. I heard you. Make it two dozen. Here's the dust."

The man pulled out a healthy gold sack the size of a small sausage and knocked it negligently against the gee-pole. Rasmunsen felt a strange trembling in the pit of his stomach, a tickling of the nostrils, and an almost overwhelming desire to sit down and cry. But a curious, wide-eyed crowd was beginning to collect, and man after man was calling out for eggs. He was without scales, but the man with the bearskin coat fetched a pair and obligingly weighed in the dust while Rasmunsen passed out the goods. Soon there was a pushing and shoving and shouldering, and a great clamor. Everybody wanted to buy and to be served first. And as the excitement grew, Rasmunsen cooled down. This would never do. There must be something behind the fact of their buying so eagerly. It would be wiser if he rested first and sized up the market. Perhaps eggs were worth two dollars apiece. Anyway, whenever he wished to sell, he was sure of a dollar and a half. "Stop!" he cried, when a couple of hundred had been sold. "No more now. I'm played out. I've got to get a cabin, and then you can come and see me."

A groan went up at this, but the man with the bearskin coat approved. Twenty-four of the frozen eggs went rattling in his capacious pockets and he didn't care whether the rest of the town ate or not. Besides, he could see Rasmunsen was on his last legs.

"There's a cabin right around the second corner from the Monte Carlo," he told him—"the one with the sody-bottle window. It ain't mine, but I've got charge of it. Rents for ten a day and cheap for the money. You move right in, and I'll see you later. Don't forget the sody-bottle window."

"Tra-la-loo!" he called back a moment later. "I'm goin' up the hill to eat eggs and dream of home."

On his way to the cabin, Rasmunsen recollected he was hungry and bought a small supply of provisions at the N. A. T. & T. store—also a beefsteak at the butcher shop and dried salmon for the dogs. He found the cabin without difficulty and left the dogs in the harness while he started the fire and got the coffee under way.

"A dollar'n a half apiece—one thousand dozen—eighteen thousand dollars!" He kept muttering it to himself, over and over, as he went about his work.

As he flopped the steak into the frying-pan the door opened. He turned. It was the man with the bearskin coat. He seemed to come in with determination, as though bound on some explicit errand, but as he looked at Rasmunsen an expression of perplexity came into his face.

"I say—now I say—" he began, then halted.

Rasmunsen wondered if he wanted the rent.

"I say, damn it, you know, them eggs is bad."

Rasmunsen staggered. He felt as though some one had struck him an astounding blow between the eyes. The walls of the cabin reeled and tilted up. He put out his hand to steady himself and rested it on the stove. The sharp pain and the smell of the burning flesh brought him back to himself.

"I see," he said slowly, fumbling in his pocket for the sack. "You want your money back."

"It ain't the money," the man said, "but hain't you got any eggs—good?"

Rasmunsen shook his head. "You'd better take the money."

But the man refused and backed away. "I'll come back," he said, "when you've taken stock, and get what's comin'."

Rasmunsen rolled the chopping-block into the cabin and carried in the eggs. He went about it quite calmly. He took up the hand-axe, and, one by one, chopped the eggs in half. These halves he examined carefully and let fall to the floor. At first he sampled from the different cases, then deliberately emptied one case at a time. The heap on the floor grew larger. The coffee boiled over and the smoke of the burning beef-steak filled the cabin. He chopped steadfastly and monotonously till the last case was finished.

Somebody knocked at the door, knocked again, and let himself in.

"What a mess!" he remarked, as he paused and surveyed the scene.

The severed eggs were beginning to thaw in the heat of the stove, and a miserable odor was growing stronger.

"Must a-happened on the steamer," he suggested.

Rasmunsen looked at him long and blankly.

"I'm Murray, Big Jim Murray, everybody knows me," the man volunteered. "I'm just hearin' your eggs is rotten, and I'm offerin' you two hundred for the batch. They ain't good as salmon, but still they're fair scoffin's for dogs."

Rasmunsen seemed turned to stone. He did not move. "You go to hell," he said passionlessly.

"Now just consider. I pride myself it's a decent price for a mess like that, and it's better'n nothin'. Two hundred. What you say?"

"You go to hell," Rasmunsen repeated softly, "and get out of here."

Murray gaped with a great awe, then went out carefully, backward, with his eyes fixed on the other's face.

Rasmunsen followed him out and turned the dogs loose. He threw them all the salmon he had bought, and coiled a sled-lashing up in his hand. Then he reëntered the cabin and drew the latch in after him. The smoke from the cindered steak made his eyes smart. He stood on the bunk, passed the lashing over the ridge-pole, and measured the swing-off with his eye. It did not seem to satisfy, for he put the stool on the bunk and climbed upon the stool. He drove a noose in the end of the lashing and slipped his head through. The other end he made fast. Then he kicked the stool out from under.

TO BUILD A FIRE (1902)

For land travel or seafaring, the world over, a companion is usually considered desirable. In the Klondike, as Tom Vincent found out, such a companion is absolutely essential. But he found it out, not by precept, but through bitter experience.

"Never travel alone," is a precept of the north. He had heard it many times and laughed; for he was a strapping young fellow, big-boned and big-muscled, with faith in himself and in the strength of his head and hands.

It was on a bleak January day when the experience came that taught him respect for the frost, and for the wisdom of the men who had battled with it.

He had left Calumet Camp on the Yukon with a light pack on his back, to go up Paul Creek to the divide between it and Cherry Creek, where his party was prospecting and hunting moose.

The frost was sixty degrees below zero, and he had thirty miles of lonely trail to cover, but he did not mind. In fact, he enjoyed it, swinging along through the silence, his blood pounding warmly through his veins, and his mind carefree and happy. For he and his comrades were certain they had struck "pay" up there on the Cherry Creek Divide; and, further, he was returning to them from Dawson with cheery home letters from the States.

At seven o'clock, when he turned the heels of his moccasins toward Calumet Camp, it was still black night. And when day broke at half past nine he had made the four-mile cut-off across the flats and was six miles up Paul Creek. The trail, which had seen little travel, followed the bed of the creek, and there was no possibility of his getting lost. He had gone to Dawson by way of Cherry Creek and Indian River, so Paul Creek was new and strange. By half past eleven he was at the forks, which had been described to him, and he knew he had covered fifteen miles, half the distance.

He knew that in the nature of things the trail was bound to grow worse from there on, and thought that, considering the good time he had made, he merited lunch. Casting off his pack and taking a seat on a fallen tree, he unmittened his right hand, reached inside his shirt next to the skin, and fished out a couple of biscuits sandwiched with sliced bacon and wrapped in a handkerchief—the only way they could be carried without freezing solid.

He had barely chewed the first mouthful when his numbing fingers warned him to put his mitten on again. This he did, not without surprise at the bitter swiftness with which the frost bit in. Undoubtedly it was the coldest snap he had ever experienced, he thought.

He spat upon the snow,—a favorite northland trick,—and the sharp crackle of the instantly congealed spittle startled him. The spirit thermometer at Calumet had registered sixty below when he left, but he was certain it had grown much colder, how much colder he could not imagine.

Half of the first biscuit was yet untouched, but he could feel himself beginning to chill—a thing most unusual for him. This would never do, he decided, and slipping the pack-straps across his shoulders, he leaped to his feet and ran briskly up the trail.

A few minutes of this made him warm again, and he settled down to a steady stride, munching the biscuits as he went along. The moisture that exhaled with his breath crusted his lips and mustache with pendent ice and formed a miniature glacier on his chin. Now and again sensation forsook his nose and cheeks, and he rubbed them till they burned with the returning blood.

Most men wore nose-straps; his partners did, but he had scorned such "feminine contraptions," and till now had never felt the need of them. Now he did feel the need, for he was rubbing constantly.

Nevertheless he was aware of a thrill of joy, of exultation. He was doing something, achieving something, mastering the elements. Once he laughed aloud in sheer strength of life, and with his clenched fist defied the frost. He was its master. What he did he did in spite of it. It could not stop him. He was going on to the Cherry Creek Divide.

Strong as were the elements, he was stronger. At such times animals crawled away into their holes and remained in hiding. But he did not hide. He was out in it, facing it, fighting it. He was a man, a master of things.

In such fashion, rejoicing proudly, he tramped on. After half an hour he rounded a bend, where the creek ran close to the mountainside, and came upon one of the most insignificant-appearing but most formidable dangers in northern travel.

The creek itself was frozen solid to its rocky bottom, but from the mountain came the outflow of several springs. These springs never froze, and the only effect of the severest cold snaps was to lessen their discharge. Protected from the frost by the blanket of snow, the water of these springs seeped down into the creek, and, on top of the creek ice, formed shallow pools.

The surface of these pools, in turn, took on a skin of ice which grew thicker and thicker, until the water overran, and so formed a second ice-skinned pool above the first.

Thus at the bottom was the solid creek ice, then probably six to eight inches of water, then a thin ice-skin, then another six inches of water and another ice-skin. And on top of this last skin was about an inch of recent snow to make the trap complete.

To Tom Vincent's eye the unbroken snow surface gave no warning of the lurking danger. As the crust was thicker at the edge, he was well toward the middle before he broke through.

In itself it was a very insignificant mishap,—a man does not drown in twelve inches of water,—but in its consequences as serious an accident as could possibly befall him.

At the instant he broke through he felt the cold water strike his feet and ankles, and with half a dozen lunges he made the bank. He was quite cool and collected. The thing to do, and the only thing to do, was to build a fire. For another precept of the north runs: *Travel with wet socks down to twenty below zero; after that build a fire.* And it was three times twenty below and colder, and he knew it.

He knew, further, that great care must be exercised; that with failure at the first attempt, the chance was made greater for failure at the second attempt. In short, he knew that there must be no failure. The moment before a strong, exulting man, boastful of his mastery of the elements, he was now fighting for his life against those same elements—such was the difference caused by the injection of a quart of water into a north-land traveller's calculations.

In a clump of pines on the rim of the bank the spring high-water had lodged many twigs and small branches. Thoroughly dried by the summer sun, they now waited the match.

It is impossible to build a fire with heavy Alaskan mittens on one's hands, so Vincent bared his, gathered a sufficient number of twigs, and knocking the snow from them, knelt down to kindle his fire. From an inside pocket he drew out his matches and a strip of thin birch bark. The matches were of the Klondike kind, sulphur matches, one hundred in a bunch.

He noticed how quickly his fingers had chilled as he separated one match from the bunch and scratched it on his trousers. The birch bark, like the dryest of paper, burst into bright flame. This he carefully fed with the smallest twigs and finest débris, cherishing the flame with the utmost care. It did not do to hurry things, as he well knew, and although his fingers were now quite stiff, he did not hurry.

After the first quick, biting sensation of cold, his feet had ached with a heavy, dull ache and were rapidly growing numb. But the fire, although a very young one, was now a success, and he knew that a little snow, briskly rubbed, would speedily cure his feet.

But at the moment he was adding the first thick twigs to the fire a grievous thing happened. The pine boughs above his head were burdened with a four months' snowfall, and so finely adjusted were the burdens that his slight movements in collecting the twigs had been sufficient to disturb the balance.

The snow from the topmost bough was the first to fall, striking and dislodging the snow on the boughs beneath. And all this snow, accumulating as it fell, smote Tom Vincent's head and shoulders and blotted out his fire.

He still kept his presence of mind, for he knew how great his danger was. He started at once to rebuild the fire, but his fingers were now so cold that he could not bend them, and he was forced to pick up each twig and splinter between the tips of the fingers of either hand.

When he came to the match he encountered great difficulty in separating one from the bunch. This he succeeded in managing, however, and also, by a great effort, in clutching the match between his thumb and forefinger. But in scratching it, he dropped it in the snow and could not pick it up again.

He stood up, desperate. He could not feel even his weight on his feet, although the ankles were aching painfully. Putting on his mittens, he stepped to one side, so that the snow would not fall upon the new fire he was to build, and beat his hands violently against a tree-trunk.

This enabled him to separate and strike a second match and to set fire to the remaining fragment of birch bark. But his body had now begun to chill and he was shivering, so that when he tried to add the first twigs his hand shook and the tiny flame was quenched.

The frost had beaten him. His hands were worthless. But he had the foresight to drop the bunch of matches into his wide-mouthed outside pocket before he slipped on his mittens in despair, and started to run up the trail. One cannot run the frost out of wet feet at sixty below and colder, however, as he quickly discovered.

He came round a sharp turn of the creek to where he could look ahead for a mile. But there was no help, no sign of help, only the white trees and the white hills, the quiet cold and the brazen silence! If only he had a comrade whose feet were not freezing, he thought, only such a comrade to start the fire that could save him!

Then his eyes chanced upon another high-water lodgment of twigs and leaves and branches. If he could strike a match, all might yet be well. With stiff fingers which he could not bend, he got out a bunch of matches, but found it impossible to separate them.

He sat down and awkwardly shuffled the bunch about on his knees, until he got it resting on his palm with the sulphur ends projecting, somewhat in the manner the blade of a hunting-knife would project when clutched in the fist.

But his fingers stood straight out. They could not clutch. This he overcame by pressing the wrist of the other hand against them, and so forcing them down upon the bunch. Time and again, holding thus by both hands, he scratched the bunch on his leg and finally ignited it. But the flame burned into the flesh of his hand, and he involuntarily relaxed his hold. The bunch fell into the snow, and while he tried vainly to pick it up, sizzled and went out.

Again he ran, by this time badly frightened. His feet were utterly devoid of sensation. He stubbed his toes once on a buried log, but beyond pitching him into the snow and wrenching his back, it gave him no feelings.

His fingers were helpless and his wrists were beginning to grow numb. His nose and cheeks he knew were freezing, but they did not count. It was his feet and hands that were to save him, if he was to be saved.

He recollected being told of a camp of moose-hunters somewhere above the forks of Paul Creek. He must be somewhere near it, he thought, and if he could find it he yet might be saved. Five minutes later he came upon it, lone and deserted, with drifted snow sprinkled inside the pine-bough shelter in which the hunters had slept. He sank down, sobbing. All was over. In an hour at best, in that terrific temperature, he would be an icy corpse.

But the love of life was strong in him, and he sprang again to his feet. He was thinking quickly. What if the matches did burn his hands? Burned hands were better than dead hands. No hands at all were better than death. He floundered along the trail till he came upon another high-water lodgment. There were twigs and branches, leaves and grasses, all dry and waiting the fire.

Again he sat down and shuffled the bunch of matches on his knees, got it into place on his palm, with the wrist of his other hand forced the nerveless fingers down against the bunch, and with the wrist kept them there. At the second scratch the bunch caught fire, and he knew that if he could stand the pain he was saved. He choked with the sulphur fumes, and the blue flame licked the flesh of his hands.

At first he could not feel it, but it burned quickly in through the frosted surface. The odor of the burning flesh—his flesh—was strong in his nostrils. He writhed about in his torment, yet held on. He set his teeth and swayed back and forth, until the clear white flame of the burning match shot up, and he had applied that flame to the leaves and grasses.

An anxious five minutes followed, but the fire gained steadily. Then he set to work to save himself. Heroic measures were necessary, such was his extremity, and he took them.

Alternately rubbing his hands with snow and thrusting them into the flames, and now and again beating them against the hard trees, he restored their circulation sufficiently for them to be of use to him. With his hunting-knife he slashed the straps from his pack, unrolled his blanket, and got out dry socks and foot-gear.

Then he cut away his moccasins and bared his feet. But while he had taken liberties with his hands, he kept his feet fairly away from the fire and rubbed them with snow. He rubbed till his hands grew numb, when he would cover his feet with the blanket, warm his hands by the fire, and return to the rubbing.

For three hours he worked, till the worst effects of the freezing had been counteracted. All that night he stayed by the fire, and it was late the next day when he limped pitifully into the camp on the Cherry Creek Divide.

In a month's time he was able to be about on his feet, although the toes were destined always after that to be very sensitive to frost. But the scars on his hands he knows he will carry to the grave. And— "*Never travel alone!*" he now lays down the precept of the north.

MOON-FACE

John Claverhouse was a moon-faced man. You know the kind, cheek-bones wide apart, chin and forehead melting into the cheeks to complete the perfect round, and the nose, broad and pudgy, equidistant from the circumference, flattened against the very centre of the face like a dough-ball upon the ceiling. Perhaps that is why I hated him, for truly he had become an offence to my eyes, and I believed the earth to be cumbered with his presence. Perhaps my mother may have been superstitious of the moon and looked upon it over the wrong shoulder at the wrong time.

Be that as it may, I hated John Claverhouse. Not that he had done me what society would consider a wrong or an ill turn. Far from it. The evil was of a deeper, subtler sort; so elusive, so intangible, as to defy clear, definite analysis in words. We all experience such things at some period in our lives. For the first time we see a certain individual, one who the very instant before we did not dream existed; and yet, at the first moment of meeting, we say: "I do not like that man." Why do we not like him? Ah, we do not know why; we know only that we do not. We have taken a dislike, that is all. And so I with John Claverhouse.

What right had such a man to be happy? Yet he was an optimist. He was always gleeful and laughing. All things were always all right, curse him! Ah! how it grated on my soul that he should be so happy! Other men could laugh, and it did not bother me. I even used to laugh myself—before I met John Claverhouse.

But his laugh! It irritated me, maddened me, as nothing else under the sun could irritate or madden me. It haunted me, gripped hold of me, and would not let me go. It was a huge, Gargantuan laugh. Waking or sleeping it was always with me, whirring and jarring across my heart-strings like an enormous rasp. At break of day it came whooping across the fields to spoil my pleasant morning revery. Under the aching noon-day glare, when the green things drooped and the birds withdrew to the depths of the forest, and all nature drowsed, his great "Ha! ha!" and "Ho! ho!" rose up to the sky and challenged the sun. And at black midnight, from the lonely cross-roads where he turned from town into his own place, came his plaguey cachinnations to rouse me from my sleep and make me writhe and clench my nails into my palms.

I went forth privily in the night-time, and turned his cattle into his fields, and in the morning heard his whooping laugh as he drove them out again. "It is nothing," he said; "the poor, dumb beasties are not to be blamed for straying into fatter pastures."

He had a dog he called "Mars," a big, splendid brute, part deer-hound and part blood-hound, and resembling both. Mars was a great delight to him, and they were always together. But I bided my time, and one day, when opportunity was ripe, lured the animal away and settled for him with strychnine and beefsteak. It made positively no impression on John Claverhouse. His laugh was as hearty and frequent as ever, and his face as much like the full moon as it always had been.

Then I set fire to his haystacks and his barn. But the next morning, being Sunday, he went forth blithe and cheerful.

"Where are you going?" I asked him, as he went by the cross-roads.

"Trout," he said, and his face beamed like a full moon. "I just dote on trout."

Was there ever such an impossible man! His whole harvest had gone up in his haystacks and barn. It was uninsured, I knew. And yet, in the face of famine and the rigorous winter, he went out gayly in quest of a mess of trout, forsooth, because he "doted" on them! Had gloom but rested, no matter how lightly, on his brow, or had his bovine countenance grown long and serious and less like the moon, or had he removed that smile but once from off his face, I am sure I could have forgiven him for existing. But no, he grew only more cheerful under misfortune.

I insulted him. He looked at me in slow and smiling surprise.

"I fight you? Why?" he asked slowly. And then he laughed. "You are so funny! Ho! ho! You'll be the death of me! He! he! he! Oh! Ho! ho! ho!"

What would you? It was past endurance. By the blood of Judas, how I hated him! Then there was that name—Claverhouse! What a name! Wasn't it absurd? Claverhouse! Merciful heaven, *why* Claverhouse? Again and again I asked myself that question. I should not have minded Smith, or Brown, or Jones—but *Claverhouse!* I leave it to you. Repeat it to yourself—Claverhouse. Just listen to the ridiculous sound of it—Claverhouse! Should a man live with such a name? I ask of you. "No," you say. And "No" said I.

But I bethought me of his mortgage. What of his crops and barn destroyed, I knew he would be unable to meet it. So I got a shrewd, close-mouthed, tight-fisted money-lender to get the mortgage transferred to him. I did not appear, but through this agent I forced the foreclosure, and but few days (no more, believe me, than the law allowed) were given John Claverhouse to remove his goods and chattels from the premises. Then I strolled down to see how he took it, for he had lived there upward of twenty years. But he met me with his saucer-eyes twinkling, and the light glowing and spreading in his face till it was as a full-risen moon.

"Ha! ha! ha!" he laughed. "The funniest tike, that youngster of mine! Did you ever hear the like? Let me tell you. He was down playing by the edge of the river when a piece of the bank caved in and splashed him. 'O papa!' he cried; 'a great big puddle flewed up and hit me.'"

He stopped and waited for me to join him in his infernal glee.

"I don't see any laugh in it," I said shortly, and I know my face went sour.

He regarded me with wonderment, and then came the damnable light, glowing and spreading, as I have described it, till his face shone soft and warm, like the summer moon, and then the laugh—"Ha! ha! That's funny! You don't see it, eh? He! he! Ho! ho! ho! He doesn't see it! Why, look here. You know a puddle—"

But I turned on my heel and left him. That was the last. I could stand it no longer. The thing must end right there, I thought, curse him! The earth should be quit of him. And as I went over the hill, I could hear his monstrous laugh reverberating against the sky.

Now, I pride myself on doing things neatly, and when I resolved to kill John Claverhouse I had it in mind to do so in such fashion that I should not look back upon it and feel ashamed. I hate bungling, and I hate brutality. To me there is something repugnant in merely striking a man with one's naked fist—faugh! it is sickening! So, to shoot, or stab, or club John Claverhouse (oh, that name!) did not appeal to me. And not only was I impelled to do it neatly and artistically, but also in such manner that not the slightest possible suspicion could be directed against me.

To this end I bent my intellect, and, after a week of profound incubation, I hatched the scheme. Then I set to work. I bought a water spaniel bitch, five months old, and devoted my whole attention to her training. Had any one spied upon me, they would have remarked that this training consisted entirely of one thing—*retrieving*. I taught the dog, which I called "Bellona," to fetch sticks I threw into the water, and not only to fetch, but to fetch at once, without mouthing or playing with them. The point was that she was to stop for nothing, but to deliver the stick in all haste. I made a practice of running away and leaving her to chase me, with the stick in her mouth, till she caught me. She was a bright animal, and took to the game with such eagerness that I was soon content.

After that, at the first casual opportunity, I presented Bellona to John Claverhouse. I knew what I was about, for I was aware of a little weakness of his, and of a little private sinning of which he was regularly and inveterately guilty.

"No," he said, when I placed the end of the rope in his hand. "No, you don't mean it." And his mouth opened wide and he grinned all over his damnable moon-face.

"I—I kind of thought, somehow, you didn't like me," he explained. "Wasn't it funny for me to make such a mistake?" And at the thought he held his sides with laughter.

"What is her name?" he managed to ask between paroxysms.

"Bellona," I said.

"He! he!" he tittered. "What a funny name!"

I gritted my teeth, for his mirth put them on edge, and snapped out between them, "She was the wife of Mars, you know."

Then the light of the full moon began to suffuse his face, until he exploded with: "That was my other dog. Well, I guess she's a widow now. Oh! Ho! ho! E! he! he! Ho!" he whooped after me, and I turned and fled swiftly over the hill.

The week passed by, and on Saturday evening I said to him, "You go away Monday, don't you?"

He nodded his head and grinned.

"Then you won't have another chance to get a mess of those trout you just 'dote' on."

But he did not notice the sneer. "Oh, I don't know," he chuckled. "I'm going up to-morrow to try pretty hard."

Thus was assurance made doubly sure, and I went back to my house hugging myself with rapture.

Early next morning I saw him go by with a dip-net and gunnysack, and Bellona trotting at his heels. I knew where he was bound, and cut out by the back pasture and climbed through the underbrush to the top of the mountain. Keeping carefully out of sight, I followed the crest along for a couple of miles to a natural amphitheatre in the hills, where the little river raced down out of a gorge and stopped for breath in a large and placid rock-bound pool. That was the spot! I sat down on the croup of the mountain, where I could see all that occurred, and lighted my pipe.

Ere many minutes had passed, John Claverhouse came plodding up the bed of the stream. Bellona was ambling about him, and they were in high feather, her short, snappy barks mingling with his deeper chest-notes. Arrived at the pool, he threw down the dip-net and sack, and drew from his hip-pocket what looked like a large, fat candle. But I knew it to be a stick of "giant"; for such was his method of catching trout. He dynamited them. He attached the fuse by wrapping the "giant" tightly in a piece of cotton. Then he ignited the fuse and tossed the explosive into the pool.

Like a flash, Bellona was into the pool after it. I could have shrieked aloud for joy. Claverhouse yelled at her, but without avail. He pelted her with clods and rocks, but she swam steadily on till she got the stick of "giant" in her mouth, when she whirled about and headed for shore. Then, for the first time, he realized his danger, and started to run. As foreseen and planned by me, she made the bank and took out after him. Oh, I tell you, it was great! As I have said, the pool lay in a sort of amphitheatre. Above and below, the stream could be crossed on stepping-stones. And around and around, up and down and across the stones, raced Claverhouse and Bellona. I could never have believed that such an ungainly man could run so fast. But run he did, Bellona hot-footed after him, and gaining. And then, just as she caught up, he in full stride, and she leaping with nose at his knee, there was a sudden flash, a burst of smoke, a terrific detonation, and where man and dog had been the instant before there was naught to be seen but a big hole in the ground.

"Death from accident while engaged in illegal fishing." That was the verdict of the coroner's jury; and that is why I pride myself on the neat and artistic way in which I finished off John Claverhouse. There was no bungling, no brutality; nothing of which to be ashamed in the whole transaction, as I am sure you will agree. No more does his infernal laugh go echoing among the hills, and no more does his fat moon-face rise up to vex me. My days are peaceful now, and my night's sleep deep.

BÂTARD

Bâtard was a devil. This was recognized throughout the Northland. "Hell's Spawn" he was called by many men, but his master, Black Leclère, chose for him the shameful name "Bâtard." Now Black Leclère was also a devil, and the twain were well matched. There is a saying that when two devils come together, hell is to pay. This is to be expected, and this certainly was to be expected when Bâtard and Black Leclère came together. The first time they met, Bâtard was a part-grown puppy, lean and hungry, with bitter eyes; and they met with snap and snarl, and wicked looks, for Leclère's upper lip had a wolfish way of lifting and showing the white, cruel teeth. And it lifted then, and his eyes glinted viciously, as he reached for Bâtard and dragged him out from the squirming litter. It was certain that they divined each other, for on the instant Bâtard had buried his puppy fangs in Leclère's hand, and Leclère, thumb and finger, was coolly choking his young life out of him.

"*Sacredam,*" the Frenchman said softly, flirting the quick blood from his bitten hand and gazing down on the little puppy choking and gasping in the snow.

Leclère turned to John Hamlin, storekeeper of the Sixty Mile Post. "Dat fo' w'at Ah lak heem. 'Ow moch, eh, you, *M'sieu'?* 'Ow moch? Ah buy heem, now; Ah buy heem queek."

And because he hated him with an exceeding bitter hate, Leclère bought Bâtard and gave him his shameful name. And for five years the twain adventured across the Northland, from St. Michael's and the Yukon delta to the head-reaches of the Pelly and even so far as the Peace River, Athabasca, and the Great Slave. And they acquired a reputation for uncompromising wickedness, the like of which never before attached itself to man and dog.

Bâtard did not know his father,—hence his name,—but, as John

Hamlin knew, his father was a great gray timber wolf. But the mother of Bâtard, as he dimly remembered her, was snarling, bickering, obscene, husky, full-fronted and heavy-chested, with a malign eye, a cat-like grip on life, and a genius for trickery and evil. There was neither faith nor trust in her. Her treachery alone could be relied upon, and her wild-wood amours attested her general depravity. Much of evil and much of strength were there in these, Bâtard's progenitors, and, bone and flesh of their bone and flesh, he had inherited it all. And then came Black Leclère, to lay his heavy hand on the bit of pulsating puppy life, to press and prod and mould till it became a big bristling beast, acute in knavery, overspilling with hate, sinister, malignant, diabolical. With a proper master Bâtard might have made an ordinary, fairly efficient sled-dog. He never got the chance: Leclère but confirmed him in his congenital iniquity.

The history of Bâtard and Leclère is a history of war—of five cruel, relentless years, of which their first meeting is fit summary. To begin with, it was Leclère's fault, for he hated with understanding and intelligence, while the long-legged, ungainly puppy hated only blindly, instinctively, without reason or method. At first there were no refinements of cruelty (these were to come later), but simple beatings and crude brutalities. In one of these Bâtard had an ear injured. He never regained control of the riven muscles, and ever after the ear drooped limply down to keep keen the memory of his tormentor. And he never forgot.

His puppyhood was a period of foolish rebellion. He was always worsted, but he fought back because it was his nature to fight back. And he was unconquerable. Yelping shrilly from the pain of lash and club, he none the less contrived always to throw in the defiant snarl, the bitter vindictive menace of his soul which fetched without fail more blows and beatings. But his was his mother's tenacious grip on life. Nothing could kill him. He flourished under misfortune, grew fat with famine, and out of his terrible struggle for life developed a preternatural intelligence. His were the stealth and cunning of the husky, his mother, and the fierceness and valor of the wolf, his father.

Possibly it was because of his father that he never wailed. His puppy yelps passed with his lanky legs, so that he became grim and taciturn, quick to strike, slow to warn. He answered curse with snarl, and blow with snap, grinning the while his implacable hatred; but never again, under the extremest agony, did Leclère bring from him the cry of fear nor of pain. This unconquerableness but fanned Leclère's wrath and stirred him to greater deviltries.

Did Leclère give Bâtard half a fish and to his mates whole ones, Bâtard went forth to rob other dogs of their fish. Also he robbed cachés and expressed himself in a thousand rogueries, till he became a terror to all dogs and masters of dogs. Did Leclère beat Bâtard and fondle Babette,—Babette who was not half the worker he was,—why, Bâtard threw her down in the snow and broke her hind leg in his heavy jaws, so that Leclère was forced to shoot her. Likewise, in bloody battles, Bâtard mastered all his team-mates, set them the law of trail and forage, and made them live to the law he set.

In five years he heard but one kind word, received but one soft stroke of a hand, and then he did not know what manner of things they were. He leaped like the untamed thing he was, and his jaws were together in a flash. It was the missionary at Sunrise, a newcomer in the country, who spoke the kind word and gave the soft stroke of the hand. And for six months after, he wrote no letters home to the States, and the surgeon at McQuestion travelled two hundred miles on the ice to save him from blood-poisoning.

Men and dogs looked askance at Bâtard when he drifted into their camps and posts. The men greeted him with feet threateningly lifted for the kick, the dogs with bristling manes and bared fangs. Once a man did kick Bâtard, and Bâtard, with quick wolf snap, closed his jaws like a steel trap on the man's calf and crunched down to the bone. Whereat the man was determined to have his life, only Black Leclère, with ominous eyes and naked hunting-knife, stepped in between. The killing of Bâtard—ah, *sacredam, that* was a pleasure Leclère reserved for himself. Some day it would happen, or else—bah! who was to know? Anyway, the problem would be solved.

For they had become problems to each other. The very breath each drew was a challenge and a menace to the other. Their hate bound them together as love could never bind. Leclère was bent on the coming of the day when Bâtard should wilt in spirit and cringe and whimper at his feet. And Bâtard—Leclère knew what was in Bâtard's mind, and more than once had read it in Bâtard's eyes. And so clearly had he read, that when Bâtard was at his back, he made it a point to glance often over his shoulder.

Men marvelled when Leclère refused large money for the dog. "Some day you'll kill him and be out his price," said John Hamlin once, when Bâtard lay panting in the snow where Leclère had kicked him, and no one knew whether his ribs were broken, and no one dared look to see.

"Dat," said Leclère, dryly, "dat is my biz'ness, *M'sieu'.*"

And the men marvelled that Bâtard did not run away. They did not understand. But Leclère understood. He was a man who lived much in the open, beyond the sound of human tongue, and he had learned the voices of wind and storm, the sigh of night, the whisper of dawn, the clash of day. In a dim way he could hear the green things growing, the running of the sap, the bursting of the bud. And he knew the subtle speech of the things that moved, of the rabbit in the snare, the moody raven beating the air with hollow wing, the baldface shuffling under the moon, the wolf like a gray shadow gliding betwixt the twilight and the dark. And to him Bâtard spoke clear and direct. Full well he understood why Bâtard did not run away, and he looked more often over his shoulder.

When in anger, Bâtard was not nice to look upon, and more than once had he leapt for Leclère's throat, to be stretched quivering and senseless in the snow, by the butt of the ever ready dogwhip. And so Bâtard learned to bide his time. When he reached his full strength and prime of youth, he thought the time had come. He was broad-chested, powerfully muscled, of far more than ordinary size, and his neck from head to shoulders was a mass of bristling hair—to all appearances a full-blooded wolf. Leclère was lying asleep in his furs when Bâtard deemed the time to be ripe. He crept upon him stealthily, head low to earth and lone ear laid back, with a feline softness of tread. Bâtard breathed gently, very gently, and not till he was close at hand did he raise his head. He paused for a moment, and looked at the bronzed bull throat, naked and knotty, and swelling to a deep and steady pulse. The slaver dripped down his fangs and slid off his tongue at the sight, and in that moment he remembered his drooping ear, his uncounted blows and prodigious wrongs, and without a sound sprang on the sleeping man.

Leclère awoke to the pang of the fangs in his throat, and, perfect animal that he was, he awoke clear-headed and with full comprehension. He closed on Bâtard's windpipe with both his hands, and rolled out of his furs to get his weight uppermost. But the thousands of Bâtard's ancestors had clung at the throats of unnumbered moose and caribou and dragged them down, and the wisdom of those ancestors was his. When Leclère's weight came on top of him, he drove his hind legs upward and in, and clawed down chest and abdomen, ripping and tearing through skin and muscle. And when he felt the man's body wince above him and lift, he worried and shook at the man's throat. His teammates closed around in a snarling circle, and Bâtard, with failing breath and fading sense, knew that their jaws were hungry for him. But that did not matter—it was the man, the man above him, and he ripped and clawed, and shook and worried, to the last ounce of his strength. But Leclère choked him with both his hands, till Bâtard's chest heaved and writhed for the air denied, and his eyes glazed and set, and his jaws slowly loosened, and his tongue protruded black and swollen.

"Eh? *Bon,* you devil!" Leclère gurgled, mouth and throat clogged with his own blood, as he shoved the dizzy dog from him.

And then Leclère cursed the other dogs off as they fell upon Bâtard. They drew back into a wider circle, squatting alertly on their haunches and licking their chops, the hair on every neck bristling and erect.

Bâtard recovered quickly, and at sound of Leclère's voice, tottered to his feet and swayed weakly back and forth.

"A-h-ah! You beeg devil!" Leclère spluttered. "Ah fix you; Ah fix you plentee, by *Gar!*"

Bâtard, the air biting into his exhausted lungs like wine, flashed full into the man's face, his jaws missing and coming together with a metallic clip. They rolled over and over on the snow, Leclère striking madly with his fists. Then they separated, face to face, and circled back and forth before each other. Leclère could have drawn his knife. His rifle was at his feet. But the beast in him was up and raging. He would do the thing with his hands—and his teeth. Bâtard sprang in, but Leclère knocked him over with a blow of the fist, fell upon him, and buried his teeth to the bone in the dog's shoulder.

It was a primordial setting and a primordial scene, such as might have been in the savage youth of the world. An open space in a dark forest, a ring of grinning wolf-dogs, and in the centre two beasts, locked in combat, snapping and snarling, raging madly about, panting, sobbing, cursing, straining, wild with passion, in a fury of murder, ripping and tearing and clawing in elemental brutishness.

But Leclère caught Bâtard behind the ear, with a blow from his fist, knocking him over, and, for the instant, stunning him. Then Leclère leaped upon him with his feet, and sprang up and down, striving to grind him into the earth. Both Bâtard's hind legs were broken ere Leclère ceased that he might catch breath.

"A-a-ah! A-a-ah!" he screamed, incapable of speech, shaking his fist, through sheer impotence of throat and larynx.

But Bâtard was indomitable. He lay there in a helpless welter, his lip feebly lifting and writhing to the snarl he had not the strength to utter. Leclère kicked him, and the tired jaws closed on the ankle, but could not break the skin.

Then Leclère picked up the whip and proceeded almost to cut him to pieces, at each stroke of the lash crying: "Dis taim Ah break you! Eh? By *Gar!* Ah break you!"

In the end, exhausted, fainting from loss of blood, he crumpled up and fell by his victim, and when the wolf-dogs closed in to take their vengeance, with his last consciousness dragged his body on top Bâtard to shield him from their fangs.

This occurred not far from Sunrise, and the missionary, opening the door to Leclère a few hours later, was surprised to note the absence of Bâtard from the team. Nor did his surprise lessen when Leclère threw back the robes from the sled, gathered Bâtard into his arms, and staggered across the threshold. It happened that the surgeon of McQuestion, who was something of a gadabout, was up on a gossip, and between them they proceeded to repair Leclère.

"*Merci, non,*" said he. "Do you fix firs' de dog. To die? *Non.* Eet is not good. Becos' heem Ah mus' yet break. Dat fo' w'at he mus' not die."

The surgeon called it a marvel, the missionary a miracle, that Leclère pulled through at all; and so weakened was he, that in the spring the fever got him, and he went on his back again. Bâtard had been in even worse plight, but his grip on life prevailed, and the bones of his hind legs knit, and his organs righted themselves, during the several weeks he lay strapped to the floor. And by the time Leclère, finally convalescent, sallow and shaky, took the sun by the cabin door, Bâtard had reasserted his supremacy among his kind, and brought not only his own team-mates but the missionary's dogs into subjection.

He moved never a muscle, nor twitched a hair, when, for the first time, Leclère tottered out on the missionary's arm, and sank down slowly and with infinite caution on the three-legged stool.

"*Bon!*" he said. "*Bon!* De good sun!" And he stretched out his wasted hands and washed them in the warmth.

Then his gaze fell on the dog, and the old light blazed back in his eyes. He touched the missionary lightly on the arm. "*Mon père,* dat is one beeg devil, dat Bâtard. You will bring me one pistol, so, dat Ah drink de sun in peace."

And thenceforth for many days he sat in the sun before the cabin door. He never dozed, and the pistol lay always across his knees. Bâtard had a way, the first thing each day, of looking for the weapon in its wonted place. At sight of it he would lift his lip faintly in token that he understood, and Leclère would lift his own lip in an answering grin. One day the missionary took note of the trick.

"Bless me!" he said. "I really believe the brute comprehends."

Leclère laughed softly. "Look you, *mon père.* Dat w'at Ah now spik, to dat does he lissen."

As if in confirmation, Bâtard just perceptibly wriggled his lone ear up to catch the sound.

"Ah say 'keel.'"

Bâtard growled deep down in his throat, the hair bristled along his neck, and every muscle went tense and expectant.

"Ah lift de gun, so, like dat." And suiting action to word, he sighted the pistol at Bâtard.

Bâtard, with a single leap, sideways, landed around the corner of the cabin out of sight.

"Bless me!" he repeated at intervals.

Leclère grinned proudly.

"But why does he not run away?"

The Frenchman's shoulders went up in the racial shrug that means all things from total ignorance to infinite understanding.

"Then why do you not kill him?"

Again the shoulders went up.

"*Mon père,*" he said after a pause, "de taim is not yet. He is one beeg devil. Some taim Ah break heem, so, an' so, all to leetle bits. Hey? Some taim. *Bon!*"

A day came when Leclère gathered his dogs together and floated down in a bateau to Forty Mile, and on to the Porcupine, where he took a commission from the P. C. Company, and went exploring for the better part of a year. After that he poled up the Koyokuk to deserted Arctic City, and later came drifting back, from camp to camp, along the Yukon. And during the long months Bâtard was well lessoned. He learned many tortures, and, notably, the torture of hunger, the torture of thirst, the torture of fire, and, worst of all, the torture of music.

Like the rest of his kind, he did not enjoy music. It gave him exquisite anguish, racking him nerve by nerve, and ripping apart every fibre of his being. It made him howl, long and wolf-like, as when the wolves bay the stars on frosty nights. He could not help howling. It was his one weakness in the contest with Leclère, and it was his shame. Leclère, on the other hand, passionately loved music—as passionately as he loved strong drink. And when his soul clamored for expression, it usually uttered itself in one or the other of the two ways, and more usually in both ways. And when he had drunk, his brain a-lilt with unsung song and the devil in him aroused and rampant, his soul found its supreme utterance in torturing Bâtard.

"Now we will haf a leetle museek," he would say. "Eh? W'at you t'ink, Bâtard?"

It was only an old and battered harmonica, tenderly treasured and patiently repaired; but it was the best that money could buy, and out of its silver reeds he drew weird vagrant airs that men had never heard · before. Then Bâtard, dumb of throat, with teeth tight clenched, would back away, inch by inch, to the farthest cabin corner. And Leclère, playing, playing, a stout club tucked under his arm, followed the animal up, inch by inch, step by step, till there was no further retreat.

At first Bâtard would crowd himself into the smallest possible space, grovelling close to the floor; but as the music came nearer and nearer, he was forced to uprear, his back jammed into the logs, his fore legs fanning the air as though to beat off the rippling waves of sound. He still kept his teeth together, but severe muscular contractions attacked his body, strange twitchings and jerkings, till he was all a-quiver and writhing in silent torment. As he lost control, his jaws spasmodically wrenched apart, and deep throaty vibrations issued forth, too low in the register of sound for human ear to catch. And then, nostrils distended, eyes dilated, hair bristling in helpless rage, arose the long wolf howl. It came with a slurring rush upward, swelling to a great heart-breaking burst of sound, and dying away in sadly cadenced woe—then the next rush upward, octave upon octave; the bursting heart; and the infinite sorrow and misery, fainting, fading, falling, and dying slowly away.

It was fit for hell. And Leclère, with fiendish ken, seemed to divine each particular nerve and heartstring, and with long wails and tremblings and sobbing minors to make it yield up its last shred of grief. It was frightful, and for twenty-four hours after, Bâtard was nervous and unstrung, starting at common sounds, tripping over his own shadow, but, withal, vicious and masterful with his team-mates. Nor did he show signs of a breaking spirit. Rather did he grow more grim and taciturn, biding his time with an inscrutable patience that began to puzzle and weigh upon Leclère. The dog would lie in the firelight, motionless, for hours, gazing straight before him at Leclère, and hating him with his bitter eyes.

Often the man felt that he had bucked against the very essence of life—the unconquerable essence that swept the hawk down out of the sky like a feathered thunderbolt, that drove the great gray goose across the zones, that hurled the spawning salmon through two thousand miles of boiling Yukon flood. At such times he felt impelled to express his own unconquerable essence; and with strong drink, wild music, and Bâtard, he indulged in vast orgies, wherein he pitted his puny strength in the face of things, and challenged all that was, and had been, and was yet to be.

"Dere is somet'ing dere," he affirmed, when the rhythmed vagaries of his mind touched the secret chords of Bâtard's being and brought forth the long lugubrious howl. "Ah pool eet out wid bot' my han's, so, an' so. Ha! Ha! Eet is fonee! Eet is ver' fonee! De priest chant, de womans pray, de mans swear, de leetle bird go *peep-peep*, Bâtard, heem go *yow-yow*—an' eet is all de ver' same t'ing. Ha! Ha!"

Father Gautier, a worthy priest, once reproved him with instances of concrete perdition. He never reproved him again.

"Eet may be so, *mon père,*" he made answer. "An' Ah t'ink Ah go troo hell a-snappin', lak de hemlock troo de fire. Eh, *mon père?*"

But all bad things come to an end as well as good, and so with Black Leclère. On the summer low water, in a poling boat, he left McDougall for Sunrise. He left McDougall in company with Timothy Brown, and arrived at Sunrise by himself. Further, it was known that they had quarrelled just previous to pulling out; for the *Lizzie,* a wheezy ten-ton stern-wheeler, twenty-four hours behind, beat Leclère in by three days. And when he did get in, it was with a clean-drilled bullet-hole through his shoulder muscle, and a tale of ambush and murder.

A strike had been made at Sunrise, and things had changed considerably. With the infusion of several hundred gold-seekers, a deal of whiskey, and half a dozen equipped gamblers, the missionary had seen the page of his years of labor with the Indians wiped clean. When the squaws became preoccupied with cooking beans and keeping the fire going for the wifeless miners, and the bucks with swapping their warm furs for black bottles and broken timepieces, he took to his bed, said "bless me" several times, and departed to his final accounting in a rough-hewn, oblong box. Whereupon the gamblers moved their roulette and faro tables into the mission house, and the click of chips and clink of glasses went up from dawn till dark and to dawn again.

Now Timothy Brown was well beloved among these adventurers of the north. The one thing against him was his quick temper and ready fist,—a little thing, for which his kind heart and forgiving hand more than atoned. On the other hand, there was nothing to atone for Black Leclère. He was "black," as more than one remembered deed bore witness, while he was as well hated as the other was beloved. So the men of Sunrise put an antiseptic dressing on his shoulder and haled him before Judge Lynch.

It was a simple affair. He had quarrelled with Timothy Brown at McDougall. With Timothy Brown he had left McDougall. Without Timothy Brown he had arrived at Sunrise. Considered in the light of his evilness, the unanimous conclusion was that he had killed Timothy Brown. On the other hand, Leclère acknowledged their facts, but challenged their conclusion, and gave his own explanation. Twenty miles out of Sunrise he and Timothy Brown were poling the boat along the rocky shore. From that shore two rifle-shots rang out. Timothy Brown pitched out of the boat and went down bubbling red, and that was the last of Timothy Brown. He, Leclère, pitched into the bottom of the boat with a stinging shoulder. He lay very quiet, peeping at the shore. After a time two Indians stuck up their heads and came out to the water's edge, carrying between them a birch-bark canoe. As they launched it,

Leclère let fly. He potted one, who went over the side after the manner of Timothy Brown. The other dropped into the bottom of the canoe, and then canoe and poling boat went down the stream in a drifting battle. After that they hung up on a split current, and the canoe passed on one side of an island, the poling boat on the other. That was the last of the canoe, and he came on into Sunrise. Yes, from the way the Indian in the canoe jumped, he was sure he had potted him. That was all.

This explanation was not deemed adequate. They gave him ten hours' grace while the *Lizzie* steamed down to investigate. Ten hours later she came wheezing back to Sunrise. There had been nothing to investigate. No evidence had been found to back up his statements. They told him to make his will, for he possessed a fifty-thousand-dollar Sunrise claim, and they were a law-abiding as well as a law-giving breed.

Leclère shrugged his shoulders. "Bot one t'ing," he said; "a leetle, w'at you call, favor—a leetle favor, dat is eet. I gif my feefty t'ousan' dollair to de church. I gif my husky dog, Bâtard, to de devil. De leetle favor? Firs' you hang heem, an' den you hang me. Eet is good, eh?"

Good it was, they agreed, that Hell's Spawn should break trail for his master across the last divide, and the court was adjourned down to the river bank, where a big spruce tree stood by itself. Slackwater Charley put a hangman's knot in the end of a hauling-line, and the noose was slipped over Leclère's head and pulled tight around his neck. His hands were tied behind his back, and he was assisted to the top of a cracker box. Then the running end of the line was passed over an overhanging branch, drawn taut, and made fast. To kick the box out from under would leave him dancing on the air.

"Now for the dog," said Webster Shaw, sometime mining engineer. "You'll have to rope him, Slackwater."

Leclère grinned. Slackwater took a chew of tobacco, rove a running noose, and proceeded leisurely to coil a few turns in his hand. He paused once or twice to brush particularly offensive mosquitoes from off his face. Everybody was brushing mosquitoes, except Leclère, about whose head a small cloud was visible. Even Bâtard, lying full-stretched on the ground, with his fore paws rubbed the pests away from eyes and mouth.

But while Slackwater waited for Bâtard to lift his head, a faint call came down the quiet air, and a man was seen waving his arms and running across the flat from Sunrise. It was the storekeeper.

"C-call 'er off, boys," he panted, as he came in among them.

"Little Sandy and Bernadotte's jes' got in," he explained with return-ing breath. "Landed down below an' come up by the short cut. Got the Beaver with 'm. Picked 'm up in his canoe, stuck in a back channel, with a couple of bullet holes in 'm. Other buck was Klok-Kutz, the one that knocked spots out of his squaw and dusted."

"Eh? W'at Ah say? Eh?" Leclère cried exultantly. "Dat de one fo' sure! Ah know. Ah spik true."

"The thing to do is teach these damned Siwashes a little manners," spoke Webster Shaw. "They're getting fat and sassy, and we'll have to bring them down a peg. Round in all the bucks and string up the Beaver for an object lesson. That's the programme. Come on and let's see what he's got to say for himself."

"Heh, M'sieu'!" Leclère called, as the crowd began to melt away through the twilight in the direction of Sunrise. "Ah lak ver' moch to see de fon."

"Oh, we'll turn you loose when we come back," Webster Shaw shouted over his shoulder. "In the meantime meditate on your sins and the ways of providence. It will do you good, so be grateful."

As is the way with men who are accustomed to great hazards, whose nerves are healthy and trained to patience, so it was with Leclère, who settled himself to the long wait—which is to say that he reconciled his mind to it. There was no settling of the body, for the taut rope forced him to stand rigidly erect. The least relaxation of the leg muscles pressed the rough-fibred noose into his neck, while the upright position caused him much pain in his wounded shoulder. He projected his under lip and expelled his breath upward along his face to blow the mosquitoes away from his eyes. But the situation had its compensation. To be snatched from the maw of death was well worth a little bodily suffering, only it was unfortunate that he should miss the hanging of the Beaver.

And so he mused, till his eyes chanced to fall upon Bâtard, head between fore paws and stretched on the ground asleep. And then Leclère ceased to muse. He studied the animal closely, striving to sense if the sleep were real or feigned. Bâtard's sides were heaving regularly, but Leclère felt that the breath came and went a shade too quickly; also he felt that there was a vigilance or alertness to every hair that belied unshackling sleep. He would have given his Sunrise claim to be assured that the dog was not awake, and once, when one of his joints cracked, he looked quickly and guiltily at Bâtard to see if he roused. He did not rouse then, but a few minutes later he got up slowly and lazily, stretched, and looked carefully about him.

"*Sacredam,*" said Leclère, under his breath.

Assured that no one was in sight or hearing, Bâtard sat down, curled his upper lip almost into a smile, looked up at Leclère, and licked his chops.

"Ah see my feenish," the man said, and laughed sardonically aloud.

Bâtard came nearer, the useless ear wabbling, the good ear cocked forward with devilish comprehension. He thrust his head on one side quizzically, and advanced with mincing, playful steps. He rubbed his body gently against the box till it shook and shook again. Leclère teetered carefully to maintain his equilibrium.

"Bâtard," he said calmly, "look out. Ah keel you."

Bâtard snarled at the word, and shook the box with greater force. Then he upreared, and with his fore paws threw his weight against it higher up. Leclère kicked out with one foot, but the rope bit into his neck and checked so abruptly as nearly to overbalance him.

"Hi, ya! *Chook! Mush-on!*" he screamed.

Bâtard retreated, for twenty feet or so, with a fiendish levity in his bearing that Leclère could not mistake. He remembered the dog often breaking the scum of ice on the water hole, by lifting up and throwing his weight upon it; and, remembering, he understood what he now had in mind. Bâtard faced about and paused. He showed his white teeth in a grin, which Leclère answered; and then hurled his body through the air, in full charge, straight for the box.

Fifteen minutes later, Slackwater Charley and Webster Shaw, returning, caught a glimpse of a ghostly pendulum swinging back and forth in the dim light. As they hurriedly drew in closer, they made out the man's inert body, and a live thing that clung to it, and shook and worried, and gave to it the swaying motion.

"Hi, ya! *Chook!* you Spawn of Hell," yelled Webster Shaw.

But Bâtard glared at him, and snarled threateningly, without loosing his jaws.

Slackwater Charley got out his revolver, but his hand was shaking, as with a chill, and he fumbled.

"Here, you take it," he said, passing the weapon over.

Webster Shaw laughed shortly, drew a sight between the gleaming eyes, and pressed the trigger. Bâtard's body twitched with the shock, threshed the ground spasmodically for a moment, and went suddenly limp. But his teeth still held fast locked.

THE STORY OF JEES UCK

There have been renunciations, and renunciations. But, in its essence, renunciation is ever the same. And the paradox of it is that men and women forego the dearest thing in the world for something dearer. It was never otherwise. Thus it was when Abel brought of the firstlings of his flock and of the fat thereof. The firstlings and the fat thereof were to him the dearest things in the world; yet he gave them over that he might be on good terms with God. So it was with Abraham when he prepared to offer up his son Isaac on a stone. Isaac was very dear to him; but God, in incomprehensible ways, was yet dearer. It may be that Abraham feared the Lord. But whether that be true or not, it has since been determined by a few billion people that he loved the Lord and desired to serve Him.

And since it has been determined that love is service, and since to renounce is to serve, then Jees Uck, who was merely a woman of a swart-skinned breed, loved with a great love. She was unversed in history, having learned to read only the signs of weather and of game; so she had never heard of Abel, nor of Abraham; nor, having escaped the good sisters at Holy Cross, had she been told the story of Ruth, the Moabitess, who renounced her very God for the sake of a stranger woman from a strange land. Jees Uck had learned only one way of renouncing, and that was with a club as the dynamic factor, in much the same manner as a dog is made to renounce a stolen marrow-bone. Yet, when the time came, she proved herself capable of rising to the height of the fair-faced royal races and of renouncing in right regal fashion.

So this is the story of Jees Uck, which is also the story of Neil Bonner, and Kitty Bonner, and a couple of Neil Bonner's progeny. Jees Uck was of a swart-skinned breed, it is true, but she was not an Indian; nor was she an Eskimo; nor even an Innuit. Going backward into mouth tradition, there appears the figure of one Skolkz, a Toyaat Indian of the Yukon, who journeyed down in his youth to the Great Delta where dwell the Innuits, and where he forgathered with a woman remembered as Olillie. Now the woman Olillie had been bred from an Eskimo mother by an Innuit man. And from Skolkz and Olillie came Halie, who was one-half Toyaat Indian, one-quarter Innuit, and one-quarter Eskimo. And Halie was the grandmother of Jees Uck.

Now Halie, in whom three stocks had been bastardized, who cherished no prejudice against further admixture, mated with a Russian fur trader called Shpack, also known in his time as the Big Fat. Shpack is herein classed Russian for lack of a more adequate term; for Shpack's father, a Slavonic convict from the Lower Provinces, had escaped from the quicksilver mines into Northern Siberia, where he knew Zimba, who was a woman of the Deer People and who became the mother of Shpack, who became the grandfather of Jees Uck.

Now had not Shpack been captured in his boyhood by the Sea People, who fringe the rim of the Arctic Sea with their misery, he would not have become the grandfather of Jees Uck and there would be no story at all. But he *was* captured by the Sea People, from whom he escaped to Kamchatka, and thence, on a Norwegian whale-ship, to the Baltic. Not long after that he turned up in St. Petersburg, and the years were not many till he went drifting east over the same weary road his father had measured with blood and groans a half-century before. But Shpack was a free man, in the employ of the great Russian Fur Company. And in that employ he fared farther and farther east, until he crossed Bering Sea into Russian America; and at Pastolik, which is hard by the Great Delta of the Yukon, became the husband of Halie, who was the grandmother of Jees Uck. Out of this union came the woman-child, Tukesan.

Shpack, under the orders of the company, made a canoe voyage of a few hundred miles up the Yukon to the post of Nulato. With him he took Halie and the babe Tukesan. This was in 1850, and in 1850 it was that the river Indians fell upon Nulato and wiped it from the face of the earth. And that was the end of Shpack and Halie. On that terrible night Tukesan disappeared. To this day the Toyaats aver they had no hand in the trouble; but, be that as it may, the fact remains that the babe Tukesan grew up among them.

Tukesan was married successively to two Toyaat brothers, to both of whom she was barren. Because of this, other women shook their heads, and no third Toyaat man could be found to dare matrimony with the childless widow. But at this time, many hundred miles above, at Fort Yukon, was a man, Spike O'Brien. Fort Yukon was a Hudson Bay Company post, and Spike O'Brien one of the company's servants. He was a good servant, but he achieved an opinion that the service was bad, and in the course of time vindicated that opinion by deserting. It was a year's journey, by the chain of posts, back to York Factory on Hudson's Bay. Further, being company posts, he knew he could not evade the company's clutches. Nothing remained but to go down the Yukon. It was true no white man had ever gone down the Yukon, and no white man knew whether the Yukon emptied into the Arctic Ocean or Bering Sea; but Spike O'Brien was a Celt, and the promise of danger was a lure he had ever followed.

A few weeks later, somewhat battered, rather famished, and about dead with river-fever, he drove the nose of his canoe into the earth bank by the village of the Toyaats and promptly fainted away. While getting his strength back, in the weeks that followed, he looked upon Tukesan and found her good. Like the father of Shpack, who lived to a ripe old age among the Siberian Deer People, Spike O'Brien might have left his aged bones with the Toyaats. But romance gripped his heart-strings and would not let him stay. As he had journeyed from York Factory to Fort Yukon, so, first among men, might he journey from Fort Yukon to the sea and win the honor of being the first man to make the Northwest Passage by land. So he departed down the river, won the honor, and was unannaled and unsung. In after years he ran a sailors' boarding-house in San Francisco, where he became esteemed a most remarkable liar by virtue of the gospel truths he told. But a child was born to Tukesan, who had been childless. And this child was Jees Uck. Her lineage has been traced at length to show that she was neither Indian, nor Eskimo, nor Innuit, nor much of anything else; also to show what waifs of the generations we are, all of us, and the strange meanderings of the seed from which we spring.

What with the vagrant blood in her and the heritage compounded of many races, Jees Uck developed a wonderful young beauty. Bizarre, perhaps, it was, and Oriental enough to puzzle any passing ethnologist. A lithe and slender grace characterized her. Beyond a quickened lilt to the imagination, the contribution of the Celt was in no wise apparent. It might possibly have put the warm blood under her skin, which made her face less swart and her body fairer; but that, in turn, might have come from Shpack, the Big Fat, who inherited the color of his Slavonic father. And, finally, she had great, blazing black eyes—the half-caste eye, round, full-orbed, and sensuous, which marks the collision of the dark races with the light. Also, the white blood in her, combined with her knowledge that it was in her, made her, in a way, ambitious. Otherwise, by upbringing and in outlook on life, she was wholly and utterly a Toyaat Indian.

One winter, when she was a young woman, Neil Bonner came into her life. But he came into her life, as he had come into the country, somewhat reluctantly. In fact, it was very much against his will, coming into the country. Between a father who clipped coupons and cultivated roses, and a mother who loved the social round, Neil Bonner had gone rather wild. He was not vicious, but a man with meat in his belly and without work in the world has to expend his energy somehow, and Neil Bonner was such a man. And he expended his energy in such fashion and to such extent that when the inevitable climax came, his father, Neil Bonner, senior, crawled out of his roses in a panic and looked on his son with a wondering eye. Then he hied himself away to a crony of kindred pursuits, with whom he was wont to confer over coupons and roses, and between the two the destiny of young Neil Bonner was made manifest. He must go away, on probation, to live down his harmless follies in order that he might live up to their own excellent standard.

This determined upon, and young Neil a little repentant and a great deal ashamed, the rest was easy. The cronies were heavy stockholders in the P. C. Company. The P. C. Company owned fleets of river-steamers and ocean-going craft, and, in addition to farming the sea, exploited a hundred thousand square miles or so of the land that, on the maps of geographers, usually occupies the white spaces. So the P. C. Company sent young Neil Bonner north, where the white spaces are, to do its work and to learn to be good like his father. "Five years of simplicity, close to the soil and far from temptation, will make a man of him," said old Neil Bonner, and forthwith crawled back among his roses. Young Neil set his jaw, pitched his chin at the proper angle, and went to work. As an underling he did his work well and gained the commendation of his superiors. Not that he delighted in the work, but that it was the one thing that prevented him from going mad.

The first year he wished he was dead. The second year he cursed God. The third year he was divided between the two emotions, and in the confusion quarrelled with a man in authority. He had the best of the quarrel, though the man in authority had the last word,—a word that sent Neil Bonner into an exile that made his old billet appear as paradise. But he went without a whimper, for the North had succeeded in making him into a man.

Here and there, on the white spaces on the map, little circlets like the letter "o" are to be found, and, appended to these circlets, on one side or the other, are names such as "Fort Hamilton," "Yanana Station," "Twenty Mile," thus leading one to imagine that the white spaces are plentifully besprinkled with towns and villages. But it is a vain imagining. Twenty Mile, which is very like the rest of the posts, is a log building the size of a corner grocery with rooms to let upstairs. A long-legged caché on stilts may be found in the back yard; also a couple of outhouses. The back yard is unfenced, and extends to the sky-line and an unascertainable bit beyond. There are no other houses in sight, though the Toyaats sometimes pitch a winter camp a mile or two down the Yukon. And this is Twenty Mile, one tentacle of the many-tentacled P. C. Company. Here the agent, with an assistant, barters with the Indians for their furs, and does an erratic trade on a gold-dust basis with the wandering miners. Here, also, the agent and his assistant yearn all winter for the spring, and when the spring comes, camp blasphemously on the roof while the Yukon washes out the establishment. And here, also, in the fourth year of his sojourn in the land, came Neil Bonner to take charge.

He had displaced no agent; for the man that previously ran the post had made away with himself; "because of the rigors of the place," said the assistant, who still remained; though the Toyaats, by their fires, had another version. The assistant was a shrunken-shouldered, hollow-chested man, with a cadaverous face and cavernous cheeks that his sparse black beard could not hide. He coughed much, as though consumption gripped his lungs, while his eyes had that mad, fevered light common to consumptives in the last stage. Pentley was his name,—Amos Pentley,—and Bonner did not like him, though he felt a pity for the forlorn and hopeless devil. They did not get along together, these two men who, of all men, should have been on good terms in the face of the cold and silence and darkness of the long winter.

In the end, Bonner concluded that Amos was partly demented, and left him alone, doing all the work himself except the cooking. Even then, Amos had nothing but bitter looks and an undisguised hatred for him. This was a great loss to Bonner; for the smiling face of one of his own kind, the cheery word, the sympathy of comradeship shared with misfortune—these things meant much; and the winter was yet young when he began to realize the added reasons, with such an assistant, that the previous agent had found to impel his own hand against his life.

It was very lonely at Twenty Mile. The bleak vastness stretched away on every side to the horizon. The snow, which was really frost, flung its mantle over the land and buried everything in the silence of death. For days it was clear and cold, the thermometer steadily recording forty to fifty degrees below zero. Then a change came over the face of things. What little moisture had oozed into the atmosphere gathered into dull gray, formless clouds; it became quite warm, the thermometer rising to twenty below; and the moisture fell out of the sky in hard frost-granules that hissed like dry sugar or driving sand when kicked underfoot. After that it became clear and cold again, until enough moisture had gathered to blanket the earth from the cold of outer space. That was all. Nothing happened. No storms, no churning waters and threshing forests, nothing but the machine-like precipitation of accumulated moisture. Possibly the most notable thing that occurred through the weary weeks was the gliding of the temperature up to the unprecedented height of fifteen below. To atone for this, outer space smote the earth with its cold till the mercury froze and the spirit thermometer remained more than seventy below for a fortnight, when it burst. There was no telling how much colder it was after that. Another occurrence, monotonous in its regularity, was the lengthening of the nights, till day became a mere blink of light between the darknesses.

Neil Bonner was a social animal. The very follies for which he was doing penance had been bred of his excessive sociability. And here, in the fourth year of his exile, he found himself in company—which were to travesty the word—with a morose and speechless creature in whose sombre eyes smouldered a hatred as bitter as it was unwarranted. And Bonner, to whom speech and fellowship were as the breath of life, went about as a ghost might go, tantalized by the gregarious revelries of some former life. In the day his lips were compressed, his face stern; but in the night he clenched his hands, rolled about in his blankets, and cried aloud like a little child. And he would remember a certain man in authority and curse him through the long hours. Also, he cursed God. But God understands. He cannot find it in His heart to blame weak mortals who blaspheme in Alaska.

And here, to the post of Twenty Mile, came Jees Uck, to trade for flour and bacon, and beads, and bright scarlet cloths for her fancy work. And further, and unwittingly, she came to the post of Twenty Mile to make a lonely man more lonely, make him reach out empty arms in his sleep. For Neil Bonner was only a man. When she first came into the store, he looked at her long, as a thirsty man may look at a flowing well. And she, with the heritage bequeathed her by Spike O'Brien, imagined daringly and smiled up into his eyes, not as the swart-skinned peoples should smile at the royal races, but as a woman smiles at a man. The thing was inevitable; only, he did not see it, and fought against her as fiercely and passionately as he was drawn toward her. And she? She was Jees Uck, by upbringing wholly and utterly a Toyaat Indian woman.

She came often to the post to trade. And often she sat by the big wood stove and chatted in broken English with Neil Bonner. And he came to look for her coming; and on the days she did not come he was worried and restless. Sometimes he stopped to think, and then she was met coldly, with a reserve that perplexed and piqued her, and which, she was convinced, was not sincere. But more often he did not dare to think, and then all went well and there were smiles and laughter. And Amos Pentley, gasping like a stranded catfish, his hollow cough a-reek with the grave, looked upon it all and grinned. He, who loved life, could not live, and it rankled his soul that others should be able to live. Wherefore he hated Bonner, who was so very much alive and into whose eyes sprang joy at the sight of Jees Uck. As for Amos, the very thought of the girl was sufficient to send his blood pounding up into a hemorrhage.

Jees Uck, whose mind was simple, who thought elementally and was unused to weighing life in its subtler quantities, read Amos Pentley like a book. She warned Bonner, openly and bluntly, in few words; but the complexities of higher existence confused the situation to him, and he laughed at her evident anxiety. To him, Amos was a poor, miserable devil, tottering desperately into the grave. And Bonner, who had suffered much, found it easy to forgive greatly.

But one morning, during a bitter snap, he got up from the breakfast table and went into the store. Jees Uck was already there, rosy from the trail, to buy a sack of flour. A few minutes later, he was out in the snow lashing the flour on her sled. As he bent over he noticed a stiffness in his neck and felt a premonition of impending physical misfortune. And as he put the last half-hitch into the lashing and attempted to straighten up, a quick spasm seized him and he sank into the snow. Tense and quivering, head jerked back, limbs extended, back arched and mouth twisted and distorted, he appeared as though being racked limb from limb. Without cry or sound, Jees Uck was in the snow beside him; but he clutched both her wrists spasmodically, and as long as the convulsion endured she was helpless. In a few moments the spasm relaxed and he was left weak and fainting, his forehead beaded with sweat, his lips flecked with foam.

"Quick!" he muttered, in a strange, hoarse voice. "Quick! Inside!"

He started to crawl on hands and knees, but she raised him up, and, supported by her young arm, he made faster progress. As he entered the store the spasm seized him again, and his body writhed irresistibly away from her and rolled and curled on the floor. Amos Pentley came and looked on with curious eyes.

"Oh, Amos!" she cried in an agony of apprehension and helplessness, "him die, you think?" But Amos shrugged his shoulders and continued to look on.

Bonner's body went slack, the tense muscles easing down and an expression of relief coming into his face. "Quick!" he gritted between his teeth, his mouth twisting with the on-coming of the next spasm and with his effort to control it. "Quick, Jees Uck! The medicine! Never mind! Drag me!"

She knew where the medicine-chest stood, at the rear of the room, beyond the stove, and thither, by the legs, she dragged the struggling man. As the spasm passed, he began, very faint and very sick, to overhaul the chest. He had seen dogs die exhibiting symptoms similar to his own, and he knew what should be done. He held up a vial of chloral hydrate, but his fingers were too weak and nerveless to draw the cork. This Jees Uck did for him, while he was plunged into another convulsion. As he came out of it he found the open bottle proffered him and looked into the great black eyes of the woman and read what men have always read in the Mate-woman's eyes. Taking a full dose of the stuff, he sank back until another spasm had passed. Then he raised himself limply on his elbow.

"Listen, Jees Uck!" he said very slowly, as though aware of the necessity for haste and yet afraid to hasten. "Do what I say. Stay by my side, but do not touch me. I must be very quiet, but you must not go away." His jaw began to set and his face to quiver and distort with the forerunning pangs, but he gulped and struggled to master them. "Do not go away. And do not let Amos go away. Understand! Amos must stay right here."

She nodded her head, and he passed off into the first of many convulsions, which gradually diminished in force and frequency. Jees Uck hung over him, remembering his injunction and not daring to touch him. Once Amos grew restless and made as though to go into the kitchen; but a quick blaze from her eyes quelled him, and after that, save for his labored breathing and charnel cough, he was very quiet.

Bonner slept. The blink of light that marked the day disappeared. Amos, followed about by the woman's eyes, lighted the kerosene lamps. Evening came on. Through the north window the heavens were emblazoned with an auroral display, which flamed and flared and died down into blackness. Some time after that, Neil Bonner roused. First he looked to see that Amos was still there, then smiled at Jees Uck and pulled himself up. Every muscle was stiff and sore, and he smiled ruefully, pressing and prodding himself as if to ascertain the extent of the ravage. Then his face went stern and businesslike.

"Jees Uck," he said, "take a candle. Go into the kitchen. There is food on the table—biscuits and beans and bacon; also, coffee in the pot on the stove. Bring it here on the counter. Also, bring tumblers and water and whiskey, which you will find on the top shelf of the locker. Do not forget the whiskey."

Having swallowed a stiff glass of the whiskey, he went carefully through the medicine chest, now and again putting aside, with definite purpose, certain bottles and vials. Then he set to work on the food, attempting a crude analysis. He had not been unused to the laboratory in his college days and was possessed of sufficient imagination to achieve results with his limited materials. The condition of tetanus, which had marked his paroxysms, simplified matters, and he made but one test. The coffee yielded nothing; nor did the beans. To the biscuits he devoted the utmost care. Amos, who knew nothing of chemistry, looked on with steady curiosity. But Jees Uck, who had boundless faith in the white man's wisdom, and especially in Neil Bonner's wisdom, and who not only knew nothing but knew that she knew nothing, watched his face rather than his hands.

Step by step he eliminated possibilities, until he came to the final test. He was using a thin medicine vial for a tube, and this he held between him and the light, watching the slow precipitation of a salt through the solution contained in the tube. He said nothing, but he saw what he had expected to see. And Jees Uck, her eyes riveted on his face, saw something, too,—something that made her spring like a tigress upon Amos and with splendid suppleness and strength bend his body back across her knee. Her knife was out of its sheath and uplifted, glinting in the lamplight. Amos was snarling; but Bonner intervened ere the blade could fall.

"That's a good girl, Jees Uck. But never mind. Let him go!"

She dropped the man obediently, though with protest writ large on her face; and his body thudded to the floor. Bonner nudged him with his moccasined foot.

"Get up, Amos!" he commanded. "You've got to pack an outfit yet to-night and hit the trail."

"You don't mean to say—" Amos blurted savagely.

"I mean to say that you tried to kill me," Neil went on in cold, even tones. "I mean to say that you killed Birdsall, for all the company believes he killed himself. You used strychnine in my case. God knows with what you fixed him. Now I can't hang you. You're too near dead, as it is. But Twenty Mile is too small for the pair of us, and you've got to mush. It's two hundred miles to Holy Cross. You can make it if you're careful not to overexert. I'll give you grub, a sled, and three dogs. You'll be as safe as if you were in jail, for you can't get out of the country. And I'll give you one chance. You're almost dead. Very well. I shall send no word to the company until the spring. In the meantime, the thing for you to do is to die. Now, *mush!*"

"You go to bed!" Jees Uck insisted, when Amos had churned away into the night toward Holy Cross. "You sick man yet, Neil."

"And you're a good girl, Jees Uck," he answered. "And here's my hand on it. But you must go home."

"You don't like me," she said simply.

He smiled, helped her on with her *parka*, and led her to the door. "Only too well, Jees Uck," he said softly; "only too well."

After that the pall of the Arctic night fell deeper and blacker on the land. Neil Bonner discovered that he had failed to put proper valuation upon even the sullen face of the murderous and death-stricken Amos. It became very lonely at Twenty Mile. "For the love of God, Prentiss, send me a man," he wrote to the agent at Fort Hamilton, three hundred miles up river. Six weeks later the Indian messenger brought back a reply. It was characteristic: "Hell. Both feet frozen. Need him myself— Prentiss."

To make matters worse, most of the Toyaats were in the back country on the flanks of a caribou herd, and Jees Uck was with them. Removing to a distance seemed to bring her closer than ever, and Neil Bonner found himself picturing her, day by day, in camp and on trail. It is not good to be alone. Often he went out of the quiet store, bareheaded and frantic, and shook his fist at the blink of day that came over the southern sky-line. And on still, cold nights he left his bed and stumbled into the frost, where he assaulted the silence at the top of his lungs, as though it were some tangible, sentient thing that he might arouse; or he shouted at the sleeping dogs till they howled and howled again. One shaggy brute he brought into the post, playing that it was the new man sent by Prentiss. He strove to make it sleep decently under blankets at night and to sit at table and eat as a man should; but the beast, mere domesticated wolf that it was, rebelled, and sought out dark corners and snarled and bit him in the leg, and was finally beaten and driven forth.

Then the trick of personification seized upon Neil Bonner and mastered him. All the forces of his environment metamorphosed into living, breathing entities and came to live with him. He re-created the primitive pantheon; reared an altar to the sun and burned candle fat and bacon grease thereon; and in the unfenced yard, by the long-legged caché, made a frost devil, which he was wont to make faces at and mock when the mercury oozed down into the bulb. All this in play, of course. He said it to himself that it was in play, and repeated it over and over to make sure, unaware that madness is ever prone to express itself in make-believe and play.

One midwinter day, Father Champreau, a Jesuit missionary, pulled into Twenty Mile. Bonner fell upon him and dragged him into the post, and clung to him and wept, until the priest wept with him from sheer compassion. Then Bonner became madly hilarious and made lavish entertainment, swearing valiantly that his guest should not depart. But Father Champreau was pressing to Salt Water on urgent business for his order, and pulled out next morning, with Bonner's blood threatened on his head.

And the threat was in a fair way toward realization, when the Toyaats returned from their long hunt to the winter camp. They had many furs, and there was much trading and stir at Twenty Mile. Also, Jees Uck came to buy beads and scarlet cloths and things, and Bonner began to find himself again. He fought for a week against her. Then the end came one night when she rose to leave. She had not forgotten her repulse, and the pride that drove Spike O'Brien on to complete the Northwest Passage by land was her pride.

"I go now," she said; "good night, Neil."

But he came up behind her. "Nay, it is not well," he said.

And as she turned her face toward his with a sudden joyful flash, he bent forward, slowly and gravely, as it were a sacred thing, and kissed her on the lips. The Toyaats had never taught her the meaning of a kiss upon the lips, but she understood and was glad.

With the coming of Jees Uck, at once things brightened up. She was regal in her happiness, a source of unending delight. The elemental workings of her mind and her naïve little ways made an immense sum of pleasurable surprise to the overcivilized man that had stooped to catch her up. Not alone was she solace to his loneliness, but her primitiveness rejuvenated his jaded mind. It was as though, after long wandering, he had returned to pillow his head in the lap of Mother Earth. In short, in Jees Uck he found the youth of the world—the youth and the strength and the joy.

And to fill the full round of his need, and that they might not see overmuch of each other, there arrived at Twenty Mile one Sandy MacPherson, as companionable a man as ever whistled along the trail or raised a ballad by a camp-fire. A Jesuit priest had run into his camp, a couple of hundred miles up the Yukon, in the nick of time to say a last word over the body of Sandy's partner. And on departing, the priest had said, "My son, you will be lonely now." And Sandy had bowed his head brokenly. "At Twenty Mile," the priest added, "there is a lonely man. You have need of each other, my son."

So it was that Sandy became a welcome third at the post, brother to the man and woman that resided there. He took Bonner moose-hunting and wolf-trapping; and, in return, Bonner resurrected a battered and wayworn volume and made him friends with Shakespeare, till Sandy declaimed iambic pentameters to his sled-dogs whenever they waxed mutinous. And of the long evenings they played cribbage and talked and disagreed about the universe, the while Jees Uck rocked matronly in an easy-chair and darned their moccasins and socks.

Spring came. The sun shot up out of the south. The land exchanged its austere robes for the garb of a smiling wanton. Everywhere light laughed and life invited. The days stretched out their balmy length and the nights passed from blinks of darkness to no darkness at all. The river bared its bosom, and snorting steamboats challenged the wilderness. There were stir and bustle, new faces, and fresh facts. An assistant arrived at Twenty Mile, and Sandy MacPherson wandered off with a bunch of prospectors to invade the Koyokuk country. And there were newspapers and magazines and letters for Neil Bonner. And Jees Uck looked on in worriment, for she knew his kindred talked with him across the world.

Without much shock, it came to him that his father was dead. There was a sweet letter of forgiveness, dictated in his last hours. There were official letters from the company, graciously ordering him to turn the post over to the assistant and permitting him to depart at his earliest pleasure. A long, legal affair from the lawyers informed him of interminable lists of stocks and bonds, real estate, rents, and chattels that were his by his father's will. And a dainty bit of stationery, sealed and monogrammed, implored dear Neil's return to his heart-broken and loving mother.

Neil Bonner did some swift thinking, and when the *Yukon Belle* coughed in to the bank on her way down to Bering Sea, he departed— departed with the ancient lie of quick return young and blithe on his lips.

"I'll come back, dear Jees Uck, before the first snow flies," he promised her, between the last kisses at the gang-plank.

And not only did he promise, but, like the majority of men under the same circumstances, he really meant it. To John Thompson, the new agent, he gave orders for the extension of unlimited credit to his wife, Jees Uck. Also, with his last look from the deck of the *Yukon Belle,* he saw a dozen men at work rearing the logs that were to make the most comfortable house along a thousand miles of river front—the house of Jess Uck, and likewise the house of Neil Bonner—ere the first flurry of snow. For he fully and fondly meant to come back. Jees Uck was dear to him, and, further, a golden future awaited the North. With his father's money he intended to verify that future. An ambitious dream allured him. With his four years of experience, and aided by the friendly coöperation of the P. C. Company, he would return to become the Rhodes of Alaska. And he would return, fast as steam could drive, as soon as he had put into shape the affairs of his father, whom he had never known, and comforted his mother, whom he had forgotten.

There was much ado when Neil Bonner came back from the Arctic. The fires were lighted and the fleshpots slung, and he took of it all and called it good. Not only was he bronzed and creased, but he was a new man under his skin, with a grip on things and a seriousness and control. His old companions were amazed when he declined to hit up the pace in the good old way, while his father's crony rubbed hands gleefully, and became an authority upon the reclamation of wayward and idle youth.

For four years Neil Bonner's mind had lain fallow. Little that was new had been added to it, but it had undergone a process of selection. It had, so to say, been purged of the trivial and superfluous. He had lived quick years, down in the world; and, up in the wilds, time had been given him to organize the confused mass of his experiences. His superficial standards had been flung to the winds and new standards erected on deeper and broader generalizations. Concerning civilization, he had gone away with one set of values, had returned with another set of values. Aided, also, by the earth smells in his nostrils and the earth sights in his eyes, he laid hold of the inner significance of civilization, beholding with clear vision its futilities and powers. It was a simple little philosophy he evolved. Clean living was the way to grace. Duty performed was sanctification. One must live clean and do his duty in order that he might work. Work was salvation. And to work toward life abundant, and more abundant, was to be in line with the scheme of things and the will of God.

Primarily, he was of the city. And his fresh earth grip and virile conception of humanity gave him a finer sense of civilization and endeared civilization to him. Day by day the people of the city clung closer to him and the world loomed more colossal. And, day by day, Alaska grew more remote and less real. And then he met Kitty Sharon—a woman of his own flesh and blood and kind; a woman who put her hand into his hand and drew him to her, till he forgot the day and hour and the time of the year the first snow flies on the Yukon.

Jees Uck moved into her grand log-house and dreamed away three golden summer months. Then came the autumn, post-haste before the down rush of winter. The air grew thin and sharp, the days thin and short. The river ran sluggishly, and skin ice formed in the quiet eddies. All migratory life departed south, and silence fell upon the land. The first snow flurries came, and the last homing steamboat bucked desperately into the running mush ice. Then came the hard ice, solid cakes and sheets, till the Yukon ran level with its banks. And when all this ceased the river stood still and the blinking days lost themselves in the darkness.

John Thompson, the new agent, laughed; but Jees Uck had faith in the mischances of sea and river. Neil Bonner might be frozen in any-where between Chilkoot Pass and St. Michael's, for the last travellers of the year are always caught by the ice, when they exchange boat for sled and dash on through the long hours behind the flying dogs.

But no flying dogs came up the trail, nor down the trail, to Twenty Mile. And John Thompson told Jees Uck, with a certain gladness ill concealed, that Bonner would never come back again. Also, and bru-tally, he suggested his own eligibility. Jees Uck laughed in his face and went back to her grand log-house. But when midwinter came, when hope dies down and life is at its lowest ebb, Jees Uck found she had no credit at the store. This was Thompson's doing, and he rubbed his hands, and walked up and down, and came to his door and looked up at Jees Uck's house, and waited. And he continued to wait. She sold her dog-team to a party of miners and paid cash for her food. And when Thompson refused to honor even her coin, Toyaat Indians made her purchases, and sledded them up to her house in the dark.

In February the first post came in over the ice, and John Thompson read in the society column of a five months' old paper of the marriage of Neil Bonner and Kitty Sharon. Jees Uck held the door ajar and him outside while he imparted the information; and, when he had done, laughed pridefully and did not believe. In March, and all alone, she gave birth to a man-child, a brave bit of new life at which she marvelled. And at that hour, a year later, Neil Bonner sat by another bed, marvelling at another bit of new life that had fared into the world.

The snow went off the ground and the ice broke out of the Yukon. The sun journeyed north, and journeyed south again; and, the money from the dogs being spent, Jees Uck went back to her own people. Oche Ish, a shrewd hunter, proposed to kill the meat for her and her babe, and catch the salmon, if she would marry him. And Imego and Hah Yo and Wy Nooch, husky young hunters all, made similar proposals. But she elected to live alone and seek her own meat and fish. She sewed moccasins and *parkas* and mittens—warm, serviceable things, and pleas-ing to the eye, withal, what of the ornamental hair-tufts and bead work. These she sold to the miners, who were drifting faster into the land each year. And not only did she win food that was good and plentiful, but she laid money by, and one day took passage on the *Yukon Belle* down the river.

At St. Michael's she washed dishes in the kitchen of the post. The servants of the company wondered at the remarkable woman with the remarkable child, though they asked no questions and she vouchsafed nothing. But just before Bering Sea closed in for the year, she bought a passage south on a strayed sealing schooner. That winter she cooked for Captain Markheim's household at Unalaska, and in the spring continued south to Sitka on a whiskey sloop. Later, she appeared at Metlakahtla, which is near to St. Mary's on the end of the Pan-Handle, where she worked in the cannery through the salmon season. When autumn came and the Siwash fishermen prepared to return to Puget Sound, she embarked with a couple of families in a big cedar canoe; and with them she threaded the hazardous chaos of the Alaskan and Canadian coasts, till the Straits of Juan de Fuca were passed and she led her boy by the hand up the hard pave of Seattle.

There she met Sandy MacPherson, on a windy corner, very much surprised and, when he had heard her story, very wroth—not so wroth as he might have been, had he known of Kitty Sharon; but of her Jees Uck breathed no word, for she had never believed. Sandy, who read commonplace and sordid desertion into the circumstance, strove to dissuade her from her trip to San Francisco, where Neil Bonner was supposed to live when he was at home. And, having striven, he made her comfortable, bought her tickets and saw her off, the while smiling in her face and muttering "damshame" into his beard.

With roar and rumble, through daylight and dark, swaying and lurching between the dawns, soaring into the winter snows and sinking to summer valleys, skirting depths, leaping chasms, piercing mountains, Jees Uck and her boy were hurled south. But she had no fear of the iron stallion; nor was she stunned by this masterful civilization of Neil Bonner's people. It seemed, rather, that she saw with greater clearness the wonder that a man of such godlike race had held her in his arms. The screaming medley of San Francisco, with its restless shipping, belching factories, and thundering traffic, did not confuse her; instead, she comprehended swiftly the pitiful sordidness of Twenty Mile and the skin-lodged Toyaat village. And she looked down at the boy that clutched her hand and wondered that she had borne him by such a man.

She paid the hack-driver five prices and went up the stone steps to Neil Bonner's front door. A slant-eyed Japanese parleyed with her for a fruitless space, then led her inside and disappeared. She remained in the hall, which to her simple fancy seemed to be the guest room—the show-place wherein were arrayed all the household treasures with the frank purpose of parade and dazzlement. The walls and ceiling were of oiled and panelled redwood. The floor was more glassy than glare ice, and she sought standing place on one of the great skins that gave a sense of security to the polished surface. A huge fireplace—an extravagant fireplace, she deemed it—yawned in the farther wall. A flood of light, mellowed by stained glass, fell across the room, and from the far end came the white gleam of a marble figure.

This much she saw, and more, when the slant-eyed servant led the way past another room—of which she caught a fleeting glance—and into a third, both of which dimmed the brave show of the entrance hall. And to her eyes the great house seemed to hold out a promise of endless similar rooms. There was such length and breadth to them, and the ceilings were so far away! For the first time since her advent into the white man's civilization, a feeling of awe laid hold of her. Neil, her Neil, lived in this house, breathed the air of it, and lay down at night and slept! It was beautiful, all this that she saw, and it pleased her; but she felt, also, the wisdom and mastery behind. It was the concrete expression of power in terms of beauty, and it was the power that she unerringly divined.

And then came a woman, queenly tall, crowned with a glory of hair that was like a golden sun. She seemed to come toward Jees Uck as a ripple of music across still water; her sweeping garment itself a song, her body playing rhythmically beneath. Jees Uck was herself a man compeller. There were Oche Ish and Imego and Hah Yo and Wy Nooch, to say nothing of Neil Bonner and John Thompson and other white men that had looked upon her and felt her power. But she gazed upon the wide blue eyes and rose-white skin of this woman that advanced to meet her, and she measured her with woman's eyes looking through man's eyes; and as a man compeller she felt herself diminish and grow insignificant before this radiant and flashing creature.

"You wish to see my husband?" the woman asked; and Jees Uck gasped at the liquid silver of a voice that had never sounded harsh cries at snarling wolf dogs, nor moulded itself to a guttural speech, nor toughened in storm and frost and camp smoke.

"No," Jees Uck answered slowly and gropingly, in order that she might do justice to her English. "I come to see Neil Bonner."

"He is my husband," the woman laughed.

Then it was true! John Thompson had not lied that bleak February day, when she laughed pridefully and shut the door in his face. As once she had thrown Amos Pentley across her knee and ripped her knife into the air, so now she felt impelled to spring upon this woman and bear her back and down, and tear the life out of her fair body. But Jees Uck was thinking quickly and gave no sign, and Kitty Bonner little dreamed how intimately she had for an instant been related with sudden death.

Jees Uck nodded her head that she understood, and Kitty Bonner explained that Neil was expected at any moment. Then they sat down on ridiculously comfortable chairs, and Kitty sought to entertain her strange visitor, and Jees Uck strove to help her.

"You knew my husband in the North?" Kitty asked, once.

"Sure. I wash um clothes," Jees Uck had answered, her English abruptly beginning to grow atrocious.

"And this is your boy? I have a little girl."

Kitty caused her daughter to be brought, and while the children, after their manner, struck an acquaintance, the mothers indulged in the talk of mothers and drank tea from cups so fragile that Jees Uck feared lest hers should crumble to pieces between her fingers. Never had she seen such cups, so delicate and dainty. In her mind she compared them with the woman who poured the tea, and there uprose in contrast the gourds and pannikins of the Toyaat village and the clumsy mugs of Twenty Mile, to which she likened herself. And in such fashion and such terms the problem presented itself. She was beaten. There was a woman other than herself better fitted to bear and upbring Neil Bonner's children. Just as his people exceeded her people, so did his womenkind exceed her. They were the man compellers, as their men were the world compellers. She looked at the rose-white tenderness of Kitty Bonner's skin and remembered the sun-beat on her own face. Likewise she looked from brown hand to white—the one, work-worn and hardened by whip handle and paddle, the other as guiltless of toil and soft as a newborn babe's. And, for all the obvious softness and apparent weakness, Jees Uck looked into the blue eyes and saw the mastery she had seen in Neil Bonner's eyes and in the eyes of Neil Bonner's people.

"Why, it's Jees Uck!" Neil Bonner said, when he entered. He said it calmly, with even a ring of joyful cordiality, coming over to her and shaking both her hands, but looking into her eyes with a worry in his own that she understood.

"Hello, Neil!" she said. "You look much good."

"Fine, fine, Jees Uck," he answered heartily, though secretly studying Kitty for some sign of what had passed between the two. Yet he knew his wife too well to expect, even though the worst had passed, such a sign.

"Well, I can't say how glad I am to see you," he went on. "What's happened? Did you strike a mine? And when did you get in?"

"Oo-a, I get in to-day," she replied, her voice instinctively seeking its guttural parts. "I no strike it, Neil. You know Cap'n Markheim, Unalaska? I cook, his house, long time. No spend money. Bime-by, plenty. Pretty good, I think, go down and see White Man's Land. Very fine, White Man's Land, very fine," she added. Her English puzzled him, for Sandy and he had sought, constantly, to better her speech, and she had proved an apt pupil. Now it seemed that she had sunk back into her race. Her face was guileless, stolidly guileless, giving no cue. Kitty's untroubled brow likewise baffled him. What had happened? How much had been said? and how much guessed?

While he wrestled with these questions and while Jees Uck wrestled with her problem—never had he looked so wonderful and great—a silence fell.

"To think that you knew my husband in Alaska!" Kitty said softly.

Knew him! Jees Uck could not forbear a glance at the boy she had borne him, and his eyes followed hers mechanically to the window where played the two children. An iron band seemed to tighten across his forehead. His knees went weak and his heart leaped up and pounded like a fist against his breast. His boy! He had never dreamed it!

Little Kitty Bonner, fairylike in gauzy lawn, with pinkest of cheeks and bluest of dancing eyes, arms outstretched and lips puckered in invitation, was striving to kiss the boy. And the boy, lean and lithe, sunbeaten and browned, skin-clad and in hair-fringed and hair-tufted *muclucs* that showed the wear of the sea and rough work, coolly withstood her advances, his body straight and stiff with the peculiar erectness common to children of savage people. A stranger in a strange land, unabashed and unafraid, he appeared more like an untamed animal, silent and watchful, his black eyes flashing from face to face, quiet so long as quiet endured, but prepared to spring and fight and tear and scratch for life, at the first sign of danger.

The contrast between boy and girl was striking, but not pitiful. There was too much strength in the boy for that, waif that he was of the generations of Shpack, Spike O'Brien, and Bonner. In his features, clean cut as a cameo and almost classic in their severity, there were the power and achievement of his father, and his grandfather, and the one known as the Big Fat, who was captured by the Sea People and escaped to Kamchatka.

Neil Bonner fought his emotion down, swallowed it down, and choked over it, though his face smiled with good humor and the joy with which one meets a friend.

"Your boy, eh, Jees Uck?" he said. And then turning to Kitty: "Handsome fellow! He'll do something with those two hands of his in this our world."

Kitty nodded concurrence. "What is your name?" she asked.

The young savage flashed his quick eyes upon her and dwelt over her for a space, seeking out, as it were, the motive beneath the question.

"Neil," he answered deliberately when the scrutiny had satisfied him.

"Injun talk," Jees Uck interposed, glibly manufacturing languages on the spur of the moment. "Him Injun talk, *nee-al,* all the same 'cracker.' Him baby, him like cracker; him cry for cracker. Him say, '*Nee-al, nee-al,*' all time him say, '*Nee-al.*' Then I say that um name. So um name all time Nee-al."

Never did sound more blessed fall upon Neil Bonner's ear than that lie from Jees Uck's lips. It was the cue, and he knew there was reason for Kitty's untroubled brow.

"And his father?" Kitty asked. "He must be a fine man."

"Oo-a, yes," was the reply. "Um father fine man. Sure!"

"Did you know him, Neil?" queried Kitty.

"Know him? Most intimately," Neil answered, and harked back to dreary Twenty Mile and the man alone in the silence with his thoughts.

And here might well end the story of Jees Uck, but for the crown she put upon her renunciation. When she returned to the North to dwell in her grand log-house, John Thompson found that the P. C. Company could make a shift somehow to carry on its business without his aid. Also, the new agent and the succeeding agents received instructions that the woman Jees Uck should be given whatsoever goods and grub she desired, in whatsoever quantities she ordered, and that no charge should be placed upon the books. Further, the company paid yearly to the woman Jees Uck a pension of five thousand dollars.

When he had attained suitable age, Father Champreau laid hands upon the boy, and the time was not long when Jees Uck received letters regularly from the Jesuit college in Maryland. Later on these letters came from Italy, and still later from France. And in the end there returned to Alaska one Father Neil, a man mighty for good in the land, who loved his mother and who ultimately went into a wider field and rose to high authority in the order.

Jees Uck was a young woman when she went back into the North, and men still looked upon her and yearned. But she lived straight, and no breath was ever raised save in commendation. She stayed for a while with the good sisters at Holy Cross, where she learned to read and write and became versed in practical medicine and surgery. After that she returned to her grand log-house and gathered about her the young girls of the Toyaat village, to show them the way of their feet in the world. It is neither Protestant nor Catholic, this school in the house built by Neil Bonner for Jees Uck, his wife; but the missionaries of all the sects look upon it with equal favor. The latch-string is always out, and tired prospectors and trail-weary men turn aside from the flowing river or frozen trail to rest there for a space and be warm by her fire. And, down in the States, Kitty Bonner is pleased at the interest her husband takes in Alaskan education and the large sums he devotes to that purpose; and, though she often smiles and chaffs, deep down and secretly she is but the prouder of him.

THE LEAGUE OF
THE OLD MEN

At the Barracks a man was being tried for his life. He was an old man, a native from the Whitefish River, which empties into the Yukon below Lake Le Barge. All Dawson was wrought up over the affair, and likewise the Yukon-dwellers for a thousand miles up and down. It has been the custom of the land-robbing and sea-robbing Anglo-Saxon to give the law to conquered peoples, and ofttimes this law is harsh. But in the case of Imber the law for once seemed inadequate and weak. In the mathematical nature of things, equity did not reside in the punishment to be accorded him. The punishment was a foregone conclusion, there could be no doubt of that; and though it was capital, Imber had but one life, while the tale against him was one of scores.

In fact, the blood of so many was upon his hands that the killings attributed to him did not permit of precise enumeration. Smoking a pipe by the trailside or lounging around the stove, men made rough estimates of the numbers that had perished at his hand. They had been whites, all of them, these poor murdered people, and they had been slain singly, in pairs, and in parties. And so purposeless and wanton had been these killings, that they had long been a mystery to the mounted police, even in the time of the captains, and later, when the creeks realized, and a governor came from the Dominion to make the land pay for its prosperity.

But more mysterious still was the coming of Imber to Dawson to give himself up. It was in the late spring, when the Yukon was growling and writhing under its ice, that the old Indian climbed painfully up the bank from the river trail and stood blinking on the main street. Men who had witnessed his advent, noted that he was weak and tottery, and that he staggered over to a heap of cabin-logs and sat down. He sat there a full day, staring straight before him at the unceasing tide of white men that flooded past. Many a head jerked curiously to the side to meet his stare, and more than one remark was dropped anent the old Siwash with so strange a look upon his face. No end of men remembered afterward that they had been struck by his extraordinary figure, and forever afterward prided themselves upon their swift discernment of the unusual.

But it remained for Dickensen, Little Dickensen, to be the hero of the occasion. Little Dickensen had come into the land with great dreams and a pocketful of cash; but with the cash the dreams vanished, and to earn his passage back to the States he had accepted a clerical position with the brokerage firm of Holbrook and Mason. Across the street from the office of Holbrook and Mason was the heap of cabin-logs upon which Imber sat. Dickensen looked out of the window at him before he went to lunch; and when he came back from lunch he looked out of the window, and the old Siwash was still there.

Dickensen continued to look out of the window, and he, too, forever afterward prided himself upon his swiftness of discernment. He was a romantic little chap, and he likened the immobile old heathen to the genius of the Siwash race, gazing calm-eyed upon the hosts of the invading Saxon. The hours swept along, but Imber did not vary his posture, did not by a hair's-breadth move a muscle; and Dickensen remembered the man who once sat upright on a sled in the main street where men passed to and fro. They thought the man was resting, but later, when they touched him, they found him stiff and cold, frozen to death in the midst of the busy street. To undouble him, that he might fit into a coffin, they had been forced to lug him to a fire and thaw him out a bit. Dickensen shivered at the recollection.

Later on, Dickensen went out on the sidewalk to smoke a cigar and cool off; and a little later Emily Travis happened along. Emily Travis was dainty and delicate and rare, and whether in London or Klondike she gowned herself as befitted the daughter of a millionnaire mining engineer. Little Dickensen deposited his cigar on an outside window ledge where he could find it again, and lifted his hat.

They chatted for ten minutes or so, when Emily Travis, glancing past Dickensen's shoulder, gave a startled little scream. Dickensen turned about to see, and was startled, too. Imber had crossed the street and was standing there, a gaunt and hungry-looking shadow, his gaze riveted upon the girl.

"What do you want?" Little Dickensen demanded, tremulously plucky.

Imber grunted and stalked up to Emily Travis. He looked her over, keenly and carefully, every square inch of her. Especially did he appear interested in her silky brown hair, and in the color of her cheek, faintly sprayed and soft, like the downy bloom of a butterfly wing. He walked around her, surveying her with the calculating eye of a man who studies the lines upon which a horse or a boat is builded. In the course of his circuit the pink shell of her ear came between his eye and the westering sun, and he stopped to contemplate its rosy transparency. Then he returned to her face and looked long and intently into her blue eyes. He grunted and laid a hand on her arm midway between the shoulder and elbow. With his other hand he lifted her forearm and doubled it back. Disgust and wonder showed in his face, and he dropped her arm with a contemptuous grunt. Then he muttered a few guttural syllables, turned his back upon her, and addressed himself to Dickensen.

Dickensen could not understand his speech, and Emily Travis laughed. Imber turned from one to the other, frowning, but both shook their heads. He was about to go away, when she called out:

"Oh, Jimmy! Come here!"

Jimmy came from the other side of the street. He was a big, hulking Indian clad in approved white-man style, with an Eldorado king's sombrero on his head. He talked with Imber, haltingly, with throaty spasms. Jimmy was a Sitkan, possessed of no more than a passing knowledge of the interior dialects.

"Him Whitefish man," he said to Emily Travis. "Me savve um talk no very much. Him want to look see chief white man."

"The Governor," suggested Dickensen.

Jimmy talked some more with the Whitefish man, and his face went grave and puzzled.

"I t'ink um want Cap'n Alexander," he explained. "Him say um kill white man, white woman, white boy, plenty kill um white people. Him want to die."

"Insane, I guess," said Dickensen.

"What you call dat?" queried Jimmy.

Dickensen thrust a finger figuratively inside his head and imparted a rotary motion thereto.

"Mebbe so, mebbe so," said Jimmy, returning to Imber, who still demanded the chief man of the white men.

A mounted policeman (unmounted for Klondike service) joined the group and heard Imber's wish repeated. He was a stalwart young fellow, broad-shouldered, deep-chested, legs cleanly built and stretched wide apart, and tall though Imber was, he towered above him by half a head. His eyes were cool, and gray, and steady, and he carried himself with the peculiar confidence of power that is bred of blood and tradition. His splendid masculinity was emphasized by his excessive boyishness,—he was a mere lad,—and his smooth cheek promised a blush as willingly as the cheek of a maid.

Imber was drawn to him at once. The fire leaped into his eyes at sight of a sabre slash that scarred his cheek. He ran a withered hand down the young fellow's leg and caressed the swelling thew. He smote the broad chest with his knuckles, and pressed and prodded the thick muscle-pads that covered the shoulders like a cuirass. The group had been added to by curious passers-by—husky miners, mountaineers, and frontiersmen, sons of the long-legged and broad-shouldered generations. Imber glanced from one to another, then he spoke aloud in the Whitefish tongue.

"What did he say?" asked Dickensen.

"Him say um all the same one man, dat p'liceman," Jimmy interpreted.

Little Dickensen was little, and what of Miss Travis, he felt sorry for having asked the question.

The policeman was sorry for him and stepped into the breach. "I fancy there may be something in his story. I'll take him up to the captain for examination. Tell him to come along with me, Jimmy."

Jimmy indulged in more throaty spasms, and Imber grunted and looked satisfied.

"But ask him what he said, Jimmy, and what he meant when he took hold of my arm."

So spoke Emily Travis, and Jimmy put the question and received the answer.

"Him say you no afraid," said Jimmy.

Emily Travis looked pleased.

"Him say you no *skookum*, no strong, all the same very soft like little baby. Him break you, in um two hands, to little pieces. Him t'ink much funny, very strange, how you can be mother of men so big, so strong, like dat p'liceman."

Emily Travers kept her eyes up and unfaltering, but her cheeks were sprayed with scarlet. Little Dickensen blushed and was quite embarrassed. The policeman's face blazed with his boy's blood.

"Come along, you," he said gruffly, setting his shoulder to the crowd and forcing a way.

Thus it was that Imber found his way to the Barracks, where he made full and voluntary confession, and from the precincts of which he never emerged.

*   *   *

Imber looked very tired. The fatigue of hopelessness and age was in his face. His shoulders drooped depressingly, and his eyes were lack-lustre. His mop of hair should have been white, but sun and weatherbeat had burned and bitten it so that it hung limp and lifeless and colorless. He took no interest in what went on around him. The courtroom was jammed with the men of the creeks and trails, and there was an ominous note in the rumble and grumble of their low-pitched voices, which came to his ears like the growl of the sea from deep caverns.

He sat close by a window, and his apathetic eyes rested now and again on the dreary scene without. The sky was overcast, and a gray drizzle was falling. It was flood-time on the Yukon. The ice was gone, and the river was up in the town. Back and forth on the main street, in canoes and poling-boats, passed the people that never rested. Often he saw these boats turn aside from the street and enter the flooded square that marked the Barracks' parade-ground. Sometimes they disappeared beneath him, and he heard them jar against the house-logs and their occupants scramble in through the window. After that came the slush of water against men's legs as they waded across the lower room and mounted the stairs. Then they appeared in the doorway, with doffed hats and dripping sea-boots, and added themselves to the waiting crowd.

And while they centred their looks on him, and in grim anticipation enjoyed the penalty he was to pay, Imber looked at them, and mused on their ways, and on their Law that never slept, but went on unceasing, in good times and bad, in flood and famine, through trouble and terror and death, and which would go on unceasing, it seemed to him, to the end of time.

A man rapped sharply on a table, and the conversation droned away into silence. Imber looked at the man. He seemed one in authority, yet Imber divined the square-browed man who sat by a desk farther back to be the one chief over them all and over the man who had rapped. Another man by the same table uprose and began to read aloud from many fine sheets of paper. At the top of each sheet he cleared his throat, at the bottom moistened his fingers. Imber did not understand his speech, but the others did, and he knew that it made them angry. Sometimes it made them very angry, and once a man cursed him, in single syllables, stinging and tense, till a man at the table rapped him to silence.

For an interminable period the man read. His monotonous, sing-song utterance lured Imber to dreaming, and he was dreaming deeply when the man ceased. A voice spoke to him in his own Whitefish tongue, and he roused up, without surprise, to look upon the face of his sister's son, a young man who had wandered away years agone to make his dwelling with the whites.

"Thou dost not remember me," he said by way of greeting.

"Nay," Imber answered. "Thou art Howkan who went away. Thy mother be dead."

"She was an old woman," said Howkan.

But Imber did not hear, and Howkan, with hand upon his shoulder, roused him again.

"I shall speak to thee what the man has spoken, which is the tale of the troubles thou hast done and which thou hast told, O fool, to the Captain Alexander. And thou shalt understand and say if it be true talk or talk not true. It is so commanded."

Howkan had fallen among the mission folk and been taught by them to read and write. In his hands he held the many fine sheets from which the man had read aloud, and which had been taken down by a clerk when Imber first made confession, through the mouth of Jimmy, to Captain Alexander. Howkan began to read. Imber listened for a space, when a wonderment rose up in his face and he broke in abruptly.

"That be my talk, Howkan. Yet from thy lips it comes when thy ears have not heard."

Howkan smirked with self-appreciation. His hair was parted in the middle. "Nay, from the paper it comes, O Imber. Never have my ears heard. From the paper it comes, through my eyes, into my head, and out of my mouth to thee. Thus it comes."

"Thus it comes? It be there in the paper?" Imber's voice sank in whisperful awe as he crackled the sheets 'twixt thumb and finger and stared at the charactery scrawled thereon. "It be a great medicine, Howkan, and thou art a worker of wonders."

"It be nothing, it be nothing," the young man responded carelessly and pridefully. He read at hazard from the document: *"In that year, before the break of the ice, came an old man, and a boy who was lame of one foot. These also did I kill, and the old man made much noise—"*

"It be true," Imber interrupted breathlessly. "He made much noise and would not die for a long time. But how dost thou know, Howkan? The chief man of the white men told thee, mayhap? No one beheld me, and him alone have I told."

Howkan shook his head with impatience. "Have I not told thee it be there in the paper, O fool?"

Imber stared hard at the ink-scrawled surface. "As the hunter looks upon the snow and says, Here but yesterday there passed a rabbit; and here by the willow scrub it stood and listened, and heard, and was afraid; and here it turned upon its trail; and here it went with great swiftness, leaping wide; and here, with greater swiftness and wider leapings, came a lynx; and here, where the claws cut deep into the snow, the lynx made a very great leap; and here it struck, with the rabbit under and rolling belly up; and here leads off the trail of the lynx alone, and there is no more rabbit,—as the hunter looks upon the markings of the snow and says thus and so and here, dost thou, too, look upon the paper and say thus and so and here be the things old Imber hath done?"

"Even so," said Howkan. "And now do thou listen, and keep thy woman's tongue between thy teeth till thou art called upon for speech."

Thereafter, and for a long time, Howkan read to him the confession, and Imber remained musing and silent. At the end, he said:

"It be my talk, and true talk, but I am grown old, Howkan, and forgotten things come back to me which were well for the head man there to know. First, there was the man who came over the Ice Mountains, with cunning traps made of iron, who sought the beaver of the Whitefish. Him I slew. And there were three men seeking gold on the Whitefish long ago. Them also I slew, and left them to the wolverines. And at the Five Fingers there was a man with a raft and much meat."

At the moments when Imber paused to remember, Howkan translated and a clerk reduced to writing. The courtroom listened stolidly to each unadorned little tragedy, till Imber told of a red-haired man whose eyes were crossed and whom he had killed with a remarkably long shot.

"Hell," said a man in the forefront of the onlookers. He said it soulfully and sorrowfully. He was red-haired. "Hell," he repeated. "That was my brother Bill." And at regular intervals throughout the session, his solemn "Hell" was heard in the courtroom; nor did his comrades check him, nor did the man at the table rap him to order.

Imber's head drooped once more, and his eyes went dull, as though a film rose up and covered them from the world. And he dreamed as only age can dream upon the colossal futility of youth.

Later, Howkan roused him again, saying: "Stand up, O Imber. It be commanded that thou tellest why you did these troubles, and slew these people, and at the end journeyed here seeking the Law."

Imber rose feebly to his feet and swayed back and forth. He began to speak in a low and faintly rumbling voice, but Howkan interrupted him.

"This old man, he is damn crazy," he said in English to the square-browed man. "His talk is foolish and like that of a child."

"We will hear his talk which is like that of a child," said the square-browed man. "And we will hear it, word for word, as he speaks it. Do you understand?"

Howkan understood, and Imber's eyes flashed, for he had witnessed the play between his sister's son and the man in authority. And then began the story, the epic of a bronze patriot which might well itself be wrought into bronze for the generations unborn. The crowd fell strangely silent, and the square-browed judge leaned head on hand and pondered his soul and the soul of his race. Only was heard the deep tones of Imber, rhythmically alternating with the shrill voice of the interpreter, and now and again, like the bell of the Lord, the wondering and meditative "Hell" of the red-haired man.

"I am Imber of the Whitefish people." So ran the interpretation of Howkan, whose inherent barbarism gripped hold of him, and who lost his mission culture and veneered civilization as he caught the savage ring and rhythm of old Imber's tale. "My father was Otsbaok, a strong man. The land was warm with sunshine and gladness when I was a boy. The people did not hunger after strange things, nor hearken to new voices, and the ways of their fathers were their ways. The women found favor in the eyes of the young men, and the young men looked upon them with content. Babes hung at the breasts of the women, and they were heavy-hipped with increase of the tribe. Men were men in those days. In peace and plenty, and in war and famine, they were men.

"At that time there was more fish in the water than now, and more meat in the forest. Our dogs were wolves, warm with thick hides and hard to the frost and storm. And as with our dogs so with us, for we were likewise hard to the frost and storm. And when the Pellys came into our land we slew them and were slain. For we were men, we Whitefish, and our fathers and our fathers' fathers had fought against the Pellys and determined the bounds of the land.

"As I say, with our dogs, so with us. And one day came the first white man. He dragged himself, so, on hand and knee, in the snow. And his skin was stretched tight, and his bones were sharp beneath. Never was such a man, we thought, and we wondered of what strange tribe he was, and of its land. And he was weak, most weak, like a little child, so that we gave him a place by the fire, and warm furs to lie upon, and we gave him food as little children are given food.

"And with him was a dog, large as three of our dogs, and very weak. The hair of this dog was short, and not warm, and the tail was frozen so that the end fell off. And this strange dog we fed, and bedded by the fire, and fought from it our dogs, which else would have killed him. And what of the moose meat and the sun-dried salmon, the man and dog took strength to themselves; and what of the strength they became big and unafraid. And the man spoke loud words and laughed at the old men and young men, and looked boldly upon the maidens. And the dog fought with our dogs, and for all of his short hair and softness slew three of them in one day.

"When we asked the man concerning his people, he said, 'I have many brothers,' and laughed in a way that was not good. And when he was in his full strength he went away, and with him went Noda, daughter to the chief. First, after that, was one of our bitches brought to pup. And never was there such a breed of dogs,—big-headed, thick-jawed, and short-haired, and helpless. Well do I remember my father, Otsbaok, a strong man. His face was black with anger at such helplessness, and he took a stone, so, and so, and there was no more helplessness. And two summers after that came Noda back to us with a man-child in the hollow of her arm.

"And that was the beginning. Came a second white man, with short-haired dogs, which he left behind him when he went. And with him went six of our strongest dogs, for which, in trade, he had given Koo-So-Tee, my mother's brother, a wonderful pistol that fired with great swiftness six times. And Koo-So-Tee was very big, what of the pistol, and laughed at our bows and arrows. 'Woman's things,' he called them, and went forth against the bald-face grizzly, with the pistol in his hand. Now it be known that it is not good to hunt the bald-face with a pistol, but how were we to know? and how was Koo-So-Tee to know? So he went against the bald-face, very brave, and fired the pistol with great swiftness six times; and the bald-face but grunted and broke in his breast like it were an egg, and like honey from a bee's nest dripped the brains of Koo-So-Tee upon the ground. He was a good hunter, and there was no one to bring meat to his squaw and children. And we were bitter, and we said, 'That which for the white men is well, is for us not well.' And this be true. There be many white men and fat, but their ways have made us few and lean.

"Came the third white man, with great wealth of all manner of wonderful foods and things. And twenty of our strongest dogs he took from us in trade. Also, what of presents and great promises, ten of our young hunters did he take with him on a journey which fared no man knew where. It is said they died in the snow of the Ice Mountains where man has never been, or in the Hills of Silence which are beyond the edge of the earth. Be that as it may, dogs and young hunters were seen never again by the Whitefish people.

"And more white men came with the years, and ever, with pay and presents, they led the young men away with them. And sometimes the young men came back with strange tales of dangers and toils in the lands beyond the Pellys, and sometimes they did not come back. And we said: 'If they be unafraid of life, these white men, it is because they have many lives; but we be few by the Whitefish, and the young men shall go away no more.' But the young men did go away; and the young women went also; and we were very wroth.

"It be true, we ate flour, and salt pork, and drank tea which was a great delight; only, when we could not get tea, it was very bad and we became short of speech and quick of anger. So we grew to hunger for the things the white men brought in trade. Trade! trade! all the time was it trade! One winter we sold our meat for clocks that would not go, and watches with broken guts, and files worn smooth, and pistols without cartridges and worthless. And then came famine, and we were without meat, and two score died ere the break of spring.

" 'Now are we grown weak,' we said; 'and the Pellys will fall upon us, and our bounds be overthrown.' But as it fared with us, so had it fared with the Pellys, and they were too weak to come against us.

"My father, Otsbaok, a strong man, was now old and very wise. And he spoke to the chief, saying: 'Behold, our dogs be worthless. No longer are they thick-furred and strong, and they die in the frost and harness. Let us go into the village and kill them, saving only the wolf ones, and these let us tie out in the night that they may mate with the wild wolves of the forest. Thus shall we have dogs warm and strong again.'

"And his word was harkened to, and we Whitefish became known for our dogs, which were the best in the land. But known we were not for ourselves. The best of our young men and women had gone away with the white men to wander on trail and river to far places. And the young women came back old and broken, as Noda had come, or they came not at all. And the young men came back to sit by our fires for a time, full of ill speech and rough ways, drinking evil drinks and gambling through long nights and days, with a great unrest always in their hearts, till the call of the white men came to them and they went away again to the unknown places. And they were without honor and respect, jeering the old-time customs and laughing in the faces of chief and shamans.

"As I say, we were become a weak breed, we Whitefish. We sold our warm skins and furs for tobacco and whiskey and thin cotton things that left us shivering in the cold. And the coughing sickness came upon us, and men and women coughed and sweated through the long nights, and the hunters on trail spat blood upon the snow. And now one, and now another, bled swiftly from the mouth and died. And the women bore few children, and those they bore were weak and given to sickness.

And other sicknesses came to us from the white men, the like of which we had never known and could not understand. Smallpox, likewise measles, have I heard these sicknesses named, and we died of them as die the salmon in the still eddies when in the fall their eggs are spawned and there is no longer need for them to live.

"And yet, and here be the strangeness of it, the white men come as the breath of death; all their ways lead to death, their nostrils are filled with it; and yet they do not die. Theirs the whiskey, and tobacco, and short-haired dogs; theirs the many sicknesses, the smallpox and measles, the coughing and mouth-bleeding; theirs the white skin, and softness to the frost and storm; and theirs the pistols that shoot six times very swift and are worthless. And yet they grow fat on their many ills, and prosper, and lay a heavy hand over all the world and tread mightily upon its peoples. And their women, too, are soft as little babes, most breakable and never broken, the mothers of men. And out of all this softness, and sickness, and weakness, come strength, and power, and authority. They be gods, or devils, as the case may be. I do not know. What do I know, I, old Imber of the Whitefish? Only do I know that they are past understanding, these white men, far-wanderers and fighters over the earth that they be.

"As I say, the meat in the forest became less and less. It be true, the white man's gun is most excellent and kills a long way off; but of what worth the gun, when there is no meat to kill? When I was a boy on the Whitefish there was moose on every hill, and each year came the caribou uncountable. But now the hunter may take the trail ten days and not one moose gladden his eyes, while the caribou uncountable come no more at all. Small worth the gun, I say, killing a long way off, when there be nothing to kill.

"And I, Imber, pondered upon these things, watching the while the Whitefish, and the Pellys, and all the tribes of the land, perishing as perished the meat of the forest. Long I pondered. I talked with the shamans and the old men who were wise. I went apart that the sounds of the village might not disturb me, and I ate no meat so that my belly should not press upon me and make me slow of eye and ear. I sat long and sleepless in the forest, wide-eyed for the sign, my ears patient and keen for the word that was to come. And I wandered alone in the blackness of night to the river bank, where was wind-moaning and sobbing of water, and where I sought wisdom from the ghosts of old shamans in the trees and dead and gone.

"And in the end, as in a vision, came to me the short-haired and detestable dogs, and the way seemed plain. By the wisdom of Otsbaok, my father and a strong man, had the blood of our own wolf-dogs been kept clean, wherefore had they remained warm of hide and strong in the harness. So I returned to my village and made oration to the men. 'This be a tribe, these white men,' I said. 'A very large tribe, and doubtless there is no longer meat in their land, and they are come among us to make a new land for themselves. But they weaken us, and we die. They are a very hungry folk. Already has our meat gone from us, and it were well, if we would live, that we deal by them as we have dealt by their dogs.'

"And further oration I made, counselling fight. And the men of the Whitefish listened, and some said one thing, and some spoke of other and worthless things, and no man made brave talk of deeds and war. But while the young men were weak as water and afraid, I watched that the old men sat silent, and that in their eyes fires came and went. And later, when the village slept and no one knew, I drew the old men away into the forest and made more talk. And now we were agreed, and we remembered the good young days, and the free land, and the times of plenty, and the gladness and sunshine; and we called ourselves brothers, and swore great secrecy, and a mighty oath to cleanse the land of the evil breed that had come upon it. It be plain we were fools, but how were we to know, we old men of the Whitefish?

"And to hearten the others, I did the first deed. I kept guard upon the Yukon till the first canoe came down. In it were two white men, and when I stood upright upon the bank and raised my hand they changed their course and drove in to me. And as the man in the bow lifted his head, so, that he might know wherefore I wanted him, my arrow sang through the air straight to his throat, and he knew. The second man, who held paddle in the stern, had his rifle half to his shoulder when the first of my three spear-casts smote him.

" 'These be the first,' I said, when the old men had gathered to me. 'Later we will bind together all the old men of all the tribes, and after that the young men who remain strong, and the work will become easy.'

"And then the two dead white men we cast into the river. And of the canoe, which was a very good canoe, we made a fire, and a fire, also, of the things within the canoe. But first we looked at the things, and they were pouches of leather which we cut open with our knives. And inside these pouches were many papers, like that from which thou hast read, O Howkan, with markings on them which we marvelled at and could not understand. Now, I am become wise, and I know them for the speech of men as thou hast told me."

A whisper and buzz went around the courtroom when Howkan finished interpreting the affair of the canoe, and one man's voice spoke up: "That was the lost '91 mail, Peter James and Delaney bringing it in and last spoken at Le Barge by Matthews going out." The clerk scratched steadily away, and another paragraph was added to the history of the North.

"There be little more," Imber went on slowly. "It be there on the paper, the things we did. We were old men, and we did not understand. Even I, Imber, do not understand. Secretly we slew, and continued to slay, for with our years we were crafty and we had learned the swiftness of going without haste. When white men came among us with black looks and rough words, and took away six of the young men with irons binding them helpless, we knew we must slay wider and farther. And one by one we old men departed up river and down to the unknown lands. It was a brave thing. Old we were, and unafraid, but the fear of far places is a terrible fear to men who are old.

"So we slew, without haste and craftily. On the Chilcoot and in the Delta we slew, from the passes to the sea, wherever the white men camped or broke their trails. It be true, they died, but it was without worth. Ever did they come over the mountains, ever did they grow and grow, while we, being old, became less and less. I remember, by the Caribou Crossing, the camp of a white man. He was a very little white man, and three of the old men came upon him in his sleep. And the next day I came upon the four of them. The white man alone still breathed, and there was breath in him to curse me once and well before he died.

"And so it went, now one old man, and now another. Sometimes the word reached us long after of how they died, and sometimes it did not reach us. And the old men of the other tribes were weak and afraid, and would not join with us. As I say, one by one, till I alone was left. I am Imber, of the Whitefish people. My father was Otsbaok, a strong man. There are no Whitefish now. Of the old men I am the last. The young men and young women are gone away, some to live with the Pellys, some with the Salmons, and more with the white men. I am very old, and very tired, and it being vain fighting the Law, as thou sayest, Howkan, I am come seeking the Law."

"O Imber, thou art indeed a fool," said Howkan.

But Imber was dreaming. The square-browed judge likewise dreamed, and all his race rose up before him in a mighty phantasmagoria—his steel-shod, mail-clad race, the lawgiver and world-maker among the families of men. He saw it dawn red-flickering across the dark forests and sullen seas; he saw it blaze, bloody and red, to full and triumphant noon; and down the shaded slope he saw the blood-red sands dropping into night. And through it all he observed the Law, pitiless and potent, ever unswerving and ever ordaining, greater than the motes of men who fulfilled it or were crushed by it, even as it was greater than he, his heart speaking for softness.

LOVE OF LIFE

"This out of all will remain—
They have lived and have tossed:
So much of the game will be gain,
Though the gold of the dice has been lost."

They limped painfully down the bank, and once the foremost of the two men staggered among the rough-strewn rocks. They were tired and weak, and their faces had the drawn expression of patience which comes of hardship long endured. They were heavily burdened with blanket packs which were strapped to their shoulders. Head-straps, passing across the forehead, helped support these packs. Each man carried a rifle. They walked in a stooped posture, the shoulders well forward, the head still farther forward, the eyes bent upon the ground.

"I wish we had just about two of them cartridges that's layin' in that cache of ourn," said the second man.

His voice was utterly and drearily expressionless. He spoke without enthusiasm; and the first man, limping into the milky stream that foamed over the rocks, vouchsafed no reply.

The other man followed at his heels. They did not remove their foot-gear, though the water was icy cold—so cold that their ankles ached and their feet went numb. In places the water dashed against their knees, and both men staggered for footing.

The man who followed slipped on a smooth boulder, nearly fell, but recovered himself with a violent effort, at the same time uttering a sharp exclamation of pain. He seemed faint and dizzy and put out his free hand while he reeled, as though seeking support against the air. When he had steadied himself he stepped forward, but reeled again and nearly fell. Then he stood still and looked at the other man, who had never turned his head.

The man stood still for fully a minute, as though debating with himself. Then he called out:

"I say, Bill, I've sprained my ankle."

Bill staggered on through the milky water. He did not look around. The man watched him go, and though his face was expressionless as ever, his eyes were like the eyes of a wounded deer.

The other man limped up the farther bank and continued straight on without looking back. The man in the stream watched him. His lips trembled a little, so that the rough thatch of brown hair which covered them was visibly agitated. His tongue even strayed out to moisten them.

"Bill!" he cried out.

It was the pleading cry of a strong man in distress, but Bill's head did not turn. The man watched him go, limping grotesquely and lurching forward with stammering gait up the slow slope toward the soft sky-line of the low-lying hill. He watched him go till he passed over the crest and disappeared. Then he turned his gaze and slowly took in the circle of the world that remained to him now that Bill was gone.

Near the horizon the sun was smouldering dimly, almost obscured by formless mists and vapors, which gave an impression of mass and density without outline or tangibility. The man pulled out his watch, the while resting his weight on one leg. It was four o'clock, and as the season was near the last of July or first of August,—he did not know the precise date within a week or two,—he knew that the sun roughly marked the northwest. He looked to the south and knew that somewhere beyond those bleak hills lay the Great Bear Lake; also, he knew that in that direction the Arctic Circle cut its forbidding way across the Canadian Barrens. This stream in which he stood was a feeder to the Coppermine River, which in turn flowed north and emptied into Coronation Gulf and the Arctic Ocean. He had never been there, but he had seen it, once, on a Hudson Bay Company chart.

Again his gaze completed the circle of the world about him. It was not a heartening spectacle. Everywhere was soft sky-line. The hills were all low-lying. There were no trees, no shrubs, no grasses—naught but a tremendous and terrible desolation that sent fear swiftly dawning into his eyes.

"Bill!" he whispered, once and twice; "Bill!"

He cowered in the midst of the milky water, as though the vastness were pressing in upon him with overwhelming force, brutally crushing him with its complacent awfulness. He began to shake as with an ague-fit, till the gun fell from his hand with a splash. This served to rouse him. He fought with his fear and pulled himself together, groping in the water and recovering the weapon. He hitched his pack farther over on his left shoulder, so as to take a portion of its weight from off the injured ankle. Then he proceeded, slowly and carefully, wincing with pain, to the bank.

He did not stop. With a desperation that was madness, unmindful of the pain, he hurried up the slope to the crest of the hill over which his comrade had disappeared—more grotesque and comical by far than that limping, jerking comrade. But at the crest he saw a shallow valley, empty of life. He fought with his fear again, overcame it, hitched the pack still farther over on his left shoulder, and lurched on down the slope.

The bottom of the valley was soggy with water, which the thick moss held, spongelike, close to the surface. This water squirted out from under his feet at every step, and each time he lifted a foot the action culminated in a sucking sound as the wet moss reluctantly released its grip. He picked his way from muskeg to muskeg, and followed the other man's footsteps along and across the rocky ledges which thrust like islets through the sea of moss.

Though alone, he was not lost. Farther on he knew he would come to where dead spruce and fir, very small and weazened, bordered the shore of a little lake, the *titchin-nichilie,* in the tongue of the country, the "land of little sticks." And into that lake flowed a small stream, the water of which was not milky. There was rush-grass on that stream—this he remembered well—but no timber, and he would follow it till its first trickle ceased at a divide. He would cross this divide to the first trickle of another stream, flowing to the west, which he would follow until it emptied into the river Dease, and here he would find a cache under an upturned canoe and piled over with many rocks. And in this cache would be ammunition for his empty gun, fish-hooks and lines, a small net—all the utilities for the killing and snaring of food. Also, he would find flour,—not much,—a piece of bacon, and some beans.

Bill would be waiting for him there, and they would paddle away south down the Dease to the Great Bear Lake. And south across the lake they would go, ever south, till they gained the Mackenzie. And south, still south, they would go, while the winter raced vainly after them, and the ice formed in the eddies, and the days grew chill and crisp, south to some warm Hudson Bay Company post, where timber grew tall and generous and there was grub without end.

These were the thoughts of the man as he strove onward. But hard as he strove with his body, he strove equally hard with his mind, trying to think that Bill had not deserted him, that Bill would surely wait for him at the cache. He was compelled to think this thought, or else there would not be any use to strive, and he would have lain down and died. And as the dim ball of the sun sank slowly into the northwest he covered every inch—and many times—of his and Bill's flight south before the downcoming winter. And he conned the grub of the cache and the grub of the Hudson Bay Company post over and over again. He had not eaten for two days; for a far longer time he had not had all he wanted to eat. Often he stooped and picked pale muskeg berries, put them into his mouth, and chewed and swallowed them. A muskeg berry is a bit of seed enclosed in a bit of water. In the mouth the water melts away and the seed chews sharp and bitter. The man knew there was no nourishment in the berries, but he chewed them patiently with a hope greater than knowledge and defying experience.

At nine o'clock he stubbed his toe on a rocky ledge, and from sheer weariness and weakness staggered and fell. He lay for some time, without movement, on his side. Then he slipped out of the pack-straps and clumsily dragged himself into a sitting posture. It was not yet dark, and in the lingering twilight he groped about among the rocks for shreds of dry moss. When he had gathered a heap he built a fire,—a smouldering, smudgy fire,—and put a tin pot of water on to boil.

He unwrapped his pack and the first thing he did was to count his matches. There were sixty-seven. He counted them three times to make sure. He divided them into several portions, wrapping them in oil paper, disposing of one bunch in his empty tobacco pouch, of another bunch in the inside band of his battered hat, of a third bunch under his shirt on the chest. This accomplished, a panic came upon him, and he unwrapped them all and counted them again. There were still sixty-seven.

He dried his wet foot-gear by the fire. The moccasins were in soggy shreds. The blanket socks were worn through in places, and his feet were raw and bleeding. His ankle was throbbing, and he gave it an examination. It had swollen to the size of his knee. He tore a long strip from one of his two blankets and bound the ankle tightly. He tore other strips and bound them about his feet to serve for both moccasins and socks. Then he drank the pot of water, steaming hot, wound his watch, and crawled between his blankets.

He slept like a dead man. The brief darkness around midnight came and went. The sun arose in the northeast—at least the day dawned in that quarter, for the sun was hidden by gray clouds.

At six o'clock he awoke, quietly lying on his back. He gazed straight up into the gray sky and knew that he was hungry. As he rolled over on his elbow he was startled by a loud snort, and saw a bull caribou regarding him with alert curiosity. The animal was not more than fifty feet away, and instantly into the man's mind leaped the vision and the savor of a caribou steak sizzling and frying over a fire. Mechanically he reached for the empty gun, drew a bead, and pulled the trigger. The bull snorted and leaped away, his hoofs rattling and clattering as he fled across the ledges.

The man cursed and flung the empty gun from him. He groaned aloud as he started to drag himself to his feet. It was a slow and arduous task. His joints were like rusty hinges. They worked harshly in their sockets, with much friction, and each bending or unbending was accomplished only through a sheer exertion of will. When he finally gained his feet, another minute or so was consumed in straightening up, so that he could stand erect as a man should stand.

He crawled up a small knoll and surveyed the prospect. There were no trees, no bushes, nothing but a gray sea of moss scarcely diversified by gray rocks, gray lakelets, and gray streamlets. The sky was gray. There was no sun nor hint of sun. He had no idea of north, and he had forgotten the way he had come to this spot the night before. But he was not lost. He knew that. Soon he would come to the land of the little sticks. He felt that it lay off to the left somewhere, not far—possibly just over the next low hill.

He went back to put his pack into shape for travelling. He assured himself of the existence of his three separate parcels of matches, though he did not stop to count them. But he did linger, debating, over a squat moose-hide sack. It was not large. He could hide it under his two hands. He knew that it weighed fifteen pounds,—as much as all the rest of the pack,—and it worried him. He finally set it to one side and proceeded to roll the pack. He paused to gaze at the squat moose-hide sack. He picked it up hastily with a defiant glance about him, as though the desolation were trying to rob him of it; and when he rose to his feet to stagger on into the day, it was included in the pack on his back.

He bore away to the left, stopping now and again to eat muskeg berries. His ankle had stiffened, his limp was more pronounced, but the pain of it was as nothing compared with the pain of his stomach. The hunger pangs were sharp. They gnawed and gnawed until he could not keep his mind steady on the course he must pursue to gain the land of little sticks. The muskeg berries did not allay this gnawing, while they made his tongue and the roof of his mouth sore with their irritating bite.

He came upon a valley where rock ptarmigan rose on whirring wings from the ledges and muskegs. Ker—ker—ker was the cry they made. He threw stones at them, but could not hit them. He placed his pack on the ground and stalked them as a cat stalks a sparrow. The sharp rocks cut through his pants' legs till his knees left a trail of blood; but the hurt was lost in the hurt of his hunger. He squirmed over the wet moss, saturating his clothes and chilling his body; but he was not aware of it, so great was his fever for food. And always the ptarmigan rose, whirring, before him, till their ker—ker—ker became a mock to him, and he cursed them and cried aloud at them with their own cry.

Once he crawled upon one that must have been asleep. He did not see it till it shot up in his face from its rocky nook. He made a clutch as startled as was the rise of the ptarmigan, and there remained in his hand three tail-feathers. As he watched its flight he hated it, as though it had done him some terrible wrong. Then he returned and shouldered his pack.

As the day wore along he came into valleys or swales where game was more plentiful. A band of caribou passed by, twenty and odd animals, tantalizingly within rifle range. He felt a wild desire to run after them, a certitude that he could run them down. A black fox came toward him, carrying a ptarmigan in his mouth. The man shouted. It was a fearful cry, but the fox, leaping away in fright, did not drop the ptarmigan.

Late in the afternoon he followed a stream, milky with lime, which ran through sparse patches of rush-grass. Grasping these rushes firmly near the root, he pulled up what resembled a young onion-sprout no larger than a shingle-nail. It was tender, and his teeth sank into it with a crunch that promised deliciously of food. But its fibers were tough. It was composed of stringy filaments saturated with water, like the berries, and devoid of nourishment. He threw off his pack and went into the rush-grass on hands and knees, crunching and munching, like some bovine creature.

He was very weary and often wished to rest—to lie down and sleep; but he was continually driven on—not so much by his desire to gain the land of little sticks as by his hunger. He searched little ponds for frogs and dug up the earth with his nails for worms, though he knew in spite that neither frogs nor worms existed so far north.

He looked into every pool of water vainly, until, as the long twilight came on, he discovered a solitary fish, the size of a minnow, in such a pool. He plunged his arm in up to the shoulder, but it eluded him. He reached for it with both hands and stirred up the milky mud at the bottom. In his excitement he fell in, wetting himself to the waist. Then the water was too muddy to admit of his seeing the fish, and he was compelled to wait until the sediment had settled.

The pursuit was renewed, till the water was again muddied. But he could not wait. He unstrapped the tin bucket and began to bale the pool. He baled wildly at first, splashing himself and flinging the water so short a distance that it ran back into the pool. He worked more carefully, striving to be cool, though his heart was pounding against his chest and his hands were trembling. At the end of half an hour the pool was nearly dry. Not a cupful of water remained. And there was no fish. He found a hidden crevice among the stones through which it had escaped to the adjoining and larger pool—a pool which he could not empty in a night and a day. Had he known of the crevice, he could have closed it with a rock at the beginning and the fish would have been his.

Thus he thought, and crumpled up and sank down upon the wet earth. At first he cried softly to himself, then he cried loudly to the pitiless desolation that ringed him around; and for a long time after he was shaken by great dry sobs.

He built a fire and warmed himself by drinking quarts of hot water, and made camp on a rocky ledge in the same fashion he had the night before. The last thing he did was to see that his matches were dry and to wind his watch. The blankets were wet and clammy. His ankle pulsed with pain. But he knew only that he was hungry, and through his restless sleep he dreamed of feasts and banquets and of food served and spread in all imaginable ways.

He awoke chilled and sick. There was no sun. The gray of earth and sky had become deeper, more profound. A raw wind was blowing, and the first flurries of snow were whitening the hilltops. The air about him thickened and grew white while he made a fire and boiled more water. It was wet snow, half rain, and the flakes were large and soggy. At first they melted as soon as they came in contact with the earth, but ever more fell, covering the ground, putting out the fire, spoiling his supply of moss-fuel.

This was a signal for him to strap on his pack and stumble onward, he knew not where. He was not concerned with the land of little sticks, nor with Bill and the cache under the upturned canoe by the river Dease. He was mastered by the verb "to eat." He was hunger-mad. He took no heed of the course he pursued, so long as that course led him through the swale bottoms. He felt his way through the wet snow to the watery muskeg berries, and went by feel as he pulled up the rush-grass by the roots. But it was tasteless stuff and did not satisfy. He found a weed that tasted sour and he ate all he could find of it, which was not much, for it was a creeping growth, easily hidden under the several inches of snow.

He had no fire that night, nor hot water, and crawled under his blanket to sleep the broken hunger-sleep. The snow turned into a cold rain. He awakened many times to feel it falling on his upturned face. Day came—a gray day and no sun. It had ceased raining. The keenness of his hunger had departed. Sensibility, as far as concerned the yearning for food, had been exhausted. There was a dull, heavy ache in his stomach, but it did not bother him so much. He was more rational, and once more he was chiefly interested in the land of little sticks and the cache by the river Dease.

He ripped the remnant of one of his blankets into strips and bound his bleeding feet. Also, he recinched the injured ankle and prepared himself for a day of travel. When he came to his pack, he paused long over the squat moose-hide sack, but in the end it went with him.

The snow had melted under the rain, and only the hilltops showed white. The sun came out, and he succeeded in locating the points of the compass, though he knew now that he was lost. Perhaps, in his previous days' wanderings, he had edged away too far to the left. He now bore off to the right to counteract the possible deviation from his true course.

Though the hunger pangs were no longer so exquisite, he realized that he was weak. He was compelled to pause for frequent rests, when he attacked the muskeg berries and rush-grass patches. His tongue felt dry and large, as though covered with a fine hairy growth, and it tasted bitter in his mouth. His heart gave him a great deal of trouble. When he had travelled a few minutes it would begin a remorseless thump, thump, thump, and then leap up and away in a painful flutter of beats that choked him and made him go faint and dizzy.

In the middle of the day he found two minnows in a large pool. It was impossible to bale it, but he was calmer now and managed to catch them in his tin bucket. They were no longer than his little finger, but he was not particularly hungry. The dull ache in his stomach had been growing duller and fainter. It seemed almost that his stomach was dozing. He ate the fish raw, masticating with painstaking care, for the eating was an act of pure reason. While he had no desire to eat, he knew that he must eat to live.

In the evening he caught three more minnows, eating two and saving the third for breakfast. The sun had dried stray shreds of moss, and he was able to warm himself with hot water. He had not covered more than ten miles that day; and the next day, travelling whenever his heart permitted him, he covered no more than five miles. But his stomach did not give him the slightest uneasiness. It had gone to sleep. He was in a strange country, too, and the caribou were growing more plentiful, also the wolves. Often their yelps drifted across the desolation, and once he saw three of them slinking away before his path.

Another night; and in the morning, being more rational, he untied the leather string that fastened the squat moose-hide sack. From its open mouth poured a yellow stream of coarse gold-dust and nuggets. He roughly divided the gold in halves, caching one half on a prominent ledge, wrapped in a piece of blanket, and returning the other half to the sack. He also began to use strips of the one remaining blanket for his feet. He still clung to his gun, for there were cartridges in that cache by the river Dease.

This was a day of fog, and this day hunger awoke in him again. He was very weak and was afflicted with a giddiness which at times blinded him. It was no uncommon thing now for him to stumble and fall; and stumbling once, he fell squarely into a ptarmigan nest. There were four newly hatched chicks, a day old—little specks of pulsating life no more than a mouthful; and he ate them ravenously, thrusting them alive into his mouth and crunching them like egg-shells between his teeth. The mother ptarmigan beat about him with great outcry. He used his gun as a club with which to knock her over, but she dodged out of reach. He threw stones at her and with one chance shot broke a wing. Then she fluttered away, running, trailing the broken wing, with him in pursuit.

The little chicks had no more than whetted his appetite. He hopped and bobbed clumsily along on his injured ankle, throwing stones and screaming hoarsely at times; at other times hopping and bobbing silently along, picking himself up grimly and patiently when he fell, or rubbing his eyes with his hand when the giddiness threatened to overpower him.

The chase led him across swampy ground in the bottom of the valley, and he came upon footprints in the soggy moss. They were not his own—he could see that. They must be Bill's. But he could not stop, for the mother ptarmigan was running on. He would catch her first, then he would return and investigate.

He exhausted the mother ptarmigan; but he exhausted himself. She lay panting on her side. He lay panting on his side, a dozen feet away, unable to crawl to her. And as he recovered she recovered, fluttering out of reach as his hungry hand went out to her. The chase was resumed. Night settled down and she escaped. He stumbled from weakness and pitched head foremost on his face, cutting his cheek, his pack upon his back. He did not move for a long while; then he rolled over on his side, wound his watch, and lay there until morning.

Another day of fog. Half of his last blanket had gone into foot-wrappings. He failed to pick up Bill's trail. It did not matter. His hunger was driving him too compellingly—only—only he wondered if Bill, too, were lost. By midday the irk of his pack became too oppressive. Again he divided the gold, this time merely spilling half of it on the ground. In the afternoon he threw the rest of it away, there remaining to him only the half-blanket, the tin bucket, and the rifle.

An hallucination began to trouble him. He felt confident that one cartridge remained to him. It was in the chamber of the rifle and he had overlooked it. On the other hand, he knew all the time that the chamber was empty. But the hallucination persisted. He fought it off for hours, then threw his rifle open and was confronted with emptiness. The disappointment was as bitter as though he had really expected to find the cartridge.

He plodded on for half an hour, when the hallucination arose again. Again he fought it, and still it persisted, till for very relief he opened his rifle to unconvince himself. At times his mind wandered farther afield, and he plodded on, a mere automaton, strange conceits and whimsicalities gnawing at his brain like worms. But these excursions out of the real were of brief duration, for ever the pangs of the hunger-bite called him back. He was jerked back abruptly once from such an excursion by a sight that caused him nearly to faint. He reeled and swayed, doddering like a drunken man to keep from falling. Before him stood a horse. A horse! He could not believe his eyes. A thick mist was in them, intershot with sparkling points of light. He rubbed his eyes savagely to clear his vision, and beheld, not a horse, but a great brown bear. The animal was studying him with bellicose curiosity.

The man had brought his gun halfway to his shoulder before he realized. He lowered it and drew his hunting-knife from its beaded sheath at his hip. Before him was meat and life. He ran his thumb along the edge of his knife. It was sharp. The point was sharp. He would fling himself upon the bear and kill it. But his heart began its warning thump, thump, thump. Then followed the wild upward leap and tattoo of flutters, the pressing as of an iron band about his forehead, the creeping of the dizziness into his brain.

His desperate courage was evicted by a great surge of fear. In his weakness, what if the animal attacked him? He drew himself up to his most imposing stature, gripping the knife and staring hard at the bear. The bear advanced clumsily a couple of steps, reared up, and gave vent to a tentative growl. If the man ran, he would run after him; but the man did not run. He was animated now with the courage of fear. He, too, growled, savagely, terribly, voicing the fear that is to life germane and that lies twisted about life's deepest roots.

The bear edged away to one side, growling menacingly, himself appalled by this mysterious creature that appeared upright and unafraid. But the man did not move. He stood like a statue till the danger was past, when he yielded to a fit of trembling and sank down into the wet moss.

He pulled himself together and went on, afraid now in a new way. It was not the fear that he should die passively from lack of food, but that he should be destroyed violently before starvation had exhausted the last particle of the endeavor in him that made toward surviving. There were the wolves. Back and forth across the desolation drifted their howls, weaving the very air into a fabric of menace that was so tangible that he found himself, arms in the air, pressing it back from him as it might be the walls of a wind-blown tent.

Now and again the wolves, in packs of two and three, crossed his path. But they sheered clear of him. They were not in sufficient numbers, and besides they were hunting the caribou, which did not battle, while this strange creature that walked erect might scratch and bite.

In the late afternoon he came upon scattered bones where the wolves had made a kill. The débris had been a caribou calf an hour before, squawking and running and very much alive. He contemplated the bones, clean-picked and polished, pink with the cell-life in them which had not yet died. Could it possibly be that he might be that ere the day was done! Such was life, eh? A vain and fleeting thing. It was only life that pained. There was no hurt in death. To die was to sleep. It meant cessation, rest. Then why was he not content to die?

But he did not moralize long. He was squatting in the moss, a bone in his mouth, sucking at the shreds of life that still dyed it faintly pink. The sweet meaty taste, thin and elusive almost as a memory, maddened him. He closed his jaws on the bones and crunched. Sometimes it was the bone that broke, sometimes his teeth. Then he crushed the bones between rocks, pounded them to a pulp, and swallowed them. He pounded his fingers, too, in his haste, and yet found a moment in which to feel surprise at the fact that his fingers did not hurt much when caught under the descending rock.

Came frightful days of snow and rain. He did not know when he made camp, when he broke camp. He travelled in the night as much as in the day. He rested wherever he fell, crawled on whenever the dying life in him flickered up and burned less dimly. He, as a man, no longer strove. It was the life in him, unwilling to die, that drove him on. He did not suffer. His nerves had become blunted, numb, while his mind was filled with weird visions and delicious dreams.

But ever he sucked and chewed on the crushed bones of the caribou calf, the least remnants of which he had gathered up and carried with him. He crossed no more hills or divides, but automatically followed a large stream which flowed through a wide and shallow valley. He did not see this stream nor this valley. He saw nothing save visions. Soul and body walked or crawled side by side, yet apart, so slender was the thread that bound them.

He awoke in his right mind, lying on his back on a rocky ledge. The sun was shining bright and warm. Afar off he heard the squawking of caribou calves. He was aware of vague memories of rain and wind and snow, but whether he had been beaten by the storm for two days or two weeks he did not know.

For some time he lay without movement, the genial sunshine pouring upon him and saturating his miserable body with its warmth. A fine day, he thought. Perhaps he could manage to locate himself. By a painful effort he rolled over on his side. Below him flowed a wide and sluggish river. Its unfamiliarity puzzled him. Slowly he followed it with his eyes, winding in wide sweeps among the bleak, bare hills, bleaker and barer and lower-lying than any hills he had yet encountered. Slowly, deliberately, without excitement or more than the most casual interest, he followed the course of the strange stream toward the skyline and saw it emptying into a bright and shining sea. He was still unexcited. Most unusual, he thought, a vision or a mirage—more likely a vision, a trick of his disordered mind. He was confirmed in this by sight of a ship lying at anchor in the midst of the shining sea. He closed his eyes for a while, then opened them. Strange how the vision persisted! Yet not strange. He knew there were no seas or ships in the heart of the barren lands, just as he had known there was no cartridge in the empty rifle.

He heard a snuffle behind him—a half-choking gasp or cough. Very slowly, because of his exceeding weakness and stiffness, he rolled over on his other side. He could see nothing near at hand, but he waited patiently. Again came the snuffle and cough, and outlined between two jagged rocks not a score of feet away he made out the gray head of a wolf. The sharp ears were not pricked so sharply as he had seen them on other wolves; the eyes were bleared and bloodshot, the head seemed to droop limply and forlornly. The animal blinked continually in the sunshine. It seemed sick. As he looked it snuffled and coughed again.

This, at least, was real, he thought, and turned on the other side so that he might see the reality of the world which had been veiled from him before by the vision. But the sea still shone in the distance and the ship was plainly discernible. Was it reality, after all? He closed his eyes for a long while and thought, and then it came to him. He had been making north by east, away from the Dease Divide and into the Coppermine Valley. This wide and sluggish river was the Coppermine. That shining sea was the Arctic Ocean. That ship was a whaler, strayed east, far east, from the mouth of the Mackenzie, and it was lying at anchor in Coronation Gulf. He remembered the Hudson Bay Company chart he had seen long ago, and it was all clear and reasonable to him.

He sat up and turned his attention to immediate affairs. He had worn through the blanket-wrappings, and his feet were shapeless lumps of raw meat. His last blanket was gone. Rifle and knife were both missing. He had lost his hat somewhere, with the bunch of matches in the band, but the matches against his chest were safe and dry inside the tobacco pouch and oil paper. He looked at his watch. It marked eleven o'clock and was still running. Evidently he had kept it wound.

He was calm and collected. Though extremely weak, he had no sensation of pain. He was not hungry. The thought of food was not even pleasant to him, and whatever he did was done by his reason alone. He ripped off his pants' legs to the knees and bound them about his feet. Somehow he had succeeded in retaining the tin bucket. He would have some hot water before he began what he foresaw was to be a terrible journey to the ship.

His movements were slow. He shook as with a palsy. When he started to collect dry moss, he found he could not rise to his feet. He tried again and again, then contented himself with crawling about on hands and knees. Once he crawled near to the sick wolf. The animal dragged itself reluctantly out of his way, licking its chops with a tongue which seemed hardly to have the strength to curl. The man noticed that the tongue was not the customary healthy red. It was a yellowish brown and seemed coated with a rough and half-dry mucus.

After he had drunk a quart of hot water the man found he was able to stand, and even to walk as well as a dying man might be supposed to walk. Every minute or so he was compelled to rest. His steps were feeble and uncertain, just as the wolf's that trailed him were feeble and uncertain; and that night, when the shining sea was blotted out by blackness, he knew he was nearer to it by no more than four miles.

Throughout the night he heard the cough of the sick wolf, and now and then the squawking of the caribou calves. There was life all around him, but it was strong life, very much alive and well, and he knew the sick wolf clung to the sick man's trail in the hope that the man would die first. In the morning, on opening his eyes, he beheld it regarding him with a wistful and hungry stare. It stood crouched, with tail between its legs, like a miserable and woe-begone dog. It shivered in the chill morning wind, and grinned dispiritedly when the man spoke to it in a voice that achieved no more than a hoarse whisper.

The sun rose brightly, and all morning the man tottered and fell toward the ship on the shining sea. The weather was perfect. It was the brief Indian Summer of the high latitudes. It might last a week. To-morrow or next day it might be gone.

In the afternoon the man came upon a trail. It was of another man, who did not walk, but who dragged himself on all fours. The man thought it might be Bill, but he thought in a dull, uninterested way. He had no curiosity. In fact, sensation and emotion had left him. He was no longer susceptible to pain. Stomach and nerves had gone to sleep. Yet the life that was in him drove him on. He was very weary, but it refused to die. It was because it refused to die that he still ate muskeg berries and minnows, drank his hot water, and kept a wary eye on the sick wolf.

He followed the trail of the other man who dragged himself along, and soon came to the end of it—a few fresh-picked bones where the soggy moss was marked by the foot-pads of many wolves. He saw a squat moose-hide sack, mate to his own, which had been torn by sharp teeth. He picked it up, though its weight was almost too much for his feeble fingers. Bill had carried it to the last. Ha! ha! He would have the laugh on Bill. He would survive and carry it to the ship in the shining sea. His mirth was hoarse and ghastly, like a raven's croak, and the sick wolf joined him, howling lugubriously. The man ceased suddenly. How could he have the laugh on Bill if that were Bill; if those bones, so pinky-white and clean, were Bill?

He turned away. Well, Bill had deserted him; but he would not take the gold, nor would he suck Bill's bones. Bill would have, though, had it been the other way around, he mused as he staggered on.

He came to a pool of water. Stooping over in quest of minnows, he jerked his head back as though he had been stung. He had caught sight of his reflected face. So horrible was it that sensibility awoke long enough to be shocked. There were three minnows in the pool, which was too large to drain; and after several ineffectual attempts to catch them in the tin bucket he forbore. He was afraid, because of his great weakness, that he might fall in and drown. It was for this reason that he did not trust himself to the river astride one of the many drift-logs which lined its sand-spits.

That day he decreased the distance between him and the ship by three miles; the next day by two—for he was crawling now as Bill had crawled; and the end of the fifth day found the ship still seven miles away and him unable to make even a mile a day. Still the Indian Summer held on, and he continued to crawl and faint, turn and turn about; and even the sick wolf coughed and wheezed at his heels. His knees had become raw meat like his feet, and though he padded them with the shirt from his back it was a red track he left behind him on the moss and stones. Once, glancing back, he saw the wolf licking hungrily his bleeding trail, and he saw sharply what his own end might be—unless —unless he could get the wolf. Then began as grim a tragedy of existence as was ever played—a sick man that crawled, a sick wolf that limped, two creatures dragging their dying carcasses across the desolation and hunting each other's lives.

Had it been a well wolf, it would not have mattered so much to the man; but the thought of going to feed the maw of that loathsome and all but dead thing was repugnant to him. He was finicky. His mind had begun to wander again, and to be perplexed by hallucinations, while his lucid intervals grew rarer and shorter.

He was awakened once from a faint by a wheeze close in his ear. The wolf leaped lamely back, losing its footing and falling in its weakness. It was ludicrous, but he was not amused. Nor was he even afraid. He was too far gone for that. But his mind was for the moment clear, and he lay and considered. The ship was no more than four miles away. He could see it quite distinctly when he rubbed the mists out of his eyes, and he could see the white sail of a small boat cutting the water of the shining sea. But he could never crawl those four miles. He knew that, and was very calm in the knowledge. He knew that he could not crawl half a mile. And yet he wanted to live. It was unreasonable that he should die after all he had undergone. Fate asked too much of him. And, dying, he declined to die. It was stark madness, perhaps, but in the very grip of Death he defied Death and refused to die.

He closed his eyes and composed himself with infinite precaution. He steeled himself to keep above the suffocating languor that lapped like a rising tide through all the wells of his being. It was very like a sea, this deadly languor, that rose and rose and drowned his consciousness bit by bit. Sometimes he was all but submerged, swimming through oblivion with a faltering stroke; and again, by some strange alchemy of soul, he would find another shred of will and strike out more strongly.

Without movement he lay on his back, and he could hear, slowly drawing near and nearer, the wheezing intake and output of the sick wolf's breath. It drew closer, ever closer, through an infinitude of time, and he did not move. It was at his ear. The harsh dry tongue grated like sandpaper against his cheek. His hands shot out—or at least he willed them to shoot out. The fingers were curved like talons, but they closed on empty air. Swiftness and certitude require strength, and the man had not this strength.

The patience of the wolf was terrible. The man's patience was no less terrible. For half a day he lay motionless, fighting off unconsciousness and waiting for the thing that was to feed upon him and upon which he wished to feed. Sometimes the languid sea rose over him and he dreamed long dreams; but ever through it all, waking and dreaming, he waited for the wheezing breath and the harsh caress of the tongue.

He did not hear the breath, and he slipped slowly from some dream to the feel of the tongue along his hand. He waited. The fangs pressed softly; the pressure increased; the wolf was exerting its last strength in an effort to sink teeth in the food for which it had waited so long. But the man had waited long, and the lacerated hand closed on the jaw. Slowly, while the wolf struggled feebly and the hand clutched feebly, the other hand crept across to a grip. Five minutes later the whole weight of the man's body was on top of the wolf. The hands had not sufficient strength to choke the wolf, but the face of the man was pressed close to the throat of the wolf and the mouth of the man was full of hair. At the end of half an hour the man was aware of a warm trickle in his throat. It was not pleasant. It was like molten lead being forced into his stomach, and it was forced by his will alone. Later the man rolled over on his back and slept.

There were some members of a scientific expedition on the whale-ship *Bedford.* From the deck they remarked a strange object on the shore. It was moving down the beach toward the water. They were unable to classify it, and, being scientific men, they climbed into the whale-boat alongside and went ashore to see. And they saw something that was alive but which could hardly be called a man. It was blind, unconscious. It squirmed along the ground like some monstrous worm. Most of its efforts were ineffectual, but it was persistent, and it writhed and twisted and went ahead perhaps a score of feet an hour.

Three weeks afterward the man lay in a bunk on the whale-ship *Bedford,* and with tears streaming down his wasted cheeks told who he was and what he had undergone. He also babbled incoherently of his mother, of sunny Southern California, and a home among the orange groves and flowers.

The days were not many after that when he sat at table with the scientific men and ship's officers. He gloated over the spectacle of so much food, watching it anxiously as it went into the mouths of others. With the disappearance of each mouthful an expression of deep regret came into his eyes. He was quite sane, yet he hated those men at meal-time. He was haunted by a fear that the food would not last. He inquired of the cook, the cabin-boy, the captain, concerning the food stores. They reassured him countless times; but he could not believe them, and pried cunningly about the lazarette to see with his own eyes.

It was noticed that the man was getting fat. He grew stouter with each day. The scientific men shook their heads and theorized. They limited the man at his meals, but still his girth increased and he swelled prodigiously under his shirt.

The sailors grinned. They knew. And when the scientific men set a watch on the man, they knew too. They saw him slouch for'ard after breakfast, and, like a mendicant, with outstretched palm, accost a sailor. The sailor grinned and passed him a fragment of sea biscuit. He clutched it avariciously, looked at it as a miser looks at gold, and thrust it into his shirt bosom. Similar were the donations from other grinning sailors.

The scientific men were discreet. They let him alone. But they privily examined his bunk. It was lined with hardtack; the mattress was stuffed with hardtack; every nook and cranny was filled with hardtack. Yet he was sane. He was taking precautions against another possible famine— that was all. He would recover from it, the scientific men said; and he did, ere the *Bedford's* anchor rumbled down in San Francisco Bay.

THE SUN-DOG TRAIL

Sitka Charley smoked his pipe and gazed thoughtfully at the *Police Gazette* illustration on the wall. For half an hour he had been steadily regarding it, and for half an hour I had been slyly watching him. Something was going on in that mind of his, and, whatever it was, I knew it was well worth knowing. He had lived life, and seen things, and performed that prodigy of prodigies, namely, the turning of his back upon his own people, and, in so far as it was possible for an Indian, becoming a white man even in his mental processes. As he phrased it himself, he had come into the warm, sat among us, by our fires, and become one of us. He had never learned to read nor write, but his vocabulary was remarkable, and more remarkable still was the completeness with which he had assumed the white man's point of view, the white man's attitude toward things.

We had struck this deserted cabin after a hard day on trail. The dogs had been fed, the supper dishes washed, the beds made, and we were now enjoying that most delicious hour that comes each day, and but once each day, on the Alaskan trail, the hour when nothing intervenes between the tired body and bed save the smoking of the evening pipe. Some former denizen of the cabin had decorated its walls with illustrations torn from magazines and newspapers, and it was these illustrations that had held Sitka Charley's attention from the moment of our arrival two hours before. He had studied them intently, ranging from one to another and back again, and I could see that there was uncertainty in his mind, and bepuzzlement.

"Well?" I finally broke the silence.

He took the pipe from his mouth and said simply, "I do not understand."

He smoked on again, and again removed the pipe, using it to point at the *Police Gazette* illustration.

"That picture—what does it mean? I do not understand."

I looked at the picture. A man, with a preposterously wicked face, his right hand pressed dramatically to his heart, was falling backward to the floor. Confronting him, with a face that was a composite of destroying angel and Adonis, was a man holding a smoking revolver.

"One man is killing the other man," I said, aware of a distinct be-puzzlement of my own and of failure to explain.

"Why?" asked Sitka Charley.

"I do not know," I confessed.

"That picture is all end," he said. "It has no beginning."

"It is life," I said.

"Life has beginning," he objected.

I was silenced for the moment, while his eyes wandered on to an adjoining decoration, a photographic reproduction of somebody's "Leda and the Swan."

"That picture," he said, "has no beginning. It has no end. I do not understand pictures."

"Look at that picture," I commanded, pointing to a third decoration. "It means something. Tell me what it means to you."

He studied it for several minutes.

"The little girl is sick," he said finally. "That is the doctor looking at her. They have been up all night—see, the oil is low in the lamp, the first morning light is coming in at the window. It is a great sickness; maybe she will die, that is why the doctor looks so hard. That is the mother. It is a great sickness, because the mother's head is on the table and she is crying."

"How do you know she is crying?" I interrupted. "You cannot see her face. Perhaps she is asleep."

Sitka Charley looked at me in swift surprise, then back at the picture. It was evident that he had not reasoned the impression.

"Perhaps she is asleep," he repeated. He studied it closely. "No, she is not asleep. The shoulders show that she is not asleep. I have seen the shoulders of a woman who cried. The mother is crying. It is a very great sickness."

"And now you understand the picture," I cried.

He shook his head, and asked, "The little girl—does it die?"

It was my turn for silence.

"Does it die?" he reiterated. "You are a painter-man. Maybe you know."

"No, I do not know," I confessed.

"It is not life," he delivered himself dogmatically. "In life little girl die or get well. Something happen in life. In picture nothing happen. No, I do not understand pictures."

His disappointment was patent. It was his desire to understand all things that white men understand, and here, in this matter, he failed. I felt, also, that there was challenge in his attitude. He was bent upon compelling me to show him the wisdom of pictures. Besides, he had remarkable powers of visualization. I had long since learned this. He visualized everything. He saw life in pictures, felt life in pictures, generalized life in pictures; and yet he did not understand pictures when seen through other men's eyes and expressed by those men with color and line upon canvas.

"Pictures are bits of life," I said. "We paint life as we see it. For instance, Charley, you are coming along the trail. It is night. You see a cabin. The window is lighted. You look through the window for one second, or for two seconds, you see something, and you go on your way. You saw maybe a man writing a letter. You saw something without beginning or end. Nothing happened. Yet it was a bit of life you saw. You remember it afterward. It is like a picture in your memory. The window is the frame of the picture."

I could see that he was interested, and I knew that as I spoke he had looked through the window and seen the man writing the letter.

"There is a picture you have painted that I understand," he said. "It is a true picture. It has much meaning. It is in your cabin at Dawson. It is a faro table. There are men playing. It is a large game. The limit is off."

"How do you know the limit is off?" I broke in excitedly, for here was where my work could be tried out on an unbiassed judge who knew life only, and not art, and who was a sheer master of reality. Also, I was very proud of that particular piece of work. I had named it "The Last Turn," and I believed it to be one of the best things I had ever done.

"There are no chips on the table," Sitka Charley explained. "The men are playing with markers. That means the roof is the limit. One man play yellow markers—maybe one yellow marker worth one thousand dollars, maybe two thousand dollars. One man play red markers. Maybe they are worth five hundred dollars, maybe one thousand dollars. It is a very big game. Everybody play very high, up to the roof. How do I know? You make the dealer with blood little bit warm in face." (I was delighted.) "The lookout, you make him lean forward in his chair. Why he lean forward? Why his face very much quiet? Why his eyes very much bright? Why dealer warm with blood a little bit in the face? Why all men very quiet?—the man with yellow markers? the man with white markers? the man with red markers? Why nobody talk? Because very much money. Because last turn."

"How do you know it is the last turn?" I asked.

"The king is coppered, the seven is played open," he answered. "Nobody bet on other cards. Other cards all gone. Everybody one mind. Everybody play king to lose, seven to win. Maybe bank lose twenty thousand dollars, maybe bank win. Yes, that picture I understand."

"Yet you do not know the end!" I cried triumphantly. "It is the last turn, but the cards are not yet turned. In the picture they will never be turned. Nobody will ever know who wins nor who loses."

"And the men will sit there and never talk," he said, wonder and awe growing in his face. "And the lookout will lean forward, and the blood will be warm in the face of the dealer. It is a strange thing. Always will they sit there, always; and the cards will never be turned."

"It is a picture," I said. "It is life. You have seen things like it yourself."

He looked at me and pondered, then said, very slowly: "No, as you say, there is no end to it. Nobody will ever know the end. Yet is it a true thing. I have seen it. It is life."

For a long time he smoked on in silence, weighing the pictorial wisdom of the white man and verifying it by the facts of life. He nodded his head several times, and grunted once or twice. Then he knocked the ashes from his pipe, carefully refilled it, and, after a thoughtful pause, lighted it again.

"Then have I, too, seen many pictures of life," he began; "pictures not painted, but seen with the eyes. I have looked at them like through the window at the man writing the letter. I have seen many pieces of life, without beginning, without end, without understanding."

With a sudden change of position he turned his eyes full upon me and regarded me thoughtfully.

"Look you," he said; "you are a painter-man. How would you paint this which I saw, a picture without beginning, the ending of which I do not understand, a piece of life with the northern lights for a candle and Alaska for a frame."

"It is a large canvas," I murmured.

But he ignored me, for the picture he had in mind was before his eyes and he was seeing it.

"There are many names for this picture," he said. "But in the picture there are many sun-dogs, and it comes into my mind to call it 'The Sun-Dog Trail.' It was a long time ago, seven years ago, the fall of '97, when I saw the woman first time. At Lake Linderman I had one canoe, very good Peterborough canoe. I came over Chilcoot Pass with two thousand letters for Dawson. I was letter carrier. Everybody rush to Klondike at that time. Many people on trail. Many people chop down trees and make boats. Last water, snow in the air, snow on the ground, ice on the lake, on the river ice in the eddies. Every day more snow, more ice. Maybe one day, maybe three days, maybe six days, any day maybe freeze-up come, then no more water, all ice, everybody walk, Dawson six hundred miles, long time walk. Boat go very quick. Everybody want to go boat. Everybody say, 'Charley, two hundred dollars you take me in canoe,' 'Charley, three hundred dollars,' 'Charley, four hundred dollars.' I say no, all the time I say no. I am letter carrier.

"In morning I get to Lake Linderman. I walk all night and am much tired. I cook breakfast, I eat, then I sleep on the beach three hours. I wake up. It is ten o'clock. Snow is falling. There is wind, much wind that blows fair. Also, there is a woman who sit in the snow alongside. She is white woman, she is young, very pretty, maybe she is twenty years old, maybe twenty-five years old. She look at me. I look at her. She is very tired. She is no dance-woman. I see that right away. She is good woman, and she is very tired.

" 'You are Sitka Charley,' she says. I get up quick and roll blankets so snow does not get inside. 'I go to Dawson,' she says. 'I go in your canoe—how much?'

"I do not want anybody in my canoe. I do not like to say no. So I say, 'One thousand dollars.' Just for fun I say it, so woman cannot come with me, much better than say no. She look at me very hard, then she says, 'When you start?' I say right away. Then she says all right, she will give me one thousand dollars.

"What can I say? I do not want the woman, yet have I given my word that for one thousand dollars she can come. I am surprised. Maybe she make fun, too, so I say, 'Let me see thousand dollars.' And that woman, that young woman, all alone on the trail, there in the snow, she take out one thousand dollars, in greenbacks, and she put them in my hand. I look at money, I look at her. What can I say? I say, 'No, my canoe very small. There is no room for outfit.' She laugh. She says, 'I am great traveller. This is my outfit.' She kick one small pack in the snow. It is two fur robes, canvas outside, some woman's clothes inside. I pick it up. Maybe thirty-five pounds. I am surprised. She take it away from me. She says, 'Come, let us start.' She carries pack into canoe. What can I say? I put my blankets into canoe. We start.

"And that is the way I saw the woman first time. The wind was fair. I put up small sail. The canoe went very fast, it flew like a bird over the high waves. The woman was much afraid. 'What for you come Klondike much afraid?' I ask. She laugh at me, a hard laugh, but she is still much afraid. Also is she very tired. I run canoe through rapids to Lake Bennett. Water very bad, and woman cry out because she is afraid. We go down Lake Bennett, snow, ice, wind like a gale, but woman is very tired and go to sleep.

"That night we make camp at Windy Arm. Woman sit by fire and eat supper. I look at her. She is pretty. She fix hair. There is much hair, and it is brown, also sometimes it is like gold in the firelight, when she turn her head, so, and flashes come from it like golden fire. The eyes are large and brown, sometimes warm like a candle behind a curtain, sometimes very hard and bright like broken ice when sun shines upon it. When she smile—how can I say?—when she smile I know white man like to kiss her, just like that, when she smile. She never do hard work. Her hands are soft, like baby's hand. She is soft all over, like baby. She is not thin, but round like baby; her arm, her leg, her muscles, all soft and round like baby. Her waist is small, and when she stand up, when she walk, or move her head or arm, it is—I do not know the word—but it is nice to look at, like—maybe I say she is built on lines like the lines of a good canoe, just like that, and when she move she is like the movement of the good canoe sliding through still water or leaping through water when it is white and fast and angry. It is very good to see.

"Why does she come into Klondike, all alone, with plenty of money? I do not know. Next day I ask her. She laugh and says: 'Sitka Charley, that is none of your business. I give you one thousand dollars take me to Dawson. That only is your business.' Next day after that I ask her what is her name. She laugh, then she says, 'Mary Jones, that is my name.' I do not know her name, but I know all the time that Mary Jones is not her name.

"It is very cold in canoe, and because of cold sometimes she not feel good. Sometimes she feel good and she sing. Her voice is like a silver bell, and I feel good all over like when I go into church at Holy Cross Mission, and when she sing I feel strong and paddle like hell. Then she laugh and says, 'You think we get to Dawson before freeze-up, Charley?' Sometimes she sit in canoe and is thinking far away, her eyes like that, all empty. She does not see Sitka Charley, nor the ice, nor the snow. She is far away. Very often she is like that, thinking far away. Sometimes, when she is thinking far away, her face is not good to see. It looks like a face that is angry, like the face of one man when he want to kill another man.

"Last day to Dawson very bad. Shore-ice in all the eddies, mush-ice in the stream. I cannot paddle. The canoe freeze to ice. I cannot get to shore. There is much danger. All the time we go down Yukon in the ice. That night there is much noise of ice. Then ice stop, canoe stop, everything stop. 'Let us go to shore,' the woman says. I say no, better wait. By and by, everything start down-stream again. There is much snow. I cannot see. At eleven o'clock at night, everything stop. At one o'clock everything start again. At three o'clock everything stop. Canoe is smashed like eggshell, but is on top of ice and cannot sink. I hear dogs howling. We wait. We sleep. By and by morning come. There is no more snow. It is the freeze-up, and there is Dawson. Canoe smash and stop right at Dawson. Sitka Charley has come in with two thousand letters on very last water.

"The woman rent a cabin on the hill, and for one week I see her no more. Then, one day, she come to me. 'Charley,' she says, 'how do you like to work for me? You drive dogs, make camp, travel with me.' I say that I make too much money carrying letters. She says, 'Charley, I will pay you more money.' I tell her that pick-and-shovel man get fifteen dollars a day in the mines. She says, 'That is four hundred and fifty dollars a month.' And I say, 'Sitka Charley is no pick-and-shovel man.' Then she says, 'I understand, Charley. I will give you seven hundred and fifty dollars each month.' It is a good price, and I go to work for her. I buy for her dogs and sled. We travel up Klondike, up Bonanza and Eldorado, over to Indian River, to Sulphur Creek, to Dominion, back across divide to Gold Bottom and to Too Much Gold, and back to Dawson. All the time she look for something, I do not know what. I am puzzled. 'What thing you look for?' I ask. She laugh. 'You look for gold?' I ask. She laugh. Then she says, 'That is none of your business, Charley.' And after that I never ask any more.

"She has a small revolver which she carries in her belt. Sometimes, on trail, she makes practice with revolver. I laugh. 'What for you laugh, Charley?' she ask. 'What for you play with that?' I say. 'It is no good. It is too small. It is for a child, a little plaything.' When we get back to Dawson she ask me to buy good revolver for her. I buy a Colt's 44. It is very heavy, but she carry it in her belt all the time.

"At Dawson comes the man. Which way he come I do not know. Only do I know he is *che-cha-quo*—what you call tenderfoot. His hands are soft, just like hers. He never do hard work. He is soft all over. At first I think maybe he is her husband. But he is too young. Also, they make two beds at night. He is maybe twenty years old. His eyes blue, his hair yellow, he has a little mustache which is yellow. His name is John Jones. Maybe he is her brother. I do not know. I ask questions no more. Only I think his name not John Jones. Other people call him Mr. Girvan. I do not think that is his name. I do not think her name is Miss Girvan, which other people call her. I think nobody know their names.

"One night I am asleep at Dawson. He wake me up. He says, 'Get the dogs ready; we start.' No more do I ask questions, so I get the dogs ready and we start. We go down the Yukon. It is night-time, it is November, and it is very cold—sixty-five below. She is soft. He is soft. The cold bites. They get tired. They cry under their breaths to themselves. By and by I say better we stop and make camp. But they say that they will go on. Three times I say better to make camp and rest, but each time they say they will go on. After that I say nothing. All the time, day after day, is it that way. They are very soft. They get stiff and sore. They do not understand moccasins, and their feet hurt very much. They limp, they stagger like drunken people, they cry under their breaths; and all the time they say, 'On! on! We will go on!'

"They are like crazy people. All the time do they go on, and on. Why do they go on? I do not know. Only do they go on. What are they after? I do not know. They are not after gold. There is no stampede. Besides, they spend plenty of money. But I ask questions no more. I, too, go on and on, because I am strong on the trail and because I am greatly paid.

"We make Circle City. That for which they look is not there. I think now that we will rest, and rest the dogs. But we do not rest, not for one day do we rest. 'Come,' says the woman to the man, 'let us go on.' And we go on. We leave the Yukon. We cross the divide to the west and swing down into the Tanana Country. There are new diggings there. But that for which they look is not there, and we take the back trail to Circle City.

"It is a hard journey. December is most gone. The days are short. It is very cold. One morning it is seventy below zero. 'Better that we do not travel to-day,' I say, 'else will the frost be unwarmed in the breathing and bite all the edges of our lungs. After that we will have bad cough, and maybe next spring will come pneumonia.' But they are *che-cha-quo*. They do not understand the trail. They are like dead people they are so tired, but they say, 'Let us go on.' We go on. The frost bites their lungs, and they get the dry cough. They cough till the tears run down their cheeks. When bacon is frying they must run away from the fire and cough half an hour in the snow. They freeze their cheeks a little bit, so that the skin turns black and is very sore. Also, the man freezes his thumb till the end is like to come off, and he must wear a large thumb on his mitten to keep it warm. And sometimes, when the frost bites hard and the thumb is very cold, he must take off the mitten and put the hand between his legs next to the skin, so that the thumb may get warm again.

"We limp into Circle City, and even I, Sitka Charley, am tired. It is

Christmas Eve. I dance, drink, make a good time, for to-morrow is Christmas Day and we will rest. But no. It is five o'clock in the morning—Christmas morning. I am two hours asleep. The man stand by my bed. 'Come, Charley,' he says, 'harness the dogs. We start.'

"Have I not said that I ask questions no more? They pay me seven hundred and fifty dollars each month. They are my masters. I am their man. If they say, 'Charley, come, let us start for hell,' I will harness the dogs, and snap the whip, and start for hell. So I harness the dogs, and we start down the Yukon. Where do we go? They do not say. Only do they say, 'On! on! We will go on!'

"They are very weary. They have travelled many hundreds of miles, and they do not understand the way of the trail. Besides, their cough is very bad—the dry cough that makes strong men swear and weak men cry. But they go on. Every day they go on. Never do they rest the dogs. Always do they buy new dogs. At every camp, at every post, at every Indian village, do they cut out the tired dogs and put in fresh dogs. They have much money, money without end, and like water they spend it. They are crazy? Sometimes I think so, for there is a devil in them that drives them on and on, always on. What is it that they try to find? It is not gold. Never do they dig in the ground. I think a long time. Then I think it is a man they try to find. But what man? Never do we see the man. Yet are they like wolves on the trail of the kill. But they are funny wolves, soft wolves, baby wolves who do not understand the way of the trail. They cry aloud in their sleep at night. In their sleep they moan and groan with the pain of their weariness. And in the day, as they stagger along the trail, they cry under their breaths. They are funny wolves.

"We pass Fort Yukon. We pass Fort Hamilton. We pass Minook. January has come and nearly gone. The days are very short. At nine o'clock comes daylight. At three o'clock comes night. And it is cold. And even I, Sitka Charley, am tired. Will we go on forever this way without end? I do not know. But always do I look along the trail for that which they try to find. There are few people on the trail. Sometimes we travel one hundred miles and never see a sign of life. It is very quiet. There is no sound. Sometimes it snows, and we are like wandering ghosts. Sometimes it is clear, and at midday the sun looks at us for a moment over the hills to the south. The northern lights flame in the sky, and the sun-dogs dance, and the air is filled with frost-dust.

"I am Sitka Charley, a strong man. I was born on the trail, and all my days have I lived on the trail. And yet have these two baby wolves made me very tired. I am lean, like a starved cat, and I am glad of my bed at night, and in the morning am I greatly weary. Yet ever are we hitting the trail in the dark before daylight, and still on the trail does the dark after nightfall find us. These two baby wolves! If I am lean like a starved cat, they are lean like cats that have never eaten and have died. Their eyes are sunk deep in their heads, bright sometimes as with fever, dim and cloudy sometimes like the eyes of the dead. Their cheeks are hollow like caves in a cliff. Also are their cheeks black and raw from many freezings. Sometimes it is the woman in the morning who says, 'I cannot get up. I cannot move. Let me die.' And it is the man who stands beside her and says, 'Come, let us go on.' And they go on. And sometimes it is the man who cannot get up, and the woman says, 'Come, let us go on.' But the one thing they do, and always do, is to go on. Always do they go on.

"Sometimes, at the trading posts, the man and woman get letters. I do not know what is in the letters. But it is the scent that they follow, these letters themselves are the scent. One time an Indian gives them a letter. I talk with him privately. He says it is a man with one eye who gives him the letter, a man who travels fast down the Yukon. That is all. But I know that the baby wolves are after the man with the one eye.

"It is February, and we have travelled fifteen hundred miles. We are getting near Bering Sea, and there are storms and blizzards. The going is hard. We come to Anvig. I do not know, but I think sure they get a letter at Anvig, for they are much excited, and they say, 'Come, hurry, let us go on.' But I say we must buy grub, and they say we must travel light and fast. Also, they say that we can get grub at Charley McKeon's cabin. Then do I know that they take the big cut-off, for it is there that Charley McKeon lives where the Black Rock stands by the trail.

"Before we start, I talk maybe two minutes with the priest at Anvig. Yes, there is a man with one eye who has gone by and who travels fast. And I know that for which they look is the man with the one eye. We leave Anvig with little grub, and travel light and fast. There are three fresh dogs bought in Anvig, and we travel very fast. The man and woman are like mad. We start earlier in the morning, we travel later at night. I look sometimes to see them die, these two baby wolves, but they will not die. They go on and on. When the dry cough take hold of them hard, they hold their hands against their stomach and double up in the snow, and cough, and cough, and cough. They cannot walk, they cannot talk. Maybe for ten minutes they cough, maybe for half an hour, and then they straighten up, the tears from the coughing frozen on their faces, and the words they say are, 'Come, let us go on.'

"Even I, Sitka Charley, am greatly weary, and I think seven hundred and fifty dollars is a cheap price for the labor I do. We take the big cut-off, and the trail is fresh. The baby wolves have their noses down to the trail, and they say, 'Hurry!' All the time do they say, 'Hurry! Faster! Faster!' It is hard on the dogs. We have not much food and we cannot give them enough to eat, and they grow weak. Also, they must work hard. The woman has true sorrow for them, and often, because of them, the tears are in her eyes. But the devil in her that drives her on will not let her stop and rest the dogs.

"And then we come upon the man with the one eye. He is in the snow by the trail, and his leg is broken. Because of the leg he has made a poor camp, and has been lying on his blankets for three days and keeping a fire going. When we find him he is swearing. He swears like hell. Never have I heard a man swear like that man. I am glad. Now that they have found that for which they look, we will have rest. But the woman says, 'Let us start. Hurry!'

"I am surprised. But the man with the one eye says, 'Never mind me. Give me your grub. You will get more grub at McKeon's cabin to-morrow. Send McKeon back for me. But do you go on.' Here is another wolf, an old wolf, and he, too, thinks but the one thought, to go on. So we give him our grub, which is not much, and we chop wood for his fire, and we take his strongest dogs and go on. We left the man with one eye there in the snow, and he died there in the snow, for McKeon never went back for him. And who that man was, and why he came to be there, I do not know. But I think he was greatly paid by the man and the woman, like me, to do their work for them.

"That day and that night we had nothing to eat, and all next day we travelled fast, and we were weak with hunger. Then we came to the Black Rock, which rose five hundred feet above the trail. It was at the end of the day. Darkness was coming, and we could not find the cabin of McKeon. We slept hungry, and in the morning looked for the cabin. It was not there, which was a strange thing, for everybody knew that McKeon lived in a cabin at Black Rock. We were near to the coast, where the wind blows hard and there is much snow. Everywhere there were small hills of snow where the wind had piled it up. I have a thought, and I dig in one and another of the hills of snow. Soon I find the walls of the cabin, and I dig down to the door. I go inside. McKeon is dead. Maybe two or three weeks he is dead. A sickness had come upon him so that he could not leave the cabin. The wind and the snow had covered the cabin. He had eaten his grub and died. I looked for his cache, but there was no grub in it.

" 'Let us go on,' said the woman. Her eyes were hungry, and her hand was upon her heart, as with the hurt of something inside. She bent back and forth like a tree in the wind as she stood there. 'Yes, let us go on,' said the man. His voice was hollow, like the *klonk* of an old raven, and he was hunger-mad. His eyes were like live coals of fire, and as his body rocked to and fro, so rocked his soul inside. And I, too, said, 'Let us go on.' For that one thought, laid upon me like a lash for every mile of fifteen hundred miles, had burned itself into my soul, and I think that I, too, was mad. Besides, we could only go on, for there was no grub. And we went on, giving no thought to the man with the one eye in the snow.

"There is little travel on the big cut-off. Sometimes two or three months and nobody goes by. The snow had covered the trail, and there was no sign that men had ever come or gone that way. All day the wind blew and the snow fell, and all day we travelled, while our stomachs gnawed their desire and our bodies grew weaker with every step they took. Then the woman began to fall. Then the man. I did not fall, but my feet were heavy and I caught my toes and stumbled many times.

"That night is the end of February. I kill three ptarmigan with the woman's revolver, and we are made somewhat strong again. But the dogs have nothing to eat. They try to eat their harness, which is of leather and walrus-hide, and I must fight them off with a club and hang all the harness in a tree. And all night they howl and fight around that tree. But we do not mind. We sleep like dead people, and in the morning get up like dead people out of their graves and go on along the trail.

"That morning is the 1st of March, and on that morning I see the first sign of that after which the baby wolves are in search. It is clear weather, and cold. The sun stay longer in the sky, and there are sun-dogs flashing on either side, and the air is bright with frost-dust. The snow falls no more upon the trail, and I see the fresh sign of dogs and sled. There is one man with that outfit, and I see in the snow that he is not strong. He, too, has not enough to eat. The young wolves see the fresh sign, too, and they are much excited. 'Hurry!' they say. All the time they say, 'Hurry! Faster, Charley, faster!'

"We make hurry very slow. All the time the man and the woman fall down. When they try to ride on sled the dogs are too weak, and the dogs fall down. Besides, it is so cold that if they ride on the sled they will freeze. It is very easy for a hungry man to freeze. When the woman fall down, the man help her up. Sometimes the woman help the man up. By and by both fall down and cannot get up, and I must help them up all the time, else they will not get up and will die there in the snow. This is very hard work, for I am greatly weary, and as well I must drive the dogs, and the man and woman are very heavy with no strength in their bodies. So, by and by, I, too, fall down in the snow, and there is no one to help me up. I must get up by myself. And always do I get up by myself, and help them up, and make the dogs go on.

"That night I get one ptarmigan, and we are very hungry. And that night the man says to me, 'What time start to-morrow, Charley?' It is like the voice of a ghost. I say, 'All the time you make start at five o'clock.' 'To-morrow,' he says, 'we will start at three o'clock.' I laugh in great bitterness, and I say, 'You are dead man.' And he says, 'To-morrow we will start at three o'clock.'

"And we start at three o'clock, for I am their man, and that which they say is to be done, I do. It is clear and cold, and there is no wind. When daylight comes we can see a long way off. And it is very quiet. We can hear no sound but the beat of our hearts, and in the silence that is a very loud sound. We are like sleep-walkers, and we walk in dreams until we fall down; and then we know we must get up, and we see the trail once more and hear the beating of our hearts. Sometimes, when I am walking in dreams this way, I have strange thoughts. Why does Sitka Charley live? I ask myself. Why does Sitka Charley work hard, and go hungry, and have all this pain? For seven hundred and fifty dollars a month, I make the answer, and I know it is a foolish answer. Also is it a true answer. And after that never again do I care for money. For that day a large wisdom came to me. There was a great light, and I saw clear, and I knew that it was not for money that a man must live, but for a happiness that no man can give, or buy, or sell, and that is beyond all value of all money in the world.

"In the morning we come upon the last-night camp of the man who is before us. It is a poor camp, the kind a man makes who is hungry and without strength. On the snow there are pieces of blanket and of canvas, and I know what has happened. His dogs have eaten their harness, and he has made new harness out of his blankets. The man and woman stare hard at what is to be seen, and as I look at them my back feels the chill as of a cold wind against the skin. Their eyes are toil-mad and hunger-mad, and burn like fire deep in their heads. Their faces are like the faces of people who have died of hunger, and their cheeks are black with the dead flesh of many freezings. 'Let us go on,' says the man. But the woman coughs and falls in the snow. It is the dry cough where the frost has bitten the lungs. For a long time she coughs, then like a woman crawling out of her grave she crawls to her feet. The tears are ice upon her cheeks, and her breath makes a noise as it comes and goes, and she says, 'Let us go on.'

"We go on. And we walk in dreams through the silence. And every time we walk is a dream and we are without pain; and every time we fall down is an awakening, and we see the snow and the mountains and the fresh trail of the man who is before us, and we know all our pain

again. We come to where we can see a long way over the snow, and
that for which they look is before them. A mile away there are black
spots upon the snow. The black spots move. My eyes are dim, and I
must stiffen my soul to see. And I see one man with dogs and a sled.
The baby wolves see, too. They can no longer talk, but they whisper,
'On, on. Let us hurry!'

"And they fall down, but they go on. The man who is before us, his
blanket harness breaks often, and he must stop and mend it. Our harness
is good, for I have hung it in trees each night. At eleven o'clock the
man is half a mile away. At one o'clock he is a quarter of a mile away.
He is very weak. We see him fall down many times in the snow. One
of his dogs can no longer travel, and he cuts it out of the harness. But
he does not kill it. I kill it with the axe as I go by, as I kill one of my
dogs which loses its legs and can travel no more.

"Now we are three hundred yards away. We go very slow. Maybe
in two, three hours we go one mile. We do not walk. All the time we
fall down. We stand up and stagger two steps, maybe three steps, then
we fall down again. And all the time I must help up the man and
woman. Sometimes they rise to their knees and fall forward, maybe four
or five times before they can get to their feet again and stagger two or
three steps and fall. But always do they fall forward. Standing or kneel-
ing, always do they fall forward, gaining on the trail each time by the
length of their bodies.

"Sometimes they crawl on hands and knees like animals that live in
the forest. We go like snails, like snails that are dying we go so slow.
And yet we go faster than the man who is before us. For he, too, falls
all the time, and there is no Sitka Charley to lift him up. Now he is two
hundred yards away. After a long time he is one hundred yards away.

"It is a funny sight. I want to laugh out loud, Ha! ha! just like that,
it is so funny. It is a race of dead men and dead dogs. It is like in a
dream when you have a nightmare and run away very fast for your life
and go very slow. The man who is with me is mad. The woman is mad.
I am mad. All the world is mad, and I want to laugh, it is so funny.

"The stranger-man who is before us leaves his dogs behind and goes
on alone across the snow. After a long time we come to the dogs. They
lie helpless in the snow, their harness of blanket and canvas on them,
the sled behind them, and as we pass them they whine to us and cry
like babies that are hungry.

"Then we, too, leave our dogs and go on alone across the snow. The
man and the woman are nearly gone, and they moan and groan and
sob, but they go on. I, too, go on. I have but one thought. It is to come

up to the stranger-man. Then it is that I shall rest, and not until then shall I rest, and it seems that I must lie down and sleep for a thousand years, I am so tired.

"The stranger-man is fifty yards away, all alone in the white snow. He falls and crawls, staggers, and falls and crawls again. He is like an animal that is sore wounded and trying to run from the hunter. By and by he crawls on hands and knees. He no longer stands up. And the man and woman no longer stand up. They, too, crawl after him on hands and knees. But I stand up. Sometimes I fall, but always do I stand up again.

"It is a strange thing to see. All about is the snow and the silence, and through it crawl the man and the woman, and the stranger-man who goes before. On either side the sun are sun-dogs, so that there are three suns in the sky. The frost-dust is like the dust of diamonds, and all the air is filled with it. Now the woman coughs, and lies still in the snow until the fit has passed, when she crawls on again. Now the man looks ahead, and he is blear-eyed as with old age and must rub his eyes so that he can see the stranger-man. And now the stranger-man looks back over his shoulder. And Sitka Charley, standing upright, maybe falls down and stands upright again.

"After a long time the stranger-man crawls no more. He stands slowly upon his feet and rocks back and forth. Also does he take off one mitten and wait with revolver in his hand, rocking back and forth as he waits. His face is skin and bones and frozen black. It is a hungry face. The eyes are deep-sunk in his head, and the lips are snarling. The man and woman, too, get upon their feet and they go toward him very slowly. And all about is the snow and the silence. And in the sky are three suns, and all the air is flashing with the dust of diamonds.

"And thus it was that I, Sitka Charley, saw the baby wolves make their kill. No word is spoken. Only does the stranger-man snarl with his hungry face. Also does he rock to and fro, his shoulders drooping, his knees bent, and his legs wide apart so that he does not fall down. The man and the woman stop maybe fifty feet away. Their legs, too, are wide apart so that they do not fall down, and their bodies rock to and fro. The stranger-man is very weak. His arm shakes, so that when he shoots at the man his bullet strikes in the snow. The man cannot take off his mitten. The stranger-man shoots at him again, and this time the bullet goes by in the air. Then the man takes the mitten in his teeth and pulls it off. But his hand is frozen and he cannot hold the revolver, and it falls in the snow. I look at the woman. Her mitten is off, and the big Colt's revolver is in her hand. Three times she shoot, quick, just like that. The hungry face of the stranger-man is still snarling as he falls forward into the snow.

"They do not look at the dead man. 'Let us go on,' they say. And we go on. But now that they have found that for which they look, they are like dead. The last strength has gone out of them. They can stand no more upon their feet. They will not crawl, but desire only to close their eyes and sleep. I see not far away a place for camp. I kick them. I have my dog-whip, and I give them the lash of it. They cry aloud, but they must crawl. And they do crawl to the place for camp. I build fire so that they will not freeze. Then I go back for sled. Also, I kill the dogs of the stranger-man so that we may have food and not die. I put the man and woman in blankets and they sleep. Sometimes I wake them and give them little bit of food. They are not awake, but they take the food. The woman sleep one day and a half. Then she wake up and go to sleep again. The man sleep two days and wake up and go to sleep again. After that we go down to the coast at St. Michaels. And when the ice goes out of Bering Sea, the man and woman go away on a steamship. But first they pay me my seven hundred and fifty dollars a month. Also, they make me a present of one thousand dollars. And that was the year that Sitka Charley gave much money to the Mission at Holy Cross."

"But why did they kill the man?" I asked.

Sitka Charley delayed reply until he had lighted his pipe. He glanced at the *Police Gazette* illustration and nodded his head at it familiarly. Then he said, speaking slowly and ponderingly:

"I have thought much. I do not know. It is something that happened. It is a picture I remember. It is like looking in at the window and seeing the man writing a letter. They came into my life and they went out of my life, and the picture is as I have said, without beginning, the end without understanding."

"You have painted many pictures in the telling," I said.

"Ay," he nodded his head. "But they were without beginning and without end."

"The last picture of all had an end," I said.

"Ay," he answered. "But what end?"

"It was a piece of life," I said.

"Ay," he answered. "It was a piece of life."

ALL GOLD CANYON

It was the green heart of the canyon, where the walls swerved back from the rigid plan and relieved their harshness of line by making a little sheltered nook and filling it to the brim with sweetness and roundness and softness. Here all things rested. Even the narrow stream ceased its turbulent down-rush long enough to form a quiet pool. Knee-deep in the water, with drooping head and half-shut eyes, drowsed a red-coated, many-antlered buck.

On one side, beginning at the very lip of the pool, was a tiny meadow, a cool, resilient surface of green that extended to the base of the frowning wall. Beyond the pool a gentle slope of earth ran up and up to meet the opposing wall. Fine grass covered the slope—grass that was spangled with flowers, with here and there patches of color, orange and purple and golden. Below, the canyon was shut in. There was no view. The walls leaned together abruptly and the canyon ended in a chaos of rocks, moss-covered and hidden by a green screen of vines and creepers and boughs of trees. Up the canyon rose far hills and peaks, the big foothills, pine-covered and remote. And far beyond, like clouds upon the border of the sky, towered minarets of white, where the Sierra's eternal snows flashed austerely the blazes of the sun.

There was no dust in the canyon. The leaves and flowers were clean and virginal. The grass was young velvet. Over the pool three cottonwoods sent their snowy fluffs fluttering down the quiet air. On the slope the blossoms of the wine-wooded manzanita filled the air with springtime odors, while the leaves, wise with experience, were already beginning their vertical twist against the coming aridity of summer. In the open spaces on the slope, beyond the farthest shadow-reach of the manzanita, poised the mariposa lilies, like so many flights of jewelled moths suddenly arrested and on the verge of trembling into flight again. Here and there that woods harlequin, the madrone, permitting itself to be caught in the act of changing its pea-green trunk to madder-red, breathed its fragrance into the air from great clusters of waxen bells. Creamy white were these bells, shaped like lilies-of-the-valley, with the sweetness of perfume that is of the springtime.

There was not a sigh of wind. The air was drowsy with its weight of perfume. It was a sweetness that would have been cloying had the air been heavy and humid. But the air was sharp and thin. It was as starlight transmuted into atmosphere, shot through and warmed by sunshine, and flower-drenched with sweetness.

An occasional butterfly drifted in and out through the patches of light and shade. And from all about rose the low and sleepy hum of mountain bees—feasting Sybarites that jostled one another good-naturedly at the board, nor found time for rough discourtesy. So quietly did the little stream drip and ripple its way through the canyon that it spoke only in faint and occasional gurgles. The voice of the stream was as a drowsy whisper, ever interrupted by dozings and silences, ever lifted again in the awakenings.

The motion of all things was a drifting in the heart of the canyon. Sunshine and butterflies drifted in and out among the trees. The hum of the bees and the whisper of the stream were a drifting of sound. And the drifting sound and drifting color seemed to weave together in the making of a delicate and intangible fabric which was the spirit of the place. It was a spirit of peace that was not of death, but of smooth-pulsing life, of quietude that was not silence, of movement that was not action, of repose that was quick with existence without being violent with struggle and travail. The spirit of the place was the spirit of the peace of the living, somnolent with the easement and content of prosperity, and undisturbed by rumors of far wars.

The red-coated, many-antlered buck acknowledged the lordship of the spirit of the place and dozed knee-deep in the cool, shaded pool. There seemed no flies to vex him and he was languid with rest. Sometimes his ears moved when the stream awoke and whispered; but they moved lazily, with foreknowledge that it was merely the stream grown garrulous at discovery that it had slept.

But there came a time when the buck's ears lifted and tensed with swift eagerness for sound. His head was turned down the canyon. His sensitive, quivering nostrils scented the air. His eyes could not pierce the green screen through which the stream rippled away, but to his ears came the voice of a man. It was a steady, monotonous, singsong voice. Once the buck heard the harsh clash of metal upon rock. At the sound he snorted with a sudden start that jerked him through the air from water to meadow, and his feet sank into the young velvet, while he pricked his ears and again scented the air. Then he stole across the tiny meadow, pausing once and again to listen, and faded away out of the canyon like a wraith, soft-footed and without sound.

The clash of steel-shod soles against the rocks began to be heard, and the man's voice grew louder. It was raised in a sort of chant and became distinct with nearness, so that the words could be heard:

> *"Tu'n around an' tu'n yo' face*
> *Untoe them sweet hills of grace*
> *(D' pow'rs of sin yo' am scornin'!).*
> *Look about an' look aroun',*
> *Fling yo' sin-pack on d' groun'*
> *(Yo' will meet wid d' Lord in d' mornin'!)."*

A sound of scrambling accompanied the song, and the spirit of the place fled away on the heels of the red-coated buck. The green screen was burst asunder, and a man peered out at the meadow and the pool and the sloping side-hill. He was a deliberate sort of man. He took in the scene with one embracing glance, then ran his eyes over the details to verify the general impression. Then, and not until then, did he open his mouth in vivid and solemn approval:

"Smoke of life an' snakes of purgatory! Will you just look at that! Wood an' water an' grass an' a side-hill! A pocket-hunter's delight an' a cayuse's paradise! Cool green for tired eyes! Pink pills for pale people ain't in it. A secret pasture for prospectors and a resting-place for tired burros, by damn!"

He was a sandy-complexioned man in whose face geniality and humor seemed the salient characteristics. It was a mobile face, quick-changing to inward mood and thought. Thinking was in him a visible process. Ideas chased across his face like wind-flaws across the surface of a lake. His hair, sparse and unkempt of growth, was as indeterminate and colorless as his complexion. It would seem that all the color of his frame had gone into his eyes, for they were startlingly blue. Also, they were laughing and merry eyes, within them much of the naïveté and wonder of the child; and yet, in an unassertive way, they contained much of calm self-reliance and strength of purpose founded upon self-experience and experience of the world.

From out the screen of vines and creepers he flung ahead of him a miner's pick and shovel and gold-pan. Then he crawled out himself into the open. He was clad in faded overalls and black cotton shirt, with hobnailed brogans on his feet, and on his head a hat whose shapelessness and stains advertised the rough usage of wind and rain and sun and camp-smoke. He stood erect, seeing wide-eyed the secrecy of the scene and sensuously inhaling the warm, sweet breath of the canyon-garden through nostrils that dilated and quivered with delight. His eyes narrowed to laughing slits of blue, his face wreathed itself in joy, and his mouth curled in a smile as he cried aloud:

"Jumping dandelions and happy hollyhocks, but that smells good to me! Talk about your attar o' roses an' cologne factories! They ain't in it!"

He had the habit of soliloquy. His quick-changing facial expressions might tell every thought and mood, but the tongue, perforce, ran hard after, repeating, like a second Boswell.

The man lay down on the lip of the pool and drank long and deep of its water. "Tastes good to me," he murmured, lifting his head and gazing across the pool at the side-hill, while he wiped his mouth with the back of his hand. The side-hill attracted his attention. Still lying on his stomach, he studied the hill formation long and carefully. It was a practised eye that travelled up the slope to the crumbling canyon-wall and back and down again to the edge of the pool. He scrambled to his feet and favored the side-hill with a second survey.

"Looks good to me," he concluded, picking up his pick and shovel and gold-pan.

He crossed the stream below the pool, stepping agilely from stone to stone. Where the side-hill touched the water he dug up a shovelful of dirt and put it into the gold-pan. He squatted down, holding the pan in his two hands, and partly immersing it in the stream. Then he imparted to the pan a deft circular motion that sent the water sluicing in and out through the dirt and gravel. The larger and the lighter particles worked to the surface, and these, by a skilful dipping movement of the pan, he spilled out and over the edge. Occasionally, to expedite matters, he rested the pan and with his fingers raked out the large pebbles and pieces of rock.

The contents of the pan diminished rapidly until only fine dirt and the smallest bits of gravel remained. At this stage he began to work very deliberately and carefully. It was fine washing, and he washed fine and finer, with a keen scrutiny and delicate and fastidious touch. At last the pan seemed empty of everything but water; but with a quick semi-circular flirt that sent the water flying over the shallow rim into the stream, he disclosed a layer of black sand on the bottom of the pan. So thin was this layer that it was like a streak of paint. He examined it closely. In the midst of it was a tiny golden speck. He dribbled a little water in over the depressed edge of the pan. With a quick flirt he sent the water sluicing across the bottom, turning the grains of black sand over and over. A second tiny golden speck rewarded his effort.

The washing had now become very fine—fine beyond all need of ordinary placer-mining. He worked the black sand, a small portion at a time, up the shallow rim of the pan. Each small portion he examined sharply, so that his eyes saw every grain of it before he allowed it to slide over the edge and away. Jealously, bit by bit, he let the black sand slip away. A golden speck, no larger than a pin-point, appeared on the rim, and by his manipulation of the water it returned to the bottom of the pan. And in such fashion another speck was disclosed, and another. Great was his care of them. Like a shepherd he herded his flock of golden specks so that not one should be lost. At last, of the pan of dirt nothing remained but his golden herd. He counted it, and then, after all his labor, sent it flying out of the pan with one final swirl of water.

But his blue eyes were shining with desire as he rose to his feet. "Seven," he muttered aloud, asserting the sum of the specks for which he had toiled so hard and which he had so wantonly thrown away. "Seven," he repeated, with the emphasis of one trying to impress a number on his memory.

He stood still a long while, surveying the hillside. In his eyes was a curiosity, new-aroused and burning. There was an exultance about his bearing and a keenness like that of a hunting animal catching the fresh scent of game.

He moved down the stream a few steps and took a second panful of dirt.

Again came the careful washing, the jealous herding of the golden specks, and the wantonness with which he sent them flying into the stream when he had counted their number.

"Five," he muttered, and repeated, "five."

He could not forbear another survey of the hill before filling the pan farther down the stream. His golden herds diminished. "Four, three, two, two, one," were his memory-tabulations as he moved down the stream. When but one speck of gold rewarded his washing, he stopped and built a fire of dry twigs. Into this he thrust the gold-pan and burned it till it was blue-black. He held up the pan and examined it critically. Then he nodded approbation. Against such a color-background he could defy the tiniest yellow speck to elude him.

Still moving down the stream, he panned again. A single speck was his reward. A third pan contained no gold at all. Not satisfied with this, he panned three times again, taking his shovels of dirt within a foot of one another. Each pan proved empty of gold, and the fact, instead of discouraging him, seemed to give him satisfaction. His elation increased with each barren washing, until he arose, exclaiming jubilantly:

"If it ain't the real thing, may God knock off my head with sour apples!"

Returning to where he had started operations, he began to pan up the stream. At first his golden herds increased—increased prodigiously. "Fourteen, eighteen, twenty-one, twenty-six," ran his memory tabulations. Just above the pool he struck his richest pan—thirty-five colors.

"Almost enough to save," he remarked regretfully as he allowed the water to sweep them away.

The sun climbed to the top of the sky. The man worked on. Pan by pan, he went up the stream, the tally of results steadily decreasing.

"It's just booful, the way it peters out," he exulted when a shovelful of dirt contained no more than a single speck of gold.

And when no specks at all were found in several pans, he straightened up and favored the hillside with a confident glance.

"Ah, ha! Mr. Pocket!" he cried out, as though to an auditor hidden somewhere above him beneath the surface of the slope. "Ah, ha! Mr. Pocket! I'm a-comin', I'm a-comin', an' I'm shorely gwine to get yer! You heah me, Mr. Pocket? I'm gwine to get yer as shore as punkins ain't cauliflowers!"

He turned and flung a measuring glance at the sun poised above him in the azure of the cloudless sky. Then he went down the canyon, following the line of shovel-holes he had made in filling the pans. He crossed the stream below the pool and disappeared through the green screen. There was little opportunity for the spirit of the place to return with its quietude and repose, for the man's voice, raised in ragtime song, still dominated the canyon with possession.

After a time, with a greater clashing of steel-shod feet on rock, he returned. The green screen was tremendously agitated. It surged back and forth in the throes of a struggle. There was a loud grating and clanging of metal. The man's voice leaped to a higher pitch and was sharp with imperativeness. A large body plunged and panted. There was a snapping and ripping and rending, and amid a shower of falling leaves a horse burst through the screen. On its back was a pack, and from this trailed broken vines and torn creepers. The animal gazed with astonished eyes at the scene into which it had been precipitated, then dropped its head to the grass and began contentedly to graze. A second horse scrambled into view, slipping once on the mossy rocks and regaining equilibrium when its hoofs sank into the yielding surface of the meadow. It was riderless, though on its back was a high-horned Mexican saddle, scarred and discolored by long usage.

The man brought up the rear. He threw off pack and saddle, with an eye to camp location, and gave the animals their freedom to graze. He unpacked his food and got out frying-pan and coffee-pot. He gathered an armful of dry wood, and with a few stones made a place for his fire.

"My!" he said, "but I've got an appetite. I could scoff iron-filings an' horseshoe nails an' thank you kindly, ma'am, for a second helpin'."

He straightened up, and, while he reached for matches in the pocket of his overalls, his eyes travelled across the pool to the side-hill. His fingers had clutched the match-box, but they relaxed their hold and the hand came out empty. The man wavered perceptibly. He looked at his preparations for cooking and he looked at the hill.

"Guess I'll take another whack at her," he concluded, starting to cross the stream.

"They ain't no sense in it, I know," he mumbled apologetically. "But keepin' grub back an hour ain't goin' to hurt none, I reckon."

A few feet back from his first line of test-pans he started a second line. The sun dropped down the western sky, the shadows lengthened, but the man worked on. He began a third line of test-pans. He was cross-cutting the hillside, line by line, as he ascended. The centre of each line produced the richest pans, while the ends came where no colors showed in the pan. And as he ascended the hillside the lines grew perceptibly shorter. The regularity with which their length diminished served to indicate that somewhere up the slope the last line would be so short as to have scarcely length at all, and that beyond could come only a point. The design was growing into an inverted "V." The converging sides of this "V" marked the boundaries of the gold-bearing dirt.

The apex of the "V" was evidently the man's goal. Often he ran his eye along the converging sides and on up the hill, trying to divine the apex, the point where the gold-bearing dirt must cease. Here resided "Mr. Pocket"—for so the man familiarly addressed the imaginary point above him on the slope, crying out:

"Come down out o' that, Mr. Pocket! Be right smart an' agreeable, an' come down!"

"All right," he would add later, in a voice resigned to determination. "All right, Mr. Pocket. It's plain to me I got to come right up an' snatch you out bald-headed. An' I'll do it! I'll do it!" he would threaten still later.

Each pan he carried down to the water to wash, and as he went higher up the hill the pans grew richer, until he began to save the gold in an empty baking-powder can which he carried carelessly in his hip-pocket. So engrossed was he in his toil that he did not notice the long twilight of oncoming night. It was not until he tried vainly to see the gold colors in the bottom of the pan that he realized the passage of time. He straightened up abruptly. An expression of whimsical wonderment and awe overspread his face as he drawled:

"Gosh darn my buttons! if I didn't plumb forget dinner!"

He stumbled across the stream in the darkness and lighted his long-delayed fire. Flapjacks and bacon and warmed-over beans constituted his supper. Then he smoked a pipe by the smouldering coals, listening to the night noises and watching the moonlight stream through the canyon. After that he unrolled his bed, took off his heavy shoes, and pulled the blankets up to his chin. His face showed white in the moonlight, like the face of a corpse. But it was a corpse that knew its resurrection, for the man rose suddenly on one elbow and gazed across at his hillside.

"Good night, Mr. Pocket," he called sleepily. "Good night."

He slept through the early gray of morning until the direct rays of the sun smote his closed eyelids, when he awoke with a start and looked about him until he had established the continuity of his existence and identified his present self with the days previously lived.

To dress, he had merely to buckle on his shoes. He glanced at his fireplace and at his hillside, wavered, but fought down the temptation and started the fire.

"Keep yer shirt on, Bill; keep yer shirt on," he admonished himself. "What's the good of rushin'? No use in gettin' all het up an' sweaty. Mr. Pocket'll wait for you. He ain't a-runnin' away before you can get yer breakfast. Now, what you want, Bill, is something fresh in yer bill o' fare. So it's up to you to go an' get it."

He cut a short pole at the water's edge and drew from one of his pockets a bit of line and a draggled fly that had once been a royal coachman.

"Mebbe they'll bite in the early morning," he muttered, as he made his first cast into the pool. And a moment later he was gleefully crying: "What'd I tell you, eh? What'd I tell you?"

He had no reel, nor any inclination to waste time, and by main strength, and swiftly, he drew out of the water a flashing ten-inch trout. Three more, caught in rapid succession, furnished his breakfast. When he came to the stepping-stones on his way to his hillside, he was struck by a sudden thought, and paused.

"I'd just better take a hike down-stream a ways," he said. "There's no tellin' what cuss may be snoopin' around."

But he crossed over on the stones, and with a "I really oughter take that hike," the need of the precaution passed out of his mind and he fell to work.

At nightfall he straightened up. The small of his back was stiff from stooping toil, and as he put his hand behind him to soothe the protesting muscles, he said:

"Now what d'ye think of that, by damn? I clean forgot my dinner again! If I don't watch out, I'll sure be degeneratin' into a two-meal-a-day crank."

"Pockets is the damnedest things I ever see for makin' a man absent-minded," he communed that night, as he crawled into his blankets. Nor did he forget to call up the hillside, "Good night, Mr. Pocket! Good night!"

Rising with the sun, and snatching a hasty breakfast, he was early at work. A fever seemed to be growing in him, nor did the increasing richness of the test-pans allay this fever. There was a flush in his cheek other than that made by the heat of the sun, and he was oblivious to fatigue and the passage of time. When he filled a pan with dirt, he ran down the hill to wash it; nor could he forbear running up the hill again, panting and stumbling profanely, to refill the pan.

He was now a hundred yards from the water, and the inverted "V" was assuming definite proportions. The width of the pay-dirt steadily decreased, and the man extended in his mind's eye the sides of the "V" to their meeting-place far up the hill. This was his goal, the apex of the "V," and he panned many times to locate it.

"Just about two yards above that manzanita bush an' a yard to the right," he finally concluded.

Then the temptation seized him. "As plain as the nose on your face," he said, as he abandoned his laborious cross-cutting and climbed to the indicated apex. He filled a pan and carried it down the hill to wash. It contained no trace of gold. He dug deep, and he dug shallow, filling and washing a dozen pans, and was unrewarded even by the tiniest golden speck. He was enraged at having yielded to the temptation, and cursed himself blasphemously and pridelessly. Then he went down the hill and took up the cross-cutting.

"Slow an' certain, Bill; slow an' certain," he crooned. "Short-cuts to fortune ain't in your line, an' it's about time you know it. Get wise, Bill; get wise. Slow an' certain's the only hand you can play; so go to it, an' keep to it, too."

As the cross-cuts decreased, showing that the sides of the "V" were converging, the depth of the "V" increased. The gold-trace was dipping into the hill. It was only at thirty inches beneath the surface that he could get colors in his pan. The dirt he found at twenty-five inches from the surface, and at thirty-five inches, yielded barren pans. At the base of the "V," by the water's edge, he had found the gold colors at the grass roots. The higher he went up the hill, the deeper the gold dipped. To dig a hole three feet deep in order to get one test-pan was a task of no mean magnitude; while between the man and the apex intervened an untold number of such holes to be dug. "An' there's no tellin' how much deeper it'll pitch," he sighed, in a moment's pause, while his fingers soothed his aching back.

Feverish with desire, with aching back and stiffening muscles, with pick and shovel gouging and mauling the soft brown earth, the man toiled up the hill. Before him was the smooth slope, spangled with flowers and made sweet with their breath. Behind him was devastation. It looked like some terrible eruption breaking out on the smooth skin of the hill. His slow progress was like that of a slug, befouling beauty with a monstrous trail.

Though the dipping gold-trace increased the man's work, he found consolation in the increasing richness of the pans. Twenty cents, thirty cents, fifty cents, sixty cents, were the values of the gold found in the pans, and at nightfall he washed his banner pan, which gave him a dollar's worth of gold-dust from a shovelful of dirt.

"I'll just bet it's my luck to have some inquisitive cuss come buttin' in here on my pasture," he mumbled sleepily that night as he pulled the blankets up to his chin.

Suddenly he sat upright. "Bill!" he called sharply. "Now, listen to me, Bill; d'ye hear! It's up to you, to-morrow mornin', to mosey round an' see what you can see. Understand? Tomorrow morning, an' don't you forget it!"

He yawned and glanced across at his side-hill. "Good night, Mr. Pocket," he called.

In the morning he stole a march on the sun, for he had finished breakfast when its first rays caught him, and he was climbing the wall of the canyon where it crumbled away and gave footing. From the outlook at the top he found himself in the midst of loneliness. As far as he could see, chain after chain of mountains heaved themselves into his vision. To the east his eyes, leaping the miles between range and range and between many ranges, brought up at last against the white-peaked Sierras—the main crest, where the backbone of the Western world reared itself against the sky. To the north and south he could see more distinctly the cross-systems that broke through the main trend of the sea of mountains. To the west the ranges fell away, one behind the other, diminishing and fading into the gentle foothills that, in turn, descended into the great valley which he could not see.

And in all that mighty sweep of earth he saw no sign of man nor of the handiwork of man—save only the torn bosom of the hillside at his feet. The man looked long and carefully. Once, far down his own canyon, he thought he saw in the air a faint hint of smoke. He looked again and decided that it was the purple haze of the hills made dark by a convolution of the canyon wall at its back.

"Hey, you, Mr. Pocket!" he called down into the canyon. "Stand out from under! I'm a-comin', Mr. Pocket! I'm a-comin'!"

The heavy brogans on the man's feet made him appear clumsy-footed, but he swung down from the giddy height as lightly and airily as a mountain goat. A rock, turning under his foot on the edge of the precipice, did not disconcert him. He seemed to know the precise time required for the turn to culminate in disaster, and in the meantime he utilized the false footing itself for the momentary earth-contact necessary to carry him on into safety. Where the earth sloped so steeply that it was impossible to stand for a second upright, the man did not hesitate. His foot pressed the impossible surface for but a fraction of the fatal second and gave him the bound that carried him onward. Again, where even the fraction of a second's footing was out of the question, he would swing his body past by a moment's hand-grip on a jutting knob of rock, a crevice, or a precariously rooted shrub. At last, with a wild leap and yell, he exchanged the face of the wall for an earth-slide and finished the descent in the midst of several tons of sliding earth and gravel.

His first pan of the morning washed out over two dollars in coarse gold. It was from the centre of the "V." To either side the diminution in the values of the pans was swift. His lines of cross-cutting holes were growing very short. The converging sides of the inverted "V" were only a few yards apart. Their meeting-point was only a few yards above him. But the pay-streak was dipping deeper and deeper into the earth. By early afternoon he was sinking the test-holes five feet before the pans could show the gold-trace.

For that matter, the gold-trace had become something more than a trace; it was a placer mine in itself, and the man resolved to come back after he had found the pocket and work over the ground. But the increasing richness of the pans began to worry him. By late afternoon the worth of the pans had grown to three and four dollars. The man scratched his head perplexedly and looked a few feet up the hill at the manzanita bush that marked approximately the apex of the "V." He nodded his head and said oracularly:

"It's one o' two things, Bill; one o' two things. Either Mr. Pocket's spilled himself all out an' down the hill, or else Mr. Pocket's that damned rich you maybe won't be able to carry him all away with you. And that'd be hell, wouldn't it, now?" He chuckled at contemplation of so pleasant a dilemma.

Nightfall found him by the edge of the stream, his eyes wrestling with the gathering darkness over the washing of a five-dollar pan.

"Wisht I had an electric light to go on working," he said.

He found sleep difficult that night. Many times he composed himself and closed his eyes for slumber to overtake him; but his blood pounded with too strong desire, and as many times his eyes opened and he murmured wearily, "Wisht it was sun-up."

Sleep came to him in the end, but his eyes were open with the first paling of the stars, and the gray of dawn caught him with breakfast finished and climbing the hillside in the direction of the secret abiding-place of Mr. Pocket.

The first cross-cut the man made, there was space for only three holes, so narrow had become the pay-streak and so close was he to the fountainhead of the golden stream he had been following for four days.

"Be ca'm, Bill; be ca'm," he admonished himself, as he broke ground for the final hole where the sides of the "V" had at last come together in a point.

"I've got the almighty cinch on you, Mr. Pocket, an' you can't lose me," he said many times as he sank the hole deeper and deeper.

Four feet, five feet, six feet, he dug his way down into the earth. The digging grew harder. His pick grated on broken rock. He examined the rock. "Rotten quartz," was his conclusion as, with the shovel, he cleared the bottom of the hole of loose dirt. He attacked the crumbling quartz with the pick, bursting the disintegrating rock asunder with every stroke.

He thrust his shovel into the loose mass. His eye caught a gleam of yellow. He dropped the shovel and squatted suddenly on his heels. As a farmer rubs the clinging earth from fresh-dug potatoes, so the man, a piece of rotten quartz held in both hands, rubbed the dirt away.

"Sufferin' Sardanopolis!" he cried. "Lumps an' chunks of it! Lumps an' chunks of it!"

It was only half rock he held in his hand. The other half was virgin gold. He dropped it into his pan and examined another piece. Little yellow was to be seen, but with his strong fingers he crumbled the rotten quartz away till both hands were filled with glowing yellow. He rubbed the dirt away from fragment after fragment, tossing them into the gold-pan. It was a treasure-hole. So much had the quartz rotted

away that there was less of it than there was of gold. Now and again
he found a piece to which no rock clung—a piece that was all gold. A
chunk, where the pick had laid open the heart of the gold, glittered like
a handful of yellow jewels, and he cocked his head at it and slowly
turned it around and over to observe the rich play of the light upon it.

"Talk about yer Too Much Gold diggin's!" the man snorted contemptuously. "Why, this diggin' 'd make it look like thirty cents. This
diggin' is All Gold. An' right here an' now I name this yere canyon 'All
Gold Canyon,' b' gosh!"

Still squatting on his heels, he continued examining the fragments
and tossing them into the pan. Suddenly there came to him a premonition of danger. It seemed a shadow had fallen upon him. But there was
no shadow. His heart had given a great jump up into his throat and was
choking him. Then his blood slowly chilled and he felt the sweat of his
shirt cold against his flesh.

He did not spring up nor look around. He did not move. He was
considering the nature of the premonition he had received, trying to
locate the source of the mysterious force that had warned him, striving
to sense the imperative presence of the unseen thing that threatened
him. There is an aura of things hostile, made manifest by messengers
too refined for the senses to know; and this aura he felt, but knew not
how he felt it. His was the feeling as when a cloud passes over the sun.
It seemed that between him and life had passed something dark and
smothering and menacing; a gloom, as it were, that swallowed up life
and made for death—his death.

Every force of his being impelled him to spring up and confront the
unseen danger, but his soul dominated the panic, and he remained
squatting on his heels, in his hands a chunk of gold. He did not dare to
look around, but he knew by now that there was something behind him
and above him. He made believe to be interested in the gold in his hand.
He examined it critically, turned it over and over, and rubbed the dirt
from it. And all the time he knew that something behind him was looking at the gold over his shoulder.

Still feigning interest in the chunk of gold in his hand, he listened
intently and he heard the breathing of the thing behind him. His eyes
searched the ground in front of him for a weapon, but they saw only
the uprooted gold, worthless to him now in his extremity. There was
his pick, a handy weapon on occasion; but this was not such an occasion. The man realized his predicament. He was in a narrow hole that
was seven feet deep. His head did not come to the surface of the ground.
He was in a trap.

He remained squatting on his heels. He was quite cool and collected;

but his mind, considering every factor, showed him only his helplessness. He continued rubbing the dirt from the quartz fragments and throwing the gold into the pan. There was nothing else for him to do. Yet he knew that he would have to rise up, sooner or later, and face the danger that breathed at his back. The minutes passed, and with the passage of each minute he knew that by so much he was nearer the time when he must stand up, or else—and his wet shirt went cold against his flesh again at the thought—or else he might receive death as he stooped there over his treasure.

Still he squatted on his heels, rubbing dirt from gold and debating in just what manner he should rise up. He might rise up with a rush and claw his way out of the hole to meet whatever threatened on the even footing above ground. Or he might rise up slowly and carelessly, and feign casually to discover the thing that breathed at his back. His instinct and every fighting fibre of his body favored the mad, clawing rush to the surface. His intellect, and the craft thereof, favored the slow and cautious meeting with the thing that menaced and which he could not see. And while he debated, a loud, crashing noise burst on his ear. At the same instant he received a stunning blow on the left side of the back, and from the point of impact felt a rush of flame through his flesh. He sprang up in the air, but halfway to his feet collapsed. His body crumpled in like a leaf withered in sudden heat, and he came down, his chest across his pan of gold, his face in the dirt and rock, his legs tangled and twisted because of the restricted space at the bottom of the hole. His legs twitched convulsively several times. His body was shaken as with a mighty ague. There was a slow expansion of the lungs, accompanied by a deep sigh. Then the air was slowly, very slowly, exhaled, and his body as slowly flattened itself down into inertness.

Above, revolver in hand, a man was peering down over the edge of the hole. He peered for a long time at the prone and motionless body beneath him. After a while the stranger sat down on the edge of the hole so that he could see into it, and rested the revolver on his knee. Reaching his hand into a pocket, he drew out a wisp of brown paper. Into this he dropped a few crumbs of tobacco. The combination became a cigarette, brown and squat, with the ends turned in. Not once did he take his eyes from the body at the bottom of the hole. He lighted the cigarette and drew its smoke into his lungs with a caressing intake of the breath. He smoked slowly. Once the cigarette went out and he relighted it. And all the while he studied the body beneath him.

In the end he tossed the cigarette stub away and rose to his feet. He moved to the edge of the hole. Spanning it, a hand resting on each edge, and with the revolver still in the right hand, he muscled his body down into the hole. While his feet were yet a yard from the bottom he released his hands and dropped down.

At the instant his feet struck bottom he saw the pocket-miner's arm leap out, and his own legs knew a swift, jerking grip that overthrew him. In the nature of the jump his revolver-hand was above his head. Swiftly as the grip had flashed about his legs, just as swiftly he brought the revolver down. He was still in the air, his fall in process of completion, when he pulled the trigger. The explosion was deafening in the confined space. The smoke filled the hole so that he could see nothing. He struck the bottom on his back, and like a cat's the pocket-miner's body was on top of him. Even as the miner's body passed on top, the stranger crooked in his right arm to fire; and even in that instant the miner, with a quick thrust of elbow, struck his wrist. The muzzle was thrown up and the bullet thudded into the dirt of the side of the hole.

The next instant the stranger felt the miner's hand grip his wrist. The struggle was now for the revolver. Each man strove to turn it against the other's body. The smoke in the hole was clearing. The stranger, lying on his back, was beginning to see dimly. But suddenly he was blinded by a handful of dirt deliberately flung into his eyes by his antagonist. In that moment of shock his grip on the revolver was broken. In the next moment he felt a smashing darkness descend upon his brain, and in the midst of the darkness even the darkness ceased.

But the pocket-miner fired again and again, until the revolver was empty. Then he tossed it from him and, breathing heavily, sat down on the dead man's legs.

The miner was sobbing and struggling for breath. "Measly skunk!" he panted; "a-campin' on my trail an' lettin' me do the work, an' then shootin' me in the back!"

He was half crying from anger and exhaustion. He peered at the face of the dead man. It was sprinkled with loose dirt and gravel, and it was difficult to distinguish the features.

"Never laid eyes on him before," the miner concluded his scrutiny. "Just a common an' ordinary thief, damn him! An' he shot me in the back! He shot me in the back!"

He opened his shirt and felt himself, front and back, on his left side.

"Went clean through, and no harm done!" he cried jubilantly. "I'll bet he aimed all right all right; but he drew the gun over when he pulled the trigger—the cuss! But I fixed 'm! Oh, I fixed 'm!"

His fingers were investigating the bullet-hole in his side, and a shade of regret passed over his face. "It's goin' to be stiffer'n hell," he said. "An' it's up to me to get mended an' get out o' here."

He crawled out of the hole and went down the hill to his camp. Half an hour later he returned, leading his pack-horse. His open shirt disclosed the rude bandages with which he had dressed his wound. He was slow and awkward with his left-hand movements, but that did not prevent his using the arm.

The bight of the pack-rope under the dead man's shoulders enabled him to heave the body out of the hole. Then he set to work gathering up his gold. He worked steadily for several hours, pausing often to rest his stiffening shoulder and to exclaim:

"He shot me in the back, the measly skunk! He shot me in the back!"

When his treasure was quite cleaned up and wrapped securely into a number of blanket-covered parcels, he made an estimate of its value.

"Four hundred pounds, or I'm a Hottentot," he concluded. "Say two hundred in quartz an' dirt—that leaves two hundred pounds of gold. Bill! Wake up! Two hundred pounds of gold! Forty thousand dollars! An' it's yourn—all yourn!"

He scratched his head delightedly and his fingers blundered into an unfamiliar groove. They quested along it for several inches. It was a crease through his scalp where the second bullet had ploughed.

He walked angrily over to the dead man.

"You would, would you?" he bullied. "You would, eh? Well, I fixed you good an' plenty, an' I'll give you decent burial, too. That's more'n you'd have done for me."

He dragged the body to the edge of the hole and toppled it in. It struck the bottom with a dull crash, on its side, the face twisted up to the light. The miner peered down at it.

"An' you shot me in the back!" he said accusingly.

With pick and shovel he filled the hole. Then he loaded the gold on his horse. It was too great a load for the animal, and when he had gained his camp he transferred part of it to his saddle-horse. Even so, he was compelled to abandon a portion of his outfit—pick and shovel and gold-pan, extra food and cooking utensils, and divers odds and ends.

The sun was at the zenith when the man forced the horses at the screen of vines and creepers. To climb the huge boulders the animals were compelled to uprear and struggle blindly through the tangled mass of vegetation. Once the saddle-horse fell heavily and the man removed the pack to get the animal on its feet. After it started on its way again the man thrust his head out from among the leaves and peered up at the hillside.

"The measly skunk!" he said, and disappeared.

There was a ripping and tearing of vines and boughs. The trees surged back and forth, marking the passage of the animals through the midst of them. There was a clashing of steel-shod hoofs on stone, and

now and again an oath or a sharp cry of command. Then the voice of
the man was raised in song:—

> *"Tu'n around an' tu'n yo' face*
> *Untoe them sweet hills of grace*
> *(D' pow'rs of sin yo' am scornin'!).*
> *Look about an' look aroun',*
> *Fling yo' sin-pack on d' groun'*
> *(Yo' will meet wid d' Lord in d' mornin'!)."*

The song grew faint and fainter, and through the silence crept back
the spirit of the place. The stream once more drowsed and whispered;
the hum of the mountain bees rose sleepily. Down through the perfume-
weighted air fluttered the snowy fluffs of the cottonwoods. The butterflies drifted in and out among the trees, and over all blazed the quiet
sunshine. Only remained the hoof-marks in the meadow and the torn
hillside to mark the boisterous trail of the life that had broken the peace
of the place and passed on.

A DAY'S LODGING

It was the gosh-dangdest stampede I ever seen. A thousand dog-teams hittin' the ice. You couldn't see 'm fer smoke. Two white men an' a Swede froze to death that night, an' there was a dozen busted their lungs. But didn't I see with my own eyes the bottom of the water-hole? It was yellow with gold like a mustard-plaster. That's why I staked the Yukon for a minin' claim. That's what made the stampede. An' then there was nothin' to it. That's what I said—NOTHIN' to it. An' I ain't got over guessin' yet.

—Narrative of Shorty.

John Messner clung with mittened hand to the bucking gee-pole and held the sled in the trail. With the other mittened hand he rubbed his cheeks and nose. He rubbed his cheeks and nose every little while. In point of fact, he rarely ceased from rubbing them, and sometimes, as their numbness increased, he rubbed fiercely. His forehead was covered by the visor of his fur cap, the flaps of which went over his ears. The rest of his face was protected by a thick beard, golden-brown under its coating of frost.

Behind him churned a heavily loaded Yukon sled, and before him toiled a string of five dogs. The rope by which they dragged the sled rubbed against the side of Messner's leg. When the dogs swung on a bend in the trail, he stepped over the rope. There were many bends, and he was compelled to step over it often. Sometimes he tripped on the rope, or stumbled, and at all times he was awkward, betraying a weariness so great that the sled now and again ran upon his heels.

When he came to a straight piece of trail, where the sled could get along for a moment without guidance, he let go the gee-pole and batted his right hand sharply upon the hard wood. He found it difficult to keep up the circulation in that hand. But while he pounded the one hand, he never ceased from rubbing his nose and cheeks with the other.

"It's too cold to travel, anyway," he said. He spoke aloud, after the manner of men who are much by themselves. "Only a fool would travel at such a temperature. If it isn't eighty below, it's because it's seventy-nine."

He pulled out his watch, and after some fumbling got it back into the breast pocket of his thick woollen jacket. Then he surveyed the heavens and ran his eye along the white sky-line to the south.

"Twelve o'clock," he mumbled, "A clear sky, and no sun."

He plodded on silently for ten minutes, and then, as though there had been no lapse in his speech, he added:

"And no ground covered, and it's too cold to travel."

Suddenly he yelled "Whoa!" at the dogs, and stopped. He seemed in a wild panic over his right hand, and proceeded to hammer it furiously against the gee-pole.

"You—poor—devils!" he addressed the dogs, which had dropped down heavily on the ice to rest. His was a broken, jerky utterance, caused by the violence with which he hammered his numb hand upon the wood. "What have you done anyway that a two-legged other animal should come along, break you to harness, curb all your natural proclivities, and make slave-beasts out of you?"

He rubbed his nose, not reflectively, but savagely in order to drive the blood into it, and urged the dogs to their work again. He travelled on the frozen surface of a great river. Behind him it stretched away in a mighty curve of many miles, losing itself in a fantastic jumble of mountains, snow-covered and silent. Ahead of him the river split into many channels to accommodate the freight of islands it carried on its breast. These islands were silent and white. No animals nor humming insects broke the silence. No birds flew in the chill air. There was no sound of man, no mark of the handiwork of man. The world slept, and it was like the sleep of death.

John Messner seemed succumbing to the apathy of it all. The frost was benumbing his spirit. He plodded on with bowed head, unobservant, mechanically rubbing nose and cheeks, and batting his steering hand against the gee-pole in the straight trail-stretches.

But the dogs were observant, and suddenly they stopped, turning their heads and looking back at their master out of eyes that were wistful and questioning. Their eyelashes were frosted white, as were their muzzles, and they had all the seeming of decrepit old age, what of the frost-rime and exhaustion.

The man was about to urge them on, when he checked himself,

roused up with an effort, and looked around. The dogs had stopped beside a water-hole, not a fissure, but a hole man-made, chopped laboriously with an axe through three and a half feet of ice. A thick skin of new ice showed that it had not been used for some time. Messner glanced about him. The dogs were already pointing the way, each wistful and hoary muzzle turned toward the dim snow-path that left the main river trail and climbed the bank of the island.

"All right, you sore-footed brutes," he said. "I'll investigate. You're not a bit more anxious to quit than I am."

He climbed the bank and disappeared. The dogs did not lie down, but on their feet eagerly waited his return. He came back to them, took a hauling-rope from the front of the sled, and put it around his shoulders. Then he *gee'd* the dogs to the right and put them at the bank on the run. It was a stiff pull, but their weariness fell from them as they crouched low to the snow, whining with eagerness and gladness as they struggled upward to the last ounce of effort in their bodies. When a dog slipped or faltered, the one behind nipped his hind quarters. The man shouted encouragement and threats, and threw all his weight on the hauling-rope.

They cleared the bank with a rush, swung to the left, and dashed up to a small log cabin. It was a deserted cabin of a single room, eight feet by ten on the inside. Messner unharnessed the animals, unloaded his sled and took possession. The last chance wayfarer had left a supply of firewood. Messner set up his light sheet-iron stove and started a fire. He put five sun-cured salmon into the oven to thaw out for the dogs, and from the water-hole filled his coffee-pot and cooking-pail.

While waiting for the water to boil, he held his face over the stove. The moisture from his breath had collected on his beard and frozen into a great mass of ice, and this he proceeded to thaw out. As it melted and dropped upon the stove it sizzled and rose about him in steam. He helped the process with his fingers, working loose small ice-chunks that fell rattling to the floor.

A wild outcry from the dogs without did not take him from his task. He heard the wolfish snarling and yelping of strange dogs and the sound of voices. A knock came on the door.

"Come in," Messner called, in a voice muffled because at the moment he was sucking loose a fragment of ice from its anchorage on his upper lip.

The door opened, and, gazing out of his cloud of steam, he saw a man and a woman pausing on the threshold.

"Come in," he said peremptorily, "and shut the door!"

Peering through the steam, he could make out but little of their personal appearance. The nose and cheek strap worn by the woman and the trail-wrappings about her head allowed only a pair of black eyes to be seen. The man was dark-eyed and smooth-shaven all except his mustache, which was so iced up as to hide his mouth.

"We just wanted to know if there is any other cabin around here," he said, at the same time glancing over the unfurnished state of the room. "We thought this cabin was empty."

"It isn't my cabin," Messner answered. "I just found it a few minutes ago. Come right in and camp. Plenty of room, and you won't need your stove. There's room for all."

At the sound of his voice the woman peered at him with quick curiousness.

"Get your things off," her companion said to her. "I'll unhitch and get the water so we can start cooking."

Messner took the thawed salmon outside and fed his dogs. He had to guard them against the second team of dogs, and when he had reëntered the cabin the other man had unpacked the sled and fetched water. Messner's pot was boiling. He threw in the coffee, settled it with half a cup of cold water, and took the pot from the stove. He thawed some sourdough biscuits in the oven, at the same time heating a pot of beans he had boiled the night before and that had ridden frozen on the sled all morning.

Removing his utensils from the stove, so as to give the newcomers a chance to cook, he proceeded to take his meal from the top of his grub-box, himself sitting on his bed-roll. Between mouthfuls he talked trail and dogs with the man, who, with head over the stove, was thawing the ice from his mustache. There were two bunks in the cabin, and into one of them, when he had cleared his lip, the stranger tossed his bed-roll.

"We'll sleep here," he said, "unless you prefer this bunk. You're the first comer and you have first choice, you know."

"That's all right," Messner answered. "One bunk's just as good as the other."

He spread his own bedding in the second bunk, and sat down on the edge. The stranger thrust a physician's small travelling case under his blankets at one end to serve for a pillow.

"Doctor?" Messner asked.

"Yes," came the answer, "but I assure you I didn't come into the Klondike to practise."

The woman busied herself with cooking, while the man sliced bacon and fired the stove. The light in the cabin was dim, filtering through in a small window made of onion-skin writing paper and oiled with bacon grease, so that John Messner could not make out very well what the woman looked like. Not that he tried. He seemed to have no interest in her. But she glanced curiously from time to time into the dark corner where he sat.

"Oh, it's a great life," the doctor proclaimed enthusiastically, pausing from sharpening his knife on the stovepipe. "What I like about it is the struggle, the endeavor with one's own hands, the primitiveness of it, the realness."

"The temperature is real enough," Messner laughed.

"Do you know how cold it actually is?" the doctor demanded.

The other shook his head.

"Well, I'll tell you. Seventy-four below zero by spirit thermometer on the sled."

"That's one hundred and six below freezing point—too cold for travelling, eh?"

"Practically suicide," was the doctor's verdict. "One exerts himself. He breathes heavily, taking into his lungs the frost itself. It chills his lungs, freezes the edges of the tissues. He gets a dry, hacking cough as the dead tissue sloughs away, and dies the following summer of pneumonia, wondering what it's all about. I'll stay in this cabin for a week, unless the thermometer rises at least to fifty below."

"I say, Tess," he said, the next moment, "don't you think that coffee's boiled long enough!"

At the sound of the woman's name, John Messner became suddenly alert. He looked at her quickly, while across his face shot a haunting expression, the ghost of some buried misery achieving swift resurrection. But the next moment, and by an effort of will, the ghost was laid again. His face was as placid as before, though he was still alert, dissatisfied with what the feeble light had shown him of the woman's face.

Automatically, her first act had been to set the coffee-pot back. It was not until she had done this that she glanced at Messner. But already he had composed himself. She saw only a man sitting on the edge of the bunk and incuriously studying the toes of his moccasins. But, as she turned casually to go about her cooking, he shot another swift look at her, and she, glancing as swiftly back, caught his look. He shifted on past her to the doctor, though the slightest smile curled his lip in appreciation of the way she had trapped him.

She drew a candle from the grub-box and lighted it. One look at her illuminated face was enough for Messner. In the small cabin the widest limit was only a matter of several steps, and the next moment she was alongside of him. She deliberately held the candle close to his face and stared at him out of eyes wide with fear and recognition. He smiled quietly back at her.

"What are you looking for, Tess?" the doctor called.

"Hairpins," she replied, passing on and rummaging in a clothes-bag on the bunk.

They served their meal on their grub-box, sitting on Messner's grub-box, and facing him. He had stretched out on his bunk to rest, lying on his side, his head on his arm. In the close quarters it was as though the three were together at table.

"What part of the States do you come from?" Messner asked.

"San Francisco," answered the doctor. "I've been in here two years, though."

"I hail from California myself," was Messner's announcement.

The woman looked at him appealingly, but he smiled and went on: "Berkeley, you know."

The other man was becoming interested.

"U. C.?" he asked.

"Yes, Class of '86."

"I meant faculty," the doctor explained. "You remind me of the type."

"Sorry to hear you say so," Messner smiled back. "I'd prefer being taken for a prospector or a dog-musher."

"I don't think he looks any more like a professor than you do a doctor," the woman broke in.

"Thank you," said Messner. Then, turning to her companion, "By the way, Doctor, what is your name, if I may ask?"

"Haythorne, if you'll take my word for it. I gave up cards with civilization."

"And Mrs. Haythorne," Messner smiled and bowed.

She flashed a look at him that was more anger than appeal.

Haythorne was about to ask the other's name. His mouth had opened to form the question when Messner cut him off.

"Come to think of it, Doctor, you may possibly be able to satisfy my curiosity. There was a sort of scandal in faculty circles some two or three years ago. The wife of one of the English professors—er, if you will pardon me, Mrs. Haythorne—disappeared with some San Francisco doctor, I understood, though his name does not just now come to my lips. Do you remember the incident?"

Haythorne nodded his head. "Made quite a stir at the time. His name was Womble—Graham Womble. He had a magnificent practice. I knew him somewhat."

"Well, what I was trying to get at was what had become of them. I was wondering if you had heard. They left no trace, hide nor hair."

"He covered his tracks cunningly." Haythorne cleared his throat. "There was rumor that they went to the South Seas—were lost on a trading schooner in a typhoon, or something like that."

"I never heard that," Messner said. "You remember the case, Mrs. Haythorne?"

"Perfectly," she answered, in a voice the control of which was in amazing contrast to the anger that blazed in the face she turned aside so that Haythorne might not see.

The latter was again on the verge of asking his name, when Messner remarked:

"This Dr. Womble, I've heard he was very handsome, and—er—quite a success, so to say, with the ladies."

"Well, if he was, he finished himself off by that affair," Haythorne grumbled.

"And the woman was a termagant—at least so I've been told. It was generally accepted in Berkeley that she made life—er—not exactly paradise for her husband."

"I never heard that," Haythorne rejoined. "In San Francisco the talk was all the other way."

"Woman sort of a martyr, eh?—crucified on the cross of matrimony?"

The doctor nodded. Messner's gray eyes were mildly curious as he went on:

"That was to be expected—two sides to the shield. Living in Berkeley I only got the one side. She was a great deal in San Francisco, it seems."

"Some coffee, please," Haythorne said.

The woman refilled his mug, at the same time breaking into light laughter.

"You're gossiping like a pair of beldames," she chided them.

"It's so interesting," Messner smiled at her, then returned to the doctor. "The husband seems then to have had a not very savory reputation in San Francisco?"

"On the contrary, he was a moral prig," Haythorne blurted out, with apparently undue warmth. "He was a little scholastic shrimp without a drop of red blood in his body."

"Did you know him?"

"Never laid eyes on him. I never knocked about in university circles."

"One side of the shield again," Messner said, with an air of weighing the matter judicially. "While he did not amount to much, it is true—that is, physically—I'd hardly say he was as bad as all that. He did take an active interest in student athletics. And he had some talent. He once wrote a Nativity play that brought him quite a bit of local appreciation. I have heard, also, that he was slated for the head of the English department, only the affair happened and he resigned and went away. It quite broke his career, or so it seemed. At any rate, on our side the shield, it was considered a knock-out blow to him. It was thought he cared a great deal for his wife."

Haythorne, finishing his mug of coffee, grunted uninterestedly and lighted his pipe.

"It was fortunate they had no children," Messner continued.

But Haythorne, with a glance at the stove, pulled on his cap and mittens.

"I'm going out to get some wood," he said. "Then I can take off my moccasins and be comfortable."

The door slammed behind him. For a long minute there was silence. The man continued in the same position on the bed. The woman sat on the grub-box, facing him.

"What are you going to do?" she asked abruptly.

Messner looked at her with lazy indecision. "What do you think I ought to do? Nothing scenic, I hope. You see I am stiff and trail-sore, and this bunk is so restful."

She gnawed her lower lip and fumed dumbly.

"But—" she began vehemently, then clenched her hands and stopped.

"I hope you don't want me to kill Mr.—er—Haythorne," he said gently, almost pleadingly. "It would be most distressing, and, I assure you, really it is unnecessary."

"But you must do something," she cried.

"On the contrary, it is quite conceivable that I do not have to do anything."

"You would stay here?"

He nodded.

She glanced desperately around the cabin and at the bed unrolled on the other bunk. "Night is coming on. You can't stop here. You can't! I tell you, you simply can't!"

"Of course I can. I might remind you that I found this cabin first and that you are my guests."

Again her eyes travelled around the room, and the terror in them leaped up at sight of the other bunk.

"Then we'll have to go," she announced decisively.

"Impossible. You have a dry, hacking cough—the sort Mr.—er— Haythorne so aptly described. You've already slightly chilled your lungs. Besides, he is a physician and knows. He would never permit it."

"Then what are you going to do?" she demanded again, with a tense, quiet utterance that boded an outbreak.

Messner regarded her in a way that was almost paternal, what of the profundity of pity and patience with which he contrived to suffuse it.

"My dear Theresa, as I told you before, I don't know. I really haven't thought about it."

"Oh! You drive me mad!" She sprang to her feet, wringing her hands in impotent wrath. "You never used to be this way."

"I used to be all softness and gentleness," he nodded concurrence. "Was that why you left me?"

"You are so different, so dreadfully calm. You frighten me. I feel you have something terrible planned all the while. But whatever you do, don't do anything rash. Don't get excited—"

"I don't get excited any more," he interrupted. "Not since you went away."

"You have improved—remarkably," she retorted.

He smiled acknowledgment. "While I am thinking about what I shall do, I'll tell you what you will have to do—tell Mr.—er—Haythorne who I am. It may make our stay in this cabin more—may I say, sociable?"

"Why have you followed me into this frightful country?" she asked irrelevantly.

"Don't think I came here looking for you, Theresa. Your vanity shall not be tickled by any such misapprehension. Our meeting is wholly fortuitous. I broke with the life academic and I had to go somewhere. To be honest, I came into the Klondike because I thought it the place you were least liable to be in."

There was a fumbling at the latch, then the door swung in and Haythorne entered with an armful of firewood. At the first warning, Theresa began casually to clear away the dishes. Haythorne went out again after more wood.

"Why didn't you introduce us?" Messner queried.

"I'll tell him," she replied, with a toss of her head. "Don't think I'm afraid."

"I never knew you to be afraid, very much, of anything."

"And I'm not afraid of confession, either," she said, with softening face and voice.

"In your case, I fear, confession is exploitation by indirection, profit-making by ruse, self-aggrandizement at the expense of God."

"Don't be literary," she pouted, with growing tenderness. "I never did like epigrammatic discussion. Besides, I'm not afraid to ask you to forgive me."

"There is nothing to forgive, Theresa. I really should thank you. True, at first I suffered; and then, with all the graciousness of spring, it dawned upon me that I was happy, very happy. It was a most amazing discovery."

"But what if I should return to you?" she asked.

"I should" (he looked at her whimsically) "be greatly perturbed."

"I am your wife. You know you have never got a divorce."

"I see," he meditated. "I have been careless. It will be one of the first things I attend to."

She came over to his side, resting her hand on his arm. "You don't want me, John?" Her voice was soft and caressing, her hand rested like a lure. "If I told you I had made a mistake? If I told you that I was very unhappy?—and I am. And I did make a mistake."

Fear began to grow on Messner. He felt himself wilting under the lightly laid hand. The situation was slipping away from him, all his beautiful calmness was going. She looked at him with melting eyes, and he, too, seemed all dew and melting. He felt himself on the edge of an abyss, powerless to withstand the force that was drawing him over.

"I am coming back to you, John. I am coming back to-day . . . now."

As in a nightmare, he strove under the hand. While she talked, he seemed to hear, rippling softly, the song of the Lorelei. It was as though, somewhere, a piano were playing and the actual notes were impinging on his ear-drums.

Suddenly he sprang to his feet, thrust her from him as her arms attempted to clasp him, and retreated backward to the door. He was in a panic.

"I'll do something desperate!" he cried.

"I warned you not to get excited." She laughed mockingly, and went about washing the dishes. "Nobody wants you. I was just playing with you. I am happier where I am."

But Messner did not believe. He remembered her facility in changing front. She had changed front now. It was exploitation by indirection. She was not happy with the other man. She had discovered her mistake. The flame of his ego flared up at the thought. She wanted to come back to him, which was the one thing he did not want. Unwittingly, his hand rattled the door-latch.

"Don't run away," she laughed. "I won't bite you."

"I am not running away," he replied with child-like defiance, at the same time pulling on his mittens. "I'm only going to get some water."

He gathered the empty pails and cooking pots together and opened the door. He looked back at her.

"Don't forget you're to tell Mr.—er—Haythorne who I am."

Messner broke the skin that had formed on the water-hole within the hour, and filled his pails. But he did not return immediately to the cabin. Leaving the pails standing in the trail, he walked up and down, rapidly, to keep from freezing, for the frost bit into the flesh like fire. His beard was white with his frozen breath when the perplexed and frowning brows relaxed and decision came into his face. He had made up his mind to his course of action, and his frigid lips and cheeks cracked into a chuckle over it. The pails were already skinned over with young ice when he picked them up and made for the cabin.

When he entered he found the other man waiting, standing near the stove, a certain stiff awkwardness and indecision in his manner. Messner set down his water-pails.

"Glad to meet you, Graham Womble," he said in conventional tones, as though acknowledging an introduction.

Messner did not offer his hand. Womble stirred uneasily, feeling for the other the hatred one is prone to feel for one he has wronged.

"And so you're the chap," Messner said in marvelling accents. "Well, well. You see, I really *am* glad to meet you. I have been—er—curious to know what Theresa found in you—where, I may say, the attraction lay. Well, well."

And he looked the other up and down as a man would look a horse up and down.

"I know how you must feel about me," Womble began.

"Don't mention it," Messner broke in with exaggerated cordiality of voice and manner. "Never mind that. What I want to know is how do you find her? Up to expectations? Has she worn well? Life been all a happy dream ever since?"

"Don't be silly," Theresa interjected.

"I can't help being natural," Messner complained.

"You can be expedient at the same time, and practical," Womble said sharply. "What we want to know is what are you going to do?"

Messner made a well-feigned gesture of helplessness. "I really don't know. It is one of those impossible situations against which there can be no prevision."

"All three of us cannot remain the night in this cabin."

Messner nodded affirmation.

"Then somebody must get out."

"That also is incontrovertible," Messner agreed. "When three bodies cannot occupy the same space at the same time, one must get out."

"And you're that one," Womble announced grimly. "It's a ten-mile pull to the next camp, but you can make it all right."

"And that's the first flaw in your reasoning," the other objected.

"Why, necessarily, should I be the one to get out? I found this cabin first."

"But Tess can't get out," Womble explained. "Her lungs are already slightly chilled."

"I agree with you. She can't venture ten miles of frost. By all means she must remain."

"Then it is as I said," Womble announced with finality.

Messner cleared his throat. "Your lungs are all right, aren't they?"

"Yes, but what of it?"

Again the other cleared his throat and spoke with painstaking and judicial slowness. "Why, I may say, nothing of it, except, ah, according to your own reasoning, there is nothing to prevent your getting out, hitting the frost, so to speak, for a matter of ten miles. You can make it all right."

Womble looked with quick suspicion at Theresa and caught in her eyes a glint of pleased surprise.

"Well?" he demanded of her.

She hesitated, and a surge of anger darkened his face. He turned upon Messner.

"Enough of this. You can't stop here."

"Yes, I can."

"I won't let you." Womble squared his shoulders. "I'm running things."

"I'll stay anyway," the other persisted.

"I'll put you out."

"I'll come back."

Womble stopped a moment to steady his voice and control himself. Then he spoke slowly, in a low, tense voice.

"Look here, Messner, if you refuse to get out, I'll thrash you. This isn't California. I'll beat you to a jelly with my two fists."

Messner shrugged his shoulders. "If you do, I'll call a miners' meeting and see you strung up to the nearest tree. As you said, this is not California. They're a simple folk, these miners, and all I'll have to do will be to show them the marks of the beating, tell them the truth about you, and present my claim for my wife."

The woman attempted to speak, but Womble turned upon her fiercely.

"You keep out of this," he cried.

In marked contrast was Messner's "Please don't intrude, Theresa."

What of her anger and pent feelings, her lungs were irritated into the dry, hacking cough, and with blood-suffused face and one hand clenched against her chest, she waited for the paroxysm to pass.

Womble looked gloomily at her, noting her cough.

"Something must be done," he said. "Yet her lungs can't stand the exposure. She can't travel till the temperature rises. And I'm not going to give her up."

Messner hemmed, cleared his throat, and hemmed again, semi-apologetically, and said, "I need some money."

Contempt showed instantly in Womble's face. At last, beneath him in vileness, had the other sunk himself.

"You've got a fat sack of dust," Messner went on. "I saw you unload it from the sled."

"How much do you want?" Womble demanded, with a contempt in his voice equal to that in his face.

"I made an estimate of the sack, and I—ah—should say it weighed about twenty pounds. What do you say we call it four thousand?"

"But it's all I've got, man!" Womble cried out.

"You've got her," the other said soothingly. "She must be worth it. Think what I'm giving up. Surely it is a reasonable price."

"All right." Womble rushed across the floor to the gold-sack. "Can't put this deal through too quick for me, you—you little worm!"

"Now, there you err," was the smiling rejoinder. "As a matter of ethics isn't the man who gives a bribe as bad as the man who takes a bribe? The receiver is as bad as the thief, you know; and you needn't console yourself with any fictitious moral superiority concerning this little deal."

"To hell with your ethics!" the other burst out. "Come here and watch the weighing of this dust. I might cheat you."

And the woman, leaning against the bunk, raging and impotent, watched herself weighed out in yellow dust and nuggets in the scales erected on the grub-box. The scales were small, making necessary many weighings, and Messner with precise care verified each weighing.

"There's too much silver in it," he remarked as he tied up the gold-sack. "I don't think it will run quite sixteen to the ounce. You got a trifle the better of me, Womble."

He handled the sack lovingly, and with due appreciation of its preciousness carried it out to his sled. Returning, he gathered his pots and pans together, packed his grub-box, and rolled up his bed. When the sled was lashed and the complaining dogs harnessed, he returned into the cabin for his mittens.

"Good-by, Tess," he said, standing at the open door.

She turned on him, struggling for speech but too frantic to word the passion that burned in her.

"Good-by, Tess," he repeated gently.

"Beast!" she managed to articulate.

She turned and tottered to the bunk, flinging herself face down upon it, sobbing: "You beasts! You beasts!"

John Messner closed the door softly behind him, and, as he started the dogs, looked back at the cabin with a great relief in his face. At the bottom of the bank, beside the water-hole, he halted the sled. He worked the sack of gold out between the lashings and carried it to the water-hole. Already a new skin of ice had formed. This he broke with his fist. Untying the knotted mouth with his teeth, he emptied the contents of the sack into the water. The river was shallow at that point, and two feet beneath the surface he could see the bottom dull-yellow in the fading light. At the sight of it, he spat into the hole.

He started the dogs along the Yukon trail. Whining spiritlessly, they were reluctant to work. Clinging to the gee-pole with his right hand and with his left rubbing cheeks and nose, he stumbled over the rope as the dogs swung on a bend.

"Mush-on, you poor, sore-footed brutes!" he cried. "That's it, mush-on!"

THE APOSTATE

Now I wake me up to work;
I pray the Lord I may not shirk.
If I should die before the night,
I pray the Lord my work's all right.
                                    Amen.

"If you don't git up, Johnny, I won't give you a bite to eat!"

The threat had no effect on the boy. He clung stubbornly to sleep, fighting for its oblivion as the dreamer fights for his dream. The boy's hands loosely clenched themselves, and he made feeble, spasmodic blows at the air. These blows were intended for his mother, but she betrayed practised familiarity in avoiding them as she shook him roughly by the shoulder.

"Lemme 'lone!"

It was a cry that began, muffled, in the deeps of sleep, that swiftly rushed upward, like a wail, into passionate belligerence, and that died away and sank down into an inarticulate whine. It was a bestial cry, as of a soul in torment, filled with infinite protest and pain.

But she did not mind. She was a sad-eyed, tired-faced woman, and she had grown used to this task, which she repeated every day of her life. She got a grip on the bed-clothes and tried to strip them down; but the boy, ceasing his punching, clung to them desperately. In a huddle, at the foot of the bed, he still remained covered. Then she tried dragging the bedding to the floor. The boy opposed her. She braced herself. Hers was the superior weight, and the boy and bedding gave, the former instinctively following the latter in order to shelter against the chill of the room that bit into his body.

As he toppled on the edge of the bed it seemed that he must fall head-first to the floor. But consciousness fluttered up in him. He righted himself and for a moment perilously balanced. Then he struck the floor on his feet. On the instant his mother seized him by the shoulders and shook him. Again his fists struck out, this time with more force and directness. At the same time his eyes opened. She released him. He was awake.

"All right," he mumbled.

She caught up the lamp and hurried out, leaving him in darkness.

"You'll be docked," she warned back to him.

He did not mind the darkness. When he had got into his clothes, he went out into the kitchen. His tread was very heavy for so thin and light a boy. His legs dragged with their own weight, which seemed unreasonable because they were such skinny legs. He drew a broken-bottomed chair to the table.

"Johnny!" his mother called sharply.

He arose as sharply from the chair, and, without a word, went to the sink. It was a greasy, filthy sink. A smell came up from the outlet. He took no notice of it. That a sink should smell was to him part of the natural order, just as it was a part of the natural order that the soap should be grimy with dish-water and hard to lather. Nor did he try very hard to make it lather. Several splashes of the cold water from the running faucet completed the function. He did not wash his teeth. For that matter he had never seen a toothbrush, nor did he know that there existed beings in the world who were guilty of so great a foolishness as tooth washing.

"You might wash yourself wunst a day without bein' told," his mother complained.

She was holding a broken lid on the pot as she poured two cups of coffee. He made no remark, for this was a standing quarrel between them, and the one thing upon which his mother was hard as adamant. "Wunst" a day it was compulsory that he should wash his face. He dried himself on a greasy towel, damp and dirty and ragged, that left his face covered with shreds of lint.

"I wish we didn't live so far away," she said, as he sat down. "I try to do the best I can. You know that. But a dollar on the rent is such a savin', an' we've more room here. You know that."

He scarcely followed her. He had heard it all before, many times. The range of her thought was limited, and she was ever harking back to the hardship worked upon them by living so far from the mills.

"A dollar means more grub," he remarked sententiously. "I'd sooner do the walkin' an' git the grub."

He ate hurriedly, half chewing the bread and washing the unmasticated chunks down with coffee. The hot and muddy liquid went by the name of coffee. Johnny thought it was coffee—and excellent coffee. That was one of the few of life's illusions that remained to him. He had never drunk real coffee in his life.

In addition to the bread, there was a small piece of cold pork. His mother refilled his cup with coffee. As he was finishing the bread, he began to watch if more was forthcoming. She intercepted his questioning glance.

"Now, don't be hoggish, Johnny," was her comment. "You've had your share. Your brothers an' sisters are smaller'n you."

He did not answer the rebuke. He was not much of a talker. Also, he ceased his hungry glancing for more. He was uncomplaining, with a patience that was as terrible as the school in which it had been learned. He finished his coffee, wiped his mouth on the back of his hand, and started to rise.

"Wait a second," she said hastily. "I guess the loaf kin stand you another slice—a thin un."

There was legerdemain in her actions. With all the seeming of cutting a slice from the loaf for him, she put loaf and slice back in the bread box and conveyed to him one of her own two slices. She believed she had deceived him, but he had noted her sleight-of-hand. Nevertheless, he took the bread shamelessly. He had a philosophy that his mother, what of her chronic sickliness, was not much of an eater anyway.

She saw that he was chewing the bread dry, and reached over and emptied her coffee cup into his.

"Don't set good somehow on my stomach this morning," she explained.

A distant whistle, prolonged and shrieking, brought both of them to their feet. She glanced at the tin alarm-clock on the shelf. The hands stood at half-past five. The rest of the factory world was just arousing from sleep. She drew a shawl about her shoulders, and on her head put a dingy hat, shapeless and ancient.

"We've got to run," she said, turning the wick of the lamp and blowing down the chimney.

They groped their way out and down the stairs. It was clear and cold, and Johnny shivered at the first contact with the outside air. The stars had not yet begun to pale in the sky, and the city lay in blackness. Both Johnny and his mother shuffled their feet as they walked. There was no ambition in the leg muscles to swing the feet clear of the ground.

After fifteen silent minutes, his mother turned off to the right.

"Don't be late," was her final warning from out of the dark that was swallowing her up.

He made no response, steadily keeping on his way. In the factory quarter, doors were opening everywhere, and he was soon one of a multitude that pressed onward through the dark. As he entered the factory gate the whistle blew again. He glanced at the east. Across a ragged sky-line of housetops a pale light was beginning to creep. This much he saw of the day as he turned his back upon it and joined his work gang.

He took his place in one of many long rows of machines. Before him, above a bin filled with small bobbins, were large bobbins revolving rapidly. Upon these he wound the jute-twine of the small bobbins. The work was simple. All that was required was celerity. The small bobbins were emptied so rapidly, and there were so many large bobbins that did the emptying, that there were no idle moments.

He worked mechanically. When a small bobbin ran out, he used his left hand for a brake, stopping the large bobbin and at the same time, with thumb and forefinger, catching the flying end of twine. Also, at the same time, with his right hand, he caught up the loose twine-end of a small bobbin. These various acts with both hands were performed simultaneously and swiftly. Then there would come a flash of his hands as he looped the weaver's knot and released the bobbin. There was nothing difficult about weaver's knots. He once boasted he could tie them in his sleep. And for that matter, he sometimes did, toiling centuries long in a single night at tying an endless succession of weaver's knots.

Some of the boys shirked, wasting time and machinery by not replacing the small bobbins when they ran out. And there was an overseer to prevent this. He caught Johnny's neighbor at the trick, and boxed his ears.

"Look at Johnny there—why ain't you like him?" the overseer wrathfully demanded.

Johnny's bobbins were running full blast, but he did not thrill at the indirect praise. There had been a time ... but that was long ago, very long ago. His apathetic face was expressionless as he listened to himself being held up as a shining example. He was the perfect worker. He knew that. He had been told so, often. It was a commonplace, and besides it didn't seem to mean anything to him any more. From the perfect worker he had evolved into the perfect machine. When his work went wrong, it was with him as with the machine, due to faulty material. It would have been as possible for a perfect nail-die to cut imperfect nails as for him to make a mistake.

And small wonder. There had never been a time when he had not been in intimate relationship with machines. Machinery had almost been bred into him, and at any rate he had been brought up on it. Twelve years before, there had been a small flutter of excitement in the loom room of this very mill. Johnny's mother had fainted. They stretched her out on the floor in the midst of the shrieking machines. A couple of elderly women were called from their looms. The foreman assisted. And in a few minutes there was one more soul in the loom room than had entered by the doors. It was Johnny, born with the pounding, crashing roar of the looms in his ears, drawing with his first breath the warm, moist air that was thick with flying lint. He had coughed that first day in order to rid his lungs of the lint; and for the same reason he had coughed ever since.

The boy alongside of Johnny whimpered and sniffed. The boy's face was convulsed with hatred for the overseer who kept a threatening eye on him from a distance; but every bobbin was running full. The boy yelled terrible oaths into the whirling bobbins before him; but the sound did not carry half a dozen feet, the roaring of the room holding it in and containing it like a wall.

Of all this Johnny took no notice. He had a way of accepting things. Besides, things grow monotonous by repetition, and this particular happening he had witnessed many times. It seemed to him as useless to oppose the overseer as to defy the will of a machine. Machines were made to go in certain ways and to perform certain tasks. It was the same with the overseer.

But at eleven o'clock there was excitement in the room. In an apparently occult way the excitement instantly permeated everywhere. The one-legged boy who worked on the other side of Johnny bobbed swiftly across the floor to a bin truck that stood empty. Into this he dived out of sight, crutch and all. The superintendent of the mill was coming along, accompanied by a young man. He was well dressed and wore a starched shirt—a gentleman, in Johnny's classification of men, and also, "the Inspector."

He looked sharply at the boys as he passed along. Sometimes he stopped and asked questions. When he did so, he was compelled to shout at the top of his lungs, at which moments his face was ludicrously contorted with the strain of making himself heard. His quick eye noted the empty machine alongside of Johnny's, but he said nothing. Johnny also caught his eye, and he stopped abruptly. He caught Johnny by the arm to draw him back a step from the machine; but with an exclamation of surprise he released the arm.

"Pretty skinny," the superintendent laughed anxiously.

"Pipe stems," was the answer. "Look at those legs. The boy's got the rickets—incipient, but he's got them. If epilepsy doesn't get him in the end, it will be because tuberculosis gets him first."

Johnny listened, but did not understand. Furthermore he was not interested in future ills. There was an immediate and more serious ill that threatened him in the form of the inspector.

"Now, my boy, I want you to tell me the truth," the inspector said, or shouted, bending close to the boy's ear to make him hear. "How old are you?"

"Fourteen," Johnny lied, and he lied with the full force of his lungs. So loudly did he lie that it started him off in a dry, hacking cough that lifted the lint which had been settling in his lungs all morning.

"Looks sixteen at least," said the superintendent.

"Or sixty," snapped the inspector.

"He's always looked that way."

"How long?" asked the inspector, quickly.

"For years. Never gets a bit older."

"Or younger, I dare say. I suppose he's worked here all those years?"

"Off and on—but that was before the new law was passed," the superintendent hastened to add.

"Machine idle?" the inspector asked, pointing at the unoccupied machine beside Johnny's, in which the part-filled bobbins were flying like mad.

"Looks that way." The superintendent motioned the overseer to him and shouted in his ear and pointed at the machine. "Machine's idle," he reported back to the inspector.

They passed on, and Johnny returned to his work, relieved in that the ill had been averted. But the one-legged boy was not so fortunate. The sharp-eyed inspector haled him out at arm's length from the bin truck. His lips were quivering, and his face had all the expression of one upon whom was fallen profound and irremediable disaster. The overseer looked astounded, as though for the first time he had laid eyes on the boy, while the superintendent's face expressed shock and displeasure.

"I know him," the inspector said. "He's twelve years old. I've had him discharged from three factories inside the year. This makes the fourth."

He turned to the one-legged boy. "You promised me, word and honor, that you'd go to school."

The one-legged boy burst into tears. "Please, Mr. Inspector, two babies died on us, and we're awful poor."

"What makes you cough that way?" the inspector demanded, as though charging him with crime.

And as in denial of guilt, the one-legged boy replied: "It ain't nothin'. I jes' caught a cold last week, Mr. Inspector, that's all."

In the end the one-legged boy went out of the room with the inspector, the latter accompanied by the anxious and protesting superintendent. After that monotony settled down again. The long morning and the longer afternoon wore away and the whistle blew for quitting time. Darkness had already fallen when Johnny passed out through the factory gate. In the interval the sun had made a golden ladder of the sky, flooded the world with its gracious warmth, and dropped down and disappeared in the west behind a ragged sky-line of housetops.

Supper was the family meal of the day—the one meal at which Johnny encountered his younger brothers and sisters. It partook of the nature of an encounter, to him, for he was very old, while they were distressingly young. He had no patience with their excessive and amazing juvenility. He did not understand it. His own childhood was too far behind him. He was like an old and irritable man, annoyed by the turbulence of their young spirits that was to him arrant silliness. He glowered silently over his food, finding compensation in the thought that they would soon have to go to work. That would take the edge off of them and make them sedate and dignified—like him. Thus it was, after the fashion of the human, that Johnny made of himself a yardstick with which to measure the universe.

During the meal, his mother explained in various ways and with infinite repetition that she was trying to do the best she could; so that it was with relief, the scant meal ended, that Johnny shoved back his chair and arose. He debated for a moment between bed and the front door, and finally went out the latter. He did not go far. He sat down on the stoop, his knees drawn up and his narrow shoulders drooping forward, his elbows on his knees and the palms of his hands supporting his chin.

As he sat there, he did no thinking. He was just resting. So far as his mind was concerned, it was asleep. His brothers and sisters came out, and with other children played noisily about him. An electric globe on the corner lighted their frolics. He was peevish and irritable, that they knew; but the spirit of adventure lured them into teasing him. They joined hands before him, and, keeping time with their bodies, chanted in his face weird and uncomplimentary doggerel. At first he snarled curses at them—curses he had learned from the lips of various foremen. Finding this futile, and remembering his dignity, he relapsed into dogged silence.

His brother Will, next to him in age, having just passed his tenth birthday, was the ringleader. Johnny did not possess particularly kindly feelings toward him. His life had early been embittered by continual giving over and giving way to Will. He had a definite feeling that Will was greatly in his debt and was ungrateful about it. In his own playtime, far back in the dim past, he had been robbed of a large part of that playtime by being compelled to take care of Will. Will was a baby then, and then, as now, their mother had spent her days in the mills. To Johnny had fallen the part of little father and little mother as well.

Will seemed to show the benefit of the giving over and the giving way. He was well-built, fairly rugged, as tall as his elder brother and even heavier. It was as though the life-blood of the one had been diverted into the other's veins. And in spirits it was the same. Johnny was jaded, worn out, without resilience, while his younger brother seemed bursting and spilling over with exuberance.

The mocking chant rose louder and louder. Will leaned closer as he danced, thrusting out his tongue. Johnny's left arm shot out and caught the other around the neck. At the same time he rapped his bony fist to the other's nose. It was a pathetically bony fist, but that it was sharp to hurt was evidenced by the squeal of pain it produced. The other children were uttering frightened cries, while Johnny's sister, Jennie, had dashed into the house.

He thrust Will from him, kicked him savagely on the shins, then reached for him and slammed him face downward in the dirt. Nor did he release him till the face had been rubbed into the dirt several times. Then the mother arrived, an anæmic whirlwind of solicitude and maternal wrath.

"Why can't he leave me alone?" was Johnny's reply to her upbraiding. "Can't he see I'm tired?"

"I'm as big as you," Will raged in her arms, his face a mess of tears, dirt, and blood. "I'm as big as you now, an' I'm goin' to git bigger. Then I'll lick you—see if I don't."

"You ought to be to work, seein' how big you are," Johnny snarled. "That's what's the matter with you. You ought to be to work. An' it's up to your ma to put you to work."

"But he's too young," she protested. "He's only a little boy."

"I was younger'n him when I started to work."

Johnny's mouth was open, further to express the sense of unfairness that he felt, but the mouth closed with a snap. He turned gloomily on his heel and stalked into the house and to bed. The door of his room was open to let in warmth from the kitchen. As he undressed in the semi-darkness he could hear his mother talking with a neighbor woman who had dropped in. His mother was crying, and her speech was punctuated with spiritless sniffles.

"I can't make out what's gittin' into Johnny," he could hear her say. "He didn't used to be this way. He was a patient little angel."

"An' he *is* a good boy," she hastened to defend. "He's worked faithful, an' he did go to work too young. But it wasn't my fault. I do the best I can, I'm sure."

Prolonged sniffling from the kitchen, and Johnny murmured to himself as his eyelids closed down, "You betcher life I've worked faithful."

The next morning he was torn bodily by his mother from the grip of sleep. Then came the meagre breakfast, the tramp through the dark, and the pale glimpse of day across the housetops as he turned his back on it and went in through the factory gate. It was another day, of all the days, and all the days were alike.

And yet there had been variety in his life—at the times he changed from one job to another, or was taken sick. When he was six, he was little mother and father to Will and the other children still younger. At seven he went into the mills—winding bobbins. When he was eight, he got work in another mill. His new job was marvellously easy. All he had to do was to sit down with a little stick in his hand and guide a stream of cloth that flowed past him. This stream of cloth came out of the maw of a machine, passed over a hot roller, and went on its way elsewhere. But he sat always in the one place, beyond the reach of daylight, a gas-jet flaring over him, himself part of the mechanism.

He was very happy at that job, in spite of the moist heat, for he was still young and in possession of dreams and illusions. And wonderful dreams he dreamed as he watched the steaming cloth streaming endlessly by. But there was no exercise about the work, no call upon his mind, and he dreamed less and less, while his mind grew torpid and drowsy. Nevertheless, he earned two dollars a week, and two dollars represented the difference between acute starvation and chronic underfeeding.

But when he was nine, he lost his job. Measles was the cause of it. After he recovered, he got work in a glass factory. The pay was better, and the work demanded skill. It was piece-work, and the more skilful he was, the bigger wages he earned. Here was incentive. And under this incentive he developed into a remarkable worker.

It was simple work, the tying of glass stoppers into small bottles. At his waist he carried a bundle of twine. He held the bottles between his knees so that he might work with both hands. Thus, in a sitting position and bending over his own knees, his narrow shoulders grew humped and his chest was contracted for ten hours each day. This was not good for the lungs, but he tied three hundred dozen bottles a day.

The superintendent was very proud of him, and brought visitors to look at him. In ten hours three hundred dozen bottles passed through his hands. This meant that he had attained machine-like perfection. All waste movements were eliminated. Every motion of his thin arms, every movement of a muscle in the thin fingers, was swift and accurate. He worked at high tension, and the result was that he grew nervous. At night his muscles twitched in his sleep, and in the daytime he could not relax and rest. He remained keyed up and his muscles continued to twitch. Also he grew sallow and his lint-cough grew worse. Then pneumonia laid hold of the feeble lungs within the contracted chest, and he lost his job in the glass-works.

Now he had returned to the jute mills where he had first begun with winding bobbins. But promotion was waiting for him. He was a good worker. He would next go on the starcher, and later he would go into the loom room. There was nothing after that except increased efficiency.

The machinery ran faster than when he had first gone to work, and his mind ran slower. He no longer dreamed at all, though his earlier years had been full of dreaming. Once he had been in love. It was when he first began guiding the cloth over the hot roller, and it was with the daughter of the superintendent. She was much older than he, a young woman, and he had seen her at a distance only a paltry half-dozen times. But that made no difference. On the surface of the cloth stream that poured past him, he pictured radiant futures wherein he performed prodigies of toil, invented miraculous machines, won to the mastership of the mills, and in the end took her in his arms and kissed her soberly on the brow.

But that was all in the long ago, before he had grown too old and tired to love. Also, she had married and gone away, and his mind had gone to sleep. Yet it had been a wonderful experience, and he used often to look back upon it as other men and women look back upon the time they believed in fairies. He had never believed in fairies nor Santa Claus; but he had believed implicitly in the smiling future his imagination had wrought into the steaming cloth stream.

He had become a man very early in life. At seven, when he drew his first wages, began his adolescence. A certain feeling of independence crept up in him, and the relationship between him and his mother changed. Somehow, as an earner and breadwinner, doing his own work in the world, he was more like an equal with her. Manhood, full-blown manhood, had come when he was eleven, at which time he had gone to work on the night shift for six months. No child works on the night shift and remains a child.

There had been several great events in his life. One of these had been when his mother bought some California prunes. Two others had been the two times when she cooked custard. Those had been events. He remembered them kindly. And at that time his mother had told him of a blissful dish she would sometime make—"floating island," she had called it, "better than custard." For years he had looked forward to the day when he would sit down to the table with floating island before him, until at last he had relegated the idea of it to the limbo of unattainable ideals.

Once he found a silver quarter lying on the sidewalk. That, also, was a great event in his life, withal a tragic one. He knew his duty on the instant the silver flashed on his eyes, before even he had picked it up. At home, as usual, there was not enough to eat, and home he should have taken it as he did his wages every Saturday night. Right conduct in this case was obvious; but he never had any spending of his money, and he was suffering from candy hunger. He was ravenous for the sweets that only on red-letter days he had ever tasted in his life.

He did not attempt to deceive himself. He knew it was sin, and deliberately he sinned when he went on a fifteen-cent candy debauch. Ten cents he saved for a future orgy; but not being accustomed to the carrying of money, he lost the ten cents. This occurred at the time when he was suffering all the torments of conscience, and it was to him an act of divine retribution. He had a frightened sense of the closeness of an awful and wrathful God. God had seen, and God had been swift to punish, denying him even the full wages of sin.

In memory he always looked back upon that event as the one great criminal deed of his life, and at the recollection his conscience always awoke and gave him another twinge. It was the one skeleton in his closet. Also, being so made and circumstanced, he looked back upon the deed with regret. He was dissatisfied with the manner in which he had spent the quarter. He could have invested it better, and, out of his later knowledge of the quickness of God, he would have beaten God out by spending the whole quarter at one fell swoop. In retrospect he spent the quarter a thousand times, and each time to better advantage.

There was one other memory of the past, dim and faded, but stamped into his soul everlasting by the savage feet of his father. It was more like a nightmare than a remembered vision of a concrete thing—more like the race-memory of man that makes him fall in his sleep and that goes back to his arboreal ancestry.

This particular memory never came to Johnny in broad daylight when he was wide awake. It came at night, in bed, at the moment that his consciousness was sinking down and losing itself in sleep. It always aroused him to frightened wakefulness, and for the moment, in the first sickening start, it seemed to him that he lay crosswise on the foot of the bed. In the bed were the vague forms of his father and mother. He never saw what his father looked like. He had but one impression of his father, and that was that he had savage and pitiless feet.

His earlier memories lingered with him, but he had no late memories. All days were alike. Yesterday or last year were the same as a thousand years—or a minute. Nothing ever happened. There were no events to mark the march of time. Time did not march. It stood always still. It was only the whirling machines that moved, and they moved nowhere —in spite of the fact that they moved faster.

When he was fourteen, he went to work on the starcher. It was a colossal event. Something had at last happened that could be remembered beyond a night's sleep or a week's pay-day. It marked an era. It was a machine Olympiad, a thing to date from. "When I went to work on the starcher," or, "after," or "before I went to work on the starcher," were sentences often on his lips.

He celebrated his sixteenth birthday by going into the loom room and taking a loom. Here was an incentive again, for it was piece-work. And he excelled, because the clay of him had been moulded by the mills into the perfect machine. At the end of three months he was running two looms, and, later, three and four.

At the end of his second year at the looms he was turning out more yards than any other weaver, and more than twice as much as some of the less skilful ones. And at home things began to prosper as he approached the full stature of his earning power. Not, however, that his increased earnings were in excess of need. The children were growing up. They ate more. And they were going to school, and school-books cost money. And somehow, the faster he worked, the faster climbed the prices of things. Even the rent went up, though the house had fallen from bad to worse disrepair.

He had grown taller; but with his increased height he seemed leaner than ever. Also, he was more nervous. With the nervousness increased his peevishness and irritability. The children had learned by many bitter lessons to fight shy of him. His mother respected him for his earning power, but somehow her respect was tinctured with fear.

There was no joyousness in life for him. The procession of the days he never saw. The nights he slept away in twitching unconsciousness. The rest of the time he worked, and his consciousness was machine consciousness. Outside this his mind was a blank. He had no ideals, and but one illusion; namely, that he drank excellent coffee. He was a work-beast. He had no mental life whatever; yet deep down in the crypts of his mind, unknown to him, were being weighed and sifted every hour of his toil, every movement of his hands, every twitch of his muscles, and preparations were making for a future course of action that would amaze him and all his little world.

It was in the late spring that he came home from work one night aware of unusual tiredness. There was a keen expectancy in the air as he sat down to the table, but he did not notice. He went through the meal in moody silence, mechanically eating what was before him. The children um'd and ah'd and made smacking noises with their mouths. But he was deaf to them.

"D'ye know what you're eatin'?" his mother demanded at last, desperately.

He looked vacantly at the dish before him, and vacantly at her.

"Floatin' island," she announced triumphantly.

"Oh," he said.

"Floating island!" the children chorussed loudly.

"Oh," he said. And after two or three mouthfuls, he added, "I guess I ain't hungry to-night."

He dropped the spoon, shoved back his chair, and arose wearily from the table.

"An' I guess I'll go to bed."

His feet dragged more heavily than usual as he crossed the kitchen floor. Undressing was a Titan's task, a monstrous futility, and he wept weakly as he crawled into bed, one shoe still on. He was aware of a rising, swelling something inside his head that made his brain thick and fuzzy. His lean fingers felt as big as his wrist, while in the ends of them was a remoteness of sensation vague and fuzzy like his brain. The small of his back ached intolerably. All his bones ached. He ached everywhere. And in his head began the shrieking, pounding, crashing, roaring of a million looms. All space was filled with flying shuttles. They darted in and out, intricately, amongst the stars. He worked a thousand looms himself, and ever they speeded up, faster and faster, and his brain unwound, faster and faster, and became the thread that fed the thousand flying shuttles.

He did not go to work next morning. He was too busy weaving colossally on the thousand looms that ran inside his head. His mother went to work, but first she sent for the doctor. It was a severe attack of la grippe, he said. Jennie served as nurse and carried out his instructions.

It was a very severe attack, and it was a week before Johnny dressed and tottered feebly across the floor. Another week, the doctor said, and he would be fit to return to work. The foreman of the loom room visited him on Sunday afternoon, the first day of his convalescence. The best weaver in the room, the foreman told his mother. His job would be held for him. He could come back to work a week from Monday.

"Why don't you thank 'im, Johnny?" his mother asked anxiously.

"He's ben that sick he ain't himself yet," she explained apologetically to the visitor.

Johnny sat hunched up and gazing steadfastly at the floor. He sat in the same position long after the foreman had gone. It was warm outdoors, and he sat on the stoop in the afternoon. Sometimes his lips moved. He seemed lost in endless calculations.

Next morning, after the day grew warm, he took his seat on the stoop. He had pencil and paper this time with which to continue his calculations, and he calculated painfully and amazingly.

"What comes after millions?" he asked at noon, when Will came home from school. "An' how d'ye work 'em?"

That afternoon finished his task. Each day, but without paper and pencil, he returned to the stoop. He was greatly absorbed in the one tree that grew across the street. He studied it for hours at a time, and was unusually interested when the wind swayed its branches and fluttered its leaves. Throughout the week he seemed lost in a great communion with himself. On Sunday, sitting on the stoop, he laughed aloud, several times, to the perturbation of his mother, who had not heard him laugh in years.

Next morning, in the early darkness, she came to his bed to rouse him. He had had his fill of sleep all week, and awoke easily. He made no struggle, nor did he attempt to hold on to the bedding when she stripped it from him. He lay quietly, and spoke quietly.

"It ain't no use, ma."

"You'll be late," she said, under the impression that he was still stupid with sleep.

"I'm awake, ma, an' I tell you it ain't no use. You might as well lemme alone. I ain't goin' to git up."

"But you'll lose your job!" she cried.

"I ain't goin' to git up," he repeated in a strange, passionless voice.

She did not go to work herself that morning. This was sickness beyond any sickness she had ever known. Fever and delirium she could understand; but this was insanity. She pulled the bedding up over him and sent Jennie for the doctor.

When that person arrived, Johnny was sleeping gently, and gently he awoke and allowed his pulse to be taken.

"Nothing the matter with him," the doctor reported. "Badly debilitated, that's all. Not much meat on his bones."

"He's always been that way," his mother volunteered.

"Now go 'way, ma, an' let me finish my snooze."

Johnny spoke sweetly and placidly, and sweetly and placidly he rolled over on his side and went to sleep.

At ten o'clock he awoke and dressed himself. He walked out into the kitchen, where he found his mother with a frightened expression on her face.

"I'm goin' away, ma," he announced, "an' I jes' want to say good-by."

She threw her apron over her head and sat down suddenly and wept. He waited patiently.

"I might a-known it," she was sobbing.

"Where?" she finally asked, removing the apron from her head and gazing up at him with a stricken face in which there was little curiosity.

"I don't know—anywhere."

As he spoke, the tree across the street appeared with dazzling brightness on his inner vision. It seemed to lurk just under his eyelids, and he could see it whenever he wished.

"An' your job?" she quavered.

"I ain't never goin' to work again."

"My God, Johnny!" she wailed, "don't say that!"

What he had said was blasphemy to her. As a mother who hears her child deny God, was Johnny's mother shocked by his words.

"What's got into you, anyway?" she demanded, with a lame attempt at imperativeness.

"Figures," he answered. "Jes' figures. I've ben doin' a lot of figurin' this week, an' it's most surprisin'."

"I don't see what that's got to do with it," she sniffled.

Johnny smiled patiently, and his mother was aware of a distinct shock at the persistent absence of his peevishness and irritability.

"I'll show you," he said. "I'm plum' tired out. What makes me tired? Moves. I've ben movin' ever since I was born. I'm tired of movin', an' I ain't goin' to move any more. Remember when I worked in the glass-house? I used to do three hundred dozen a day. Now I reckon I made about ten different moves to each bottle. That's thirty-six thousan' moves a day. Ten days, three hundred an' sixty thousan' moves a day. One month, one million an' eighty thousan' moves. Chuck out the eighty thousan'—" he spoke with the complacent beneficence of a philanthropist—"chuck out the eighty thousan', that leaves a million moves a month—twelve million moves a year.

"At the looms I'm movin' twic'st as much. That makes twenty-five million moves a year, an' it seems to me I've ben a movin' that way 'most a million years.

"Now this week I ain't moved at all. I ain't made one move in hours an' hours. I tell you it was swell, jes' settin' there, hours an' hours, an' doin' nothin'. I ain't never ben happy before. I never had any time. I've ben movin' all the time. That ain't no way to be happy. An' I ain't goin' to do it any more. I'm jes' goin' to set, an' set, an' rest, an' rest, and then rest some more."

"But what's goin' to come of Will an' the children?" she asked despairingly.

"That's it, 'Will an' the children,' " he repeated.

But there was no bitterness in his voice. He had long known his mother's ambition for the younger boy, but the thought of it no longer rankled. Nothing mattered any more. Not even that.

"I know, ma, what you've ben plannin' for Will—keepin' him in school to make a bookkeeper out of him. But it ain't no use, I've quit. He's got to go to work."

"An' after I have brung you up the way I have," she wept, starting to cover her head with the apron and changing her mind.

"You never brung me up," he answered with sad kindliness. "I brung myself up, ma, an' I brung up Will. He's bigger'n me, an' heavier, an' taller. When I was a kid, I reckon I didn't git enough to eat. When he come along an' was a kid, I was workin' an' earnin' grub for him too. But that's done with. Will can go to work, same as me, or he can go to hell, I don't care which. I'm tired. I'm goin' now. Ain't you goin' to say good-by?"

She made no reply. The apron had gone over her head again, and she was crying. He paused a moment in the doorway.

"I'm sure I done the best I knew how," she was sobbing.

He passed out of the house and down the street. A wan delight came into his face at the sight of the lone tree. "Jes' ain't goin' to do nothin'," he said to himself, half aloud, in a crooning tone. He glanced wistfully up at the sky, but the bright sun dazzled and blinded him.

It was a long walk he took, and he did not walk fast. It took him past the jute-mill. The muffled roar of the loom room came to his ears, and he smiled. It was a gentle, placid smile. He hated no one, not even the pounding, shrieking machines. There was no bitterness in him, nothing but an inordinate hunger for rest.

The houses and factories thinned out and the open spaces increased as he approached the country. At last the city was behind him, and he was walking down a leafy lane beside the railroad track. He did not walk like a man. He did not look like a man. He was a travesty of the human. It was a twisted and stunted and nameless piece of life that shambled like a sickly ape, arms loose-hanging, stoop-shouldered, narrow-chested, grotesque and terrible.

He passed by a small railroad station and lay down in the grass under a tree. All afternoon he lay there. Sometimes he dozed, with muscles that twitched in his sleep. When awake, he lay without movement, watching the birds or looking up at the sky through the branches of the tree above him. Once or twice he laughed aloud, but without relevance to anything he had seen or felt.

After twilight had gone, in the first darkness of the night, a freight train rumbled into the station. When the engine was switching cars on to the side-track, Johnny crept along the side of the train. He pulled open the side-door of an empty box-car and awkwardly and laboriously climbed in. He closed the door. The engine whistled. Johnny was lying down, and in the darkness he smiled.

THE WIT OF PORPORTUK

El-Soo had been a Mission girl. Her mother had died when she was very small, and Sister Alberta had plucked El-Soo as a brand from the burning, one summer day, and carried her away to Holy Cross Mission and dedicated her to God. El-Soo was a full-blooded Indian, yet she exceeded all the half-breed and quarter-breed girls. Never had the good sisters dealt with a girl so adaptable and at the same time so spirited.

El-Soo was quick, and deft, and intelligent; but above all she was fire, the living flame of life, a blaze of personality that was compounded of will, sweetness, and daring. Her father was a chief, and his blood ran in her veins. Obedience, on the part of El-Soo, was a matter of terms and arrangement. She had a passion for equity, and perhaps it was because of this that she excelled in mathematics.

But she excelled in other things. She learned to read and write English as no girl had ever learned in the Mission. She led the girls in singing, and into song she carried her sense of equity. She was an artist, and the fire of her flowed toward creation. Had she from birth enjoyed a more favorable environment, she would have made literature or music.

Instead, she was El-Soo, daughter of Klakee-Nah, a chief, and she lived in the Holy Cross Mission where were no artists, but only pure-souled Sisters who were interested in cleanliness and righteousness and the welfare of the spirit in the land of immortality that lay beyond the skies.

The years passed. She was eight years old when she entered the Mission; she was sixteen, and the Sisters were corresponding with their superiors in the Order concerning the sending of El-Soo to the United States to complete her education, when a man of her own tribe arrived at Holy Cross and had talk with her. El-Soo was somewhat appalled by him. He was dirty. He was a Caliban-like creature, primitively ugly, with a mop of hair that had never been combed. He looked at her disapprovingly and refused to sit down.

"Thy brother is dead," he said, shortly.

El-Soo was not particularly shocked. She remembered little of her brother. "Thy father is an old man, and alone," the messenger went on. "His house is large and empty, and he would hear thy voice and look upon thee."

Him she remembered—Klakee-Nah, the head-man of the village, the friend of the missionaries and the traders, a large man thewed like a giant, with kindly eyes and masterful ways, and striding with a consciousness of crude royalty in his carriage.

"Tell him that I will come," was El-Soo's answer.

Much to the despair of the Sisters, the brand plucked from the burning went back to the burning. All pleading with El-Soo was vain. There was much argument, expostulation, and weeping. Sister Alberta even revealed to her the project of sending her to the United States. El-Soo stared wide-eyed into the golden vista thus opened up to her, and shook her head. In her eyes persisted another vista. It was the mighty curve of the Yukon at Tana-naw Station, with the St. George Mission on one side, and the trading post on the other, and midway between the Indian village and a certain large log house where lived an old man tended upon by slaves.

All dwellers on the Yukon bank for twice a thousand miles knew the large log house, the old man and the tending slaves; and well did the Sisters know the house, its unending revelry, its feasting and its fun. So there was weeping at Holy Cross when El-Soo departed.

There was a great cleaning up in the large house when El-Soo arrived. Klakee-Nah, himself masterful, protested at this masterful conduct of his young daughter; but in the end, dreaming barbarically of magnificence, he went forth and borrowed a thousand dollars from old Porportuk, than whom there was no richer Indian on the Yukon. Also, Klakee-Nah ran up a heavy bill at the trading post. El-Soo re-created the large house. She invested it with new splendor, while Klakee-Nah maintained its ancient traditions of hospitality and revelry.

All this was unusual for a Yukon Indian, but Klakee-Nah was an unusual Indian. Not alone did he like to render inordinate hospitality, but, what of being a chief and of acquiring much money, he was able to do it. In the primitive trading days he had been a power over his people, and he had dealt profitably with the white trading companies. Later on, with Porportuk, he had made a gold-strike on the Koyokuk River. Klakee-Nah was by training and nature an aristocrat. Porportuk was bourgeois, and Porportuk bought him out of the gold-mine. Porportuk was content to plod and accumulate. Klakee-Nah went back to his large house and proceeded to spend. Porportuk was known as the richest Indian in Alaska. Klakee-Nah was known as the whitest. Porportuk was a money-lender and a usurer. Klakee-Nah was an anachronism—a mediæval ruin, a fighter and a feaster, happy with wine and song.

El-Soo adapted herself to the large house and its ways as readily as she had adapted herself to Holy Cross Mission and its ways. She did not try to reform her father and direct his footsteps toward God. It is true, she reproved him when he drank overmuch and profoundly, but that was for the sake of his health and the direction of his footsteps on solid earth.

The latchstring to the large house was always out. What with the coming and the going, it was never still. The rafters of the great living-room shook with the roar of wassail and of song. At table sat men from all the world and chiefs from distant tribes—Englishmen and Colonials, lean Yankee traders and rotund officials of the great companies, cow-boys from the Western ranges, sailors from the sea, hunters and dog-mushers of a score of nationalities.

El-Soo drew breath in a cosmopolitan atmosphere. She could speak English as well as she could her native tongue, and she sang English songs and ballads. The passing Indian ceremonials she knew, and the perishing traditions. The tribal dress of the daughter of a chief she knew how to wear upon occasion. But for the most part she dressed as white women dress. Not for nothing was her needlework at the Mission and her innate artistry. She carried her clothes like a white woman, and she made clothes that could be so carried.

In her way she was as unusual as her father, and the position she occupied was as unique as his. She was the one Indian woman who was the social equal with the several white women at Tana-naw Station. She was the one Indian woman to whom white men honorably made proposals of marriage. And she was the one Indian woman whom no white man ever insulted.

For El-Soo was beautiful—not as white women are beautiful, not as Indian women are beautiful. It was the flame of her, that did not depend upon feature, that was her beauty. So far as mere line and feature went, she was the classic Indian type. The black hair and the fine bronze were hers, and the black eyes, brilliant and bold, keen as sword-light, proud; and hers the delicate eagle nose with the thin, quivering nostrils, the high cheek-bones that were not broad apart, and the thin lips that were not too thin. But over all and through all poured the flame of her—the unanalyzable something that was fire and that was the soul of her, that lay mellow-warm or blazed in her eyes, that sprayed the cheeks of her, that distended the nostrils, that curled the lip, or, when the lip was in repose, that was still there in the lip, the lip palpitant with its presence.

And El-Soo had wit—rarely sharp to hurt, yet quick to search out forgivable weakness. The laughter of her mind played like lambent flame over all about her, and from all about her arose answering laughter. Yet she was never the centre of things. This she would not permit. The large house, and all of which it was significant, was her father's; and through it, to the last, moved his heroic figure—host, master of the revels, and giver of the law. It is true, as the strength oozed from him, that she caught up responsibilities from his failing hands. But in appearance he still ruled, dozing ofttimes at the board, a bacchanalian ruin, yet in all seeming the ruler of the feast.

And through the large house moved the figure of Porportuk, ominous, with shaking head, coldly disapproving, paying for it all. Not that he really paid, for he compounded interest in weird ways, and year by year absorbed the properties of Klakee-Nah. Porportuk once took it upon himself to chide El-Soo upon the wasteful way of life in the large house—it was when he had about absorbed the last of Klakee-Nah's wealth—but he never ventured so to chide again. El-Soo, like her father, was an aristocrat, as disdainful of money as he, and with an equal sense of honor as finely strung.

Porportuk continued grudgingly to advance money, and ever the money flowed in golden foam away. Upon one thing El-Soo was resolved—her father should die as he had lived. There should be for him no passing from high to low, no diminution of the revels, no lessening of the lavish hospitality. When there was famine, as of old, the Indians came groaning to the large house and went away content. When there was famine and no money, money was borrowed from Porportuk, and the Indians still went away content. El-Soo might well have repeated, after the aristocrats of another time and place, that after her came the deluge. In her case the deluge was old Porportuk. With every advance of money, he looked upon her with a more possessive eye, and felt bourgeoning within him ancient fires.

But El-Soo had no eyes for him. Nor had she eyes for the white men who wanted to marry her at the Mission with ring and priest and book. For at Tana-naw Station was a young man, Akoon, of her own blood, and tribe, and village. He was strong and beautiful to her eyes, a great hunter, and, in that he had wandered far and much, very poor; he had been to all the unknown wastes and places; he had journeyed to Sitka and to the United States; he had crossed the continent to Hudson Bay and back again, and as seal-hunter on a ship he had sailed to Siberia and for Japan.

When he returned from the gold-strike in Klondike he came, as was his wont, to the large house to make report to old Klakee-Nah of all the world that he had seen; and there he first saw El-Soo, three years back from the Mission. Thereat, Akoon wandered no more. He refused a wage of twenty dollars a day as pilot on the big steamboats. He hunted some and fished some, but never far from Tana-naw Station, and he was at the large house often and long. And El-Soo measured him against many men and found him good. He sang songs to her, and was ardent and glowed until all Tana-naw Station knew he loved her. And Porportuk but grinned and advanced more money for the upkeep of the large house.

Then came the death table of Klakee-Nah. He sat at feast, with death in his throat, that he could not drown with wine. And laughter and joke and song went around, and Akoon told a story that made the rafters echo. There were no tears or sighs at that table. It was no more than fit that Klakee-Nah should die as he had lived, and none knew this better than El-Soo, with her artist sympathy. The old roystering crowd was there, and, as of old, three frost-bitten sailors were there, fresh from the long traverse from the Arctic, survivors of a ship's company of seventy-four. At Klakee-Nah's back were four old men, all that were left him of the slaves of his youth. With rheumy eyes they saw to his needs, with palsied hands filling his glass or striking him on the back between the shoulders when death stirred and he coughed and gasped.

It was a wild night, and as the hours passed and the fun laughed and roared along, death stirred more restlessly in Klakee-Nah's throat. Then it was that he sent for Porportuk. And Porportuk came in from the outside frost to look with disapproving eyes upon the meat and wine on the table for which he had paid. But as he looked down the length of flushed faces to the far end and saw the face of El-Soo, the light in his eyes flared up, and for a moment the disapproval vanished.

Place was made for him at Klakee-Nah's side, and a glass placed before him. Klakee-Nah, with his own hands, filled the glass with fervent spirits. "Drink!" he cried. "Is it not good?"

And Porportuk's eyes watered as he nodded his head and smacked his lips.

"When, in your own house, have you had such drink?" Klakee-Nah demanded.

"I will not deny that the drink is good to this old throat of mine," Porportuk made answer, and hesitated for the speech to complete the thought.

"But it costs overmuch," Klakee-Nah roared, completing it for him.

Porportuk winced at the laughter that went down the table. His eyes burned malevolently. "We were boys together, of the same age," he said. "In your throat is death. I am still alive and strong."

An ominous murmur arose from the company. Klakee-Nah coughed and strangled, and the old slaves smote him between the shoulders. He emerged gasping, and waved his hand to still the threatening rumble.

"You have grudged the very fire in your house because the wood cost overmuch!" he cried. "You have grudged life. To live cost overmuch, and you have refused to pay the price. Your life has been like a cabin where the fire is out and there are no blankets on the floor." He signalled to a slave to fill his glass, which he held aloft. "But I have lived. And I have been warm with life as you have never been warm. It is true, you shall live long. But the longest nights are the cold nights when a man shivers and lies awake. My nights have been short, but I have slept warm."

He drained the glass. The shaking hand of a slave failed to catch it as it crashed to the floor. Klakee-Nah sank back, panting, watching the upturned glasses at the lips of the drinkers, his own lips slightly smiling to the applause. At a sign, two slaves attempted to help him sit upright again. But they were weak, his frame was mighty, and the four old men tottered and shook as they helped him forward.

"But manner of life is neither here nor there," he went on. "We have other business, Porportuk, you and I, to-night. Debts are mischances, and I am in mischance with you. What of my debt, and how great is it?"

Porportuk searched in his pouch and brought forth a memorandum. He sipped at his glass and began. "There is the note of August, 1889, for three hundred dollars. The interest has never been paid. And the note of the next year for five hundred dollars. This note was included in the note of two months later for a thousand dollars. Then there is the note—"

"Never mind the many notes!" Klakee-Nah cried out impatiently. "They make my head go around and all the things inside my head. The whole! The round whole! How much is it?"

Porportuk referred to his memorandum. "Fifteen thousand nine hundred and sixty-seven dollars and seventy-five cents," he read with careful precision.

"Make it sixteen thousand, make it sixteen thousand," Klakee-Nah said grandly. "Odd numbers were ever a worry. And now—and it is for this that I have sent for you—make me out a new note for sixteen thousand, which I shall sign. I have no thought of the interest. Make it as large as you will, and make it payable in the next world, when I shall meet you by the fire of the Great Father of all Indians. Then the note will be paid. This I promise you. It is the word of Klakee-Nah."

Porportuk looked perplexed, and loudly the laughter arose and shook the room. Klakee-Nah raised his hands. "Nay," he cried. "It is not a joke. I but speak in fairness. It was for this I sent for you, Porportuk. Make out the note."

"I have no dealings with the next world," Porportuk made answer slowly.

"Have you no thought to meet me before the Great Father!" Klakee-Nah demanded. Then he added, "I shall surely be there."

"I have no dealings with the next world," Porportuk repeated sourly.

The dying man regarded him with frank amazement.

"I know naught of the next world," Porportuk explained. "I do business in this world."

Klakee-Nah's face cleared. "This comes of sleeping cold of nights," he laughed. He pondered for a space, then said, "It is in this world that you must be paid. There remains to me this house. Take it, and burn the debt in the candle there."

"It is an old house and not worth the money," Porportuk made answer.

"There are my mines on the Twisted Salmon."

"They have never paid to work," was the reply.

"There is my share in the steamer *Koyokuk*. I am half owner."

"She is at the bottom of the Yukon."

Klakee-Nah started. "True, I forgot. It was last spring when the ice went out." He mused for a time, while the glasses remained untasted, and all the company waited upon his utterance.

"Then it would seem I owe you a sum of money which I cannot pay ... in this world?" Porportuk nodded and glanced down the table.

"Then it would seem that you, Porportuk, are a poor business man," Klakee-Nah said slyly. And boldly Porportuk made answer, "No; there is security yet untouched."

"What!" cried Klakee-Nah. "Have I still property? Name it, and it is yours, and the debt is no more."

"There it is." Porportuk pointed at El-Soo.

Klakee-Nah could not understand. He peered down the table, brushed his eyes, and peered again.

"Your daughter, El-Soo—her will I take and the debt be no more. I will burn the debt there in the candle."

Klakee-Nah's great chest began to heave. "Ho! ho!—a joke—Ho! ho!

ho!" he laughed Homerically. "And with your cold bed and daughters old enough to be the mother of El-Soo! Ho! ho! ho!" He began to cough and strangle, and the old slaves smote him on the back. "Ho! ho!" he began again, and went off into another paroxysm.

Porportuk waited patiently, sipping from his glass and studying the double row of faces down the board. "It is no joke," he said finally. "My speech is well meant."

Klakee-Nah sobered and looked at him, then reached for his glass, but could not touch it. A slave passed it to him, and glass and liquor he flung into the face of Porportuk.

"Turn him out!" Klakee-Nah thundered to the waiting table that strained like a pack of hounds in leash. "And roll him in the snow!"

As the mad riot swept past him and out of doors, he signalled to the slaves, and the four tottering old men supported him on his feet as he met the returning revellers, upright, glass in hand, pledging them a toast to the short night when a man sleeps warm.

It did not take long to settle the estate of Klakee-Nah. Tommy, the little Englishman, clerk at the trading post, was called in by El-Soo to help. There was nothing but debts, notes overdue, mortgaged properties, and properties mortgaged but worthless. Notes and mortgages were held by Porportuk. Tommy called him a robber many times as he pondered the compounding of the interest.

"Is it a debt, Tommy?" El-Soo asked.

"It is a robbery," Tommy answered.

"Nevertheless, it is a debt," she persisted.

The winter wore away, and the early spring, and still the claims of Porportuk remained unpaid. He saw El-Soo often and explained to her at length, as he had explained to her father, the way the debt could be cancelled. Also, he brought with him old medicine-men, who elaborated to her the everlasting damnation of her father if the debt were not paid. One day, after such an elaboration, El-Soo made final announcement to Porportuk.

"I shall tell you two things," she said. "First, I shall not be your wife. Will you remember that? Second, you shall be paid the last cent of the sixteen thousand dollars—"

"Fifteen thousand nine hundred and sixty-seven dollars and seventy-five cents," Porportuk corrected.

"My father said sixteen thousand," was her reply. "You shall be paid."

"How?"

"I know not how, but I shall find out how. Now go, and bother me no more. If you do"—she hesitated to find fitting penalty—"if you do, I shall have you rolled in the snow again as soon as the first snow flies."

This was still in the early spring, and a little later El-Soo surprised the country. Word went up and down the Yukon from Chilcoot to the Delta, and was carried from camp to camp to the farthermost camps, that in June, when the first salmon ran, El-Soo, daughter of Klakee-Nah, would sell herself at public auction to satisfy the claims of Porportuk. Vain were the attempts to dissuade her. The missionary at St. George wrestled with her, but she replied:—

"Only the debts to God are settled in the next world. The debts of men are of this world, and in this world are they settled."

Akoon wrestled with her, but she replied: "I do love thee, Akoon; but honor is greater than love, and who am I that I should blacken my father?" Sister Alberta journeyed all the way up from Holy Cross on the first steamer, and to no better end.

"My father wanders in the thick and endless forests," said El-Soo. "And there will he wander, with the lost souls crying, till the debt be paid. Then, and not until then, may he go on to the house of the Great Father."

"And you believe this?" Sister Alberta asked.

"I do not know," El-Soo made answer. "It was my father's belief."

Sister Alberta shrugged her shoulders incredulously.

"Who knows but that the things we believe come true?" El-Soo went on. "Why not? The next world to you may be heaven and harps ... because you have believed heaven and harps; to my father the next world may be a large house where he will sit always at table feasting with God."

"And you?" Sister Alberta asked. "What is your next world?"

El-Soo hesitated but for a moment. "I should like a little of both," she said. "I should like to see your face as well as the face of my father."

The day of the auction came. Tana-naw Station was populous. As was their custom, the tribes had gathered to await the salmon-run, and in the meantime spent the time in dancing and frolicking, trading and gossiping. Then there was the ordinary sprinkling of white adventurers, traders, and prospectors, and, in addition, a large number of white men who had come because of curiosity or interest in the affair.

It had been a backward spring, and the salmon were late in running. This delay but keyed up the interest. Then, on the day of the auction, the situation was made tense by Akoon. He arose and made public and solemn announcement that whosoever bought El-Soo would forthwith and immediately die. He flourished the Winchester in his hand to indicate the manner of the taking-off. El-Soo was angered thereat; but he refused to speak with her, and went to the trading post to lay in extra ammunition.

The first salmon was caught at ten o'clock in the evening, and at midnight the auction began. It took place on top of the high bank along-side the Yukon. The sun was due north just below the horizon, and the sky was lurid red. A great crowd gathered about the table and the two chairs that stood near the edge of the bank. To the fore were many white men and several chiefs. And most prominently to the fore, rifle in hand, stood Akoon. Tommy, at El-Soo's request, served as auctioneer, but she made the opening speech and described the goods about to be sold. She was in native costume, in the dress of a chief's daughter, splendid and barbaric, and she stood on a chair, that she might be seen to advantage.

"Who will buy a wife?" she asked. "Look at me. I am twenty years old and a maid. I will be a good wife to the man who buys me. If he is a white man, I shall dress in the fashion of white women; if he is an Indian, I shall dress as"—she hesitated a moment—"a squaw. I can make my own clothes, and sew, and wash, and mend. I was taught for eight years to do these things at Holy Cross Mission. I can read and write English, and I know how to play the organ. Also I can do arithmetic and some algebra—a little. I shall be sold to the highest bidder, and to him I will make out a bill of sale of myself. I forgot to say that I can sing very well, and that I have never been sick in my life. I weigh one hundred and thirty-two pounds; my father is dead and I have no relatives. Who wants me?"

She looked over the crowd with flaming audacity and stepped down. At Tommy's request she stood upon the chair again, while he mounted the second chair and started the bidding.

Surrounding El-Soo stood the four old slaves of her father. They were age-twisted and palsied, faithful to their meat, a generation out of the past that watched unmoved the antics of younger life. In the front of the crowd were several Eldorado and Bonanza kings from the Upper Yukon, and beside them, on crutches, swollen with scurvy, were two broken prospectors. From the midst of the crowd, thrust out by its own vividness, appeared the face of a wild-eyed squaw from the remote regions of the Upper Tana-naw; a strayed Sitkan from the coast stood side by side with a Stick from Lake Le Barge, and, beyond, a half-dozen French-Canadian voyageurs, grouped by themselves. From afar came the faint cries of myriads of wild-fowl on the nesting-grounds. Swallows were skimming up overhead from the placid surface of the Yukon, and robins were singing. The oblique rays of the hidden sun shot through the smoke, high-dissipated from forest fires a thousand miles away, and turned the heavens to sombre red, while the earth shone red in the reflected glow. This red glow shone in the faces of all, and made everything seem unearthly and unreal.

The bidding began slowly. The Sitkan, who was a stranger in the land and who had arrived only half an hour before, offered one hundred dollars in a confident voice, and was surprised when Akoon turned threateningly upon him with the rifle. The bidding dragged. An Indian from the Tozikakat, a pilot, bid one hundred and fifty, and after some time a gambler, who had been ordered out of the Upper Country, raised the bid to two hundred. El-Soo was saddened; her pride was hurt; but the only effect was that she flamed more audaciously upon the crowd.

There was a disturbance among the onlookers as Porportuk forced his way to the front. "Five hundred dollars!" he bid in a loud voice, then looked about him proudly to note the effect.

He was minded to use his great wealth as a bludgeon with which to stun all competition at the start. But one of the voyageurs, looking on El-Soo with sparkling eyes, raised the bid a hundred.

"Seven hundred!" Porportuk returned promptly.

And with equal promptness came the "Eight hundred," of the voyageur.

Then Porportuk swung his club again. "Twelve hundred!" he shouted.

With a look of poignant disappointment, the voyageur succumbed. There was no further bidding. Tommy worked hard, but could not elicit a bid.

El-Soo spoke to Porportuk. "It were good, Porportuk, for you to weigh well your bid. Have you forgotten the thing I told you—that I would never marry you!"

"It is a public auction," he retorted. "I shall buy you with a bill of sale. I have offered twelve hundred dollars. You come cheap."

"Too damned cheap!" Tommy cried. "What if I am auctioneer? That does not prevent me from bidding. I'll make it thirteen hundred."

"Fourteen hundred," from Porportuk.

"I'll buy you in to be my—my sister," Tommy whispered to El-Soo, then called aloud, "Fifteen hundred!"

At two thousand, one of the Eldorado kings took a hand, and Tommy dropped out.

A third time Porportuk swung the club of his wealth, making a clean raise of five hundred dollars. But the Eldorado king's pride was touched. No man could club him. And he swung back another five hundred.

El-Soo stood at three thousand. Porportuk made it thirty-five hundred, and gasped when the Eldorado king raised it a thousand dollars. Porportuk again raised it five hundred, and again gasped when the king raised a thousand more.

Porportuk became angry. His pride was touched; his strength was challenged, and with him strength took the form of wealth. He would not be ashamed for weakness before the world. El-Soo became incidental. The savings and scrimpings from the cold nights of all his years were ripe to be squandered. El-Soo stood at six thousand. He made it seven thousand. And then, in thousand-dollar bids, as fast as they could be uttered, her price went up. At fourteen thousand the two men stopped for breath.

Then the unexpected happened. A still heavier club was swung. In the pause that ensued, the gambler, who had scented a speculation and formed a syndicate with several of his fellows, bid sixteen thousand dollars.

"Seventeen thousand," Porportuk said weakly.

"Eighteen thousand," said the king.

Porportuk gathered his strength. "Twenty thousand."

The syndicate dropped out. The Eldorado king raised a thousand, and Porportuk raised back; and as they bid, Akoon turned from one to the other, half menacingly, half curiously, as though to see what manner of man it was that he would have to kill. When the king prepared to make his next bid, Akoon having pressed closer, the king first loosed the revolver at his hip, then said:—

"Twenty-three thousand."

"Twenty-four thousand," said Porportuk. He grinned viciously, for the certitude of his bidding had at last shaken the king. The latter moved over close to El-Soo. He studied her carefully, for a long while.

"And five hundred," he said at last.

"Twenty-five thousand," came Porportuk's raise.

The king looked for a long space, and shook his head. He looked again, and said reluctantly, "And five hundred."

"Twenty-six thousand," Porportuk snapped.

The king shook his head and refused to meet Tommy's pleading eye. In the meantime Akoon had edged close to Porportuk. El-Soo's quick eye noted this, and, while Tommy wrestled with the Eldorado king for another bid, she bent, and spoke in a low voice in the ear of a slave. And while Tommy's "Going—going—going—" dominated the air, the slave went up to Akoon and spoke in a low voice in his ear. Akoon made no sign that he had heard, though El-Soo watched him anxiously.

"Gone!" Tommy's voice rang out. "To Porportuk, for twenty-six thousand dollars."

Porportuk glanced uneasily at Akoon. All eyes were centred upon Akoon, but he did nothing.

"Let the scales be brought," said El-Soo.

"I shall make payment at my house," said Porportuk.

"Let the scales be brought," El-Soo repeated. "Payment shall be made here where all can see."

So the gold-scales were brought from the trading post, while Porportuk went away and came back with a man at his heels, on whose shoulders was a weight of gold-dust in moose-hide sacks. Also, at Porportuk's back, walked another man with a rifle, who had eyes only for Akoon.

"Here are the notes and mortgages," said Porportuk, "for fifteen thousand nine hundred and sixty-seven dollars and seventy-five cents."

El-Soo received them into her hands and said to Tommy, "Let them be reckoned as sixteen thousand."

"There remains ten thousand dollars to be paid in gold," Tommy said.

Porportuk nodded, and untied the mouths of the sacks. El-Soo, standing at the edge of the bank, tore the papers to shreds and sent them fluttering out over the Yukon. The weighing began, but halted.

"Of course, at seventeen dollars," Porportuk had said to Tommy, as he adjusted the scales.

"At sixteen dollars," El-Soo said sharply.

"It is the custom of all the land to reckon gold at seventeen dollars for each ounce," Porportuk replied. "And this is a business transaction."

El-Soo laughed. "It is a new custom," she said. "It began this spring. Last year, and the years before, it was sixteen dollars an ounce. When my father's debt was made, it was sixteen dollars. When he spent at the store the money he got from you, for one ounce he was given sixteen dollars' worth of flour, not seventeen. Wherefore, shall you pay for me at sixteen, and not at seventeen." Porportuk grunted and allowed the weighing to proceed.

"Weigh it in three piles, Tommy," she said. "A thousand dollars here, three thousand here, and here six thousand."

It was slow work, and, while the weighing went on, Akoon was closely watched by all.

"He but waits till the money is paid," one said; and the word went around and was accepted, and they waited for what Akoon should do when the money was paid. And Porportuk's man with the rifle waited and watched Akoon.

The weighing was finished, and the gold-dust lay on the table in three dark-yellow heaps. "There is a debt of my father to the Company for three thousand dollars," said El-Soo. "Take it, Tommy, for the Company. And here are four old men, Tommy. You know them. And here is one thousand dollars. Take it, and see that the old men are never hungry and never without tobacco."

Tommy scooped the gold into separate sacks. Six thousand dollars remained on the table. El-Soo thrust the scoop into the heap, and with a sudden turn whirled the contents out and down to the Yukon in a golden shower. Porportuk seized her wrist as she thrust the scoop a second time into the heap.

"It is mine," she said calmly. Porportuk released his grip, but he gritted his teeth and scowled darkly as she continued to scoop the gold into the river till none was left.

The crowd had eyes for naught but Akoon, and the rifle of Porportuk's man lay across the hollow of his arm, the muzzle directed at Akoon a yard away, the man's thumb on the hammer. But Akoon did nothing.

"Make out the bill of sale," Porportuk said grimly.

And Tommy made out the bill of sale, wherein all right and title in the woman El-Soo was vested in the man Porportuk. El-Soo signed the document, and Porportuk folded it and put it away in his pouch. Suddenly his eyes flashed, and in sudden speech he addressed El-Soo.

"But it was not your father's debt," he said. "What I paid was the price for you. Your sale is business of to-day and not of last year and the years before. The ounces paid for you will buy at the post to-day seventeen dollars of flour, and not sixteen. I have lost a dollar on each ounce. I have lost six hundred and twenty-five dollars."

El-Soo thought for a moment, and saw the error she had made. She smiled, and then she laughed.

"You are right," she laughed "I made a mistake. But it is too late. You have paid, and the gold is gone. You did not think quick. It is your loss. Your wit is slow these days, Porportuk. You are getting old."

He did not answer. He glanced uneasily at Akoon, and was reassured. His lips tightened, and a hint of cruelty came into his face. "Come," he said, "we will go to my house."

"Do you remember the two things I told you in the spring?" El-Soo asked, making no movement to accompany him.

"My head would be full with the things women say, did I heed them," he answered.

"I told you that you would be paid," El-Soo went on carefully. "And I told you that I would never be your wife."

"But that was before the bill of sale." Porportuk crackled the paper between his fingers inside the pouch. "I have bought you before all the world. You belong to me. You will not deny that you belong to me."

"I belong to you," El-Soo said steadily.

"I own you."

"You own me."

Porportuk's voice rose slightly and triumphantly. "As a dog, I own you."

"As a dog you own me," El-Soo continued calmly. "But, Porportuk, you forget the thing I told you. Had any other man bought me, I should have been that man's wife. I should have been a good wife to that man. Such was my will. But my will with you was that I should never be your wife. Wherefore, I am your dog."

Porportuk knew that he played with fire, and he resolved to play firmly. "Then I speak to you, not as El-Soo, but as a dog," he said; "and I tell you to come with me." He half reached to grip her arm, but with a gesture she held him back.

"Not so fast, Porportuk. You buy a dog. The dog runs away. It is your loss. I am your dog. What if I run away?"

"As the owner of the dog, I shall beat you—"

"When you catch me?"

"When I catch you."

"Then catch me."

He reached swiftly for her, but she eluded him. She laughed as she circled around the table. "Catch her!" Porportuk commanded the Indian with the rifle, who stood near to her. But as the Indian stretched forth his arm to her, the Eldorado king felled him with a fist blow under the ear. The rifle clattered to the ground. Then was Akoon's chance. His eyes glittered, but he did nothing.

Porportuk was an old man, but his cold nights retained for him his activity. He did not circle the table. He came across suddenly, over the top of the table. El-Soo was taken off her guard. She sprang back with a sharp cry of alarm, and Porportuk would have caught her had it not been for Tommy. Tommy's leg went out. Porportuk tripped and pitched forward on the ground. El-Soo got her start.

"Then catch me," she laughed over her shoulder, as she fled away.

She ran lightly and easily, but Porportuk ran swiftly and savagely. He outran her. In his youth he had been swiftest of all the young men. But El-Soo dodged in a willowy, elusive way. Being in native dress, her feet were not cluttered with skirts, and her pliant body curved a flight that defied the gripping fingers of Porportuk.

With laughter and tumult, the great crowd scattered out to see the chase. It led through the Indian encampment; and ever dodging, circling, and reversing, El-Soo and Porportuk appeared and disappeared among the tents. El-Soo seemed to balance herself against the air with her arms, now one side, now on the other, and sometimes her body, too, leaned out upon the air far from the perpendicular as she achieved her sharpest curves. And Porportuk, always a leap behind, or a leap this side or that, like a lean hound strained after her.

They crossed the open ground beyond the encampment and disappeared in the forest. Tana-naw Station waited their reappearance, and long and vainly it waited.

In the meantime Akoon ate and slept, and lingered much at the steamboat landing, deaf to the rising resentment of Tana-naw Station in that he did nothing. Twenty-four hours later Porportuk returned. He was tired and savage. He spoke to no one but Akoon, and with him tried to pick a quarrel. But Akoon shrugged his shoulders and walked away. Porportuk did not waste time. He outfitted half a dozen of the young men, selecting the best trackers and travellers, and at their head plunged into the forest.

Next day the steamer *Seattle*, bound up river, pulled in to the shore and wooded up. When the lines were cast off and she churned out from the bank, Akoon was on board in the pilot-house. Not many hours afterward, when it was his turn at the wheel, he saw a small birch-bark canoe put off from the shore. There was only one person in it. He studied it carefully, put the wheel over, and slowed down.

The captain entered the pilot-house. "What's the matter?" he demanded. "The water's good."

Akoon grunted. He saw a larger canoe leaving the bank, and in it were a number of persons. As the *Seattle* lost headway, he put the wheel over some more.

The captain fumed. "It's only a squaw," he protested.

Akoon did not grunt. He was all eyes for the squaw and the pursuing canoe. In the latter six paddles were flashing, while the squaw paddled slowly.

"You'll be aground," the captain protested, seizing the wheel.

But Akoon countered his strength on the wheel and looked him in the eyes. The captain slowly released the spokes.

"Queer beggar," he sniffed to himself.

Akoon held the *Seattle* on the edge of the shoal water and waited till he saw the squaw's fingers clutch the forward rail. Then he signalled for full speed ahead and ground the wheel over. The large canoe was very near, but the gap between it and the steamer was widening.

The squaw laughed and leaned over the rail. "Then catch me, Porportuk!" she cried.

Akoon left the steamer at Fort Yukon. He outfitted a small poling-boat and went up the Porcupine River. And with him went El-Soo. It was a weary journey, and the way led across the backbone of the world; but Akoon had travelled it before. When they came to the head-waters of the Porcupine, they left the boat and went on foot across the Rocky Mountains.

Akoon greatly liked to walk behind El-Soo and watch the movement of her. There was a music in it that he loved. And especially he loved the well-rounded calves in their sheaths of soft-tanned leather, the slim ankles, and the small moccasined feet that were tireless through the longest days.

"You are light as air," he said, looking up at her. "It is no labor for you to walk. You almost float, so lightly do your feet rise and fall. You are like a deer, El-Soo; you are like a deer, and your eyes are like deer's eyes, sometimes when you look at me, or when you hear a quick sound and wonder if it be danger that stirs. Your eyes are like a deer's eyes now as you look at me."

And El-Soo, luminous and melting, bent and kissed Akoon.

"When we reach the Mackenzie, we will not delay," Akoon said later. "We will go south before the winter catches us. We will go to the sunlands where there is no snow. But we will return. I have seen much of the world, and there is no land like Alaska, no sun like our sun, and the snow is good after the long summer."

"And you will learn to read," said El-Soo.

And Akoon said, "I will surely learn to read."

But there was delay when they reached the Mackenzie. They fell in with a band of Mackenzie Indians and, hunting, Akoon was shot by accident. The rifle was in the hands of a youth. The bullet broke Akoon's right arm and, ranging farther, broke two of his ribs. Akoon knew rough surgery, while El-Soo had learned some refinements at Holy Cross. The bones were finally set, and Akoon lay by the fire for them to knit. Also, he lay by the fire so that the smoke would keep the mosquitoes away.

Then it was that Porportuk, with his six young men, arrived. Akoon groaned in his helplessness and made appeal to the Mackenzies. But Porportuk made demand, and the Mackenzies were perplexed. Porportuk was for seizing upon El-Soo, but this they would not permit. Judgment must be given, and, as it was an affair of man and woman, the council of the old men was called—this that warm judgment might not be given by the young men, who were warm of heart.

The old men sat in a circle about the smudge-fire. Their faces were lean and wrinkled, and they gasped and panted for air. The smoke was not good for them. Occasionally they struck with withered hands at the mosquitoes that braved the smoke. After such exertion they coughed hollowly and painfully. Some spat blood, and one of them sat a bit apart with head bowed forward, and bled slowly and continuously at the mouth; the coughing sickness had gripped them. They were as dead men; their time was short. It was a judgment of the dead.

"And I paid for her a heavy price," Porportuk concluded his complaint. "Such a price you have never seen. Sell all that is yours—sell your spears and arrows and rifles, sell your skins and furs, sell your tents and boats and dogs, sell everything, and you will not have maybe a thousand dollars. Yet did I pay for the woman, El-Soo, twenty-six times the price of all your spears and arrows and rifles, your skins and furs, your tents and boats and dogs. It was a heavy price."

The old men nodded gravely, though their weazened eye-slits widened with wonder that any woman should be worth such a price. The one that bled at the mouth wiped his lips. "Is it true talk?" he asked each of Porportuk's six young men. And each answered that it was true.

"Is it true talk?" he asked El-Soo, and she answered, "It is true."

"But Porportuk has not told that he is an old man," Akoon said, "and that he has daughters older than El-Soo."

"It is true, Porportuk is an old man," said El-Soo.

"It is for Porportuk to measure the strength of his age," said he who bled at the mouth. "We be old men. Behold! Age is never so old as youth would measure it."

And the circle of old men champed their gums, and nodded approvingly, and coughed.

"I told him that I would never be his wife," said El-Soo.

"Yet you took from him twenty-six times all that we possess?" asked a one-eyed old man.

El-Soo was silent.

"It is true?" And his one eye burned and bored into her like a fiery gimlet.

"It is true," she said.

"But I will run away again," she broke out passionately, a moment later. "Always will I run away."

"That is for Porportuk to consider," said another of the old men. "It is for us to consider the judgment."

"What price did you pay for her?" was demanded of Akoon.

"No price did I pay for her," he answered. "She was above price. I did not measure her in gold-dust, nor in dogs, and tents, and furs."

The old men debated among themselves and mumbled in undertones. "These old men are ice," Akoon said in English. "I will not listen to their judgment, Porportuk. If you take El-Soo, I will surely kill you."

The old men ceased and regarded him suspiciously. "We do not know the speech you make," one said.

"He but said that he would kill me," Porportuk volunteered. "So it were well to take from him his rifle, and to have some of your young men sit by him, that he may not do me hurt. He is a young man, and what are broken bones to youth!"

Akoon, lying helpless, had rifle and knife taken from him, and to either side of his shoulders sat young men of the Mackenzies. The one-eyed old man arose and stood upright. "We marvel at the price paid for one mere woman," he began; "but the wisdom of the price is no concern of ours. We are here to give judgment, and judgment we give. We have no doubt. It is known to all that Porportuk paid a heavy price for the woman El-Soo. Wherefore does the woman El-Soo belong to Porportuk and none other." He sat down heavily, and coughed. The old men nodded and coughed.

"I will kill you," Akoon cried in English.

Porportuk smiled and stood up. "You have given true judgment," he said to the council, "and my young men will give to you much tobacco. Now let the woman be brought to me."

Akoon gritted his teeth. The young men took El-Soo by the arms. She did not resist, and was led, her face a sullen flame, to Porportuk.

"Sit there at my feet till I have made my talk," he commanded. He paused a moment. "It is true," he said, "I am an old man. Yet can I understand the ways of youth. The fire has not all gone out of me. Yet am I no longer young, nor am I minded to run these old legs of mine through all the years that remain to me. El-Soo can run fast and well. She is a deer. This I know, for I have seen and run after her. It is not good that a wife should run so fast. I paid for her a heavy price, yet does she run away from me. Akoon paid no price at all, yet does she run to him.

"When I came among you people of the Mackenzie, I was of one mind. As I listened in the council and thought of the swift legs of El-Soo, I was of many minds. Now am I of one mind again, but it is a different mind from the one I brought to the council. Let me tell you my mind. When a dog runs once away from a master, it will run away again. No matter how many times it is brought back, each time it will run away again. When we have such dogs, we sell them. El-Soo is like a dog that runs away. I will sell her. Is there any man of the council that will buy?"

The old men coughed and remained silent.

"Akoon would buy," Porportuk went on, "but he has no money.

Wherefore I will give El-Soo to him, as he said, without price. Even now will I give her to him."

Reaching down, he took El-Soo by the hand and led her across the space to where Akoon lay on his back.

"She has a bad habit, Akoon," he said, seating her at Akoon's feet. "As she has run away from me in the past, in the days to come she may run away from you. But there is no need to fear that she will ever run away, Akoon. I shall see to that. Never will she run away from you—this the word of Porportuk. She has great wit. I know, for often has it bitten into me. Yet am I minded myself to give my wit play for once. And by my wit will I secure her to you, Akoon."

Stooping, Porportuk crossed El-Soo's feet, so that the instep of one lay over that of the other; and then, before his purpose could be divined, he discharged his rifle through the two ankles. As Akoon struggled to rise against the weight of the young men, there was heard the crunch of the broken bone rebroken.

"It is just," said the old men, one to another.

El-Soo made no sound. She sat and looked at her shattered ankles, on which she would never walk again.

"My legs are strong, El-Soo," Akoon said. "But never will they bear me away from you."

El-Soo looked at him, and for the first time in all the time he had known her, Akoon saw tears in her eyes.

"Your eyes are like deer's eyes, El-Soo," he said.

"Is it just?" Porportuk asked, and grinned from the edge of the smoke as he prepared to depart.

"It is just," the old men said. And they sat on in the silence.

THE UNPARALLELED
INVASION

It was in the year 1976 that the trouble between the world and China reached its culmination. It was because of this that the celebration of the Second Centennial of American Liberty was deferred. Many other plans of the nations of the earth were twisted and tangled and postponed for the same reason. The world awoke rather abruptly to its danger; but for over seventy years, unperceived, affairs had been shaping toward this very end.

The year 1904 logically marks the beginning of the development that, seventy years later, was to bring consternation to the whole world. The Japanese-Russian War took place in 1904, and the historians of the time gravely noted it down that that event marked the entrance of Japan into the comity of nations. What it really did mark was the awakening of China. This awakening, long expected, had finally been given up. The Western nations had tried to arouse China, and they had failed. Out of their native optimism and race-egotism they had therefore concluded that the task was impossible, that China would never awaken.

What they had failed to take into account was this: *that between them and China was no common psychological speech.* Their thought-processes were radically dissimilar. There was no intimate vocabulary. The Western mind penetrated the Chinese mind but a short distance when it found itself in a fathomless maze. The Chinese mind penetrated the Western mind an equally short distance when it fetched up against a blank, incomprehensible wall. It was all a matter of language. There was no way to communicate Western ideas to the Chinese mind. China remained asleep. The material achievement and progress of the West was a closed book to her; nor could the West open the book. Back and deep down on the tie-ribs of consciousness, in the mind, say, of the English-speaking race, was a capacity to thrill to short, Saxon words; back and deep-down on the tie-ribs of consciousness of the Chinese mind was a capacity to thrill to its own hieroglyphics; but the Chinese mind could not thrill to short, Saxon words; nor could the English-speaking mind thrill to hieroglyphics. The fabrics of their minds were woven from totally different stuffs. They were mental aliens. And so it was that Western material achievement and progress made no dent on the rounded sleep of China.

Came Japan and her victory over Russia in 1904. Now the Japanese race was the freak and paradox among Eastern peoples. In some strange way Japan was receptive to all the West had to offer. Japan swiftly assimilated the Western ideas, and digested them, and so capably applied them that she suddenly burst forth, full-panoplied, a world-power. There is no explaining this peculiar openness of Japan to the alien culture of the West. As well might be explained any biological sport in the animal kingdom.

Having decisively thrashed the great Russian Empire, Japan promptly set about dreaming a colossal dream of empire for herself. Korea she had made into a granary and a colony; treaty privileges and vulpine diplomacy gave her the monopoly of Manchuria. But Japan was not satisfied. She turned her eyes upon China. There lay a vast territory, and in that territory were the hugest deposits in the world of iron and coal—the backbone of industrial civilization. Given natural resources, the other great factor in industry is labor. In that territory was a population of 400,000,000 souls—one quarter of the then total population of the earth. Furthermore, the Chinese were excellent workers, while their fatalistic philosophy (or religion) and their stolid nervous organization constituted them splendid soldiers—if they were properly managed. Needless to say, Japan was prepared to furnish that management.

But best of all, from the standpoint of Japan, the Chinese was a kindred race. The baffling enigma of the Chinese character to the West was no baffling enigma to the Japanese. The Japanese understood as we could never school ourselves or hope to understand. Their mental processes were the same. The Japanese thought with the same thought-symbols as did the Chinese, and they thought in the same peculiar grooves. Into the Chinese mind the Japanese went on where we were balked by the obstacle of incomprehension. They took the turning which we could not perceive, twisted around the obstacle, and were out of sight in the ramifications of the Chinese mind where we could not follow. They were brothers. Long ago one had borrowed the other's written language, and, untold generations before that, they had diverged from the common Mongol stock. There had been changes, differentiations brought about by diverse conditions and infusions of other blood; but down at the bottom of their beings, twisted into the fibers of them,

was a heritage in common, a sameness in kind that time had not oblit-
erated.

And so Japan took upon herself the management of China. In the
years immediately following the war with Russia, her agents swarmed
over the Chinese Empire. A thousand miles beyond the last mission
station toiled her engineers and spies, clad as coolies, under the guise
of itinerant merchants or proselyting Buddhist priests, noting down the
horsepower of every waterfall, the likely sites for factories, the heights
of mountains and passes, the strategic advantages and weaknesses, the
wealth of the farming valleys, the number of bullocks in a district or the
number of laborers that could be collected by forced levies. Never was
there such a census, and it could have been taken by no other people
than the dogged, patient, patriotic Japanese.

But in short time secrecy was thrown to the winds. Japan's officers
reorganized the Chinese army; her drill sergeants made the mediæval
warriors over into twentieth century soldiers, accustomed to all the
modern machinery of war and with a higher average of marksmanship
than the soldiers of any Western nation. The engineers of Japan deepened and widened the intricate system of canals, built factories and foun-
dries, netted the empire with telegraphs and telephones, and inaugurated
the era of railroad-building. It was these same protagonists of machine-
civilization that discovered the great oil deposits of Chunsan, the iron
mountains of Whang-Sing, the copper ranges of Chinchi, and they sank
the gas wells of Wow-Wee, that most marvelous reservoir of natural
gas in all the world.

In China's councils of empire were the Japanese emissaries. In the
ears of the statesmen whispered the Japanese statesmen. The political
reconstruction of the Empire was due to them. They evicted the scholar
class, which was violently reactionary, and put into office progressive
officials. And in every town and city of the Empire newspapers were
started. Of course, Japanese editors ran the policy of these papers, which
policy they got direct from Tokio. It was these papers that educated and
made progressive the great mass of the population.

China was at last awake. Where the West had failed, Japan succeeded.
She had transmuted Western culture and achievement into terms that
were intelligible to the Chinese understanding. Japan herself, when she
so suddenly awakened, had astounded the world. But at the time she
was only forty millions strong. China's awakening, what of her four
hundred millions and the scientific advance of the world, was frightfully
astounding. She was the colossus of the nations, and swiftly her voice
was heard in no uncertain tones in the affairs and councils of the na-

tions. Japan egged her on, and the proud Western peoples listened with respectful ears.

China's swift and remarkable rise was due, perhaps more than to anything else, to the superlative quality of her labor. The Chinese was the perfect type of industry. He had always been that. For sheer ability to work, no worker in the world could compare with him. Work was the breath of his nostrils. It was to him what wandering and fighting in far lands and spiritual adventure had been to other peoples. Liberty, to him, epitomized itself in access to the means of toil. To till the soil and labor interminably was all he asked of life and the powers that be. And the awakening of China had given its vast population not merely free and unlimited access to the means of toil, but access to the highest and most scientific machine-means of toil.

China rejuvenescent! It was but a step to China rampant. She discovered a new pride in herself and a will of her own. She began to chafe under the guidance of Japan, but she did not chafe long. On Japan's advice, in the beginning, she had expelled from the Empire all Western missionaries, engineers, drill sergeants, merchants, and teachers. She now began to expel the similar representatives of Japan. The latter's advisory statesmen were showered with honors and decorations, and sent home. The West had awakened Japan, and, as Japan had then requited the West, Japan was now requited by China. Japan was thanked for her kindly aid and flung out bag and baggage by her gigantic protégé. The Western nations chuckled. Japan's rainbow dream had gone glimmering. She grew angry. China laughed at her. The blood and the swords of the Samurai would out, and Japan rashly went to war. This occurred in 1922, and in seven bloody months Manchuria, Korea, and Formosa were taken away from her and she was hurled back, bankrupt, to stifle in her tiny, crowded islands. Exit Japan from the world drama. Thereafter she devoted herself to art, and her task became to please the world greatly with her creations of wonder and beauty.

Contrary to expectation, China did not prove warlike. She had no Napoleonic dream, and was content to devote herself to the arts of peace. After a time of disquiet, the idea was accepted that China was to be feared, not in war, but in commerce. It will be seen that the real danger was not apprehended. China went on consummating her machine-civilization. Instead of a large standing army, she developed an immensely larger and splendidly efficient militia. Her navy was so small that it was the laughing stock of the world; nor did she attempt to strengthen her navy. The treaty ports of the world were never entered by her visiting battleships.

The real danger lay in the fecundity of her loins, and it was in 1970 that the first cry of alarm was raised. For some time all territories adjacent to China had been grumbling at Chinese immigration; but now it suddenly came home to the world that China's population was 500,000,000. She had increased by a hundred millions since her awakening. Burchaldter called to attention the fact that there were more Chinese in existence than white-skinned people. He performed a simple sum in arithmetic. He added together the populations of the United States, Canada, New Zealand, Australia, South Africa, England, France, Germany, Italy, Austria, European Russia, and all Scandinavia. The result was 495,000,000. And the population of China over-topped this tremendous total by 5,000,000. Burchaldter's figures went around the world, and the world shivered.

For many centuries China's population had been constant. Her territory had been saturated with population; that is to say, her territory, with the primitive method of production, had supported the maximum limit of population. But when she awoke and inaugurated the machine-civilization, her productive power had been enormously increased. Thus, on the same territory, she was able to support a far larger population. At once the birth rate began to rise and the death rate to fall. Before, when population pressed against the means of subsistence, the excess population had been swept away by famine. But now, thanks to the machine-civilization, China's means of subsistence had been enormously extended, and there were no famines; her population followed on the heels of the increase in the means of subsistence.

During this time of transition and development of power, China had entertained no dreams of conquest. The Chinese was not an imperial race. It was industrious, thrifty, and peace-loving. War was looked upon as an unpleasant but necessary task that at times must be performed. And so, while the Western races had squabbled and fought, and world-adventured against one another, China had calmly gone on working at her machines and growing. Now she was spilling over the boundaries of her Empire—that was all, just spilling over into the adjacent territories with all the certainty and terrifying slow momentum of a glacier.

Following upon the alarm raised by Burchaldter's figures, in 1970, France made a long-threatened stand. French Indo-China had been over-run, filled up, by Chinese immigrants. France called a halt. The Chinese wave flowed on. France assembled a force of a hundred thousand on the boundary between her unfortunate colony and China, and China sent down an army of militia-soldiers a million strong. Behind came the wives and sons and daughters and relatives, with their personal household luggage, in a second army. The French force was brushed aside like a fly. The Chinese militia-soldiers, along with their families, over five millions all told, coolly took possession of French Indo-China and settled down to stay for a few thousand years.

Outraged France was in arms. She hurled fleet after fleet against the coast of China, and nearly bankrupted herself by the effort. China had no navy. She withdrew like a turtle into her shell. For a year the French fleets blockaded the coast and bombarded exposed towns and villages. China did not mind. She did not depend upon the rest of the world for anything. She calmly kept out of range of the French guns and went on working. France wept and wailed, wrung her impotent hands and appealed to the dumbfounded nations. Then she landed a punitive expedition to march to Peking. It was two hundred and fifty thousand strong, and it was the flower of France. It landed without opposition and marched into the interior. And that was the last ever seen of it. The line of communication was snapped on the second day. Not a survivor came back to tell what had happened. It had been swallowed up in China's cavernous maw, that was all.

In the five years that followed, China's expansion, in all land directions, went on apace. Siam was made part of the Empire, and, in spite of all that England could do, Burma and the Malay Peninsula were overrun; while all along the long south boundary of Siberia, Russia was pressed severely by China's advancing hordes. The process was simple. First came the Chinese immigration (or, rather, it was already there, having come there slowly and insidiously during the previous years). Next came the clash at arms and the brushing away of all opposition by a monster army of militia-soldiers, followed by their families and household baggage. And finally came their settling down as colonists in the conquered territory. Never was there so strange and effective a method of world conquest.

Napal and Bhutan were over-run, and the whole northern boundary of India pressed against by this fearful tide of life. To the west, Bokhara, and, even to the south and west, Afghanistan, were swallowed up. Persia, Turkestan, and all Central Asia felt the pressure of the flood. It was at this time that Burchaldter revised his figures. He had been mistaken. China's population must be seven hundred millions, eight hundred millions, nobody knew how many millions, but at any rate it would soon be a billion. There were two Chinese for every white-skinned human in the world, Burchaldter announced, and the world trembled. China's increase must have begun immediately, in 1904. It was remembered that since that date there had not been a single famine. At 5,000,000 a year increase, her total increase in the intervening seventy years must be 350,000,000. But who was to know? It might be more. Who was to know anything of this strange new menace of the twentieth century—China, old China, rejuvenescent, fruitful, and militant!

The Convention of 1975 was called at Philadelphia. All the Western nations, and some few of the Eastern, were represented. Nothing was accomplished. There was talk of all countries putting bounties on children to increase the birth rate, but it was laughed to scorn by the arithmeticians, who pointed out that China was too far in the lead in that direction. No feasible way of coping with China was suggested. China was appealed to and threatened by the United Powers, and that was all the Convention of Philadelphia came to; and the Convention and the Powers were laughed at by China. Li Tang Fwung, the power behind the Dragon Throne, deigned to reply.

"What does China care for the comity of nations?" said Li Tang Fwung. "We are the most ancient, honorable, and royal of races. We have our own destiny to accomplish. It is unpleasant that our destiny does not jibe with the destiny of the rest of the world, but what would you? You have talked windily about the royal races and the heritage of the earth, and we can only reply that that remains to be seen. You cannot invade us. Never mind about your navies. Don't shout. We know our navy is small. You see, we use it for police purposes. We do not care for the sea. Our strength is in our population, which will soon be a billion. Thanks to you, we are equipped with all modern war-machinery. Send your navies. We will not notice them. Send your punitive expeditions, but first remember France. To land half a million soldiers on our shores would strain the resources of any of you. And our thousand millions would swallow them down in a mouthful. Send a million; send five million, and we will swallow them down just as readily. Pouf! A mere nothing, a meager morsel. Destroy, as you have threatened, you United States, the ten million coolies we have forced upon your shores—why, the amount scarcely equals half of our excess birth rate for a year."

So spoke Li Tang Fwung. The world was nonplussed, helpless, terrified. Truly had he spoken. There was no combating China's amazing birth rate. If her population was a billion, and was increasing twenty millions a year, in twenty-five years it would be a billion and a half—equal to the total population of the world in 1904. And nothing could be done. There was no way to dam up the over-spilling monstrous flood of life. War was futile. China laughed at a blockade of her coasts. She welcomed invasion. In her capacious maw was room for all the hosts of earth that could be hurled at her. And in the meantime her flood of yellow life poured out and on over Asia. China laughed and read in their magazines the learned lucubrations of the distracted Western scholars.

But there was one scholar China failed to reckon on—Jacobus Laningdale. Not that he was a scholar, except in the widest sense. Primarily, Jacobus Laningdale was a scientist, and, up to that time, a very obscure scientist, a professor employed in the laboratories of the Health Office of New York City. Jacobus Laningdale's head was very like any other head, but in that head was evolved an idea. Also, in that head was the wisdom to keep that idea secret. He did not write an article for the magazines. Instead, he asked for a vacation. On September 19, 1975, he arrived in Washington. It was evening, but he proceeded straight to the White House, for he had already arranged an audience with the President. He was closeted with President Moyer for three hours. What passed between them was not learned by the rest of the world until long after; in fact, at that time the world was not interested in Jacobus Laningdale. Next day the President called in his Cabinet. Jacobus Laningdale was present. The proceedings were kept secret. But that very afternoon Rufus Cowdery, Secretary of State, left Washington and early the following morning sailed for England. The secret that he carried began to spread, but it spread only among the heads of governments. Possibly half a dozen men in a nation were intrusted with the idea that had formed in Jacobus Laningdale's head. Following the spread of the secret, sprang up great activity in all the dock-yards, arsenals, and navy-yards. The people of France and Austria became suspicious, but so sincere were their governments' calls for confidence that they acquiesced in the unknown project that was afoot.

This was the time of the Great Truce. All countries pledged themselves solemnly not to go to war with any other country. The first definite action was the gradual mobilization of the armies of Russia, Germany, Austria, Italy, Greece, and Turkey. Then began the eastward movement. All railroads into Asia were glutted with troop trains. China was the objective, that was all that was known. A little later began the great sea movement. Expeditions of war ships were launched from all countries. Fleet followed fleet, and all proceeded to the coast of China. The nations cleaned out their navy-yards. They sent their revenue cutters and dispatch boats and lighthouse tenders, and they sent their last antiquated cruisers and battleships. Not content with this, they impressed the merchant marine. The statistics show that 58,640 merchant steamers, equipped with searchlights and rapid-fire guns, were dispatched by the various nations to China.

And China smiled and waited. On her land side, along her boundaries, were millions of the warriors of Europe. She mobilized five times as many millions of her militia and waited the invasion. On her sea coasts she did the same. But China was puzzled. After all this enormous preparation, there was no invasion. She could not understand. Along the great Siberian frontier all was quiet. Along her coasts the towns and villages were not even shelled. Never, in the history of the world, had there been so mighty a gathering of war fleets. The fleets of all the world were there, and day and night millions of tons of battleships plowed the brine of her coasts, and nothing happened. Nothing was attempted. Did they think to make her emerge from her shell? China smiled. Did they think to tire her out, or starve her out? China smiled again.

But on May 1, 1976, had the reader been in the imperial city of Peking, with its then population of eleven millions, he would have witnessed a curious sight. He would have seen the streets filled with the chattering yellow populace, every queued head tilted back, every slant eye turned skyward. And high up in the blue he would have beheld a tiny dot of black, which, because of its orderly evolutions, he would have identified as an airship. From this airship, as it curved its flight back and forth over the city, fell missiles—strange, harmless missiles, tubes of fragile glass that shattered into thousands of fragments on the streets and house-tops. But there was nothing deadly about these tubes of glass. Nothing happened. There were no explosions. It is true, several Chinese were killed by the tubes dropping on their heads from so enormous a height; but what were three Chinese against an excess birth rate of twenty millions? One tube struck perpendicularly in a fish pond in a garden and was not broken. It was dragged ashore by the master of the house. He did not dare to open it, but, accompanied by his friends, and surrounded by an ever-increasing crowd, he carried the mysterious tube to the magistrate of the district. The latter was a brave man. With all eyes upon him, he shattered the tube with a blow from his brass-bowled pipe. Nothing happened. Of those who were very near, one or two thought they saw some mosquitos fly out. That was all. The crowd set up a great laugh and dispersed.

As Peking was bombarded by glass tubes, so was all China. The tiny airships, dispatched from the warships, contained but two men each, and over all cities, towns, and villages they wheeled and curved, one man directing the ship, the other man throwing over the glass tubes.

Had the reader again been in Peking, six weeks later, he would have looked in vain for the eleven million inhabitants. Some few of them he would have found, a few hundred thousand, perhaps, their carcasses festering in the houses and in the deserted streets, and piled high on the abandoned death wagons. But for the rest he would have had to seek along the highways and byways of the Empire. And not all would he have found fleeing from plague-stricken Peking, for behind them, by hundreds and thousands of unburied corpses by the wayside, he could have marked their flight. And as it was with Peking, so was it with all the cities, towns, and villages of the Empire. The plague smote them all. Nor was it one plague, nor two plagues; it was a score of plagues. Every virulent form of infectious death stalked through the land. Too late the Chinese government apprehended the meaning of the colossal preparations, the marshaling of the world hosts, the flights of the tiny airships, and the rain of the tubes of glass. The proclamations of the government were vain. They could not stop the eleven million plague-stricken wretches, fleeing from the one city of Peking to spread disease through all the land. The physicians and health officers died at their posts; and death, the all-conqueror, rode over the decrees of the Emperor and Li Tang Fwung. It rode over them as well, for Li Tang Fwung died in the second week, and the Emperor, hidden away in the Summer Palace, died in the fourth week.

Had there been one plague, China might have coped with it. But from a score of plagues no creature was immune. The man who escaped smallpox went down before scarlet fever. The man who was immune to yellow fever was carried away by cholera; and if he were immune to that, too, the Black Death, which was the bubonic plague, swept him away. For it was these bacteria, and germs, and microbes, and bacilli, cultured in the laboratories of the West, that had come down upon China in the rain of glass.

All organization vanished. The government crumbled away. Decrees and proclamations were useless when the men who made them and signed them one moment were dead the next. Nor could the maddened millions, spurred on to flight by death, pause to heed anything. They fled from the cities to infect the country, and wherever they fled they carried the plagues with them. The hot summer was on—Jacobus Laningdale had selected the time shrewdly—and the plague festered everywhere. Much is conjectured of what occurred, and much has been learned from the stories of the few survivors. The wretched creatures stormed across the Empire in many-millioned flight. The vast armies China had collected on her frontiers melted away. The farms were ravaged for food, and no more crops were planted, while the crops already in were left unattended and never came to harvest. The most remarkable thing, perhaps, was the flights. Many millions engaged in them, charging to the bounds of the Empire to be met and turned back by the gigantic armies of the West. The slaughter of the mad hosts on the boundaries was stupendous. Time and again the guarding line was drawn back twenty or thirty miles to escape the contagion of the multitudinous dead.

Once the plague broke through and seized upon the German and Austrian soldiers who were guarding the borders of Turkestan. Preparations had been made for such a happening, and though sixty thousand soldiers of Europe were carried off, the international corps of physicians isolated the contagion and dammed it back. It was during this struggle that it was suggested that a new plague-germ had originated, that in some way or other a sort of hybridization between plague-germs had taken place, producing a new and frightfully virulent germ. First suspected by Vomberg, who became infected with it and died, it was later isolated and studied by Stevens, Hazenfelt, Norman, and Landers.

Such was the unparalleled invasion of China. For that billion of people there was no hope. Pent in their vast and festering charnel house, all organization and cohesion lost, they could do naught but die. They could not escape. As they were flung back from their land frontiers, so were they flung back from the sea. Seventy-five thousand vessels patroled the coasts. By day their smoking funnels dimmed the sea-rim, and by night their flashing searchlights plowed the dark and harrowed it for the tiniest escaping junk. The attempts of the immense fleets of junks were pitiful. Not one ever got by the guarding sea-hounds. Modern war-machinery held back the disorganized mass of China, while the plagues did the work.

But old War was made a thing of laughter. Naught remained to him but patrol duty. China had laughed at war, and war she was getting, but it was ultra-modern war, twentieth century war, the war of the scientist and the laboratory, the war of Jacobus Laningdale. Hundred-ton guns were toys compared with the micro-organic projectiles hurled from the laboratories, the messengers of death, the destroying angels that stalked through the empire of a billion souls.

During all the summer and fall of 1976 China was an inferno. There was no eluding the microscopic projectiles that sought out the remotest hiding places. The hundreds of millions of dead remained unburied and the germs multiplied themselves, and, toward the last, millions died daily of starvation. Besides, starvation weakened the victims and destroyed their natural defences against the plagues. Cannibalism, murder, and madness reigned. And so perished China.

Not until the following February, in the coldest weather, were the first expeditions made. These expeditions were small, composed of scientists and bodies of troops; but they entered China from every side. In spite of the most elaborate precautions against infection, numbers of soldiers and a few of the physicians were stricken. But the exploration went bravely on. They found China devastated, a howling wilderness through which wandered bands of wild dogs and desperate bandits who had survived. All survivors were put to death wherever found. And then began the great task, the sanitation of China. Five years and hundreds of millions of treasure were consumed, and then the world moved in— not in zones, as was the idea of Baron Albrecht, but heterogeneously, according to the democratic American program. It was a vast and happy intermingling of nationalities that settled down in China in 1982 and the years that followed—a tremendous and successful experiment in cross-fertilization. We know to-day the splendid mechanical, intellectual, and art output that followed.

It was in 1987, the Great Truce having been dissolved, that the ancient quarrel between France and Germany over Alsace and Lorraine recrudesced. The war-cloud grew dark and threatening in April, and on April 17 the Convention of Copenhagen was called. The representatives of the nations of the world being present, all nations solemnly pledged themselves never to use against one another the laboratory methods of warfare they had employed in the invasion of China.

—Excerpt from Walt Mervin's
"Certain Essays in History."

TO BUILD A FIRE (1908)

Day had broken cold and gray, exceedingly cold and gray, when the man turned aside from the main Yukon trail and climbed the high earth-bank, where a dim and little-travelled trail led eastward through the fat spruce timberland. It was a steep bank, and he paused for breath at the top, excusing the act to himself by looking at his watch. It was nine o'clock. There was no sun nor hint of sun, though there was not a cloud in the sky. It was a clear day, and yet there seemed an intangible pall over the face of things, a subtle gloom that made the day dark, and that was due to the absence of sun. This fact did not worry the man. He was used to the lack of sun. It had been days since he had seen the sun, and he knew that a few more days must pass before that cheerful orb, due south, would just peep above the sky-line and dip immediately from view.

The man flung a look back along the way he had come. The Yukon lay a mile wide and hidden under three feet of ice. On top of this ice were as many feet of snow. It was all pure white, rolling in gentle, undulations where the ice-jams of the freeze-up had formed. North and south, as far as his eye could see, it was unbroken white, save for a dark hair-line that curved and twisted from around the spruce-covered island to the south, and that curved and twisted away into the north, where it disappeared behind another spruce-covered island. This dark hair-line was the trail—the main trail—that led south five hundred miles to the Chilcoot Pass, Dyea, and salt water; and that led north seventy miles to Dawson, and still on to the north a thousand miles to Nulato, and finally to St. Michael on Bering Sea, a thousand miles and half a thousand more.

But all this—the mysterious, far-reaching hair-line trail, the absence of sun from the sky, the tremendous cold, and the strangeness and weirdness of it all—made no impression on the man. It was not because he was long used to it. He was a newcomer in the land, a *chechaquo,* and this was his first winter. The trouble with him was that he was without imagination. He was quick and alert in the things of life, but only in the things, and not in the significances. Fifty degrees below zero meant eighty-odd degrees of frost. Such fact impressed him as being cold and uncomfortable, and that was all. It did not lead him to meditate upon his frailty as a creature of temperature, and upon man's frailty in general, able only to live within certain narrow limits of heat and cold; and from there on it did not lead him to the conjectural field of immortality and man's place in the universe. Fifty degrees below zero stood for a bite of frost that hurt and that must be guarded against by the use of mittens, ear-flaps, warm moccasins, and thick socks. Fifty degrees below zero was to him just precisely fifty degrees below zero. That there should be anything more to it than that was a thought that never entered his head.

As he turned to go on, he spat speculatively. There was a sharp, explosive crackle that startled him. He spat again. And again, in the air, before it could fall to the snow, the spittle crackled. He knew that at fifty below spittle crackled on the snow, but this spittle had crackled in the air. Undoubtedly it was colder than fifty below—how much colder he did not know. But the temperature did not matter. He was bound for the old claim on the left fork of Henderson Creek, where the boys were already. They had come over across the divide from the Indian Creek country, while he had come the roundabout way to take a look at the possibilities of getting out logs in the spring from the islands in the Yukon. He would be in to camp by six o'clock; a bit after dark, it was true, but the boys would be there, a fire would be going, and a hot supper would be ready. As for lunch, he pressed his hand against the protruding bundle under his jacket. It was also under his shirt, wrapped up in a handkerchief and lying against the naked skin. It was the only way to keep the biscuits from freezing. He smiled agreeably to himself as he thought of those biscuits, each cut open and sopped in bacon grease, and each enclosing a generous slice of fried bacon.

He plunged in among the big spruce trees. The trail was faint. A foot of snow had fallen since the last sled had passed over, and he was glad he was without a sled, travelling light. In fact, he carried nothing but the lunch wrapped in the handkerchief. He was surprised, however, at the cold. It certainly was cold, he concluded, as he rubbed his numb nose and cheek-bones with his mittened hand. He was a warm-whiskered man, but the hair on his face did not protect the high cheek-bones and the eager nose that thrust itself aggressively into the frosty air.

At the man's heels trotted a dog, a big native husky, the proper wolf-dog, gray-coated and without any visible or temperamental difference from its brother, the wild wolf. The animal was depressed by the tremendous cold. It knew that it was no time for travelling. Its instinct told it a truer tale than was told to the man by the man's judgment. In reality, it was not merely colder than fifty below zero; it was colder than sixty below, than seventy below. It was seventy-five below zero. Since the freezing-point is thirty-two above zero, it meant that one hundred and seven degrees of frost obtained. The dog did not know anything about thermometers. Possibly in its brain there was no sharp consciousness of a condition of very cold such as was in the man's brain. But the brute had its instinct. It experienced a vague but menacing apprehension that subdued it and made it slink along at the man's heels, and that made it question eagerly every unwonted movement of the man as if expecting him to go into camp or to seek shelter somewhere and build a fire. The dog had learned fire, and it wanted fire, or else to burrow under the snow and cuddle its warmth away from the air.

The frozen moisture of its breathing had settled on its fur in a fine powder of frost, and especially were its jowls, muzzle, and eyelashes whitened by its crystalled breath. The man's red beard and mustache were likewise frosted, but more solidly, the deposit taking the form of ice and increasing with every warm, moist breath he exhaled. Also, the man was chewing tobacco, and the muzzle of ice held his lips so rigidly that he was unable to clear his chin when he expelled the juice. The result was that a crystal beard of the color and solidity of amber was increasing its length on his chin. If he fell down it would shatter itself, like glass, into brittle fragments. But he did not mind the appendage. It was the penalty all tobacco-chewers paid in that country, and he had been out before in two cold snaps. They had not been so cold as this, he knew, but by the spirit thermometer at Sixty Mile he knew they had been registered at fifty below and at fifty-five.

He held on through the level stretch of woods for several miles, crossed a wide flat of nigger-heads, and dropped down a bank to the frozen bed of a small stream. This was Henderson Creek, and he knew he was ten miles from the forks. He looked at his watch. It was ten o'clock. He was making four miles an hour, and he calculated that he would arrive at the forks at half-past twelve. He decided to celebrate that event by eating his lunch there.

The dog dropped in again at his heels, with a tail drooping discouragement, as the man swung along the creek-bed. The furrow of the old sled-trail was plainly visible, but a dozen inches of snow covered the marks of the last runners. In a month no man had come up or down that silent creek. The man held steadily on. He was not much given to thinking, and just then particularly he had nothing to think about save that he would eat lunch at the forks and that at six o'clock he would be in camp with the boys. There was nobody to talk to; and, had there been, speech would have been impossible because of the ice-muzzle on his mouth. So he continued monotonously to chew tobacco and to increase the length of his amber beard.

Once in a while the thought reiterated itself that it was very cold and that he had never experienced such cold. As he walked along he rubbed his cheek-bones and nose with the back of his mittened hand. He did this automatically, now and again changing hands. But rub as he would, the instant he stopped his cheek-bones went numb, and the following instant the end of his nose went numb. He was sure to frost his cheeks; he knew that, and experienced a pang of regret that he had not devised a nose-strap of the sort Bud wore in cold snaps. Such a strap passed across the cheeks, as well, and saved them. But it didn't matter much, after all. What were frosted cheeks? A bit painful, that was all; they were never serious.

Empty as the man's mind was of thoughts, he was keenly observant, and he noticed the changes in the creek, the curves and bends and timber-jams, and always he sharply noted where he placed his feet. Once, coming around a bend, he shied abruptly, like a startled horse, curved away from the place where he had been walking, and retreated several paces back along the trail. The creek he knew was frozen clear to the bottom,—no creek could contain water in that arctic winter,—but he knew also that there were springs that bubbled out from the hillsides and ran along under the snow and on top the ice of the creek. He knew that the coldest snaps never froze these springs, and he knew likewise their danger. They were traps. They hid pools of water under the snow that might be three inches deep, or three feet. Sometimes a skin of ice half an inch thick covered them, and in turn was covered by the snow. Sometimes there were alternate layers of water and ice-skin, so that when one broke through he kept on breaking through for a while, sometimes wetting himself to the waist.

That was why he had shied in such panic. He had felt the give under his feet and heard the crackle of a snow-hidden ice-skin. And to get his feet wet in such a temperature meant trouble and danger. At the very least it meant delay, for he would be forced to stop and build a fire, and under its protection to bare his feet while he dried his socks and moccasins. He stood and studied the creek-bed and its banks, and decided that the flow of water came from the right. He reflected awhile, rubbing his nose and cheeks, then skirted to the left, stepping gingerly and test-ing the footing for each step. Once clear of the danger, he took a fresh chew of tobacco and swung along at his four-mile gait.

In the course of the next two hours he came upon several similar traps. Usually the snow above the hidden pools had a sunken, candied appearance that advertised the danger. Once again, however, he had a close call; and once, suspecting danger, he compelled the dog to go on in front. The dog did not want to go. It hung back until the man shoved it forward, and then it went quickly across the white, unbroken surface. Suddenly it broke through, floundered to one side, and got away to firmer footing. It had wet its forefeet and legs, and almost immediately the water that clung to it turned to ice. It made quick efforts to lick the ice off its legs, then dropped down in the snow and began to bite out the ice that had formed between the toes. This was a matter of instinct. To permit the ice to remain would mean sore feet. It did not know this. It merely obeyed the mysterious prompting that arose from the deep crypts of its being. But the man knew, having achieved a judgment on the subject, and he removed the mitten from his right hand and helped tear out the ice-particles. He did not expose his fingers more than a minute, and was astonished at the swift numbness that smote them. It certainly was cold. He pulled on the mitten hastily, and beat the hand savagely across his chest.

At twelve o'clock the day was at its brightest. Yet the sun was too far south on its winter journey to clear the horizon. The bulge of the earth intervened between it and Henderson Creek, where the man walked under a clear sky at noon and cast no shadow. At half-past twelve, to the minute, he arrived at the forks of the creek. He was pleased at the speed he had made. If he kept it up, he would certainly be with the boys by six. He unbuttoned his jacket and shirt and drew forth his lunch. The action consumed no more than a quarter of a min-ute, yet in that brief moment the numbness laid hold of the exposed fingers. He did not put the mitten on, but, instead, struck the fingers a dozen sharp smashes against his leg. Then he sat down on a snow-covered log to eat. The sting that followed upon the striking of his fingers against his leg ceased so quickly that he was startled. He had had no chance to take a bite of biscuit. He struck the fingers repeatedly and returned them to the mitten, baring the other hand for the purpose of eating. He tried to take a mouthful, but the ice-muzzle prevented. He had forgotten to build a fire and thaw out. He chuckled at his foolish-ness, and as he chuckled he noted the numbness creeping into the ex-posed fingers. Also, he noted that the stinging which had first come to his toes when he sat down was already passing away. He wondered whether the toes were warm or numb. He moved them inside the moc-casins and decided that they were numb.

He pulled the mitten on hurriedly and stood up. He was a bit fright-ened. He stamped up and down until the stinging returned into the feet. It certainly was cold, was his thought. That man from Sulphur Creek had spoken the truth when telling how cold it sometimes got in the country. And he had laughed at him at the time! That showed one must not be too sure of things. There was no mistake about it, it *was* cold. He strode up and down, stamping his feet and threshing his arms, until reassured by the returning warmth. Then he got out matches and pro-ceeded to make a fire. From the undergrowth, where high water of the previous spring had lodged a supply of seasoned twigs, he got his fire-wood. Working carefully from a small beginning, he soon had a roaring fire, over which he thawed the ice from his face and in the protection of which he ate his biscuits. For the moment the cold of space was outwitted. The dog took satisfaction in the fire, stretching out close enough for warmth and far enough away to escape being singed.

When the man had finished, he filled his pipe and took his comfort-able time over a smoke. Then he pulled on his mittens, settled the ear-flaps of his cap firmly about his ears, and took the creek trail up the left fork. The dog was disappointed and yearned back toward the fire. This man did not know cold. Possibly all the generations of his ancestry had been ignorant of cold, of real cold, of cold one hundred and seven de-grees below freezing-point. But the dog knew; all its ancestry knew, and it had inherited the knowledge. And it knew that it was not good to walk abroad in such fearful cold. It was the time to lie snug in a hole in the snow and wait for a curtain of cloud to be drawn across the face of outer space whence this cold came. On the other hand, there was no keen intimacy between the dog and the man. The one was the toil-slave of the other, and the only caresses it had ever received were the caresses of the whip-lash and of harsh and menacing throat-sounds that threat-ened the whip-lash. So the dog made no effort to communicate its ap-prehension to the man. It was not concerned in the welfare of the man; it was for its own sake that it yearned back toward the fire. But the man whistled, and spoke to it with the sound of whip-lashes, and the dog swung in at the man's heels and followed after.

The man took a chew of tobacco and proceeded to start a new amber beard. Also, his moist breath quickly powdered with white his mustache, eyebrows, and lashes. There did not seem to be so many springs on the left fork of the Henderson, and for half an hour the man saw no signs of any. And then it happened. At a place where there were no signs, where the soft, unbroken snow seemed to advertise solidity beneath, the man broke through. It was not deep. He wet himself halfway to the knees before he floundered out to the firm crust.

He was angry, and cursed his luck aloud. He had hoped to get into camp with the boys at six o'clock, and this would delay him an hour, for he would have to build a fire and dry out his foot-gear. This was imperative at that low temperature—he knew that much; and he turned aside to the bank, which he climbed. On top, tangled in the underbrush about the trunks of several small spruce trees, was a high-water deposit of dry fire-wood—sticks and twigs, principally, but also larger portions of seasoned branches and fine, dry, last-year's grasses. He threw down several large pieces on top of the snow. This served for a foundation and prevented the young flame from drowning itself in the snow it otherwise would melt. The flame he got by touching a match to a small shred of birch-bark that he took from his pocket. This burned even more readily than paper. Placing it on the foundation, he fed the young flame with wisps of dry grass and with the tiniest dry twigs.

He worked slowly and carefully, keenly aware of his danger. Gradually, as the flame grew stronger, he increased the size of the twigs with which he fed it. He squatted in the snow, pulling the twigs out from their entanglement in the brush and feeding directly to the flame. He knew there must be no failure. When it is seventy-five below zero, a man must not fail in his first attempt to build a fire—that is, if his feet are wet. If his feet are dry, and he fails, he can run along the trail for half a mile and restore his circulation. But the circulation of wet and freezing feet cannot be restored by running when it is seventy-five below. No matter how fast he runs, the wet feet will freeze the harder.

All this the man knew. The old-timer on Sulphur Creek had told him about it the previous fall, and now he was appreciating the advice. Already all sensation had gone out of his feet. To build the fire he had been forced to remove his mittens, and the fingers had quickly gone numb. His pace of four miles an hour had kept his heart pumping blood to the surface of his body and to all the extremities. But the instant he stopped, the action of the pump eased down. The cold of space smote the unprotected tip of the planet, and he, being on that unprotected tip, received the full force of the blow. The blood of his body recoiled before it. The blood was alive, like the dog, and like the dog it wanted to hide away and cover itself up from the fearful cold. So long as he walked four miles and hour, he pumped that blood, willy-nilly, to the surface; but now it ebbed away and sank down into the recesses of his body. The extremities were the first to feel its absence. His wet feet froze the faster, and his exposed fingers numbed the faster, though they had not yet begun to freeze. Nose and cheeks were already freezing, while the skin of all his body chilled as it lost its blood.

But he was safe. Toes and nose and cheeks would be only touched by the frost, for the fire was beginning to burn with strength. He was feeding it with twigs the size of his finger. In another minute he would be able to feed it with branches the size of his wrist, and then he could remove his wet foot-gear, and, while it dried, he could keep his naked feet warm by the fire, rubbing them at first, of course, with snow. The fire was a success. He was safe. He remembered the advice of the old-timer on Sulphur Creek, and smiled. The old-timer had been very serious in laying down the law that no man must travel alone in the Klondike after fifty below. Well, here he was; he had had the accident; he was alone; and he had saved himself. Those old-timers were rather womanish, some of them, he thought. All a man had to do was to keep his head, and he was all right. Any man who was a man could travel alone. But it was surprising, the rapidity with which his cheeks and nose were freezing. And he had not thought his fingers could go lifeless in so short a time. Lifeless they were, for he could scarcely make them move together to grip a twig, and they seemed remote from his body and from him. When he touched a twig, he had to look and see whether or not he had hold of it. The wires were pretty well down between him and his finger-ends.

All of which counted for little. There was the fire, snapping and crackling and promising life with every dancing flame. He started to untie his moccasins. They were coated with ice; the thick German socks were like sheaths of iron halfway to the knees; and the moccasin strings were like rods of steel all twisted and knotted as by some conflagration. For a moment he tugged with his numb fingers, then, realizing the folly of it, he drew his sheath-knife.

But before he could cut the strings, it happened. It was his own fault or, rather, his mistake. He should not have built the fire under the spruce tree. He should have built it in the open. But it had been easier to pull the twigs from the brush and drop them directly on the fire. Now the tree under which he had done this carried a weight of snow on its boughs. No wind had blown for weeks, and each bough was fully freighted. Each time he had pulled a twig he had communicated a slight agitation to the tree—an imperceptible agitation, so far as he was concerned, but an agitation sufficient to bring about the disaster. High up in the tree one bough capsized its load of snow. This fell on the boughs beneath, capsizing them. This process continued, spreading out and involving the whole tree. It grew like an avalanche, and it descended without warning upon the man and the fire, and the fire was blotted out! Where it had burned was a mantle of fresh and disordered snow.

The man was shocked. It was as though he had just heard his own sentence of death. For a moment he sat and stared at the spot where the fire had been. Then he grew very calm. Perhaps the old-timer on Sulphur Creek was right. If he had only had a trail-mate he would have been in no danger now. The trail-mate could have built the fire. Well, it was up to him to build the fire over again, and this second time there must be no failure. Even if he succeeded, he would most likely lose some toes. His feet must be badly frozen by now, and there would be some time before the second fire was ready.

Such were his thoughts, but he did not sit and think them. He was busy all the time they were passing through his mind. He made a new foundation for a fire, this time in the open, where no treacherous tree could blot it out. Next, he gathered dry grasses and tiny twigs from the high-water flotsam. He could not bring his fingers together to pull them out, but he was able to gather them by the handful. In this way he got many rotten twigs and bits of green moss that were undesirable, but it was the best he could do. He worked methodically, even collecting an armful of the larger branches to be used later when the fire gathered strength. And all the while the dog sat and watched him, a certain yearning wistfulness in its eyes, for it looked upon him as the fire-provider, and the fire was slow in coming.

When all was ready, the man reached in his pocket for a second piece of birch-bark. He knew the bark was there, and, though he could not feel it with his fingers, he could hear its crisp rustling as he fumbled for it. Try as he would, he could not clutch hold of it. And all the time, in his consciousness, was the knowledge that each instant his feet were freezing. This thought tended to put him in a panic, but he fought against it and kept calm. He pulled on his mittens with his teeth, and threshed his arms back and forth, beating his hands with all his might against his sides. He did this sitting down, and he stood up to do it; and all the while the dog sat in the snow, its wolf-brush of a tail curled around warmly over its forefeet, its sharp wolf-ears pricked forward intently as it watched the man. And the man, as he beat and threshed with his arms and hands, felt a great surge of envy as he regarded the creature that was warm and secure in its natural covering.

After a time he was aware of the first faraway signals of sensation in his beaten fingers. The faint tingling grew stronger till it evolved into a stinging ache that was excruciating, but which the man hailed with satisfaction. He stripped the mitten from his right hand and fetched forth the birch-bark. The exposed fingers were quickly going numb again.

Next he brought out his bunch of sulphur matches. But the tremendous cold had already driven the life out of his fingers. In his effort to separate one match from the others, the whole bunch fell in the snow. He tried to pick it out of the snow, but failed. The dead fingers could neither touch nor clutch. He was very careful. He drove the thought of his freezing feet, and nose, and cheeks, out of his mind, devoting his whole soul to the matches. He watched, using the sense of vision in place of that of touch, and when he saw his fingers on each side the bunch, he closed them—that is, he willed to close them, for the wires were down, and the fingers did not obey. He pulled the mitten on the right hand, and beat it fiercely against his knee. Then, with both mittened hands, he scooped the bunch of matches, along with much snow, into his lap. Yet he was no better off.

After some manipulation he managed to get the bunch between the heels of his mittened hands. In this fashion he carried it to his mouth. The ice crackled and snapped when by a violent effort he opened his mouth. He drew the lower jaw in, curled the upper lip out of the way, and scraped the bunch with his upper teeth in order to separate a match. He succeeded in getting one, which he dropped on his lap. He was no better off. He could not pick it up. Then he devised a way. He picked it up in his teeth and scratched it on his leg. Twenty times he scratched before he succeeded in lighting it. As it flamed he held it with his teeth to the birch-bark. But the burning brimstone went up his nostrils and into his lungs, causing him to cough spasmodically. The match fell into the snow and went out.

The old-timer on Sulphur Creek was right, he thought in the moment of controlled despair that ensued: after fifty below, a man should travel with a partner. He beat his hands, but failed in exciting any sensation. Suddenly he bared both hands, removing the mittens with his teeth. He caught the whole bunch between the heels of his hands. His arm-muscles not being frozen enabled him to press the hand-heels tightly against the matches. Then he scratched the bunch along his leg. It flared into flame, seventy sulphur matches at once! There was no wind to blow them out. He kept his head to one side to escape the strangling fumes, and held the blazing bunch to the birch-bark. As he so held it, he became aware of sensation in his hand. His flesh was burning. He could smell it. Deep down below the surface he could feel it. The sensation developed into pain that grew acute. And still he endured it, holding the flame of the matches clumsily to the bark that would not light readily because his own burning hands were in the way, absorbing most of the flame.

At last, when he could endure no more, he jerked his hands apart. The blazing matches fell sizzling into the snow, but the birch-bark was alight. He began laying dry grasses and the tiniest twigs on the flame. He could not pick and choose, for he had to lift the fuel between the heels of his hands. Small pieces of rotten wood and green moss clung to the twigs, and he bit them off as well as he could with his teeth. He cherished the flame carefully and awkwardly. It meant life, and it must not perish. The withdrawal of blood from the surface of his body now made him begin to shiver, and he grew more awkward. A large piece of green moss fell squarely on the little fire. He tried to poke it out with his fingers, but his shivering frame made him poke too far, and he disrupted the nucleus of the little fire, the burning grasses and tiny twigs separating and scattering. He tried to poke them together again, but in spite of the tenseness of the effort, his shivering got away with him, and the twigs were hopelessly scattered. Each twig gushed a puff of smoke and went out. The fire-provider had failed. As he looked apathetically about him, his eyes chanced on the dog, sitting across the ruins of the fire from him, in the snow, making restless, hunching movements, slightly lifting one forefoot and then the other, shifting its weight back and forth on them with wistful eagerness.

The sight of the dog put a wild idea into his head. He remembered the tale of the man, caught in a blizzard, who killed a steer and crawled inside the carcass, and so was saved. He would kill the dog and bury his hands in the warm body until the numbness went out of them. Then he could build another fire. He spoke to the dog, calling it to him; but in his voice was a strange note of fear that frightened the animal, who had never known the man to speak in such way before. Something was the matter, and its suspicious nature sensed danger—it knew not what danger, but somewhere, somehow, in its brain arose an apprehension of the man. It flattened its ears down at the sound of the man's voice, and its restless, hunching movements and the liftings and shiftings of its forefeet became more pronounced; but it would not come to the man. He got on his hands and knees and crawled toward the dog. This unusual posture again excited suspicion, and the animal sidled mincingly away.

The man sat up in the snow for a moment and struggled for calmness. Then he pulled on his mittens, by means of his teeth, and got upon his feet. He glanced down at first in order to assure himself that he was really standing up, for the absence of sensation in his feet left him unrelated to the earth. His erect position in itself started to drive the webs of suspicion from the dog's mind; and when he spoke peremptorily, with the sound of whip-lashes in his voice, the dog rendered its customary allegiance and came to him. As it came within reaching distance, the man lost his control. His arms flashed out to the dog, and he experienced genuine surprise when he discovered that his hands could not clutch, that there was neither bend nor feeling in the fingers. He had forgotten for the moment that they were frozen and that they were freezing more and more. All this happened quickly, and before the animal could get away, he encircled its body with his arms. He sat down in the snow, and in this fashion held the dog, while it snarled and whined and struggled.

But it was all he could do, hold its body encircled in his arms and sit there. He realized that he could not kill the dog. There was no way to do it. With his helpless hands he could neither draw nor hold his sheath-knife nor throttle the animal. He released it, and it plunged wildly away, with tail between its legs, and still snarling. It halted forty feet away and surveyed him curiously, with ears sharply pricked forward. The man looked down at his hands in order to locate them, and found them hanging on the ends of his arms. It struck him as curious that one should have to use his eyes in order to find out where his hands were. He began threshing his arms back and forth, beating the mittened hands against his sides. He did this for five minutes, violently, and his heart pumped enough blood up to the surface to put a stop to his shivering. But no sensation was aroused in the hands. He had an impression that they hung like weights on the ends of his arms, but when he tried to run the impression down, he could not find it.

A certain fear of death, dull and oppressive, came to him. This fear quickly became poignant as he realized that it was no longer a mere matter of freezing his fingers and toes, or of losing his hands and feet, but that it was a matter of life and death with the chances against him. This threw him into a panic, and he turned and ran up the creek-bed along the old, dim trail. The dog joined in behind and kept up with him. He ran blindly, without intention, in fear such as he had never known in his life. Slowly, as he ploughed and floundered through the snow, he began to see things again,—the banks of the creek, the old timber-jams, the leafless aspens, and the sky. The running made him feel better. He did not shiver. Maybe, if he ran on, his feet would thaw out; and, anyway, if he ran far enough, he would reach camp and the boys. Without doubt he would lose some fingers and toes and some of his face; but the boys would take care of him, and save the rest of him when he got there. And at the same time there was another thought in his mind that said he would never get to the camp and the boys; that it was too many miles away, that the freezing had too great a start on him, and that he would soon be stiff and dead. This thought he kept in the background and refused to consider. Sometimes it pushed itself forward and demanded to be heard, but he thrust it back and strove to think of other things.

It struck him as curious that he could run at all on feet so frozen that he could not feel them when they struck the earth and took the weight of his body. He seemed to himself to skim along above the surface, and to have no connection with the earth. Somewhere he had once seen a winged Mercury, and he wondered if Mercury felt as he felt when skimming over the earth.

His theory of running until he reached camp and the boys had one flaw in it: he lacked the endurance. Several times he stumbled, and finally he tottered, crumpled up, and fell. When he tried to rise, he failed. He must sit and rest, he decided, and next time he would merely walk and keep on going. As he sat and regained his breath, he noted that he was feeling quite warm and comfortable. He was not shivering, and it even seemed that a warm glow had come to his chest and trunk. And yet, when he touched his nose or cheeks, there was no sensation. Running would not thaw them out. Nor would it thaw out his hands and feet. Then the thought came to him that the frozen portions of his body must be extending. He tried to keep this thought down, to forget it, to think of something else; he was aware of the panicky feeling that it caused, and he was afraid of the panic. But the thought asserted itself, and persisted, until it produced a vision of his body totally frozen. This was too much, and he made another wild run along the trail. Once he slowed down to a walk, but the thought of the freezing extending itself made him run again.

And all the time the dog ran with him, at his heels. When he fell down a second time, it curled its tail over its forefeet and sat in front of him, facing him, curiously eager and intent. The warmth and security of the animal angered him, and he cursed it till it flattened down its ears appeasingly. This time the shivering came more quickly upon the man. He was losing in his battle with the frost. It was creeping into his body from all sides. The thought of it drove him on, but he ran no more than a hundred feet, when he staggered and pitched headlong. It was his last panic. When he had recovered his breath and control, he sat up and entertained in his mind the conception of meeting death with dignity. However, the conception did not come to him in such terms. His idea of it was that he had been making a fool of himself, running around like a chicken with its head cut off—such was the simile that occurred to him. Well, he was bound to freeze anyway, and he might as well take it decently. With this new-found peace of mind came the first glimmerings of drowsiness. A good idea, he thought, to sleep off to death.

It was like taking an anæsthetic. Freezing was not so bad as people thought. There were lots worse ways to die.

He pictured the boys finding his body next day. Suddenly he found himself with them, coming along the trail and looking for himself. And, still with them, he came around a turn in the trail and found himself lying in the snow. He did not belong with himself any more, for even then he was out of himself, standing with the boys and looking at himself in the snow. It certainly was cold, was his thought. When he got back to the States he could tell the folks what real cold was. He drifted on from this to a vision of the old-timer on Sulphur Creek. He could see him quite clearly, warm and comfortable, and smoking a pipe.

"You were right, old hoss; you were right," the man mumbled to the old-timer of Sulphur Creek.

Then the man drowsed off into what seemed to him the most comfortable and satisfying sleep he had ever known. The dog sat facing him and waiting. The brief day drew to a close in a long, slow twilight. There were no signs of a fire to be made, and, besides, never in the dog's experience had it known a man to sit like that in the snow and make no fire. As the twilight drew on, its eager yearning for the fire mastered it, and with a great lifting and shifting of forefeet, it whined softly, then flattened its ears down in anticipation of being chidden by the man. But the man remained silent. Later, the dog whined loudly. And still later it crept close to the man and caught the scent of death. This made the animal bristle and back away. A little longer it delayed, howling under the stars that leaped and danced and shone brightly in the cold sky. Then it turned and trotted up the trail in the direction of the camp it knew, where were the other food-providers and fire-providers.

THE HOUSE OF PRIDE

Percival Ford wondered why he had come. He did not dance. He did not care much for army people. Yet he knew them all—gliding and revolving there on the broad *lanai* of the Seaside, the officers in their fresh-starched uniforms of white, the civilians in white and black, and the women bare of shoulders and arms. After two years in Honolulu the Twentieth was departing to its new station in Alaska, and Percival Ford, as one of the big men of the Islands, could not help knowing the officers and their women.

But between knowing and liking was a vast gulf. The army women frightened him just a little. They were in ways quite different from the women he liked best—the elderly women, the spinsters and the bespectacled maidens, and the very serious women of all ages whom he met on church and library and kindergarten committees, who came meekly to him for contributions and advice. He ruled those women by virtue of his superior mentality, his great wealth, and the high place he occupied in the commercial baronage of Hawaii. And he was not afraid of them in the least. Sex, with them, was not obtrusive. Yes, that was it. There was in them something else, or more, than the assertive grossness of life. He was fastidious; he acknowledged that to himself; and these army women, with their bare shoulders and naked arms, their straight-looking eyes, their vitality and challenging femaleness, jarred upon his sensibilities.

Nor did he get on better with the army men, who took life lightly, drinking and smoking and swearing their way through life and asserting the essential grossness of flesh no less shamelessly than their women. He was always uncomfortable in the company of the army men. They seemed uncomfortable, too. And he felt, always, that they were laughing at him up their sleeves, or pitying him, or tolerating him. Then, too, they seemed, by mere contiguity, to emphasize a lack in him, to call attention to that in them which he did not possess and which he thanked God he did not possess. Faugh! They were like their women!

In fact, Percival Ford was no more a woman's man than he was a man's man. A glance at him told the reason. He had a good constitution, never was on intimate terms with sickness, nor even mild disorders; but he lacked vitality. His was a negative organism. No blood with a ferment in it could have nourished and shaped that long and narrow face, those thin lips, lean cheeks, and the small, sharp eyes. The thatch of hair, dust-colored, straight and sparse, advertised the niggard soil, as did the nose, thin, delicately modeled, and just hinting the suggestion of a beak. His meagre blood had denied him much of life, and permitted him to be an extremist in one thing only, which thing was righteousness. Over right conduct he pondered and agonized, and that he should do right was as necessary to his nature as loving and being loved were necessary to commoner clay.

He was sitting under the algaroba trees between the *lanai* and the beach. His eyes wandered over the dancers and he turned his head away and gazed seaward across the mellow-sounding surf to the Southern Cross burning low on the horizon. He was irritated by the bare shoulders and arms of the women. If he had a daughter he would never permit it, never. But his hypothesis was the sheerest abstraction. The thought process had been accompanied by no inner vision of that daughter. He did not see a daughter with arms and shoulders. Instead, he smiled at the remote contingency of marriage. He was thirty-five, and, having had no personal experience of love, he looked upon it, not as mythical, but as bestial. Anybody could marry. The Japanese and Chinese coolies, toiling on the sugar plantations and in the rice-fields, married. They invariably married at the first opportunity. It was because they were so low in the scale of life. There was nothing else for them to do. They were like the army men and women. But for him there were other and higher things. He was different from them—from all of them. He was proud of how he happened to be. He had come of no petty love-match. He had come of lofty conception of duty and of devotion to a cause. His father had not married for love. Love was a madness that had never perturbed Isaac Ford. When he answered the call to go to the heathen with the message of life, he had had no thought and no desire for marriage. In this they were alike, his father and he. But the Board of Missions was economical. With New England thrift it weighed and measured and decided that married missionaries were less expensive per capita and more efficacious. So the Board commanded Isaac Ford to marry. Furthermore, it furnished him with a wife, another zealous soul with no thought of marriage, intent only on doing the

Lord's work among the heathen. They saw each other for the first time in Boston. The Board brought them together, arranged everything, and by the end of the week they were married and started on the long voyage around the Horn.

Percival Ford was proud that he had come of such a union. He had been born high, and he thought of himself as a spiritual aristocrat. And he was proud of his father. It was a passion with him. The erect, austere figure of Isaac Ford had burned itself upon his pride. On his desk was a miniature of that soldier of the Lord. In his bedroom hung the portrait of Isaac Ford, painted at the time when he had served under the Monarchy as prime minister. Not that Isaac Ford had coveted place and worldly wealth, but that, as prime minister, and, later, as banker, he had been of greater service to the missionary cause. The German crowd, and the English crowd, and all the rest of the trading crowd, had sneered at Isaac Ford as a commercial soul-saver; but he, his son, knew different. When the natives, emerging abruptly from their feudal system, with no conception of the nature and significance of property in land, were letting their broad acres slip through their fingers, it was Isaac Ford who had stepped in between the trading crowd and its prey and taken possession of fat, vast holdings. Small wonder the trading crowd did not like his memory. But he had never looked upon his enormous wealth as his own. He had considered himself God's steward. Out of the revenues he had built schools, and hospitals, and churches. Nor was it his fault that sugar, after the slump, had paid forty per cent; that the bank he founded had prospered into a railroad; and that, among other things, fifty thousand acres of Oahu pasture land, which he had bought for a dollar an acre, grew eight tons of sugar to the acre every eighteen months. No, in all truth Isaac Ford was an heroic figure, fit, so Percival Ford thought privately, to stand beside the statue of Kamehameha I in front of the Judiciary Building. Isaac Ford was gone, but he, his son, carried on the good work at least as inflexibly if not as masterfully.

He turned his eyes back to the *lanai*. What was the difference, he asked himself, between the shameless, grass-girdled *hula* dances and the décolleté dances of the women of his own race? Was there an essential difference? or was it a matter of degree?

As he pondered the problem a hand rested on his shoulder.

"Hello, Ford, what are you doing here? Isn't this a bit festive?"

"I try to be lenient, Dr. Kennedy, even as I look on," Percival Ford answered gravely. "Won't you sit down?"

Dr. Kennedy sat down, clapping his palms sharply. A white-clad Japanese servant answered swiftly.

Scotch and soda was Kennedy's order; then, turning to the other, he said:—

"Of course, I don't ask you."

"But I will take something," Ford said firmly. The doctor's eyes showed surprise, and the servant waited. "Boy, a lemonade, please."

The doctor laughed at it heartily, as a joke on himself, and glanced at the musicians under the hau tree.

"Why, it's the Aloha Orchestra," he said. "I thought they were with the Hawaiian Hotel on Tuesday nights. Some rumpus, I guess."

His eyes paused for a moment and dwelt upon the one who was playing a guitar and singing a Hawaiian song to the accompaniment of all the instruments. His face became grave as he looked at the singer, and it was still grave as he turned it to his companion.

"Look here, Ford, isn't it time you let up on Joe Garland? I understand you are in opposition to the Promotion Committee's sending him to the States on this surf-board proposition, and I've been wanting to speak to you about it. I should have thought you'd be glad to get him out of the country. It would be a good way to end your persecution of him."

"Persecution?" Percival Ford's eyebrows lifted interrogatively.

"Call it by any name you please," Kennedy went on. "You've hounded that poor devil for years. It's not his fault. Even you will admit that."

"Not his fault?" Percival Ford's thin lips drew tightly together for the moment. "Joe Garland is dissolute and idle. He has always been a wastrel, a profligate."

"But that's no reason you should keep on after him the way you do. I've watched you from the beginning. The first thing you did when you returned from college and found him working on the plantation as outside *luna* was to fire him—you with your millions, and he with his sixty dollars a month."

"Not the first thing," Percival Ford said judicially, in the tone he was accustomed to use in committee meetings. "I gave him his warning. The superintendent said he was a capable *luna*. I had no objection to him on that ground. It was what he did outside working hours. He undid my work faster than I could build it up. Of what use were the Sunday schools, the night schools, and the sewing classes, when in the evenings there was Joe Garland with his infernal and eternal tum-tumming of guitar and *ukulele*, his strong drink, and his *hula* dancing? After I warned him, I came upon him—I shall never forget it—came upon him, down at the cabins. It was evening. I could hear the *hula* songs before I saw the scene. And when I did see it, there were the girls, shameless in the moonlight and dancing—the girls upon whom I had worked to teach clean living and right conduct. And there were three girls there, I remember, just graduated from the mission school. Of course I discharged Joe Garland. I know it was the same at Hilo. People said I went out of my way when I persuaded Mason and Fitch to discharge him. But it was the missionaries who requested me to do so. He was undoing their work by his reprehensible example."

"Afterwards, when he got on the railroad, your railroad, he was discharged without cause," Kennedy challenged.

"Not so," was the quick answer. "I had him into my private office and talked with him for half an hour."

"You discharged him for inefficiency?"

"For immoral living, if you please."

Dr. Kennedy laughed with a grating sound. "Who the devil gave it to you to be judge and jury? Does landlordism give you control of the immortal souls of those that toil for you? I have been your physician. Am I to expect to-morrow your ukase that I give up Scotch and soda or your patronage? Bah! Ford, you take life too seriously. Besides, when Joe got into that smuggling scrape (he wasn't in your employ, either), and he sent word to you, asked you to pay his fine, you left him to do his six months hard labor on the reef. Don't forget, you left Joe Garland in the lurch that time. You threw him down, hard; and yet I remember the first day you came to school—we boarded, you were only a day scholar—you had to be initiated. Three times under in the swimming tank—you remember, it was the regular dose every new boy got. And you held back. You denied that you could swim. You were frightened, hysterical—"

"Yes, I know," Percival Ford said slowly. "I was frightened. And it was a lie, for I could swim. . . . And I was frightened."

"And you remember who fought for you? who lied for you harder than you could lie and swore he knew you couldn't swim? Who jumped into the tank and pulled you out after the first under and was nearly drowned for it by the other boys, who had discovered by that time that you *could* swim?"

"Of course I know," the other rejoined coldly. "But a generous act as a boy does not excuse a lifetime of wrong living."

"He has never done wrong to you?—personally and directly, I mean?"

"No," was Percival Ford's answer. "That is what makes my position impregnable. I have no personal spite against him. He is bad, that is all. His life is bad—"

"Which is another way of saying that he does not agree with you in the way life should be lived," the doctor interrupted.

"Have it that way. It is immaterial. He is an idler—"

"With reason," was the interruption, "considering the jobs out of which you have knocked him."

"He is immoral—"

"Oh, hold on now, Ford. Don't go harping on that. You are pure New England stock. Joe Garland is half Kanaka. Your blood is thin. His is warm. Life is one thing to you, another thing to him. He laughs and sings and dances through life, genial, unselfish, childlike, everybody's friend. You go through life like a perambulating prayer-wheel, a friend of nobody but the righteous, and the righteous are those who agree with you as to what is right. And after all, who shall say? You live like an anchorite. Joe Garland lives like a good fellow. Who has extracted the most from life? We are paid to live, you know. When the wages are too meagre we throw up the job, which is the cause, believe me, of all rational suicide. Joe Garland would starve to death on the wages you get from life. You see, he is made differently. So would you starve on his wages, which are singing, and love—"

"Lust, if you will pardon me," was the interruption.

Dr. Kennedy smiled.

"Love, to you, is a word of four letters and a definition which you have extracted from the dictionary. But love, real love, dewy and palpitant and tender, you do not know. If God made you and me, and men and women, believe me he made love, too. But to come back. It's about time you quit hounding Joe Garland. It is not worthy of you, and it is cowardly. The thing for you to do is to reach out and lend him a hand."

"Why I, any more than you?" the other demanded. "Why don't you reach him a hand?"

"I have. I'm reaching him a hand now. I'm trying to get you not to down the Promotion Committee's proposition of sending him away. I got him the job at Hilo with Mason and Fitch. I've got him half a dozen jobs, out of every one of which you drove him. But never mind that. Don't forget one thing—and a little frankness won't hurt you—it is not fair play to saddle another's fault on Joe Garland; and you know that you, least of all, are the man to do it. Why, man, it's not good taste. It's positively indecent."

"Now I don't follow you," Percival Ford answered. "You're up in the air with some obscure scientific theory of heredity and personal irresponsibility. But how any theory can hold Joe Garland irresponsible for his wrongdoings and at the same time hold me personally responsible for them—more responsible than any one else, including Joe Garland—is beyond me."

"It's a matter of delicacy, I suppose, or of taste, that prevents you from following me," Dr. Kennedy snapped out. "It's all very well, for the sake of society, tacitly to ignore some things, but you do more than tacitly ignore."

"What is it, pray, that I tacitly ignore!"

Dr. Kennedy was angry. A deeper red than that of constitutional Scotch and soda suffused his face, as he answered:

"Your father's son."

"Now just what do you mean?"

"Damn it, man, you can't ask me to be plainer spoken than that. But if you will, all right—Isaac's Ford's son—Joe Garland—your brother."

Percival Ford sat quietly, an annoyed and shocked expression on his face. Kennedy looked at him curiously, then, as the slow minutes dragged by, became embarrassed and frightened.

"My God!" he cried finally, "you don't mean to tell me that you didn't know!"

As in answer, Percival Ford's cheeks turned slowly gray.

"It's a ghastly joke," he said; "a ghastly joke."

The doctor had got himself in hand.

"Everybody knows it," he said. "I thought you knew it. And since you don't know it, it's time you did, and I'm glad of the chance of setting you straight. Joe Garland and you are brothers—half-brothers."

"It's a lie," Ford cried. "You don't mean it. Joe Garland's mother was Eliza Kunilio." (Dr. Kennedy nodded.) "I remember her well, with her duck pond and *taro* patch. His father was Joseph Garland, the beach-comber." (Dr. Kennedy shook his head.) "He died only two or three years ago. He used to get drunk. There's where Joe got his dissolute-ness. There's the heredity for you."

"And nobody told you," Kennedy said wonderingly, after a pause.

"Dr. Kennedy, you have said something terrible, which I cannot al-low to pass. You must either prove or, or . . ."

"Prove it yourself. Turn around and look at him. You've got him in profile. Look at his nose. That's Isaac Ford's. Yours is a thin edition of it. That's right. Look. The lines are fuller, but they are all there."

Percival Ford looked at the Kanaka half-breed who played under the *hau* tree, and it seemed, as by some illumination, that he was gazing on a wraith of himself. Feature after feature flashed up an unmistakable resemblance. Or, rather, it was he who was the wraith of that other full-muscled and generously moulded man. And his features, and that other man's features, were all reminiscent of Isaac Ford. And nobody had told him. Every line of Isaac Ford's face he knew. Miniatures, portraits, and photographs of his father were passing in review through his mind, and here and there, over and again, in the face before him, he caught resemblances and vague hints of likeness. It was devil's work that could reproduce the austere features of Isaac Ford in the loose and sensuous features before him. Once, the man turned, and for one flashing instant it seemed to Percival Ford that he saw his father, dead and gone, peering at him out of the face of Joe Garland.

"It's nothing at all," he could faintly hear Dr. Kennedy saying. "They were all mixed up in the old days. You know that. You've seen it all your life. Sailors married queens and begat princesses and all the rest of it. It was the usual thing in the Islands."

"But not with my father," Percival Ford interrupted.

"There you are." Kennedy shrugged his shoulders. "Cosmic sap and smoke of life. Old Isaac Ford was straightlaced and all the rest, and I know there's no explaining it, least of all to himself. He understood it no more than you do. Smoke of life, that's all. And don't forget one thing, Ford. There was a dab of unruly blood in old Isaac Ford, and Joe Garland inherited it—all of it, smoke of life and cosmic sap; while you inherited all of old Isaac's ascetic blood. And just because your blood is cold, well-ordered, and well-disciplined, is no reason that you should frown upon Joe Garland. When Joe Garland undoes the work you do, remember that it is only old Isaac Ford on both sides, undoing with one hand what he does with the other. You are Isaac Ford's right hand, let us say; Joe Garland is his left hand."

Percival Ford made no answer, and in the silence Dr. Kennedy finished his forgotten Scotch and soda. From across the grounds an automobile hooted imperatively.

"There's the machine," Dr. Kennedy said, rising. "I've got to run. I'm sorry I've shaken you up, and at the same time I'm glad. And know one thing, Isaac Ford's dab of unruly blood was remarkably small, and Joe Garland got it all. And one other thing. If your father's left hand offend you, don't smite it off. Besides, Joe is all right. Frankly, if I could choose between you and him to live with me on a desert isle, I'd choose Joe."

Little bare-legged children ran about him, playing, on the grass; but Percival Ford did not see them. He was gazing steadily at the singer under the *hau* tree. He even changed his position once, to get closer. The clerk of the Seaside went by, limping with age and dragging his reluctant feet. He had lived forty years on the Islands. Percival Ford beckoned to him, and the clerk came respectfully, and wondering that he should be noticed by Percival Ford.

"John," Ford said, "I want you to give me some information. Won't you sit down?"

The clerk sat down awkwardly, stunned by the unexpected honor. He blinked at the other and mumbled, "Yes, sir, thank you."

"John, who is Joe Garland?"

The clerk stared at him, blinked, cleared his throat, and said nothing.

"Go on," Percival Ford commanded. "Who is he?"

"You're joking me, sir," the other managed to articulate.

"I spoke to you seriously."

The clerk recoiled from him.

"You don't mean to say you don't know?" he questioned, his question in itself the answer.

"I want to know."

"Why, he's—" John broke off and looked about him helplessly. "Hadn't you better ask somebody else? Everybody thought you knew. We always thought . . ."

"Yes, go ahead."

"We always thought that that was why you had it in for him."

Photographs and miniatures of Isaac Ford were trooping through his son's brain, and ghosts of Isaac Ford seemed in the air about him. "I wish you good night, sir," he could hear the clerk saying, and he saw him beginning to limp away.

"John," he called abruptly.

John came back and stood near him, blinking and nervously moistening his lips.

"You haven't told me yet, you know."

"Oh, about Joe Garland?"

"Yes, about Joe Garland. Who is he?"

"He's your brother, sir, if I say it who shouldn't."

"Thank you, John. Good night."

"And you didn't know?" the old man queried, content to linger, now that the crucial point was past.

"Thank you, John. Good night," was the response.

"Yes, sir, thank you, sir. I think it's going to rain. Good night, sir."

Out of a clear sky, filled only with stars and moonlight, fell a rain so fine and attenuated as to resemble a vapor spray. Nobody minded it; the children played on, running bare-legged over the grass and leaping into the sand; and in a few minutes it was gone. In the southeast, Diamond Head, a black blot, sharply defined, silhouetted its crater-form against the stars. At sleepy intervals the surf flung its foam across the sand to the grass, and far out could be seen the black specks of swimmers under the moon. The voices of the singers, singing a waltz, died away; and in the silence, from somewhere under the trees, arose the laugh of a woman that was a love-cry. It startled Percival Ford, and it reminded him of Dr. Kennedy's phrase. Down by the outrigger canoes, where they lay hauled out on the sand, he saw men and women, Kanakas, reclining languorously, like lotus-eaters, the women in white *holokus;* and against one such *holoku* he saw the dark head of the steersman of the canoe resting upon the woman's shoulder. Farther down, where the strip of sand widened at the entrance to the lagoon, he saw a man and woman walking side by side. As they drew near the light *lanai,* he saw the woman's hand go down to her waist and disengage a girdling arm. And as they passed him, Percival Ford nodded to a captain he knew, and to a major's daughter. Smoke of life, that was it, an ample phrase. And again, from under the dark algaroba tree arose the laugh of a woman that was a love-cry; and past his chair, on the way to bed, a bare-legged youngster was led by a chiding Japanese nurse-maid. The voices of the singers broke softly and meltingly into an Hawaiian love song, and officers and women, with encircling arms, were gliding and whirling on the *lanai;* and once again the woman laughed under the algaroba trees.

And Percival Ford knew only disapproval of it all. He was irritated by the love-laugh of the woman, by the steersman with pillowed head on the white *holoku,* by the couples that walked on the beach, by the officers and women that danced, and by the voices of the singers singing of love, and his brother singing there with them under the *hau* tree. The woman that laughed especially irritated him. A curious train of thought was aroused. He was Isaac Ford's son, and what had happened with Isaac Ford might happen with him. He felt in his cheeks the faint heat of a blush at the thought, and experienced a poignant sense of shame. He was appalled by what was in his blood. It was like learning suddenly that his father had been a leper and that his own blood might bear the taint of that dread disease. Isaac Ford, the austere soldier of the Lord— the old hypocrite! What difference between him and any beach-comber? The house of pride that Percival Ford had builded was tumbling about his ears.

The hours passed, the army people laughed and danced, the native orchestra played on, and Percival Ford wrestled with the abrupt and overwhelming problem that had been thrust upon him. He prayed quietly, his elbow on the table, his head bowed upon his hand, with all the appearance of any tired onlooker. Between the dances the army men and women and the civilians fluttered up to him and buzzed conventionally, and when they went back to the *lanai* he took up his wrestling where he had left it off.

He began to patch together his shattered ideal of Isaac Ford, and for cement he used a cunning and subtle logic. It was of the sort that is compounded in the brain laboratories of egotists, and it worked. It was incontrovertible that his father had been made of finer clay than those about him; but still, old Isaac had been only in the process of becoming, while he, Percival Ford, had become. As proof of it, he rehabilitated his father and at the same time exalted himself. His lean little ego waxed to colossal proportions. He was great enough to forgive. He glowed at the thought of it. Isaac Ford had been great, but he was greater, for he could forgive Isaac Ford and even restore him to the holy place in his memory, though the place was not quite so holy as it had been. Also, he applauded Isaac Ford for having ignored the outcome of his one step aside. Very well, he, too, would ignore it.

The dance was breaking up. The orchestra had finished "Aloha Oe" and was preparing to go home. Percival Ford clapped his hands for the Japanese servant.

"You tell that man I want to see him," he said, pointing out Joe Garland. "Tell him come here, now."

Joe Garland approached and halted respectfully several paces away, nervously fingering the guitar which he still carried. The other did not ask him to sit down.

"You are my brother," he said.

"Why, everybody knows that," was the reply, in tones of wonderment.

"Yes, so I understand," Percival Ford said dryly. "But I did not know it till this evening."

The half-brother waited uncomfortably in the silence that followed, during which Percival Ford coolly considered his next utterance.

"You remember that first time I came to school and the boys ducked me?" he asked. "Why did you take my part."

The half-brother smiled bashfully.

"Because you knew?"

"Yes, that was why."

"But I didn't know," Percival Ford said in the same dry fashion.

"Yes," the other said.

Another silence fell. Servants were beginning to put out the lights on the *lanai*.

"You know ... now," the half-brother said simply.

Percival Ford frowned. Then he looked the other over with a considering eye.

"How much will you take to leave the Islands and never come back?" he demanded.

"And never come back?" Joe Garland faltered. "It is the only land I know. Other lands are cold. I do not know other lands. I have many friends here. In other lands there would not be one voice to say, '*Aloha*, Joe, my boy.'"

"I said never to come back," Percival Ford reiterated. "The *Alameda* sails to-morrow for San Francisco."

Joe Garland was bewildered.

"But why?" he asked. "You know now that we are brothers."

"That is why," was the retort. "As you said yourself, everybody knows. I will make it worth your while."

All awkwardness and embarrassment disappeared from Joe Garland. Birth and station were bridged and reversed.

"You want me to go?" he demanded.

"I want you to go and never to come back," Percival Ford answered.

And in that moment, flashing and fleeting, it was given him to see his brother tower above him like a mountain, and to feel himself dwindle and dwarf to microscopic insignificance. But it is not well for one to see himself truly, nor can one so see himself for long and live; and only for that flashing moment did Percival Ford see himself and his brother in true perspective. The next moment he was mastered by his meagre and insatiable ego.

"As I said, I will make it worth your while. You will not suffer. I will pay you well."

"All right," Joe Garland said. "I'll go."

He started to turn away.

"Joe," the other called. "You see my lawyer to-morrow morning. Five hundred down and two hundred a month as long as you stay away."

"You are very kind," Joe Garland answered softly. "You are too kind. And anyway, I guess I don't want your money. I go to-morrow on the *Alameda*."

He walked away, but did not say good-by.

Percival Ford clapped his hands.

"Boy," he said to the Japanese, "a lemonade."

And over the lemonade he smiled long and contentedly to himself.

THE HOUSE OF MAPUHI

Despite the heavy clumsiness of her lines, the *Aorai* handled easily in the light breeze, and her captain ran her well in before he hove to just outside the suck of the surf. The atoll of Hikueru lay low on the water, a circle of pounded coral sand a hundred yards wide, twenty miles in circumference, and from three to five feet above high-water mark. On the bottom of the huge and glassy lagoon was much pearl shell, and from the deck of the schooner, across the slender ring of the atoll, the divers could be seen at work. But the lagoon had no entrance for even a trading schooner. With a favoring breeze cutters could win in through the tortuous and shallow channel, but the schooners lay off and on outside and sent in their small boats.

The *Aorai* swung out a boat smartly, into which sprang half a dozen brown-skinned sailors clad only in scarlet loincloths. They took the oars, while in the stern-sheets, at the steering sweep, stood a young man garbed in the tropic white that marks the European. But he was not all European. The golden strain of Polynesia betrayed itself in the sun-gilt of his fair skin and cast up golden sheens and lights through the glimmering blue of his eyes. Raoul he was, Alexandré Raoul, youngest son of Marie Raoul, the wealthy quarter-caste, who owned and managed half a dozen trading schooners similar to the *Aorai*. Across an eddy just outside the entrance, and in and through and over a boiling tide-rip, the boat fought its way to the mirrored calm of the lagoon. Young Raoul leaped out upon the white sand and shook hands with a tall native. The man's chest and shoulders were magnificent, but the stump of a right arm, beyond the flesh of which the age-whitened bone projected several inches, attested the encounter with a shark that had put an end to his diving days and made him a fawner and an intriguer for small favors.

"Have you heard, Alec?" were his first words. "Mapuhi has found a

pearl—such a pearl. Never was there one like it ever fished up in Hikueru, nor in all the Paumotus, nor in all the world. Buy it from him. He
has it now. And remember that I told you first. He is a fool and you
can get it cheap. Have you any tobacco?"

Straight up the beach to a shack under a pandanus-tree Raoul headed.
He was his mother's supercargo, and his business was to comb all the
Paumotus for the wealth of copra, shell, and pearls that they yielded up.

He was a young supercargo, it was his second voyage in such capacity, and he suffered much secret worry from his lack of experience in
pricing pearls. But when Mapuhi exposed the pearl to his sight he managed to suppress the startle it gave him, and to maintain a careless,
commercial expression on his face. For the pearl had struck him a blow.
It was large as a pigeon egg, a perfect sphere, of a whiteness that reflected opalescent lights from all colors about it. It was alive. Never had
he seen anything like it. When Mapuhi dropped it into his hand he was
surprised by the weight of it. That showed that it was a good pearl. He
examined it closely, through a pocket magnifying-glass. It was without
flaw or blemish. The purity of it seemed almost to melt into the atmosphere out of his hand. In the shade it was softly luminous, gleaming
like a tender moon. So translucently white was it, that when he dropped
it into a glass of water he had difficulty in finding it. So straight and
swiftly had it sunk to the bottom that he knew its weight was excellent.

"Well, what do you want for it?" he asked, with a fine assumption of
nonchalance.

"I want—" Mapuhi began, and behind him, framing his own dark
face, the dark faces of two women and a girl nodded concurrence in
what he wanted. Their heads were bent forward, they were animated
by a suppressed eagerness, their eyes flashed avariciously.

"I want a house," Mapuhi went on. "It must have a roof of galvanized
iron and an octagon-drop-clock. It must be six fathoms long with a
porch all around. A big room must be in the centre, with a round table
in the middle of it and the octagon-drop-clock on the wall. There must
be four bedrooms, two on each side of the big room, and in each bedroom must be an iron bed, two chairs, and a wash-stand. And back of
the house must be a kitchen, a good kitchen, with pots and pans and a
stove. And you must build the house on my island, which is Fakarava."

"Is that all?" Raoul asked incredulously.

"There must be a sewing-machine," spoke up Tefara, Mapuhi's wife.

"Not forgetting the octagon-drop-clock," added Nauri, Mapuhi's
mother.

"Yes, that is all," said Mapuhi.

Young Raoul laughed. He laughed long and heartily. But while he laughed he secretly performed problems in mental arithmetic. He had never built a house in his life, and his notions concerning house building were hazy. While he laughed, he calculated the cost of the voyage to Tahiti for materials, of the materials themselves, of the voyage back again to Fakarava, and the cost of landing the materials and of building the house. It would come to four thousand French dollars, allowing a margin for safety—four thousand French dollars were equivalent to twenty thousand francs. It was impossible. How was he to know the value of such a pearl? Twenty thousand francs was a lot of money—and of his mother's money at that.

"Mapuhi," he said, "you are a big fool. Set a money price."

But Mapuhi shook his head, and the three heads behind him shook with his.

"I want the house," he said. "It must be six fathoms long with a porch all around—"

"Yes, yes," Raoul interrupted. "I know all about your house, but it won't do. I'll give you a thousand Chili dollars."

The four heads chorused a silent negative.

"And a hundred Chili dollars in trade."

"I want the house," Mapuhi began.

"What good will the house do you?" Raoul demanded. "The first hurricane that comes along will wash it away. You ought to know. Captain Raffy says it looks like a hurricane right now."

"Not on Fakarava," said Mapuhi. "The land is much higher there. On this island, yes. Any hurricane can sweep Hikueru. I will have the house on Fakarava. It must be six fathoms long with a porch all around—"

And Raoul listened again to the tale of the house. Several hours he spent in the endeavor to hammer the house-obsession out of Mapuhi's mind; but Mapuhi's mother and wife, and Ngakura, Mapuhi's daughter, bolstered him in his resolve for the house. Through the open doorway, while he listened for the twentieth time to the detailed description of the house that was wanted, Raoul saw his schooner's second boat draw up on the beach. The sailors rested on the oars, advertising haste to be gone. The first mate of the *Aorai* sprang ashore, exchanged a word with the one-armed native, then hurried toward Raoul. The day grew suddenly dark, as a squall obscured the face of the sun. Across the lagoon Raoul could see approaching the ominous line of the puff of wind.

"Captain Raffy says you've got to get to hell outa here," was the mate's greeting. "If there's any shell, we've got to run the risk of picking it up later on—so he says. The barometer's dropped to twenty-nine-seventy."

The gust of wind struck the pandanus-tree overhead and tore through the palms beyond, flinging half a dozen ripe cocoanuts with heavy thuds to the ground. Then came the rain out of the distance, advancing with the roar of a gale of wind and causing the water of the lagoon to smoke in driven windrows. The sharp rattle of the first drops was on the leaves when Raoul sprang to his feet.

"A thousand Chili dollars, cash down, Mapuhi," he said. "And two hundred Chili dollars in trade."

"I want a house—" the other began.

"Mapuhi!" Raoul yelled, in order to make himself heard. "You are a fool!"

He flung out of the house, and, side by side with the mate, fought his way down the beach toward the boat. They could not see the boat. The tropic rain sheeted about them so that they could see only the beach under their feet and the spiteful little waves from the lagoon that snapped and bit at the sand. A figure appeared through the deluge. It was Huru-Huru, the man with the one arm.

"Did you get the pearl?" he yelled in Raoul's ear.

"Mapuhi is a fool!" was the answering yell, and the next moment they were lost to each other in the descending water.

Half an hour later, Huru-Huru, watching from the seaward side of the atoll, saw the two boats hoisted in and the *Aorai* pointing her nose out to sea. And near her, just come in from the sea on the wings of the squall, he saw another schooner hove to and dropping a boat into the water. He knew her. It was the *Orohena*, owned by Toriki, the half-caste trader, who served as his own supercargo and who doubtlessly was even then in the stern-sheets of the boat. Huru-Huru chuckled. He knew that Mapuhi owed Toriki for trade-goods advanced the year before.

The squall had passed. The hot sun was blazing down, and the lagoon was once more a mirror. But the air was sticky like mucilage, and the weight of it seemed to burden the lungs and make breathing difficult.

"Have you heard the news, Toriki?" Huru-Huru asked. "Mapuhi has found a pearl. Never was there a pearl like it ever fished up in Hikueru, nor anywhere in the Paumotus, nor anywhere in all the world. Mapuhi is a fool. Besides, he owes you money. Remember that I told you first. Have you any tobacco?"

And to the grass-shack of Mapuhi went Toriki. He was a masterful man, withal a fairly stupid one. Carelessly he glanced at the wonderful pearl—glanced for a moment only; and carelessly he dropped it into his pocket.

"You are lucky," he said. "It is a nice pearl. I will give you credit on the books."

"I want a house," Mapuhi began, in consternation. "It must be six fathoms—"

"Six fathoms your grandmother!" was the trader's retort. "You want to pay up your debts, that's what you want. You owed me twelve hundred dollars Chili. Very well; you owe them no longer. The amount is squared. Besides, I will give you credit for two hundred Chili. If, when I get to Tahiti, the pearl sells well, I will give you credit for another hundred—that will make three hundred. But mind, only if the pearl sells well. I may even lose money on it."

Mapuhi folded his arms in sorrow and sat with bowed head. He had been robbed of his pearl. In place of the house, he had paid a debt. There was nothing to show for the pearl.

"You are a fool," said Tefara.

"You are a fool," said Nauri, his mother. "Why did you let the pearl into his hand?"

"What was I to do?" Mapuhi protested. "I owed him the money. He knew I had the pearl. You heard him yourself ask to see it. I had not told him. He knew. Somebody else told him. And I owed him the money."

"Mapuhi is a fool," mimicked Ngakura.

She was twelve years old and did not know any better. Mapuhi relieved his feelings by sending her reeling from a box on the ear; while Tefara and Nauri burst into tears and continued to upbraid him after the manner of women.

Huru-Huru, watching on the beach, saw a third schooner that he knew heave to outside the entrance and drop a boat. It was the *Hira,* well named, for she was owned by Levy, the German Jew, the greatest pearl-buyer of them all, and, as was well known, Hira was the Tahitian god of fishermen and thieves.

"Have you heard the news?" Huru-Huru asked, as Levy, a fat man with massive asymmetrical features, stepped out upon the beach. "Mapuhi has found a pearl. There was never a pearl like it in Hikueru, in all the Paumotus, in all the world. Mapuhi is a fool. He has sold it to Toriki for fourteen hundred Chili—I listened outside and heard. Toriki is likewise a fool. You can buy it from him cheap. Remember that I told you first. Have you any tobacco?"

"Where is Toriki?"

"In the house of Captain Lynch, drinking absinthe. He has been there an hour."

And while Levy and Toriki drank absinthe and chaffered over the pearl, Huru-Huru listened and heard the stupendous price of twenty-five thousand francs agreed upon.

It was at this time that both the *Orohena* and the *Hira*, running in close to the shore, began firing guns and signalling frantically. The three men stepped outside in time to see the two schooners go hastily about and head off shore, dropping mainsails and flying-jibs on the run in the teeth of the squall that heeled them far over on the whitened water. Then the rain blotted them out.

"They'll be back after it's over," said Toriki. "We'd better be getting out of here."

"I reckon the glass has fallen some more," said Captain Lynch.

He was a white-bearded sea-captain, too old for service, who had learned that the only way to live on comfortable terms with his asthma was on Hikueru. He went inside to look at the barometer.

"Great God!" they heard him exclaim, and rushed in to join him at staring at a dial, which marked twenty-nine-twenty.

Again they came out, this time anxiously to consult sea and sky. The squall had cleared away, but the sky remained overcast. The two schooners, under all sail and joined by a third, could be seen making back. A veer in the wind induced them to slack off sheets, and five minutes afterward a sudden veer from the opposite quarter caught all three schooners aback, and those on shore could see the boom-tackles being slacked away or cast off on the jump. The sound of the surf was loud, hollow, and menacing, and a heavy swell was setting in. A terrible sheet of lightning burst before their eyes, illuminating the dark day, and the thunder rolled wildly about them.

Toriki and Levy broke into a run for their boats, the latter ambling along like a panic-stricken hippopotamus. As their two boats swept out the entrance, they passed the boat of the *Aorai* coming in. In the stern-sheets, encouraging the rowers, was Raoul. Unable to shake the vision of the pearl from his mind, he was returning to accept Mapuhi's price of a house.

He landed on the beach in the midst of a driving thunder squall that was so dense that he collided with Huru-Huru before he saw him.

"Too late," yelled Huru-Huru. "Mapuhi sold it to Toriki for fourteen hundred Chili, and Toriki sold it to Levy for twenty-five thousand francs. And Levy will sell it in France for a hundred thousand francs. Have you any tobacco?"

Raoul felt relieved. His troubles about the pearl were over. He need not worry any more, even if he had not got the pearl. But he did not believe Huru-Huru. Mapuhi might well have sold it for fourteen hundred Chili, but that Levy, who knew pearls, should have paid twenty-five thousand francs was too wide a stretch. Raoul decided to interview Captain Lynch on the subject, but when he arrived at that ancient mariner's house, he found him looking wide-eyed at the barometer.

"What do you read it?" Captain Lynch asked anxiously, rubbing his spectacles and staring again at the instrument.

"Twenty-nine-ten," said Raoul. "I have never seen it so low before."

"I should say not!" snorted the captain. "Fifty years boy and man on all the seas, and I've never seen it go down to that. Listen!"

They stood for a moment, while the surf rumbled and shook the house. Then they went outside. The squall had passed. They could see the *Aorai* lying becalmed a mile away and pitching and tossing madly in the tremendous seas that rolled in stately procession down out of the northeast and flung themselves furiously upon the coral shore. One of the sailors from the boat pointed at the mouth of the passage and shook his head. Raoul looked and saw a white anarchy of foam and surge.

"I guess I'll stay with you to-night, Captain," he said; then turned to the sailor and told him to haul the boat out and to find shelter for himself and fellows.

"Twenty-nine flat," Captain Lynch reported, coming out from another look at the barometer, a chair in his hand.

He sat down and stared at the spectacle of the sea. The sun came out, increasing the sultriness of the day, while the dead calm still held. The seas continued to increase in magnitude.

"What makes that sea is what gets me," Raoul muttered petulantly. "There is no wind, yet look at it, look at that fellow there!"

Miles in length, carrying tens of thousands of tons in weight, its impact shook the frail atoll like an earthquake. Captain Lynch was startled.

"Gracious!" he exclaimed, half-rising from his chair, then sinking back.

"But there is no wind," Raoul persisted. "I could understand it if there was wind along with it."

"You'll get the wind soon enough without worryin' for it," was the grim reply.

The two men sat on in silence. The sweat stood out on their skin in myriads of tiny drops that ran together, forming blotches of moisture, which, in turn, coalesced into rivulets that dripped to the ground. They panted for breath, the old man's efforts being especially painful. A sea swept up the beach, licking around the trunks of the cocoanuts and subsiding almost at their feet.

"'Way past high-water mark," Captain Lynch remarked; "and I've been here eleven years." He looked at his watch. "It is three o'clock."

A man and woman, at their heels a motley following of brats and curs, trailed disconsolately by. They came to a halt beyond the house, and, after much irresolution, sat down in the sand. A few minutes later another family trailed in from the opposite direction, the men and women carrying a heterogeneous assortment of possessions. And soon several hundred persons of all ages and sexes were congregated about the captain's dwelling. He called to one new arrival, a woman with a nursing babe in her arms, and in answer received the information that her house had just been swept into the lagoon.

This was the highest spot of land in miles, and already, in many places on either hand, the great seas were making a clean breach of the slender ring of the atoll and surging into the lagoon. Twenty miles around stretched the ring of the atoll, and in no place was it more than fifty fathoms wide. It was the height of the diving season, and from all the islands around, even as far as Tahiti, the natives had gathered.

"There are twelve hundred men, women, and children here," said Captain Lynch. "I wonder how many will be here to-morrow morning."

"But why don't it blow?—that's what I want to know," Raoul demanded.

"Don't worry, young man, don't worry; you'll get your troubles fast enough."

Even as Captain Lynch spoke, a great watery mass smote the atoll. The sea-water churned about them three inches deep under their chairs. A low wail of fear went up from the many women. The children with clasped hands stared at the immense rollers and cried piteously. Chickens and cats, wading perturbedly in the water, as by common consent, with flight and scramble took refuge on the roof of the captain's house. A Paumotan, with a litter of new-born puppies in a basket, climbed into a cocoanut tree and twenty feet above the ground made the basket fast. The mother floundered about in the water beneath, whining and yelping.

And still the sun shone brightly and the dead calm continued. They sat and watched the seas and the insane pitching of the *Aorai.* Captain Lynch gazed at the huge mountains of water sweeping in until he could gaze no more. He covered his face with his hands to shut out the sight; then went into the house.

"Twenty-eight-sixty," he said quietly when he returned.

In his arm was a coil of small rope. He cut it into two-fathom lengths, giving one to Raoul and, retaining one for himself, distributed the remainder among the women with the advice to pick out a tree and climb.

A light air began to blow out of the northeast, and the fan of it on his cheek seemed to cheer Raoul up. He could see the *Aorai* trimming her sheets and heading off shore, and he regretted that he was not on her. She would get away at any rate, but as for the atoll— A sea breached across, almost sweeping him off his feet, and he selected a tree. Then he remembered the barometer and ran back to the house. He encountered Captain Lynch on the same errand and together they went in.

"Twenty-eight-twenty," said the old mariner. "It's going to be fair hell around here—what was that?"

The air seemed filled with the rush of something. The house quivered and vibrated, and they heard the thrumming of a mighty note of sound. The windows rattled. Two panes crashed; a draught of wind tore in, striking them and making them stagger. The door opposite banged shut, shattering the latch. The white doorknob crumbled in fragments to the floor. The room's walls bulged like a gas balloon in the process of sudden inflation. Then came a new sound like the rattle of musketry, as the spray from a sea struck the wall of the house. Captain Lynch looked at his watch. It was four o'clock. He put on a coat of pilot cloth, unhooked the barometer, and stowed it away in a capacious pocket. Again a sea struck the house, with a heavy thud, and the light building tilted, twisted quarter-around on its foundation, and sank down, its floor at an angle of ten degrees.

Raoul went out first. The wind caught him and whirled him away. He noted that it had hauled around to the east. With a great effort he threw himself on the sand, crouching and holding his own. Captain Lynch, driven like a wisp of straw, sprawled over him. Two of the *Aorai's* sailors, leaving a cocoanut tree to which they had been clinging, came to their aid, leaning against the wind at impossible angles and fighting and clawing every inch of the way.

The old man's joints were stiff and he could not climb, so the sailors, by means of short ends of rope tied together, hoisted him up the trunk, a few feet at a time, till they could make him fast, at the top of the tree, fifty feet from the ground. Raoul passed his length of rope around the base of an adjacent tree and stood looking on. The wind was frightful. He had never dreamed it could blow so hard. A sea breached across the atoll, wetting him to the knees ere it subsided into the lagoon. The sun had disappeared, and a lead-colored twilight settled down. A few drops of rain, driving horizontally, struck him. The impact was like that of leaden pellets. A splash of salt spray struck his face. It was like the slap of a man's hand. His cheeks stung, and involuntary tears of pain were in his smarting eyes. Several hundred natives had taken to the trees, and he could have laughed at the bunches of human fruit clustering in the tops. Then, being Tahitian-born, he doubled his body at the waist, clasped the trunk of his tree with his hands, pressed the soles of his feet against the near surface of the trunk, and began to walk up the tree. At the top he found two women, two children, and a man. One little girl clasped a house-cat in her arms.

From his eyrie he waved his hand to Captain Lynch, and that doughty patriarch waved back. Raoul was appalled at the sky. It had approached much nearer—in fact, it seemed just over his head; and it had turned from lead to black. Many people were still on the ground grouped about the bases of the trees and holding on. Several such clusters were praying, and in one the Mormon missionary was exhorting. A weird sound, rhythmical, faint as the faintest chirp of a far cricket, enduring but for a moment, but in that moment suggesting to him vaguely the thought of heaven and celestial music, came to his ear. He glanced about him and saw, at the base of another tree, a large cluster of people holding on by ropes and by one another. He could see their faces working and their lips moving in unison. No sound came to him, but he knew that they were singing hymns.

Still the wind continued to blow harder. By no conscious process could he measure it, for it had long since passed beyond all his experience of wind; but he knew somehow, nevertheless, that it was blowing harder. Not far away a tree was uprooted, flinging its load of human beings to the ground. A sea washed across the strip of sand, and they were gone. Things were happening quickly. He saw a brown shoulder and a black head silhouetted against the churning white of the lagoon. The next instant that, too, had vanished. Other trees were going, falling and criss-crossing like matches. He was amazed at the power of the wind. His own tree was swaying perilously, one woman was wailing and clutching the little girl, who in turn still hung on to the cat.

The man, holding the other child, touched Raoul's arm and pointed. He looked and saw the Mormon church careering drunkenly a hundred feet away. It had been torn from its foundations, and wind and sea were heaving and shoving it toward the lagoon. A frightful wall of water caught it, tilted it, and flung it against half a dozen cocoanut trees. The bunches of human fruit fell like ripe cocoanuts. The subsiding wave showed them on the ground, some lying motionless, others squirming and writhing. They reminded him strangely of ants. He was not shocked. He had risen above horror. Quite as a matter of course he noted the succeeding wave sweep the sand clean of the human wreckage. A third wave, more colossal than any he had yet seen, hurled the church into the lagoon, where it floated off into the obscurity to leeward, half-submerged, reminding him for all the world of a Noah's ark.

He looked for Captain Lynch's house, and was surprised to find it gone. Things certainly were happening quickly. He noticed that many of the people in the trees that still held had descended to the ground.

The wind had yet again increased. His own tree showed that. It no longer swayed or bent over and back. Instead, it remained practically stationary, curved in a rigid angle from the wind and merely vibrating. But the vibration was sickening. It was like that of a tuning-fork or the tongue of a jew's-harp. It was the rapidity of the vibration that made it so bad. Even though its roots held, it could not stand the strain for long. Something would have to break.

Ah, there was one that had gone. He had not seen it go, but there it stood, the remnant, broken off half-way up the trunk. One did not know what happened unless he saw it. The mere crashing of trees and wails of human despair occupied no place in that mighty volume of sound. He chanced to be looking in Captain Lynch's direction when it happened. He saw the trunk of the tree, half-way up, splinter and part without noise. The head of the tree, with three sailors of the *Aorai* and the old captain, sailed off over the lagoon. It did not fall to the ground, but drove through the air like a piece of chaff. For a hundred yards he followed its flight, when it struck the water. He strained his eyes, and was sure that he saw Captain Lynch wave farewell.

Raoul did not wait for anything more. He touched the native and made signs to descend to the ground. The man was willing, but his women were paralyzed from terror, and he elected to remain with them. Raoul passed his rope around the tree and slid down. A rush of salt water went over his head. He held his breath and clung desperately to the rope. The water subsided, and in the shelter of the trunk he breathed once more. He fastened the rope more securely, and then was put under by another sea. One of the women slid down and joined him, the native remaining by the other woman, the two children, and the cat.

The supercargo had noticed how the groups clinging at the bases of the other trees continually diminished. Now he saw the process work out alongside him. It required all his strength to hold on, and the woman who had joined him was growing weaker. Each time he emerged from a sea he was surprised to find himself still there, and next, surprised to find the woman still there. At last he emerged to find himself alone. He looked up. The top of the tree had gone as well. At half its original height, a splintered end vibrated. He was safe. The roots still held, while the tree had been shorn of its windage. He began to climb up. He was so weak that he went slowly, and sea after sea caught him before he was above them. Then he tied himself to the trunk and stiffened his soul to face the night and he knew not what.

He felt very lonely in the darkness. At times it seemed to him that it was the end of the world and that he was the last one left alive. Still the wind increased. Hour after hour it increased. By what he calculated was eleven o'clock, the wind had become unbelievable. It was a horrible, monstrous thing, a screaming fury, a wall that smote and passed on but that continued to smite and pass on—a wall without end. It seemed to him that he had become light and ethereal; that it was he that was in motion; that he was being driven with inconceivable velocity through unending solidity. The wind was no longer air in motion. It had become substantial as water or quicksilver. He had a feeling that he could reach into it and tear it out in chunks as one might do with the meat in the carcass of a steer; that he could seize hold of the wind and hang on to it as a man might hang on to the face of a cliff.

The wind strangled him. He could not face it and breathe, for it rushed in through his mouth and nostrils, distending his lungs like bladders. At such moments it seemed to him that his body was being packed and swollen with solid earth. Only by pressing his lips to the trunk of the tree could he breathe. Also, the ceaseless impact of the wind exhausted him. Body and brain became wearied. He no longer observed, no longer thought, and was but semiconscious. One idea constituted his consciousness: *So this was a hurricane.* That one idea persisted irregularly. It was like a feeble flame that flickered occasionally. From a state of stupor he would return to it—*So this was a hurricane.* Then he would go off into another stupor.

The height of the hurricane endured from eleven at night till three in the morning, and it was at eleven that the tree in which clung Mapuhi and his women snapped off. Mapuhi rose to the surface of the lagoon, still clutching his daughter Ngakura. Only a South Sea islander could have lived in such a driving smother. The pandanus-tree, to which he attached himself, turned over and over in the froth and churn; and it was only by holding on at times and waiting, and at other times shifting his grips rapidly, that he was able to get his head and Ngakura's to the surface at intervals sufficiently near together to keep the breath in them. But the air was mostly water, what with flying spray and sheeted rain that poured along at right angles to the perpendicular.

It was ten miles across the lagoon to the farther ring of sand. Here, tossing tree-trunks, timbers, wrecks of cutters, and wreckage of houses, killed nine out of ten of the miserable beings who survived the passage of the lagoon. Half-drowned, exhausted, they were hurled into this mad mortar of the elements and battered into formless flesh. But Mapuhi was fortunate. His chance was the one in ten; it fell to him by the freakage of fate. He emerged upon the sand, bleeding from a score of wounds. Ngakura's left arm was broken; the fingers of her right hand were crushed; and cheek and forehead were laid open to the bone. He clutched a tree that yet stood, and clung on, holding the girl and sobbing for air, while the waters of the lagoon washed by knee-high and at times waist-high.

At three in the morning the backbone of the hurricane broke. By five no more than a stiff breeze was blowing. And by six it was dead calm and the sun was shining. The sea had gone down. On the yet restless edge of the lagoon, Mapuhi saw the broken bodies of those that had failed in the landing. Undoubtedly Tefara and Nauri were among them. He went along the beach examining them, and came upon his wife, lying half in and half out of the water. He sat down and wept, making harsh animal-noises after the manner of primitive grief. Then she stirred uneasily, and groaned. He looked more closely. Not only was she alive, but she was uninjured. She was merely sleeping. Hers also had been the one chance in ten.

Of the twelve hundred alive the night before but three hundred remained. The Mormon missionary and a gendarme made the census. The lagoon was cluttered with corpses. Not a house nor a hut was standing. In the whole atoll not two stones remained one upon another. One in fifty of the cocoanut palms still stood, and they were wrecks, while on not one of them remained a single nut. There was no fresh water. The shallow wells that caught the surface seepage of the rain were filled with salt. Out of the lagoon a few soaked bags of flour were recovered. The survivors cut the hearts out of the fallen cocoanut trees and ate them. Here and there they crawled into tiny hutches, made by hollowing out the sand and covering over with fragments of metal roofing. The missionary made a crude still, but he could not distill water for three hundred persons. By the end of the second day, Raoul, taking a bath in the lagoon, discovered that his thirst was somewhat relieved. He cried out the news, and thereupon three hundred men, women, and children could have been seen, standing up to their necks in the lagoon and trying to drink water in through their skins. Their dead floated about them, or were stepped upon where they still lay upon the bottom. On the third day the people buried their dead and sat down to wait for the rescue steamers.

In the meantime, Nauri, torn from her family by the hurricane, had been swept away on an adventure of her own. Clinging to a rough plank that wounded and bruised her and that filled her body with splinters, she was thrown clear over the atoll and carried away to sea. Here, under the amazing buffets of mountains of water, she lost her plank. She was an old woman nearly sixty; but she was Paumotan-born, and she had never been out of sight of the sea in her life. Swimming in the darkness, strangling, suffocating, fighting for air, she was struck a heavy blow on the shoulder by a cocoanut. On the instant her plan was formed, and she seized the nut. In the next hour she captured seven more. Tied together, they formed a lifebuoy that preserved her life while at the same time it threatened to pound her to a jelly. She was a fat woman, and she bruised easily; but she had had experience of hurricanes, and, while she prayed to her shark god for protection from sharks, she waited for the wind to break. But at three o'clock she was in such a stupor that she did not know. Nor did she know at six o'clock when the dead calm settled down. She was shocked into consciousness when she was thrown upon the sand. She dug in with raw and bleeding hands and feet and clawed against the backwash until she was beyond the reach of the waves.

She knew where she was. This land could be no other than the tiny islet of Takokota. It had no lagoon. No one lived upon it. Hikueru was fifteen miles away. She could not see Hikueru, but she knew that it lay to the south. The days went by, and she lived on the cocoanuts that had kept her afloat. They supplied her with drinking water and with food. But she did not drink all she wanted, nor eat all she wanted. Rescue was problematical. She saw the smoke of the rescue steamers on the horizon, but what steamer could be expected to come to lonely, uninhabited Takokota?

From the first she was tormented by corpses. The sea persisted in flinging them upon her bit of sand, and she persisted, until her strength failed, in thrusting them back into the sea where the sharks tore at them and devoured them. When her strength failed, the bodies festooned her beach with ghastly horror, and she withdrew from them as far as she could, which was not far.

By the tenth day her last cocoanut was gone, and she was shrivelling from thirst. She dragged herself along the sand, looking for cocoanuts. It was strange that so many bodies floated up, and no nuts. Surely, there were more cocoanuts afloat than dead men! She gave up at last, and lay exhausted. The end had come. Nothing remained but to wait for death.

Coming out of a stupor, she became slowly aware that she was gazing at a patch of sandy-red hair on the head of a corpse. The sea flung the body toward her, then drew it back. It turned over, and she saw that it had no face. Yet there was something familiar about that patch of sandy-red hair. An hour passed. She did not exert herself to make the identification. She was waiting to die, and it mattered little to her what man that thing of horror once might have been.

But at the end of the hour she sat up slowly and stared at the corpse. An unusually large wave had thrown it beyond the reach of the lesser waves. Yes, she was right; that patch of red hair could belong to but one man in the Paumotus. It was Levy, the German Jew, the man who had bought the pearl and carried it away on the *Hira*. Well, one thing was evident: the *Hira* had been lost. The pearl-buyer's god of fishermen and thieves had gone back on him.

She crawled down to the dead man. His shirt had been torn away, and she could see the leather money-belt about his waist. She held her breath and tugged at the buckles. They gave easier than she had expected, and she crawled hurriedly away across the sand, dragging the belt after her. Pocket after pocket she unbuckled in the belt and found empty. Where could he have put it? In the last pocket of all she found it, the first and only pearl he had bought on the voyage. She crawled a few feet farther, to escape the pestilence of the belt, and examined the pearl. It was the one Mapuhi had found and been robbed of by Toriki. She weighed it in her hand and rolled it back and forth caressingly. But in it she saw no intrinsic beauty. What she did see was the house Mapuhi and Tefara and she had builded so carefully in their minds. Each time she looked at the pearl she saw the house in all its details, including the octagon-drop-clock on the wall. That was something to live for.

She tore a strip from her *ahu* and tied the pearl securely about her neck. Then she went on along the beach, panting and groaning, but resolutely seeking for cocoanuts. Quickly she found one, and, as she glanced around, a second. She broke one, drinking its water, which was mildewy, and eating the last particle of the meat. A little later she found a shattered dugout. Its outrigger was gone, but she was hopeful, and, before the day was out, she found the outrigger. Every find was an augury. The pearl was a talisman. Late in the afternoon she saw a wooden box floating low in the water. When she dragged it out on the beach its contents rattled, and inside she found ten tins of salmon. She opened one by hammering it on the canoe. When a leak was started, she drained the tin. After that she spent several hours in extracting the salmon, hammering and squeezing it out a morsel at a time.

Eight days longer she waited for rescue. In the meantime she fastened the outrigger back on the canoe, using for lashings all the cocoanut-fibre she could find, and also what remained of her *ahu*. The canoe was badly cracked, and she could not make it water-tight; but a calabash made from a cocoanut she stored on board for a bailer. She was hard put for a paddle. With a piece of tin she sawed off all her hair close to the scalp. Out of the hair she braided a cord; and by means of the cord she lashed a three-foot piece of broom-handle to a board from the salmon case. She gnawed wedges with her teeth and with them wedged the lashing.

On the eighteenth day, at midnight, she launched the canoe through the surf and started back for Hikueru. She was an old woman. Hardship had stripped her fat from her till scarcely more than bones and skin and a few stringy muscles remained. The canoe was large and should have been paddled by three strong men. But she did it alone, with a makeshift paddle. Also, the canoe leaked badly, and one-third of her time was devoted to bailing. By clear daylight she looked vainly for Hikueru. Astern, Takokota had sunk beneath the sea-rim. The sun blazed down on her nakedness, compelling her body to surrender its moisture. Two tins of salmon were left, and in the course of the day she battered holes in them and drained the liquid. She had no time to waste in extracting the meat. A current was setting to the westward, she made westing whether she made southing or not.

In the early afternoon, standing upright in the canoe, she sighted Hikueru. Its wealth of cocoanut palms was gone. Only here and there, at wide intervals, could she see the ragged remnants of trees. The sight cheered her. She was nearer than she had thought. The current was setting her to the westward. She bore up against it and paddled on. The wedges in the paddle-lashing worked loose, and she lost much time, at frequent intervals, in driving them tight. Then there was the bailing. One hour in three she had to cease paddling in order to bail. And all the time she drifted to the westward.

By sunset Hikueru bore southeast from her, three miles away. There was a full moon, and by eight o'clock the land was due east and two miles away. She struggled on for another hour, but the land was as far away as ever. She was in the main grip of the current; the canoe was too large; the paddle was too inadequate; and too much of her time and strength was wasted in bailing. Besides, she was very weak and growing weaker. Despite her efforts, the canoe was drifting off to the westward.

She breathed a prayer to her shark god, slipped over the side, and began to swim. She was actually refreshed by the water, and quickly left the canoe astern. At the end of an hour the land was perceptibly nearer. Then came her fright. Right before her eyes, not twenty feet away, a large fin cut the water. She swam steadily toward it, and slowly it glided away, curving off toward the right and circling around her. She kept her eyes on the fin and swam on. When the fin disappeared, she lay face downward on the water and watched. When the fin reappeared she resumed her swimming. The monster was lazy—she could see that. Without doubt he had been well fed since the hurricane. Had he been very hungry, she knew he would not have hesitated from making a dash for her. He was fifteen feet long, and one bite, she knew, could cut her in half.

But she did not have any time to waste on him. Whether she swam or not, the current drew away from the land just the same. A half-hour went by, and the shark began to grow bolder. Seeing no harm in her he drew closer, in narrowing circles, cocking his eyes at her impudently as he slid past. Sooner or later, she knew well enough, he would get up sufficient courage to dash at her. She resolved to play first. It was a desperate act she meditated. She was an old woman, alone in the sea and weak from starvation and hardship; and yet she, in the face of this sea-tiger, must anticipate his dash by herself dashing at him. She swam on, waiting her chance. At last he passed languidly by, barely eight feet away. She rushed at him suddenly, feigning that she was attacking him. He gave a wild flirt of his tail as he fled away, and his sandpaper hide, striking her, took off her skin from elbow to shoulder. He swam rapidly, in a widening circle, and at last disappeared.

In the hole in the sand, covered over by fragments of metal roofing, Mapuhi and Tefara lay disputing.

"If you had done as I said," charged Tefara, for the thousandth time, "and hidden the pearl and told no one, you would have it now."

"But Huru-Huru was with me when I opened the shell—have I not told you so times and times and times without end?"

"And now we shall have no house. Raoul told me to-day that if you had not sold the pearl to Toriki—"

"I did not sell it. Toriki robbed me."

"—that if you had not sold the pearl, he would give you five thousand French dollars, which is ten thousand Chili."

"He has been talking to his mother," Mapuhi explained. "She has an eye for a pearl."

"And now the pearl is lost," Tefara complained.

"It paid my debt with Toriki. That is twelve hundred I have made, anyway."

"Toriki is dead," she cried. "They have heard no word of his schooner. She was lost along with the *Aorai* and the *Hira*. Will Toriki pay you the three hundred credit he promised? No, because Toriki is dead. And had you found no pearl, would you to-day owe Toriki the twelve hundred? No, because Toriki is dead, and you cannot pay dead men."

"But Levy did not pay Toriki," Mapuhi said. "He gave him a piece of paper that was good for the money in Papeete; and now Levy is dead and cannot pay; and Toriki is dead and the paper lost with him, and the pearl is lost with Levy. You are right, Tefara. I have lost the pearl, and got nothing for it. Now let us sleep."

He held up his hand suddenly and listened. From without came a noise, as of one who breathed heavily and with pain. A hand fumbled against the mat that served for a door.

"Who is there?" Mapuhi cried.

"Nauri," came the answer. "Can you tell me where is my son, Mapuhi?"

Tefara screamed and gripped her husband's arm.

"A ghost!" she chattered. "A ghost!"

Mapuhi's face was a ghastly yellow. He clung weakly to his wife.

"Good woman," he said in faltering tones, striving to disguise his voice, "I know your son well. He is living on the east side of the lagoon."

From without came the sound of a sigh. Mapuhi began to feel elated. He had fooled the ghost.

"But where do you come from, old woman?" he asked.

"From the sea," was the dejected answer.

"I knew it! I knew it!" screamed Tefara, rocking to and fro.

"Since when has Tefara bedded in a strange house?" came Nauri's voice through the matting.

Mapuhi looked fear and reproach at his wife. It was her voice that had betrayed them.

"And since when has Mapuhi, my son, denied his old mother?" the voice went on.

"No, no, I have not—Mapuhi has not denied you," he cried. "I am not Mapuhi. He is on the east end of the lagoon, I tell you."

Ngakura sat up in bed and began to cry. The matting started to shake.

"What are you doing?" Mapuhi demanded.

"I am coming in," said the voice of Nauri.

One end of the matting lifted. Tefara tried to dive under the blankets, but Mapuhi held on to her. He had to hold on to something. Together, struggling with each other, with shivering bodies and chattering teeth, they gazed with protruding eyes at the lifting mat. They saw Nauri, dripping with sea-water, without her *ahu,* creep in. They rolled over backward from her and fought for Ngakura's blanket with which to cover their heads.

"You might give your old mother a drink of water," the ghost said plaintively.

"Give her a drink of water," Tefara commanded in a shaking voice.

"Give her a drink of water," Mapuhi passed on the command to Ngakura.

And together they kicked out Ngakura from under the blanket. A minute later, peeping, Mapuhi saw the ghost drinking. When it reached out a shaking hand and laid it on his, he felt the weight of it and was convinced that it was no ghost. Then he emerged, dragging Tefara after him, and in a few minutes all were listening to Nauri's tale. And when she told of Levy, and dropped the pearl into Tefara's hand, even she was reconciled to the reality of her mother-in-law.

"In the morning," said Tefara, "you will sell the pearl to Raoul for five thousand French."

"The house?" objected Nauri.

"He will build the house," Tefara answered. "He says it will cost four thousand French. Also will he give one thousand French in credit, which is two thousand Chili."

"And it will be six fathoms long?" Nauri queried.

"Ay," answered Mapuhi, "six fathoms."

"And in the middle room will be the octagon-drop-clock?"

"Ay, and the round table as well."

"Then give me something to eat, for I am hungry," said Nauri, complacently. "And after that we will sleep, for I am weary. And to-morrow we will have more talk about the house before we sell the pearl. It will be better if we take the thousand French in cash. Money is ever better than credit in buying goods from the traders."

THE CHINAGO

"The coral waxes, the palm grows, but man departs."
—TAHITIAN PROVERB.

Ah Cho did not understand French. He sat in the crowded court room, very weary and bored, listening to the unceasing, explosive French that now one official and now another uttered. It was just so much gabble to Ah Cho, and he marvelled at the stupidity of the Frenchmen who took so long to find out the murderer of Chung Ga, and who did not find him at all. The five hundred coolies on the plantation knew that Ah San had done the killing, and here was Ah San not even arrested. It was true that all the coolies had agreed secretly not to testify against one another; but then, it was so simple, the Frenchmen should have been able to discover that Ah San was the man. They were very stupid, these Frenchmen.

Ah Cho had done nothing of which to be afraid. He had had no hand in the killing. It was true he had been present at it, and Schemmer, the overseer on the plantation, had rushed into the barracks immediately afterward and caught him there, along with four or five others; but what of that? Chung Ga had been stabbed only twice. It stood to reason that five or six men could not inflict two stab wounds. At the most, if a man had struck but once, only two men could have done it.

So it was that Ah Cho reasoned, when he, along with his four companions, had lied and blocked and obfuscated in their statements to the court concerning what had taken place. They had heard the sounds of the killing, and, like Schemmer, they had run to the spot. They had got there before Schemmer—that was all. True, Schemmer had testified that, attracted by the sound of quarrelling as he chanced to pass by, he had stood for at least five minutes outside; that then, when he entered, he found the prisoners already inside; and that they had not entered just before, because he had been standing by the one door to the barracks. But what of that? Ah Cho and his four fellow-prisoners had testified that Schemmer was mistaken. In the end they would be let go. They were all confident of that. Five men could not have their heads cut off for two stab wounds. Besides, no foreign devil had seen the killing. But these Frenchmen were so stupid. In China, as Ah Cho well knew, the magistrate would order all of them to the torture and learn the truth. The truth was very easy to learn under torture. But these Frenchmen did not torture—bigger fools they! Therefore they would never find out who killed Chung Ga.

But Ah Cho did not understand everything. The English Company that owned the plantation had imported into Tahiti, at great expense, the five hundred coolies. The stockholders were clamoring for dividends, and the Company had not yet paid any; wherefore the Company did not want its costly contract laborers to start the practice of killing one another. Also, there were the French, eager and willing to impose upon the Chinagos the virtues and excellences of French law. There was nothing like setting an example once in a while; and, besides, of what use was New Caledonia except to send men to live out their days in misery and pain in payment of the penalty for being frail and human?

Ah Cho did not understand all this. He sat in the court room and waited for the baffled judgment that would set him and his comrades free to go back to the plantation and work out the terms of their contracts. This judgment would soon be rendered. Proceedings were drawing to a close. He could see that. There was no more testifying, no more gabble of tongues. The French devils were tired, too, and evidently waiting for the judgment. And as he waited he remembered back in his life to the time when he had signed the contract and set sail in the ship for Tahiti. Times had been hard in his seacoast village, and when he indentured himself to labor for five years in the South Seas at fifty cents Mexican a day, he had thought himself fortunate. There were men in his village who toiled a whole year for ten dollars Mexican, and there were women who made nets all the year round for five dollars, while in the houses of shopkeepers there were maid-servants who received four dollars for a year of service. And here he was to receive fifty cents a day; for one day, only one day, he was to receive that princely sum! What if the work were hard? At the end of the five years he would return home—that was in the contract—and he would never have to work again. He would be a rich man for life, with a house of his own, a wife, and children growing up to venerate him. Yes, and back of the house he would have a small garden, a place of meditation and repose, with goldfish in a tiny lakelet, and wind bells tinkling in the several trees, and there would be a high wall all around so that his meditation and repose should be undisturbed.

Well, he had worked out three of those five years. He was already a wealthy man (in his own country), through his earnings, and only two years more intervened between the cotton plantation on Tahiti and the meditation and repose that awaited him. But just now he was losing money because of the unfortunate accident of being present at the killing of Chung Ga. He had lain three weeks in prison, and for each day of those three weeks he had lost fifty cents. But now judgment would soon be given, and he would go back to work.

Ah Cho was twenty-two years old. He was happy and good-natured, and it was easy for him to smile. While his body was slim in the Asiatic way, his face was rotund. It was round, like the moon, and it irradiated a gentle complacence and a sweet kindliness of spirit that was unusual among his countrymen. Nor did his looks belie him. He never caused trouble, never took part in wrangling. He did not gamble. His soul was not harsh enough for the soul that must belong to a gambler. He was content with little things and simple pleasures. The hush and quiet in the cool of the day after the blazing toil in the cotton field was to him an infinite satisfaction. He could sit for hours gazing at a solitary flower and philosophizing about the mysteries and riddles of being. A blue heron on a tiny crescent of sandy beach, a silvery splatter of flying fish, or a sunset of pearl and rose across the lagoon, could entrance him to all forgetfulness of the procession of wearisome days and of the heavy lash of Schemmer.

Schemmer, Karl Schemmer, was a brute, a brutish brute. But he earned his salary. He got the last particle of strength out of the five hundred slaves; for slaves they were until their term of years was up. Schemmer worked hard to extract the strength from those five hundred sweating bodies and to transmute it into bales of fluffy cotton ready for export. His dominant, iron-clad, primeval brutishness was what enabled him to effect the transmutation. Also, he was assisted by a thick leather belt, three inches wide and a yard in length, with which he always rode and which, on occasion, could come down on the naked back of a stooping coolie with a report like a pistol-shot. These reports were frequent when Schemmer rode down the furrowed field.

Once, at the beginning of the first year of contract labor, he had killed a coolie with a single blow of his fist. He had not exactly crushed the man's head like an egg-shell, but the blow had been sufficient to addle what was inside, and, after being sick for a week, the man had died. But the Chinese had not complained to the French devils that ruled over

Tahiti. It was their own lookout. Schemmer was their problem. They must avoid his wrath as they avoided the venom of the centipedes that lurked in the grass or crept into the sleeping quarters on rainy nights. The Chinagos—such they were called by the indolent, brown-skinned island folk—saw to it that they did not displease Schemmer too greatly. This was equivalent to rendering up to him a full measure of efficient toil. That blow of Schemmer's fist had been worth thousands of dollars to the Company, and no trouble ever came of it to Schemmer.

The French, with no instinct for colonization, futile in their childish playgame of developing the resources of the island, were only too glad to see the English Company succeed. What matter of Schemmer and his redoubtable fist? The Chinago that died? Well, he was only a Chinago. Besides, he died of sunstroke, as the doctor's certificate attested. True, in all the history of Tahiti no one had ever died of sunstroke. But it was that, precisely that, which made the death of this Chinago unique. The doctor said as much in his report. He was very candid. Dividends must be paid, or else one more failure would be added to the long history of failure in Tahiti.

There was no understanding these white devils. Ah Cho pondered their inscrutableness as he sat in the court room waiting the judgment. There was no telling what went on at the back of their minds. He had seen a few of the white devils. They were all alike—the officers and sailors on the ship, the French officials, the several white men on the plantation, including Schemmer. Their minds all moved in mysterious ways there was no getting at. They grew angry without apparent cause, and their anger was always dangerous. They were like wild beasts at such times. They worried about little things, and on occasion could out-toil even a Chinago. They were not temperate as Chinagos were temperate; they were gluttons, eating prodigiously and drinking more prodigiously. A Chinago never knew when an act would please them or arouse a storm of wrath. A Chinago could never tell. What pleased one time, the very next time might provoke an outburst of anger. There was a curtain behind the eyes of the white devils that screened the backs of their minds from the Chinago's gaze. And then, on top of it all, was that terrible efficiency of the white devils, that ability to do things, to make things go, to work results, to bend to their wills all creeping, crawling things, and the powers of the very elements themselves. Yes, the white men were strange and wonderful, and they were devils. Look at Schemmer.

Ah Cho wondered why the judgment was so long in forming. Not a man on trial had laid hand on Chung Ga. Ah San alone had killed him. Ah San had done it, bending Chung Ga's head back with one hand by a grip of his queue, and with the other hand, from behind, reaching over and driving the knife into his body. Twice had he driven it in. There in the court room, with closed eyes, Ah Cho saw the killing acted over again—the squabble, the vile words bandied back and forth, the filth and insult flung upon venerable ancestors, the curses laid upon unbegotten generations, the leap of Ah San, the grip on the queue of Chung Ga, the knife that sank twice into his flesh, the bursting open of the door, the irruption of Schemmer, the dash for the door, the escape of Ah San, the flying belt of Schemmer that drove the rest into the corner, and the firing of the revolver as a signal that brought help to Schemmer. Ah Cho shivered as he lived it over. One blow of the belt had bruised his cheek, taking off some of the skin. Schemmer had pointed to the bruises when, on the witness-stand, he had identified Ah Cho. It was only just now that the marks had become no longer visible. That had been a blow. Half an inch nearer the centre and it would have taken out his eye. Then Ah Cho forgot the whole happening in a vision he caught of the garden of meditation and repose that would be his when he returned to his own land.

He sat with impassive face, while the magistrate rendered the judgment. Likewise were the faces of his four companions impassive. And they remained impassive when the interpreter explained that the five of them had been found guilty of the murder of Chung Ga, and that Ah Chow should have his head cut off, Ah Cho serve twenty years in prison in New Caledonia, Wong Li twelve years, and Ah Tong ten years. There was no use in getting excited about it. Even Ah Chow remained expressionless as a mummy, though it was his head that was to be cut off. The magistrate added a few words, and the interpreter explained that Ah Chow's face having been most severely bruised by Schemmer's strap had made his identification so positive that, since one man must die, he might as well be that man. Also, the fact that Ah Cho's face likewise had been severely bruised, conclusively proving his presence at the murder and his undoubted participation, had merited him the twenty years of penal servitude. And down to the ten years of Ah Tong, the proportioned reason for each sentence was explained. Let the Chinagos take the lesson to heart, the Court said finally, for they must learn that the law would be fulfilled in Tahiti though the heavens fell.

The five Chinagos were taken back to jail. They were not shocked nor grieved. The sentences being unexpected was quite what they were accustomed to in their dealings with the white devils. From them a Chinago rarely expected more than the unexpected. The heavy punishment for a crime they had not committed was no stranger than the countless strange things that white devils did. In the weeks that followed, Ah Cho often contemplated Ah Chow with mild curiosity. His head was to be cut off by the guillotine that was being erected on the plantation. For him there would be no declining years, no gardens of tranquillity. Ah Cho philosophized and speculated about life and death. As for himself, he was not perturbed. Twenty years were merely twenty years. By that much was his garden removed from him—that was all. He was young, and the patience of Asia was in his bones. He could wait those twenty years, and by that time the heats of his blood would be assuaged and he would be better fitted for that garden of calm delight. He thought of a name for it; he would call it The Garden of the Morning Calm. He was made happy all day by the thought, and he was inspired to devise a moral maxim on the virtue of patience, which maxim proved a great comfort, especially to Wong Li and Ah Tong. Ah Chow, however, did not care for the maxim. His head was to be separated from his body in so short a time that he had no need for patience to wait for that event. He smoked well, ate well, slept well, and did not worry about the slow passage of time.

Cruchot was a gendarme. He had seen twenty years of service in the colonies, from Nigeria and Senegal to the South Seas, and those twenty years had not perceptibly brightened his dull mind. He was as slow-witted and stupid as in his peasant days in the south of France. He knew discipline and fear of authority, and from God down to the sergeant of gendarmes the only difference to him was the measure of slavish obedience which he rendered. In point of fact, the sergeant bulked bigger in his mind than God, except on Sundays when God's mouthpieces had their say. God was usually very remote, while the sergeant was ordinarily very close at hand.

Cruchot it was who received the order from the Chief Justice to the jailer commanding that functionary to deliver over to Cruchot the person of Ah Chow. Now, it happened that the Chief Justice had given a dinner the night before to the captain and officers of the French man-of-war. His hand was shaking when he wrote out the order, and his eyes were aching so dreadfully that he did not read over the order. It was only a Chinago's life he was signing away, anyway. So he did not notice that he had omitted the final letter in Ah Chow's name. The order read "Ah Cho," and, when Cruchot presented the order, the jailer turned over to him the person of Ah Cho. Cruchot took that person beside him on the seat of a wagon, behind two mules, and drove away.

Ah Cho was glad to be out in the sunshine. He sat beside the gendarme and beamed. He beamed more ardently than ever when he noted the mules headed south toward Atimaono. Undoubtedly Schemmer had sent for him to be brought back. Schemmer wanted him to work. Very well, he would work well. Schemmer would never have cause to complain. It was a hot day. There had been a stoppage of the trades. The mules sweated, Cruchot sweated, and Ah Cho sweated. But it was Ah Cho that bore the heat with the least concern. He had toiled three years under that sun on the plantation. He beamed and beamed with such genial good nature that even Cruchot's heavy mind was stirred to wonderment.

"You are very funny," he said at last.

Ah Cho nodded and beamed more ardently. Unlike the magistrate, Cruchot spoke to him in the Kanaka tongue, and this, like all Chinagos and all foreign devils, Ah Cho understood.

"You laugh too much," Cruchot chided. "One's heart should be full of tears on a day like this."

"I am glad to get out of the jail."

"Is that all?" The gendarme shrugged his shoulders.

"Is it not enough?" was the retort.

"Then you are not glad to have your head cut off?"

Ah Cho looked at him in abrupt perplexity and said:—

"Why, I am going back to Atimaono to work on the plantation for Schemmer. Are you not taking me to Atimaono?"

Cruchot stroked his long mustaches reflectively. "Well, well," he said finally, with a flick of the whip at the off mule, "so you don't know?"

"Know what?" Ah Cho was beginning to feel a vague alarm. "Won't Schemmer let me work for him any more?"

"Not after to-day." Cruchot laughed heartily. It was a good joke. "You see, you won't be able to work after to-day. A man with his head off can't work, eh?" He poked the Chinago in the ribs, and chuckled.

Ah Cho maintained silence while the mules trotted a hot mile. Then he spoke: "Is Schemmer going to cut off my head?"

Cruchot grinned as he nodded.

"It is a mistake," said Ah Cho, gravely. "I am not the Chinago that is to have his head cut off. I am Ah Cho. The honorable judge has determined that I am to stop twenty years in New Caledonia."

The gendarme laughed. It was a good joke, this funny Chinago trying to cheat the guillotine. The mules trotted through a cocoanut grove and for half a mile beside the sparkling sea before Ah Cho spoke again.

"I tell you I am not Ah Chow. The honorable judge did not say that my head was to go off."

"Don't be afraid," said Cruchot, with the philanthropic intention of making it easier for his prisoner. "It is not difficult to die that way." He snapped his fingers. "It is quick—like that. It is not like hanging on the end of a rope and kicking and making faces for five minutes. It is like killing a chicken with a hatchet. You cut its head off, that is all. And it is the same with a man. Pouf!—it is over. It doesn't hurt. You don't even think it hurts. You don't think. Your head is gone, so you cannot think. It is very good. That is the way I want to die—quick, ah, quick. You are lucky to die that way. You might get the leprosy and fall to pieces slowly, a finger at a time, and now and again a thumb, also the toes. I knew a man who was burned by hot water. It took him two days to die. You could hear him yelling a kilometre away. But you? Ah! so easy! Chck!—the knife cuts your neck like that. It is finished. The knife may even tickle. Who can say? Nobody who died that way ever came back to say."

He considered this last an excruciating joke, and permitted himself to be convulsed with laughter for half a minute. Part of his mirth was assumed, but he considered it his humane duty to cheer up the Chinago.

"But I tell you I am Ah Cho," the other persisted. "I don't want my head cut off."

Cruchot scowled. The Chinago was carrying the foolishness too far.

"I am not Ah Chow—" Ah Cho began.

"That will do," the gendarme interrupted. He puffed up his cheeks and strove to appear fierce.

"I tell you I am not—" Ah Cho began again.

"Shut up!" bawled Cruchot.

After that they rode along in silence. It was twenty miles from Papeete to Atimaono, and over half the distance was covered by the time the Chinago again ventured into speech.

"I saw you in the court room, when the honorable judge sought after our guilt," he began. "Very good. And do you remember that Ah Chow, whose head is to be cut off—do you remember that he—Ah Chow— was a tall man? Look at me."

He stood up suddenly, and Cruchot saw that he was a short man. And just as suddenly Cruchot caught a glimpse of a memory picture of Ah Chow, and in that picture Ah Chow was tall. To the gendarme all Chinagos looked alike. One face was like another. But between tallness and shortness he could differentiate, and he knew that he had the wrong man beside him on the seat. He pulled up the mules abruptly, so that the pole shot ahead of them, elevating their collars.

"You see, it was a mistake," said Ah Cho, smiling pleasantly.

But Cruchot was thinking. Already he regretted that he had stopped the wagon. He was unaware of the error of the Chief Justice, and he had no way of working it out; but he did know that he had been given this Chinago to take to Atimaono and that it was his duty to take him to Atimaono. What if he was the wrong man and they cut his head off? It was only a Chinago when all was said, and what was a Chinago, anyway? Besides, it might not be a mistake. He did not know what went on in the minds of his superiors. They knew their business best. Who was he to do their thinking for them? Once, in the long ago, he had attempted to think for them, and the sergeant had said: "Cruchot, you are a fool! The quicker you know that, the better you will get on. You are not to think; you are to obey and leave thinking to your betters." He smarted under the recollection. Also, if he turned back to Papeete, he would delay the execution at Atimaono, and if he were wrong in turning back, he would get a reprimand from the sergeant who was waiting for the prisoner. And, furthermore, he would get a reprimand at Papeete as well.

He touched the mules with the whip and drove on. He looked at his watch. He would be half an hour late as it was, and the sergeant was bound to be angry. He put the mules into a faster trot. The more Ah Cho persisted in explaining the mistake, the more stubborn Cruchot became. The knowledge that he had the wrong man did not make his temper better. The knowledge that it was through no mistake of his confirmed him in the belief that the wrong he was doing was the right. And, rather than incur the displeasure of the sergeant, he would willingly have assisted a dozen wrong Chinagos to their doom.

As for Ah Cho, after the gendarme had struck him over the head with the butt of the whip and commanded him in a loud voice to shut up, there remained nothing for him to do but to shut up. The long ride continued in silence. Ah Cho pondered the strange ways of the foreign devils. There was no explaining them. What they were doing with him was of a piece with everything they did. First they found guilty five innocent men, and next they cut off the head of the man that even they, in their benighted ignorance, had deemed meritorious of no more than twenty years' imprisonment. And there was nothing he could do. He could only sit idly and take what these lords of life measured out to him. Once, he got in a panic, and the sweat upon his body turned cold; but he fought his way out of it. He endeavored to resign himself to his fate by remembering and repeating certain passages from the "Yin Chih Wen" ("The Tract of the Quiet Way"); but, instead, he kept seeing his dream-garden of meditation and repose. This bothered him, until he abandoned himself to the dream and sat in his garden listening to the tinkling of the wind-bells in the several trees. And lo! sitting thus, in the dream, he was able to remember and repeat the passages from "The Tract of the Quiet Way."

So the time passed nicely until Atimaono was reached and the mules trotted up to the foot of the scaffold, in the shade of which stood the impatient sergeant. Ah Cho was hurried up the ladder of the scaffold. Beneath him on one side he saw assembled all the coolies of the plantation. Schemmer had decided that the event would be a good object-lesson, and so had called in the coolies from the fields and compelled them to be present. As they caught sight of Ah Cho they gabbled among themselves in low voices. They saw the mistake; but they kept it to themselves. The inexplicable white devils had doubtlessly changed their minds. Instead of taking the life of one innocent man, they were taking the life of another innocent man. Ah Chow or Ah Cho—what did it matter which? They could never understand the white dogs any more than could the white dogs understand them. Ah Cho was going to have his head cut off, but they, when their two remaining years of servitude were up, were going back to China.

Schemmer had made the guillotine himself. He was a handy man, and though he had never seen a guillotine, the French officials had explained the principle to him. It was on his suggestion that they had ordered the execution to take place at Atimaono instead of at Papeete. The scene of the crime, Schemmer had argued, was the best possible place for the punishment, and, in addition, it would have a salutary influence upon the half-thousand Chinagos on the plantation. Schemmer had also volunteered to act as executioner, and in that capacity he was now on the scaffold, experimenting with the instrument he had made. A banana tree, of the size and consistency of a man's neck, lay under the guillotine. Ah Cho watched with fascinated eyes. The German, turning a small crank, hoisted the blade to the top of the little derrick he had rigged. A jerk on a stout piece of cord loosed the blade and it dropped with a flash, neatly severing the banana trunk.

"How does it work?" The sergeant, coming out on top the scaffold, had asked the question.

"Beautifully," was Schemmer's exultant answer. "Let me show you."

Again he turned the crank that hoisted the blade, jerked the cord, and sent the blade crashing down on the soft tree. But this time it went no more than two-thirds of the way through.

The sergeant scowled. "That will not serve," he said.

Schemmer wiped the sweat from his forehead. "What it needs is more weight," he announced. Walking up to the edge of the scaffold, he called his orders to the blacksmith for a twenty-five-pound piece of iron. As he stooped over to attach the iron to the broad top of the blade, Ah Cho glanced at the sergeant and saw his opportunity.

"The honorable judge said that Ah Chow was to have his head cut off," he began.

The sergeant nodded impatiently. He was thinking of the fifteen-mile ride before him that afternoon, to the windward side of the island, and of Berthe, the pretty half-caste daughter of Lafière, the pearl-trader, who was waiting for him at the end of it.

"Well, I am not Ah Chow. I am Ah Cho. The honorable jailer has made a mistake. Ah Chow is a tall man, and you see I am short."

The sergeant looked at him hastily and saw the mistake. "Schemmer!" he called, imperatively. "Come here."

The German grunted, but remained bent over his task till the chunk of iron was lashed to his satisfaction. "Is your Chinago ready?" he demanded.

"Look at him," was the answer. "Is he the Chinago?"

Schemmer was surprised. He swore tersely for a few seconds, and looked regretfully across at the thing he had made with his own hands and which he was eager to see work. "Look here," he said finally, "we can't postpone this affair. I've lost three hours' work already out of those five hundred Chinagos. I can't afford to lose it all over again for the right man. Let's put the performance through just the same. It is only a Chinago."

The sergeant remembered the long ride before him, and the pearl-trader's daughter, and debated with himself.

"They will blame it on Cruchot—if it is discovered," the German urged. "But there's little chance of its being discovered. Ah Chow won't give it away, at any rate."

"The blame won't lie with Cruchot, anyway," the sergeant said. "It must have been the jailer's mistake."

"Then let's go on with it. They can't blame us. Who can tell one Chinago from another? We can say that we merely carried out instructions with the Chinago that was turned over to us. Besides, I really can't take all those coolies a second time away from their labor."

They spoke in French, and Ah Cho, who did not understand a word of it, nevertheless knew that they were determining his destiny. He knew, also, that the decision rested with the sergeant, and he hung upon that official's lips.

"All right," announced the sergeant. "Go ahead with it. He is only a Chinago."

"I'm going to try it once more, just to make sure." Schemmer moved the banana trunk forward under the knife, which he had hoisted to the top of the derrick.

Ah Cho tried to remember maxims from "The Tract of the Quiet Way." "Live in concord," came to him; but it was not applicable. He was not going to live. He was about to die. No, that would not do.

"Forgive malice"—yes, but there was no malice to forgive. Schemmer and the rest were doing this thing without malice. It was to them merely a piece of work that had to be done, just as clearing the jungle, ditching the water, and planting cotton were pieces of work that had to be done. Schemmer jerked the cord, and Ah Cho forgot "The Tract of the Quiet Way." The knife shot down with a thud, making a clean slice of the tree.

"Beautiful!" exclaimed the sergeant, pausing in the act of lighting a cigarette. "Beautiful, my friend."

Schemmer was pleased at the praise.

"Come on, Ah Chow," he said, in the Tahitian tongue.

"But I am not Ah Chow—" Ah Cho began.

"Shut up!" was the answer. "If you open your mouth again, I'll break your head."

The overseer threatened him with a clenched fist, and he remained silent. What was the good of protesting? Those foreign devils always had their way. He allowed himself to be lashed to the vertical board that was the size of his body. Schemmer drew the buckles tight—so tight that the straps cut into his flesh and hurt. But he did not complain. The hurt would not last long. He felt the board tilting over in the air toward the horizontal, and closed his eyes. And in that moment he caught a last glimpse of his garden of meditation and repose. It seemed to him that he sat in the garden. A cool wind was blowing, and the bells in the several trees were tinkling softly. Also, birds were making sleepy noises, and from beyond the high wall came the subdued sound of village life.

Then he was aware that the board had come to rest, and from muscular pressures and tensions he knew that he was lying on his back. He opened his eyes. Straight above him he saw the suspended knife blazing in the sunshine. He saw the weight which had been added, and noted that one of Schemmer's knots had slipped. Then he heard the sergeant's voice in sharp command. Ah Cho closed his eyes hastily. He did not want to see that knife descend. But he felt it—for one great fleeting instant. And in that instant he remembered Cruchot and what Cruchot had said. But Cruchot was wrong. The knife did not tickle. That much he knew before he ceased to know.

LOST FACE

It was the end. Subienkow had travelled a long trail of bitterness and horror, homing like a dove for the capitals of Europe, and here, farther away than ever, in Russian America, the trail ceased. He sat in the snow, arms tied behind him, waiting the torture. He stared curiously before him at a huge Cossack, prone in the snow, moaning in his pain. The men had finished handling the giant and turned him over to the women. That they exceeded the fiendishness of the men, the man's cries attested.

Subienkow looked on, and shuddered. He was not afraid to die. He had carried his life too long in his hands, on that weary trail from Warsaw to Nulato, to shudder at mere dying. But he objected to the torture. It offended his soul. And this offence, in turn, was not due to the mere pain he must endure, but to the sorry spectacle the pain would make of him. He knew that he would pray, and beg, and entreat, even as Big Ivan and the others that had gone before. This would not be nice. To pass out bravely and cleanly, with a smile and a jest—ah! that would have been the way. But to lose control, to have his soul upset by the pangs of the flesh, to screech and gibber like an ape, to become the veriest beast—ah, that was what was so terrible.

There had been no chance to escape. From the beginning, when he dreamed the fiery dream of Poland's independence, he had become a puppet in the hands of Fate. From the beginning, at Warsaw, at St. Petersburg, in the Siberian mines, in Kamtchatka, on the crazy boats of the fur-thieves, Fate had been driving him to this end. Without doubt, in the foundations of the world was graved this end for him—for him, who was so fine and sensitive, whose nerves scarcely sheltered under his skin, who was a dreamer, and a poet, and an artist. Before he was dreamed of, it had been determined that the quivering bundle of sensitiveness that constituted him should be doomed to live in raw and howling savagery, and to die in this far land of night, in this dark place beyond the last boundaries of the world.

He sighed. So that thing before him was Big Ivan—Big Ivan the giant, the man without nerves, the man of iron, the Cossack turned freebooter of the seas, who was as phlegmatic as an ox, with a nervous system so low that what was pain to ordinary men was scarcely a tickle to him. Well, well, trust these Nulato Indians to find Big Ivan's nerves and trace them to the roots of his quivering soul. They were certainly doing it. It was inconceivable that a man could suffer so much and yet live. Big Ivan was paying for his low order of nerves. Already he had lasted twice as long as any of the others.

Subienkow felt that he could not stand the Cossack's sufferings much longer. Why didn't Ivan die? He would go mad if that screaming did not cease. But when it did cease, his turn would come. And there was Yakaga awaiting him, too, grinning at him even now in anticipation— Yakaga, whom only last week he had kicked out of the fort, and upon whose face he had laid the lash of his dog-whip. Yakaga would attend to him. Doubtlessly Yakaga was saving for him more refined tortures, more exquisite nerve-racking. Ah! that must have been a good one, from the way Ivan screamed. The squaws bending over him stepped back with laughter and clapping of hands. Subienkow saw the monstrous thing that had been perpetrated, and began to laugh hysterically. The Indians looked at him in wonderment that he should laugh. But Subienkow could not stop.

This would never do. He controlled himself, the spasmodic twitchings slowly dying away. He strove to think of other things, and began reading back in his own life. He remembered his mother and his father, and the little spotted pony, and the French tutor who had taught him dancing and sneaked him an old worn copy of Voltaire. Once more he saw Paris, and dreary London, and gay Vienna, and Rome. And once more he saw that wild group of youths who had dreamed, even as he, the dream of an independent Poland with a king of Poland on the throne at Warsaw. Ah, there it was that the long trail began. Well, he had lasted longest. One by one, beginning with the two executed at St. Petersburg, he took up the count of the passing of those brave spirits. Here one had been beaten to death by a jailer, and there, on that blood-stained highway of the exiles, where they had marched for endless months, beaten and maltreated by their Cossack guards, another had dropped by the way. Always it had been savagery—brutal, bestial savagery. They had died—of fever, in the mines, under the knout. The last two had died after the escape, in the battle with the Cossacks, and he alone had won to Kamtchatka with the stolen papers and the money of a traveller he had left lying in the snow.

It had been nothing but savagery. All the years, with his heart in studios, and theatres, and courts, he had been hemmed in by savagery. He had purchased his life with blood. Everybody had killed. He had killed that traveller for his passports. He had proved that he was a man of parts by duelling with two Russian officers on a single day. He had had to prove himself in order to win to a place among the fur-thieves. He had had to win to that place. Behind him lay the thousand-years-long road across all Siberia and Russia. He could not escape that way. The only way was ahead, across the dark and icy sea of Behring to Alaska. The way had led from savagery to deeper savagery. On the scurvy-rotten ships of the fur-thieves, out of food and out of water, buffeted by the interminable storms of that stormy sea, men had become animals. Thrice he had sailed east from Kamtchatka. And thrice, after all manner of hardship and suffering, the survivors had come back to Kamtchatka. There had been no outlet for escape, and he could not go back the way he had come, for the mines and the knout awaited him.

Again, the fourth and last time, he had sailed east. He had been with those who first found the fabled Seal Islands; but he had not returned with them to share the wealth of furs in the mad orgies of Kamtchatka. He had sworn never to go back. He knew that to win to those dear capitals of Europe he must go on. So he had changed ships and remained in the dark new land. His comrades were Slavonian hunters and Russian adventurers, Mongols and Tartars and Siberian aborigines; and through the savages of the new world they had cut a path of blood. They had massacred whole villages that refused to furnish the fur-tribute; and they, in turn, had been massacred by ships' companies. He, with one Finn, had been the sole survivors of such a company. They had spent a winter of solitude and starvation on a lonely Aleutian isle, and their rescue in the spring by another fur-ship had been one chance in a thousand.

But always the terrible savagery had hemmed him in. Passing from ship to ship, and ever refusing to return, he had come to the ship that explored south. All down the Alaska coast they had encountered nothing but hosts of savages. Every anchorage among the beetling islands or under the frowning cliffs of the mainland had meant a battle or a storm. Either the gales blew, threatening destruction, or the war canoes came off, manned by howling natives with the war-paint on their faces, who came to learn the bloody virtues of the sea-rovers' gunpowder. South, south they had coasted, clear to the myth-land of California. Here, it was said, were Spanish adventurers who had fought their way up from Mexico. He had had hopes of those Spanish adventurers. Escaping to them, the rest would have been easy—a year or two, what did it matter more or less—and he would win to Mexico, then a ship, and Europe would be his. But they had met no Spaniards. Only had they encountered the same impregnable wall of savagery. The denizens of the confines of the world, painted for war, had driven them back from the shores. At last, when one boat was cut off and every man killed, the commander had abandoned the quest and sailed back to the north.

The years had passed. He had served under Tebenkoff when Michaelovski Redoubt was built. He had spent two years in the Kuskokwim country. Two summers, in the month of June, he had managed to be at the head of Kotzebue Sound. Here, at this time, the tribes assembled for barter; here were to be found spotted deerskins from Siberia, ivory from the Diomedes, walrus skins from the shores of the Arctic, strange stone lamps, passing in trade from tribe to tribe, no one knew whence, and, once, a hunting-knife of English make; and here, Subienkow knew, was the school in which to learn geography. For he met Eskimos from Norton Sound, from King Island and St. Lawrence Island, from Cape Prince of Wales, and Point Barrow. Such places had other names, and their distances were measured in days.

It was a vast region these trading savages came from, and a vaster region from which, by repeated trade, their stone lamps and that steel knife had come. Subienkow bullied, and cajoled, and bribed. Every far-journeyer or strange tribesman was brought before him. Perils unaccountable and unthinkable were mentioned, as well as wild beasts, hostile tribes, impenetrable forests, and mighty mountain ranges; but always from beyond came the rumor and the tale of white-skinned men, blue of eye and fair of hair, who fought like devils and who sought always for furs. They were to the east—far, far to the east. No one had seen them. It was the word that had been passed along.

It was a hard school. One could not learn geography very well through the medium of strange dialects, from dark minds that mingled fact and fable and that measured distances by "sleeps" that varied according to the difficulty of the going. But at last came the whisper that gave Subienkow courage. In the east lay a great river where were these blue-eyed men. The river was called the Yukon. South of Michaelovski Redoubt emptied another great river which the Russians knew as the Kwikpak. These two rivers were one, ran the whisper.

Subienkow returned to Michaelovski. For a year he urged an expedition up the Kwikpak. Then arose Malakoff, the Russian half-breed, to lead the wildest and most ferocious of the hell's broth of mongrel ad-

venturers who had crossed from Kamtchatka. Subienkow was his lieutenant. They threaded the mazes of the great delta of the Kwikpak,
picked up the first low hills on the northern bank, and for half a thousand miles, in skin canoes loaded to the gunwales with trade-goods and
ammunition, fought their way against the five-knot current of a river
that ran from two to ten miles wide in a channel many fathoms deep.
Malakoff decided to build the fort at Nulato. Subienkow urged to go
farther. But he quickly reconciled himself to Nulato. The long winter
was coming on. It would be better to wait. Early the following summer,
when the ice was gone, he would disappear up the Kwikpak and work
his way to the Hudson Bay Company's posts. Malakoff had never heard
the whisper that the Kwikpak was the Yukon, and Subienkow did not
tell him.

Came the building of the fort. It was enforced labor. The tiered walls
of logs arose to the sighs and groans of the Nulato Indians. The lash
was laid upon their backs, and it was the iron hand of the freebooters
of the sea that laid on the lash. There were Indians that ran away, and
when they were caught they were brought back and spread-eagled before the fort, where they and their tribe learned the efficacy of the knout.
Two died under it; others were injured for life; and the rest took the
lesson to heart and ran away no more. The snow was flying ere the fort
was finished, and then it was the time for furs. A heavy tribute was laid
upon the tribe. Blows and lashings continued, and that the tribute should
be paid, the women and children were held as hostages and treated with
the barbarity that only the fur-thieves knew.

Well, it had been a sowing of blood, and now was come the harvest.
The fort was gone. In the light of its burning, half the fur-thieves had
been cut down. The other half had passed under the torture. Only Subienkow remained, or Subienkow and Big Ivan, if that whimpering,
moaning thing in the snow could be called Big Ivan. Subienkow caught
Yakaga grinning at him. There was no gainsaying Yakaga. The mark
of the lash was still on his face. After all, Subienkow could not blame
him, but he disliked the thought of what Yakaga would do to him. He
thought of appealing to Makamuk, the head-chief; but his judgment told
him that such appeal was useless. Then, too, he thought of bursting his
bonds and dying fighting. Such an end would be quick. But he could
not break his bonds. Caribou thongs were stronger than he. Still devis-
ing, another thought came to him. He signed for Makamuk, and that an
interpreter who knew the coast dialect should be brought.

"Oh, Makamuk," he said, "I am not minded to die. I am a great man,
and it were foolishness for me to die. In truth, I shall not die. I am not
like these other carrion."

He looked at the moaning thing that had once been Big Ivan, and stirred it contemptuously with his toe.

"I am too wise to die. Behold, I have a great medicine. I alone know this medicine. Since I am not going to die, I shall exchange this medicine with you."

"What is this medicine?" Makamuk demanded.

"It is a strange medicine."

Subienkow debated with himself for a moment, as if loath to part with the secret.

"I will tell you. A little bit of this medicine rubbed on the skin makes the skin hard like a rock, hard like iron, so that no cutting weapon can cut it. The strongest blow of a cutting weapon is a vain thing against it. A bone knife becomes like a piece of mud; and it will turn the edge of the iron knives we have brought among you. What will you give me for the secret of the medicine?"

"I will give you your life," Makamuk made answer through the interpreter.

Subienkow laughed scornfully.

"And you shall be a slave in my house until you die."

The Pole laughed more scornfully.

"Untie my hands and feet and let us talk," he said.

The chief made the sign; and when he was loosed Subienkow rolled a cigarette and lighted it.

"This is foolish talk," said Makamuk. "There is no such medicine. It cannot be. A cutting edge is stronger than any medicine."

The chief was incredulous, and yet he wavered. He had seen too many deviltries of fur-thieves that worked. He could not wholly doubt.

"I will give you your life; but you shall not be a slave," he announced.

"More than that."

Subienkow played his game as coolly as if he were bartering for a foxskin.

"It is a very great medicine. It has saved my life many times. I want a sled and dogs, and six of your hunters to travel with me down the river and give me safety to one day's sleep from Michaelovski Redoubt."

"You must live here, and teach us all of your deviltries," was the reply.

Subienkow shrugged his shoulders and remained silent. He blew cigarette smoke out on the icy air, and curiously regarded what remained of the big Cossack.

"That scar!" Makamuk said suddenly, pointing to the Pole's neck, where a livid mark advertised the slash of a knife in a Kamtchatkan brawl. "The medicine is not good. The cutting edge was stronger than the medicine."

"It was a strong man that drove the stroke." (Subienkow considered.) "Stronger than you, stronger than your strongest hunter, stronger than he."

Again, with the toe of his moccasin, he touched the Cossack—a grisly spectacle, no longer conscious—yet in whose dismembered body the pain-racked life clung and was loath to go.

"Also, the medicine was weak. For at that place there were no berries of a certain kind, of which I see you have plenty in this country. The medicine here will be strong."

"I will let you go down river," said Makamuk; "and the sled and the dogs and the six hunters to give you safety shall be yours."

"You are slow," was the cool rejoinder. "You have committed an offence against my medicine in that you did not at once accept my terms. Behold, I now demand more. I want one hundred beaver skins." (Makamuk sneered.) "I want one hundred pounds of dried fish." (Makamuk nodded, for fish were plentiful and cheap.) "I want two sleds—one for me and one for my furs and fish. And my rifle must be returned to me. If you do not like the price, in a little while the price will grow."

Yakaga whispered to the chief.

"But how can I know your medicine is true medicine?" Makamuk asked.

"It is very easy. First, I shall go into the woods—"

Again Yakaga whispered to Makamuk, who made a suspicious dissent.

"You can send twenty hunters with me," Subienkow went on. "You see, I must get the berries and the roots with which to make the medicine. Then, when you have brought the two sleds and loaded on them the fish and the beaver skins and the rifle, and when you have told off the six hunters who will go with me—then, when all is ready, I will rub the medicine on my neck, so, and lay my neck there on that log. Then can your strongest hunter take the axe and strike three times on my neck. You yourself can strike the three times."

Makamuk stood with gaping mouth, drinking in this latest and most wonderful magic of the fur-thieves.

"But first," the Pole added hastily, "between each blow I must put on fresh medicine. The axe is heavy and sharp, and I want no mistakes."

"All that you have asked shall be yours," Makamuk cried in a rush of acceptance. "Proceed to make your medicine."

Subienkow concealed his elation. He was playing a desperate game, and there must be no slips. He spoke arrogantly.

"You have been slow. My medicine is offended. To make the offence clean you must give me your daughter."

He pointed to the girl, an unwholesome creature, with a cast in one eye and a bristling wolf-tooth. Makamuk was angry, but the Pole remained imperturbable, rolling and lighting another cigarette.

"Make haste," he threatened. "If you are not quick, I shall demand yet more."

In the silence that followed, the dreary northland scene faded from before him, and he saw once more his native land, and France, and, once, as he glanced at the wolf-toothed girl, he remembered another girl, a singer and a dancer, whom he had known when first as a youth he came to Paris.

"What do you want with the girl?" Makamuk asked.

"To go down the river with me." Subienkow glanced her over critically. "She will make a good wife, and it is an honor worthy of my medicine to be married to your blood."

Again he remembered the singer and dancer and hummed aloud a song she had taught him. He lived the old life over, but in a detached, impersonal sort of way, looking at the memory-pictures of his own life as if they were pictures in a book of anybody's life. The chief's voice, abruptly breaking the silence, startled him.

"It shall be done," said Makamuk. "The girl shall go down the river with you. But be it understood that I myself strike the three blows with the axe on your neck."

"But each time I shall put on the medicine," Subienkow answered, with a show of ill-concealed anxiety.

"You shall put the medicine on between each blow. Here are the hunters who shall see you do not escape. Go into the forest and gather your medicine."

Makamuk had been convinced of the worth of the medicine by the Pole's rapacity. Surely nothing less than the greatest of medicines could enable a man in the shadow of death to stand up and drive an old-woman's bargain.

"Besides," whispered Yakaga, when the Pole, with his guard, had disappeared among the spruce trees, "when you have learned the medicine you can easily destroy him."

"But how can I destroy him?" Makamuk argued. "His medicine will not let me destroy him."

"There will be some part where he has not rubbed the medicine," was Yakaga's reply. "We will destroy him through that part. It may be his ears. Very well; we will thrust a spear in one ear and out the other.

Or it may be his eyes. Surely the medicine will be much too strong to rub on his eyes."

The chief nodded. "You are wise, Yakaga. If he possesses no other devil-things, we will then destroy him."

Subienkow did not waste time in gathering the ingredients for his medicine. He selected whatsoever came to hand such as spruce needles, the inner bark of the willow, a strip of birch bark, and a quantity of moss-berries, which he made the hunters dig up for him from beneath the snow. A few frozen roots completed his supply, and he led the way back to camp.

Makamuk and Yakaga crouched beside him, noting the quantities and kinds of the ingredients he dropped into the pot of boiling water.

"You must be careful that the moss-berries go in first," he explained.

"And—oh, yes, one other thing—the finger of a man. Here, Yakaga, let me cut off your finger."

But Yakaga put his hands behind him and scowled.

"Just a small finger," Subienkow pleaded.

"Yakaga, give him your finger," Makamuk commanded.

"There be plenty of fingers lying around," Yakaga grunted, indicating the human wreckage in the snow of the score of persons who had been tortured to death.

"It must be the finger of a live man," the Pole objected.

"Then shall you have the finger of a live man." Yakaga strode over to the Cossack and sliced off a finger.

"He is not yet dead," he announced, flinging the bloody trophy in the snow at the Pole's feet. "Also, it is a good finger, because it is large."

Subienkow dropped it into the fire under the pot and began to sing. It was a French love-song that with great solemnity he sang into the brew.

"Without these words I utter into it, the medicine is worthless," he explained. "The words are the chiefest strength of it. Behold, it is ready."

"Name the words slowly, that I may know them," Makamuk commanded.

"Not until after the test. When the axe flies back three times from my neck, then will I give you the secret of the words."

"But if the medicine is not good medicine?" Makamuk queried anxiously.

Subienkow turned upon him wrathfully.

"My medicine is always good. However, if it is not good, then do by me as you have done to the others. Cut me up a bit at a time, even as you have cut him up." He pointed to the Cossack. "The medicine is now cool. Thus, I rub it on my neck, saying this further medicine."

With great gravity he slowly intoned a line of the "Marseillaise," at the same time rubbing the villainous brew thoroughly into his neck.

An outcry interrupted his play-acting. The giant Cossack, with a last resurgence of his tremendous vitality, had arisen to his knees. Laughter and cries of surprise and applause arose from the Nulatos, as Big Ivan began flinging himself about in the snow with mighty spasms.

Subienkow was made sick by the sight, but he mastered his qualms and made believe to be angry.

"This will not do," he said. "Finish him, and then we will make the test. Here, you, Yakaga, see that his noise ceases."

While this was being done, Subienkow turned to Makamuk.

"And remember, you are to strike hard. This is not baby-work. Here, take the axe and strike the log, so that I can see you strike like a man."

Makamuk obeyed, striking twice, precisely and with vigor, cutting out a large chip.

"It is well." Subienkow looked about him at the circle of savage faces that somehow seemed to symbolize the wall of savagery that had hemmed him about ever since the Czar's police had first arrested him in Warsaw. "Take your axe, Makamuk, and stand so. I shall lie down. When I raise my hand, strike, and strike with all your might. And be careful that no one stands behind you. The medicine is good, and the axe may bounce from off my neck and right out of your hands."

He looked at the two sleds, with the dogs in harness, loaded with furs and fish. His rifle lay on top of the beaver skins. The six hunters who were to act as his guard stood by the sleds.

"Where is the girl?" the Pole demanded. "Bring her up to the sleds before the test goes on."

When this had been carried out, Subienkow lay down in the snow, resting his head on the log like a tired child about to sleep. He had lived so many dreary years that he was indeed tired.

"I laugh at you and your strength, O Makamuk," he said. "Strike, and strike hard."

He lifted his hand. Makamuk swung the axe, a broadaxe for the squaring of logs. The bright steel flashed through the frosty air, poised for a perceptible instant above Makamuk's head, then descended upon Subienkow's bare neck. Clear through flesh and bone it cut its way, biting deeply into the log beneath. The amazed savages saw the head bounce a yard away from the blood-spouting trunk.

There was a great bewilderment and silence, while slowly it began to dawn in their minds that there had been no medicine. The fur-thief had outwitted them. Alone, of all their prisoners, he had escaped the torture. That had been the stake for which he played. A great roar of laughter went up. Makamuk bowed his head in shame. The fur-thief had fooled him. He had lost face before all his people. Still they continued to roar out their laughter. Makamuk turned, and with bowed head stalked away. He knew that thenceforth he would be no longer known as Makamuk. He would be Lost Face; the record of his shame would be with him until he died; and whenever the tribes gathered in the spring for the salmon, or in the summer for the trading, the story would pass back and forth across the camp-fires of how the fur-thief died peaceably, at a single stroke, by the hand of Lost Face.

"Who was Lost Face?" he could hear, in anticipation, some insolent young buck demand. "Oh, Lost Face," would be the answer, "he who once was Makamuk in the days before he cut off the fur-thief's head."

KOOLAU THE LEPER

"Because we are sick they take away our liberty. We have obeyed the law. We have done no wrong. And yet they would put us in prison. Molokai is a prison. That you know. Niuli, there, his sister was sent to Molokai seven years ago. He has not seen her since. Nor will he ever see her. She must stay there until she dies. This is not her will. It is not Niuli's will. It is the will of the white men who rule the land. And who are these white men?

"We know. We have it from our fathers and our fathers' fathers. They came like lambs, speaking softly. Well might they speak softly, for we were many and strong, and all the islands were ours. As I say, they spoke softly. They were of two kinds. The one kind asked our permission, our gracious permission, to preach to us the word of God. The other kind asked our permission, our gracious permission, to trade with us. That was the beginning. To-day all the islands are theirs, all the land, all the cattle—everything is theirs. They that preached the word of God and they that preached the word of Rum have fore-gathered and become great chiefs. They live like kings in houses of many rooms, with multitudes of servants to care for them. They who had nothing have everything, and if you, or I, or any Kanaka be hungry, they sneer and say, 'Well, why don't you work? There are the plantations.'"

Koolau paused. He raised one hand, and with gnarled and twisted fingers lifted up the blazing wreath of hibiscus that crowned his black hair. The moonlight bathed the scene in silver. It was a night of peace, though those who sat about him and listened had all the seeming of battle-wrecks. Their faces were leonine. Here a space yawned in a face where should have been a nose, and there an arm-stump showed where a hand had rotted off. They were men and women beyond the pale, the thirty of them, for upon them had been placed the mark of the beast.

They sat, flower-garlanded, in the perfumed, luminous night, and their lips made uncouth noises and their throats rasped approval of Koolau's speech. They were creatures who once had been men and women. But they were men and women no longer. They were monsters—in face and form grotesque caricatures of everything human. They were hideously maimed and distorted, and had the seeming of creatures that had been racked in millenniums of hell. Their hands, when they possessed them, were like harpy-claws. Their faces were the misfits and slips, crushed and bruised by some mad god at play in the machinery of life. Here and there were features which the mad god had smeared half away, and one woman wept scalding tears from twin pits of horror, where her eyes once had been. Some were in pain and groaned from their chests. Others coughed, making sounds like the tearing of tissue. Two were idiots, more like huge apes marred in the making, until even an ape were an angel. They mowed and gibbered in the moonlight, under crowns of drooping, golden blossoms. One, whose bloated ear-lobe flapped like a fan upon his shoulder, caught up a gorgeous flower of orange and scarlet and with it decorated the monstrous ear that flip-flapped with his every movement.

And over these things Koolau was king. And this was his kingdom, —a flower-throttled gorge, with beetling cliffs and crags, from which floated the blattings of wild goats. On three sides the grim walls rose, festooned in fantastic draperies of tropic vegetation and pierced by cave-entrances—the rocky lairs of Koolau's subjects. On the fourth side the earth fell away into a tremendous abyss, and, far below, could be seen the summits of lesser peaks and crags, at whose bases foamed and rumbled the Pacific surge. In fine weather a boat could land on the rocky beach that marked the entrance of Kalalau Valley, but the weather must be very fine. And a cool-headed mountaineer might climb from the beach to the head of Kalalau Valley, to this pocket among the peaks where Koolau ruled; but such a mountaineer must be very cool of head, and he must know the wild-goat trails as well. The marvel was that the mass of human wreckage that constituted Koolau's people should have been able to drag its helpless misery over the giddy goat-trails to this inaccessible spot.

"Brothers," Koolau began.

But one of the mowing, apelike travesties emitted a wild shriek of madness, and Koolau waited while the shrill cachination was tossed back and forth among the rocky walls and echoed distantly through the pulseless night.

"Brothers, is it not strange? Ours was the land, and behold, the land is not ours. What did these preachers of the word of God and the word of Rum give us for the land? Have you received one dollar, as much as one dollar, any one of you, for the land? Yet it is theirs, and in return they tell us we can go to work on the land, their land, and that what we produce by our toil shall be theirs. Yet in the old days we did not have to work. Also, when we are sick, they take away our freedom."

"Who brought the sickness, Koolau?" demanded Kiloliana, a lean and wiry man with a face so like a laughing faun's that one might expect to see the cloven hoofs under him. They were cloven, it was true, but the cleavages were great ulcers and livid putrefactions. Yet this was Kiloliana, the most daring climber of them all, the man who knew every goat-trail and who had led Koolau and his wretched followers into the recesses of Kalalau.

"Ay, well questioned," Koolau answered. "Because we would not work the miles of sugar-cane where once our horses pastured, they brought the Chinese slaves from over seas. And with them came the Chinese sickness—that which we suffer from and because of which they would imprison us on Molokai. We were born on Kauai. We have been to the other islands, some here and some there, to Oahu, to Maui, to Hawaii, to Honolulu. Yet always did we come back to Kauai. Why did we come back? There must be a reason. Because we love Kauai. We were born here. Here we have lived. And here shall we die—unless—unless—there be weak hearts amongst us. Such we do not want. They are fit for Molokai. And if there be such, let them not remain. To-morrow the soldiers land on the shore. Let the weak hearts go down to them. They will be sent swiftly to Molokai. As for us, we shall stay and fight. But know that we will not die. We have rifles. You know the narrow trails where men must creep, one by one. I, alone, Koolau, who was once a cowboy on Niihau, can hold the trail against a thousand men. Here is Kapalei, who was once a judge over men and a man with honor, but who is now a hunted rat, like you and me. Hear him. He is wise."

Kapalei arose. Once he had been a judge. He had gone to college at Punahou. He had sat at meat with lords and chiefs and the high representatives of alien powers who protected the interests of traders and missionaries. Such had been Kapalei. But now, as Koolau had said, he was a hunted rat, a creature outside the law, sunk so deep in the mire of human horror that he was above the law as well as beneath it. His face was featureless, save for gaping orifices and for the lidless eyes that burned under hairless brows.

"Let us not make trouble," he began. "We ask to be left alone. But if they do not leave us alone, then is the trouble theirs, and the penalty. My fingers are gone, as you see." He held up his stumps of hands that all might see. "Yet have I the joint of one thumb left, and it can pull a trigger as firmly as did its lost neighbor in the old days. We love Kauai. Let us live here, or die here, but do not let us go to the prison of Molokai. The sickness is not ours. We have not sinned. The men who preached the word of God and the word of Rum brought the sickness with the coolie slaves who work the stolen land. I have been a judge. I know the law and the justice, and I say to you it is unjust to steal a man's land, to make that man sick with the Chinese sickness, and then to put that man in prison for life."

"Life is short, and the days are filled with pain," said Koolau. "Let us drink and dance and be happy as we can."

From one of the rocky lairs calabashes were produced and passed around. The calabashes were filled with the fierce distillation of the root of the *ti*-plant; and as the liquid fire coursed through them and mounted to their brains, they forgot that they had once been men and women, for they were men and women once more. The woman who wept scalding tears from open eye-pits was indeed a woman apulse with life as she plucked the strings of an *ukulele* and lifted her voice in a barbaric love-call such as might have come from the dark forest-depths of the primeval world. The air tingled with her cry, softly imperious and seductive. Upon a mat, timing his rhythm to the woman's song, Kiloliana danced. It was unmistakable. Love danced in all his movements, and, next, dancing with him on the mat, was a woman whose heavy hips and generous breast gave the lie to her disease-corroded face. It was a dance of the living dead, for in their disintegrating bodies life still loved and longed. Ever the woman whose sightless eyes ran scalding tears chanted her love-cry, ever the dancers danced of love in the warm night, and ever the calabashes went around till in all their brains were maggots crawling of memory and desire. And with the woman on the mat danced a slender maid whose face was beautiful and unmarred, but whose twisted arms that rose and fell marked the disease's ravage. And the two idiots, gibbering and mouthing strange noises, danced apart, grotesque, fantastic, travestying love as they themselves had been travestied by life.

But the woman's love-cry broke midway, the calabashes were lowered, and the dancers ceased, as all gazed into the abyss above the sea, where a rocket flared like a wan phantom through the moonlit air.

"It is the soldiers," said Koolau. "Tomorrow there will be fighting. It is well to sleep and be prepared."

The lepers obeyed, crawling away to their lairs in the cliff, until only Koolau remained, sitting motionless in the moonlight, his rifle across his knees, as he gazed far down to the boats landing on the beach.

The far head of Kalalau Valley had been well chosen as a refuge.

Except Kiloliana, who knew back-trails up the precipitous walls, no man could win to the gorge save by advancing across a knife-edged ridge. This passage was a hundred yards in length. At best, it was a scant twelve inches wide. On either side yawned the abyss. A slip, and to right or left the man would fall to his death. But once across he would find himself in an earthly paradise. A sea of vegetation laved the landscape, pouring its green billows from wall to wall, dripping from the cliff-lips in great vine-masses, and flinging a spray of ferns and airplants into the multitudinous crevices. During the many months of Koolau's rule, he and his followers had fought with this vegetable sea. The choking jungle, with its riot of blossoms, had been driven back from the bananas, oranges, and mangoes that grew wild. In little clearings grew the wild arrowroot; on stone terraces, filled with soil scrapings, were the *taro* patches and the melons; and in every open space where the sunshine penetrated, were *papaia* trees burdened with their golden fruit.

Koolau had been driven to this refuge from the lower valley by the beach. And if he were driven from it in turn, he knew of gorges among the jumbled peaks of the inner fastnesses where he could lead his subjects and live. And now he lay with his rifle beside him, peering down through a tangled screen of foliage at the soldiers on the beach. He noted that they had large guns with them, from which the sunshine flashed as from mirrors. The knife-edged passage lay directly before him. Crawling upward along the trail that led to it he could see tiny specks of men. He knew they were not the soldiers, but the police. When they failed, then the soldiers would enter the game.

He affectionately rubbed a twisted hand along his rifle barrel and made sure that the sights were clean. He had learned to shoot as a wild-cattle hunter on Niihau, and on that island his skill as a marksman was unforgotten. As the toiling specks of men grew nearer and larger, he estimated the range, judged the deflection of the wind that swept at right angles across the line of fire, and calculated the chances of over-shooting marks that were so far below his level. But he did not shoot. Not until they reached the beginning of the passage did he make his presence known. He did not disclose himself, but spoke from the thicket.

"What do you want?" he demanded.

"We want Koolau, the leper," answered the man who led the native police, himself a blue-eyed American.

"You must go back," Koolau said.

He knew the man, a deputy sheriff, for it was by him that he had been harried out of Niihau, across Kauai, to Kalalau Valley, and out of the valley to the gorge.

"Who are you?" the sheriff asked.

"I am Koolau, the leper," was the reply.

"Then come out. We want you. Dead or alive, there is a thousand dollars on your head. You cannot escape."

Koolau laughed aloud in the thicket.

"Come out!" the sheriff commanded, and was answered by silence.

He conferred with the police, and Koolau saw that they were preparing to rush him.

"Koolau," the sheriff called. "Koolau, I am coming across to get you."

"Then look first and well about you at the sun and sea and sky, for it will be the last time you behold them."

"That's all right, Koolau," the sheriff said soothingly. "I know you're a dead shot. But you won't shoot me. I have never done you any wrong."

Koolau grunted in the thicket.

"I say, you know, I've never done you any wrong, have I?" the sheriff persisted.

"You do me wrong when you try to put me in prison," was the reply. "And you do me wrong when you try for the thousand dollars on my head. If you will live, stay where you are."

"I've got to come across and get you. I'm sorry. But it is my duty."

"You will die before you get across."

The sheriff was no coward. Yet was he undecided. He gazed into the gulf on either side, and ran his eyes along the knife-edge he must travel. Then he made up his mind.

"Koolau," he called.

But the thicket remained silent.

"Koolau, don't shoot. I am coming."

The sheriff turned, gave some orders to the police, then started on his perilous way. He advanced slowly. It was like walking a tight rope. He had nothing to lean upon but the air. The lava rock crumbled under his feet, and on either side the dislodged fragments pitched downward through the depths. The sun blazed upon him, and his face was wet with sweat. Still he advanced, until the halfway point was reached.

"Stop!" Koolau commanded from the thicket. "One more step and I shoot."

The sheriff halted, swaying for balance as he stood poised above the void. His face was pale, but his eyes were determined. He licked his dry lips before he spoke.

"Koolau, you won't shoot me. I know you won't."

He started once more. The bullet whirled him half about. On his face was an expression of querulous surprise as he reeled to the fall. He tried to save himself by throwing his body across the knife-edge; but at that moment he knew death. The next moment the knife-edge was vacant. Then came the rush, five policemen, in single file, with superb steadiness, running along the knife-edge. At the same instant the rest of the posse opened fire on the thicket. It was madness. Five times Koolau pulled the trigger, so rapidly that his shots constituted a rattle. Changing his position and crouching low under the bullets that were biting and singing through the bushes, he peered out. Four of the police had followed the sheriff. The fifth lay across the knife-edge, still alive. On the farther side, no longer firing, were the surviving police. On the naked rock there was no hope for them. Before they could clamber down Koolau could have picked off the last man. But he did not fire, and, after a conference, one of them took off a white undershirt and waved it as a flag. Followed by another, he advanced along the knife-edge to their wounded comrade. Koolau gave no sign, but watched them slowly withdraw and become specks as they descended into the lower valley.

Two hours later, from another thicket, Koolau watched a body of police trying to make the ascent from the opposite side of the valley. He saw the wild goats flee before them as they climbed higher and higher, until he doubted his judgment and sent for Kiloliana who crawled in beside him.

"No, there is no way," said Kiloliana.

"The goats?" Koolau questioned.

"They come over from the next valley, but they cannot pass to this. There is no way. Those men are not wiser than goats. They may fall to their deaths. Let us watch."

"They are brave men," said Koolau. "Let us watch."

Side by side they lay among the morning-glories, with the yellow blossoms of the *hau* dropping upon them from overhead, watching the motes of men toil upward, till the thing happened, and three of them, slipping, rolling, sliding, dashed over a cliff-lip and fell sheer half a thousand feet.

Kiloliana chuckled.

"We will be bothered no more," he said.

"They have war guns," Koolau made answer. "The soldiers have not yet spoken."

In the drowsy afternoon, most of the lepers lay in their rock dens asleep. Koolau, his rifle on his knees, fresh-cleaned and ready, dozed in the entrance to his own den. The maid with the twisted arm lay below in the thicket and kept watch on the knife-edge passage. Suddenly Koolau was startled wide awake by the sound of an explosion on the beach. The next instant the atmosphere was incredibly rent asunder. The terrible sound frightened him. It was as if all the gods had caught the envelope of the sky in their hands and were ripping it apart as a woman rips apart a sheet of cotton cloth. But it was such an immense ripping, growing swiftly nearer. Koolau glanced up apprehensively, as if expecting to see the thing. Then high up on the cliff overhead the shell burst in a fountain of black smoke. The rock was shattered, the fragments falling to the foot of the cliff.

Koolau passed his hand across his sweaty brow. He was terribly shaken. He had had no experience with shell-fire, and this was more dreadful than anything he had imagined.

"One," said Kapahei, suddenly bethinking himself to keep count.

A second and a third shell flew screaming over the top of the wall, bursting beyond view. Kapahei methodically kept the count. The lepers crowded into the open space before the caves. At first they were frightened, but as the shells continued their flight overhead the leper folk became reassured and began to admire the spectacle. The two idiots shrieked with delight, prancing wild antics as each air-tormenting shell went by. Koolau began to recover his confidence. No damage was being done. Evidently they could not aim such large missiles at such long range with the precision of a rifle.

But a change came over the situation. The shells began to fall short. One burst below in the thicket by the knife-edge. Koolau remembered the maid who lay there on watch, and ran down to see. The smoke was still rising from the bushes when he crawled in. He was astounded. The branches were splintered and broken. Where the girl had lain was a hole in the ground. The girl herself was in shattered fragments. The shell had burst right on her.

First peering out to make sure no soldiers were attempting the passage, Koolau started back on the run for the caves. All the time the shells were moaning, whining, screaming by, and the valley was rumbling and reverberating with the explosions. As he came in sight of the caves, he saw the two idiots cavorting about, clutching each other's hands with their stumps of fingers. Even as he ran, Koolau saw a spout of black smoke rise from the ground, near to the idiots. They were flung apart bodily by the explosion. One lay motionless, but the other was dragging himself by his hands toward the cave. His legs trailed out helplessly behind him, while the blood was pouring from his body. He seemed bathed in blood, and as he crawled he cried like a little dog. The rest of the lepers, with the exception of Kapahei, had fled into the caves.

"Seventeen," said Kapahei. "Eighteen," he added.

This last shell had fairly entered into one of the caves. The explosion caused all the caves to empty. But from the particular cave no one emerged. Koolau crept in through the pungent, acrid smoke. Four bodies, frightfully mangled, lay about. One of them was the sightless woman whose tears till now had never ceased.

Outside, Koolau found his people in a panic and already beginning to climb the goat trail that led out of the gorge and on among the jumbled heights and chasms. The wounded idiot, whining feebly and dragging himself along on the ground by his hands, was trying to follow. But at the first pitch of the wall his helplessness overcame him and he fell back.

"It would be better to kill him," said Koolau to Kapahei, who still sat in the same place.

"Twenty-two," Kapahei answered. "Yes, it would be a wise thing to kill him. Twenty-three—twenty-four."

The idiot whined sharply when he saw the rifle leveled at him. Koolau hesitated, then lowered the gun.

"It is a hard thing to do," he said.

"You are a fool, twenty-six, twenty-seven," said Kapahei. "Let me show you."

He arose and, with a heavy fragment of rock in his hand, approached the wounded thing. As he lifted his arm to strike, a shell burst full upon him, relieving him of the necessity of the act and at the same time putting an end to his count.

Koolau was alone in the gorge. He watched the last of his people drag their crippled bodies over the brow of the height and disappear. Then he turned and went down to the thicket where the maid had been killed. The shell-fire still continued, but he remained; for far below he could see the soldiers climbing up. A shell burst twenty feet away. Flattening himself into the earth, he heard the rush of the fragments above his body. A shower of *hau* blossoms rained upon him. He lifted his head to peer down the trail, and sighed. He was very much afraid. Bullets from rifles would not have worried him, but this shell-fire was abominable. Each time a shell shrieked by he shivered and crouched; but each time he lifted his head again to watch the trail.

At last the shells ceased. This, he reasoned, was because the soldiers were drawing near. They crept along the trail in single file, and he tried to count them until he lost track. At any rate, there were a hundred or so of them—all come after Koolau the leper. He felt a fleeting prod of pride. With war guns and rifles, police and soldiers, they came for him, and he was only one man, a crippled wreck of a man at that. They offered a thousand dollars for him, dead or alive. In all his life he had never possessed that much money. The thought was a bitter one. Kapahei had been right. He, Koolau, had done no wrong. Because the *haoles* wanted labor with which to work the stolen land, they had brought in the Chinese coolies, and with them had come the sickness. And now, because he had caught the sickness, he was worth a thousand dollars—but not to himself. It was his worthless carcass, rotten with disease or dead from a bursting shell, that was worth all that money.

When the soldiers reached the knife-edged passage, he was prompted to warn them. But his gaze fell upon the body of the murdered maid, and he kept silent. When six had ventured on the knife-edge, he opened fire. Nor did he cease when the knife-edge was bare. He emptied his magazine, reloaded, and emptied it again. He kept on shooting. All his wrongs were blazing in his brain, and he was in a fury of vengeance. All down the goat trail the soldiers were firing, and though they lay flat and sought to shelter themselves in the shallow inequalities of the surface, they were exposed marks to him. Bullets whistled and thudded about him, and an occasional ricochet sang sharply through the air. One bullet ploughed a crease through his scalp, and a second burned across his shoulder-blade without breaking the skin.

It was a massacre, in which one man did the killing. The soldiers began to retreat, helping along their wounded. As Koolau picked them off he became aware of the smell of burnt meat. He glanced about him at first, and then discovered that it was his own hands. The heat of the rifle was doing it. The leprosy had destroyed most of the nerves in his hands. Though his flesh burned and he smelled it, there was no sensation.

He lay in the thicket, smiling, until he remembered the war guns. Without doubt they would open up on him again, and this time upon the very thicket from which he had inflicted the damage. Scarcely had he changed his position to a nook behind a small shoulder of the wall where he had noted that no shells fell, than the bombardment recommenced. He counted the shells. Sixty more were thrown into the gorge before the war-guns ceased. The tiny area was pitted with their explosions, until it seemed impossible that any creature could have survived. So the soldiers thought, for, under the burning afternoon sun, they climbed the goat trail again. And again the knife-edged passage was disputed, and again they fell back to the beach.

For two days longer Koolau held the passage, though the soldiers contented themselves with flinging shells into his retreat. Then Pahau, a leper boy, came to the top of the wall at the back of the gorge and shouted down to him that Kiloliana, hunting goats that they might eat, had been killed by a fall, and that the women were frightened and knew not what to do. Koolau called the boy down and left him with a spare gun with which to guard the passage. Koolau found his people disheartened. The majority of them were too helpless to forage food for themselves under such forbidding circumstances, and all were starving. He selected two women and a man who were not too far gone with the disease, and sent them back to the gorge to bring up food and mats. The rest he cheered and consoled until even the weakest took a hand in building rough shelters for themselves.

But those he had dispatched for food did not return, and he started back for the gorge. As he came out on the brow of the wall, half a dozen rifles cracked. A bullet tore through the fleshy part of his shoulder, and his cheek was cut by a sliver of rock where a second bullet smashed against the cliff. In the moment that this happened, and he leaped back, he saw that the gorge was alive with soldiers. His own people had betrayed him. The shell-fire had been too terrible, and they had preferred the prison of Molokai.

Koolau dropped back and unslung one of his heavy cartridge-belts. Lying among the rocks, he allowed the head and shoulders of the first soldier to rise clearly into view before pulling trigger. Twice this happened, and then, after some delay, in place of a head and shoulders a white flag was thrust above the edge of the wall.

"What do you want?" he demanded.

"I want you, if you are Koolau the leper," came the answer.

Koolau forgot where he was, forgot everything, as he lay and marvelled at the strange persistence of these *haoles* who would have their will though the sky fell in. Aye, they would have their will over all men and all things, even though they died in getting it. He could not but admire them, too, what of that will in them that was stronger than life and that bent all things to their bidding. He was convinced of the hopelessness of his struggle. There was no gainsaying that terrible will of the *haoles*. Though he killed a thousand, yet would they rise like the sands of the sea and come upon him, ever more and more. They never knew when they were beaten. That was their fault and their virtue. It was where his own kind lacked. He could see, now, how the handful of the preachers of God and the preachers of Rum had conquered the land. It was because—

"Well, what have you got to say? Will you come with me?"

It was the voice of the invisible man under the white flag. There he was, like any *haole,* driving straight toward the end determined.

"Let us talk," said Koolau.

The man's head and shoulders arose, then his whole body. He was a smooth-faced, blue-eyed youngster of twenty-five, slender and natty in his captain's uniform. He advanced until halted, then seated himself a dozen feet away:—

"You are a brave man," said Koolau wonderingly. "I could kill you like a fly."

"No, you couldn't," was the answer.

"Why not?"

"Because you are a man, Koolau, though a bad one. I know your story. You kill fairly."

Koolau grunted, but was secretly pleased.

"What have you done with my people?" he demanded. "The boy, the two women, and the man?"

"They gave themselves up, as I have now come for you to do."

Koolau laughed incredulously.

"I am a free man," he announced. "I have done no wrong. All I ask is to be left alone. I have lived free, and I shall die free. I will never give myself up."

"Then your people are wiser than you," answered the young captain. "Look—they are coming now."

Koolau turned and watched the remnant of his band approach. Groaning and sighing, a ghastly procession, it dragged its wretchedness past. It was given to Koolau to taste a deeper bitterness, for they hurled imprecations and insults at him as they went by; and the panting hag who brought up the rear halted, and with skinny, harpy-claws extended, shaking her snarling death's head from side to side, she laid a curse upon him. One by one they dropped over the lip-edge and surrendered to the hiding soldiers.

"You can go now," said Koolau to the captain. "I will never give myself up. That is my last word. Good-by."

The captain slipped over the cliff to his soldiers. The next moment, and without a flag of truce, he hoisted his hat on his scabbard, and Koolau's bullet tore through it. That afternoon they shelled him out from the beach, and as he retreated into the high inaccessible pockets beyond, the soldiers followed him.

For six weeks they hunted him from pocket to pocket, over the volcanic peaks and along the goat trails. When he hid in the lantana jungle, they formed lines of beaters, and through lantana jungle and guava scrub they drove him like a rabbit. But ever he turned and doubled and eluded. There was no cornering him. When pressed too closely, his sure rifle held them back and they carried their wounded down the goat trails to the beach. There were times when they did the shooting as his brown body showed for a moment through the underbrush. Once, five of them caught him on an exposed goat trail between pockets. They emptied their rifles at him as he limped and climbed along his dizzy way. Afterward they found blood-stains and knew that he was wounded. At the end of six weeks they gave up. The soldiers and police returned to Honolulu, and Kalalau Valley was left to him for his own, though head-hunters ventured after him from time to time and to their own undoing.

Two years later, and for the last time, Koolau crawled unto a thicket and lay down among the *ti*-leaves and wild ginger blossoms. Free he had lived, and free he was dying. A slight drizzle of rain began to fall, and he drew a ragged blanket about the distorted wreck of his limbs. His body was covered with an oilskin coat. Across his chest he laid his Mauser rifle, lingering affectionately for a moment to wipe the dampness from the barrel. The hand with which he wiped had no fingers left upon it with which to pull the trigger.

He closed his eyes, for, from the weakness in his body and the fuzzy turmoil in his brain, he knew that his end was near. Like a wild animal he had crept into hiding to die. Half-conscious, aimless and wandering, he lived back in his life to his early manhood on Niihau. As life faded and the drip of the rain grew dim in his ears, it seemed to him that he was once more in the thick of the horse-breaking, with raw colts rearing and bucking under him, his stirrups tied together beneath, or charging madly about the breaking corral and driving the helping cowboys over the rails. The next instant, and with seeming naturalness, he found himself pursuing the wild bulls of the upland pastures, roping them and leading them down to the valleys. Again the sweat and dust of the branding pen stung his eyes and bit his nostrils.

All his lusty, whole-bodied youth was his, until the sharp pangs of impending dissolution brought him back. He lifted his monstrous hands and gazed at them in wonder. But how? Why? Why should the wholeness of that wild youth of his change to this? Then he remembered, and once again, and for a moment, he was Koolau, the leper. His eyelids fluttered wearily down and the drip of the rain ceased in his ears. A prolonged trembling set up in his body. This, too, ceased. He half-lifted his head, but it fell back. Then his eyes opened, and did not close. His last thought was of his Mauser, and he pressed it against his chest with his folded, fingerless hands.

CHUN AH CHUN

There was nothing striking in the appearance of Chun Ah Chun. He was rather undersized, as Chinese go, and the Chinese narrow shoulders and spareness of flesh were his. The average tourist, casually glimpsing him on the streets of Honolulu, would have concluded that he was a good-natured little Chinese, probably the proprietor of a prosperous laundry or tailorshop. In so far as good nature and prosperity went, the judgment would be correct, though beneath the mark; for Ah Chun was as good-natured as he was prosperous, and of the latter no man knew a tithe the tale. It was well known that he was enormously wealthy, but in his case "enormous" was merely the symbol for the unknown.

Ah Chun had shrewd little eyes, black and beady and so very little that they were like gimlet-holes. But they were wide apart, and they sheltered under a forehead that was patently the forehead of a thinker. For Ah Chun had his problems, and had had them all his life. —Not that he ever worried over them. He was essentially a philosopher, and whether as coolie, or multi-millionnaire and master of many men, his poise of soul was the same. He lived always in the high equanimity of spiritual repose, undeterred by good fortune, unruffled by ill fortune. All things went well with him, whether they were blows from the overseer in the cane field or a slump in the price of sugar when he owned those cane fields himself. Thus, from the steadfast rock of his sure content he mastered problems such as are given to few men to consider, much less to a Chinese peasant.

He was precisely that—a Chinese peasant, born to labor in the fields all his days like a beast, but fated to escape from the fields like the prince in a fairy tale. Ah Chun did not remember his father, a small farmer in a district not far from Canton; nor did he remember much of his mother, who had died when he was six. But he did remember his respected uncle, Ah Kow, for him had he served as a slave from his

sixth year to his twenty-fourth. It was then that he escaped by contracting himself as a coolie to labor for three years on the sugar plantations
of Hawaii for fifty cents a day.

Ah Chun was observant. He perceived little details that not one man
in a thousand ever noticed. Three years he worked in the field, at the
end of which time he knew more about cane-growing than the overseers
or even the superintendent, while the superintendent would have been
astounded at the knowledge the weazened little coolie possessed of the
reduction processes in the mill. But Ah Chun did not study only sugar
processes. He studied to find out how men came to be owners of sugar
mills and plantations. One judgment he achieved early, namely, that
men did not become rich from the labor of their own hands. He knew,
for he had labored for a score of years himself. The men who grew rich
did so from the labor of the hands of others. That man was richest who
had the greatest number of his fellow-creatures toiling for him.

So, when his term of contract was up, Ah Chun invested his savings
in a small importing store, going into partnership with one, Ah Yung.
The firm ultimately became the great one of "Ah Chun & Ah Yung,"
which handled anything from India silks and ginseng to guano islands
and blackbird brigs. In the meantime, Ah Chun hired out as cook. He
was a good cook, and in three years he was the highest-paid chef in
Honolulu. His career was assured, and he was a fool to abandon it, as
Dantin, his employer, told him; but Ah Chun knew his own mind best,
and for knowing it was called a triple-fool and given a present of fifty
dollars over and above the wages due him.

The firm of Ah Chun & Ah Yung was prospering. There was no
need for Ah Chun longer to be a cook. There were boom times in
Hawaii. Sugar was being extensively planted, and labor was needed. Ah
Chun saw the chance, and went into the labor-importing business. He
brought thousands of Cantonese coolies into Hawaii, and his wealth
began to grow. He made investments. His beady black eyes saw bar-
gains where other men saw bankruptcy. He bought a fish-pond for a
song, which later paid five hundred per cent and was the opening wedge
by which he monopolized the fish market of Honolulu. He did not talk
for publication, nor figure in politics, nor play at revolutions, but he
forecast events more clearly and farther ahead than did the men who
engineered them. In his mind's eye he saw Honolulu a modern, electric-
lighted city at a time when it straggled, unkempt and sand-tormented,
over a barren reef of uplifted coral rock. So he bought land. He bought
land from merchants who needed ready cash, from impecunious natives,
from riotous traders' sons, from widows and orphans and the lepers
deported to Molokai; and, somehow, as the years went by, the pieces

of land he had bought proved to be needed for warehouses, or office buildings, or hotels. He leased, and rented, sold and bought, and resold again.

But there were other things as well. He put his confidence and his money into Parkinson, the renegade captain whom nobody would trust. And Parkinson sailed away on mysterious voyages in the little *Vega*. Parkinson was taken care of until he died, and years afterward Honolulu was astonished when the news leaked out that the Drake and Acorn guano islands had been sold to the British Phosphate Trust for three-quarters of a million. Then there were the fat, lush days of King Kala-kaua, when Ah Chun paid three hundred thousand dollars for the opium license. If he paid a third of a million for the drug monopoly, the investment was nevertheless a good one, for the dividends bought him the Kalalau Plantation, which, in turn, paid him thirty per cent for seventeen years and was ultimately sold by him for a million and a half.

It was under the Kamehamehas, long before, that he had served his own country as Chinese Consul—a position that was not altogether unlucrative; and it was under Kamehameha IV that he changed his citizenship, becoming an Hawaiian subject in order to marry Stella Allendale, herself a subject of the brown-skinned king, though more of Anglo-Saxon blood ran in her veins than of Polynesian. In fact, the random breeds in her were so attenuated that they were valued at eights and sixteenths. In the latter proportion was the blood of her great-grandmother, Paahao—the Princess Paahao, for she came of the royal line. Stella Allendale's great-grandfather had been a Captain Blunt, an English adventurer who took service under Kamehameha I and was made a tabu chief himself. Her grandfather had been a New Bedford whaling captain, while through her own father had been introduced a remote blend of Italian and Portuguese which had been grafted upon his own English stock. Legally a Hawaiian, Ah Chun's spouse was more of any one of three other nationalities.

And into this conglomerate of the races, Ah Chun introduced the Mongolian mixture. Thus, his children by Mrs. Ah Chun were one thirty-second Polynesian, one-sixteenth Italian, one-sixteenth Portuguese, one-half Chinese, and eleven thirty-seconds English and American. It might well be that Ah Chun would have refrained from matrimony could he have foreseen the wonderful family that was to spring from this union. It was wonderful in many ways. First, there was its size. There were fifteen sons and daughters, mostly daughters. The sons had come first, three of them, and then had followed, in unswerving sequence, a round dozen of girls. The blend of the races was excellent. Not alone fruitful did it prove, for the progeny, without exception, was healthy and without blemish. But the most amazing thing about the family was its beauty. All the girls were beautiful—delicately, ethereally beautiful. Mama Ah Chun's rotund lines seemed to modify papa Ah Chun's lean angles, so that the daughters were willowy without being lathy, round-muscled without being chubby. In every feature of every face were haunting reminiscences of Asia, all manipulated over and disguised by old England, New England, and South of Europe. No observer, without information, would have guessed the heavy Chinese strain in their veins; nor could any observer, after being informed, fail to note immediately the Chinese traces.

As beauties, the Ah Chun girls were something new. Nothing like them had been seen before. They resembled nothing so much as they resembled one another, and yet each girl was sharply individual. There was no mistaking one for another. On the other hand, Maud, who was blue-eyed and yellow-haired, would remind one instantly of Henrietta, an olive brunette with large, languishing dark eyes and hair that was blue-black. The hint of resemblance that ran through them all, reconciling every differentiation, was Ah Chun's contribution. He had furnished the groundwork upon which had been traced the blended patterns of the races. He had furnished the slim-boned Chinese frame, upon which had been builded the delicacies and subtleties of Saxon, Latin, and Polynesian flesh.

Mrs. Ah Chun had ideas of her own to which Ah Chun gave credence, though never permitting them expression when they conflicted with his own philosophic calm. She had been used all her life to living in European fashion. Very well. Ah Chun gave her a European mansion. Later, as his sons and daughters grew able to advise, he built the bungalow, a spacious, rambling affair, as unpretentious as it was magnificent. Also, as time went by, there arose a mountain house on Tantalus, to which the family could flee when the "sick wind" blew from the south. And at Waikiki he built a beach residence on an extensive site so well chosen that later on, when the United States government condemned it for fortification purposes, an immense sum accompanied the condemnation. In all his houses were billiard and smoking rooms and guest rooms galore, for Ah Chun's wonderful progeny was given to lavish entertainment. The furnishing was extravagantly simple. Kings' ransoms were expended without display—thanks to the educated tastes of the progeny.

Ah Chun had been liberal in the matter of education. "Never mind expense," he had argued in the old days with Parkinson when that slack mariner could see no reason for making the *Vega* seaworthy; "you sail the schooner, I pay the bills." And so with his sons and daughters. It had been for them to get the education and never mind the expense. Harold, the eldest-born, had gone to Harvard and Oxford; Albert and Charles had gone through Yale in the same classes. And the daughters, from the eldest down, had undergone their preparation at Mills Seminary in California and passed on to Vassar, Wellesley, or Bryn Mawr. Several, having so desired, had had the finishing touches put on in Europe. And from all the world Ah Chun's sons and daughters returned to him to suggest and advise in the garnishment of the chaste magnificence of his residences. Ah Chun himself preferred the voluptuous glitter of Oriental display; but he was a philosopher, and he clearly saw that his children's tastes were correct according to Western standards.

Of course, his children were not known as the Ah Chun children. As he had evolved from a coolie laborer to a multi-millionnaire, so had his name evolved. Mama Ah Chun had spelled it A'Chun, but her wiser offspring had elided the apostrophe and spelled it Achun. Ah Chun did not object. The spelling of his name interfered no whit with his comfort nor his philosophic calm. Besides, he was not proud. But when his children arose to the height of a starched shirt, a stiff collar, and a frock coat, they did interfere with his comfort and calm. Ah Chun would have none of it. He preferred the loose-flowing robes of China, and neither could they cajole nor bully him into making the change. They tried both courses, and in the latter one failed especially disastrously. They had not been to America for nothing. They had learned the virtues of the boycott as employed by organized labor, and he, their father, Chun Ah Chun, they boycotted in his own house, Mama Achun aiding and abetting. But Ah Chun himself, while unversed in Western culture, was thoroughly conversant with Western labor conditions. An extensive employer of labor himself, he knew how to cope with its tactics. Promptly he imposed a lockout on his rebellious progeny and erring spouse. He discharged his scores of servants, locked up his stables, closed his houses, and went to live in the Royal Hawaiian Hotel, in which enterprise he happened to be the heaviest stockholder. The family fluttered distractedly on visits about with friends, while Ah Chun calmly managed his many affairs, smoked his long pipe with the tiny silver bowl, and pondered the problem of his wonderful progeny.

This problem did not disturb his calm. He knew in his philosopher's soul that when it was ripe he would solve it. In the meantime he enforced the lesson that, complacent as he might be, he was nevertheless the absolute dictator of the Achun destinies. The family held out for a week, then returned, along with Ah Chun and the many servants to occupy the bungalow once more. And thereafter no question was raised when Ah Chun elected to enter his brilliant drawing-room in blue silk robe, wadded slippers, and black silk skull-cap with red button peak, or when he chose to draw at his slender-stemmed silver-bowled pipe among the cigarette- and cigar-smoking officers and civilians on the broad verandas or in the smoking room.

Ah Chun occupied a unique position in Honolulu. Though he did not appear in society, he was eligible anywhere. Except among the Chinese merchants of the city, he never went out; but he received, and he was always the centre of his household and the head of his table. Himself peasant-born Chinese, he presided over an atmosphere of culture and refinement second to none in all the islands. Nor were there any in all the islands too proud to cross his threshold and enjoy his hospitality. First of all, the Achun bungalow was of irreproachable tone. Next, Ah Chun was a power. And, finally, Ah Chun was a moral paragon and an honest business man. Despite the fact that business morality was higher than on the mainland, Ah Chun outshone the business men of Honolulu in the scrupulous rigidity of his honesty. It was a saying that his word was as good as his bond. His signature was never needed to bind him. He never broke his word. Twenty years after Hotchkiss, of Hotchkiss, Morterson Company, died, they found among mislaid papers a memorandum of a loan of thirty thousand dollars to Ah Chun. It had been incurred when Ah Chun was privy counsellor to Kamehameha II. In the bustle and confusion of those heyday, money-making times, the affair had slipped Ah Chun's mind. There was no note, no legal claim against him, but he settled in full with the Hotchkiss' Estate, voluntarily paying a compound interest that dwarfed the principal. Likewise, when he verbally guaranteed the disastrous Kakiku Ditch Scheme, at a time when the least sanguine did not dream a guarantee necessary—"Signed his check for two hundred thousand without a quiver, gentlemen, without a quiver," was the report of the secretary of the defunct enterprise, who had been sent on the forlorn hope of finding out Ah Chun's intentions. And on top of the many similar actions that were true of his word, there was scarcely a man of repute in the islands that at one time or another had not experienced the helping financial hand of Ah Chun.

So it was that Honolulu watched his wonderful family grow up into a perplexing problem and secretly sympathized with him, for it was beyond any of them to imagine what he was going to do with it. But Ah Chun saw the problem more clearly than they. No one knew as he knew the extent to which he was an alien in his family. His own family did not guess it. He saw that there was no place for him amongst this marvellous seed of his loins, and he looked forward to his declining years and knew that he would grow more and more alien. He did not understand his children. Their conversation was of things that did not interest him and about which he knew nothing. The culture of the West had passed him by. He was Asiatic to the last fibre, which meant that he was heathen. Their Christianity was to him so much nonsense. But all this he would have ignored as extraneous and irrelevant, could he have but understood the young people themselves. When Maud, for instance, told him that the housekeeping bills for the month were thirty thousand—that he understood, as he understood Albert's request for five thousand with which to buy the schooner yacht *Muriel* and become a member of the Hawaiian Yacht Club. But it was their remoter, complicated desires and mental processes that obfuscated him. He was not slow in learning that the mind of each son and daughter was a secret labyrinth which he could never hope to tread. Always he came upon the wall that divides East from West. Their souls were inaccessible to him, and by the same token he knew that his soul was inaccessible to them.

Besides, as the years came upon him, he found himself harking back more and more to his own kind. The reeking smells of the Chinese quarter were spicy to him. He sniffed them with satisfaction as he passed along the street, for in his mind they carried him back to the narrow tortuous alleys of Canton swarming with life and movement. He regretted that he had cut off his queue to please Stella Allendale in the prenuptial days, and he seriously considered the advisability of shaving his crown and growing a new one. The dishes his highly paid chef concocted for him failed to tickle his reminiscent palate in the way that the weird messes did in the stuffy restaurant down in the Chinese quarter. He enjoyed vastly more a half-hour's smoke and chat with two or three Chinese chums, than to preside at the lavish and elegant dinners for which his bungalow was famed, where the pick of the Americans and Europeans sat at the long table, men and women on equality, the women with jewels that blazed in the subdued light against white necks and arms, the men in evening dress, and all chattering and laughing over topics and witticisms that, while they were not exactly Greek to him, did not interest him nor entertain.

But it was not merely his alienness and his growing desire to return to his Chinese flesh-pots that constituted the problem. There was also his wealth. He had looked forward to a placid old age. He had worked hard. His reward should have been peace and repose. But he knew that with his immense fortune peace and repose could not possibly be his. Already there were signs and omens. He had seen similar troubles before. There was his old employer, Dantin, whose children had wrested from him, by due process of law, the management of his property, having the Court appoint guardians to administer it for him. Ah Chun knew, and knew thoroughly well, that had Dantin been a poor man, it would have been found that he could quite rationally manage his own affairs. And old Dantin had had only three children and half a million, while he, Chun Ah Chun, had fifteen children and no one but himself knew how many millions.

"Our daughters are beautiful women," he said to his wife, one evening. "There are many young men. The house is always full of young men. My cigar bills are very heavy. Why are there no marriages?"

Mama Achun shrugged her shoulders and waited.

"Women are women and men are men—it is strange there are no marriages. Perhaps the young men do not like our daughters."

"Ah, they like them well enough," Mama Achun answered; "but you see, they cannot forget that you are your daughters' father."

"Yet you forgot who my father was," Ah Chun said gravely. "All you asked was for me to cut off my queue."

"The young men are more particular than I was, I fancy."

"What is the greatest thing in the world?" Ah Chun demanded with abrupt irrelevance.

Mama Achun pondered for a moment, then replied: "God."

He nodded. "There are gods and gods. Some are paper, some are wood, some are bronze. I use a small one in the office for a paper-weight. In the Bishop Museum are many gods of coral rock and lava-stone."

"But there is only one God," she announced decisively, stiffening her ample frame argumentatively.

Ah Chun noted the danger signal and sheered off.

"What is greater than God, then?" he asked. "I will tell you. It is money. In my time I have had dealings with Jews and Christians, Mohammedans and Buddhists, and with little black men from the Solomons and New Guinea who carried their god about them, wrapped in oiled paper. They possessed various gods, these men, but they all worshipped money. There is that Captain Higginson. He seems to like Henrietta."

"He will never marry her," retorted Mama Achun. "He will be an admiral before he dies—"

"A rear admiral," Ah Chun interpolated. "Yes, I know. That is the way they retire.

"His family in the United States is a high one. They would not like it if he married . . . if he did not marry an American girl."

Ah Chun knocked the ashes out of his pipe and thoughtfully refilled the silver bowl with a tiny pleget of tobacco. He lighted it and smoked it out before he spoke.

"Henrietta is the oldest girl. The day she marries I will give her three hundred thousand dollars. That will fetch that Captain Higginson and his high family along with him. Let the word go out to him. I leave it to you."

And Ah Chun sat and smoked on, and in the curling smoke-wreaths he saw take shape the face and figure of Toy Shuey—Toy Shuey, the maid of all work in his uncle's house in the Cantonese village, whose work was never done and who received for a whole year's work one dollar. And he saw his youthful self arise in the curling smoke, his youthful self who had toiled eighteen years in his uncle's field for little more. And now he, Ah Chun, the peasant, dowered his daughter with three hundred thousand years of such toil. And she was but one daughter of a dozen. He was not elated at the thought. It struck him that it was a funny, whimsical world, and he chuckled aloud and startled Mama Achun from a revery which he knew lay deep in the hidden crypts of her being where he had never penetrated.

But Ah Chun's word went forth, as a whisper, and Captain Higginson forgot his rear-admiralship and his high family and took to wife three hundred thousand dollars and a refined and cultured girl who was one thirty-second Polynesian, one-sixteenth Italian, one-sixteenth Portuguese, eleven thirty-seconds English and Yankee, and one-half Chinese.

Ah Chun's munificence had its effect. His daughters became suddenly eligible and desirable. Clara was the next, but when the Secretary of the Territory formally proposed for her, Ah Chun informed him that he must await his turn, that Maud was the oldest and that she must be married first. It was shrewd policy. The whole family was made vitally interested in marrying off Maud, which it did in three months, to Ned Humphreys, the United States immigration commissioner. Both he and Maud complained, for the dowry was only two hundred thousand. Ah Chun explained that his initial generosity had been to break the ice, and that after that his daughters could not expect otherwise than to go more cheaply.

Clara followed Maud, and thereafter, for a space of two years, there was a continuous round of weddings in the bungalow. In the meantime Ah Chun had not been idle. Investment after investment was called in. He sold out his interests in a score of enterprises, and step by step, so as not to cause a slump in the market, he disposed of his large holdings in real estate. Toward the last he did precipitate a slump and sold at sacrifice. What caused this haste were the squalls he saw already rising above the horizon. By the time Lucille was married, echoes of bickerings and jealousies were already rumbling in his ears. The air was thick with schemes and counter schemes to gain his favor and to prejudice him against one or another or all but one of his sons-in-law. All of which was not conducive to the peace and repose he had planned for his old age.

He hastened his efforts. For a long time he had been in correspondence with the chief banks in Shangai and Macao. Every steamer for several years had carried away drafts drawn in favor of one, Chun Ah Chun, for deposit in those Far Eastern banks. The drafts now became heavier. His two youngest daughters were not yet married. He did not wait, but dowered them with a hundred thousand each, which sums lay in the Bank of Hawaii, drawing interest and awaiting their wedding day. Albert took over the business of the firm of Ah Chun & Ah Yung, Harold, the eldest, having elected to take a quarter of a million and go to England to live. Charles, the youngest, took a hundred thousand, a legal guardian, and a course in a Keeley institute. To Mama Achun was given the bungalow, the mountain House on Tantalus, and a new sea-side residence in place of the one Ah Chun sold to the government. Also, to Mama Achun was given half a million in money well invested.

Ah Chun was now ready to crack the nut of the problem. One fine morning when the family was at breakfast—he had seen to it that all his sons-in-law and their wives were present—he announced that he was returning to his ancestral soil. In a neat little homily he explained that he had made ample provision for his family, and he laid down various maxims that he was sure, he said, would enable them to dwell together in peace and harmony. Also, he gave business advice to his sons-in-law, preached the virtues of temperate living and safe invest-ments, and gave them the benefit of his encyclopedic knowledge of industrial and business conditions in Hawaii. Then he called for his carriage, and, in the company of the weeping Mama Achun, was driven down to the Pacific Mail steamer, leaving behind him a panic in the bungalow. Captain Higginson clamored wildly for an injunction. The daughters shed copious tears. One of their husbands, an ex-Federal judge, questioned Ah Chun's sanity, and hastened to the proper author-ities to inquire into it. He returned with the information that Ah Chun had appeared before the commission the day before, demanded an ex-amination, and passed with flying colors. There was nothing to be done, so they went down and said good-by to the little old man, who waved farewell from the promenade deck as the big steamer poked her nose seaward through the coral reef.

But the little old man was not bound for Canton. He knew his own country too well, and the squeeze of the Mandarins, to venture into it with the tidy bulk of wealth that remained to him. He went to Macao. Now Ah Chun had long exercised the power of a king and he was as imperious as a king. When he landed at Macao and went into the office of the biggest European hotel to register, the clerk closed the book on him. Chinese were not permitted. Ah Chun called for the manager and was treated with contumely. He drove away, but in two hours he was back again. He called the clerk and manager in, gave them a month's salary, and discharged them. He had made himself the owner of the hotel; and in the finest suite he settled down during the many months the gorgeous palace in the suburbs was building for him. In the meantime, with the inevitable ability that was his, he increased the earnings of his big hotel from three per cent to thirty.

The troubles Ah Chun had flown began early. There were sons-in-law that made bad investments, others that played ducks and drakes with the Achun dowries. Ah Chun being out of it, they looked at Mama Ah Chun and her half million, and, looking, engendered not the best of feeling toward one another. Lawyers waxed fat in the striving to ascertain the construction of trust deeds. Suits, cross-suits, and counter-suits cluttered the Hawaiian courts. Nor did the police courts escape. There were angry encounters in which harsh words and harsher blows were struck. There were such things as flower-pots being thrown to add emphasis to winged words. And suits for libel arose that dragged their way through the courts and kept Honolulu agog with excitement over the revelations of the witnesses.

In his palace, surrounded by all dear delights of the Orient, Ah Chun smokes his placid pipe and listens to the turmoil overseas. Each mail steamer, in faultless English, typewritten on an American machine, a letter goes from Macao to Honolulu, in which, by admirable texts and precepts, Ah Chun advises his family to live in unity and harmony. As for himself, he is out of it all and well content. He has won to peace and repose. At times he chuckles and rubs his hands, and his slant little black eyes twinkle merrily at the thought of the funny world. For out of all his living and philosophizing that remains to him—the conviction that it is a very funny world.

THE HEATHEN

I met him first in a hurricane; and though we had gone through the hurricane on the same schooner, it was not until the schooner had gone to pieces under us that I first laid eyes on him. Without doubt I had seen him with the rest of the kanaka crew on board, but I had not consciously been aware of his existence, for the *Petite Jeanne* was rather overcrowded. In addition to her eight or ten kanaka seamen, her white captain, mate, and supercargo, and her six cabin passengers, she sailed from Rangiroa with something like eighty-five deck passengers—Paumotans and Tahitians, men, women, and children each with a trade box, to say nothing of sleeping-mats, blankets, and clothes-bundles.

The pearling season in the Paumotus was over, and all hands were returning to Tahiti. The six of us cabin passengers were pearl-buyers. Two were Americans, one was Ah Choon (the whitest Chinese I have ever known), one was a German, one was a Polish Jew, and I completed the half dozen.

It had been a prosperous season. Not one of us had cause for complaint, nor one of the eighty-five deck passengers either. All had done well, and all were looking forward to a rest-off and a good time in Papeete.

Of course, the *Petite Jeanne* was over-loaded. She was only seventy tons, and she had no right to carry a tithe of the mob she had on board. Beneath her hatches she was crammed and jammed with pearl-shell and copra. Even the trade room was packed full with shell. It was a miracle that the sailors could work her. There was no moving about the decks. They simply climbed back and forth along the rails.

In the night-time they walked upon the sleepers, who carpeted the deck, I'll swear, two deep. Oh! and there were pigs and chickens on deck, and sacks of yams, while every conceivable place was festooned with strings of drinking cocoanuts and bunches of bananas. On both sides, between the fore and main shrouds, guys had been stretched, just low enough for the fore-boom to swing clear; and from each of these guys at least fifty bunches of bananas were suspended.

It promised to be a messy passage, even if we did make it in the two or three days that would have been required if the southeast trades had been blowing fresh. But they weren't blowing fresh. After the first five hours the trade died away in a dozen or so gasping fans. The calm continued all that night and the next day—one of those glaring, glassy, calms, when the very thought of opening one's eyes to look at it is sufficient to cause a headache.

The second day a man died—an Easter Islander, one of the best divers that season in the lagoon. Smallpox—that is what it was; though how smallpox could come on board, when there had been no known cases ashore when we left Rangiroa, is beyond me. There it was, though—smallpox, a man dead, and three others down on their backs.

There was nothing to be done. We could not segregate the sick, nor could we care for them. We were packed like sardines. There was nothing to do but rot and die—that is, there was nothing to do after the night that followed the first death. On that night, the mate, the super-cargo, the Polish Jew, and four native divers sneaked away in the large whale-boat. They were never heard of again. In the morning the captain promptly scuttled the remaining boats, and there we were.

That day there were two deaths; the following day three; then it jumped to eight. It was curious to see how we took it. The natives, for instance, fell into a condition of dumb, stolid fear. The captain—Oudouse, his name was, a Frenchman—became very nervous and voluble. He actually got the twitches. He was a large, fleshy man, weighing at least two hundred pounds, and he quickly became a faithful representation of a quivering jelly-mountain of fat.

The German, the two Americans, and myself bought up all the Scotch whiskey, and proceeded to stay drunk. The theory was beautiful—namely, if we kept ourselves soaked in alcohol, every smallpox germ that came into contact with us would immediately be scorched to a cinder. And the theory worked, though I must confess that neither Captain Oudouse nor Ah Choon were attacked by the disease either. The Frenchman did not drink at all, while Ah Choon restricted himself to one drink daily.

It was a pretty time. The sun, going into northern declination, was straight overhead. There was no wind, except for frequent squalls, which blew fiercely for from five minutes to half an hour, and wound up by deluging us with rain. After each squall, the awful sun would come out, drawing clouds of steam from the soaked decks.

The steam was not nice. It was the vapor of death, freighted with millions and millions of germs. We always took another drink when we saw it going up from the dead and dying, and usually we took two or three more drinks, mixing them exceptionally stiff. Also, we made it a rule to take an additional several each time they hove the dead over to the sharks that swarmed about us.

We had a week of it, and then the whiskey gave out. It is just as well, or I shouldn't be alive now. It took a sober man to pull through what followed, as you will agree when I mention the little fact that only two men did pull through. The other man was the heathen—at least, that was what I heard Captain Oudouse call him at the moment I first became aware of the heathen's existence. But to come back.

It was at the end of the week, with the whiskey gone, and the pearl-buyers sober, that I happened to glance at the barometer that hung in the cabin companionway. Its normal register in the Paumotus was 29.90, and it was quite customary to see it vacillate between 29.85 and 30.00, or even 30.05; but to see it as I saw it, down to 29.62, was sufficient to sober the most drunken pearl-buyer that ever incinerated smallpox microbes in Scotch whiskey.

I called Captain Oudouse's attention to it, only to be informed that he had watched it going down for several hours. There was little to do, but that little he did very well, considering the circumstances. He took off the light sails, shortened right down to storm canvas, spread life-lines, and waited for the wind. His mistake lay in what he did after the wind came. He hove to on the port tack, which was the right thing to do south of the Equator, if—and there was the rub—*if* one were *not* in the direct path of the hurricane.

We were in the direct path. I could see that by the steady increase of the wind and the equally steady fall of the barometer. I wanted him to turn and run with the wind on the port quarter until the barometer ceased falling, and then to heave to. We argued till he was reduced to hysteria, but budge he would not. The worst of it was that I could not get the rest of the pearl-buyers to back me up. Who was I, anyway, to know more about the sea and its ways than a properly qualified captain? was what was in their minds, I knew.

Of course the sea rose with the wind frightfully; and I shall never forget the first three seas the *Petite Jeanne* shipped. She had fallen off, as vessels do at times when hove to, and the first sea made a clean breach. The life-lines were only for the strong and well, and little good were they even for them when the women and children, the bananas and cocoanuts, the pigs and trade boxes, the sick and the dying, were swept along in a solid, screeching, groaning mass.

The second sea filled the *Petite Jeanne*'s decks flush with the rails; and, as her stern sank down and her bow tossed skyward, all the miserable dunnage of life and luggage poured aft. It was a human torrent. They came head-first, feet-first, sidewise, rolling over and over, twisting, squirming, writhing, and crumpling up. Now and again one caught a grip on a stanchion or a rope; but the weight of the bodies behind tore such grips loose.

One man I noticed fetch up, head on and square on, with the starboard-bitt. His head cracked like an egg. I saw what was coming, sprang on top of the cabin, and from there into the mainsail itself. Ah Choon and one of the Americans tried to follow me, but I was one jump ahead of them. The American was swept away and over the stern like a piece of chaff. Ah Choon caught a spoke of the wheel, and swung in behind it. But a strapping Raratonga vahine (woman)—she must have weighed two hundred and fifty—brought up against him, and got an arm around his neck. He clutched the kanaka steersman with his other hand; and just at that moment the schooner flung down to starboard.

The rush of bodies and sea that was coming along the port runway between the cabin and the rail turned abruptly and poured to starboard. Away they went—vahine, Ah Choon, and steersman; and I swear I saw Ah Choon grin at me with philosophic resignation as he cleared the rail and went under.

The third sea—the biggest of the three—did not do so much damage. By the time it arrived nearly everybody was in the rigging. On deck perhaps a dozen gasping, half-drowned, and half-stunned wretches were rolling about or attempting to crawl into safety. They went by the board, as did the wreckage of the two remaining boats. The other pearl-buyers and myself, between seas, managed to get about fifteen women and children into the cabin, and battened down. Little good it did the poor creatures in the end.

Wind? Out of all my experience I could not have believed it possible for the wind to blow as it did. There is no describing it. How can one describe a nightmare? It was the same way with that wind. It tore the clothes off our bodies. I say *tore them off,* and I mean it. I am not asking you to believe it. I am merely telling something that I saw and felt. There are times when I do not believe it myself. I went through it, and that is enough. One could not face that wind and live. It was a monstrous thing, and the most monstrous thing about it was that it increased and continued to increase.

Imagine countless millions and billions of tons of sand. Imagine this sand tearing along at ninety, a hundred, a hundred and twenty, or any other number of miles per hour. Imagine, further, this sand to be invisible, impalpable, yet to retain all the weight and density of sand. Do all this, and you may get a vague inkling of what that wind was like.

Perhaps sand is not the right comparison. Consider it mud, invisible, impalpable, but heavy as mud. Nay, it goes beyond that. Consider every molecule of air to be a mud-bank in itself. Then try to imagine the multitudinous impact of mud-banks. No; it is beyond me. Language may be adequate to express the ordinary conditions of life, but it cannot possibly express any of the conditions of so enormous a blast of wind. It would have been better had I stuck by my original intention of not attempting a description.

I will say this much: The sea, which had risen at first, was beaten down by that wind. More: it seemed as if the whole ocean had been sucked up in the maw of the hurricane, and hurled on through that portion of space which previously had been occupied by the air.

Of course, our canvas had gone long before. But Captain Oudouse had on the *Petite Jeanne* something I had never before seen on a South Sea schooner—a sea-anchor. It was a conical canvas bag, the mouth of which was kept open by a huge hoop of iron. The sea-anchor was bridled something like a kite, so that it bit into the water as a kite bites into the air, but with a difference. The sea-anchor remained just under the surface of the ocean in a perpendicular position. A long line, in turn, connected it with the schooner. As a result, the *Petite Jeanne* rode bow on to the wind and to what sea there was.

The situation really would have been favorable had we not been in the path of the storm. True, the wind itself tore our canvas out of the gaskets, jerked out our topmasts, and made a raffle of our running-gear, but still we would have come through nicely had we not been square in front of the advancing storm-centre. That was what fixed us. I was in a state of stunned, numbed, paralysed collapse from enduring the impact of the wind, and I think I was just about ready to give up and die when the centre smote us. The blow we received was an absolute lull. There was not a breath of air. The effect on one was sickening.

Remember that for hours we had been at terrific muscular tension, withstanding the awful pressure of that wind. And then, suddenly, the pressure was removed. I know that I felt as though I was about to expand, to fly apart in all directions. It seemed as if every atom composing my body was repelling every other atom and was on the verge of rushing off irresistibly into space. But that lasted only for a moment. Destruction was upon us.

In the absence of the wind and pressure the sea rose. It jumped, it leaped, it soared straight toward the clouds. Remember, from every point of the compass that inconceivable wind was blowing in toward the centre of calm. The result was that the seas sprang up from every point of the compass. There was no wind to check them. They popped up like corks released from the bottom of a pail of water. There was no system to them, no stability. They were hollow, maniacal seas. They were eighty feet high at the least. They were not seas at all. They resembled no sea a man had ever seen.

They were splashes, monstrous splashes—that is all. Splashes that were eighty feet high. Eighty! They were more than eighty. They went over our mastheads. They were spouts, explosions. They were drunken. They fell anywhere, anyhow. They jostled one another; they collided. They rushed together and collapsed upon one another, or fell apart like a thousand waterfalls all at once. It was no ocean any man had ever dreamed of, that hurricane centre. It was confusion thrice confounded. It was anarchy. It was a hell-pit of sea-water gone mad.

The *Petite Jeanne?* I don't know. The heathen told me afterwards that he did not know. She was literally torn apart, ripped wide open, beaten into a pulp, smashed into kindling wood, annihilated. When I came to I was in the water, swimming automatically, though I was about two-thirds drowned. How I got there I had no recollection. I remembered seeing the *Petite Jeanne* fly to pieces at what must have been the instant that my own consciousness was buffeted out of me. But there I was, with nothing to do but make the best of it, and in that best there was little promise. The wind was blowing again, the sea was much smaller and more regular, and I knew that I had passed through the centre. Fortunately, there were no sharks about. The hurricane had dissipated the ravenous horde that had surrounded the death ship and fed off the dead.

It was about midday when the *Petite Jeanne* went to pieces, and it must have been two hours afterwards when I picked up with one of her hatch-covers. Thick rain was driving at the time; and it was the merest chance that flung me and the hatch-cover together. A short length of line was trailing from the rope handle; and I knew that I was good for a day, at least, if the sharks did not return. Three hours later, possibly a little longer, sticking close to the cover, and, with closed eyes, concentrating my whole soul upon the task of breathing in enough air to keep me going and at the same time of avoiding breathing in enough water to drown me, it seemed to me that I heard voices. The rain had ceased, and wind and sea were easing marvellously. Not twenty feet away from me, on another hatch-cover, were Captain Oudouse and the heathen. They were fighting over the possession of the cover—at least, the Frenchman was.

"Païen noir!" I heard him scream, and at the same time I saw him kick the kanaka.

Now, Captain Oudouse had lost all his clothes, except his shoes, and they were heavy brogans. It was a cruel blow, for it caught the heathen on the mouth and the point of the chin, half stunning him. I looked for him to retaliate, but he contented himself with swimming about forlornly a safe ten feet away. Whenever a fling of the sea threw him closer, the Frenchman, hanging on with his hands, kicked out at him with both feet. Also, at the moment of delivering each kick, he called the kanaka a black heathen.

"For two centimes I'd come over there and drown you, you white beast!" I yelled.

The only reason I did not go was that I felt too tired. The very thought of the effort to swim over was nauseating. So I called to the kanaka to come to me, and proceeded to share the hatch-cover with him. Otoo, he told me his name was (pronounced ō-tō-ō); also, he told me that he was a native of Bora Bora, the most westerly of the Society Group. As I learned afterward, he had got the hatch-cover first, and, after some time, encountering Captain Oudouse, had offered to share it with him, and had been kicked off for his pains.

And that was how Otoo and I first came together. He was no fighter. He was all sweetness and gentleness, a love-creature, though he stood nearly six feet tall and was muscled like a gladiator. He was no fighter, but he was also no coward. He had the heart of a lion; and in the years that followed I have seen him run risks that I would never dream of taking. What I mean is that while he was no fighter, and while he always avoided precipitating a row, he never ran away from trouble when it started. And it was "'Ware shoal!" when once Otoo went into action. I shall never forget what he did to Bill King. It occurred in German Samoa. Bill King was hailed the champion heavyweight of the American Navy. He was a big brute of a man, a veritable gorilla, one of those hard-hitting, rough-housing chaps, and clever with his fists as well. He picked the quarrel, and he kicked Otoo twice and struck him once before Otoo felt it to be necessary to fight. I don't think it lasted four minutes, at the end of which time Bill King was the unhappy possessor of four broken ribs, a broken forearm, and a dislocated shoulder-blade. Otoo knew nothing of scientific boxing. He was merely a man-handler; and Bill King was something like three months in recovering from the bit of manhandling he received that afternoon on Apia beach.

But I am running ahead of my yarn. We shared the hatch-cover between us. We took turn and turn about, one lying flat on the cover and resting, while the other, submerged to the neck, merely held on with his hands. For two days and nights, spell and spell, on the cover and in the water, we drifted over the ocean. Towards the last I was delirious most of the time; and there were times, too, when I heard Otoo babbling and raving in his native tongue. Our continuous immersion prevented us from dying of thirst, though the sea-water and the sunshine gave us the prettiest imaginable combination of salt pickle and sunburn.

In the end, Otoo saved my life; for I came to lying on the beach twenty feet from the water, sheltered from the sun by a couple of cocoanut leaves. No one but Otoo could have dragged me there and stuck up the leaves for shade. He was lying beside me. I went off again; and the next time I came round, it was cool and starry night, and Otoo was pressing a drinking cocoanut to my lips.

We were the sole survivors of the *Petite Jeanne*. Captain Oudouse must have succumbed to exhaustion, for several days later his hatch-cover drifted ashore without him. Otoo and I lived with the natives of the atoll for a week, when we were rescued by the French cruiser and taken to Tahiti. In the meantime, however, we had performed the ceremony of exchanging names. In the South Seas such a ceremony binds two men closer together than blood-brothership. The initiative had been mine; and Otoo was rapturously delighted when I suggested it.

"It is well," he said, in Tahitian. "For we have been mates together for two days on the lips of Death."

"But Death stuttered," I smiled.

"It was a brave deed you did, master," he replied, "and Death was not vile enough to speak."

"Why do you 'master' me?" I demanded, with a show of hurt feelings. "We have exchanged names. To you I am Otoo. To me you are Charley. And between you and me, forever and forever, you shall be Charley, and I shall be Otoo. It is the way of the custom. And when we die, if it does happen that we live again somewhere beyond the stars and the sky, still shall you be Charley to me, and I Otoo to you."

"Yes, master," he answered, his eyes luminous and soft with joy.

"There you go!" I cried indignantly.

"What does it matter what my lips utter?" he argued. "They are only my lips. But I shall think Otoo always. Whenever I think of myself, I shall think of you. Whenever men call me by name, I shall think of you. And beyond the sky and beyond the stars, always and forever, you shall be Otoo to me. Is it well, master?"

I hid my smile, and answered that it was well.

We parted at Papeete. I remained ashore to recuperate; and he went on in a cutter to his own island, Bora Bora. Six weeks later he was back. I was surprised, for he had told me of his wife, and said that he was returning to her, and would give over sailing on far voyages.

"Where do you go, master?" he asked, after our first greetings.

I shrugged my shoulders. It was a hard question.

"All the world," was my answer—"all the world, all the sea, and all the islands that are in the sea."

"I will go with you," he said simply. "My wife is dead."

I never had a brother; but from what I have seen of other men's brothers, I doubt if any man ever had a brother that was to him what Otoo was to me. He was brother and father and mother as well. And this I know: I lived a straighter and better man because of Otoo. I cared little for other men, but I had to live straight in Otoo's eyes. Because of him I dared not tarnish myself. He made me his ideal, compounding me, I fear, chiefly out of his own love and worship; and there were times when I stood close to the steep pitch of hell, and would have taken the plunge had not the thought of Otoo restrained me. His pride in me entered into me, until it became one of the major rules in my personal code to do nothing that would diminish that pride of his.

Naturally, I did not learn right away what his feelings were toward me. He never criticised, never censured; and slowly the exalted place I held in his eyes dawned upon me, and slowly I grew to comprehend the hurt I could inflict upon him by being anything less than my best.

For seventeen years we were together; for seventeen years he was at my shoulder, watching while I slept, nursing me through fever and wounds—ay, and receiving wounds in fighting for me. He signed on the same ships with me; and together we ranged the Pacific from Hawaii to Sydney Head, and from Torres Straits to the Galapagos. We black-birded from the New Hebrides and the Line Islands over to the westward clear through the Louisades, New Britain, New Ireland, and New Hanover. We were wrecked three times—in the Gilberts, in the Santa Cruz group, and in the Fijis. And we traded and slaved wherever a dollar promised in the way of pearl and pearl-shell, copra, bêche-de-mer, hawkbill turtle-shell, and stranded wrecks.

It began in Papeete, immediately after his announcement that he was going with me over all the sea, and the islands in the midst thereof. There was a club in those days in Papeete, where the pearlers, traders, captains, and riffraff of South Sea adventurers forgathered. The play ran high, and the drink ran high; and I am very much afraid that I kept later hours than were becoming or proper. No matter what the hour was when I left the club, there was Otoo waiting to see me safely home.

At first I smiled; next I chided him. Then I told him flatly that I stood in need of no wet-nursing. After that I did not see him when I came out of the club. Quite by accident, a week or so later, I discovered that he still saw me home, lurking across the street among the shadows of the mango-trees. What could I do? I know what I did do.

Insensibly I began to keep better hours. On wet and stormy nights, in the thick of the folly and the fun, the thought would persist in coming to me of Otoo keeping his dreary vigil under the dripping mangoes. Truly, he made a better man of me. Yet he was not strait-laced. And he knew nothing of common Christian morality. All the people on Bora Bora were Christians; but he was a heathen, the only unbeliever on the island, a gross materialist, who believed that when he died he was dead. He believed merely in fair play and square dealing. Petty meanness, in his code, was almost as serious as wanton homicide; and I do believe that he respected a murderer more than a man given to small practices.

Concerning me, personally, he objected to my doing anything that was hurtful to me. Gambling was all right. He was an ardent gambler himself. But late hours, he explained, were bad for one's health. He had seen men who did not take care of themselves die of fever. He was no teetotaller, and welcomed a stiff nip any time when it was wet work in the boats. On the other hand, he believed in liquor in moderation. He had seen many men killed or disgraced by square-face or Scotch.

Otoo had my welfare always at heart. He thought ahead for me, weighed my plans, and took a greater interest in them than I did myself. At first, when I was unaware of this interest of his in my affairs, he had to divine my intentions, as, for instance, at Papeete, when I contemplated going partners with a knavish fellow-countryman on a guano venture. I did not know he was a knave. Nor did any white man in Papeete. Neither did Otoo know, but he saw how thick we were getting, and found out for me, and without my asking him. Native sailors from the ends of the seas knock about on the beach in Tahiti; and Otoo, suspicious merely, went among them till he had gathered sufficient data to justify his suspicions. Oh, it was a nice history, that of Randolph Waters. I couldn't believe it when Otoo first narrated it; but when I sheeted it home to Waters he gave in without a murmur, and got away on the first steamer to Aukland.

At first, I am free to confess, I couldn't help resenting Otoo's poking his nose into my business. But I knew that he was wholly unselfish; and soon I had to acknowledge his wisdom and discretion. He had his eyes open always to my main chance, and he was both keen-sighted and far-sighted. In time he became my counsellor, until he knew more of my business than I did myself. He really had my interest at heart more than I did. Mine was the magnificent carelessness of youth, for I preferred romance to dollars, and adventure to a comfortable billet with all night in. So it was well that I had some one to look out for me. I know that if it had not been for Otoo, I should not be here to-day.

Of numerous instances, let me give one. I had had some experience in blackbirding before I went pearling in the Paumotus. Otoo and I were on the beach in Samoa—we really were on the beach and hard aground—when my chance came to go as recruiter on a blackbird brig. Otoo signed on before the mast; and for the next half-dozen years, in as many ships, we knocked about the wildest portions of Melanesia. Otoo saw to it that he always pulled stroke-oar in my boat. Our custom in recruiting labor was to land the recruiter on the beach. The covering boat always lay on its oars several hundred feet off shore, while the recruiter's boat, also lying on its oars, kept afloat on the edge of the beach. When I landed with my trade-goods, leaving my steering sweep apeak, Otoo left his stroke position and came into the stern-sheets, where a Winchester lay ready to hand under a flap of canvas. The boat's crew was also armed, the Sniders concealed under canvas flaps that ran the length of the gunwales. While I was busy arguing and persuading the woolly-headed cannibals to come and labor on the Queensland plantations Otoo kept watch. And often and often his low voice warned me of suspicious actions and impending treachery. Sometimes it was the quick shot from his rifle, knocking a nigger over, that was the first warning I received. And in my rush to the boat his hand was always there to jerk me flying aboard. Once, I remember, on *Santa Anna,* the boat grounded just as the trouble began. The covering boat was dashing to our assistance, but the several score of savages would have wiped us out before it arrived. Otoo took a flying leap ashore, dug both hands into the trade-goods, and scattered tobacco, beads, tomahawks, knives, and calicoes in all directions.

This was too much for the woolly-heads. While they scrambled for the treasures, the boat was shoved clear, and we were aboard and forty feet away. And I got thirty recruits off that very beach in the next four hours.

The particular instance I have in mind was on Malaita, the most savage island in the easterly Solomons. The natives had been remarkably friendly; and how were we to know that the whole village had been taking up a collection for over two years with which to buy a white man's head? The beggars are all head-hunters, and they especially esteem a white man's head. The fellow who captured the head would receive the whole collection. As I say, they appeared very friendly; and on this day I was fully a hundred yards down the beach from the boat.

Otoo had cautioned me; and, as usual when I did not heed him, I came to grief.

The first I knew, a cloud of spears sailed out of the mangrove swamp at me. At least a dozen were sticking into me. I started to run, but tripped over one that was fast in my calf, and went down. The woolly-heads made a run for me, each with a long-handled, fantail tomahawk with which to hack off my head. They were so eager for the prize that they got in one another's way. In the confusion, I avoided several hacks by throwing myself right and left on the sand.

Then Otoo arrived—Otoo the manhandler. In some way he had got hold of a heavy war club, and at close quarters it was a far more efficient weapon than a rifle. He was right in the thick of them, so that they could not spear him, while their tomahawks seemed worse than useless. He was fighting for me, and he was in a true Berserker rage. The way he handled that club was amazing. Their skulls squashed like overripe oranges. It was not until he had driven them back, picked me up in his arms, and started to run, that he received his first wounds. He arrived in the boat with four spear thrusts, got his Winchester, and with it got a man for every shot. Then we pulled aboard the schooner, and doctored up.

Seventeen years we were together. He made me. I should to-day be a supercargo, a recruiter, or a memory, if it had not been for him.

"You spend your money, and you go out and get more," he said one day. "It is easy to get money now. But when you get old, your money will be spent, and you will not be able to go out and get more. I know, master. I have studied the way of white men. On the beaches are many old men who were young once, and who could get money just like you. Now they are old, and they have nothing, and they wait about for the young men like you to come ashore and buy drinks for them.

"The black boy is a slave on the plantations. He gets twenty dollars a year. He works hard. The overseer does not work hard. He rides a horse and watches the black boy work. He gets twelve hundred dollars a year. I am a sailor on the schooner. I get fifteen dollars a month. That is because I am a good sailor. I work hard. The captain has a double awning, and drinks beer out of long bottles. I have never seen him haul a rope or pull an oar. He gets one hundred and fifty dollars a month. I am a sailor. He is a navigator. Master, I think it would be very good for you to know navigation."

Otoo spurred me on to it. He sailed with me as second mate on my first schooner, and he was far prouder of my command than I was myself. Later on it was:

"The captain is well paid, master; but the ship is in his keeping, and he is never free from the burden. It is the owner who is better paid—the owner who sits ashore with many servants and turns his money over."

"True, but a schooner costs five thousand dollars—an old schooner at that," I objected. "I should be an old man before I saved five thousand dollars."

"There be short ways for white men to make money," he went on, pointing ashore at the cocoanut-fringed beach.

We were in the Solomons at the time, picking up a cargo of ivory-nuts along the east coast of Guadalcanar.

"Between this river mouth and the next it is two miles," he said. "The flat land runs far back. It is worth nothing now. Next year—who knows?—or the year after, men will pay much money for that land. The anchorage is good. Big steamers can lie close up. You can buy the land four miles deep from the old chief for ten thousand sticks of tobacco, ten bottles of square-face, and a Snider, which will cost you, maybe, one hundred dollars. Then you place the deed with the commissioner; and the next year, or the year after, you sell and become the owner of a ship."

I followed his lead, and his words came true, though in three years, instead of two. Next came the grasslands deal on Guadalcanar—twenty thousand acres, on a governmental nine hundred and ninety-nine years' lease at a nominal sum. I owned the lease for precisely ninety days, when I sold it to a company for half a fortune. Always it was Otoo who looked ahead and saw the opportunity. He was responsible for the salving of the *Doncaster*—bought in at auction for a hundred pounds, and clearing three thousand after every expense was paid. He led me into the Savaii plantation and the cocoa venture on Upolu.

We did not go seafaring so much as in the old days. I was too well off. I married, and my standard of living rose; but Otoo remained the same old-time Otoo, moving about the house or trailing through the office, his wooden pipe in his mouth, a shilling undershirt on his back, and a four-shilling lava-lava about his loins. I could not get him to spend money. There was no way of repaying him except with love, and God knows he got that in full measure from all of us. The children worshipped him; and if he had been spoilable, my wife would surely have been his undoing.

The children! He really was the one who showed them the way of their feet in the world practical. He began by teaching them to walk. He sat up with them when they were sick. One by one, when they were scarcely toddlers, he took them down to the lagoon, and made them into amphibians. He taught them more than I ever knew of the habits of fish and the ways of catching them. In the bush it was the same thing. At seven, Tom knew more woodcraft than I ever dreamed existed. At six, Mary went over the Sliding Rock without a quiver, and I have seen strong men balk at that feat. And when Frank had just turned six he could bring up shillings from the bottom in three fathoms.

"My people in Bora Bora do not like heathen—they are all Christians; and I do not like Bora Bora Christians," he said one day, when I, with the idea of getting him to spend some of the money that was rightfully his, had been trying to persuade him to make a visit to his own island in one of our schooners—a special voyage which I had hoped to make a record breaker in the matter of prodigal expense.

I say one of *our* schooners, though legally at the time they belonged to me. I struggled long with him to enter into partnership.

"We have been partners from the day the *Petite Jeanne* went down," he said at last. "But if your heart so wishes, then shall we become partners by the law. I have no work to do, yet are my expenses large. I drink and eat and smoke in plenty—it costs much, I know. I do not pay for the playing of billiards, for I play on your table; but still the money goes. Fishing on the reef is only a rich man's pleasure. It is shocking, the cost of hooks and cotton line. Yes; it is necessary that we be partners by the law. I need the money. I shall get it from the head clerk in the office."

So the papers were made out and recorded. A year later I was compelled to complain.

"Charley," said I, "you are a wicked old fraud, a miserly skinflint, a miserable land-crab. Behold, your share for the year in all our partnership has been thousands of dollars. The head clerk has given me this paper. It says that in the year you have drawn just eighty-seven dollars and twenty cents."

"Is there any owing me?" he asked anxiously.

"I tell you thousands and thousands," I answered.

His face brightened, as with an immense relief.

"It is well," he said. "See that the head clerk keeps good account of it. When I want it, I shall want it, and there must not be a cent missing.

"If there is," he added fiercely, after a pause, "it must come out of the clerk's wages."

And all the time, as I afterwards learned, his will, drawn up by Carruthers, and making me sole beneficiary, lay in the American consul's safe.

But the end came, as the end must come to all human associations. It occurred in the Solomons, where our wildest work had been done in the wild young days, and where we were once more—principally on a holiday, incidentally to look after our holdings on Florida Island and to look over the pearling possibilities of the Mboli Pass. We were lying at Savo, having run in to trade for curios.

Now, Savo is alive with sharks. The custom of the woolly-heads of burying their dead in the sea did not tend to discourage the sharks from making the adjacent waters a hang-out. It was my luck to be coming aboard in a tiny, overloaded, native canoe, when the thing capsized. There were four woolly-heads and myself in it, or, rather, hanging to it. The schooner was a hundred yards away. I was just hailing for a boat when one of the woolly-heads began to scream. Holding on to the end of the canoe, both he and that portion of the canoe were dragged under several times. Then he loosed his clutch and disappeared. A shark had got him.

The three remaining niggers tried to climb out of the water upon the bottom of the canoe. I yelled and cursed and struck at the nearest with my fist, but it was no use. They were in a blind funk. The canoe could barely have supported one of them. Under the three it upended and rolled sidewise, throwing them back into the water.

I abandoned the canoe and started to swim toward the schooner, expecting to be picked up by the boat before I got there. One of the niggers elected to come with me, and we swam along silently, side by side, now and again putting our faces into the water and peering about for sharks. The screams of the man who stayed by the canoe informed us that he was taken. I was peering into the water when I saw a big shark pass directly beneath me. He was fully sixteen feet in length. I saw the whole thing. He got the woolly-head by the middle, and away he went, the poor devil, head, shoulders, and arms out of water all the time, screeching in a heart-rending way. He was carried along in this fashion for several hundred feet, when he was dragged beneath the surface.

I swam doggedly on, hoping that that was the last unattached shark. But there was another. Whether it was one that had attacked the natives earlier, or whether it was one that had made a good meal elsewhere, I do not know. At any rate, he was not in such haste as the others. I could not swim so rapidly now, for a large part of my effort was devoted to keeping track of him. I was watching him when he made his first attack. By good luck I got both hands on his nose, and, though his momentum nearly shoved me under, I managed to keep him off. He veered clear, and began circling about again. A second time I escaped him by the same manœuvre. The third rush was a miss on both sides. He sheered at the moment my hands should have landed on his nose, but his sandpaper hide (I had on a sleeveless undershirt) scraped the skin off one arm from elbow to shoulder.

By this time I was played out, and gave up hope. The schooner was still two hundred feet away. My face was in the water, and I was watching him manœuvre for another attempt, when I saw a brown body pass between us. It was Otoo.

"Swim for the schooner, master!" he said. And he spoke gayly, as though the affair was a mere lark. "I know sharks. The shark is my brother."

I obeyed, swimming slowly on, while Otoo swam about me, keeping always between me and the shark, foiling his rushes and encouraging me.

"The davit tackle carried away, and they are rigging the falls," he explained, a minute or so later, and then went under to head off another attack.

By the time the schooner was thirty feet away I was about done for. I could scarcely move. They were heaving lines at us from on board, but they continually fell short. The shark, finding that it was receiving no hurt, had become bolder. Several times it nearly got me, but each time Otoo was there just the moment before it was too late. Of course, Otoo could have saved himself any time. But he stuck by me.

"Good-by, Charley! I'm finished!" I just managed to gasp.

I knew that the end had come, and that the next moment I should throw up my hands and go down.

But Otoo laughed in my face, saying:

"I will show you a new trick. I will make that shark feel sick!"

He dropped in behind me, where the shark was preparing to come at me.

"A little more to the left!" he next called out. "There is a line there on the water. To the left, master—to the left!"

I changed my course and struck out blindly. I was by that time barely conscious. As my hand closed on the line I heard an exclamation from on board. I turned and looked. There was no sign of Otoo. The next instant he broke surface. Both hands were off at the wrist, the stumps spouting blood.

"Otoo!" he called softly. And I could see in his gaze the love that thrilled in his voice.

Then, and then only, at the very last of all our years, he called me by that name.

"Good-by, Otoo!" he called.

Then he was dragged under, and I was hauled aboard, where I fainted in the captain's arms.

And so passed Otoo, who saved me and made me a man, and who

saved me in the end. We met in the maw of a hurricane, and parted in the maw of a shark, with seventeen intervening years of comradeship, the like of which I dare to assert has never befallen two men, the one brown and the other white. If Jehovah be from His high place watching every sparrow fall, not least in His kingdom shall be Otoo, the one heathen of Bora Bora.

MAUKI

He weighed one hundred and ten pounds. His hair was kinky and negroid, and he was black. He was peculiarly black. He was neither blue-black nor purple-black, but plum-black. His name was Mauki, and he was the son of a chief. He had three *tambos*. *Tambo* is Melanesian for *taboo*, and is first cousin to that Polynesian word. Mauki's three *tambos* were as follows: first, he must never shake hands with a woman, nor have a woman's hand touch him or any of his personal belongings; secondly, he must never eat clams nor any food from a fire in which clams had been cooked; thirdly, he must never touch a crocodile, nor travel in a canoe that carried any part of a crocodile even if as large as a tooth.

Of a different black were his teeth, which were deep black, or, perhaps better, *lamp*-black. They had been made so in a single night, by his mother, who had compressed about them a powdered mineral which was dug from the landslide back of Port Adams. Port Adams is a salt-water village on Malaita, and Malaita is the most savage island in the Solomons—so savage that no traders nor planters have yet gained a foothold on it; while, from the time of the earliest bêche-de-mer fishers and sandalwood traders down to the latest labor recruiters equipped with automatic rifles and gasolene engines, scores of white adventurers have been passed out by tomahawks and soft-nosed Snider bullets. So Malaita remains to-day, in the twentieth century, the stamping ground of the labor recruiters, who farm its coasts for laborers who engage and contract themselves to toil on the plantations of the neighboring and more civilized islands for a wage of thirty dollars a year. The natives of those neighboring and more civilized islands have themselves become too civilized to work on plantations.

Mauki's ears were pierced, not in one place, nor two places, but in a couple of dozen places. In one of the smaller holes he carried a clay pipe. The larger holes were too large for such use. The bowl of the pipe would have fallen through. In fact, in the largest hole in each ear he habitually wore round wooden plugs that were an even four inches in diameter. Roughly speaking, the circumference of said holes was twelve and one-half inches. Mauki was catholic in his tastes. In the various smaller holes he carried such things as empty rifle cartridges, horseshoe nails, copper screws, pieces of string, braids of sennit, strips of green leaf, and, in the cool of the day, scarlet hibiscus flowers. From which it will be seen that pockets were not necessary to his well-being. Besides, pockets were impossible, for his only wearing apparel consisted of a piece of calico several inches wide. A pocket knife he wore in his hair, the blade snapped down on a kinky lock. His most prized possession was the handle of a china cup, which he suspended from a ring of turtle-shell, which, in turn, was passed through the partition-cartilage of his nose.

But in spite of embellishments, Mauki had a nice face. It was really a pretty face, viewed by any standard, and for a Melanesian it was a remarkably good-looking face. Its one fault was its lack of strength. It was softly effeminate, almost girlish. The features were small, regular, and delicate. The chin was weak, and the mouth was weak. There was no strength nor character in the jaws, forehead, and nose. In the eyes only could be caught any hint of the unknown quantities that were so large a part of his make-up and that other persons could not understand. These unknown quantities were pluck, pertinacity, fearlessness, imagination, and cunning; and when they found expression in some consistent and striking action, those about him were astounded.

Mauki's father was chief over the village at Port Adams, and thus, by birth a salt-water man, Mauki was half amphibian. He knew the way of the fishes and oysters, and the reef was an open book to him. Canoes, also, he knew. He learned to swim when he was a year old. At seven years he could hold his breath a full minute and swim straight down to bottom through thirty feet of water. And at seven years he was stolen by the bushmen, who cannot even swim and who are afraid of salt water. Thereafter Mauki saw the sea only from a distance, through rifts in the jungle and from open spaces on the high mountain sides. He became the slave of old Fanfoa, head chief over a score of scattered bush-villages on the range-lips of Malaita, the smoke of which, on calm mornings, is about the only evidence the seafaring white men have of the teeming interior population. For the whites do not penetrate Malaita. They tried it once, in the days when the search was on for gold, but they always left their heads behind to grin from the smoky rafters of the bushmen's huts.

When Mauki was a young man of seventeen, Fanfoa got out of tobacco. He got dreadfully out of tobacco. It was hard times in all his villages. He had been guilty of a mistake. Suo was a harbor so small that a large schooner could not swing at anchor in it. It was surrounded by mangroves that overhung the deep water. It was a trap, and into the trap sailed two white men in a small ketch. They were after recruits, and they possessed much tobacco and trade-goods, to say nothing of three rifles and plenty of ammunition. Now there were no salt-water men living at Suo, and it was there that the bushmen could come down to the sea. The ketch did a splendid traffic. It signed on twenty recruits the first day. Even old Fanfoa signed on. And that same day the score of new recruits chopped off the two white men's heads, killed the boat's crew, and burned the ketch. Thereafter, and for three months, there was tobacco and trade-goods in plenty and to spare in all the bush-villages. Then came the man-of-war that threw shells for miles into the hills, frightening the people out of their villages and into the deeper bush. Next the man-of-war sent landing parties ashore. The villages were all burned, along with the tobacco and trade-stuff. The cocoanuts and bananas were chopped down, the taro gardens uprooted, and the pigs and chickens killed.

It taught Fanfoa a lesson, but in the meantime he was out of tobacco. Also, his young men were too frightened to sign on with the recruiting vessels. That was why Fanfoa ordered his slave, Mauki, to be carried down and signed on for half a case of tobacco advance, along with knives, axes, calico, and beads, which he would pay for with his toil on the plantations. Mauki was sorely frightened when they brought him on board the schooner. He was a lamb led to the slaughter. White men were ferocious creatures. They had to be, or else they would not make a practice of venturing along the Malaita coast and into all harbors, two on a schooner, when each schooner carried from fifteen to twenty blacks as boat's crew, and often as high as sixty or seventy black recruits. In addition to this, there was always the danger of the shore population, the sudden attack and the cutting off of the schooner and all hands. Truly, white men must be terrible. Besides, they were possessed of such devil-devils—rifles that shot very rapidly many times, things of iron and brass that made the schooners go when there was no wind, and boxes that talked and laughed just as men talked and laughed. Ay, and he had heard of one white man whose particular devil-devil was so powerful that he could take out all his teeth and put them back at will.

Down into the cabin they took Mauki. On deck, the one white man kept guard with two revolvers in his belt. In the cabin the other white man sat with a book before him, in which he inscribed strange marks and lines. He looked at Mauki as though he had been a pig or a fowl, glanced under the hollows of his arms, and wrote in the book. Then he held out the writing stick and Mauki just barely touched it with his hand, in so doing pledging himself to toil for three years on the plantations of the Moongleam Soap Company. It was not explained to him that the will of the ferocious white men would be used to enforce the pledge, and that, behind all, for the same use, was all the power and all the warships of Great Britain.

Other blacks there were on board, from unheard-of far places, and when the white man spoke to them, they tore the long feather from Mauki's hair, cut that same hair short, and wrapped about his waist a lava-lava of bright yellow calico.

After many days on the schooner, and after beholding more land and islands than he had ever dreamed of, he was landed on New Georgia, and put to work in the field clearing jungle and cutting cane grass. For the first time he knew what work was. Even as a slave to Fanfoa he had not worked like this. And he did not like work. It was up at dawn and in at dark, on two meals a day. And the food was tiresome. For weeks at a time they were given nothing but sweet potatoes to eat, and for weeks at a time it would be nothing but rice. He cut out the cocoanut from the shells day after day; and for long days and weeks he fed the fires that smoked the copra, till his eyes got sore and he was set to felling trees. He was a good axe-man, and later he was put in the bridge-building gang. Once, he was punished by being put in the road-building gang. At times he served as boat's crew in the whale-boats, when they brought in copra from distant beaches or when the white men went out to dynamite fish.

Among other things he learned bêche-de-mer English, with which he could talk with all white men, and with all recruits who otherwise would have talked in a thousand different dialects. Also, he learned certain things about the white men, principally that they kept their word. If they told a boy he was going to receive a stick of tobacco, he got it. If they told a boy they would knock seven bells out of him if he did a certain thing, when he did that thing seven bells invariably were knocked out of him. Mauki did not know what seven bells were, but they occurred in bêche-de-mer, and he imagined them to be the blood and teeth that sometimes accompanied the process of knocking out seven bells. One other thing he learned: no boy was struck or punished unless he did wrong. Even when the white men were drunk, as they were frequently, they never struck unless a rule had been broken.

Mauki did not like the plantation. He hated work, and he was the son of a chief. Furthermore, it was ten years since he had been stolen from

Port Adams by Fanfoa, and he was homesick. He was even homesick for the slavery under Fanfoa. So he ran away. He struck back into the bush, with the idea of working southward to the beach and stealing a canoe in which to go home to Port Adams. But the fever got him, and he was captured and brought back more dead than alive.

A second time he ran away, in the company of two Malaita boys. They got down the coast twenty miles, and were hidden in the hut of a Malaita freeman, who dwelt in that village. But in the dead of night two white men came, who were not afraid of all the village people and who knocked seven bells out of the three runaways, tied them like pigs, and tossed them into the whale-boat. But the man in whose house they had hidden—seven times seven bells must have been knocked out of him from the way the hair, skin, and teeth flew, and he was discouraged for the rest of his natural life from harboring runaway laborers.

For a year Mauki toiled on. Then he was made a house-boy, and had good food and easy times, with light work in keeping the house clean and serving the white men with whiskey and beer at all hours of the day and most hours of the night. He liked it, but he liked Port Adams more. He had two years longer to serve, but two years were too long for him in the throes of homesickness. He had grown wiser with his year of service, and, being now a house-boy, he had opportunity. He had the cleaning of the rifles, and he knew where the key to the store-room was hung. He planned the escape, and one night ten Malaita boys and one boy from San Cristoval sneaked from the barracks and dragged one of the whale-boats down to the beach. It was Mauki who supplied the key that opened the padlock on the boat, and it was Mauki who equipped the boat with a dozen Winchesters, an immense amount of ammunition, a case of dynamite with detonators and fuse, and ten cases of tobacco.

The northwest monsoon was blowing, and they fled south in the night-time, hiding by day on detached and uninhabited islets, or dragging their whale-boat into the bush on the large islands. Thus they gained Guadalcanar, skirted halfway along it, and crossed the Indispensable Straits to Florida Island. It was here that they killed the San Cristoval boy, saving his head and cooking and eating the rest of him. The Malaita coast was only twenty miles away, but the last night a strong current and baffling winds prevented them from gaining across. Daylight found them still several miles from their goal. But daylight brought a cutter, in which were two white men, who were not afraid of eleven Malaita men armed with twelve rifles. Mauki and his companions were carried back to Tulagi, where lived the great white master of all the white men. And the great white master held a court, after which, one by one, the runaways were tied up and given twenty lashes each, and sentenced to a fine of fifteen dollars. Then they were sent back to New Georgia, where the white men knocked seven bells out of them all around and put them to work. But Mauki was no longer house-boy. He was put in the road-making gang. The fine of fifteen dollars had been paid by the white men from whom he had run away, and he was told that he would have to work it out, which meant six months' additional toil. Further, his share of the stolen tobacco earned him another year of toil.

Port Adams was now three years and a half away, so he stole a canoe one night, hid on the islets in Manning Straits, passed through the Straits, and began working along the eastern coast of Ysabel, only to be captured, two-thirds of the way along, by the white men on Meringe Lagoon. After a week, he escaped from them and took to the bush. There were no bush natives on Ysabel, only salt-water men, who were all Christians. The white men put up a reward of five hundred sticks of tobacco, and every time Mauki ventured down to the sea to steal a canoe he was chased by the salt-water men. Four months of this passed, when, the reward having been raised to a thousand sticks, he was caught and sent back to New Georgia and the road-building gang. Now a thousand sticks are worth fifty dollars, and Mauki had to pay the reward himself, which required a year and eight months' labor. So Port Adams was now five years away.

His homesickness was greater than ever, and it did not appeal to him to settle down and be good, work out his four years, and go home. The next time, he was caught in the very act of running away. His case was brought before Mr. Haveby, the island manager of the Moongleam Soap Company, who adjudged him an incorrigible. The Company had plantations on the Santa Cruz Islands, hundreds of miles across the sea, and there it sent its Solomon Islands' incorrigibles. And there Mauki was sent, though he never arrived. The schooner stopped at Santa Anna, and in the night Mauki swam ashore, where he stole two rifles and a case of tobacco from the trader and got away in a canoe to Cristoval. Malaita was now to the north, fifty or sixty miles away. But when he attempted the passage, he was caught by a light gale and driven back to Santa Anna, where the trader clapped him in irons and held him against the return of the schooner from Santa Cruz. The two rifles the trader recovered, but the case of tobacco was charged up to Mauki at the rate of another year. The sum of years he now owed the Company was six.

On the way back to New Georgia, the schooner dropped anchor in Marau Sound, which lies at the southeastern extremity of Guadalcanar. Mauki swam ashore with handcuffs on his wrists and got away to the bush. The schooner went on, but the Moongleam trader ashore offered a thousand sticks, and to him Mauki was brought by the bushmen with a year and eight months tacked on to his account. Again, and before the schooner called in, he got away, this time in a whale-boat accompanied by a case of the trader's tobacco. But a northwest gale wrecked him upon Ugi, where the Christian natives stole his tobacco and turned him over to the Moongleam trader who resided there. The tobacco the natives stole meant another year for him, and the tale was now eight years and a half.

"We'll send him to Lord Howe," said Mr. Haveby. "Bunster is there, and we'll let them settle it between them. It will be a case, I imagine, of Mauki getting Bunster, or Bunster getting Mauki, and good riddance in either event."

If one leaves Meringe Lagoon, on Ysabel, and steers a course due north, magnetic, at the end of one hundred and fifty miles he will lift the pounded coral beaches of Lord Howe above the sea. Lord Howe is a ring of land some one hundred and fifty miles in circumference, several hundred yards wide at its widest, and towering in places to a height of ten feet above sea-level. Inside this ring of sand is a mighty lagoon studded with coral patches. Lord Howe belongs to the Solomons neither geographically nor ethnologically. It is an atoll, while the Solomons are high islands; and its people and language are Polynesian, while the inhabitants of the Solomons are Melanesian. Lord Howe has been populated by the westward Polynesian drift which continues to this day, big out-rigger canoes being washed upon its beaches by the southeast trade. That there has been a slight Melanesian drift in the period of the northwest monsoon, is also evident.

Nobody ever comes to Lord Howe, or Ontong-Java as it is sometimes called. Thomas Cook & Son do not sell tickets to it, and tourists do not dream of its existence. Not even a white missionary has landed on its shore. Its five thousand natives are as peaceable as they are primitive. Yet they were not always peaceable. The *Sailing Directions* speak of them as hostile and treacherous. But the men who compile the *Sailing Directions* have never heard of the change that was worked in the hearts of the inhabitants, who, not many years ago, cut off a big bark and killed all hands with the exception of the second mate. This survivor carried the news to his brothers. The captains of three trading schooners returned with him to Lord Howe. They sailed their vessels right into the lagoon and proceeded to preach the white man's gospel that only white men shall kill white men and that the lesser breeds must keep hands off. The schooners sailed up and down the lagoon, harrying and destroying. There was no escape from the narrow sand-circle, no bush to which to flee. The men were shot down at sight, and there was no avoiding being sighted. The villages were burned, the canoes smashed, the chickens and pigs killed, and the precious cocoanut-trees chopped down. For a month this continued, when the schooners sailed away; but the fear of the white man had been seared into the souls of the islanders and never again were they rash enough to harm one.

Max Bunster was the one white man on Lord Howe, trading in the pay of the ubiquitous Moongleam Soap Company. And the Company billeted him on Lord Howe, because, next to getting rid of him, it was the most out-of-the-way place to be found. That the Company did not get rid of him was due to the difficulty of finding another man to take his place. He was a strapping big German, with something wrong in his brain. Semi-madness would be a charitable statement of his condition. He was a bully and a coward, and a thrice-bigger savage than any savage on the island. Being a coward, his brutality was of the cowardly order. When he first went into the Company's employ, he was stationed on Savo. When a consumptive colonial was sent to take his place, he beat him up with his fists and sent him off a wreck in the schooner that brought him.

Mr. Haveby next selected a young Yorkshire giant to relieve Bunster. The Yorkshire man had a reputation as a bruiser and preferred fighting to eating. But Bunster wouldn't fight. He was a regular little lamb—for ten days, at the end of which time the Yorkshire man was prostrated by a combined attack of dysentery and fever. Then Bunster went for him, among other things getting him down and jumping on him a score or so of times. Afraid of what would happen when his victim recovered, Bunster fled away in a cutter to Guvutu, where he signalized himself by beating up a young Englishman already crippled by a Boer bullet through both hips.

Then it was that Mr. Haveby sent Bunster to Lord Howe, the falling-off place. He celebrated his landing by mopping up half a case of gin and by thrashing the elderly and wheezy mate of the schooner which had brought him. When the schooner departed, he called the kanakas down to the beach and challenged them to throw him in a wrestling bout, promising a case of tobacco to the one who succeeded. Three kanakas he threw, but was promptly thrown by a fourth, who, instead of receiving the tobacco, got a bullet through his lungs.

And so began Bunster's reign on Lord Howe. Three thousand people lived in the principal village; but it was deserted, even in broad day, when he passed through. Men, women, and children fled before him. Even the dogs and pigs got out of the way, while the king was not above hiding under a mat. The two prime ministers lived in terror of

Bunster, who never discussed any moot subject, but struck out with his
fists instead.

And to Lord Howe came Mauki, to toil for Bunster for eight long
years and a half. There was no escaping from Lord Howe. For better
or worse, Bunster and he were tied together. Bunster weighed two
hundred pounds. Mauki weighed one hundred and ten. Bunster was a
degenerate brute. But Mauki was a primitive savage. While both had
wills and ways of their own.

Mauki had no idea of the sort of master he was to work for. He
had had no warnings, and he had concluded as a matter of course that
Bunster would be like other white men, a drinker of much whiskey, a
ruler and a lawgiver who always kept his word and who never struck a
boy undeserved. Bunster had the advantage. He knew all about Mauki,
and gloated over the coming into possession of him. The last cook was
suffering from a broken arm and a dislocated shoulder, so Bunster made
Mauki cook and general house-boy.

And Mauki soon learned that there were white men and white men.
On the very day the schooner departed he was ordered to buy a chicken
from Samisee, the native Tongan missionary. But Samisee had sailed
across the lagoon and would not be back for three days. Mauki returned
with the information. He climbed the steep stairway (the house stood
on piles twelve feet above the sand), and entered the living-room to
report. The trader demanded the chicken. Mauki opened his mouth to
explain the missionary's absence. But Bunster did not care for explanations. He struck out with his fist. The blow caught Mauki on the mouth
and lifted him into the air. Clear through the doorway he flew, across
the narrow veranda, breaking the top railing, and down to the ground.
His lips were a contused, shapeless mass, and his mouth was full of
blood and broken teeth.

"That'll teach you that back talk don't go with me," the trader
shouted, purple with rage, peering down at him over the broken railing.

Mauki had never met a white man like this, and he resolved to walk
small and never offend. He saw the boat-boys knocked about, and one
of them put in irons for three days with nothing to eat for the crime of
breaking a rowlock while pulling. Then, too, he heard the gossip of the
village and learned why Bunster had taken a third wife—by force, as
was well known. The first and second wives lay in the graveyard, under
the white coral sand, with slabs of coral rock at head and feet. They
had died, it was said, from beatings he had given them. The third wife
was certainly ill-used, as Mauki could see for himself.

But there was no way by which to avoid offending the white man,
who seemed offended with life. When Mauki kept silent, he was struck

and called a sullen brute. When he spoke, he was struck for giving back talk. When he was grave, Bunster accused him of plotting and gave him a thrashing in advance; and when he strove to be cheerful and to smile, he was charged with sneering at his lord and master and given a taste of stick. Bunster was a devil. The village would have done for him, had it not remembered the lesson of the three schooners. It might have done for him anyway, if there had been a bush to which to flee. As it was, the murder of the white men, of any white man, would bring a man-of-war that would kill the offenders and chop down the precious cocoanut-trees. Then there were the boat-boys, with minds fully made up to drown him by accident at the first opportunity to capsize the cutter. Only Bunster saw to it that the boat did not capsize.

Mauki was of a different breed, and, escape being impossible while Bunster lived, he was resolved to get the white man. The trouble was that he could never find a chance. Bunster was always on guard. Day and night his revolvers were ready to hand. He permitted nobody to pass behind his back, as Mauki learned after having been knocked down several times. Bunster knew that he had more to fear from the good-natured, even sweet-faced, Malaita boy than from the entire population of Lord Howe; and it gave added zest to the programme of torment he was carrying out. And Mauki walked small, accepted his punishments, and waited.

All other white men had respected his *tambos,* but not so Bunster. Mauki's weekly allowance of tobacco was two sticks. Bunster passed them to his woman and ordered Mauki to receive them from her hand. But this could not be, and Mauki went without his tobacco. In the same way he was made to miss many a meal, and to go hungry many a day. He was ordered to make chowder out of the big clams that grew in the lagoon. This he could not do, for clams were *tambo.* Six times in succession he refused to touch the clams, and six times he was knocked senseless. Bunster knew that the boy would die first, but called his refusal mutiny, and would have killed him had there been another cook to take his place.

One of the trader's favorite tricks was to catch Mauki's kinky locks and bat his head against the wall. Another trick was to catch Mauki unawares and thrust the live end of a cigar against his flesh. This Bunster called vaccination, and Mauki was vaccinated a number of times a week. Once, in a rage, Bunster ripped the cup handle from Mauki's nose, tearing the hole clear out of the cartilage.

"Oh, what a mug!" was his comment, when he surveyed the damage he had wrought.

The skin of a shark is like sandpaper, but the skin of a ray fish is like a rasp. In the South Seas the natives use it as a wood file in smoothing down canoes and paddles. Bunster had a mitten made of ray fish skin. The first time he tried it on Mauki, with one sweep of the hand it fetched the skin off his back from neck to armpit. Bunster was delighted. He gave his wife a taste of the mitten, and tried it out thoroughly on the boat-boys. The prime ministers came in for a stroke each, and they had to grin and take it for a joke.

"Laugh, damn you, laugh!" was the cue he gave.

Mauki came in for the largest share of the mitten. Never a day passed without a caress from it. There were times when the loss of so much cuticle kept him awake at night, and often the half-healed surface was raked raw afresh by the facetious Mr. Bunster. Mauki continued his patient wait, secure in the knowledge that sooner or later his time would come. And he knew just what he was going to do, down to the smallest detail, when the time did come.

One morning Bunster got up in a mood for knocking seven bells out of the universe. He began on Mauki, and wound up on Mauki, in the interval knocking down his wife and hammering all the boat-boys. At breakfast he called the coffee slops and threw the scalding contents of the cup into Mauki's face. By ten o'clock Bunster was shivering with ague, and half an hour later he was burning with fever. It was no ordinary attack. It quickly became pernicious, and developed into blackwater fever. The days passed, and he grew weaker and weaker, never leaving his bed. Mauki waited and watched, the while his skin grew intact once more. He ordered the boys to beach the cutter, scrub her bottom, and give her a general overhauling. They thought the order emanated from Bunster, and they obeyed. But Bunster at the time was lying unconscious and giving no orders. This was Mauki's chance, but still he waited.

When the worst was past, and Bunster lay convalescent and conscious, but weak as a baby, Mauki packed his few trinkets, including the china cup handle, into his trade box. Then he went over to the village and interviewed the king and his two prime ministers.

"This fella Bunster, him good fella you like too much?" he asked.

They explained in one voice that they liked the trader not at all. The ministers poured forth a recital of all the indignities and wrongs that had been heaped upon them. The king broke down and wept. Mauki interrupted rudely.

"You savve me—me big fella marster my country. You no like 'm this fella white marster. Me no like 'm. Plenty good you put hundred cocoanut, two hundred cocoanut, three hundred cocoanut along cutter. Him finish, you go sleep 'm good fella. Altogether kanaka sleep 'm good fella. Bime by big fella noise along house, you no savve hear 'm that fella noise. You altogether sleep strong fella too much."

In like manner Mauki interviewed the boat-boys. Then he ordered Bunster's wife to return to her family house. Had she refused, he would have been in a quandary, for his *tambo* would not have permitted him to lay hands on her.

The house deserted, he entered the sleeping-room, where the trader lay in a doze. Mauki first removed the revolvers, then placed the ray fish mitten on his hand. Bunster's first warning was a stroke of the mitten that removed the skin the full length of his nose.

"Good fella, eh?" Mauki grinned, between two strokes, one of which swept the forehead bare and the other of which cleaned off one side of his face. "Laugh, damn you, laugh."

Mauki did his work thoroughly, and the kanakas, hiding in their houses, heard the "big fella noise" that Bunster made and continued to make for an hour or more.

When Mauki was done, he carried the boat compass and all the rifles and ammunition down to the cutter, which he proceeded to ballast with cases of tobacco. It was while engaged in this that a hideous, skinless thing came out of the house and ran screaming down the beach till it fell in the sand and mowed and gibbered under the scorching sun. Mauki looked toward it and hesitated. Then he went over and removed the head, which he wrapped in a mat and stowed in the stern-locker of the cutter.

So soundly did the kanakas sleep through that long hot day that they did not see the cutter run out through the passage and head south, close-hauled on the southeast trade. Nor was the cutter ever sighted on that long tack to the shores of Ysabel, and during the tedious head-beat from there to Malaita. He landed at Port Adams with a wealth of rifles and tobacco such as no one man had ever possessed before. But he did not stop there. He had taken a white man's head, and only the bush could shelter him. So back he went to the bush-villages, where he shot old Fanfoa and half a dozen of the chief men, and made himself the chief over all the villages. When his father died, Mauki's brother ruled in Port Adams, and, joined together, salt-water men and bushmen, the resulting combination was the strongest of the ten score fighting tribes of Malaita.

More than his fear of the British government was Mauki's fear of the all-powerful Moongleam Soap Company; and one day a message came up to him in the bush, reminding him that he owed the Company eight and one-half years of labor. He sent back a favorable answer, and then appeared the inevitable white man, the captain of the schooner, the only white man during Mauki's reign who ventured the bush and came out alive. This man not only came out, but he brought with him seven hundred and fifty dollars in gold sovereigns—the money price of eight years and a half of labor plus the cost price of certain rifles and cases of tobacco.

Mauki no longer weighs one hundred and ten pounds. His stomach is three times its former girth, and he has four wives. He has many other things—rifles and revolvers, the handle of a china cup, and an excellent collection of bushmen's heads. But more precious than the entire collection is another head, perfectly dried and cured, with sandy hair and a yellowish beard, which is kept wrapped in the finest of fibre lava-lavas. When Mauki goes to war with villages beyond his realm, he invariably gets out this head, and, alone in his grass palace, contemplates it long and solemnly. At such times the hush of death falls on the village, and not even a pickaninny dares make a noise. The head is esteemed the most powerful devil-devil on Malaita, and to the possession of it is ascribed all of Mauki's greatness.

THE STRENGTH
OF THE STRONG

Parables don't lie, but liars will parable.
—LIP-KING.

Old Long Beard paused in his narrative, licked his greasy fingers, and wiped them on his naked sides where his one piece of ragged bearskin failed to cover him. Crouched around him, on their hams, were three young men, his grandsons, Deer-Runner, Yellow-Head, and Afraid-of-the-Dark. In appearance they were much the same. Skins of wild animals partly covered them. They were lean and meager of build, narrow-hipped and crooked-legged, and at the same time deep-chested, with heavy arms and enormous hands. There was much hair on their chests and shoulders, and on the outsides of their arms and legs. Their heads were matted with uncut hair, long locks of which often strayed before their eyes, beady and black and glittering like the eyes of birds. They were narrow between the eyes and broad between the cheeks, while their lower jaws were projecting and massive.

It was a night of clear starlight, and below them, stretching away remotely, lay range on range of forest-covered hills. In the distance the heavens were red from the glow of a volcano. At their backs yawned the black mouth of a cave, out of which, from time to time, blew draughty gusts of wind. Immediately in front of them blazed a fire. At one side, partly devoured, lay the carcass of a bear, with about it, at a respectable distance, several large dogs, shaggy and wolf-like. Beside each man lay his bow and arrows and a huge club. In the cave-mouth a number of rude spears leaned against the rock.

"So that was how we moved from the cave to the tree," old Long Beard spoke up.

They laughed boisterously, like big children, at recollection of a previous story his words called up. Long Beard laughed, too, the five-inch bodkin of bone, thrust midway through the cartilage of his nose, leaping and dancing and adding to his ferocious appearance. He did not exactly say the words recorded, but he made animal-like sounds with his mouth that meant the same thing.

"And that is the first I remember of the Sea Valley," Long Beard went on. "We were a very foolish crowd. We did not know the secret of strength. For, behold, each family lived by itself, and took care of itself. There were thirty families, but we got no strength from one another. We were in fear of each other all the time. No one ever paid visits. In the top of our tree we built a grass house, and on the platform outside was a pile of rocks, which were for the heads of any that might chance to try to visit us. Also, we had our spears and arrows. We never walked under the trees of the other families, either. My brother did, once, under old Boo-oogh's tree, and he got his head broken and that was the end of him.

"Old Boo-oogh was very strong. It was said he could pull a grown man's head right off. I never heard of him doing it, because no man would give him a chance. Father wouldn't. One day, when father was down on the beach, Boo-oogh took after mother. She couldn't run fast, for the day before she had got her leg clawed by a bear when she was up on the mountain gathering berries. So Boo-oogh caught her and carried her up into his tree. Father never got her back. He was afraid. Old Boo-oogh made faces at him.

"But father did not mind. Strong-Arm was another strong man. He was one of the best fishermen. But one day, climbing after seagull eggs, he had a fall from the cliff. He was never strong after that. He coughed a great deal, and his shoulders drew near to each other. So father took Strong-Arm's wife. When he came around and coughed under our tree, father laughed at him and threw rocks at him. It was our way in those days. We did not know how to add strength together and become strong."

"Would a brother take a brother's wife?" Deer-Runner demanded.

"Yes, if he had gone to live in another tree by himself."

"But we do not do such things now," Afraid-of-the-Dark objected.

"It is because I have taught your fathers better." Long Beard thrust his hairy paw into the bear meat and drew out a handful of suet, which he sucked with a meditative air. Again he wiped his hands on his naked sides and went on. "What I am telling you happened in the long ago, before we knew any better."

"You must have been fools not to know better," was Deer-Runner's comment, Yellow-Head grunting approval.

"So we were, but we became bigger fools, as you shall see. Still, we did learn better, and this was the way of it. We Fish-Eaters had not learned to add our strength until our strength was the strength of all of us. But the Meat-Eaters, who lived across the divide in the Big Valley, stood together, hunted together, fished together, and fought together. One day they came into our valley. Each family of us got into its own cave and tree. There were only ten Meat-Eaters, but they fought together, and we fought each family by itself."

Long Beard counted long and perplexedly on his fingers.

"There were sixty men of us," was what he managed to say with fingers and lips combined. "And we were very strong, only we did not know it. So we watched the ten men attack Boo-oogh's tree. He made a good fight, but he had no chance. We looked on. When some of the Meat-Eaters tried to climb the tree, Boo-oogh had to show himself in order to drop stones on their heads, whereupon the other Meat-Eaters, who were waiting for that very thing, shot him full of arrows. And that was the end of Boo-oogh.

"Next, the Meat-Eaters got One-Eye and his family in his cave. They built a fire in the mouth and smoked him out, like we smoked out the bear there to-day. Then they went after Six-Fingers, up his tree, and, while they were killing him and his grown son, the rest of us ran away. They caught some of our women, and killed two old men who could not run fast and several children. The women they carried away with them to the Big Valley.

"After that the rest of us crept back, and, somehow, perhaps because we were in fear and felt the need for one another, we talked the thing over. It was our first council—our first real council. And in that council we formed our first tribe. For we had learned the lesson. Of the ten Meat-Eaters, each man had had the strength of ten, for the ten had fought as one man. They had added their strength together. But of the thirty families and the sixty men of us, we had had the strength of but one man, for each had fought alone.

"It was a great talk we had, and it was hard talk, for we did not have the words then as now with which to talk. The Bug made some of the words long afterward, and so did others of us make words from time to time. But in the end we agreed to add our strength together and to be as one man when the Meat-Eaters came over the divide to steal our women. And that was the tribe.

"We set two men on the divide, one for the day and one for the night, to watch if the Meat-Eaters came. These were the eyes of the tribe. Then, also, day and night, there were to be ten men awake with their clubs and spears and arrows in their hands, ready to fight. Before, when a man went after fish, or clams, or gull-eggs, he carried his weapons with him, and half the time he was getting food and half the time watching for fear some other man would get him. Now that was all changed. The men went out without their weapons and spent all their time getting food. Likewise, when the women went into the mountains after roots and berries, five of the ten men went with them to guard them. While all the time, day and night, the eyes of the tribe watched from the top of the divide.

"But troubles came. As usual, it was about the women. Men without wives wanted other men's wives, and there was much fighting between men, and now and again one got his head smashed or a spear through his body. While one of the watchers was on top the divide, another man stole his wife, and he came down to fight. Then the other watcher was in fear that someone would take his wife, and he came down likewise. Also, there was trouble among the ten men who carried always their weapons, and they fought five against five, till some ran away down the coast and the others ran after them.

"So it was that the tribe was left without eyes or guards. We had not the strength of sixty. We had no strength at all. So we held a council and made our first laws. I was but a cub at the time, but I remember. We said that, in order to be strong, we must not fight one another, and we made a law that when a man killed another him would the tribe kill. We made another law that whoso stole another man's wife him would the tribe kill. We said that whatever man had too great strength, and by that strength hurt his brothers in the tribe, him would we kill that his strength might hurt no more. For, if we let his strength hurt, the brothers would become afraid and the tribe would fall apart, and we would be as weak as when the Meat-Eaters first came upon us and killed Boo-oogh.

"Knuckle-Bone was a strong man, a very strong man, and he knew not law. He knew only his own strength, and in the fullness thereof he went forth and took the wife of Three-Clams. Three-Clams tried to fight, but Knuckle-Bone clubbed out his brains. Yet had Knuckle-Bone forgotten that all the men of us had added our strength to keep the law among us, and him we killed, at the foot of his tree, and hung his body on a branch as a warning that the law was stronger than any man. For we were the law, all of us, and no man was greater than the law.

"Then there were other troubles, for know, O Deer-Runner, and Yellow-Head, and Afraid-of-the-Dark, that it is not easy to make a tribe. There were many things, little things, that it was a great trouble to call all the men together to have a council about. We were having councils morning, noon, and night, and in the middle of the night. We could find little time to go out and get food, what of the councils, for there was always some little thing to be settled, such as naming two new watchers to take the place of the old ones on the hill, or naming how much food should fall to the share of the men who kept their weapons always in their hands and got no food for themselves.

"We stood in need of a chief man to do these things, who would be the voice of the council, and who would account to the council for the things he did. So we named Fith-Fith the chief man. He was a strong man, too, and very cunning, and when he was angry he made noises just like that, *fith-fith*, like a wildcat.

"The ten men who guarded the tribe were set to work making a wall of stones across the narrow part of the valley. The women and large children helped, as did other men, until the wall was strong. After that, all the families came down out of their caves and trees and built grass houses behind the shelter of the wall. These houses were large and much better than the caves and trees, and everybody had a better time of it because the men had added their strength together and become a tribe. Because of the wall and the guards and the watchers, there was more time to hunt and fish and pick roots and berries; there was more food, and better food, and no one went hungry. And Three-Legs, so named because his legs had been smashed when a boy and who walked with a stick—Three-Legs got the seed of the wild corn and planted it in the ground in the valley near his house. Also, he tried planting fat roots and other things he found in the mountain valleys.

"Because of the safety in the Sea Valley, which was because of the wall and the watchers and the guards, and because there was food in plenty for all without having to fight for it, many families came in from the coast valleys on both sides and from the high back mountains where they had lived more like wild animals than men. And it was not long before the Sea Valley filled up, and in it were countless families. But, before this happened, the land, which had been free to all and belonged to all, was divided up. Three-Legs began it when he planted corn. But most of us did not care about the land. We thought the marking of the boundaries with fences of stone was a foolishness. We had plenty to eat, and what more did we want? I remember that my father and I built stone fences for Three-Legs and were given corn in return.

"So only a few got all the land, and Three-Legs got most of it. Also, others that had taken land gave it to the few that held on, being paid in return with corn and fat roots, and bearskins, and fishes which the farmers got from the fishermen in exchange for corn. And, the first thing we knew, all the land was gone.

"It was about this time that Fith-Fith died and Dog-Tooth, his son,

was made chief. He demanded to be made chief anyway, because his
father had been chief before him. Also, he looked upon himself as a
greater chief than his father. He was a good chief at first, and worked
hard, so that the council had less and less to do. Then arose a new voice
in the Sea Valley. It was Twisted-Lip. We had never thought much of
him, until he began to talk with the spirits of the dead. Later we called
him Big-Fat, because he ate over-much, and did no work, and grew
round and large. One day Big-Fat told us that the secrets of the dead
were his, and that he was the voice of God. He became great friends
with Dog-Tooth, who commanded that we build Big-Fat a grass house.
And Big-Fat put taboos all around this house and kept God inside.

"More and more Dog-Tooth became greater than the council, and
when the council grumbled and said it would name a new chief, Big-
Fat spoke with the voice of God and said no. Also, Three-Legs and the
others who held the land stood behind Dog-Tooth. Moreover, the
strongest man in the council was Sea-Lion, and him the land-owners
gave land to secretly, along with many bearskins and baskets of corn.
So Sea-Lion said that Big-Fat's voice was truly the voice of God and
must be obeyed. And soon afterward Sea-Lion was named the voice of
Dog-Tooth and did most of his talking for him.

"Then there was Little-Belly, a little man, so thin in the middle that
he looked as if he had never had enough to eat. Inside the mouth of the
river, after the sand-bar had combed the strength of the breakers, he
built a big fish-trap. No man had ever seen or dreamed a fish-trap before. He worked weeks on it, with his son and his wife, while the rest
of us laughed at their labors. But, when it was done, the first day he
caught more fish in it than could the whole tribe in a week, whereat
there was great rejoicing. There was only one other place in the river
for a fish-trap, but, when my father and I and a dozen other men started
to make a very large trap, the guards came from the big grass-house
we had built for Dog-Tooth. And the guards poked us with their spears
and told us begone, because Little-Belly was going to build a trap there
himself on the word of Sea-Lion, who was the voice of Dog-Tooth.

"There was much grumbling, and my father called a council. But,
when he rose to speak, him the Sea-Lion thrust through the throat with
a spear and he died. And Dog-Tooth and Little-Belly, and Three-Legs
and all that held land said it was good. And Big-Fat said it was the will
of God. And after that all men were afraid to stand up in the council,
and there was no more council.

"Another man, Pig-Jaw, began to keep goats. He had heard about it
as among the Meat-Eaters, and it was not long before he had many
flocks. Other men, who had no land and no fish-traps, and who else

would have gone hungry, were glad to work for Pig-Jaw, caring for his goats, guarding them from wild dogs and tigers, and driving them to the feeding pastures in the mountains. In return, Pig-Jaw gave them goat-meat to eat and goat-skins to wear, and sometimes they traded the goat-meat for fish and corn and fat roots.

"It was this time that money came to be. Sea-Lion was the man who first thought of it, and he talked it over with Dog-Tooth and Big-Fat. You see, these three were the ones that got a share of everything in the Sea Valley. One basket out of every three of corn was theirs, one fish out of every three, one goat out of every three. In return, they fed the guards and the watchers, and kept the rest for themselves. Sometimes, when a big haul of fish was made, they did not know what to do with all their share. So Sea-Lion set the women to making money out of shell—little round pieces, with a hole in each one, and all made smooth and fine. These were strung on strings, and the strings were called money.

"Each string was of the value of thirty fish, or forty fish, but the women, who made a string a day, were given two fish each. The fish came out of the shares of Dog-Tooth, Big-Fat, and Sea-Lion, which they three did not eat. So all the money belonged to them. Then they told Three-Legs and the other land owners that they would take their share of corn and roots in money, Little-Belly that they would take their share of fish in money, the Pig-Jaw that they would take their share of goats and cheese in money. Thus, a man who had nothing, worked for one who had, and was paid in money. With this money he bought corn, and fish, and meat, and cheese. And Three-Legs and all owners of things paid Dog-Tooth and Sea-Lion and Big-Fat their share in money. And they paid the guards and watchers in money, and the guards and watchers bought their food with the money. And, because money was cheap, Dog-Tooth made many more men into guards. And, because money was cheap to make, a number of men began to make money out of shell themselves. But the guards stuck spears in them and shot them full of arrows, because they were trying to break up the tribe. It was bad to break up the tribe, for then the Meat-Eaters would come over the divide and kill them all.

"Big-Fat was the voice of God, but he took Broken-Rib and made him into a priest, so that he became the voice of Big-Fat and did most of his talking for him. And both had other men to be servants to them. So, also, did Little-Belly and Three-Legs and Pig-Jaw have other men to lie in the sun about their grass houses and carry messages for them and give commands. And more and more were men taken away from work, so that those that were left worked harder than ever before. It seemed that men desired to do no work and strove to seek out other ways whereby men should work for them. Crooked-Eyes found such a way. He made the first fire-brew out of corn. And thereafter he worked no more, for he talked secretly with Dog-Tooth and Big-Fat and the other masters, and it was agreed that he should be the only one to make fire-brew. But Crooked-Eyes did no work himself. Men made the brew for him, and he paid them in money. Then he sold the fire-brew for money, and all men bought. And many strings of money did he give Dog-Tooth and Sea-Lion and all of them.

"Big-Fat and Broken-Rib stood by Dog-Tooth when he took his second wife, and his third wife. They said Dog-Tooth was different from other men and second only to God that Big-Fat kept in his taboo house, and Dog-Tooth said so, too, and wanted to know who were they to grumble about how many wives he took. Dog-Tooth had a big canoe made, and many more men he took from work, who did nothing and lay in the sun, save only when Dog-Tooth went in the canoe, when they paddled for him. And he made Tiger-Face head man over all the guards, so that Tiger-Face became his right arm, and when he did not like a man Tiger-Face killed that man for him. And Tiger-Face, also, made another man to be his right arm, and to give commands, and to kill for him.

"But this was the strange thing: as the days went by we who were left worked harder and harder, and yet did we get less and less to eat."

"But what of the goats and the corn and the fat roots and the fish-trap," spoke up Afraid-of-the-Dark, "what of all this? Was there not more food to be gained by man's work?"

"It is so," Long-Beard agreed. "Three men on the fish-trap got more fish than the whole tribe before there was a fish-trap. But have I not said we were fools? The more food we were able to get, the less food did we have to eat."

"But was it not plain that the many men who did not work ate it all up?" Yellow-Head demanded.

Long-Beard nodded his head sadly. "Dog-Tooth's dogs were stuffed with meat, and the men who lay in the sun and did no work were rolling in fat, and, at the same time, there were little children crying themselves to sleep with hunger biting them with every wail."

Deer-Runner was spurred by the recital of famine to tear out a chunk of bear-meat and broil it on a stick over the coals. This he devoured with smacking lips, while Long-Beard went on:

"When we grumbled Big-Fat arose, and with the voice of God said that God had chosen the wise men to own the land and the goats and the fish-trap and the fire-brew, and that without these wise men we would all be animals, as in the days when we lived in trees.

"And there arose one who became a singer of songs for the king. Him they called the Bug, because he was small and ungainly of face and limb and excelled not in work or deed. He loved the fattest marrow bones, the choicest fish, the milk warm from the goats, the first corn that was ripe, and the snug place by the fire. And thus, becoming singer of songs to the king, he found a way to do nothing and be fat. And when the people grumbled more and more, and some threw stones at the king's grass house, the Bug sang a song of how good it was to be a Fish-Eater. In his song he told that the Fish-Eaters were the chosen of God and the finest men God had made. He sang of the Meat-Eaters as pigs and crows, and sang how fine and good it was for the Fish-Eater to fight and die doing God's work, which was the killing of Meat-Eaters. The words of his song were like fire in us, and we clamored to be led against the Meat-Eaters. And we forgot that we were hungry, and why we had grumbled, and were glad to be led by Tiger-Face over the divide, where we killed many Meat-Eaters and were content.

"But things were no better in the Sea Valley. The only way to get food was to work for Three-Legs or Little-Belly or Pig-Jaw; for there was no land that a man might plant with corn for himself. And often there were more men than Three-Legs and the others had work for. So these men went hungry, and so did their wives and children and their old mothers. Tiger-Face said they could become guards if they wanted to, and many of them did, and thereafter they did no work except to poke spears in the men who did work and who grumbled at feeding so many idlers.

"And when we grumbled, ever the Bug sang new songs. He said that Three-Legs and Pig-Jaw and the rest were strong men, and that that was why they had so much. He said that we should be glad to have strong men with us, else would we perish of our own worthlessness and the Meat-Eaters. Therefore, we should be glad to let such strong men have all they could lay hands on. And Big-Fat and Pig-Jaw and Tiger-Face and all the rest said it was true.

" 'All right,' said Long-Fang, 'then will I, too, be a strong man.' And he got himself corn and began to make fire-brew and sell it for strings of money. And, when Crooked-Eyes complained, Long-Fang said that he was himself a strong man, and that if Crooked-Eyes made any more noise he would bash his brains out for him. Whereat Crooked-Eyes was afraid and went and talked with Three-Legs and Pig-Jaw. And all three went and talked to Dog-Tooth. And Dog-Tooth spoke to Sea-Lion, and

Sea-Lion sent a runner with a message to Tiger-Face. And Tiger-Face sent his guards, who burned Long-Fang's house along with the fire-brew he had made. Also, they killed him and all his family. And Big-Fat said it was good, and the Bug sang another song about how good it was to observe the law, and what a fine land the Sea Valley was, and how every man who loved the Sea Valley should go forth and kill the bad Meat-Eaters. And again his song was as fire to us, and we forgot to grumble.

"It was very strange. When Little-Belly caught too many fish, so that it took a great many to sell for a little money, he threw many of the fish back into the sea, so that more money would be paid for what was left. And Three-Legs often let many large fields lie idle so as to get more money for his corn. And the women, making so much money out of shell that much money was needed to buy with, Dog-Tooth stopped the making of money. And the women had no work, so they took the places of the men. I worked on the fish-trap, getting a string of money every five days. But my sister now did my work, getting a string of money for every ten days. The women worked cheaper, and there was less food, and Tiger-Face said for us to become guards. Only I could not become a guard because I was lame of one leg and Tiger-Face would not have me. And there were many like me. We were broken men and only fit to beg for work or to take care of the babies while the women worked."

Yellow-Head, too, was made hungry by the recital and broiled a piece of bear-meat on the coals.

"But why didn't you rise up, all of you, and kill Three-Legs and Pig-Jaw and Big-Fat and the rest and get enough to eat?" Afraid-in-the-Dark demanded.

"Because we could not understand," Long-Beard answered. "There was too much to think about, and, also, there were the guards sticking spears into us, and Big-Fat talking about God, and the Bug singing new songs. And when any man did think right, and said so, Tiger-Face and the guards got him, and he was tied out to the rocks at low tide so that the rising waters drowned him.

"It was a strange thing—the money. It was like the Bug's songs. It seemed all right, but it wasn't, and we were slow to understand. Dog-Tooth began to gather the money in. He put it in a big pile, in a grass house, with guards to watch it day and night. And the more money he piled in the house the dearer money became, so that a man worked a longer time for a string of money than before. Then, too, there was always talk of war with the Meat-Eaters, and Dog-Tooth and Tiger-Face filled many houses with corn, and dried fish, and smoked goat-meat, and cheese. And with the food piled there in mountains the people had not enough to eat. But what did it matter? Whenever the people grumbled too loudly the Bug sang a new song, and Big-Fat said it was God's word that we should kill Meat-Eaters, and Tiger-Face led us over the divide to kill and be killed. I was not good enough to be a guard and lie fat in the sun, but, when we made war, Tiger-Face was glad to take me along. And when we had eaten all the food stored in the houses we stopped fighting and went back to work to pile up more food."

"Then were you all crazy," commented Deer-Runner.

"Then were we indeed all crazy," Long-Beard agreed. "It was strange, all of it. There was Split-Nose. He said everything was wrong. He said it was true that we grew strong by adding our strength together. And he said that, when we first formed the tribe, it was right that the men whose strength hurt the tribe should be shorn of their strength— men who bashed their brothers' heads and stole their brothers' wives. And now, he said, the tribe was not getting stronger, but was getting weaker, because there were men with another kind of strength that were hurting the tribe—men who had the strength of the land, like Three-Legs; who had the strength of the fish-trap, like Little-Belly; who had the strength of all the goat meat, like Pig-Jaw. The thing to do, Split-Nose said, was to shear these men of their evil strength; to make them go to work, all of them, and to let no man eat who did not work.

"And the Bug sang another song about men like Split-Nose, who wanted to go back and live in trees.

"Yet Split-Nose said no; that he did not want to go back, but ahead; that they grew strong only as they added their strength together; and that, if the Fish-Eaters would add their strength to the Meat-Eaters, there would be no more fighting and no more watchers and no more guards, and that, with all men working, there would be so much food that each man would have to work not more than two hours a day.

"Then the Bug sang again, and he sang that Split-Nose was lazy, and he sang also the 'Song of the Bees.' It was a strange song, and those who listened were made mad, as from the drinking of strong fire-brew. The song was of a swarm of bees, and of a robber wasp who had come in to live with the bees and who was stealing all their honey. The wasp was lazy and told them there was no need to work; also, he told them to make friends with the bears, who were not honey-stealers but only very good friends. And the Bug sang in crooked words, so that those who listened knew that the swarm was the Sea Valley tribe, that the bears were the Meat-Eaters, and that the lazy wasp was Split-Nose. And, when the Bug sang that the bees listened to the wasp till the swarm was near to perishing, the people growled and snarled, and when the

Bug sang that at last the good bees arose and stung the wasp to death, the people picked up stones from the ground and stoned Split-Nose to death till there was naught to be seen of him but the heap of stones they had flung on top of him. And there were many poor people who worked long and hard and had not enough to eat that helped throw the stones on Split-Nose.

"And, after the death of Split-Nose, there was but one other man that dared rise up and speak his mind, and that man was Hair-Face. 'Where is the strength of the strong?' he asked. 'We are the strong, all of us, and we are stronger than Dog-Tooth and Tiger-Face and Three-Legs and Pig-Jaw and all the rest who do nothing and eat much and weaken us by the hurt of their strength which is bad strength. Men who are slaves are not strong. If the man who first found the virtue and use of fire had used his strength we would have been his slaves, as we are the slaves to-day of Little-Belly, who found the virtue and use of the fish-trap; and of the men who found the virtue and use of the land, and the goats, and the fire-brew. Before, we lived in trees, my brothers, and no man was safe. But we fight no more with one another. We have added our strength together. Then let us fight no more with the Meat-Eaters. Let us add our strength and their strength together. Then will we be indeed strong. And then we will go out together, the Fish-Eaters and the Meat-Eaters, and we will kill the tigers and the lions and the wolves and the wild dogs, and we will pasture our goats on all the hillsides and plant our corn and fat roots in all the high mountain valleys. In that day we will be so strong that all the wild animals will flee before us and perish. And nothing will withstand us, for the strength of each man will be the strength of all men in the world.'

"So said Hair-Face, and they killed him, because, they said, he was a wild man and wanted to go back and live in a tree. It was very strange. Whenever a man arose and wanted to go forward all those that stood still said he went backward and should be killed. And the poor people helped stone him, and were fools. We were all fools, except those who were fat and did no work. The fools were called wise, and the wise were stoned. Men who worked did not get enough to eat, and the men who did not work ate too much.

"And the tribe went on losing strength. The children were weak and sickly. And, because we ate not enough, strange sicknesses came among us and we died like flies. And then the Meat-Eaters came upon us. We had followed Tiger-Face too often over the divide and killed them. And now they came to repay in blood. We were too weak and sick to man the big wall. And they killed us, all of us, except some of the women, which they took away with them. The Bug and I escaped, and I hid in the wildest places, and became a hunter of meat and went hungry no more. I stole a wife from the Meat-Eaters, and went to live in the caves of the high mountains where they could not find me. And we had three sons, and each son stole a wife from the Meat-Eaters. And the rest you know, for are you not the sons of my sons?"

"But the Bug?" queried Deer-Runner. "What became of him?"

"He went to live with the Meat-Eaters and to be a singer of songs to the king. He is an old man now, but he sings the same old songs; and, when a man rises up to go forward, he sings that that man is walking backward to live in a tree."

Long Beard dipped into the bear-carcass and sucked with toothless gums at a fist of suet.

"Some day," he said, wiping his hands on his sides, "all the fools will be dead and then all live men will go forward. The strength of the strong will be theirs, and they will add their strength together, so that, of all the men in the world, not one will fight with another. There will be no guards nor watchers on the walls. And all the hunting animals will be killed, and, as Hair-Face said, all the hillsides will be pastured with goats and all the high mountain valleys will be planted with corn and fat roots. And all men will be brothers, and no man will lie idle in the sun and be fed by his fellows. And all that will come to pass in the time when the fools are dead, and when there will be no more singers to stand still and sing the 'Song of the Bees.' Bees are not men."

SOUTH OF THE SLOT

Old San Francisco, which is the San Francisco of only the other day, the day before the Earthquake, was divided midway by the Slot. The Slot was an iron crack that ran along the center of Market street, and from the Slot arose the burr of the ceaseless, endless cable that was hitched at will to the cars it dragged up and down. In truth, there were two slots, but in the quick grammar of the West time was saved by calling them, and much more that they stood for, "The Slot." North of the Slot were the theaters, hotels, and shopping district, the banks and the staid, respectable business houses. South of the Slot were the factories, slums, laundries, machine-shops, boiler works, and the abodes of the working class.

The Slot was the metaphor that expressed the class cleavage of Society, and no man crossed this metaphor, back and forth, more successfully than Freddie Drummond. He made a practice of living in both worlds, and in both worlds he lived signally well. Freddie Drummond was a professor in the Sociology Department of the University of California, and it was as a professor of sociology that he first crossed over the Slot, lived for six months in the great labor-ghetto, and wrote "The Unskilled Laborer"—a book that was hailed everywhere as an able contribution to the literature of progress, and as a splendid reply to the literature of discontent. Politically and economically it was nothing if not orthodox. Presidents of great railway systems bought whole editions of it to give to their employees. The Manufacturers' Association alone distributed fifty thousand copies of it. In a way, it was almost as immoral as the far-famed and notorious "Message to Garcia," while in its pernicious preachment of thrift and content it ran "Mrs. Wiggs of the Cabbage Patch" a close second.

At first, Freddie Drummond found it monstrously difficult to get along among the working people. He was not used to their ways, and they certainly were not used to his. They were suspicious. He had no antecedents. He could talk of no previous jobs. His hands were soft. His extraordinary politeness was ominous. His first idea of the rôle he would play was that of a free and independent American who chose to work with his hands and no explanations given. But it wouldn't do, as he quickly discovered. At the beginning they accepted him, very provisionally, as a freak. A little later, as he began to know his way about better, he insensibly drifted into the rôle that would work—namely, he was a man who had seen better days, very much better days, but who was down in his luck, though, to be sure, only temporarily.

He learned many things, and generalized much and often erroneously, all of which can be found in the pages of "The Unskilled Laborer." He saved himself, however, after the sane and conservative manner of his kind, by labeling his generalizations as "tentative." One of his first experiences was in the great Wilmax Cannery, where he was put on piecework making small packing cases. A box factory supplied the parts, and all Freddie Drummond had to do was to fit the parts into a form and drive in the wire nails with a light hammer.

It was not skilled labor, but it was piece-work. The ordinary laborers in the cannery got a dollar and a half per day. Freddie Drummond found the other men on the same job with him jogging along and earning a dollar and seventy-five cents a day. By the third day he was able to earn the same. But he was ambitious. He did not care to jog along and, being unusually able and fit, on the fourth day earned two dollars. The next day, having keyed himself up to an exhausting high-tension, he earned two dollars and a half. His fellow workers favored him with scowls and black looks, and made remarks, slangily witty and which he did not understand, about sucking up to the boss and pace-making and holding her down when the rains set in. He was astonished at their malingering on piece-work, generalized about the inherent laziness of the unskilled laborer, and proceeded next day to hammer out three dollars' worth of boxes.

And that night, coming out of the cannery, he was interviewed by his fellow workmen, who were very angry and incoherently slangy. He failed to comprehend the motive behind their action. The action itself was strenuous. When he refused to ease down his pace and bleated about freedom of contract, independent Americanism, and the dignity of toil, they proceeded to spoil his pace-making ability. It was a fierce battle, for Drummond was a large man and an athlete, but the crowd finally jumped on his ribs, walked on his face, and stamped on his fingers, so that it was only after lying in bed for a week that he was able to get up and look for another job. All of which is duly narrated in that first book of his, in the chapter entitled "The Tyranny of Labor."

A little later, in another department of the Wilmax Cannery, lumping as a fruit-distributor among the women, he essayed to carry two boxes of fruit at a time, and was promptly reproached by the other fruit-lumpers. It was palpable malingering; but he was there, he decided, not to change conditions, but to observe. So he lumped one box thereafter, and so well did he study the art of shirking that he wrote a special chapter on it, with the last several paragraphs devoted to tentative generalizations.

In those six months he worked at many jobs and developed into a very good imitation of a genuine worker. He was a natural linguist, and he kept notebooks, making a scientific study of the workers' slang or argot, until he could talk quite intelligibly. This language also enabled him more intimately to follow their mental processes, and thereby to gather much data for a projected chapter in some future book which he planned to entitle "Synthesis of Working-Class Psychology."

Before he arose to the surface from that first plunge into the underworld he discovered that he was a good actor and demonstrated the plasticity of his nature. He was himself astonished at his own fluidity. Once having mastered the language and conquered numerous fastidious qualms, he found that he could flow into any nook of working-class life and fit it so snugly as to feel comfortably at home. As he said, in the preface to his second book, "The Toiler," he endeavored really to know the working people, and the only possible way to achieve this was to work beside them, eat their food, sleep in their beds, be amused with their amusements, think their thoughts, and feel their feelings.

He was not a deep thinker. He had no faith in new theories. All his norms and criteria were conventional. His Thesis, on the French Revolution, was noteworthy in college annals, not merely for its painstaking and voluminous accuracy, but for the fact that it was the dryest, deadest, most formal, and most orthodox screed ever written on the subject. He was a very reserved man, and his natural inhibition was large in quantity and steel-like in quality. He had but few friends. He was too undemonstrative, too frigid. He had no vices, nor had anyone ever discovered any temptations. Tobacco he detested, beer he abhorred, and he was never known to drink anything stronger than an occasional light wine at dinner.

When a freshman he had been baptized "Ice-Box" by his warmer-blooded fellows. As a member of the faculty he was known as "Cold-Storage." He had but one grief, and that was "Freddie." He had earned it when he played full-back on the 'Varsity eleven, and his formal soul had never succeeded in living it down. "Freddie" he would ever be, expect officially, and through nightmare vistas he looked into a future when his world would speak of him as "Old Freddie."

For he was very young to be a Doctor of Sociology, only twenty-seven, and he looked younger. In appearance and atmosphere he was a strapping big college man, smooth-faced and easy-mannered, clean and simple and wholesome, with a known record of being a splendid athlete and an implied vast possession of cold culture of the inhibited sort. He never talked shop out of class and committee rooms, except later on, when his books showered him with distasteful public notice and he yielded to the extent of reading occasional papers before certain literary and economic societies.

He did everything right—too right; and in dress and comportment was inevitably correct. Not that he was a dandy. Far from it. He was a college man, in dress and carriage as like as a pea to the type that of late years is being so generously turned out of our institutions of higher learning. His handshake was satisfyingly strong and stiff. His blue eyes were coldly blue and convincingly sincere. His voice, firm and masculine, clean and crisp of enunciation, was pleasant to the ear. The one drawback to Freddie Drummond was his inhibition. He never unbent. In his football days, the higher the tension of the game, the cooler he grew. He was noted as a boxer, but he was regarded as an automaton, with the inhuman precision of a machine judging distance and timing blows, guarding, blocking, and stalling. He was rarely punished himself, while he rarely punished an opponent. He was too clever and too controlled to permit himself to put a pound more weight into a punch than he intended. With him it was a matter of exercise. It kept him fit.

As time went by, Freddie Drummond found himself more frequently crossing the Slot and losing himself in South of Market. His summer and winter holidays were spent there, and, whether it was a week or a week-end, he found the time spent there to be valuable and enjoyable. And there was so much material to be gathered. His third book, "Mass and Master," became a text-book in the American universities; and almost before he knew it, he was at work on a fourth one, "The Fallacy of the Inefficient."

Somewhere in his make-up there was a strange twist or quirk. Perhaps it was a recoil from his environment and training, or from the tempered seed of his ancestors, who had been bookmen generation preceding generation; but at any rate, he found enjoyment in being down in the working-class world. In his own world he was "Cold-Storage," but down below he was "Big" Bill Totts, who could drink and smoke, and slang and fight, and be an all-around favorite. Everybody liked Bill, and more than one working girl made love to him. At first he had been merely a good actor, but as time went on, simulation became second nature. He no longer played a part, and he loved sausages, sausages and bacon, than which, in his own proper sphere, there was nothing more loathsome in the way of food.

From doing the thing for the need's sake, he came to doing the thing for the thing's sake. He found himself regretting as the time drew near for him to go back to his lecture-room and his inhibition. And he often found himself waiting with anticipation for the dreamy time to pass when he could cross the Slot and cut loose and play the devil. He was not wicked, but as "Big" Bill Totts he did a myriad things that Freddie Drummond would never have been permitted to do. Moreover, Freddie Drummond never would have wanted to do them. That was the strangest part of his discovery. Freddie Drummond and Bill Totts were two totally different creatures. The desires and tastes and impulses of each ran counter to the other's. Bill Totts could shirk at a job with clear conscience, while Freddie Drummond condemned shirking as vicious, criminal, and un-American, and devoted whole chapters to condemnation of the vice. Freddie Drummond did not care for dancing, but Bill Totts never missed the nights at the various dancing clubs, such as The Magnolia, The Western Star, and The Elite; while he won a massive silver cup, standing thirty inches high, for being the best-sustained character at the Butchers and Meat Workers' annual grand masked ball. And Bill Totts liked the girls and the girls liked him, while Freddie Drummond enjoyed playing the ascetic in this particular, was open in his opposition to equal suffrage, and cynically bitter in his secret condemnation of coeducation.

Freddie Drummond changed his manners with his dress, and without effort. When he entered the obscure little room used for his transformation scenes, he carried himself just a bit too stiffly. He was too erect, his shoulders were an inch too far back, while his face was grave, almost harsh, and practically expressionless. But when he emerged in Bill Totts's clothes he was another creature. Bill Totts did not slouch, but somehow his whole form limbered up and became graceful. The very sound of the voice was changed, and the laugh was loud and hearty, while loose speech and an occasional oath were as a matter of course on his lips. Also, Bill Totts was a trifle inclined to late hours, and at times, in saloons, to be good-naturedly bellicose with other workmen. Then, too, at Sunday picnics or when coming home from the show, either arm betrayed a practiced familiarity in stealing around girls' waists, while he displayed a wit keen and delightful in the flirtatious badinage that was expected of a good fellow in his class.

So thoroughly was Bill Totts himself, so thoroughly a workman, a genuine denizen of South of the Slot, that he was as class-conscious as the average of his kind, and his hatred for a scab even exceeded that of the average loyal union man. During the Water Front Strike, Freddie Drummond was somehow able to stand apart from the unique combination, and, coldly critical, watch Bill Totts hilariously slug scab longshoremen. For Bill Totts was a dues-paying member of the Longshoremen Union and had a right to be indignant with the usurpers of his job. "Big" Bill Totts was so very big, and so very able, that it was "Big" Bill to the front when trouble was brewing. From acting outraged feelings, Freddie Drummond, in the rôle of his other self, came to experience genuine outrage, and it was only when he returned to the classic atmosphere of the university that he was able, sanely and conservatively, to generalize upon his underworld experiences and put them down on paper as a trained sociologist should. That Bill Totts lacked the perspective to raise him above class-consciousness, Freddie Drummond clearly saw. But Bill Totts could not see it. When he saw a scab taking his job away, he saw red at the same time, and little else did he see. It was Freddie Drummond, irreproachably clothed and comported, seated at his study desk or facing his class in "Sociology 17," who saw Bill Totts, and all around Bill Totts, and all around the whole scab and union-labor problem and its relation to the economic welfare of the United States in the struggle for the world market. Bill Totts really wasn't able to see beyond the next meal and the prize-fight the following night at the Gaiety Athletic Club.

It was while gathering material for "Women and Work" that Freddie received his first warning of the danger he was in. He was too successful at living in both worlds. This strange dualism he had developed was after all very unstable, and, as he sat in his study and meditated, he saw that it could not endure. It was really a transition stage, and if he persisted he saw that he would inevitably have to drop one world or the other. He could not continue in both. And as he looked at the row of volumes that graced the upper shelf of his revolving book-case, his volumes, beginning with his Thesis and ending with "Women and Work," he decided that that was the world he would hold to and stick by. Bill Totts had served his purpose, but he had become a too dangerous accomplice. Bill Totts would have to cease.

Freddie Drummond's fright was due to Mary Condon, President of the International Glove Workers' Union No. 974. He had seen her, first, from the spectators' gallery, at the annual convention of the Northwest Federation of Labor, and he had seen her through Bill Totts' eyes, and that individual had been most favorably impressed by her. She was not

Freddie Drummond's sort at all. What if she were a royal-bodied woman, graceful and sinewy as a panther, with amazing black eyes that could fill with fire or laughter-love, as the mood might dictate? He detested women with a too exuberant vitality and a lack of . . . well, of inhibition. Freddie Drummond accepted the doctrine of evolution because it was quite universally accepted by college men, and he flatly believed that man had climbed up the ladder of life out of the weltering muck and mess of lower and monstrous organic things. But he was a trifle ashamed of this genealogy, and preferred not to think of it. Wherefore, probably, he practiced his iron inhibition and preached it to others, and preferred women of his own type, who could shake free of this bestial and regrettable ancestral line and by discipline and control emphasize the wideness of the gulf that separated them from what their dim forbears had been.

Bill Totts had none of these considerations. He had liked Mary Condon from the moment his eyes first rested on her in the convention hall, and he had made it a point, then and there, to find out who she was. The next time he met her, and quite by accident, was when he was driving an express wagon for Pat Morrissey. It was in a lodging house in Mission Street, where he had been called to take a trunk into storage. The landlady's daughter had called him and led him to the little bedroom, the occupant of which, a glove-maker, had just been removed to hospital. But Bill did not know this. He stooped, up-ended the trunk, which was a large one, got it on his shoulder, and struggled to his feet with his back toward the open door. At that moment he heard a woman's voice.

"Belong to the union?" was the question asked.

"Aw, what's it to you?" he retorted. "Run along now, an' git outa my way. I wanta turn round."

The next he knew, big as he was, he was whirled half around and sent reeling backward, the trunk overbalancing him, till he fetched up with a crash against the wall. He started to swear, but at the same instant found himself looking into Mary Condon's flashing, angry eyes.

"Of course I b'long to the union," he said. "I was only kiddin' you."

"Where's your card?" she demanded in business-like tones.

"In my pocket. But I can't git it out now. This trunk's too damn heavy. Come on down to the wagon an' I'll show it to you."

"Put that trunk down," was the command.

"What for? I got a card, I'm tellin' you."

"Put it down, that's all. No scab's going to handle that trunk. You ought to be ashamed of yourself, you big coward, scabbing on honest men. Why don't you join the union and be a man?"

Mary Condon's color had left her face, and it was apparent that she was in a rage.

"To think of a big man like you turning traitor to his class. I suppose you're aching to join the militia for a chance to shoot down union drivers the next strike. You may belong to the militia already, for that matter. You're the sort—"

"Hold on, now, that's too much!" Bill dropped the trunk to the floor with a bang, straightened up, and thrust his hand into his inside coat pocket. "I told you I was only kiddin'. There, look at that."

It was a union card properly enough.

"All right, take it along," Mary Condon said. "And the next time don't kid."

Her face relaxed as she noticed the ease with which he got the big trunk to his shoulder, and her eyes glowed as they glanced over the graceful massiveness of the man. But Bill did not see that. He was too busy with the trunk.

The next time he saw Mary Condon was during the Laundry Strike. The Laundry Workers, but recently organized, were green at the business, and had petitioned Mary Condon to engineer the strike. Freddie Drummond had had an inkling of what was coming, and had sent Bill Totts to join the union and investigate. Bill's job was in the wash-room, and the men had been called out first, that morning, in order to stiffen the courage of the girls; and Bill chanced to be near the door to the mangle-room when Mary Condon started to enter. The superintendent, who was both large and stout, barred her way. He wasn't going to have his girls called out, and he'd teach her a lesson to mind her own business. And as Mary tried to squeeze past him he thrust her back with a fat hand on her shoulder. She glanced around and saw Bill.

"Here you, Mr. Totts," she called. "Lend a hand. I want to get in."

Bill experienced a startle of warm surprise. She had remembered his name from his union card. The next moment the superintendent had been plucked from the doorway raving about rights under the law, and the girls were deserting their machines. During the rest of that short and successful strike, Bill constituted himself Mary Condon's henchman and messenger, and when it was over returned to the University to be Freddie Drummond and to wonder what Bill Totts could see in such a woman.

Freddie Drummond was entirely safe, but Bill had fallen in love. There was no getting away from the fact of it, and it was this fact that had given Freddie Drummond his warning. Well, he had done his work, and his adventures could cease. There was no need for him to cross the Slot again. All but the last three chapters of his latest, "Labor Tactics and Strategy," was finished, and he had sufficient material on hand adequately to supply those chapters.

Another conclusion he arrived at, was that in order to sheet-anchor himself as Freddie Drummond, closer ties and relations in his own social nook were necessary. It was time that he was married, anyway, and he was fully aware that if Freddie Drummond didn't get married, Bill Totts assuredly would, and the complications were too awful to contemplate. And so, enters Catherine Van Vorst. She was a college woman herself, and her father, the one wealthy member of the faculty, was the head of the Philosophy Department as well. It would be a wise marriage from every standpoint, Freddie Drummond concluded when the engagement was consummated and announced. In appearance cold and reserved, aristocratic and wholesomely conservative, Catherine Van Vorst, though warm in her way, possessed an inhibition equal to Drummond's.

All seemed well with him, but Freddie Drummond could not quite shake off the call of the underworld, the lure of the free and open, of the unhampered, irresponsible life South of the Slot. As the time of his marriage approached, he felt that he had indeed sowed wild oats, and he felt, moreover, what a good thing it would be if he could have but one wild fling more, play the good fellow and the wastrel one last time, ere he settled down to gray lecture-rooms and sober matrimony. And, further to tempt him, the very last chapter of "Labor Tactics and Strategy" remained unwritten for lack of a trifle more of essential data which he had neglected to gather.

So Freddie Drummond went down for the last time as Bill Totts, got his data, and, unfortunately, encountered Mary Condon. Once more installed in his study, it was not a pleasant thing to look back upon. It made his warning doubly imperative. Bill Totts had behaved abominably. Not only had he met Mary Condon at the Central Labor Council, but he had stopped in at a chop-house with her, on the way home, and treated her to oysters. And before they parted at her door, his arms had been about her, and he had kissed her on the lips and kissed her repeatedly. And her last words in his ear, words uttered softly with a catchy sob in the throat that was nothing more nor less than a love cry, were "Bill . . . dear, dear Bill."

Freddie Drummond shuddered at the recollection. He saw the pit yawning for him. He was not by nature a polygamist, and he was appalled at the possibilities of the situation. It would have to be put an end to, and it would end in one only of two ways: either he must become wholly Bill Totts and be married to Mary Condon, or he must remain wholly Freddie Drummond and be married to Catherine Van Vorst. Otherwise, his conduct would be beneath contempt and horrible.

In the several months that followed, San Francisco was torn with labor strife. The unions and the employers' associations had locked horns with a determination that looked as if they intended to settle the matter, one way or the other, for all time. But Freddie Drummond corrected proofs, lectured classes, and did not budge. He devoted himself to Catherine Van Vorst, and day by day found more to respect and admire in her—nay, even to love in her. The Street Car Strike tempted him, but not so severely as he would have expected; and the great Meat Strike came on and left him cold. The ghost of Bill Totts had been successfully laid, and Freddie Drummond with rejuvenescent zeal tackled a brochure, long-planned, on the topic of "diminishing returns."

The wedding was two weeks off, when, one afternoon, in San Francisco, Catherine Van Vorst picked him up and whisked him away to see a Boys' Club, recently instituted by the settlement workers with whom she was interested. It was her brother's machine, but they were alone with the exception of the chauffeur. At the junction with Kearny Street, Market and Geary Streets intersect like the sides of a sharp-angled letter "V." They, in the auto, were coming down Market with the intention of negotiating the sharp apex and going up Geary. But they did not know what was coming down Geary, timed by fate to meet them at the apex. While aware from the papers that the Meat Strike was on and that it was an exceedingly bitter one, all thought of it at that moment was farthest from Freddie Drummond's mind. Was he not seated beside Catherine? And, besides, he was carefully expositing to her his views on settlement work—views that Bill Totts' adventures had played a part in formulating.

Coming down Geary Street were six meat wagons. Beside each scab driver sat a policeman. Front and rear, and along each side of this procession, marched a protecting escort of one hundred police. Behind the police rear guard, at a respectful distance, was an orderly but vociferous mob, several blocks in length, that congested the street from sidewalk to sidewalk. The Beef Trust was making an effort to supply the hotels, and, incidentally, to begin the breaking of the strike. The St. Francis had already been supplied, at a cost of many broken windows and broken heads, and the expedition was marching to the relief of the Palace Hotel.

All unwitting, Drummond sat beside Catherine, talking settlement work, as the auto, honking methodically and dodging traffic, swung in a wide curve to get around the apex. A big coal wagon, loaded with lump coal and drawn by four huge horses, just debouching from Kearny Street as though to turn down Market, blocked their way. The driver of the wagon seemed undecided, and the chauffeur, running slow but disregarding some shouted warning from the crossing policemen, swerved the auto to the left, violating the traffic rules, in order to pass in front of the wagon.

At that moment Freddie Drummond discontinued his conversation. Nor did he resume it again, for the situation was developing with the rapidity of a transformation scene. He heard the roar of the mob at the rear, and caught a glimpse of the helmeted police and the lurching meat wagons. At the same moment, laying on his whip and standing up to his task, the coal driver rushed horses and wagon squarely in front of the advancing procession, pulled the horses up sharply, and put on the big brake. Then he made his lines fast to the brake-handle and sat down with the air of one who had stopped to stay. The auto had been brought to a stop, too, by his big panting leaders which had jammed against it.

Before the chauffeur could back clear, an old Irishman, driving a rickety express wagon and lashing his one horse to a gallop, had locked wheels with the auto. Drummond recognized both horse and wagon, for he had driven them often himself. The Irishman was Pat Morrissey. On the other side a brewery wagon was locking with the coal wagon, and an east-bound Kearny-Street car, wildly clanging its gong, the motorman shouting defiance at the crossing policeman, was dashing forward to complete the blockade. And wagon after wagon was locking and blocking and adding to the confusion. The meat wagons halted. The police were trapped. The roar at the rear increased as the mob came on to the attack, while the vanguard of the police charged the obstructing wagons.

"We're in for it," Drummond remarked coolly to Catherine.

"Yes," she nodded, with equal coolness. "What savages they are."

His admiration for her doubled on itself. She was indeed his sort. He would have been satisfied with her even if she had screamed and clung to him, but this—this was magnificent. She sat in that storm center as calmly as if it had been no more than a block of carriages at the opera.

The police were struggling to clear a passage. The driver of the coal wagon, a big man in shirt sleeves, lighted a pipe and sat smoking. He glanced down complacently at a captain of police who was raving and cursing at him, and his only acknowledgment was a shrug of the shoulders. From the rear arose the rat-tat-tat of clubs on heads and a pandemonium of cursing, yelling, and shouting. A violent accession of noise proclaimed that the mob had broken through and was dragging a scab from a wagon. The police captain reinforced from his vanguard, and the mob at the rear was repelled. Meanwhile, window after window in the high office building on the right had been opened, and the class-conscious clerks were raining a shower of office furniture down on the heads of police and scabs. Waste-baskets, ink-bottles, paper-weights, typewriters—anything and everything that came to hand was filling the air.

A policeman, under orders from his captain, clambered to the lofty seat of the coal wagon to arrest the driver. And the driver, rising leisurely and peacefully to meet him, suddenly crumpled him in his arms and threw him down on top of the captain. The driver was a young giant, and when he climbed on top his load and poised a lump of coal in both hands, a policeman, who was just scaling the wagon from the side, let go and dropped back to earth. The captain ordered half a dozen of his men to take the wagon. The teamster, scrambling over the load from side to side, beat them down with huge lumps of coal.

The crowd on the sidewalks and the teamsters on the locked wagons roared encouragement and their own delight. The motorman, smashing helmets with his controller bar, was beaten into insensibility and dragged from his platform. The captain of police, beside himself at the repulse of his men, led the next assault on the coal wagon. A score of police were swarming up the tall-sided fortress. But the teamster multiplied himself. At times there were six or eight policemen rolling on the pavement and under the wagon. Engaged in repulsing an attack on the rear end of his fortress, the teamster turned about to see the captain just in the act of stepping on to the seat from the front end. He was still in the air and in most unstable equilibrium, when the teamster hurled a thirty-pound lump of coal. It caught the captain fairly on the chest, and he went over backward, striking on a wheeler's back, tumbling on to the ground, and jamming against the rear wheel of the auto.

Catherine thought he was dead, but he picked himself up and charged back. She reached out her gloved hand and patted the flank of the snorting, quivering horse. But Drummond did not notice the action. He had eyes for nothing save the battle of the coal wagon, while somewhere in his complicated psychology, one Bill Totts was heaving and straining in an effort to come to life. Drummond believed in law and order and the maintenance of the established, but this riotous savage within him would have none of it. Then, if ever, did Freddie Drummond call upon his iron inhibition to save him. But it is written that the house divided against itself must fall. And Freddie Drummond found that he had divided all the will and force of him with Bill Totts, and between them the entity that constituted the pair of them was being wrenched in twain.

Freddie Drummond sat in the auto, quite composed, alongside Catherine Van Vorst; but looking out of Freddie Drummond's eyes was Bill Totts, and somewhere behind those eyes, battling for the control of their mutual body, were Freddie Drummond, the sane and conservative sociologist, and Bill Totts, the class-conscious and bellicose union workingman. It was Bill Totts, looking out of those eyes, who saw the inevitable end of the battle on the coal wagon. He saw a policeman gain the top of the load, a second, and a third. They lurched clumsily on the loose footing, but their long riot-clubs were out and swinging. One blow caught the teamster on the head. A second he dodged, receiving it on the shoulder. For him the game was plainly up. He dashed in suddenly, clutched two policemen in his arms, and hurled himself a prisoner to the pavement, his hold never relaxing on his two captors.

Catherine Van Vorst was sick and faint at sight of the blood and brutal fighting. But her qualms were vanquished by the sensational and most unexpected happening that followed. The man beside her emitted an unearthly and uncultured yell and rose to his feet. She saw him spring over the front seat, leap to the broad rump of the wheeler, and from there gain the wagon. His onslaught was like a whirlwind. Before the bewildered officer on top the load could guess the errand of this conventionally clad but excited-seeming gentleman, he was the recipient of a punch that arched him back through the air to the pavement. A kick in the face led an ascending policeman to follow his example. A rush of three more gained the top and locked with Bill Totts in a gigantic clinch, during which his scalp was opened up by a club, and coat, vest, and half his starched shirt were torn from him. But the three policemen were flung wide and far, and Bill Totts, raining down lumps of coal, held the fort.

The captain led gallantly to the attack, but was bowled over by a chunk of coal that burst on his head in black baptism. The need of the police was to break the blockade in front before the mob could break in at the rear, and Bill Totts' need was to hold the wagon till the mob did break through. So the battle of the coal went on.

The crowd had recognized its champion. "Big" Bill, as usual, had come to the front, and Catherine Van Vorst was bewildered by the cries of "Bill! O you Bill!" that arose on every hand. Pat Morrissey, on his wagon seat, was jumping and screaming in an ecstasy, "Eat 'em, Bill! Eat 'em! Eat 'em alive!" From the sidewalk she heard a woman's voice cry out, "Look out, Bill—front end!" Bill took the warning and with well-directed coal cleaned the front end of the wagon of assailants. Catherine Van Vorst turned her head and saw on the curb of the sidewalk a woman with vivid coloring and flashing black eyes who was staring with all her soul at the man who had been Freddie Drummond a few minutes before.

The windows of the office building became vociferous with applause. A fresh shower of office chairs and filing cabinets descended. The mob had broken through on one side the line of wagons, and was advancing, each segregated policeman the center of a fighting group. The scabs were torn from their seats, the traces of the horses cut, and the frightened animals put in flight. Many policemen crawled under the coal wagon for safety, while the loose horses, with here and there a policeman on their backs or struggling at their heads to hold them, surged across the sidewalk opposite the jam and broke into Market Street.

Catherine Van Vorst heard the woman's voice calling in warning. She was back on the curb again, and crying out:

"Beat it, Bill! Now's your time! Beat it!"

The police for the moment had been swept away. Bill Totts leaped to the pavement and made his way to the woman on the sidewalk. Catherine Van Vorst saw her throw her arms around him and kiss him on the lips; and Catherine Van Vorst watched him curiously as he went on down the sidewalk, one arm around the woman, both talking and laughing, and he with a volubility and abandon she could never have dreamed possible.

The police were back again and clearing the jam while waiting for reinforcements and new drivers and horses. The mob had done its work and was scattering, and Catherine Van Vorst, still watching, could see the man she had known as Freddie Drummond. He towered a head above the crowd. His arm was still about the woman. And she in the motorcar, watching, saw the pair cross Market Street, cross the Slot, and disappear down Third Street into the labor ghetto.

In the years that followed no more lectures were given in the University of California by one Freddie Drummond, and no more books on economics and the labor question appeared over the name of Frederick A. Drummond. On the other hand there arose a new labor leader, William Totts by name. He it was who married Mary Condon, President of the International Glove Workers' Union No. 974; and he it was who called the notorious Cooks and Waiters' Strike, which, before its successful termination, brought out with it scores of other unions, among which, of the more remotely allied, were the Chicken Pickers and the Undertakers.

SAMUEL

Margaret Henan would have been a striking figure under any circumstances, but never more so than when I first chanced upon her, a sack of grain of fully a hundred-weight on her shoulder, as she walked with sure though tottering stride from the cart-tail to the stable, pausing for an instant to gather strength at the foot of the steep steps that led to the grain-bin. There were four of these steps, and she went up them, a step at a time, slowly, unwaveringly, and with so dogged a certitude that it never entered my mind that her strength could fail her and let that hundred-weight sack fall from the lean and withered frame that well-nigh doubled under it. For she was patently an old woman, and it was her age that made me linger by the cart and watch.

Six times she went between the cart and the stable, each time with a full sack on her back, and beyond passing the time of day with me she took no notice of my presence. Then, the cart empty, she fumbled for matches and lighted a short clay pipe, pressing down the burning surface of the tobacco with a calloused and apparently nerveless thumb. The hands were noteworthy. They were large-knuckled, sinewy and malformed by labor, rimed with callouses, the nails blunt and broken, and with here and there cuts and bruises, healed and healing, such as are common to the hands of hard-working men. On the back were huge, upstanding veins, eloquent of age and toil. Looking at them, it was hard to believe that they were the hands of the woman who had once been the belle of Island McGill. This last, of course, I learned later. At the time I knew neither her history nor her identity.

She wore heavy man's brogans. Her legs were stockingless, and I had noticed when she walked that her bare feet were thrust into the crinkly, iron-like shoes that sloshed about her lean ankles at every step. Her figure, shapeless and waistless, was garbed in a rough man's shirt and in a ragged flannel petticoat that had once been red. But it was her face, wrinkled, withered and weather-beaten, surrounded by an aureole of unkempt and straggling wisps of grayish hair, that caught and held me. Neither drifted hair nor serried wrinkles could hide the splendid dome of a forehead, high and broad without verging in the slightest on the abnormal.

The sunken cheeks and pinched nose told little of the quality of the life that flickered behind those clear blue eyes of hers. Despite the minutiae of wrinkle-work that somehow failed to weazen them, her eyes were clear as a girl's—clear, out-looking, and far-seeing, and with an open and unblinking steadfastness of gaze that was disconcerting. The remarkable thing was the distance between them. It is a lucky man or woman who has the width of an eye between, but with Margaret Henan the width between her eyes was fully that of an eye and a half. Yet so symmetrically molded was her face that this remarkable feature produced no uncanny effect, and, for that matter, would have escaped the casual observer's notice. The mouth, shapeless and toothless, with down-turned corners and lips dry and parchment-like, nevertheless lacked the muscular slackness so usual with age. The lips might have been those of a mummy, save for that impression of rigid firmness they gave. Not that they were atrophied. On the contrary, they seemed tense and set with a muscular and spiritual determination. There, and in the eyes, was the secret of the certitude with which she carried the heavy sacks up the steep steps, with never a false step or over-balance, and emptied them in the grain-bin.

"You are an old woman to be working like this," I ventured.

She looked at me with that strange, unblinking gaze, and she thought and spoke with the slow deliberateness that characterized everything about her, as if well aware of an eternity that was hers and in which there was no need for haste. Again I was impressed by the enormous certitude of her. In this eternity that seemed so indubitably hers, there was time and to spare for safe-footing and stable equilibrium—for certitude, in short. No more in her spiritual life than in carrying the hundred-weights of grain, was there a possibility of a misstep or an overbalancing. The feeling produced in me was uncanny. Here was a human soul that, save for the most glimmering of contacts, was beyond the humanness of me. And the more I learned of Margaret Henan in the weeks that followed the more mysteriously remote she became. She was as alien as a far-journeyer from some other star, and no hint could she nor all the countryside give me of what norms of living, what heats of feeling, or rules of philosophic contemplation actuated her in all that she had been and was.

"I will be suvunty-two come Guid Friday a fortnight," she said in reply to my question.

"But you are an old woman to be doing this man's work, and a strong man's work at that," I insisted.

Again she seemed to immerse herself in that atmosphere of contemplative eternity, and so strangely did it affect me that I should not have been surprised to have awaked a century or so later and found her just beginning to enunciate her reply:

"The work hoz tull be done, an' I am beholden tull no one."

"But have you no children, no family relations?"

"O, ay, a-plenty o' them, but they no see fut tull be helpun' me."

She drew out her pipe for a moment, then added, with a nod of her head toward the house, "I luv' wuth meself."

I glanced at the house, straw-thatched and commodious, at the large stable, and at the large array of fields I knew must belong with the place.

"It is a big bit of land for you to farm by yourself."

"O, ay, a bug but, suvunty acres. Ut kept me old mon buzzy, along wuth a son an' a hired mon, tull say naught o' extra honds un the harvest an' a maid-servant un the house."

She clambered into the cart, gathered the reins in her hands, and quizzed me with her keen, shrewd eyes.

"Belike ye hail from over the watter—Ameruky, I'm meanun'?"

"Yes, I'm a Yankee," I answered.

"Ye wull no be findun' mony Island McGill folk stoppun' un Ameruky?"

"No; I don't remember ever meeting one in the States."

She nodded her head.

"They are home-lovun' bodies, though I wull no be sayun' they are no fair-traveled. Yet they come home ot the last, them oz are no lost ot sea or kult by fevers an' such-like un foreign parts."

"Then your sons will have gone to sea and come home again?" I queried.

"O, ay, all savun' Samuel oz was drownded."

At the mention of Samuel I could have sworn to a strange light in her eyes, and it seemed to me, as by some telepathic flash, that I divined in her a tremendous wistfulness, an immense yearning. It seemed to me that here was the key to her inscrutableness, the clew that if followed properly would make all her strangeness plain. It came to me that here was a contact and that for the moment I was glimpsing into the soul of her. The question was tickling on my tongue, but she forestalled me.

She *tckh'd* to the horse, and with a "Guid day tull you, sir," drove off.

*   *   *

A simple, homely people, are the folk of Island McGill, and I doubt if a more sober, thrifty, and industrious folk is to be found in all the world. Meeting them abroad—and to meet them abroad one must meet them on the sea, for a hybrid seafaring and farmer breed are they—one would never take them to be Irish. Irish they claim to be, speaking of the North of Ireland with pride and sneering at their Scottish brothers; yet Scotch they undoubtedly are, transplanted Scotch of long ago, it is true, but none the less Scotch, with a thousand traits, to say nothing of their tricks of speech and woolly utterance, which nothing less than their Scotch clannishness could have preserved to this late day.

A narrow loch, scarcely half a mile wide, separates Island McGill from the mainland of Ireland; and, once across this loch, one finds himself in an entirely different country. The Scotch impression is strong, and the people, to commence with, are Presbyterians. When it is considered that there is no public house in all the island and that seven thousand souls dwell therein, some idea may be gained of the temperateness of the community. Wedded to old ways, public opinion and the ministers are powerful influences, while fathers and mothers are revered and obeyed as in few other places in this modern world. Courting lasts never later than ten at night, and no girl walks out with her young man without her parents' knowledge and consent.

The young men go down to the sea and sow their wild oats in the wicked ports, returning periodically, between voyages, to live the old intensive morality, to court till ten o'clock, to sit under the minister each Sunday, and to listen at home to the same stern precepts that the elders preached to them from the time they were laddies. Much they learned of women in the ends of the earth, these seafaring sons, yet a canny wisdom was theirs and they never brought wives home with them. The one solitary exception to this had been the schoolmaster, who had been guilty of bringing a wife from half a mile the other side of the loch. For this he had never been forgiven, and he rested under a cloud for the remainder of his days. At his death the wife went back across the loch to her own people, and the blot on the escutcheon of Island McGill was erased. In the end the sailor-men married girls of their own home land and settled down to become exemplars of all the virtues for which the island was noted.

Island McGill was without a history. She boasted none of the events that go to make history. There had never been any wearing of the green, any Fenian conspiracies, any land disturbances. There had been but one eviction, and that purely technical—a test case, and on advice of the tenant's lawyer. So Island McGill was without annals. History had passed her by. She paid her taxes, acknowledged her crowned rulers, and left the world alone; all she asked in return was that the world leave her alone. The world was composed of two parts—Island McGill and the rest of it. And whatever was not Island McGill was outlandish and barbarian; and well she knew, for did not her seafaring sons bring home report of that world and its ungodly ways?

It was from the skipper of a Glasgow tramp, as passenger from Colombo to Rangoon, that I had first learned of the existence of Island McGill; and it was from him that I had carried the letter that gave me entrance to the house of Mrs. Ross, widow of a master mariner, with a daughter living with her and with two sons, master mariners themselves and out upon the sea. Mrs. Ross did not take in boarders, and it was Captain Ross's letter alone that had enabled me to get from her bed and board. In the evening, after my encounter with Margaret Henan, I questioned Mrs. Ross, and I knew on the instant that I had in truth stumbled upon mystery.

Like all Island McGill folk, as I was soon to discover, Mrs. Ross was at first averse to discussing Margaret Henan at all. Yet it was from her I learned that evening that Margaret Henan had once been one of the island belles. Herself the daughter of a well-to-do farmer, she had married Thomas Henan, equally well-to-do. Beyond the usual housewife's tasks she had never been accustomed to work. Unlike many of the island women, she had never lent a hand in the fields.

"But what of her children?" I asked.

"Two o' the sons, Jamie an' Timothy uz married an' be goun' tull sea. Thot bug house close tull the post-office uz Jamie's. The daughters thot ha' no married be luvun' wuth them as dud marry. An' the rest be dead."

"The Samuels," Clara interpolated, with what I suspected was a giggle.

She was Mrs. Ross's daughter, a strapping young woman with handsome features and remarkably handsome black eyes.

" 'Tuz naught tull be smuckerun' ot," her mother reproved her.

"The Samuels?" I intervened. "I don't understand."

"Her four sons thot died."

"And were they all named Samuel?"

"Ay."

"Strange," I commented in the lagging silence.

"Very strange," Mrs. Ross affirmed, proceeding stolidly with the knit-

ting of the woolen singlet on her knees—one of the countless under-
garments that she interminably knitted for her skipper sons.

"And it was only the Samuels that died?" I queried, in further
attempt.

"The others luv'd," was the answer. "A fine fomuly—no finer on the
island. No better lods ever sailed out of Island McGill. The munuster
held them up oz models tull pottern after. Nor was ever a whusper
breathed again' the girls."

"But why is she left alone now in her old age?" I persisted. "Why
don't her own flesh and blood look after her? Why does she live alone?
Don't they ever go to see her or care for her?"

"Never a one un twenty years an' more now. She fetch't ut on tull
herself. She drove them from the house just oz she drove old Tom
Henan, thot was her husband, tull hus death."

"Drink?" I ventured.

Mrs. Ross shook her head scornfully, as if drink was a weakness
beneath the weakest of Island McGill.

A long pause followed, during which Mrs. Ross knitted stolidly on,
only nodding permission when Clara's young man, mate on one of the
Shire Line sailing ships, came to walk out with her. I studied the half-
dozen ostrich eggs, hanging in the corner against the wall like a cluster
of some monstrous fruit. On each shell was painted precipitous and
impossible seas through which full-rigged ships foamed with a lack of
perspective only equaled by their sharp technical perfection. On the
mantelpiece stood two large pearl shells, obviously a pair, intricately
carved by the patient hands of New Caledonian convicts. In the center
of the mantel was a stuffed bird of paradise, while about the room were
scattered gorgeous shells from the southern seas, delicate sprays of coral
sprouting from barnacled *pi-pi* shells and cased in glass, assegais from
South Africa, stone-axes from New Guinea, huge Alaskan tobacco-
pouches beaded with heraldic totem designs, a boomerang from Australia, divers ships in glass bottles, a cannibal *kai-kai* bowl from the
Marquesas, and fragile cabinets from China and the Indies and inlaid
with mother-of-pearl and precious woods.

I gazed at this varied trove brought home by sailor sons, and pondered the mystery of Margaret Henan, who had driven her husband to
his death and been forsaken by all her kin. It was not the drink. Then
what was it?—some shocking cruelty? some amazing infidelity? or some
fearful, old-world peasant-crime?

I broached my theories, but to all Mrs. Ross shook her head.

"Ut was no thot," she said. "Margaret was a guid wife an' a guid
mother, an' I doubt she would harm a fly. She brought up her fomuly

God-fearin' an' decent-minded. Her trouble was thot she took lunatuc—turned eediot."

Mrs. Ross tapped significantly on her forehead to indicate a state of addlement.

"But I talked with her this afternoon," I objected, "and I found her a sensible woman—remarkably bright for one of her years."

"Ay, an' I'm grantun' all thot you say," she went on calmly. "But I am no referrun' tull thot. I am referrun' tull her wucked-headed an' vucious stubbornness. No more stubborn woman ever luv'd than Margaret Henan. Ut was all on account o' Samuel, which was the name o' her eldest an' they do say her favorut brother—hum oz died by hus own hond all through the munuster's mustake un no registerun' the new church ot Dublin. Ut was a lesson thot the name was musfortunate, but she would no take ut, an' there was talk when she called her first child Samuel—hum thot died o' the croup. An' wuth thot what does she do but call the next one Samuel, an' hum only three when he fell un tull the tub o' hot watter an' was plain cooked tull death. Ut all come, I tell you, o' her wucked-headed an' foolush stubbornness. For a Samuel she must hov; an' ut was the death of the four of her sons. After the first, dudna her own mother go down un the dirt tull her feet, a-beggun' an' pleadun' wuth her no tull name her next one Samuel? But she was no tull be turned from her purpose. Margaret Henan was always set un her ways, an' never more so thon on thot name Samuel.

"She was fair lunatuc on Samuel. Dudna her neighbors, an' all kuth an' kun savun' them thot luv'd un the house wuth her, get up an' walk out ot the christenun' of the second—hum thot was cooked? Thot they dud, an' ot the very moment the munuster asked what would the bairn's name be. 'Samuel,' says she; an' wuth thot they got up an' walked out an' left the house. An' ot the door dudna her Aunt Fannie, her mother's suster, turn an' say loud for all tull hear: 'What for wull she be wantun' tull murder the wee thung?' The munuster heard fine, an' dudna like ut, but, oz he told my Larry afterward, what could he do? Ut was the woman's wush, an' there was no law again' a mother callun' her child accordun' tull her wush.

"An' then was there no' the third Samuel? An' when he was lost ot sea of the Cape, dudna she break all laws o' nature tull hov a fourth? She was forty-seven, I'm tellun' ye, an' she hod a child ot forty-seven. Thunk on ut! Ot forty-seven! Ut was fair scand'lous."

From Clara, next morning, I got the tale of Margaret Henan's favorite brother; and from here and there, in the week that followed, I pieced together the tragedy of Margaret Henan. Samuel Dundee had been the youngest of Margaret's four brothers, and, as Clara told me, she had well-nigh worshiped him. He was going to sea at the time, skipper of one of the sailing ships of the Bank Line, when he married Agnes Hewitt. She was described as a slender wisp of a girl, delicately featured and with a nervous organization of the supersensitive order. Theirs had been the first marriage in the "new" church, and after a two-weeks' honeymoon Samuel had kissed his bride good-bye and sailed in command of the *Loughbank,* a big four-masted bark.

And it was because of the "new" church that the minister's blunder occurred. Nor was it the blunder of the minister alone, as one of the elders later explained; for it was equally the blunder of the whole Presbytery of Coughleen, which included fifteen churches on Island McGill and the mainland. The old church, beyond repair, had been torn down and the new one built on the original foundation. Looking upon the foundation stones as similar to a ship's keel, it never entered the minister's nor the Presbytery's head that the new church was legally any other than the old church.

"An' three couples was married the first week un the new church," Clara said. "First of all, Samuel Dundee an' Agnes Hewitt; the next day Albert Mahan an' Minnie Duncan; an' by the week-end Eddie Troy and Flo Mackintosh—all sailor-men, an' un sux weeks' time the last of them back tull their ships an' awa', an' no one o' them dreamin' of the wuckedness they'd been ot."

The Imp of the Perverse must have chuckled at the situation. All things favored. The marriages had taken place in the first week of May, and it was not till three months later that the minister, as required by law, made his quarterly report to the civil authorities in Dublin. Promptly came back the announcement that his church had no legal existence, not being registered according to the law's demands. This was overcome by prompt registration; but the marriages were not to be so easily remedied. The three sailor-husbands were away, and their wives, in short, were not their wives.

"But the munuster was no for alarmin' the bodies," said Clara. "He kept hus council an' bided hus time, waitin' for the lods tull be back from sea. Oz luck would have ut, he was away across the island tull a christenun' when Albert Mahan arrives home onexpected, hus shup just docked ot Dublin. Ut's nine o'clock ot night when the munuster, un hus sluppers an' dressun' gown, gets the news. Up he jumps an' calls for horse an' saddle, an' awa' he goes like the wund for Albert Mahan's. Albert uz just goun' tull bed an' hoz one shoe off when the munuster arrives.

" 'Come wuth me, the pair o' ye,' says he, breathless-like. 'What for, an' me dead weary an' goun' tull bed?' says Albert. 'Tull be lawful married,' says the munuster. Albert looks black an' says, 'Now munuster ye wull be jokin',' but tull humself, oz I've heard hum tell mony a time, he uz wonderun' thot the munuster should a-took tull whuskey ot hus time o' life.

" 'We be no married?' says Minnie. He shook his head. 'An' I om no Mussus Mahan?' 'No,' says he, 'ye are no Mussus Mahan. Ye are plain Muss Duncan.' 'But ye married us yoursel',' says she. 'I dud an' I dudna,' says he. An' wuth thot he tells them the whole upshot, an' Albert puts on hus shoe, an' they go with the munuster an' are married proper an' lawful, an' oz Albert Mahan says afterward mony's the time, ' 'Tus no every mon thot hoz two weddun' nights on Island McGill.' "

Six months later Eddie Troy came home and was promptly re-married. But Samuel Dundee was away on a three-years' voyage and his ship fell overdue. Further to complicate the situation, a baby boy, past two years old, was waiting for him in the arms of his wife. The months passed, and the wife grew thin with worrying. "Ut's no meself I'm thunkun' on," she is reported to have said many times, "but ut's the puir fatherless bairn. Uf aught happened tull Samuel where wull the bairn stond?"

Lloyds posted the *Loughbank* as missing, and the owners ceased the monthly remittance of Samuel's half-pay to his wife. It was the question of the child's legitimacy that preyed on her mind, and, when all hope of Samuel's return was abandoned, she drowned herself and the child in the loch. And here enters the greater tragedy. The *Loughbank* was not lost. By a series of sea disasters and delays too interminable to relate, she had made one of those long, unsighted passages such as occur once or twice in half a century. How the Imp must have held both his sides! Back from the sea came Samuel, and when they broke the news to him something else broke somewhere in his heart or head. Next morning they found him where he had tried to kill himself across the grave of his wife and child. Never in the history of Island McGill was there so fearful a deathbed. He spat in the minister's face and reviled him, and died blaspheming so terribly that those that tended on him did so with averted gaze and trembling hands.

And, in the face of all this, Margaret Henan named her first child Samuel.

How account for the woman's stubbornness? Or was it a morbid obses-sion that demanded a child of hers should be named Samuel? Her third child was a girl, named after herself, and the fourth was a boy again. Despite the strokes of fate that had already bereft her, and despite the loss of friends and relatives, she persisted in her resolve to name the child after her brother. She was shunned at church by those who had grown up with her. Her mother, after a final appeal, left her house with the warning that if the child were so named she would never speak to her again. And though the old lady lived thirty-odd years longer she kept her word. The minister agreed to christen the child any name but Samuel, and every other minister on Island McGill refused to christen it by the name she had chosen. There was talk on the part of Margaret Henan of going to law at the time, but in the end she carried the child to Belfast and there had it christened Samuel.

And then nothing happened. The whole island was confuted. The boy grew and prospered. The schoolmaster never ceased averring that it was the brightest lad he had ever seen. Samuel had a splendid constitution, a tremendous grip on life. To everybody's amazement he escaped the usual run of childish afflictions. Measles, whooping-cough and mumps knew him not. He was armor-clad against germs, immune to all disease. Headaches and earaches were things unknown. "Never so much oz a boil or a pumple," as one of the old bodies told me, ever marred his healthy skin. He broke school records in scholarship and athletics, and whipped every boy of his size or years on Island McGill.

It was a triumph for Margaret Henan. This paragon was hers, and it bore the cherished name. With the one exception of her mother, friends and relatives drifted back and acknowledged that they had been mistaken; though there were old crones who still abided by their opinion and who shook their heads ominously over their cups of tea. The boy was too wonderful to last. There was no escaping the curse of the name his mother had wickedly laid upon him. The young generation joined Margaret Henan in laughing at them, but the old crones continued to shake their heads.

Other children followed. Margaret Henan's fifth was a boy, whom she called Jamie, and in rapid succession followed three girls, Alice, Sara, and Nora, the boy Timothy, and two more girls, Florence and Katie. Katie was the last and eleventh, and Margaret Henan, at thirty-five, ceased from her exertions. She had done well by Island McGill and the Queen. Nine healthy children were hers. All prospered. It seemed her ill luck had shot its bolt with the deaths of her first two. Nine lived, and one of them was named Samuel.

Jamie elected to follow the sea, though it was not so much a matter of election as compulsion, for the eldest sons on Island McGill remained on the land while all other sons went to the salt plowing. Timothy followed Jamie, and by the time the latter had got his first command, a steamer in the Bay trade out of Cardiff, Timothy was mate of a big sailing ship. Samuel, however, did not take kindly to the soil. The farmer's life had no attraction for him. His brothers went to sea, not out of desire, but because it was the only way for them to gain their bread; and he, who had no need to go, envied them when, returned from far voyages, they sat by the kitchen fire and told their bold tales of the wonderlands beyond the sea-rim.

Samuel became a teacher, much to his father's disgust, and even took extra certificates, going to Belfast for his examinations. When the old master retired, Samuel took over his school. Secretly, however, he studied navigation, and it was Margaret's delight when he sat by the kitchen fire, and, despite their master's tickets, tangled up his brothers in the theoretics of their profession. Tom Henan alone was outraged when Samuel, school teacher, gentleman, and heir to the Henan farm, shipped to sea before the mast. Margaret had an abiding faith in her son's star, and whatever he did she was sure was for the best. Like everything else connected with his glorious personality, there had never been known so swift a rise as in the case of Samuel. Barely with two years' sea experience before the mast, he was taken from the forecastle and made a provisional second mate. This occurred in a fever port on the West Coast, and the committee of skippers that examined him agreed that he knew more of the science of navigation than they had remembered or forgotten. Two years later he sailed from Liverpool, mate of the *Starry Grace*, with both master's and extra-master's tickets in his possession. And then it happened—the thing the old crones had been shaking their heads over for years.

It was told me by Gavin McNab, bosun of the *Starry Grace* at the time, himself an Island McGill man.

"Wull do I remember ut," he said. "We was runnin' our Eastun' down, an' makun' heavy weather of ut. Oz fine a sailor-mon oz ever walked was Samuel Henan. I remember the look of hum wull thot last marnun', a-watchun' them bug seas curlun' up astern, an' a-watchun' the old girl an' seeun' how she took them—the skupper down below an' drunkun' for days. Ut was ot seven thot Henan brought her up on tull the wund, not darun' tull run longer un thot fearful sea. Ot eight, after havun' breakfast, he turns un, an' a half hour after up comes the skupper, bleary-eyed an' shaky an' holdun' on tull the companion. Ut was fair smokun', I om tellun' ye, an' there he stood, blunkun' an' noddun' an' talkun' tull humsel'. 'Keep off,' says he ot last tull the mon ot the wheel. 'My God!' says the second mate, standun' beside hum. The skupper never looks tull hum ot all, but keeps on mutterun' an' jabberun' tull humsel'. All of a suddent-like he straightuns up an' throws hus head back, an' says: 'Put your wheel over, me mon—now, domn ye! Are ye deef thot ye'll no be hearun' me?'

"Ut was a drunken mon's luck, for the *Starry Grace* wore off afore thot God-Almighty gale wuthout shuppun' a bucket o' watter, the second mate shoutun' orders an' the crew jumpun' like mod. An' wuth thot the skupper nods contented-like tull humself an' goes below after more whuskey. Ut was plain murder o' the lives o' all of us, for ut was no the time for the buggest shup afloat tull be runnun'. Run? Never hov I seen the like! Ut was beyond all thunkun', an' me goun' tull sea, boy an' mon, for forty year. I tell you ut was fair awesome.

"The face o' the second mate was white oz death, an' he stood ut alone for half an hour, when ut was too much for hum an' he went below an' called Samuel an' the third. Ay, a fine sailor-mon thot Samuel, but ut was too much for hum. He looked an' studied, and looked an' studied, but he could no see hus way. He durst na heave tull. She would ha' been sweeput o' all honds an' stucks an' everythung afore she could a-fetcht up. There was naught tull do but keep on runnun'. An' uf ut worsened we were lost onyway, for soon or late thot overtakun' sea was sure tull sweep us clear over poop an' all.

"Dud I say ut was a God-Almighty gale? Ut was worse nor thot. The devil himself must ha' hod a hond un the brewun' o' ut, ut was thot fearsome. I ha' looked on some sights, but I om no carun' tull look on the like o' thot again. No mon dared tull be un hus bunk. No, nor no mon on the decks. All honds of us stood on top the house an' held on an' watched. The three mates was on the poop, with two men ot the wheel, an' the only mon below was thot whuskey-blighted captain snorun' drunk.

"An' then I see ut comun', a mile away, risun' above all the waves like an island un the sea—the buggest wave ever I looked upon. The three mates stood tulgether an' watched ut comun', a-prayun' like we thot she would no break un passun' us. But ut was no tull be. Ot the last, when she rose up like a mountain, curlun' above the stern an' blottun' out the sky, the mates scottered, the second an' third runnun' for the mizzen-shrouds an' climbun' up, but the first runnun' tull the wheel tull lend a hond. He was a brave mon, thot Samuel Henan. He run straight un tull the face o' thot father o' all waves, no thunkun' on humself but thunkun' only o' the shup. The two men was lashed tull the wheel, but he would be ready tull hond un the case they was kult. An' then she took ut. We on the house could no see the poop for the thousand tons o' watter thot hod hut ut. Thot wave cleaned them out,

took everythung along wuth ut—the two mates, climbun' up the miz-
zen-ruggun', Samuel Henan runnun' tull the wheel, the two men ot the
wheel, ay, an' the wheel utself. We never saw aught o' them, for she
broached tull what o' the wheel goun', an' two men o' us was drownded
off the house, no tull mention the carpenter thot we pucked up ot the
break o' the poop wuth every bone o' hus body broke tull he was like
so much jelly."

And here enters the marvel of it, the miraculous wonder of that woman's
heroic spirit. Margaret Henan was forty-seven when the news came
home of the loss of Samuel; and it was not long after that the unbelievable rumor went around Island McGill. I say unbelievable. Island McGill
would not believe. Doctor Hall pooh-pooh'd it. Everybody laughed at
it as a good joke. They traced back the gossip to Sara Dack, servant to
the Henans', and who alone lived with Margaret and her husband. But
Sara Dack persisted in her assertion and was called a low-mouthed liar.
One or two dared question Tom Henan himself, but beyond black looks
and curses for their presumption they elicited nothing from him.

The rumor died down, and the island fell to discussing in all its ramifications the loss of the *Grenoble* in the China Seas, with all her officers
and half her crew born and married on Island McGill. But the rumor
would not stay down. Sara Dack was louder in her assertions, the looks
Tom Henan cast about him were blacker than ever, and Dr. Hall, after
a visit to the Henan house, no longer pooh-pooh'd. Then Island McGill
sat up, and there was a tremendous wagging of tongues. It was unnat-
ural and ungodly. The like had never been heard. And when, as time
passed, the truth of Sara Dack's utterances was manifest, the island folk
decided, like the bosun of the *Starry Grace,* that only the devil could have
had a hand in so untoward a happening. And the infatuated woman, so
Sara Dack reported, insisted that it would be a boy. "Eleven bairns ha'
I borne," she said; "sux o' them lossies an' five o' them loddies. An'
sunce there be balance un all thungs, so wull there be balance wuth me.
Sux o' one an' half a dozen o' the other—there uz the balance, an' oz
sure oz the sun rises un the marnun', thot sure wull ut be a boy."

And boy it was, and a prodigy. Dr. Hall raved about its unblemished
perfection and massive strength, and wrote a brochure on it for the
Dublin Medical Society as the most interesting case of the sort in his
long career. When Sara Dack gave the babe's unbelievable weight, Island McGill refused to believe and once again called her liar. But when
Doctor Hall attested that he had himself weighed it and seen it tip that

very notch, Island McGill held its breath and accepted whatever report Sara Dack made of the infant's progress or appetite. And once again Margaret Henan carried a babe to Belfast and had it christened Samuel.

"Oz good oz gold ut was," said Sara Dack to me.

Sara, at the time I met her, was a buxom, phlegmatic spinster of sixty, equipped with an experience so tragic and unusual that though her tongue ran on for decades its output would still be of imperishable interest to her cronies.

"Oz good oz gold," said Sara Dack. "Ut never fretted. Sut ut down un the sun by the hour an' never a sound ut would make oz long oz ut was no hungered. An' thot strong! The grup o' uts honds was like a mon's. I mind me, when ut was but hours old, ut grupped me so mighty thot I fetcht a scream I was thot frighted. Ut was the punk o' health. Ut slept an' ate, an' grew. Ut never bothered. Never a night's sleep ut lost tull no one, nor ever a munut's, an' thot wuth cuttin' uts teeth an' all. An' Margaret would dandle ut on her knee an' ask was there ever so fine a loddie un the three Kungdoms.

"The way ut grew! Ut was un keepun' wuth the way ut ate. Ot a year ut was the size o' a bairn of two. Ut was slow tull walk an' talk. Exceptun' for gurgly noises un uts throat an' for creepun' on all fours, ut dudna monage much un the walkun' an' talkun' line. But thot was tull be expected from the way ut grew. Ut all went tull growun' strong an' healthy. An' even old Tom Henan cheered up ot the might of ut an' said was there ever the like o' ut un the three Kungdoms. Ut was Doctor Hall thot first suspicioned, I mind me well, though ut was luttle I dreamt what he was up tull ot the time. I see hum holdun' thungs un front o' luttle Sammy's eyes, an' a-makun' noises, loud an' soft, an' far an' near, un luttle Sammy's ears. An' then I see Doctor Hall go away, wrunklun' hus eyebrows an' shakun' hus head like the bairn was ailun'. But he was no ailun', oz I could swear tull, me a-seeun' hum eat an' grow. But Doctor Hal no said a word tull Margaret an' I was no for guessun' the why he was sore-puzzled.

"I mind me when luttle Sammy first spoke. He was two years old an' the size of a child o' five, though he could no monage the walkun' yet but when around on all-fours, happy an' contented-like an' makun' no trouble oz long oz he was fed promptly, whuch was onusual often. I was hangun' the wash on the line ot the time when out he comes, on all-fours, hus bug head waggun' tull an' fro an' blunkun' un the sun. An' then, suddent, he talked. I was thot took a-back I near died o' fright, an' fine I knew ut then, the shakun' o' Doctor Hall's head. Talked?

Never a bairn on Island McGill talked so loud an' tull such purpose. There was no mustakun' ut. I stood there all tremblun' an' shakun'. Little Sammy was brayun'. I tell you, sir, he was brayun' like an ass— just like thot, loud an' long an' cheerful tull ut seemed hus lungs ud crack.

"He was a eediot—a great, awful, monster eediot. Ut was after he talked thot Doctor Hall told Margaret, but she would no believe. Ut would all come right, she said. Ut was growun' too fast for aught else. Guv ut time, said she, an' we would see. But old Tom Henan knew, an' he never held up hus head again. He could no abide the thung, an' would no brung humsel' tull touch ut, though I om no denyun' he was fair fascinated by ut. Mony the time I see hum watchun' of ut aroun' a corner, lookun' ot ut tull hus eyes fair bulged wuth the horror; an' when ut brayed old Tom ud stuck hus fungers tull hus ears an' look thot miserable I could a-puttied hum.

"An' bray ut could! Ut was the only thung ut could do besides eat an' grow. Whenever ut was hungry ut brayed, an' there was no stoppun' ut save wuth food. An' always of a marnun', when first ut crawled tull the kutchen-door an' blunked out ot the sun, ut brayed. An' ut was brayun' that brought about uts end.

"I mind me well. Ut was three years old an' oz bug oz a lod o' ten. Old Tom hed been goun' from bod tull worse, ploughun' up an' down the fields an' talkun' an' mutterun' tull humself. On the marnun' o' the day I mind me, he was suttun' on the bench outside the kutchen, a-futtun' the handle tull a puck-axe. Unbeknown, the monster eediot crawled tull the door an' brayed after hus fashion ot the sun. I see old Tom start up an' look. An' there was the monster eediot, waggun' uts bug head an' blunkun' an' brayun' like the great bug ass ut was. Ut was too much for Tom. Somethin' went wrong wuth hum suddent-like. He jumped tull hus feet an' fetcht the puck-handle down on the monster eediot's head. An' he hut ut again an' again like ut was a mod dog an' hum afeard o' ut. An' he went straight tull the stable an' hung humsel' tull a rafter. An' I was no for stoppun' on after such-like, an' I went tull stay along wuth me suster thot was married tull John Martin an' comfortable-off."

I sat on the bench by the kitchen door and regarded Margaret Henan, while with her callous thumb she pressed down the live fire of her pipe and gazed out across the twilight-sombered fields. It was the very bench Tom Henan had sat upon that last sanguinary day of life. And Margaret sat in the doorway where the monster, blinking at the sun, had so often wagged its head and brayed. We had been talking for an hour, she with that slow certitude of eternity that so befitted her; and, for the life of me, I could lay no finger on the motives that ran through the tangled warp and woof of her. Was she a martyr to Truth? Did she have it in her to worship at so abstract a shrine? Had she conceived Abstract Truth to be the one high goal of human endeavor on that day of long ago when she named her first-born Samuel? Or was hers the stubborn obstinacy of the ox? the fixity of purpose of the balky horse? the stolidity of the self-willed peasant-mind? Was it whim or fancy?—the one streak of lunacy in what was otherwise an eminently rational mind? Or, reverting, was hers the spirit of a Bruno? Was she convinced of the intellectual rightness of the stand she had taken? Was hers a steady, enlightened opposition to superstition? or—and a subtler thought—was she mastered by some vaster, profounder superstition, a fetish-worship of which the Alpha and the Omega was the cryptic *Samuel?*

"Wull ye be tellun' me," she said, "thot uf the second Samuel hod been named Larry thot he would no hov fell un the hot watter an' drownded? Atween you an' me, sir, an' ye are untellugent-lookun' tull the eye, would the name hov made ut onyways dufferent? Would the washun' no be done thot day uf he hod been Larry or Michael? Would hot watter no be hot, an' would hot watter no burn uf he hod hod ony other name but Samuel?"

I acknowledged the justice of her contention, and she went on.

"Do a wee but of a name change the plans o' God? Do the world run by hut or muss, an' be God a weak, shully-shallyun' creature thot ud alter the fate an' destiny o' thungs because the worm Margaret Henan seen fut tull name her bairn Samuel? There be my son Jamie. He wull no sign a Rooshan-Funn un hus crew because o' believun' thot Rooshan-Funns do be monajun' the wunds an' hov the makun' o' bod weather. Wull you be thunkun' so? Wull you be thunkun' thot God thot makes the wunds tull blow wull bend hus head from on high tull lussen tull the word o' a greasy Rooshan-Funn un some dirty shup's fo'c'sle?"

I said no, certainly not; but she was not to be set aside from pressing home the point of her argument.

"Then wull you be thunkun' thot God thot directs the stars un their courses, an' tull whose mighty foot the world uz but a footstool, wull you be thunkun' thot he wull take a spite again' Margaret Henan an' send a bug wave off the Cape tull wash her son un tull eternity, all because she was for namun' hum Samuel?"

"But why Samuel?" I asked.

"An' thot I dinna know. I wanted ut so."

"But *why* did you want it so?"

"An' uz ut me thot would be answerun' a such-like question? Be there ony mon luvun' or dead thot can answer? Who can tell the *why* o' like? My Jamie was fair daft on buttermilk; he would drunk ut tull, oz he said himself, hus back-teeth was awash. But my Tumothy could no abide buttermilk. I like tull lussen tull the thunder growlun' an' roarun', an' rampajun'. My Katie could no abide the noise of ut, but must scream an' flutter an' go runnun' for the mudmost o' a feather-bed. Never yet hov I heard the answer tull the *why* o' like. God alone hoz thot answer. You an' me be mortal an' we canna know. Enough for us tull know what we like an' what we duslike. I *like*—thot uz the first word an' the last. An' behind thot *like* no mon can go an' find the *why* o' ut. I *like* Samuel, an' I like ut wull. Ut uz a sweet name, an' there be a rollun' wonder un the sound o' ut thot passes onderstandun'."

The twilight deepened, and in the silence I gazed upon that splendid dome of a forehead which time could not mar, at the width between the eyes, and at the eyes themselves—clear, out-looking, and wide-seeing. She rose to her feet with an air of dismissing me, saying:

"Ut wull be a dark walk home, an' there wull be more thon a sprunkle o' wet un the sky."

"Have you any regrets, Margaret Henan?" I asked, suddenly and without forethought.

She studied me a moment.

"Ay, thot I no ha' borne another son."

"And you would . . . ?" I faltered.

"Ay, thot I would," she answered. "Ut would ha' been hus name."

I went down the dark road between the hawthorne hedges puzzling over the why of like, repeating *Samuel* to myself and aloud and listening to the rolling wonder in its sound that had charmed her soul and led her life in tragic places. *Samuel!* There was a rolling wonder in the sound. Ay, there was!

A PIECE OF STEAK

With the last morsel of bread Tom King wiped his plate clean of the last particle of flour gravy and chewed the resulting mouthful in a slow and meditative way. When he arose from the table, he was oppressed by the feeling that he was distinctly hungry. Yet he alone had eaten. The two children in the other room had been sent early to bed in order that in sleep they might forget they had gone supperless. His wife had touched nothing, and had sat silently and watched him with solicitous eyes. She was a thin, worn woman of the working-class, though signs of an earlier prettiness were not wanting in her face. The flour for the gravy she had borrowed from the neighbor across the hall. The last two ha'pennies had gone to buy the bread.

He sat down by the window on a rickety chair that protested under his weight, and quite mechanically he put his pipe in his mouth and dipped into the side pocket of his coat. The absence of any tobacco made him aware of his action, and, with a scowl for his forgetfulness, he put the pipe away. His movements were slow, almost hulking, as though he were burdened by the heavy weight of his muscles. He was a solid-bodied, stolid-looking man, and his appearance did not suffer from being overprepossessing. His rough clothes were old and slouchy. The uppers of his shoes were too weak to carry the heavy resoling that was itself of no recent date. And his cotton shirt, a cheap, two-shilling affair, showed a frayed collar and ineradicable paint stains.

But it was Tom King's face that advertised him unmistakably for what he was. It was the face of a typical prize-fighter; of one who had put in long years of service in the squared ring and, by that means, developed and emphasized all the marks of the fighting beast. It was distinctly a lowering countenance, and, that no feature of it might escape notice, it was clean-shaven. The lips were shapeless, and constituted a mouth harsh to excess, that was like a gash in his face. The jaw was aggressive,

brutal, heavy. The eyes, slow of movement and heavy-lidded, were almost expressionless under the shaggy, indrawn brows. Sheer animal that
he was, the eyes were the most animal-like feature about him. They
were sleepy, lion-like—the eyes of a fighting animal. The forehead
slanted quickly back to the hair, which, clipped close, showed every
bump of a villainous-looking head. A nose, twice broken and moulded
variously by countless blows, and a cauliflower ear, permanently swollen and distorted to twice its size, completed his adornment, while the
beard, fresh-shaven as it was, sprouted in the skin and gave the face a
blue-black stain.

All together, it was the face of a man to be afraid of in a dark alley
or lonely place. And yet Tom King was not a criminal, nor had he ever
done anything criminal. Outside of brawls, common to his walk in life,
he had harmed no one. Nor had he ever been known to pick a quarrel.
He was a professional, and all the fighting brutishness of him was reserved for his professional appearances. Outside the ring he was slow-
going, easy-natured, and, in his younger days, when money was flush,
too open-handed for his own good. He bore no grudges and had few
enemies. Fighting was a business with him. In the ring he struck to
hurt, struck to maim, struck to destroy; but there was no animus in it.
It was a plain business proposition. Audiences assembled and paid for
the spectacle of men knocking each other out. The winner took the big
end of the purse. When Tom King faced the Wool loomolloo Gouger,
twenty years before, he knew that the Gouger's jaw was only four
months healed after having been broken in a Newcastle bout. And he
had played for that jaw and broken it again in the ninth round, not
because he bore the Gouger any ill-will, but because that was the surest
way to put the Gouger out and win the big end of the purse. Nor had
the Gouger borne him any ill-will for it. It was the game, and both
knew the game and played it.

Tom King had never been a talker, and he sat by the window, morosely silent, staring at his hands. The veins stood out on the backs of
the hands, large and swollen; and the knuckles, smashed and battered
and malformed, testified to the use to which they had been put. He had
never heard that a man's life was the life of his arteries, but well he
knew the meaning of those big, upstanding veins. His heart had pumped
too much blood through them at top pressure. They no longer did the
work. He had stretched the elasticity out of them, and with their disten-
tion had passed his endurance. He tired easily now. No longer could he
do a fast twenty rounds, hammer and tongs, fight, fight, fight, from gong
to gong, with fierce rally on top of fierce rally, beaten to the ropes and
in turn beating his opponent to the ropes, and rallying fiercest and fast-

est of all in that last, twentieth round, with the house on its feet and yelling, himself rushing, striking, ducking, raining showers of blows upon showers of blows and receiving showers of blows in return, and all the time the heart faithfully pumping the surging blood through the adequate veins. The veins, swollen at the time, had always shrunk down again, though not quite—each time, imperceptibly at first, remaining just a trifle larger than before. He stared at them and at his battered knuckles, and, for the moment, caught a vision of the youthful excellence of those hands before the first knuckle had been smashed on the head of Benny Jones, otherwise known as the Welsh Terror.

The impression of his hunger came back on him.

"Blimey, but couldn't I go a piece of steak!" he muttered aloud, clenching his huge fists and spitting out a smothered oath.

"I tried both Burke's an' Sawley's," his wife said half apologetically.

"An' they wouldn't?" he demanded.

"Not a ha'penny. Burke said—" She faltered.

"G'wan! Wot'd he say?"

"As how 'e was thinkin' Sandel ud do ye to-night, an' as how yer score was comfortable big as it was."

Tom King grunted, but did not reply. He was busy thinking of the bull terrier he had kept in his younger days to which he had fed steaks without end. Burke would have given him credit for a thousand steaks—then. But times had changed. Tom King was getting old; and old men, fighting before second-rate clubs, couldn't expect to run bills of any size with the tradesmen.

He had got up in the morning with a longing for a piece of steak, and the longing had not abated. He had not had a fair training for this fight. It was a drought year in Australia, times were hard, and even the most irregular work was difficult to find. He had had no sparring partner, and his food had not been of the best nor always sufficient. He had done a few days' navvy work when he could get it, and he had run around the Domain in the early mornings to get his legs in shape. But it was hard, training without a partner and with a wife and two kiddies that must be fed. Credit with the tradesmen had undergone very slight expansion when he was matched with Sandel. The secretary of the Gayety Club had advanced him three pounds—the loser's end of the purse—and beyond that had refused to go. Now and again he had managed to borrow a few shillings from old pals, who would have lent more only that it was a drought year and they were hard put themselves. No—and there was no use in disguising the fact—his training had not been satisfactory. He should have had better food and no worries. Besides, when a man is forty, it is harder to get into condition than when he is twenty.

"What time is it, Lizzie?" he asked.

His wife went across the hall to inquire, and came back.

"Quarter before eight."

"They'll be startin' the first bout in a few minutes," he said. "Only a try-out. Then there's a four-round spar 'tween Dealer Wells an' Gridley, an' a ten-round go 'tween Starlight an' some sailor bloke. I don't come on for over an hour."

At the end of another silent ten minutes, he rose to his feet.

"Truth is, Lizzie, I ain't had proper trainin'."

He reached for his hat and started for the door. He did not offer to kiss her—he never did on going out—but on this night she dared to kiss him, throwing her arms around him and compelling him to bend down to her face. She looked quite small against the massive bulk of the man.

"Good luck, Tom," she said. "You gotter do 'im."

"Ay, I gotter do 'im," he repeated. "That's all there is to it. I jus' gotter do 'im."

He laughed with an attempt at heartiness, while she pressed more closely against him. Across her shoulders he looked around the bare room. It was all he had in the world, with the rent overdue, and her and the kiddies. And he was leaving it to go out into the night to get meat for his mate and cubs—not like a modern working-man going to his machine grind, but in the old, primitive, royal, animal way, by fighting for it.

"I gotter do 'im," he repeated, this time a hint of desperation in his voice. "If it's a win, it's thirty quid—an' I can pay all that's owin', with a lump o' money left over. If it's a lose, I get naught—not even a penny for me to ride home on the tram. The secretary's give all that's comin' from a loser's end. Good-by, old woman. I'll come straight home if it's a win."

"An' I'll be waitin' up," she called to him along the hall.

It was full two miles to the Gayety, and as he walked along he remembered how in his palmy days—he had once been the heavy-weight champion of New South Wales—he would have ridden in a cab to the fight, and how, most likely, some heavy backer would have paid for the cab and ridden with him. There were Tommy Burns and that Yankee nigger, Jack Johnson—they rode about in motor-cars. And he walked! And, as any man knew, a hard two miles was not the best preliminary to a fight. He was an old un, and the world did not wag well with old uns. He was good for nothing now except navvy work, and his broken nose and swollen ear were against him even in that. He found himself wishing that he had learned a trade. It would have been better in the long run. But no one had told him, and he knew, deep down in his heart, that he would not have listened if they had. It had been so easy. Big money—sharp, glorious fights—periods of rest and loafing in between—a following of eager flatterers, the slaps on the back, the shakes of the hand, the toffs glad to buy him a drink for the privilege of five minutes' talk—and the glory of it, the yelling houses, the whirl-wind finish, the referee's "King wins!" and his name in the sporting columns next day.

Those had been times! But he realized now, in his slow, ruminating way, that it was the old uns he had been putting away. He was Youth, rising; and they were Age, sinking. No wonder it had been easy—they with their swollen veins and battered knuckles and weary in the bones of them from the long battles they had already fought. He remembered the time he put out old Stowsher Bill, at Rush-Cutters Bay, in the eigh-teenth round, and how old Bill had cried afterward in the dressing-room like a baby. Perhaps old Bill's rent had been overdue. Perhaps he'd had at home a missus an' a couple of kiddies. And perhaps Bill, that very day of the fight, had had a hungering for a piece of steak. Bill had fought game and taken incredible punishment. He could see now, after he had gone through the mill himself, that Stowsher Bill had fought for a bigger stake, that night twenty years ago, than had young Tom King, who had fought for glory and easy money. No wonder Stowsher Bill had cried afterward in the dressing-room.

Well, a man had only so many fights in him, to begin with. It was the iron law of the game. One man might have a hundred hard fights in him, another man only twenty; each, according to the make of him and the quality of his fibre, had a definite number, and, when he had fought them, he was done. Yes, he had had more fights in him than most of them, and he had had far more than his share of the hard, gruelling fights—the kind that worked the heart and lungs to bursting, that took the elastic out of the arteries and made hard knots of muscle out of Youth's sleek suppleness, that wore out nerve and stamina and made brain and bones weary from excess of effort and endurance over-wrought. Yes, he had done better than all of them. There was none of his old fighting partners left. He was the last of the old guard. He had seen them all finished, and he had had a hand in finishing some of them.

They had tried him out against the old uns, and one after another he had put them away—laughing when, like old Stowsher Bill, they cried in the dressing-room. And now he was an old un, and they tried out the youngsters on him. There was that bloke, Sandel. He had come over from New Zealand with a record behind him. But nobody in Australia knew anything about him, so they put him up against old Tom King. If Sandel made a showing, he would be given better men to fight, with bigger purses to win; so it was to be depended upon that he would put up a fierce battle. He had everything to win by it—money and glory and career; and Tom King was the grizzled old chopping-block that guarded the highway to fame and fortune. And he had nothing to win except thirty quid, to pay to the landlord and the tradesmen. And, as Tom King thus ruminated, there came to his stolid vision the form of Youth, glorious Youth, rising exultant and invincible, supple of muscle and silken of skin, with heart and lungs that had never been tired and torn and that laughed at limitation of effort. Yes, Youth was the Nemesis. It destroyed the old uns and recked not that, in so doing, it destroyed itself. It enlarged its arteries and smashed its knuckles, and was in turn destroyed by Youth. For Youth was ever youthful. It was only Age that grew old.

At Castlereagh Street he turned to the left, and three blocks along came to the Gayety. A crowd of young larrikins hanging outside the door made respectful way for him, and he heard one say to another: "That's 'im! That's Tom King!"

Inside, on the way to his dressing-room, he encountered the secretary, a keen-eyed, shrewd-faced young man, who shook his hand.

"How are you feelin', Tom?" he asked.

"Fit as a fiddle," King answered, though he knew that he lied, and that if he had a quid, he would give it right there for a good piece of steak.

When he emerged from the dressing-room, his seconds behind him, and came down the aisle to the squared ring in the centre of the hall, a burst of greeting and applause went up from the waiting crowd. He acknowledged salutations right and left, though few of the faces did he know. Most of them were the faces of kiddies unborn when he was winning his first laurels in the squared ring. He leaped lightly to the raised platform and ducked through the ropes to his corner, where he sat down on a folding stool. Jack Ball, the referee, came over and shook his hand. Ball was a broken-down pugilist who for over ten years had not entered the ring as a principal. King was glad that he had him for referee. They were both old uns. If he should rough it with Sandel a bit beyond the rules, he knew Ball could be depended upon to pass it by.

Aspiring young heavyweights, one after another, were climbing into the ring and being presented to the audience by the referee. Also, he issued their challenges for them.

"Young Pronto," Bill announced, "from North Sydney, challenges the winner for fifty pounds side bet."

The audience applauded, and applauded again as Sandel himself sprang through the ropes and sat down in his corner. Tom King looked across the ring at him curiously, for in a few minutes they would be locked together in merciless combat, each trying with all the force of him to knock the other into unconsciousness. But little could he see, for Sandel, like himself, had trousers and sweater on over his ring costume. His face was strongly handsome, crowned with a curly mop of yellow hair, while his thick, muscular neck hinted at bodily magnificence.

Young Pronto went to one corner and then the other, shaking hands with the principals and dropping down out of the ring. The challenges went on. Ever Youth climbed through the ropes—Youth unknown, but insatiable—crying out to mankind that with strength and skill it would match issues with the winner. A few years before, in his own heyday of invincibleness, Tom King would have been amused and bored by these preliminaries. But now he sat fascinated, unable to shake the vision of Youth from his eyes. Always were these youngsters rising up in the boxing game, springing through the ropes and shouting their defiance; and always were the old uns going down before them. They climbed to success over the bodies of the old uns. And ever they came, more and more youngsters—Youth unquenchable and irresistible—and ever they put the old uns away, themselves becoming old uns and travelling the same downward path, while behind them, ever pressing on them, was Youth eternal—the new babies, grown lusty and dragging their elders down, with behind them more babies to the end of time— Youth that must have its will and that will never die.

King glanced over to the press box and nodded to Morgan, of the *Sportsman,* and Corbett, of the *Referee.* Then he held out his hands, while Sid Sullivan and Charley Bates, his seconds, slipped on his gloves and laced them tight, closely watched by one of Sandel's seconds, who first examined critically the tapes on King's knuckles. A second of his own was in Sandel's corner, performing a like office. Sandel's trousers were pulled off, and, as he stood up, his sweater was skinned off over his head. And Tom King, looking, saw Youth incarnate, deep-chested, heavy-thewed, with muscles that slipped and slid like live things under the white satin skin. The whole body was acrawl with life, and Tom King knew that it was a life that had never oozed its freshness out through the aching pores during the long fights wherein Youth paid its toll and departed not quite so young as when it entered.

The two men advanced to meet each other, and, as the gong sounded and the seconds clattered out of the ring with the folding stools, they shook hands and instantly took their fighting attitudes. And instantly, like a mechanism of steel and springs balanced on a hair trigger, Sandel was in and out and in again, landing a left to the eyes, a right to the ribs, ducking a counter, dancing lightly away and dancing menacingly back again. He was swift and clever. It was a dazzling exhibition. The house yelled its approbation. But King was not dazzled. He had fought too many fights and too many youngsters. He knew the blows for what they were—too quick and too deft to be dangerous. Evidently Sandel was going to rush things from the start. It was to be expected. It was the way of Youth, expending its splendor and excellence in wild insurgence and furious onslaught, overwhelming opposition with its own unlimited glory of strength and desire.

Sandel was in and out, here, there, and everywhere, light-footed and eager-hearted, a living wonder of white flesh and stinging muscle that wove itself into a dazzling fabric of attack, slipping and leaping like a flying shuttle from action to action through a thousand actions, all of them centred upon the destruction of Tom King, who stood between him and fortune. And Tom King patiently endured. He knew his business, and he knew Youth now that Youth was no longer his. There was nothing to do till the other lost some of his steam, was his thought, and he grinned to himself as he deliberately ducked so as to receive a heavy blow on the top of his head. It was a wicked thing to do, yet eminently fair according to the rules of the boxing game. A man was supposed to take care of his own knuckles, and, if he insisted on hitting an opponent on the top of the head, he did so at his own peril. King could have ducked lower and let the blow whiz harmlessly past, but he remembered his own early fights and how he smashed his first knuckle on the head of the Welsh Terror. He was but playing the game. That duck had accounted for one of Sandel's knuckles. Not that Sandel would mind it now. He would go on, superbly regardless, hitting as hard as ever throughout the fight. But later on, when the long ring battles had begun to tell, he would regret that knuckle and look back and remember how he smashed it on Tom King's head.

The first round was all Sandel's, and he had the house yelling with the rapidity of his whirlwind rushes. He overwhelmed King with avalanches of punches, and King did nothing. He never struck once, contenting himself with covering up, blocking and ducking and clinching to avoid punishment. He occasionally feinted, shook his head when the weight of a punch landed, and moved stolidly about, never leaping or springing or wasting an ounce of strength. Sandel must foam the froth of Youth away before discreet Age could dare to retaliate. All King's movements were slow and methodical, and his heavy-lidded, slow-moving eyes gave him the appearance of being half asleep or dazed. Yet they were eyes that saw everything, that had been trained to see everything through all his twenty years and odd in the ring. They were eyes that did not blink or waver before an impending blow, but that coolly saw and measured distance.

Seated in his corner for the minute's rest at the end of the round, he lay back with outstretched legs, his arms resting on the right angle of the ropes, his chest and abdomen heaving frankly and deeply as he gulped down the air driven by the towels of his seconds. He listened with closed eyes to the voices of the house, "Why don't yeh fight, Tom?" many were crying. "Yeh ain't afraid of 'im, are yeh?"

"Muscle-bound," he heard a man on a front seat comment. "He can't move quicker. Two to one on Sandel, in quids."

The gong struck and the two men advanced from their corners. Sandel came forward fully three-quarters of the distance, eager to begin again; but King was content to advance the shorter distance. It was in line with his policy of economy. He had not been well trained, and he had not had enough to eat, and every step counted. Besides, he had already walked two miles to the ringside. It was a repetition of the first round, with Sandel attacking like a whirlwind and with the audience indignantly demanding why King did not fight. Beyond feinting and several slowly delivered and ineffectual blows he did nothing save block and stall and clinch. Sandel wanted to make the pace fast, while King, out of his wisdom, refused to accommodate him. He grinned with a certain wistful pathos in his ring-battered countenance, and went on cherishing his strength with the jealousy of which only Age is capable. Sandel was Youth, and he threw his strength away with the munificent abandon of Youth. To King belonged the ring generalship, the wisdom bred of long, aching fights. He watched with cool eyes and head, moving slowly and waiting for Sandel's froth to foam away. To the majority of the onlookers it seemed as though King was hopelessly outclassed, and they voiced their opinion in offers of three to one on Sandel. But there were wise ones, a few, who knew King of old time, and who covered what they considered easy money.

The third round began as usual, one-sided, with Sandel doing all the leading and delivering all the punishment. A half-minute had passed when Sandel, overconfident, left an opening. King's eyes and right arm flashed in the same instant. It was his first real blow—a hook, with the twisted arch of the arm to make it rigid, and with all the weight of the half-pivoted body behind it. It was like a sleepy-seeming lion suddenly thrusting out a lightning paw. Sandel, caught on the side of the jaw, was felled like a bullock. The audience gasped and murmured awe-stricken applause. The man was not muscle-bound, after all, and he could drive a blow like a trip-hammer.

Sandel was shaken. He rolled over and attempted to rise, but the sharp yells from his seconds to take the count restrained him. He knelt on one knee, ready to rise, and waited, while the referee stood over him, counting the seconds loudly in his ear. At the ninth he rose in fighting attitude, and Tom King, facing him, knew regret that the blow had not been an inch nearer the point of the jaw. That would have been a knockout, and he could have carried the thirty quid home to the missus and the kiddies.

The round continued to the end of its three minutes, Sandel for the first time respectful of his opponent and King slow of movement and sleepy-eyed as ever. As the round neared its close, King, warned of the fact by sight of the seconds crouching outside ready for the spring in through the ropes, worked the fight around to his own corner. And when the gong struck, he sat down immediately on the waiting stool, while Sandel had to walk all the way across the diagonal of the square to his own corner. It was a little thing, but it was the sum of little things that counted. Sandel was compelled to walk that many more steps, to give up that much energy, and to lose a part of the precious minute of rest. At the beginning of every round King loafed slowly out from his corner, forcing his opponent to advance the greater distance. The end of every round found the fight manœuvred by King into his own corner so that he could immediately sit down.

Two more rounds went by, in which King was parsimonious of effort and Sandel prodigal. The latter's attempt to force a fast pace made King uncomfortable, for a fair percentage of the multitudinous blows showered upon him went home. Yet King persisted in his dogged slowness, despite the crying of the young hotheads for him to go in and fight. Again, in the sixth round, Sandel was careless, again Tom King's fearful right flashed out to the jaw, and again Sandel took the nine seconds count.

By the seventh round Sandel's pink of condition was gone, and he settled down to what he knew was to be the hardest fight in his experience. Tom King was an old un, but a better old un than he had ever encountered—an old un who never lost his head, who was remarkably able at defence, whose blows had the impact of a knotted club, and who had a knockout in either hand. Nevertheless, Tom King dared not hit often. He never forgot his battered knuckles, and knew that every hit must count if the knuckles were to last out the fight. As he sat in his corner, glancing across at his opponent, the thought came to him that the sum of his wisdom and Sandel's youth would constitute a world's champion heavyweight. But that was the trouble. Sandel would never become a world champion. He lacked the wisdom, and the only way for him to get it was to buy it with Youth; and when wisdom was his, Youth would have been spent in buying it.

King took every advantage he knew. He never missed an opportunity to clinch, and in effecting most of the clinches his shoulder drove stiffly into the other's ribs. In the philosophy of the ring a shoulder was as good as a punch so far as damage was concerned, and a great deal better so far as concerned expenditure of effort. Also, in the clinches King rested his weight on his opponent, and was loath to let go. This compelled the interference of the referee, who tore them apart, always assisted by Sandel, who had not yet learned to rest. He could not refrain from using those glorious flying arms and writhing muscles of his, and when the other rushed into a clinch, striking shoulder against ribs, and with head resting under Sandel's left arm, Sandel almost invariably swung his right behind his own back and into the projecting face. It was a clever stroke, much admired by the audience, but it was not dangerous, and was, therefore, just that much wasted strength. But Sandel was tireless and unaware of limitations, and King grinned and doggedly endured.

Sandel developed a fierce right to the body, which made it appear that King was taking an enormous amount of punishment, and it was only the old ringsters who appreciated the deft touch of King's left glove to the other's biceps just before the impact of the blow. It was true, the blow landed each time; but each time it was robbed of its power by that touch on the biceps. In the ninth round, three times inside a minute, King's right hooked its twisted arch to the jaw; and three times Sandel's body, heavy as it was, was levelled to the mat. Each time he took the nine seconds allowed him and rose to his feet, shaken and jarred, but still strong. He had lost much of his speed, and he wasted less effort. He was fighting grimly; but he continued to draw upon his chief asset, which was Youth. King's chief asset was experience. As his vitality had dimmed and his vigor abated, he had replaced them with cunning, with wisdom born of the long fights and with a careful shepherding of strength. Not alone had he learned never to make a superfluous movement, but he had learned how to seduce an opponent into throwing his strength away. Again and again, by feint of foot and hand and body he continued to inveigle Sandel into leaping back, ducking, or countering. King rested, but he never permitted Sandel to rest. It was the strategy of Age.

Early in the tenth round King began stopping the other's rushes with straight lefts to the face, and Sandel, grown wary, responded by drawing the left, then by ducking it and delivering his right in a swinging hook to the side of the head. It was too high up to be vitally effective; but when first it landed, King knew the old, familiar descent of the black veil of unconsciousness across his mind. For the instant, or for the slightest fraction of an instant, rather, he ceased. In the one moment he saw his opponent ducking out of his field of vision and the background of white, watching faces; in the next moment he again saw his opponent and the background of faces. It was as if he had slept for a time and just opened his eyes again, and yet the interval of unconsciousness was so microscopically short that there had been no time for him to fall. The audience saw him totter and his knees give, and then saw him recover and tuck his chin deeper into the shelter of his left shoulder.

Several times Sandel repeated the blow, keeping King partially dazed, and then the latter worked out his defence, which was also a counter. Feinting with his left he took a half-step backward, at the same time upper cutting with the whole strength of his right. So accurately was it timed that it landed squarely on Sandel's face in the full, downward sweep of the duck, and Sandel lifted in the air and curled backward, striking the mat on his head and shoulders. Twice King achieved this, then turned loose and hammered his opponent to the ropes. He gave Sandel no chance to rest or to set himself, but smashed blow in upon blow till the house rose to its feet and the air was filled with an unbroken roar of applause. But Sandel's strength and endurance were superb, and he continued to stay on his feet. A knockout seemed certain, and a captain of police, appalled at the dreadful punishment, arose by the ringside to stop the fight. The gong struck for the end of the round and Sandel staggered to his corner, protesting to the captain that he was sound and strong. To prove it, he threw two back air-springs, and the police captain gave in.

Tom King, leaning back in his corner and breathing hard, was disappointed. If the fight had been stopped, the referee, perforce, would have rendered him the decision and the purse would have been his. Unlike Sandel, he was not fighting for glory or career, but for thirty quid. And now Sandel would recuperate in the minute of rest.

Youth will be served—this saying flashed into King's mind, and he remembered the first time he had heard it, the night when he had put away Stowsher Bill. The toff who had bought him a drink after the fight and patted him on the shoulder had used those words. Youth will be served! The toff was right. And on that night in the long ago he had been Youth. To-night Youth sat in the opposite corner. As for himself, he had been fighting for half an hour now, and he was an old man. Had he fought like Sandel, he would not have lasted fifteen minutes. But the point was that he did not recuperate. Those upstanding arteries and that sorely tried heart would not enable him to gather strength in the intervals between the rounds. And he had not had sufficient strength in him to begin with. His legs were heavy under him and beginning to cramp. He should not have walked those two miles to the fight. And there was the steak which he had got up longing for that morning. A great and terrible hatred rose up in him for the butchers who had refused him credit. It was hard for an old man to go into a fight without enough to eat. And a piece of steak was such a little thing, a few pennies at best; yet it meant thirty quid to him.

With the gong that opened the eleventh round, Sandel rushed, making a show of freshness which he did not really possess. King knew it for what it was—a bluff as old as the game itself. He clinched to save himself, then, going free, allowed Sandel to get set. This was what King desired. He feinted with his left, drew the answering duck and swinging upward hook, then made the half-step backward, delivered the upper cut full to the face and crumpled Sandel over to the mat. After that he never let him rest, receiving punishment himself, but inflicting far more, smashing Sandel to the ropes, hooking and driving all manner of blows into him, tearing away from his clinches or punching him out of attempted clinches, and ever when Sandel would have fallen, catching him with one uplifting hand and with the other immediately smashing him into the ropes where he could not fall.

The house by this time had gone mad, and it was his house, nearly every voice yelling: "Go it, Tom!" "Get 'im! Get 'im!" "You've got 'im, Tom! You've got 'im!" It was to be a whirlwind finish, and that was what a ringside audience paid to see.

And Tom King, who for half an hour had conserved his strength, now expended it prodigally in the one great effort he knew he had in him. It was his one chance—now or not at all. His strength was waning fast, and his hope was that before the last of it ebbed out of him he would have beaten his opponent down for the count. And as he continued to strike and force, coolly estimating the weight of his blows and the quality of the damage wrought, he realized how hard a man Sandel was to knock out. Stamina and endurance were his to an extreme degree, and they were the virgin stamina and endurance of Youth. Sandel was certainly a coming man. He had it in him. Only out of such rugged fibre were successful fighters fashioned.

Sandel was reeling and staggering, but Tom King's legs were cramping and his knuckles going back on him. Yet he steeled himself to strike the fierce blows, every one of which brought anguish to his tortured hands. Though now he was receiving practically no punishment, he was weakening as rapidly as the other. His blows went home, but there was no longer the weight behind them, and each blow was the result of a severe effort of will. His legs were like lead, and they dragged visibly under him; while Sandel's backers, cheered by this symptom, began calling encouragement to their man.

King was spurred to a burst of effort. He delivered two blows in succession—a left, a trifle too high, to the solar plexus, and a right cross to the jaw. They were not heavy blows, yet so weak and dazed was Sandel that he went down and lay quivering. The referee stood over him, shouting the count of the fatal seconds in his ear. If before the tenth second was called, he did not rise, the fight was lost. The house stood in hushed silence. King rested on trembling legs. A mortal dizziness was upon him, and before his eyes the sea of faces sagged and swayed, while to his ears, as from a remote distance, came the count of the referee. Yet he looked upon the fight as his. It was impossible that a man so punished could rise.

Only Youth could rise, and Sandel rose. At the fourth second he rolled over on his face and groped blindly for the ropes. By the seventh second he had dragged himself to his knee, where he rested, his head rolling groggily on his shoulders. As the referee cried "Nine!" Sandel stood upright, in proper stalling position, his left arm wrapped about his face, his right wrapped about his stomach. Thus were his vital points guarded, while he lurched forward toward King in the hope of effecting a clinch and gaining more time.

At the instant Sandel arose, King was at him, but the two blows he delivered were muffled on the stalled arms. The next moment Sandel was in the clinch and holding on desperately while the referee strove to drag the two men apart. King helped to force himself free. He knew the rapidity with which Youth recovered, and he knew that Sandel was his if he could prevent that recovery. One stiff punch would do it. Sandel was his, indubitably his. He had outgeneralled him, outfought him, outpointed him. Sandel reeled out of the clinch, balanced on the hair line between defeat or survival. One good blow would topple him over and down and out. And Tom King, in a flash of bitterness, remembered the piece of steak and wished that he had it then behind that necessary punch he must deliver. He nerved himself for the blow, but it was not heavy enough nor swift enough. Sandel swayed, but did not fall, staggering back to the ropes and holding on. King staggered after him, and, with a pang like that of dissolution, delivered another blow. But his body had deserted him. All that was left of him was a fighting intelligence that was dimmed and clouded from exhaustion. The blow that was aimed for the jaw struck no higher than the shoulder. He had willed the blow higher, but the tired muscles had not been able to obey. And, from the impact of the blow, Tom King himself reeled back and nearly fell. Once again he strove. This time his punch missed altogether, and, from absolute weakness, he fell against Sandel and clinched, holding on to him to save himself from sinking to the floor.

King did not attempt to free himself. He had shot his bolt. He was gone. And Youth had been served. Even in the clinch he could feel Sandel growing stronger against him. When the referee thrust them apart, there, before his eyes, he saw Youth recuperate. From instant to instant Sandel grew stronger. His punches, weak and futile at first, became stiff and accurate. Tom King's bleared eyes saw the gloved fist driving at his jaw, and he willed to guard it by interposing his arm. He saw the danger, willed the act; but the arm was too heavy. It seemed burdened with a hundredweight of lead. It would not lift itself, and he strove to lift it with his soul. Then the gloved fist landed home. He experienced a sharp snap that was like an electric spark, and, simultaneously, the veil of blackness enveloped him.

When he opened his eyes again he was in his corner, and he heard the yelling of the audience like the roar of the surf at Bondi Beach. A wet sponge was being pressed against the base of his brain, and Sid Sullivan was blowing cold water in a refreshing spray over his face and chest. His gloves had already been removed, and Sandel, bending over him, was shaking his hand. He bore no ill-will toward the man who had put him out, and he returned the grip with a heartiness that made his battered knuckles protest. Then Sandel stepped to the centre of the ring and the audience hushed its pandemonium to hear him accept young Pronto's challenge and offer to increase the side bet to one hundred pounds. King looked on apathetically while his seconds mopped the streaming water from him, dried his face, and prepared him to leave the ring. He felt hungry. It was not the ordinary, gnawing kind, but a great faintness, a palpitation at the pit of the stomach that communicated itself to all his body. He remembered back into the fight to the moment when he had Sandel swaying and tottering on the hair-line balance of defeat. Ah, that piece of steak would have done it! He had lacked just that for the decisive blow, and he had lost. It was all because of the piece of steak.

His seconds were half-supporting him as they helped him through the ropes. He tore free from them, ducked through the ropes unaided, and leaped heavily to the floor, following on their heels as they forced a passage for him down the crowded centre aisle. Leaving the dressing-room for the street, in the entrance to the hall, some young fellow spoke to him.

"W'y didn't yuh go in an' get 'im when yuh 'ad 'im?" the young fellow asked.

"Aw, go to hell!" said Tom King, and passed down the steps to the sidewalk.

The doors of the public house at the corner were swinging wide, and he saw the lights and the smiling barmaids, heard the many voices discussing the fight and the prosperous chink of money on the bar. Somebody called to him to have a drink. He hesitated perceptibly, then refused and went on his way.

He had not a copper in his pocket, and the two-mile walk home seemed very long. He was certainly getting old. Crossing the Domain, he sat down suddenly on a bench, unnerved by the thought of the missus sitting up for him, waiting to learn the outcome of the fight. That was harder than any knockout, and it seemed almost impossible to face.

He felt weak and sore, and the pain of his smashed knuckles warned him that, even if he could find a job at navvy work, it would be a week before he could grip a pick handle or a shovel. The hunger palpitation at the pit of the stomach was sickening. His wretchedness overwhelmed him, and into his eyes came an unwonted moisture. He covered his face with his hands, and, as he cried, he remembered Stowsher Bill and how he had served him that night in the long ago. Poor old Stowsher Bill! He could understand now why Bill had cried in the dressing-room.

THE MADNESS OF
JOHN HARNED

I tell this for a fact. It happened in the bull-ring at Quito. I sat in the box with John Harned, and with Maria Valenzuela, and with Luis Cervallos. I saw it happen. I saw it all from first to last. I was on the steamer *Ecuadore* from Panama to Guayaquil. Maria Valenzuela is my cousin. I have known her always. She is very beautiful. I am a Spaniard—an Ecuadoriano, true, but I am descended from Pedro Patino, who was one of Pizarro's captains. They were brave men. They were heroes. Did not Pizarro lead three hundred and fifty Spanish cavaliers and four thousand Indians into the far Cordilleras in search of treasure? And did not all the four thousand Indians and three hundred of the brave cavaliers die on that vain quest? But Pedro Patino did not die. He it was that lived to found the family of the Patino. I am Ecuadoriano, true, but I am Spanish. I am Manuel de Jesus Patino. I own many haciendas, and ten thousand Indians are my slaves, though the law says they are free men who work by freedom of contract. The law is a funny thing. We Ecuadorianos laugh at it. It is our law. We make it for ourselves. I am Manuel de Jesus Patino. Remember that name. It will be written some day in history. There are revolutions in Ecuador. We call them elections. It is a good joke is it not?—what you call a pun?

John Harned was an American. I met him first at the Tivoli hotel in Panama. He had much money—this I have heard. He was going to Lima, but he met Maria Valenzuela in the Tivoli hotel. Maria Valenzuela is my cousin, and she is beautiful. It is true, she is the most beautiful woman in Ecuador. But also is she most beautiful in every country—in Paris, in Madrid, in New York, in Vienna. Always do all men look at her, and John Harned looked long at her at Panama. He loved her, that I know for a fact. She was Ecuadoriano, true—but she was of all countries; she was of all the world. She spoke many languages. She sang—ah! like an artiste. Her smile—wonderful, divine. Her eyes—ah! have I not seen men look in her eyes? They were what you English call amazing. They were promises of paradise. Men drowned themselves in her eyes.

Maria Valenzuela was rich—richer than I, who am accounted very rich in Ecuador. But John Harned did not care for her money. He had a heart—a funny heart. He was a fool. He did not go to Lima. He left the steamer at Guayaquil and followed her to Quito. She was coming home from Europe and other places. I do not see what she found in him, but she liked him. This I know for a fact, else he would not have followed her to Quito. She asked him to come. Well do I remember the occasion. She said:

"Come to Quito and I will show you the bull-fight—brave, clever, magnificent!"

But he said: "I go to Lima, not Quito. Such is my passage engaged on the steamer."

"You travel for pleasure—no?" said Maria Valenzuela; and she looked at him as only Maria Valenzuela could look, her eyes warm with the promise.

And he came. No; he did not come for the bull-fight. He came because of what he had seen in her eyes. Women like Maria Valenzuela are born once in a hundred years. They are of no country and no time. They are what you call universal. They are goddesses. Men fall down at their feet. They play with men and run them through their pretty fingers like sand. Cleopatra was such a woman they say; and so was Circe. She turned men into swine. Ha! ha! It is true—no?

It all came about because Maria Valenzuela said:

"You English people are—what shall I say?—savage—no? You prize-fight. Two men each hit the other with their fists till their eyes are blinded and their noses are broken. Hideous! And the other men who look on cry out loudly and are made glad. It is barbarous—no?"

"But they are men," said John Harned; "and they prize-fight out of desire. No one makes them prize-fight. They do it because they desire it more than anything else in the world."

Maria Valenzuela—there was scorn in her smile as she said:

"They kill each other often—is it not so? I have read it in the papers."

"But the bull," said John Harned. "The bull is killed many times in the bull-fight, and the bull does not come into the ring out of desire. It is not fair to the bull. He is compelled to fight. But the man in the prize-fight—no; he is not compelled."

"He is the more brute therefore," said Maria Valenzuela. "He is savage. He is primitive. He is animal. He strikes with his paws like a bear from a cave, and he is ferocious. But the bull-fight—ah! You have not seen the bull-fight—no? The toreador is clever. He must have skill. He is modern. He is romantic. He is only a man, soft and tender, and he faces the wild bull in conflict. And he kills with a sword, a slender sword, with one thrust, so, to the heart of the great beast. It is delicious. It makes the heart beat to behold—the small man, the great beast, the wide level sand, the thousands that look on without breath; the great beast rushes to the attack, the small man stands like a statue; he does not move, he is unafraid, and in his hand is the slender sword flashing like silver in the sun; nearer and nearer rushes the great beast with its sharp horns, the man does not move, and then—so—the sword flashes, the thrust is made, to the heart, to the hilt, the bull falls to the sand and is dead, and the man is unhurt. It is brave. It is magnificent! Ah!—I could love the toreador. But the man of the prize-fight—he is the brute, the human beast, the savage primitive, the maniac that receives many blows in his stupid face and rejoices. Come to Quito and I will show you the brave sport, the sport of men, the toreador and the bull."

But John Harned did not go to Quito for the bull-fight. He went because of Maria Valenzuela. He was a large man, more broad of shoulder than we Ecuadorianos, more tall, more heavy of limb and bone. True, he was larger even than most men of his own race. His eyes were blue, though I have seen them gray, and, sometimes, like cold steel. His features were large, too—not delicate like ours, and his jaw was very strong to look at. Also, his face was smooth-shaven like a priest's. Why should a man feel shame for the hair on his face? Did not God put it there? Yes, I believe in God. I am not a pagan like many of you English. God is good. He made me an Ecuadoriano with ten thousand slaves. And when I die I shall go to God. Yes, the priests are right.

But John Harned. He was a quiet man. He talked always in a low voice, and he never moved his hands when he talked. One would have thought his heart was a piece of ice; yet did he have a streak of warm in his blood, for he followed Maria Valenzuela to Quito. Also, and for all that he talked low without moving his hands, he was an animal, as you shall see—the beast primitive, the stupid, ferocious savage of the long ago that dressed in wild skins and lived in the caves along with the bears and wolves.

Luis Cervallos is my friend, the best of Ecuadorianos. He owns three cacao plantations at Naranjito and Chobo. At Milagro is his big sugar plantation. He has large haciendas at Ambato and Latacunga, and down the coast is he interested in oil-wells. Also has he spent much money in planting rubber along the Guayas. He is modern, like the Yankee; and, like the Yankee, full of business. He has much money, but it is in many ventures, and ever he needs more money for new ventures and for the old ones. He has been everywhere and seen everything. When he was a very young man he was in the Yankee military academy what you call West Point. There was trouble. He was made to resign. He does not like Americans. But he did like Maria Valenzuela, who was of his own country. Also, he needed her money for his ventures and for his gold mine in Eastern Ecuador where the painted Indians live. I was his friend. It was my desire that he should marry Maria Valenzuela. Further, much of my money had I invested in his ventures, more so in his gold mine which was very rich but which first required the expense of much money before it would yield forth its riches. If Luis Cervallos married Maria Valenzuela I should have more money very immediately.

But John Harned followed Maria Valenzuela to Quito, and it was quickly clear to us—to Luis Cervallos and me—that she looked upon John Harned with great kindness. It is said that a woman will have her will, but this is a case not in point, for Maria Valenzuela did not have her will—at least not with John Harned. Perhaps it would all have happened as it did, even if Luis Cervallos and I had not sat in the box that day at the bull-ring in Quito. But this I know: we *did* sit in the box that day. And I shall tell you what happened.

The four of us were in the one box, guests of Luis Cervallos. I was next to the Presidente's box. On the other side was the box of General José Eliceo Salazar. With him were Joaquin Endara and Uricisino Castillo, both generals, and Colonel Jacinto Fierro and Captain Baltazar de Echeverria. Only Luis Cervallos had the position and the influence to get that box next to the Presidente. I know for a fact that the Presidente himself expressed the desire to the management that Luis Cervallos should have that box.

The band finished playing the national hymn of Ecuador. The procession of the toreadors was over. The Presidente nodded to begin. The bugles blew, and the bull dashed in—you know the way, excited, bewildered, the darts in its shoulder burning like fire, itself seeking madly whatever enemy to destroy. The toreadors hid behind their shelters and waited. Suddenly they appeared forth, the capadors, five of them, from every side, their colored capes flinging wide. The bull paused at sight of such a generosity of enemies, unable in his own mind to know which to attack. Then advanced one of the capadors alone to meet the bull. The bull was very angry. With its fore-legs it pawed the sand of the arena till the dust rose all about it. Then it charged, with lowered head, straight for the lone capador.

It is always of interest, the first charge of the first bull. After a time it is natural that one should grow tired, a trifle, that the keenness should lose its edge. But that first charge of the first bull! John Harned was seeing it for the first time, and he could not escape the excitement—the sight of the man, armed only with a piece of cloth, and of the bull rushing upon him across the sand with sharp horns, widespreading.

"See!" cried Maria Valenzuela. "Is it not superb?"

John Harned nodded, but did not look at her. His eyes were sparkling, and they were only for the bull-ring. The capador stepped to the side, with a twirl of the cape eluding the bull and spreading the cape on his own shoulders.

"What do you think?" asked Maria Valenzuela. "Is it not a—what-you-call—sporting proposition—no?"

"It is certainly," said John Harned. "It is very clever."

She clapped her hands with delight. They were little hands. The audience applauded. The bull turned and came back. Again the capador eluded him, throwing the cape on his shoulders, and again the audience applauded. Three times did this happen. The capador was very excellent. Then he retired, and the other capador played with the bull. After that they placed the banderillos in the bull, in the shoulders, on each side of the back-bone, two at a time. Then stepped forward Ordonez, the chief matador, with the long sword and the scarlet cape. The bugles blew for the death. He is not so good as Matestini. Still he is good, and with one thrust he drove the sword to the heart, and the bull doubled his legs under him and lay down and died. It was a pretty thrust, clean and sure; and there was much applause, and many of the common people threw their hats into the ring. Maria Valenzuela clapped her hands with the rest, and John Harned, whose cold heart was not touched by the event, looked at her with curiosity.

"You like it?" he asked.

"Always," she said, still clapping her hands.

"From a little girl," said Luis Cervallos. "I remember her first fight. She was four years old. She sat with her mother, and just like now she clapped her hands. She is a proper Spanish woman."

"You have seen it," said Maria Valenzuela to John Harned, as they fastened the mules to the dead bull and dragged it out. "You have seen the bull-fight and you like it—no? What do you think?"

"I think the bull had no chance," he said. "The bull was doomed from the first. The issue was not in doubt. Every one knew, before the bull entered the ring, that it was to die. To be a sporting proposition, the issue must be in doubt. It was one stupid bull who had never fought a man against five wise men who had fought many bulls. It would be possibly a little bit fair if it were one man against one bull."

"Or one man against five bulls," said Maria Valenzuela; and we all laughed, and Luis Cervallos laughed loudest.

"Yes," said John Harned, "against five bulls, and the man, like the bulls, never in the bull-ring before—a man like yourself, Senor Cervallos."

"Yet we Spanish like the bull-fight," said Luis Cervallos; and I swear the devil was whispering then in his ear, telling him to do that which I shall relate.

"Then must it be a cultivated taste," John Harned made answer. "We kill bulls by the thousand every day in Chicago, yet no one cares to pay admittance to see."

"That is butchery," said I; "but this—ah, this is an art. It is delicate. It is fine. It is rare."

"Not always," said Luis Cervallos. "I have seen clumsy matadors, and I tell you it is not nice."

He shuddered, and his face betrayed such what-you-call disgust, that I knew, then, that the devil was whispering and that he was beginning to play a part.

"Senor Harned may be right," said Luis Cervallos. "It may not be fair to the bull. For is it not known to all of us that for twenty-four hours the bull is given no water, and that immediately before the fight he is permitted to drink his fill?"

"And he comes into the ring heavy with water?" said John Harned quickly; and I saw that his eyes were very gray and very sharp and very cold.

"It is necessary for the sport," said Luis Cervallos. "Would you have the bull so strong that he would kill the toreadors?"

"I would that he had a fighting chance," said John Harned, facing the ring to see the second bull come in.

It was not a good bull. It was frightened. It ran around the ring in search of a way to get out. The capadors stepped forth and flared their capes, but he refused to charge upon them.

"It is a stupid bull," said Maria Valenzuela.

"I beg pardon," said John Harned; "but it would seem to me a wise bull. He knows he must not fight man. See! He smells death there in the ring."

True. The bull, pausing where the last one had died, was smelling the wet sand and snorting. Again he ran around the ring, with raised head, looking at the faces of the thousands that hissed him, that threw orange-peel at him and called him names. But the smell of blood decided him, and he charged a capador, so without warning that the man just escaped. He dropped his cape and dodged into the shelter. The bull struck the wall of the ring with a crash. And John Harned said, in a quiet voice, as though he talked to himself:

"I will give one thousand sucres to the lazar-house of Quito if a bull kills a man this day."

"You like bulls?" said Maria Valenzuela with a smile.

"I like such men less," said John Harned. "A toreador is not a brave man. He surely cannot be a brave man. See, the bull's tongue is already out. He is tired and he has not yet begun."

"It is the water," said Luis Cervallos.

"Yes, it is the water," said John Harned. "Would it not be safer to hamstring the bull before he comes on?"

Maria Valenzuela was made angry by this sneer in John Harned's words. But Luis Cervallos smiled so that only I could see him, and then it broke upon my mind surely the game he was playing. He and I were to be banderilleros. The big American bull was there in the box with us. We were to stick the darts in him till he became angry, and then there might be no marriage with Maria Valenzuela. It was a good sport. And the spirit of bull-fighters was in our blood.

The bull was now angry and excited. The capadors had great game with him. He was very quick, and sometimes he turned with such sharpness that his hind legs lost their footing and he plowed the sand with his quarter. But he charged always the flung capes and committed no harm.

"He has no chance," said John Harned. "He is fighting wind."

"He thinks the cape is his enemy," explained Maria Valenzuela. "See how cleverly the capador deceives him."

"It is his nature to be deceived," said John Harned. "Wherefore he is doomed to fight wind. The toreadors know it, the audience knows it, you know it, I know it—we all know from the first that he will fight wind. He only does not know it. It is his stupid beast-nature. He has no chance."

"It is very simple," said Luis Cervallos. "The bull shuts his eyes when he charges. Therefore—"

"The man steps out of the way and the bull rushes by," John Harned interrupted.

"Yes," said Luis Cervallos; "that is it. The bull shuts his eyes, and the man knows it."

"But cows do not shut their eyes," said John Harned. "I know a cow at home that is a Jersey and gives milk, that would whip the whole gang of them."

"But the toreadors do not fight cows," said I.

"They are afraid to fight cows," said John Harned.

"Yes," said Luis Cervallos; "they are afraid to fight cows. There would be no sport in killing toreadors."

"There would be some sport," said John Harned, "if a toreador were killed once in a while. When I become an old man, and mayhap a cripple, and should I need to make a living and be unable to do hard work, then would I become a bull-fighter. It is a light vocation for elderly gentlemen and pensioners."

"But see!" said Maria Valenzuela, as the bull charged bravely and the capador eluded it with a fling of his cape. "It requires skill so to avoid the beast."

"True," said John Harned. "But believe me, it requires a thousand times more skill to avoid the many and quick punches of a prize-fighter who keeps his eyes open and strikes with intelligence. Furthermore, this bull does not want to fight. Behold, he runs away."

It was not a good bull, for again it ran around the ring, seeking to find a way out.

"Yet these bulls are sometimes the most dangerous," said Luis Cervallos. "It can never be known what they will do next. They are wise. They are half cow. The bull-fighters never like them.—See! He has turned!"

Once again, baffled and made angry by the walls of the ring that would not let him out, the bull was attacking his enemies valiantly.

"His tongue is hanging out," said John Harned. "First, they fill him with water. Then they tire him out, one man and then another, persuading him to exhaust himself by fighting wind. While some tire him, others rest. But the bull they never let rest. Afterward, when he is quite tired and no longer quick, the matador sticks the sword into him."

The time had now come for the banderillos. Three times one of the fighters endeavored to place the darts, and three times did he fail. He but stung the bull and maddened it. The banderillos must go in, you know, two at a time, into the shoulders, on each side the backbone and close to it. If but one be placed, it is a failure. The crowd hissed and called for Ordonez. And then Ordonez did a great thing. Four times he stood forth, and four times, at the first attempt, he stuck in the banderillos, so that eight of them, well placed, stood out of the back of the bull at one time. The crowd went mad, and a rain of hats and money fell upon the sand of the ring.

And just then the bull charged unexpectedly one of the capadors. The man slipped and lost his head. The bull caught him—fortunately between his wide horns. And while the audience watched, breathless and silent, John Harned stood up and yelled with gladness. Alone, in that hush of all of us, John Harned yelled. And he yelled for the bull. As you see yourself, John Harned wanted the man killed. His was a brutal heart. This bad conduct made those angry that sat in the box of General

Salazar, and they cried out against John Harned. And Urcisino Castillo told him to his face that he was a dog of a Gringo and other things. Only it was in Spanish, and John Harned did not understand. He stood and yelled, perhaps for the time of ten seconds, when the bull was enticed into charging the other capadors and the man arose unhurt.

"The bull has no chance," John Harned said with sadness as he sat down. "The man was uninjured. They fooled the bull away from him." Then he turned to Maria Valenzuela and said: "I beg your pardon. I was excited."

She smiled and in reproof tapped his arm with her fan.

"It is your first bull-fight," she said. "After you have seen more you will not cry for the death of the man. You Americans, you see, are more brutal than we. It is because of your prize-fighting. We come only to see the bull killed."

"But I would the bull had some chance," he answered. "Doubtless, in time, I shall cease to be annoyed by the men who take advantage of the bull."

The bugles blew for the death. Ordonez stood forth with the sword and the scarlet cloth. But the bull had changed again, and did not want to fight. Ordonez stamped his foot in the sand, and cried out, and waved the scarlet cloth. Then the bull charged, but without heart. There was no weight to the charge. It was a poor thrust. The sword struck a bone and bent. Ordonez took a fresh sword. The bull, again stung to fight, charged once more. Five times Ordonez essayed the thrust, and each time the sword went but part way in or struck bone. The sixth time, the sword went in to the hilt. But it was a bad thrust. The sword missed the heart and stuck out half a yard through the ribs on the opposite side. The audience hissed the matador. I glanced at John Harned. He sat silent, without movement; but I could see his teeth were set, and his hands were clenched tight on the railing of the box.

All fight was now out of the bull, and, though it was no vital thrust, he trotted lamely what of the sword that stuck through him, in one side and out the other. He ran away from the matador and the capadors, and circled the edge of the ring, looking up at the many faces.

"He is saying: 'For God's sake let me out of this; I don't want to fight,' " said John Harned.

That was all. He said no more, but sat and watched, though sometimes he looked sideways at Maria Valenzuela to see how she took it. She was angry with the matador. He was awkward, and she had desired a clever exhibition.

The bull was now very tired, and weak from loss of blood, though far from dying. He walked slowly around the wall of the ring, seeking a way out. He would not charge. He had had enough. But he must be killed. There is a place, in the neck of a bull behind the horns, where the cord of the spine is unprotected and where a short stab will immediately kill. Ordonez stepped in front of the bull and lowered his scarlet cloth to the ground. The bull would not charge. He stood still and smelled the cloth, lowering his head to do so. Ordonez stabbed between the horns at the spot in the neck. The bull jerked his head up. The stab had missed. Then the bull watched the sword. When Ordonez moved the cloth on the ground, the bull forgot the sword and lowered his head to smell the cloth. Again Ordonez stabbed, and again he failed. He tried many times. It was stupid. And John Harned said nothing. At last a stab went home, and the bull fell to the sand, dead immediately, and the mules were made fast and he was dragged out.

"The Gringos say it is a cruel sport—no?" said Luis Cervallos. "That it is not humane. That it is bad for the bull. No?"

"No," said John Harned. "The bull does not count for much. It is bad for those that look on. It is degrading to those that look on. It teaches them to delight in animal suffering. It is cowardly for five men to fight one stupid bull. Therefore those that look on learn to be cowards. The bull dies, but those that look on live and the lesson is learned. The bravery of men is not nourished by scenes of cowardice."

Maria Valenzuela said nothing. Neither did she look at him. But she heard every word and her cheeks were white with anger. She looked out across the ring and fanned herself, but I saw that her hand trembled. Nor did John Harned look at her. He went on as though she were not there. He, too, was angry, coldly angry.

"It is the cowardly sport of a cowardly people," he said.

"Ah," said Luis Cervallos softly, "you think you understand us."

"I understand now the Spanish Inquisition," said John Harned. "It must have been more delightful than bull-fighting."

Luis Cervallos smiled but said nothing. He glanced at Maria Valenzuela, and knew that the bull-fight in the box was won. Never would she have further to do with the Gringo who spoke such words. But neither Luis Cervallos nor I was prepared for the outcome of the day. I fear we do not understand the Gringos. How were we to know that John Harned, who was so coldly angry, should go suddenly mad? But mad he did go, as you shall see. The bull did not count for much—he said so himself. Then why should the horse count for so much? That I cannot understand. The mind of John Harned lacked logic. That is the only explanation.

"It is not usual to have horses in the bull-ring at Quito," said Luis Cervallos, looking up from the program. "In Spain they always have them. But to-day, by special permission we shall have them. When the next bull comes on there will be horses and picadors—you know, the men who carry lances and ride the horses."

"The bull is doomed from the first," said John Harned. "Are the horses then likewise doomed?"

"They are blindfolded so that they may not see the bull," said Luis Cervallos. "I have seen many horses killed. It is a brave sight."

"I have seen the bull slaughtered," said John Harned. "I will now see the horse slaughtered, so that I may understand more fully the fine points of this noble sport."

"They are old horses," said Luis Cervallos, "that are not good for anything else."

"I see," said John Harned.

The third bull came on, and soon against it were both capadors and picadors. One picador took his stand directly below us. I agree, it was a thin and aged horse he rode, a bag of bones covered with mangy hide.

"It is a marvel that the poor brute can hold up the weight of the rider," said John Harned. "And now that the horse fights the bull, what weapons has it?"

"The horse does not fight the bull," said Luis Cervallos.

"Oh," said John Harned, "then is the horse there to be gored? That must be why it is blind-folded, so that it shall not see the bull coming to gore it."

"Not quite so," said I. "The lance of the picador is to keep the bull from goring the horse."

"Then are horses rarely gored?" asked John Harned.

"No," said Luis Cervallos. "I have seen, at Seville, eighteen horses killed in one day, and the people clamored for more horses."

"Were they blindfolded like this horse?" asked John Harned.

"Yes," said Luis Cervallos.

After that we talked no more, but watched the fight. And John Harned was going mad all the time, and we did not know. The bull refused to charge the horse. And the horse stood still, and because it could not see it did not know that the capadors were trying to make the bull charge upon it. The capadors teased the bull with their capes, and when it charged them they ran toward the horse and into their shelters. At last the bull was well angry, and it saw the horse before it.

"The horse does not know, the horse does not know," John Harned whispered like to himself, unaware that he voiced his thought aloud.

The bull charged, and of course the horse knew nothing till the picador failed and the horse found himself impaled on the bull's horns from beneath. The bull was magnificently strong. The sight of its strength was splendid to see. It lifted the horse clear into the air; and as the horse fell to its side on the ground the picador landed on his feet and escaped, while the capadors lured the bull away. The horse was emptied of its essential organs. Yet did it rise to its feet screaming. It was the scream of the horse that did it, that made John Harned completely mad; for he, too, started to rise to his feet. I heard him curse low and deep. He never took his eyes from the horse, which, still screaming, strove to run, but fell down instead and rolled on its back so that all its four legs were kicking in the air. Then the bull charged it and gored it again and again until it was dead.

John Harned was now on his feet. His eyes were no longer cold like steel. They were blue flames. He looked at Maria Valenzuela, and she looked at him, and in his face was a great loathing. The moment of his madness was upon him. Everybody was looking, now that the horse was dead; and John Harned was a large man and easy to be seen.

"Sit down," said Luis Cervallos, "or you will make a fool of yourself."

John Harned replied nothing. He struck out his fist. He smote Luis Cervallos in the face so that he fell like a dead man across the chairs and did not rise again. He saw nothing of what followed. But I saw much. Urcisino Castillo, leaning forward from the next box, with his cane struck John Harned full across the face. And John Harned smote him with his fist so that in falling he overthrew General Salazar. John Harned was now in what-you-call Berserker rage—no? The beast primitive in him was loose and roaring—the beast primitive of the holes and caves of the long ago.

"You came for a bull-fight," I heard him say, "and by God I'll show you a man-fight!"

It was a fight. The soldiers guarding the Presidente's box leaped across, but from one of them he took a rifle and beat them on their heads with it. From the other box Colonel Jacinto Fierro was shooting at him with a revolver. The first shot killed a soldier. This I know for a fact. I saw it. But the second shot struck John Harned in the side. Whereupon he swore, and with a lunge drove the bayonet of his rifle into Colonel Jacinto Fierro's body. It was horrible to behold. The Americans and the English are a brutal race. They sneer at our bull-fighting, yet do they delight in the shedding of blood. More men were killed that day because of John Harned than were ever killed in all the history of the bull-ring of Quito, yes, and of Guayaquil and all Ecuador.

It was the scream of the horse that did it. Yet why did not John Harned go mad when the bull was killed? A beast is a beast, be it bull or horse. John Harned was mad. There is no other explanation. He was blood-mad, a beast himself. I leave it to your judgment. Which is worse—the goring of the horse by the bull, or the goring of Colonel Jacinto Fierro by the bayonet in the hands of John Harned? And John Harned gored others with that bayonet. He was full of devils. He fought with many bullets in him, and he was hard to kill. And Maria Valenzuela was a brave woman. Unlike the other women, she did not cry out nor faint. She sat still in her box, gazing out across the bull-ring. Her face was white and she fanned herself, but she never looked around.

From all sides came the soldiers and officers and the common people bravely to subdue the mad Gringo. It is true—the cry went up from the crowd to kill all the Gringos. It is an old cry in Latin-American countries, what of the dislike for the Gringos and their uncouth ways. It is true, the cry went up. But the brave Ecuadorianos killed only John Harned, and first he killed seven of them. Besides, there were many hurt. I have seen many bull-fights, but never have I seen anything so abominable as the scene in the boxes when the fight was over. It was like a field of battle. The dead lay around everywhere, while the wounded sobbed and groaned and some of them died. One man, whom John Harned had thrust through the belly with the bayonet, clutched at himself with both his hands and screamed. I tell you for a fact it was more terrible than the screaming of a thousand horses.

No, Maria Valenzuela did not marry Luis Cervallos. I am sorry for that. He was my friend, and much of my money was invested in his ventures. It was five weeks before the surgeons took the bandages from his face. And there is a scar there to this day, on the cheek, under the eye. Yet John Harned struck him but once and struck him only with his naked fist. Maria Valenzuela is in Austria now. It is said she is to marry an Arch-Duke or some high nobleman. I do not know. I think she liked John Harned before he followed her to Quito to see the bull-fight. But why the horse? That is what I desire to know. Why should he watch the bull and say that it did not count, and then go immediately and most horribly mad because a horse screamed? There is no understanding the Gringos. They are barbarians.

THE NIGHT-BORN

It was in the old Alta-Inyo Club—a warm night for San Francisco—
and through the open windows, hushed and far, came the brawl of the
streets. The talk had led on from the Graft Prosecution and the latest
signs that the town was to be run wide open, down through all the
grotesque sordidness and rottenness of man-hate and man-meanness,
until the name of O'Brien was mentioned—O'Brien, the promising
young pugilist who had been killed in the prize-ring the night before.
At once the air had seemed to freshen. O'Brien had been a clean-living
young man with ideals. He neither drank, smoked, nor swore, and his had
been the body of a beautiful young god. He had even carried his prayer-
book to the ringside. They found it in his coat pocket in the dressing-
room . . . afterward.

Here was Youth, clean and wholesome, unsullied—the thing of glory
and wonder for men to conjure with . . . after it has been lost to them
and they have turned middle-aged. And so well did we conjure, that
Romance came and for an hour led us far from the man-city and its
snarling roar. Bardwell, in a way, started it by quoting from Thoreau;
but it was old Trefethan, bald-headed and dewlapped, who took up the
quotation and for the hour to come was Romance incarnate. At first we
might have wondered how many Scotches he had consumed since dinner, but very soon all that was forgotten.

"It was in 1898—I was thirty-five then," he said. "Yes, I know you
are adding it up. You're right. I'm forty-[s]even now; look ten years
more; and the doctors say—damn the doctors anyway!"

He lifted the long glass to his lips and sipped it slowly to soothe
away his irritation.

"But I was young . . . once. I was young twelve years ago, and I had
hair on top of my head, and my stomach was lean as a runner's, and
the longest day was none too long for me. I was a husky back there in

'98. You remember me, Milner. You knew me then. Wasn't I a pretty good bit of all right?"

Milner nodded and agreed. Like Trefethan, he was another mining engineer who had cleaned up a fortune in the Klondike.

"You certainly were, old man," Milner said. "I'll never forget when you cleaned out those lumberjacks in the M. & M. that night that little newspaper man started the row. Slavin was in the country at the time,"—this to us—"and his manager wanted to get up a match with Trefethan."

"Well, look at me now," Trefethan commanded angrily. "That's what the Goldstead did to me—God knows how many millions, but nothing left in my soul . . . nor in my veins. The good red blood is gone. I am a jellyfish, a huge, gross mass of oscillating protoplasm, a—a . . ."

But language failed him, and he drew solace from the long glass.

"Women looked at me . . . then; and turned their heads to look a second time. Strange that I never married. But the girl. That's what I started to tell you about. I met her a thousand miles from anywhere, and then some. And she quoted to me those very words of Thoreau that Bardwell quoted a moment ago—the ones about the day-born gods and the night-born.

"It was after I had made my locations on Goldstead—and didn't know what a treasure-pot that creek was going to prove—that I made that trip east over the Rockies, angling across to the Great Slave. Up North there the Rockies are something more than a back-bone. They are a boundary, a dividing line, a wall impregnable and unscalable. There is no intercourse across them, though, on occasion, from the early days, wandering trappers have crossed them, though more were lost by the way than ever came through. And that was precisely why I tackled the job. It was a traverse any man would be proud to make. I am prouder of it right now than anything else I have ever done.

"It is an unknown land. Great stretches of it have never been explored. There are big valleys there where the white man has never set foot, and Indian tribes as primitive as ten thousand years . . . almost, for they have had some contact with the whites. Parties of them come out once in a while to trade, and that is all. Even the Hudson Bay Company failed to find them and farm them.

"And now the girl. I was coming up a stream—you'd call it a river in California—uncharted and unnamed. It was a noble valley, now shut in by high canyon walls, and again opening out into beautiful stretches, wide and long, with pasture shoulder-high in the bottoms, meadows dotted with flowers, and with clumps of timber—spruce—virgin and magnificent. The dogs were packing on their backs, and were sore-footed and played out; while I was looking for any bunch of Indians to get sleds and drivers from and go on with the first snow. It was late fall, but the way those flowers persisted surprised me. I was supposed to be in sub-arctic America, and high up among the buttresses of the Rockies, and yet there was that everlasting spread of flowers. Some day the white settlers will be in there and growing wheat down all that valley.

"And then I lifted a smoke, and heard the barking of the dogs— Indian dogs—and came into camp. There must have been five hundred of them, proper Indians at that, and I could see by the jerking-frames that the fall hunting had been good. And then I met her—Lucy. That was her name. Sign language—that was all we could talk with, till they led me to a big fly—you know, half a tent, open on the one side where a campfire burned. It was all of moose-skins, this fly—moose-skins, smoke-cured, hand-rubbed, and golden-brown. Under it everything was neat and orderly, as no Indian camp ever was. The bed was laid on fresh spruce boughs. There were furs galore, and on top of all was a robe of swan-skins—white swan-skins—I have never seen anything like that robe. And on top of it, sitting cross-legged, was Lucy. She was nut-brown. I have called her a girl. But she was not. She was a woman, a nut-brown woman, an Amazon, a full-blooded, full-bodied woman, and royal ripe. And her eyes were blue.

"That's what took me off my feet—her eyes—blue, not China blue, but deep blue, like the sea and sky all melted into one, and very wise. More than that, they had laughter in them—warm laughter, sun-warm and human, very human, and . . . shall I say feminine? They were. They were a woman's eyes, a proper woman's eyes. You know what that means. Can I say more? Also, in those blue eyes were, at the same time, a wild unrest, a wistful yearning, and a repose, an absolute repose, a sort of all-wise and philosophical calm."

Trefethan broke off abruptly.

"You fellows think I am screwed. I'm not. This is only my fifth since dinner. I am dead sober. I am solemn. I sit here now side by side with my sacred youth. It is not I—'old' Trefethan—that talks; it is my youth, and it is my youth that says those were the most wonderful eyes I have ever seen—so very calm, so very restless; so very wise, so very curious; so very old, so very young; so satisfied and yet yearning so wistfully. Boys, I can't describe them. When I have told you about her, you may know better for yourselves.

"She did not stand up. But she put out her hand.

" 'Stranger,' she said, 'I'm real glad to see you.'

"I leave it to you—that sharp, frontier, Western tang of speech. Picture my sensations. It was a woman, a white woman, but that tang! It was amazing that it should be a white woman, here, beyond the last boundary of the world—but the tang. I tell you, it hurt. It was like the stab of a flatted note. And yet, let me tell you, that woman was a poet. You shall see.

"She dismissed the Indians. And, by Jove, they went. They took her orders and followed her blind. She was *hi-yu skookum* chief. She told the bucks to make a camp for me and to take care of my dogs. And they did, too. And they knew enough not to get away with as much as a moccasin-lace of my outfit. She was a regular She-Who-Must-Be-Obeyed, and I want to tell you it chilled me to the marrow, sent those little thrills Marathoning up and down my spinal column, meeting a white woman out there at the head of a tribe of savages a thousand miles the other side of No Man's Land.

" 'Stranger,' she said, 'I reckon you're sure the first white that ever set foot in this valley. Set down an' talk a spell, and then we'll have a bite to eat. Which way might you be comin'?'

"There it was, that tang again. But from now to the end of the yarn I want you to forget it. I tell you I forgot it, sitting there on the edge of that swan-skin robe and listening and looking at the most wonderful woman that ever stepped out of the pages of Thoreau or of any other man's book.

"I stayed on there a week. It was on her invitation. She promised to fit me out with dogs and sleds and with Indians that would put me across the best pass of the Rockies in five hundred miles. Her fly was pitched apart from the others, on the high bank by the river, and a couple of Indian girls did her cooking for her and the camp work. And so we talked and talked, while the first snow fell and continued to fall and make a surface for my sleds. And this was her story.

"She was frontier-born, of poor settlers, and you know what that means—work, work, always work, work in plenty and without end.

" 'I never seen the glory of the world,' she said. 'I had no time. I knew it was right out there, anywhere, all around the cabin, but there was always the bread to set, the scrubbin' and the washin' and the work that was never done. I used to be plumb sick at times, jes' to get out into it all, especially in the spring when the songs of the birds drove me most clean crazy. I wanted to run out through the long pasture grass, wetting my legs with the dew of it, and to climb the rail fence, and keep on through the timber and up and up over the divide so as to get a look around. Oh, I had all kinds of hankerings—to follow up the canyon beds and slosh around from pool to pool, making friends with the water-dogs and the speckly trout; to peep on the sly and watch the squirrels and rabbits and small furry things and see what they was doing and learn the secrets of their ways. Seemed to me, if I had time, I could crawl among the flowers, and, if I was good and quiet, catch them whispering with themselves, telling all kinds of wise things that mere humans never know.'"

Trefethan paused to see that his glass had been refilled.

"Another time she said: 'I wanted to run nights like a wild thing, just to run through the moonshine and under the stars, to run white and naked in the darkness that I knew must feel like cool velvet, and to run and run and keep on running. One evening, plumb tuckered out—it had been a dreadful hard hot day, and the bread wouldn't raise and the churning had gone wrong, and I was all irritated and jerky—well, that evening I made mention to dad of this wanting to run of mine. He looked at me curious-some and a bit scared. And then he gave me two pills to take. Said to go to bed and get a good sleep and I'd be all hunky-dory in the morning. So I never mentioned my hankerings to him, or any one any more.'

"The mountain home broke up—starved out, I imagine—and the family came to Seattle to live. There she worked in a factory—long hours, you know, and all the rest, deadly work. And after a year of that she became waitress in a cheap restaurant—hash-slinger, she called it.

"She said to me once, 'Romance I guess was what I wanted. But there wan't no romance floating around in dishpans and washtubs, or in factories and hash-joints.'

"When she was eighteen she married—a man who was going up to Juneau to start a restaurant. He had a few dollars saved, and appeared prosperous. She didn't love him—she was emphatic about that; but she was all tired out, and she wanted to get away from the unending drudgery. Besides, Juneau was in Alaska, and her yearning took the form of a desire to see that wonderland. But little she saw of it. He started the restaurant, a little cheap one, and she quickly learned what he had married her for . . . to save paying wages. She came pretty close to running the joint and doing all the work from waiting to dishwashing. She cooked most of the time as well. And she had four years of it.

"Can't you picture her, this wild woods creature, quick with every old primitive instinct, yearning for the free open, and mowed up in a vile little hash-joint and toiling and moiling for four mortal years?

"'There was no meaning in anything,' she said. 'What was it all about? Why was I born? Was that all the meaning of life—just to work and work and be always tired?—to go to bed tired and to wake up tired, with every day like every other day unless it was harder?' She had heard talk of immortal life from the gospel sharps, she said, but she could not reckon that what she was doing was a likely preparation for her immortality.

"But she still had her dreams, though more rarely. She had read a few books—what, it is pretty hard to imagine, Seaside Library novels most likely; yet they had been food for fancy. 'Sometimes,' she said, 'when I was that dizzy from the heat of the cooking that if I didn't take a breath of fresh air I'd faint, I'd stick my head out of the kitchen window and close my eyes and see most wonderful things. All of a sudden I'd be traveling down a country road, and everything clean and quiet, no dust, no dirt; just streams ripplin' down sweet meadows, and lambs playing, breezes blowing the breath of flowers, and soft sunshine over everything; and lovely cows lazying knee-deep in quiet pools, and young girls bathing in a curve of stream all white and slim and natural —and I'd know I was in Arcady. I'd read about that country once, in a book. And maybe knights, all flashing in the sun, would come riding around a bend in the road, or a lady on a milk-white mare, and in the distance I could see the towers of a castle rising, or I just knew, on the next turn, that I'd come upon some palace, all white and airy and fairy-like, with fountains playing, and flowers all over everything, and peacocks on the lawn ... and then I'd open my eyes, and the heat of the cooking range would strike on me, and I'd hear Jake sayin'—he was my husband—I'd hear Jake sayin', "Why ain't you served them beans? Think I can wait here all day!" Romance!—I reckon the nearest I ever come to it was when a drunken Armenian cook got the snakes and tried to cut my throat with a potato knife and I got my arm burned on the stove before I could lay him out with the potato stomper.

" 'I wanted easy ways, and lovely things, and Romance and all that; but it just seemed I had no luck nohow and was only and expressly born for cooking and dishwashing. There was a wild crowd in Juneau them days, but I looked at the other women, and their way of life didn't excite me. I reckon I wanted to be clean. I don't know why; I just wanted to, I guess; and I reckoned I might as well die dishwashing as die their way.' "

Trefethan halted in his tale for a moment, completing to himself some thread of thought.

"And this is the woman I met up there in the Arctic, running a tribe of wild Indians and a few thousand square miles of hunting territory. And it happened simply enough, though, for that matter, she might have lived and died among the pots and pans. But 'Came the whisper, came the vision.' That was all she needed, and she got it.

" 'I woke up one day,' she said. 'Just happened on it in a scrap of newspaper. I remember every word of it, and I can give it to you.' And then she quoted Thoreau's *Cry of the Human:*

" 'The young pines springing up in the corn field from year to year are to me a refreshing fact. We talk of civilizing the Indian, but that is not the name for his improvement. By the wary independence and aloofness of his dim forest life he preserves his intercourse with his native gods and is admitted from time to time to a rare and peculiar society with nature. He has glances of starry recognition, to which our saloons are strangers. The steady illumination of his genius, dim only because distant, is like the faint but satisfying light of the stars compared with the dazzling but ineffectual and shortlived blaze of candles. The Society Islanders had their day-born gods, but they were not supposed to be of equal antiquity with the ... night-born gods.'

"That's what she did, repeated it word for word, and I forgot the tang, for it was solemn, a declaration of religion—pagan, if you will; and clothed in the living garmenture of herself.

" 'And the rest of it was torn away,' she added, a great emptiness in her voice. 'It was only a scrap of newspaper. But that Thoreau was a wise man. I wish I knew more about him.' She stopped a moment, and I swear her face was ineffably holy as she said, 'I could have made him a good wife.'

"And then she went on. 'I knew right away, as soon as I read that, what was the matter with me. I was a night-born. I, who had lived all my life with the day-born, was a night-born. That was why I had never been satisfied with cooking and dishwashing; that was why I had hankered to run naked in the moonlight. And I knew that this dirty little Juneau hash-joint was no place for me. And right there and then I said, "I quit." I packed up my few rags of clothes, and started. Jake saw me and tried to stop me.

" ' "What you doing?" he says.

" ' "Divorcin' you and me," I says. "I'm headin' for tall timber and where I belong."

" ' "No you don't," he says, reaching for me to stop me. "The cookin' has got on your head. You listen to me talk before you up and do anything brash."

" 'But I pulled a gun—a little Colt's forty-four—and says, "This does my talkin' for me."

" 'And I left.' "

Trefethan emptied his glass and called for another.

"Boys, do you know what that girl did? She was twenty-two. She had spent her life over the dish-pan and she knew no more about the world than I do of the fourth dimension, or the fifth. All roads led to her desire. No; she didn't head for the dance-halls. On the Alaskan Panhandle it is preferable to travel by water. She went down to the beach. An Indian canoe was starting for Dyea—you know the kind, carved out of a single tree, narrow and deep and sixty feet long. She gave them a couple of dollars and got on board.

" 'Romance?' she told me. 'It was Romance from the jump. There were three families altogether in that canoe, and that crowded there wasn't room to turn around, with dogs and Indian babies sprawling over everything, and everybody dipping a paddle and making that canoe go. And all around the great solemn mountains, and tangled drifts of clouds and sunshine. And oh, the silence! the great wonderful silence! And, once, the smoke of a hunter's camp, away off in the distance, trailing among the trees. It was like a picnic, a grand picnic, and I could see my dreams coming true, and I was ready for something to happen 'most any time. And it did.

" 'And that first camp, on the island! And the boys spearing fish in the mouth of the creek, and the big deer one of the bucks shot just around the point. And there were flowers everywhere, and in back from the beach the grass was thick and lush and neck-high. And some of the girls went through this with me, and we climbed the hillside behind and picked berries and roots that tasted sour and were good to eat. And we came upon a big bear in the berries making his supper, and he said "Oof!" and ran away as scared as we were. And then the camp, and the camp smoke, and the smell of fresh venison cooking. It was beautiful. I was with the night-born at last, and I knew that was where I belonged. And for the first time in my life, it seemed to me, I went to bed happy that night, looking out under a corner of the canvas at the stars cut off black by a big shoulder of mountain, and listening to the night-noises, and knowing that the same thing would go on next day and forever and ever, for I was n't going back. And I never did go back.

" 'Romance! I got it next day. We had to cross a big arm of the ocean—twelve or fifteen miles, at least; and it came on to blow when we were in the middle. That night I was along on shore, with one wolf-dog, and I was the only one left alive.'

"Picture it yourself," Trefethan broke off to say. "The canoe was wrecked and lost, and everybody pounded to death on the rocks except her. She went ashore hanging on to a dog's tail, escaping the rocks and washing up on a tiny beach, the only one in miles.

" 'Lucky for me it was the mainland,' she said. 'So I headed right away back, through the woods and over the mountains and straight on anywhere. Seemed I was looking for something and knew I'd find it. I wasn't afraid. I was night-born, and the big timber couldn't kill me. And on the second day I found it. I came upon a small clearing and a tumbledown cabin. Nobody had been there for years and years. The roof had fallen in. Rotted blankets lay in the bunks, and pots and pans were on the stove. But that was not the most curious thing. Outside, along the edge of the trees, you can't guess what I found. The skeletons of eight horses, each tied to a tree. They had starved to death, I reckon, and left only little piles of bones scattered some here and there. And each horse had had a load on its back. There the loads lay, in among the bones—painted canvas sacks, and inside moosehide sacks, and inside the moosehide sacks—what do you think?'

"She stopped, reached under a corner of the bed among the spruce boughs, and pulled out a leather sack. She untied the mouth and ran out into my hand as pretty a stream of gold as I have ever seen—coarse gold, placer gold, some large dust, but mostly nuggets, and it was so fresh and rough that it scarcely showed signs of water-wash.

" 'You say you're a mining engineer,' she said, 'and you know this country. Can you name a pay-creek that has the color of that gold?'

"I couldn't. There wasn't a trace of silver. It was almost pure, and I told her so.

" 'You bet,' she said. 'I sell that for nineteen dollars an ounce. You can't get over seventeen for Eldorado gold, and Minook gold don't fetch quite eighteen. Well, that was what I found among the bones—eight horse-loads of it, one hundred and fifty pounds to the load.'

" 'A quarter of a million dollars!' I cried out.

" 'That's what I reckoned it roughly,' she answered. 'Talk about Romance! And me a slaving the way I had all the years, when as soon as I ventured out, inside three days, this was what happened. And what became of the men that mined all that gold? Often and often I wonder about it. They left their horses, loaded and tied, and just disappeared off the face of the earth, leaving neither hide nor hair behind them. I never heard tell of them. Nobody knows anything about them. Well, being the night-born, I reckon I was their rightful heir.' "

Trefethan stopped to light a cigar.

"Do you know what that girl did? She cached the gold, saving out thirty pounds, which she carried back to the coast. Then she signaled a passing canoe, made her way to Pat Healy's trading post at Dyea, outfitted, and went over Chilcoot Pass. That was in '88—eight years before the Klondike strike, and the Yukon was a howling wilderness. She was afraid of the bucks, but she took two young squaws with her, crossed the lakes, and went down the river and to all the early camps on the Lower Yukon. She wandered several years over that country and then on in to where I met her. Liked the looks of it, she said, seeing, in her own words, 'a big bull caribou knee-deep in purple iris on the valley-bottom.' She hooked up with the Indians, doctored them, gained their confidence, and gradually took them in charge. She had only left that country once, and then, with a bunch of the young bucks, she went over Chilcoot, cleaned up her gold-cache, and brought it back with her.

" 'And here I be, stranger,' she concluded her yarn, 'and here's the most precious thing I own.'

"She pulled out a little pouch of buckskin, worn on her neck like a locket, and opened it. And inside, wrapped in oiled silk, yellowed with age and worn and thumbed, was the original scrap of newspaper containing the quotation from Thoreau.

" 'And are you happy? . . . satisfied?' I asked her. 'With a quarter of a million you wouldn't have to work down in the States. You must miss a lot.'

" 'Not much,' she answered. 'I wouldn't swop places with any woman down in the States. These are my people; this is where I belong. But there are times—' and in her eyes smoldered up that hungry yearning I've mentioned—'there are times when I wish most awful bad for that Thoreau man to happen along.'

" 'Why?' I asked.

" 'So as I could marry him. I do get mighty lonesome at spells. I'm just a woman—a real woman. I've heard tell of the other kind of women that gallivanted off like me and did queer things—the sort that become soldiers in armies and sailors on ships. But those women are queer themselves. They're more like men than women; they look like men and they don't have ordinary women's needs. They don't want love, nor little children in their arms and around their knees. I'm not that sort. I leave it to you, stranger. Do I look like a man?'

"She didn't. She was a woman, a beautiful, nut-brown woman, with a sturdy, health-rounded woman's body and with wonderful deep-blue woman's eyes.

" 'Ain't I woman?' she demanded. 'I am. I'm 'most all woman, and then some. And the funny thing is, though I'm night-born in everything else, I'm not when it comes to mating. I reckon that kind likes its own kind best. That's the way it is with me, anyway, and has been all these years.'

" 'You mean to tell me—' I began.

" 'Never,' she said, and her eyes looked into mine with the straightness of truth. 'I had one husband, only—him I call the Ox; and I reckon he's still down in Juneau running the hash-joint. Look him up, if you ever get back, and you'll find he's rightly named.'

"And look him up I did, two years afterward. He was all she said—solid and stolid, the Ox—shuffling around and waiting on the tables.

" 'You need a wife to help you,' I said.

" 'I had one once,' was his answer.

" 'Widower?'

" 'Yep. She went loco. She always said the heat of the cooking would get her, and it did. Pulled a gun on me one day and ran away with some Siwashes in a canoe. Caught a blow up the coast and all hands drowned.' "

Trefethan devoted himself to his glass and remainded silent.

"But the girl?" Milner reminded him. "You left your story just as it was getting interesting, tender. Did it?"

"It did," Trefethan replied. "As she said herself, she was savage in everything except mating, and then she wanted her own kind. She was very nice about it, but she was straight to the point. She wanted to marry me.

" 'Stranger,' she said, 'I want you bad. You like this sort of life or you wouldn't be here trying to cross the Rockies in fall weather. It's a likely spot. You'll find few likelier. Why not settle down? I'll make you a good wife.'

"And then it was up to me. And she waited. I don't mind confessing that I was sorely tempted. I was half in love with her as it was. You know I have never married. And I don't mind adding, looking back over my life, that she is the only woman that ever affected me that way. But it was too preposterous, the whole thing, and I lied like a gentleman. I told her I was already married.

" 'Is your wife waiting for you?' she asked.

"I said yes.

" 'And she loves you?'

"I said yes.

"And that was all. She never pressed her point ... except once, and then she showed a bit of fire.

" 'All I've got to do,' she said, 'is to give the word, and you don't get away from here. If I give the word, you stay on. . . . But I ain't going to give it. I wouldn't want you if you didn't want to be wanted ... and if you didn't want me.'

"She went ahead and outfitted me and started me on my way.

" 'It's a darned shame, stranger,' she said, at parting. 'I like your looks, and I like you. If you ever change your mind, come back.'

"Now there was one thing I wanted to do, and that was to kiss her good-bye, but I didn't know how to go about it nor how she would take it.—I tell you I was half in love with her. But she settled it herself.

" 'Kiss me,' she said. 'Just something to go on and remember.'

"And we kissed, there in the snow, in that valley by the Rockies, and I left her standing by the trail and went on after my dogs. I was six weeks in crossing over the pass and coming down to the first post on Great Slave Lake."

The brawl of the streets came up to us like a distant surf. A steward, moving noiselessly, brought fresh siphons. And in the silence Trefethan's voice fell like a funeral bell:

"It would have been better had I stayed. Look at me."

We saw his grizzled mustache, the bald spot on his head, the puff-sacks under his eyes, the sagging cheeks, the heavy dewlap, the general tiredness and staleness and fatness, all the collapse and ruin of a man who had once been strong but who had lived too easily and too well.

"It's not too late, old man," Bardwell said, almost in a whisper.

"By God! I wish I weren't a coward!" was Trefethan's answering cry. "I could go back to her. She's there, now. I could shape up and live many a long year . . . with her . . . up there. To remain here is to commit suicide. But I am an old man—forty-seven—look at me. The trouble is," he lifted his glass and glanced at it, "the trouble is that suicide of this sort is so easy. I am soft and tender. The thought of the long day's travel with the dogs appals me; the thought of the keen frost in the morning and of the frozen sled-lashings frightens me—"

Automatically the glass was creeping toward his lips. With a swift surge of anger he made as if to crash it down upon the floor. Next came hesitancy and second thought. The glass moved upward to his lips and paused. He laughed harshly and bitterly, but his words were solemn: "Well, here's to the Night-Born. She *was* a wonder."

WAR

He was a young man, not more than twenty-four or five, and he might have sat his horse with the careless grace of his youth had he not been so catlike and tense. His black eyes roved everywhere, catching the movements of twigs and branches where small birds hopped, questing ever onward through the changing vistas of trees and brush, and returning always to the clumps of undergrowth on either side. And as he watched, so did he listen, though he rode on in silence, save for the boom of heavy guns from far to the west. This had been sounding monotonously in his ears for hours, and only its cessation would have aroused his notice. For he had business closer to hand. Across his saddle-bow was balanced a carbine.

So tensely was he strung, that a bunch of quail, exploding into flight from under his horse's nose, startled him to such an extent that automatically, instantly, he had reined in and fetched the carbine halfway to his shoulder. He grinned sheepishly, recovered himself, and rode on. So tense was he, so bent upon the work he had to do, that the sweat stung his eyes unwiped, and unheeded rolled down his nose and spattered his saddle pommel. The band of his cavalryman's hat was fresh-stained with sweat. The roan horse under him was likewise wet. It was high noon of a breathless day of heat. Even the birds and squirrels did not dare the sun, but sheltered in shady hiding places among the trees.

Man and horse were littered with leaves and dusted with yellow pollen, for the open was ventured no more than was compulsory. They kept to the brush and trees, and invariably the man halted and peered out before crossing a dry glade or naked stretch of upland pasturage. He worked always to the north, though his way was devious, and it was from the north that he seemed most to apprehend that for which he was looking. He was no coward, but his courage was only that of the average civilized man, and he was looking to live, not die.

Up a small hillside he followed a cowpath through such dense scrub that he was forced to dismount and lead his horse. But when the path swung around to the west, he abandoned it and headed to the north again along the oak-covered top of the ridge.

The ridge ended in a steep descent—so steep that he zigzagged back and forth across the face of the slope, sliding and stumbling among the dead leaves and matted vines and keeping a watchful eye on the horse above that threatened to fall down upon him. The sweat ran from him, and the pollen-dust, settling pungently in mouth and nostrils, increased his thirst. Try as he would, nevertheless the descent was noisy, and frequently he stopped, panting in the dry heat and listening for any warning from beneath.

At the bottom he came out on a flat, so densely forested that he could not make out its extent. Here the character of the woods changed, and he was able to remount. Instead of the twisted hillside oaks, tall straight trees, big-trunked and prosperous, rose from the damp fat soil. Only here and there were thickets, easily avoided, while he encountered winding, park-like glades where the cattle had pastured in the days before war had run them off.

His progress was more rapid now, as he came down into the valley, and at the end of half an hour he halted at an ancient rail fence on the edge of a clearing. He did not like the openness of it, yet his path lay across to the fringe of trees that marked the banks of the stream. It was a mere quarter of a mile across that open, but the thought of venturing out in it was repugnant. A rifle, a score of them, a thousand, might lurk in that fringe by the stream.

Twice he essayed to start, and twice he paused. He was appalled by his own loneliness. The pulse of war that beat from the West suggested the companionship of battling thousands; here was naught but silence, and himself, and possible death-dealing bullets from a myriad ambushes. And yet his task was to find what he feared to find. He must go on, and on, till somewhere, some time, he encountered another man, or other men, from the other side, scouting, as he was scouting, to make report, as he must make report, of having come in touch.

Changing his mind, he skirted inside the woods for a distance, and again peeped forth. This time, in the middle of the clearing, he saw a small farmhouse. There were no signs of life. No smoke curled from the chimney, not a barn-yard fowl clucked and strutted. The kitchen door stood open, and he gazed so long and hard into the black aperture that it seemed almost that a farmer's wife must emerge at any moment.

He licked the pollen and dust from his dry lips, stiffened himself, mind and body, and rode out into the blazing sunshine. Nothing stirred.

He went on past the house, and approached the wall of trees and bushes by the river's bank. One thought persisted maddeningly. It was of the crash into his body of a high-velocity bullet. It made him feel very fragile and defenseless, and he crouched lower in the saddle.

Tethering his horse in the edge of the wood, he continued a hundred yards on foot till he came to the stream. Twenty feet wide it was, without perceptible current, cool and inviting, and he was very thirsty. But he waited inside his screen of leafage, his eyes fixed on the screen on the opposite side. To make the wait endurable, he sat down, his carbine resting on his knees. The minutes passed, and slowly his tenseness relaxed. At last he decided there was no danger; but just as he prepared to part the bushes and bend down to the water, a movement among the opposite bushes caught his eye.

It might be a bird. But he waited. Again there was an agitation of the bushes, and then, so suddenly that it almost startled a cry from him, the bushes parted and a face peered out. It was a face covered with several weeks' growth of ginger-colored beard. The eyes were blue and wide apart, with laughter-wrinkles in the corners that showed despite the tired and anxious expression of the whole face.

All this he could see with microscopic clearness, for the distance was no more than twenty feet. And all this he saw in such brief time, that he saw it as he lifted his carbine to his shoulder. He glanced along the sights, and knew that he was gazing upon a man who was as good as dead. It was impossible to miss at such point blank range.

But he did not shoot. Slowly he lowered the carbine and watched. A hand, clutching a water-bottle, became visible and the ginger beard bent downward to fill the bottle. He could hear the gurgle of the water. Then arm and bottle and ginger beard disappeared behind the closing bushes. A long time he waited, when, with thirst unslaked, he crept back to his horse, rode slowly across the sun-washed clearing, and passed into the shelter of the woods beyond.

· II ·

Another day, hot and breathless. A deserted farmhouse, large, with many outbuildings and an orchard, standing in a clearing. From the woods, on a roan horse, carbine across pommel, rode the young man with the quick black eyes. He breathed with relief as he gained the house. That a fight had taken place here earlier in the season was evident. Clips and empty cartridges, tarnished with verdigris, lay on the ground, which, while wet, had been torn up by the hoofs of horses. Hard by the kitchen garden were graves, tagged and numbered. From the oak tree by the kitchen door, in tattered, weather-beaten garments, hung the bodies of two men. The faces, shriveled and defaced, bore no likeness to the faces of men. The roan horse snorted beneath them, and the rider caressed and soothed it and tied it farther away.

Entering the house, he found the interior a wreck. He trod on empty cartridges as he walked from room to room to reconnoiter from the windows. Men had camped and slept everywhere, and on the floor of one room he came upon stains unmistakable where the wounded had been laid down.

Again outside, he led the horse around behind the barn and invaded the orchard. A dozen trees were burdened with ripe apples. He filled his pockets, eating while he picked. Then a thought came to him, and he glanced at the sun, calculating the time of his return to camp. He pulled off his shirt, tying the sleeves and making a bag. This he proceeded to fill with apples.

As he was about to mount his horse, the animal suddenly pricked up its ears. The man, too, listened, and heard, faintly, the thud of hoofs on soft earth. He crept to the corner of the barn and peered out. A dozen mounted men, strung out loosely, approaching from the opposite side of the clearing, were only a matter of a hundred yards or so away. They rode on to the house. Some dismounted, while others remained in the saddle as an earnest that their stay would be short. They seemed to be holding a council, for he could hear them talking excitedly in the detested tongue of the alien invader. The time passed, but they seemed unable to reach a decision. He put the carbine away in its boot, mounted, and waited impatiently, balancing the shirt of apples on the pommel.

He heard footsteps approaching, and drove his spurs so fiercely into the roan as to force a surprised groan from the animal as it leaped forward. At the corner of the barn he saw the intruder, a mere boy of nineteen or twenty for all of his uniform, jump back to escape being run down. At the same moment the roan swerved, and its rider caught a glimpse of the aroused men by the house. Some were springing from their horses, and he could see the rifles going to their shoulders. He passed the kitchen door and the dried corpses swinging in the shade, compelling his foes to run around the front of the house. A rifle cracked, and a second, but he was going fast, leaning forward, low in the saddle, one hand clutching the shirt of apples, the other guiding the horse.

The top bar of the fence was four feet high, but he knew his roan and leaped it at full career to the accompaniment of several scattered shots. Eight hundred yards straight away were the woods, and the roan was covering the distance with mighty strides. Every man was now firing. They were pumping their guns so rapidly that he no longer heard individual shots. A bullet went through his hat, but he was unaware, though he did know when another tore through the apples on the pommel. And he winced and ducked even lower when a third bullet, fired low, struck a stone between his horse's legs and ricochetted off through the air, buzzing and humming like some incredible insect.

The shots died down as the magazines were emptied, until, quickly, there was no more shooting. The young man was elated. Through that astonishing fusillade he had come unscathed. He glanced back. Yes, they had emptied their magazines. He could see several reloading. Others were running back behind the house for their horses. As he looked, two already mounted, came back into view around the corner, riding hard. And at the same moment, he saw the man with the unmistakable ginger beard kneel down on the ground, level his gun, and coolly take his time for the long shot.

The young man threw his spurs into the horse, crouched very low, and swerved in his flight in order to distract the other's aim. And still the shot did not come. With each jump of the horse, the woods sprang nearer. They were only two hundred yards away, and still the shot was delayed.

And then he heard it, the last thing he was to hear, for he was dead ere he hit the ground in the long crashing fall from the saddle. And they, watching at the house, saw him fall, saw his body bounce when it struck the earth, and saw the burst of red-cheeked apples that rolled about him. They laughed at the unexpected eruption of apples, and clapped their hands in applause of the long shot by the man with the ginger beard.

TOLD IN THE
DROOLING WARD

Me? I'm not a drooler. I'm the assistant. I don't know what Miss Jones or Miss Kelsey could do without me. There are fifty-five low-grade droolers in this ward, and how could they ever all be fed if I wasn't around? I like to feed droolers. They don't make trouble. They can't. Something's wrong with most of their legs and arms, and they can't talk. They're very low-grade. I can walk, and talk, and do things. You must be careful with the droolers and not feed them too fast. Then they choke. Miss Jones says I'm an expert. When a new nurse comes I show her how to do it. It's funny watching a new nurse try to feed them. She goes at it so slow and careful that supper time would be around before she finished shoving down their breakfast. Then I show her, because I'm an expert. Dr. Dalrymple says I am, and he ought to know. A drooler can eat twice as fast if you know how to make him.

My name's Tom. I'm twenty-eight years old. Everybody knows me in the institution. This is an institution, you know. It belongs to the State of California and is run by politics. I know. I've been here a long time. Everybody trusts me. I run errands all over the place, when I'm not busy with the droolers. I like droolers. It makes me think how lucky I am that I ain't a drooler.

I like it here in the Home. I don't like the outside. I know. I've been around a bit, and run away, and adopted. Me for the Home, and for the drooling ward best of all. I don't look like a drooler, do I? You can tell the difference soon as you look at me. I'm an assistant, expert assistant. That's going some for a feeb. Feeb? Oh, that's feeble-minded. I thought you knew. We're all feebs in here.

But I'm a high-grade feeb. Dr. Dalrymple says I'm too smart to be in the Home, but I never let on. It's a pretty good place. And I don't throw fits like lots of the feebs. You see that house up there through the trees. The high-grade epilecs all live in it by themselves. They're stuck up because they ain't just ordinary feebs. They call it the club house, and they say they're just as good as anybody outside, only they're sick. I don't like them much. They laugh at me, when they ain't busy throwing fits. But I don't care. I never have to be scared about falling down and busting my head. Sometimes they run around in circles trying to find a place to sit down quick, only they don't. Low-grade epilecs are disgusting, and high-grade epilecs put on airs. I'm glad I ain't an epilec. There ain't anything to them. They just talk big, that's all.

Miss Kelsey says I talk too much. But I talk sense, and that's more than the other feebs do. Dr. Dalrymple says I have the gift of language. I know it. You ought to hear me talk when I'm by myself, or when I've got a drooler to listen. Sometimes I think I'd like to be a politician, only it's too much trouble. They're all great talkers; that's how they hold their jobs.

Nobody's crazy in this institution. They're just feeble in their minds. Let me tell you something funny. There's about a dozen high-grade girls that set the tables in the big dining-room. Sometimes when they're done ahead of time, they all sit down in chairs in a circle and talk. I sneak up to the door and listen, and I nearly die to keep from laughing. Do you want to know what they talk? It's like this. They don't say a word for a long time. And then one says, "Thank God I'm not feeble-minded." And all the rest nod their heads and look pleased. And then nobody says anything for a time. After which the next girl in the circle says, "Thank God I'm not feeble-minded," and they nod their heads all over again. And it goes on around the circle, and they never say anything else. Now they're real feebs, ain't they? I leave it to you. I'm not that kind of a feeb, thank God.

Sometimes I don't think I'm a feeb at all. I play in the band and read music. We're all supposed to be feebs in the band except the leader. He's crazy. We know it, but we never talk about it except amongst ourselves. His job is politics, too, and we don't want him to lose it. I play the drum. They can't get along without me in this institution. I was sick once, so I know. It's a wonder the drooling ward didn't break down while I was in hospital.

I could get out of here if I wanted to. I'm not so feeble as some might think. But I don't let on. I have too good a time. Besides, everything would run down if I went away. I'm afraid some time they'll find out I'm not a feeb and send me out into the world to earn my own living. I know the world, and I don't like it. The Home is fine enough for me.

You see how I grin sometimes. I can't help that. But I can put it on a lot. I'm not bad, though. I look at myself in the glass. My mouth is funny, I know that, and it lops down, and my teeth are bad. You can tell a feeb anywhere by looking at his mouth and teeth. But that doesn't prove I'm a feeb. It's just because I'm lucky that I look like one.

I know a lot. If I told you all I know, you'd be surprised. But when I don't want to know, or when they want me to do something I don't want to do, I just let my mouth lop down and laugh and make foolish noises. I watch the foolish noises made by the low-grades, and I can fool anybody. And I know a lot of foolish noises. Miss Kelsey called me a fool the other day. She was very angry, and that was where I fooled her.

Miss Kelsey asked me once why I don't write a book about feebs. I was telling her what was the matter with little Albert. He's a drooler, you know, and I can always tell the way he twists his left eye what's the matter with him. So I was explaining it to Miss Kelsey, and, because she didn't know, it made her mad. But some day, mebbe, I'll write that book. Only it's so much trouble. Besides, I'd sooner talk.

Do you know what a micro is? It's the kind with the little heads no bigger than your fist. They're usually droolers, and they live a long time. The hydros don't drool. They have the big heads, and they're smarter. But they never grow up. They always die. I never look at one without thinking he's going to die. Sometimes, when I'm feeling lazy, or the nurse is mad at me, I wish I was a drooler with nothing to do and somebody to feed me. But I guess I'd sooner talk and be what I am.

Only yesterday Doctor Dalrymple said to me, "Tom," he said, "I just don't know what I'd do without you." And he ought to know, seeing as he's had the bossing of a thousand feebs for going on two years. Dr. Whatcomb was before him. They get appointed, you know. It's politics. I've seen a whole lot of doctors here in my time. I was here before any of them. I've been in this institution twenty-five years. No, I've got no complaints. The institution couldn't be run better.

It's a snap to be a high-grade feeb. Just look at Doctor Dalrymple. He has troubles. He holds his job by politics. You bet we high-graders talk politics. We know all about it, and it's bad. An institution like this oughtn't to be run on politics. Look at Doctor Dalrymple. He's been here two years and learned a lot. Then politics will come along and throw him out and send a new doctor who don't know anything about feebs.

I've been acquainted with just thousands of nurses in my time. Some of them are nice. But they come and go. Most of the women get married. Sometimes I think I'd like to get married. I spoke to Dr. Whatcomb about it once, but he told me he was very sorry, because feebs ain't allowed to get married. I've been in love. She was a nurse. I won't tell you her name. She had blue eyes, and yellow hair, and a kind voice, and she liked me. She told me so. And she always told me to be a good boy. And I was, too, until afterward, and then I ran away. You see, she went off and got married, and she didn't tell me about it.

I guess being married ain't what it's cracked up to be. Dr. Anglin and his wife used to fight. I've seen them. And once I heard her call him a feeb. Now nobody has a right to call anybody a feeb that ain't. Dr. Anglin got awful mad when she called him that. But he didn't last long. Politics drove him out, and Doctor Mandeville came. He didn't have a wife. I heard him talking one time with the engineer. The engineer and his wife fought like cats and dogs, and that day Doctor Mandeville told him he was damn glad he wasn't tied to no petticoats. A petticoat is a skirt. I knew what he meant, if I was a feeb. But I never let on. You hear lots when you don't let on.

I've seen a lot in my time. Once I was adopted, and went away on the railroad over forty miles to live with a man named Peter Bopp and his wife. They had a ranch. Doctor Anglin said I was strong and bright, and I said I was, too. That was because I wanted to be adopted. And Peter Bopp said he'd give me a good home, and the lawyers fixed up the papers.

But I soon made up my mind that a ranch was no place for me. Mrs. Bopp was scared to death of me and wouldn't let me sleep in the house. They fixed up the woodshed and made me sleep there. I had to get up at four o'clock and feed the horses, and milk cows, and carry the milk to the neighbours. They called it chores, but it kept me going all day. I chopped wood, and cleaned chicken houses, and weeded vegetables, and did most everything on the place. I never had any fun. I hadn't no time.

Let me tell you one thing. I'd sooner feed mush and milk to feebs than milk cows with the frost on the ground. Mrs. Bopp was scared to let me play with her children. And I was scared, too. They used to make faces at me when nobody was looking, and call me "Looney." Everybody called me Looney Tom. And the other boys in the neighbourhood threw rocks at me. You never see anything like that in the Home here. The feebs are better behaved.

Mrs. Bopp used to pinch me and pull my hair when she thought I was too slow, and I only made foolish noises and went slower. She said I'd be the death of her some day. I left the boards off the old well in the pasture, and the pretty new calf fell in and got drowned. Then Peter Bopp said he was going to give me a licking. He did, too. He took a strap halter and went at me. It was awful. I'd never had a licking in my life. They don't do such things in the Home, which is why I say the Home is the place for me.

I know the law, and I knew he had no right to lick me with a strap halter. That was being cruel, and the guardianship papers said he mustn't be cruel. I didn't say anything. I just waited, which shows you what kind of a feeb I am. I waited a long time, and got slower, and made more foolish noises; but he wouldn't send me back to the Home, which was what I wanted. But one day, it was the first of the month, Mrs. Brown gave me three dollars, which was for her milk bill with Peter Bopp. That was in the morning. When I brought the milk in the evening I was to bring back the receipt. But I didn't. I just walked down to the station, bought a ticket like any one, and rode on the train back to the Home. That's the kind of a feeb I am.

Doctor Anglin was gone then, and Doctor Mandeville had his place. I walked right into his office. He didn't know me. "Hello," he said, "this ain't visiting day." "I ain't a visitor," I said. "I'm Tom. I belong here." Then he whistled and showed he was surprised. I told him all about it, and showed him the marks of the strap halter, and he got madder and madder all the time and said he'd attend to Mr. Peter Bopp's case.

And mebbe you think some of them little droolers weren't glad to see me.

I walked right into the ward. There was a new nurse feeding little Albert. "Hold on," I said. "That ain't the way. Don't you see how he's twisting that left eye? Let me show you." Mebbe she thought I was a new doctor, for she just gave me the spoon, and I guess I filled little Albert up with the most comfortable meal he'd had since I went away. Droolers ain't bad when you understand them. I heard Miss Jones tell Miss Kelsey once that I had an amazing gift in handling droolers.

Some day, mebbe, I'm going to talk with Doctor Dalrymple and get him to give me a declaration that I ain't a feeb. Then I'll get him to make me a real assistant in the drooling ward, with forty dollars a month and my board. And then I'll marry Miss Jones and live right on here. And if she won't have me, I'll marry Miss Kelsey or some other nurse. There's lots of them that want to get married. And I won't care if my wife gets mad and calls me a feeb. What's the good? And I guess when one's learned to put up with droolers a wife won't be much worse.

I didn't tell you about when I ran away. I hadn't no idea of such a thing, and it was Charley and Joe who put me up to it. They're high-grade epilecs, you know. I'd been up to Doctor Wilson's office with a message, and was going back to the drooling ward, when I saw Charley and Joe hiding around the corner of the gymnasium and making motions to me. I went over to them.

"Hello," Joe said. "How's droolers?"

"Fine," I said. "Had any fits lately?"

That made them mad, and I was going on, when Joe said, "We're running away. Come on."

"What for?" I said.

"We're going up over the top of the mountain," Joe said.

"And find a gold mine," said Charley. "We don't have fits any more. We're cured."

"All right," I said. And we sneaked around back of the gymnasium and in among the trees. Mebbe we walked along about ten minutes, when I stopped.

"What's the matter?" said Joe.

"Wait," I said. "I got to go back."

"What for?" said Joe.

And I said, "To get little Albert."

And they said I couldn't, and got mad. But I didn't care. I knew they'd wait. You see, I've been here twenty-five years, and I know the back trails that lead up the mountain, and Charley and Joe didn't know those trails. That's why they wanted me to come.

So I went back and got little Albert. He can't walk, or talk, or do anything except drool, and I had to carry him in my arms. We went on past the last hayfield, which was as far as I'd ever gone. Then the woods and brush got so thick, and me not finding any more trail, we followed the cow-path down to a big creek and crawled through the fence which showed where the Home land stopped.

We climbed up the big hill on the other side of the creek. It was all big trees, and no brush, but it was so steep and slippery with dead leaves we could hardly walk. By and by we came to a real bad place. It was forty feet across, and if you slipped you'd fall a thousand feet, or mebbe a hundred. Anyway, you wouldn't fall—just slide. I went across first, carrying little Albert. Joe came next. But Charley got scared right in the middle and sat down.

"I'm going to have a fit," he said.

"No, you're not," said Joe. "Because if you was you wouldn't 'a' sat down. You take all your fits standing."

"This is a different kind of a fit," said Charley, beginning to cry.

He shook and shook, but just because he wanted to he couldn't scare up the least kind of a fit.

Joe got mad and used awful language. But that didn't help none. So I talked soft and kind to Charley. That's the way to handle feebs. If you get mad, they get worse. I know. I'm that way myself. That's why I was almost the death of Mrs. Bopp. She got mad.

It was getting along in the afternoon, and I knew we had to be on our way, so I said to Joe:

"Here, stop your cussing and hold Albert. I'll go back and get him."

And I did, too; but he was so scared and dizzy he crawled along on hands and knees while I helped him. When I got him across and took Albert back in my arms, I heard somebody laugh and looked down. And there was a man and woman on horseback looking up at us. He had a gun on his saddle, and it was her who was laughing.

"Who in hell's that?" said Joe, getting scared. "Somebody to catch us?"

"Shut up your cussing," I said to him. "That is the man who owns this ranch and writes books."

"How do you do, Mr. Endicott," I said down to him.

"Hello," he said. "What are you doing here?"

"We're running away," I said.

And he said, "Good luck. But be sure and get back before dark."

"But this is a real running away," I said.

And then both he and his wife laughed.

"All right," he said. "Good luck just the same. But watch out the bears and mountain lions don't get you when it gets dark."

Then they rode away laughing, pleasant like; but I wished he hadn't said that about the bears and mountain lions.

After we got around the hill, I found a trail, and we went much faster. Charley didn't have any more signs of fits, and began laughing and talking about gold mines. The trouble was with little Albert. He was almost as big as me. You see, all the time I'd been calling him little Albert, he'd been growing up. He was so heavy I couldn't keep up with Joe and Charley. I was all out of breath. So I told them they'd have to take turns in carrying him, which they said they wouldn't. Then I said I'd leave them and they'd get lost, and the mountain lions and bears would eat them. Charley looked like he was going to have a fit right there, and Joe said, "Give him to me." And after that we carried him in turn.

We kept right on up that mountain. I don't think there was any gold mine, but we might 'a' got to the top and found it, if we hadn't lost the trail, and if it hadn't got dark, and if little Albert hadn't tired us all out carrying him. Lots of feebs are scared of the dark, and Joe said he was going to have a fit right there. Only he didn't. I never saw such an unlucky boy. He never could throw a fit when he wanted to. Some of the feebs can throw fits as quick as a wink.

By and by it got real black, and we were hungry, and we didn't have no fire. You see, they don't let feebs carry matches, and all we could do was just shiver. And we'd never thought about being hungry. You see, feebs always have their food ready for them, and that's why it's better to be a feeb than earning your living in the world.

And worse than everything was the quiet. There was only one thing worse, and it was the noises. There was all kinds of noises every once in a while, with quiet spells in between. I reckon they were rabbits, but they made noises in the brush like wild animals—you know, rustle rustle, thump, bump, crackle crackle, just like that. First Charley got a fit, a real one, and Joe threw a terrible one. I don't mind fits in the Home with everybody around. But out in the woods on a dark night is different. You listen to me, and never go hunting gold mines with epilecs, even if they are high-grade.

I never had such an awful night. When Joe and Charley weren't throwing fits they were making believe, and in the darkness the shivers from the cold which I couldn't see seemed like fits, too. And I shivered so hard I thought I was getting fits myself. And little Albert, with nothing to eat, just drooled and drooled. I never seen him as bad as that before. Why, he twisted that left eye of his until it ought to have dropped out. I couldn't see it, but I could tell from the movements he made. And Joe just lay and cussed and cussed, and Charley cried and wished he was back in the Home.

We didn't die, and next morning we went right back the way we'd come. And little Albert got awful heavy. Doctor Wilson was mad as could be, and said I was the worst feeb in the institution, along with Joe and Charley. But Miss Striker, who was a nurse in the drooling ward then, just put her arms around me and cried, she was that happy I'd got back. I thought right there that mebbe I'd marry her. But only a month afterward she got married to the plumber that came up from the city to fix the gutter-pipes of the new hospital. And little Albert never twisted his eye for two days, it was that tired.

Next time I run away I'm going right over that mountain. But I ain't going to take epilecs along. They ain't never cured, and when they get scared or excited they throw fits to beat the band. But I'll take little Albert. Somehow I can't get along without him. And anyway, I ain't going to run away. The drooling ward's a better snap than gold mines, and I hear there's a new nurse coming. Besides, little Albert's bigger than I am now, and I could never carry him over a mountain. And he's growing bigger every day. It's astonishing.

THE MEXICAN

Nobody knew his history—they of the Junta least of all. He was their "little mystery," their "big patriot," and in his way he worked as hard for the coming Mexican Revolution as did they. They were tardy in recognizing this, for not one of the Junta liked him. The day he first drifted into their crowded, busy rooms, they all suspected him of being a spy—one of the bought tools of the Diaz secret service. Too many of the comrades were in civil and military prisons scattered over the United States, and others of them, in irons, were even then being taken across the border to be lined up against adobe walls and shot.

At the first sight the boy did not impress them favorably. Boy he was, not more than eighteen and not over large for his years. He announced that he was Felipe Rivera, and that it was his wish to work for the Revolution. That was all—not a wasted word, no further explanation. He stood waiting. There was no smile on his lips, no geniality in his eyes. Big dashing Paulino Vera felt an inward shudder. Here was something forbidding, terrible, inscrutable. There was something venomous and snakelike in the boy's black eyes. They burned like cold fire, as with a vast, concentrated bitterness. He flashed them from the faces of the conspirators to the typewriter which little Mrs. Sethby was industriously operating. His eyes rested on hers but an instant—she had chanced to look up—and she, too, sensed the nameless something that made her pause. She was compelled to read back in order to regain the swing of the letter she was writing.

Paulino Vera looked questioningly at Arrellano and Ramos, and questioningly they looked back and to each other. The indecision of doubt brooded in their eyes. This slender boy was the Unknown, vested with all the menace of the Unknown. He was unrecognizable, something quite beyond the ken of honest, ordinary revolutionists whose fiercest hatred for Diaz and his tyranny after all was only that of honest and ordinary patriots. Here was something else, they knew not what. But Vera, always the most impulsive, the quickest to act, stepped into the breach.

"Very well," he said coldly. "You say you want to work for the Revolution. Take off your coat. Hang it over there. I will show you—come—where are the buckets and cloths. The floor is dirty. You will begin by scrubbing it, and by scrubbing the floors of the other rooms. The spittoons need to be cleaned. Then there are the windows."

"Is it for the Revolution?" the boy asked.

"It is for the Revolution," Vera answered.

Rivera looked cold suspicion at all of them, then proceeded to take off his coat.

"It is well," he said.

And nothing more. Day after day he came to his work—sweeping, scrubbing, cleaning. He emptied the ashes from the stoves, brought up the coal and kindling, and lighted the fires before the most energetic one of them was at his desk.

"Can I sleep here?" he asked once.

Ah, ha! So that was it—the hand of Diaz showing through! To sleep in the rooms of the Junta meant access to their secrets, to the lists of names, to the addresses of comrades down on Mexican soil. The request was denied, and Rivera never spoke of it again. He slept they knew not where, and ate they knew not where nor how. Once, Arrellano offered him a couple of dollars. Rivera declined the money with a shake of the head. When Vera joined in and tried to press it upon him, he said:

"I am working for the Revolution."

It takes money to raise a modern revolution, and always the Junta was pressed. The members starved and toiled, and the longest day was none too long, and yet there were times when it appeared as if the Revolution stood or fell on no more than the matter of a few dollars. Once, the first time, when the rent of the house was two months behind and the landlord was threatening dispossession, it was Felipe Rivera, the scrub-boy in the poor, cheap clothes, worn and threadbare, who laid sixty dollars in gold on May Sethby's desk. There were other times. Three hundred letters, clicked out on the busy typewriters (appeals for assistance, for sanctions from the organized labor groups, requests for square news deals to the editors of newspapers, protests against the high-handed treatment of revolutionists by the United States courts), lay unmailed, awaiting postage. Vera's watch had disappeared—the old-fashioned gold repeater that had been his father's. Likewise had gone the plain gold band from May Sethby's third finger. Things were desperate. Ramos and Arrellano pulled their long mustaches in despair.

The letters must go off, and the Post Office allowed no credit to purchasers of stamps. Then it was that Rivera put on his hat and went out. When he came back he laid a thousand two-cent stamps on May Sethby's desk.

"I wonder if it is the cursed gold of Diaz?" said Vera to the comrades.

They elevated their brows and could not decide. And Felipe Rivera, the scrubber for the Revolution, continued, as occasion arose, to lay down gold and silver for the Junta's use.

And still they could not bring themselves to like him. They did not know him. His ways were not theirs. He gave no confidences. He repelled all probing. Youth that he was, they could never nerve themselves to dare to question him.

"A great and lonely spirit, perhaps, I do not know, I do not know," Arrellano said helplessly.

"He is not human," said Ramos.

"His soul has been seared," said May Sethby. "Light and laughter have been burned out of him. He is like one dead, and yet he is fearfully alive."

"He has been through hell," said Vera. "No man could look like that who has not been through hell—and he is only a boy."

Yet they could not like him. He never talked, never inquired, never suggested. He would stand listening, expressionless, a thing dead, save for his eyes, coldly burning, while their talk of the Revolution ran high and warm. From face to face and speaker to speaker his eyes would turn, boring like gimlets of incandescent ice, disconcerting and perturbing.

"He is no spy," Vera confided to May Sethby. "He is a patriot—mark me, the greatest patriot of us all. I know it, I feel it, here in my heart and head I feel it. But him I know not at all."

"He has a bad temper," said May Sethby.

"I know," said Vera, with a shudder. "He has looked at me with those eyes of his. They do not love; they threaten; they are savage as a wild tiger's. I know, if I should prove unfaithful to the Cause, that he would kill me. He has no heart. He is pitiless as steel, keen and cold as frost. He is like moonshine in a winter night when a man freezes to death on some lonely mountain top. I am not afraid of Diaz and all his killers; but this boy, of him am I afraid. I tell you true. I am afraid. He is the breath of death."

Yet Vera it was who persuaded the others to give the first trust to Rivera. The line of communication between Los Angeles and Lower California had broken down. Three of the comrades had dug their own graves and been shot into them. Two more were United States prisoners in Los Angeles. Juan Alvarado, the Federal commander, was a monster.

All their plans did he checkmate. They could no longer gain access to the active revolutionists, and the incipient ones, in Lower California.

Young Rivera was given his instructions and dispatched south. When he returned, the line of communication was reëstablished, and Juan Alvarado was dead. He had been found in bed, a knife hilt-deep in his breast. This had exceeded Rivera's instructions, but they of the Junta knew the times of his movements. They did not ask him. He said nothing. But they looked at one another and conjectured.

"I have told you," said Vera. "Diaz has more to fear from this youth than from any man. He is implacable. He is the hand of God."

The bad temper, mentioned by May Sethby, and sensed by them all, was evidenced by physical proofs. Now he appeared with a cut lip, a blackened cheek, or a swollen ear. It was patent that he brawled, somewhere in that outside world where he ate and slept, gained money, and moved in ways unknown to them. As the time passed, he had come to set type for the little revolutionary sheet they published weekly. There were occasions when he was unable to set type, when his knuckles were bruised and battered, when his thumbs were injured and helpless, when one arm or the other hung wearily at his side while his face was drawn with unspoken pain.

"A wastrel," said Arrellano.

"A frequenter of low places," said Ramos.

"But where does he get the money?" Vera demanded. "Only to-day, just now, have I learned that he paid the bill for white paper—one hundred and forty dollars."

"There are his absences," said May Sethby. "He never explains them."

"We should set a spy upon him," Ramos propounded.

"I should not care to be that spy," said Vera. "I fear you would never see me again, save to bury me. He has a terrible passion. Not even God would he permit to stand between him and the way of his passion."

"I feel like a child before him," Ramos confessed.

"To me he is power—he is the primitive, the wild wolf,—the striking rattlesnake, the stinging centipede," said Arrellano.

"He is the Revolution incarnate," said Vera. "He is the flame and the spirit of it, the insatiable cry for vengeance that makes no cry but that slays noiselessly. He is a destroying angel moving through the still watches of the night."

"I could weep over him," said May Sethby. "He knows nobody. He hates all people. Us he tolerates, for we are the way of his desire. He is alone . . . lonely." Her voice broke in a half sob and there was dimness in her eyes.

Rivera's ways and times were truly mysterious. There were periods when they did not see him for a week at a time. Once, he was away a month. These occasions were always capped by his return, when, without advertisement or speech, he laid gold coins on May Sethby's desk. Again, for days and weeks, he spent all his time with the Junta. And yet again, for irregular periods, he would disappear through the heart of each day, from early morning until late afternoon. At such times he came early and remained late. Arrellano had found him at midnight, setting type with fresh swollen knuckles, or mayhap it was his lip, new-split, that still bled.

· II ·

The time of the crisis approached. Whether or not the Revolution would be depended upon the Junta, and the Junta was hard-pressed. The need for money was greater than ever before, while money was harder to get. Patriots had given their last cent and now could give no more. Section gang laborers—fugitive peons from Mexico—were contributing half their scanty wages. But more than that was needed. The heart-breaking, conspiring, undermining toil of years approached fruition. The time was ripe. The Revolution hung on the balance. One shove more, one last heroic effort, and it would tremble across the scales to victory. They knew their Mexico. Once started, the Revolution would take care of itself. The whole Diaz machine would go down like a house of cards. The border was ready to rise. One Yankee, with a hundred I. W. W. men, waited the word to cross over the border and begin the conquest of Lower California. But he needed guns. And clear across to the Atlantic, the Junta in touch with them all and all of them needing guns, mere adventurers, soldiers of fortune, bandits, disgruntled American union men, socialists, anarchists, rough-necks, Mexican exiles, peons escaped from bondage, whipped miners from the bull-pens of Cœur d'Alene and Colorado who desired only the more vindictively to fight—all the flot-sam and jetsam of wild spirits from the madly complicated modern world. And it was guns and ammunition, ammunition and guns—the unceasing and eternal cry.

Fling this heterogeneous, bankrupt, vindictive mass across the border, and the Revolution was on. The custom house, the northern ports of entry, would be captured. Diaz could not resist. He dared not throw the weight of his armies against them, for he must hold the south. And through the south the flame would spread despite. The people would rise. The defenses of city after city would crumple up. State after state would totter down. And at last, from every side, the victorious armies of the Revolution would close in on the City of Mexico itself, Diaz's last stronghold.

But the money. They had the men, impatient and urgent, who would use the guns. They knew the traders who would sell and deliver the guns. But to culture the Revolution thus far had exhausted the Junta. The last dollar had been spent, the last resource and the last starving patriot milked dry, and the great adventure still trembled on the scales. Guns and ammunition! The ragged battalions must be armed. But how? Ramos lamented his confiscated estates. Arrellano wailed the spendthriftness of his youth. May Sethby wondered if it would have been different had they of the Junta been more economical in the past.

"To think that the freedom of Mexico should stand or fall on a few paltry thousands of dollars," said Paulino Vera.

Despair was in all their faces. José Amarillo, their last hope, a recent convert, who had promised money, had been apprehended at his hacienda in Chihuahua and shot against his own stable wall. The news had just come through.

Rivera, on his knees, scrubbing, looked up, with suspended brush, his bare arms flecked with soapy, dirty water.

"Will five thousand do it?" he asked.

They looked their amazement. Vera nodded and swallowed. He could not speak, but he was on the instant invested with a vast faith.

"Order the guns," Rivera said, and thereupon was guilty of the longest flow of words they had ever heard him utter. "The time is short. In three weeks I shall bring you the five thousand. It is well. The weather will be warmer for those who fight. Also, it is the best I can do."

Vera fought his faith. It was incredible. Too many fond hopes had been shattered since he had begun to play the revolution game. He believed this threadbare scrubber of the Revolution, and yet he dared not believe.

"You are crazy," he said.

"In three weeks," said Rivera. "Order the guns."

He got up, rolled down his sleeves, and put on his coat.

"Order the guns," he said. "I am going now."

· III ·

After hurrying and scurrying, much telephoning and bad language, a night session was held in Kelly's office. Kelly was rushed with business; also, he was unlucky. He had brought Danny Ward out from New York, arranged the fight for him with Billy Carthey, the date was three weeks away, and for two days now, carefully concealed from the sporting writers, Carthey had been lying up, badly injured. There was no one to take his place. Kelly had been burning the wires East to every eligible lightweight, but they were tied up with dates and contracts. And now hope had revived, though faintly.

"You've got a hell of a nerve," Kelly addressed Rivera, after one look, as soon as they got together.

Hate that was malignant was in Rivera's eyes, but his face remained impassive.

"I can lick Ward," was all he said.

"How do you know? Ever see him fight?"

Rivera shook his head.

"He can beat you up with one hand and both eyes closed."

Rivera shrugged his shoulders.

"Haven't you got anything to say?" the fight promoter snarled.

"I can lick him."

"Who'd you ever fight, anyway?" Michael Kelly demanded. Michael was the promoter's brother, and ran the Yellowstone pool rooms where he made goodly sums on the fight game.

Rivera favored him with a bitter, unanswering stare.

The promoter's secretary, a distinctively sporty young man, sneered audibly.

"Well, you know Roberts," Kelly broke the hostile silence. "He ought to be here. I've sent for him. Sit down and wait, though from the looks of you, you haven't got a chance. I can't throw the public down with a bum fight. Ringside seats are selling at fifteen dollars, you know that."

When Roberts arrived, it was patent that he was mildly drunk. He was a tall, lean, slack-jointed individual, and his walk, like his talk, was a smooth and languid drawl.

Kelly went straight to the point.

"Look here, Roberts, you've been braggin' you discovered this little Mexican. You know Carthey's broke his arm. Well, this little yellow streak has the gall to blow in to-day and say he'll take Carthey's place. What about it?"

"It's all right, Kelly," came the slow response. "He can put up a fight."

"I suppose you'll be sayin' next that he can lick Ward," Kelly snapped.

Roberts considered judicially.

"No, I won't say that. Ward's a top-notcher and a ring general. But he can't hashhouse Rivera in short order. I know Rivera. Nobody can get his goat. He ain't got a goat that I could ever discover. And he's a two-handed fighter. He can throw in the sleep-makers from any position."

"Never mind that. What kind of a show can he put up? You've been conditioning and training fighters all your life. I take off my hat to your judgment. Can he give the public a run for its money?"

"He sure can, and he'll worry Ward a mighty heap on top of it. You don't know that boy. I do. I discovered him. He ain't got a goat. He's a devil. He's a wizzy-wooz if anybody should ask you. He'll make Ward sit up with a show of local talent that'll make the rest of you sit up. I won't say he'll lick Ward, but he'll put up such a show that you'll all know he's a comer."

"All right." Kelly turned to his secretary. "Ring up Ward. I warned him to show up if I thought it worth while. He's right across at the Yellowstone, throwin' chests and doing the popular." Kelly turned back to the conditioner. "Have a drink?"

Roberts sipped his highball and unburdened himself.

"Never told you how I discovered the little cuss. It was a couple of years ago he showed up out at the quarters. I was getting Prayne ready for his fight with Delaney. Prayne's wicked. He ain't got a tickle of mercy in his make-up. He'd chopped up his pardner's something cruel, and I couldn't find a willing boy that'd work with him. I'd noticed this little starved Mexican kid hanging around, and I was desperate. So I grabbed him, slammed on the gloves, and put him in. He was tougher'n rawhide, but weak. And he didn't know the first letter in the alphabet of boxing. Prayne chopped him to ribbons. But he hung on for two sickening rounds, when he fainted. Starvation, that was all. Battered? You couldn't have recognized him. I gave him half a dollar and a square meal. You oughta seen him wolf it down. He hadn't had a bite for a couple of days. That's the end of him, thinks I. But next day he showed up, stiff an' sore, ready for another half and a square meal. And he done better as time went by. Just a born fighter, and tough beyond belief. He has n't a heart. He's a piece of ice. And he never talked eleven words in a string since I know him. He saws wood and does his work."

"I've seen 'm," the secretary said. "He's worked a lot for you."

"All the big little fellows has tried out on him," Roberts answered. "And he's learned from 'em. I've seen some of them he could lick. But his heart wasn't in it. I reckoned he never liked the game. He seemed to act that way."

"He's been fighting some before the little clubs the last few months," Kelly said.

"Sure. But I don't know what struck 'm. All of a sudden his heart got into it. He just went out like a streak and cleaned up all the little local fellows. Seemed to want the money, and he's won a bit, though his clothes don't look it. He's peculiar. Nobody knows his business. Nobody knows how he spends his time. Even when he's on the job, he plumb up and disappears most of each day soon as his work is done. Sometimes he just blows away for weeks at a time. But he don't take advice. There's a fortune in it for the fellow that gets the job of managin' him, only he won't consider it. And you watch him hold out for the cash money when you get down to terms."

It was at this stage that Danny Ward arrived. Quite a party it was. His manager and trainer were with him, and he breezed in like a gusty draught of geniality, good-nature, and all-conqueringness. Greetings flew about, a joke here, a retort there, a smile or a laugh for everybody. Yet it was his way, and only partly sincere. He was a good actor, and he had found geniality a most valuable asset in the game of getting on in the world. But down underneath he was the deliberate, cold-blooded fighter and business man. The rest was a mask. Those who knew him or trafficked with him said that when it came to brass tacks he was Danny-on-the-Spot. He was invariably present at all business discussions, and it was urged by some that his manager was a blind whose only function was to serve as Danny's mouth-piece.

Rivera's way was different. Indian blood, as well as Spanish, was in his veins, and he sat back in a corner, silent, immobile, only his black eyes passing from face to face and noting everything.

"So that's the guy," Danny said, running an appraising eye over his proposed antagonist. "How de do, old chap."

Rivera's eyes burned venomously, but he made no sign of acknowledgment. He disliked all Gringos, but this Gringo he hated with an immediacy that was unusual even in him.

"Gawd!" Danny protested facetiously to the promoter. "You ain't expectin' me to fight a deef mute." When the laughter subsided, he made another hit. "Los Angeles must be on the dink when this is the best you can scare up. What kindergarten did you get 'm from?"

"He's a good little boy, Danny, take it from me," Roberts defended. "Not as easy as he looks."

"And half the house is sold already," Kelly pleaded. "You'll have to take 'm on, Danny. It's the best we can do."

Danny ran another careless and unflattering glance over Rivera and sighed.

"I gotta be easy with 'm, I guess. If only he don't blow up."

Roberts snorted.

"You gotta be careful," Danny's manager warned. "No taking chances with a dub that's likely to sneak a lucky one across."

"Oh, I'll be careful all right, all right," Danny smiled. "I'll get 'm at the start an' nurse 'm along for the dear public's sake. What d' ye say to fifteen rounds, Kelly— An' then the hay for him?"

"That'll do," was the answer. "As long as you make it realistic."

"Then let's get down to biz." Danny paused and calculated. "Of course, sixty-five per cent. of gate receipts, same as with Carthey. But the split'll be different. Eighty will just about suit me." And to his manager, "That right?"

The manager nodded.

"Here, you, did you get that?" Kelly asked Rivera.

Rivera shook his head.

"Well, it's this way," Kelly exposited. "The purse'll be sixty-five per cent. of the gate receipts. You're a dub, and an unknown. You and Danny split, twenty per cent. goin' to you, an' eighty to Danny. That's fair, isn't it, Roberts?"

"Very fair, Rivera," Roberts agreed. "You see, you ain't got a reputation yet."

"What will sixty-five per cent. of the gate receipts be?" Rivera demanded.

"Oh, maybe five thousand, maybe as high as eight thousand," Danny broke in to explain. "Something like that. Your share'll come to something like a thousand or sixteen hundred. Pretty good for takin' a licking from a guy with my reputation. What d' ye say?"

Then Rivera took their breaths away.

"Winner takes all," he said with finality.

A dead silence prevailed.

"It's like candy from a baby," Danny's manager proclaimed.

Danny shook his head.

"I've been in the game too long," he explained. "I'm not casting reflections on the referee, or the present company. I'm not sayin' nothing about book-makers an' frame-ups that sometimes happen. But what I do say is that it's poor business for a fighter like me. I play safe. There's no tellin'. Mebbe I break my arm, eh? Or some guy slips me a bunch of dope?" He shook his head solemnly. "Win or lose, eighty is my split. What d' ye say, Mexican?"

Rivera shook his head.

Danny exploded. He was getting down to brass tacks now.

"Why, you dirty little greaser! I've a mind to knock your block off right now."

Roberts drawled his body to interposition between hostilities.

"Winner takes all," Rivera repeated sullenly.

"Why do you stand out that way?" Danny asked.

"I can lick you," was the straight answer.

Danny half started to take off his coat. But, as his manager knew, it was a grand stand play. The coat did not come off, and Danny allowed himself to be placated by the group. Everybody sympathized with him. Rivera stood alone.

"Look here, you little fool," Kelly took up the argument. "You're nobody. We know what you've been doing the last few months—putting away little local fighters. But Danny is class. His next fight after this will be for the championship. And you're unknown. Nobody ever heard of you out of Los Angeles."

"They will," Rivera answered with a shrug, "after this fight."

"You think for a second you can lick me?" Danny blurted in.

Rivera nodded.

"Oh, come; listen to reason," Kelly pleaded. "Think of the advertising."

"I want the money," was Rivera's answer.

"You couldn't win from me in a thousand years," Danny assured him.

"Then what are you holding out for?" Rivera countered. "If the money's that easy, why don't you go after it?"

"I will, so help me!" Danny cried with abrupt conviction. "I'll beat you to death in the ring, my boy—you monkeyin' with me this way. Make out the articles, Kelly. Winner take all. Play it up in the sportin' columns. Tell 'em it's a grudge fight. I'll show this fresh kid a few."

Kelly's secretary had begun to write, when Danny interrupted.

"Hold on!" He turned to Rivera. "Weights?"

"Ringside," came the answer.

"Not on your life, Fresh Kid. If winner takes all, we weigh in at ten A.M."

"And winner takes all?" Rivera queried.

Danny nodded. That settled it. He would enter the ring in his full ripeness of strength.

"Weigh in at ten," Rivera said.

The secretary's pen went on scratching.

"It means five pounds," Roberts complained to Rivera. "You've given too much away. You've thrown the fight right there. Danny'll be as strong as a bull. You're a fool. He'll lick you sure. You ain't got the chance of a dew-drop in hell."

Rivera's answer was a calculated look of hatred. Even this Gringo he despised, and him had he found the whitest Gringo of them all.

·IV·

Barely noticed was Rivera as he entered the ring. Only a very slight and very scattering ripple of half-hearted hand-clapping greeted him. The house did not believe in him. He was the lamb led to slaughter at the hands of the great Danny. Besides, the house was disappointed. It had expected a rushing battle between Danny Ward and Billy Carthey, and here it must put up with this poor little tyro. Still further, it had manifested its disapproval of the change by betting two, and even three, to one on Danny. And where a betting audience's money is, there is its heart.

The Mexican boy sat down in his corner and waited. The slow minutes lagged by. Danny was making him wait. It was an old trick, but ever it worked on the young, new fighters. They grew frightened, sitting thus and facing their own apprehensions and a callous, tobacco-smoking audience. But for once the trick failed. Roberts was right. Rivera had no goat. He, who was more delicately coördinated, more finely nerved and strung than any of them, had no nerves of this sort. The atmosphere of fore-doomed defeat in his own corner had no effect on him. His handlers were Gringos and strangers. Also they were scrubs—the dirty driftage of the fight game, without honor, without efficiency. And they were chilled, as well, with certitude that theirs was the losing corner.

"Now you gotta be careful," Spider Hagerty warned him. Spider was his chief second. "Make it last as long as you can—them's my instructions from Kelly. If you don't, the papers'll call it another bum fight and give the game a bigger black eye in Los Angeles."

All of which was not encouraging. But Rivera took no notice. He despised prize fighting. It was the hated game of the hated Gringo. He had taken up with it, as a chopping block for others in the training quarters, solely because he was starving. The fact that he was marvelously made for it, had meant nothing. He hated it. Not until he had come in to the Junta, had he fought for money, and he had found the money easy. Not first among the sons of men had he been to find himself successful at a despised vocation.

He did not analyze. He merely knew that he must win this fight. There could be no other outcome. For behind him, nerving him to this belief, were profounder forces than any the crowded house dreamed. Danny Ward fought for money, and for the easy ways of life that money would bring. But the things Rivera fought for burned in his brain—blazing and terrible visions, that, with eyes wide open, sitting lonely in the corner of the ring and waiting for his tricky antagonist, he saw as clearly as he had lived them.

He saw the white-walled, water-power factories of Rio Blanco. He saw the six thousand workers, starved and wan, and the little children, seven and eight years of age, who toiled long shifts for ten cents a day. He saw the perambulating corpses, the ghastly death's heads of men who labored in the dye-rooms. He remembered that he had heard his father call the dye-rooms the "suicide-holes," where a year was death. He saw the little patio, and his mother cooking and moiling at crude housekeeping and finding time to caress and love him. And his father he saw, large, big-moustached and deep-chested, kindly above all men, who loved all men and whose heart was so large that there was love to overflowing still left for the mother and the little muchacho playing in the corner of the patio. In those days his name had not been Felipe Rivera. It had been Fernandez, his father's and mother's name. Him had they called Juan. Later, he had changed it himself, for he had found the name of Fernandez hated by prefects of police, *jefes politicos,* and *rurales.*

Big, hearty Joaquin Fernandez! A large place he occupied in Rivera's visions. He had not understood at the time, but looking back he could understand. He could see him setting type in the little printery, or scribbling endless hasty, nervous lines on the much-cluttered desk. And he could see the strange evenings, when workmen, coming secretly in the dark like men who did ill deeds, met with his father and talked long hours where he, the muchacho, lay not always asleep in the corner.

As from a remote distance he could hear Spider Hagerty saying to him: "No layin' down at the start. Them's instructions. Take a beatin' an' earn your dough."

Ten minutes had passed, and he still sat in his corner. There were no signs of Danny, who was evidently playing the trick to the limit.

But more visions burned before the eye of Rivera's memory. The strike, or, rather, the lockout, because the workers of Rio Blanco had helped their striking brothers of Puebla. The hunger, the expeditions in the hills for berries, the roots and herbs that all ate and that twisted and pained the stomachs of all of them. And then, the nightmare; the waste of ground before the company's store; the thousands of starving workers; General Rosalio Martinez and the soldiers of Porfirio Diaz; and the death-spitting rifles that seemed never to cease spitting, while the workers' wrongs were washed and washed again in their own blood. And that night! He saw the flat cars, piled high with the bodies of the slain, consigned to Vera Cruz, food for the sharks of the bay. Again he crawled over the grisly heaps, seeking and finding, stripped and mangled, his father and his mother. His mother he especially remembered —only her face projecting, her body burdened by the weight of dozens of bodies. Again the rifles of the soldiers of Porfirio Diaz cracked, and again he dropped to the ground and slunk away like some hunted coyote of the hills.

To his ears came a great roar, as of the sea, and he saw Danny Ward, leading his retinue of trainers and seconds, coming down the center aisle. The house was in wild uproar for the popular hero who was bound to win. Everybody proclaimed him. Everybody was for him. Even Rivera's own seconds warmed to something akin to cheerfulness when Danny ducked jauntily through the ropes and entered the ring. His face continually spread to an unending succession of smiles, and when Danny smiled he smiled in every feature, even to the laughter-wrinkles of the corners of the eyes and into the depths of the eyes themselves. Never was there so genial a fighter. His face was a running advertisement of good feeling, of good fellowship. He knew everybody. He joked, and laughed, and greeted his friends through the ropes. Those farther away, unable to suppress their admiration, cried loudly: "Oh, you Danny!" It was a joyous ovation of affection that lasted a full five minutes.

Rivera was disregarded. For all that the audience noticed, he did not exist. Spider Hagerty's bloated face bent down close to his.

"No gettin' scared," the Spider warned. "An' remember instructions. You gotta last. No layin' down. If you lay down, we got instructions to beat you up in the dressing rooms. Savve? You just gotta fight."

The house began to applaud. Danny was crossing the ring to him. Danny bent over, caught Rivera's right hand in both his own and shook it with impulsive heartiness. Danny's smile-wreathed face was close to his. The audience yelled its appreciation of Danny's display of sporting spirit. He was greeting his opponent with the fondness of a brother. Danny's lips moved, and the audience, interpreting the unheard words to be those of a kindly-natured sport, yelled again. Only Rivera heard the low words.

"You little Mexican rat," hissed from between Danny's gaily smiling lips, "I'll fetch the yellow outa you."

Rivera made no move. He did not rise. He merely hated with his eyes.

"Get up, you dog!" some man yelled through the ropes from behind.

The crowd began to hiss and boo him for his unsportsmanlike conduct, but he sat unmoved. Another great outburst of applause was Danny's as he walked back across the ring.

When Danny stripped, there was ohs! and ahs! of delight. His body was perfect, alive with easy suppleness and health and strength. The skin was white as a woman's, and as smooth. All grace, and resilience, and power resided therein. He had proved it in scores of battles. His photographs were in all the physical culture magazines.

A groan went up as Spider Hagerty peeled Rivera's sweater over his head. His body seemed leaner, because of the swarthiness of the skin. He had muscles, but they made no display like his opponent's. What the audience neglected to see was the deep chest. Nor could it guess the toughness of the fiber of the flesh, the instantaneousness of the cell explosions of the muscles, the fineness of the nerves that wired every part of him into a splendid fighting mechanism. All the audience saw was a brown-skinned boy of eighteen with what seemed the body of a boy. With Danny it was different. Danny was a man of twenty-four, and his body was a man's body. The contrast was still more striking as they stood together in the center of the ring receiving the referee's last instructions.

Rivera noticed Roberts sitting directly behind the newspaper men. He was drunker than usual, and his speech was correspondingly slower.

"Take it easy, Rivera," Roberts drawled. "He can't kill you, remember that. He'll rush you at the go-off, but don't get rattled. You just cover up, and stall, and clinch. He can't hurt you much. Just make believe to yourself that he's choppin' out on you at the trainin' quarters."

Rivera made no sign that he had heard.

"Sullen little devil," Roberts muttered to the man next to him. "He always was that way."

But Rivera forgot to look his usual hatred. A vision of countless rifles blinded his eyes. Every face in the audience, far as he could see, to the high dollar-seats, was transformed into a rifle. And he saw the long Mexican border arid and sun-washed and aching, and along it he saw the ragged bands that delayed only for the guns.

Back in his corner he waited, standing up. His seconds had crawled out through the ropes, taking the canvas stool with them. Diagonally across the squared ring, Danny faced him. The gong struck, and the battle was on. The audience howled its delight. Never had it seen a battle open more convincingly. The papers were right. It was a grudge fight. Three-quarters of the distance Danny covered in the rush to get together, his intention to eat up the Mexican lad plainly advertised. He assailed with not one blow, nor two, nor a dozen. He was a gyroscope of blows, a whirlwind of destruction. Rivera was nowhere. He was overwhelmed, buried beneath avalanches of punches delivered from every angle and position by a past master in the art. He was overborne, swept back against the ropes, separated by the referee, and swept back against the ropes again.

It was not a fight. It was a slaughter, a massacre. Any audience, save a prize fighting one, would have exhausted its emotions in that first minute. Danny was certainly showing what he could do—a splendid exhibition. Such was the certainty of the audience, as well as its excitement and favoritism, that it failed to take notice that the Mexican still stayed on his feet. It forgot Rivera. It rarely saw him, so closely was he enveloped in Danny's man-eating attack. A minute of this went by, and two minutes. Then, in a separation, it caught a clear glimpse of the Mexican. His lip was cut, his nose was bleeding. As he turned and staggered into a clinch, the welts of oozing blood, from his contacts with the ropes, showed in red bars across his back. But what the audience did not notice was that his chest was not heaving and that his eyes were coldly burning as ever. Too many aspiring champions, in the cruel welter of the training camps, had practiced this man-eating attack on him. He had learned to live through for a compensation of from half a dollar a go up to fifteen dollars a week—a hard school, and he was schooled hard.

Then happened the amazing thing. The whirling, blurring mix-up ceased suddenly. Rivera stood alone. Danny, the redoubtable Danny, lay on his back. His body quivered as consciousness strove to return to it. He had not staggered and sunk down, nor had he gone over in a long slumping fall. The right hook of Rivera had dropped him in midair with the abruptness of death. The referee shoved Rivera back with one hand, and stood over the fallen gladiator counting the seconds. It is the custom of prizefighting audiences to cheer a clean knock-down blow. But this audience did not cheer. The thing had been too unexpected. It watched the toll of the seconds in tense silence, and through this silence the voice of Roberts rose exultantly:

"I told you he was a two-handed fighter!"

By the fifth second, Danny was rolling over on his face, and when seven was counted, he rested on one knee, ready to rise after the count of nine and before the count of ten. If his knee still touched the floor at "ten," he was considered "down," and also "out." The instant his knee left the floor, he was considered "up," and in that instant it was Rivera's right to try and put him down again. Rivera took no chances. The moment that knee left the floor he would strike again. He circled around, but the referee circled in between, and Rivera knew that the seconds he counted were very slow. All Gringos were against him, even the referee.

At "nine" the referee gave Rivera a sharp thrust back. It was unfair, but it enabled Danny to rise, the smile back on his lips. Doubled partly over, with arms wrapped about face and abdomen, he cleverly stumbled into a clinch. By all the rules of the game the referee should have broken it, but he did not, and Danny clung on like a surf-battered barnacle and moment by moment recuperated. The last minute of the round was going fast. If he could live to the end, he would have a full minute in his corner to revive. And live to the end he did, smiling through all desperateness and extremity.

"The smile that won't come off!" somebody yelled, and the audience laughed loudly in its relief.

"The kick that Greaser's got is something God-awful," Danny gasped in his corner to his adviser while his handlers worked frantically over him.

The second and third rounds were tame. Danny, a tricky and consummate ring general, stalled and blocked and held on, devoting himself to recovering from that dazing first-round blow. In the fourth round he was himself again. Jarred and shaken, nevertheless his good condition had enabled him to regain his vigor. But he tried no man-eating tactics. The Mexican had proved a tartar. Instead, he brought to bear his best fighting powers. In tricks and skill and experience he was the master, and though he could land nothing vital, he proceeded scientifically to chop and wear down his opponent. He landed three blows to Rivera's one, but they were punishing blows only, and not deadly. It was the sum of many of them that constituted deadliness. He was respectful of this two-handed dub with the amazing short-arm kicks in both his fists.

In defense, Rivera developed a disconcerting straight-left. Again and again, attack after attack he straight-lefted away from him with accumulated damage to Danny's mouth and nose. But Danny was protean. That was why he was the coming champion. He could change from style to style of fighting at will. He now devoted himself to infighting. In this he was particularly wicked, and it enabled him to avoid the other's straight-left. Here he set the house wild repeatedly, capping it with a marvelous lock-break and lift of an inside upper-cut that raised the Mexican in the air and dropped him to the mat. Rivera rested on one knee, making the most of the count, and in the soul of him he knew the referee was counting short seconds on him.

Again, in the seventh, Danny achieved the diabolical inside uppercut. He succeeded only in staggering Rivera, but, in the ensuing moment of defenseless helplessness, he smashed him with another blow through the ropes. Rivera's body bounced on the heads of the newspaper men below, and they boosted him back to the edge of the platform outside the ropes. Here he rested on one knee, while the referee raced off the seconds. Inside the ropes, through which he must duck to enter the ring,

Danny waited for him. Nor did the referee intervene or thrust Danny back.

The house was beside itself with delight.

"Kill 'm, Danny, kill 'm!" was the cry.

Scores of voices took it up until it was like a war-chant of wolves.

Danny did his best, but Rivera, at the count of eight, instead of nine, came unexpectedly through the ropes and safely into a clinch. Now the referee worked, tearing him away so that he could be hit, giving Danny every advantage that an unfair referee can give.

But Rivera lived, and the daze cleared from his brain. It was all of a piece. They were the hated Gringos and they were all unfair. And in the worst of it visions continued to flash and sparkle in his brain—long lines of railroad track that simmered across the desert; *rurales* and American constables; prisons and calabooses; tramps at water tanks—all the squalid and painful panorama of his odyssey after Rio Blanca and the strike. And, resplendent and glorious, he saw the great, red Revolution sweeping across his land. The guns were there before him. Every hated face was a gun. It was for the guns he fought. He was the guns. He was the Revolution. He fought for all Mexico.

The audience began to grow incensed with Rivera. Why didn't he take the licking that was appointed him? Of course he was going to be licked, but why should he be so obstinate about it? Very few were interested in him, and they were the certain, definite percentage of a gambling crowd that plays long shots. Believing Danny to be the winner, nevertheless they had put their money on the Mexican at four to ten and one to three. More than a trifle was up on the point of how many rounds Rivera could last. Wild money had appeared at the ringside proclaiming that he could not last seven rounds, or even six. The winners of this, now that their cash risk was happily settled, had joined in cheering on the favorite.

Rivera refused to be licked. Through the eighth round his opponent strove vainly to repeat the uppercut. In the ninth, Rivera stunned the house again. In the midst of a clinch he broke the lock with a quick, lithe movement, and in the narrow space between their bodies his right lifted from the waist. Danny went to the floor and took the safety of the count. The crowd was appalled. He was being bested at his own game. His famous right-uppercut had been worked back on him. Rivera made no attempt to catch him as he arose at "nine." The referee was openly blocking that play, though he stood clear when the situation was reversed and it was Rivera who desired to rise.

Twice in the tenth, Rivera put through the right-uppercut, lifted from waist to opponent's chin. Danny grew desperate. The smile never left his face, but he went back to his man-eating rushes. Whirlwind as he would, he could not damage Rivera, while Rivera, through the blur and whirl, dropped him to the mat three times in succession. Danny did not recuperate so quickly now, and by the eleventh round he was in a serious way. But from then till the fourteenth he put up the gamest exhibition of his career. He stalled and blocked, fought parsimoniously, and strove to gather strength. Also, he fought as foully as a successful fighter knows how. Every trick and device he employed, butting in the clinches with the seeming of accident, pinioning Rivera's glove between arm and body, heeling his glove on Rivera's mouth to clog his breathing. Often, in the clinches, through his cut and smiling lips he snarled insults unspeakable and vile in Rivera's ear. Everybody, from the referee to the house, was with Danny and was helping Danny. And they knew what he had in mind. Bested by this surprise-box of an unknown, he was pinning all on a single punch. He offered himself for punishment, fished, and feinted, and drew, for that one opening that would enable him to whip a blow through with all his strength and turn the tide. As another and greater fighter had done before him, he might do—a right and left, to solar plexus and across the jaw. He could do it, for he was noted for the strength of punch that remained in his arms as long as he could keep his feet.

Rivera's seconds were not half-caring for him in the intervals between rounds. Their towels made a showing, but drove little air into his panting lungs. Spider Hagerty talked advice to him, but Rivera knew it was wrong advice. Everybody was against him. He was surrounded by treachery. In the fourteenth round he put Danny down again, and himself stood resting, hands dropped at side, while the referee counted. In the other corner Rivera had been noting suspicious whisperings. He saw Michael Kelly make his way to Roberts and bend and whisper. Rivera's ears were a cat's, desert-trained, and he caught snatches of what was said. He wanted to hear more, and when his opponent arose he maneuvered the fight into a clinch over against the ropes.

"Got to," he could hear Michael, while Roberts nodded. "Danny's got to win—I stand to lose a mint—I've got a ton of money covered —my own—If he lasts the fifteenth I'm bust—The boy'll mind you. Put something across."

And thereafter Rivera saw no more visions. They were trying to job him. Once again he dropped Danny and stood resting, his hands at his side. Roberts stood up.

"That settled him," he said. "Go to your corner."

He spoke with authority, as he had often spoken to Rivera at the training quarters. But Rivera looked hatred at him and waited for Danny to rise. Back in his corner in the minute interval, Kelly, the promoter, came and talked to Rivera.

"Throw it, damn you," he rasped in a harsh low voice. "You gotta lay down, Rivera. Stick with me and I'll make your future. I'll let you lick Danny next time. But here's where you lay down."

Rivera showed with his eyes that he heard, but he made neither sign of assent nor dissent.

"Why don't you speak?" Kelly demanded angrily.

"You lose, anyway," Spider Hagerty supplemented. "The referee'll take it away from you. Listen to Kelly, and lay down."

"Lay down, kid," Kelly pleaded, "and I'll help you to the championship."

Rivera did not answer.

"I will, so help me, kid."

At the strike of the gong Rivera sensed something impending. The house did not. Whatever it was it was there inside the ring with him and very close. Danny's earlier surety seemed returned to him. The confidence of his advance frightened Rivera. Some trick was about to be worked. Danny rushed, but Rivera refused the encounter. He side-stepped away into safety. What the other wanted was a clinch. It was in some way necessary to the trick. Rivera backed and circled away, yet he knew, sooner or later, the clinch and the trick would come. Desperately he resolved to draw it. He made as if to effect the clinch with Danny's next rush. Instead, at the last instant, just as their bodies should have come together, Rivera darted nimbly back. And in the same instant Danny's corner raised a cry of foul. Rivera had fooled them. The referee paused irresolutely. The decision that trembled on his lips was never uttered, for a shrill, boy's voice from the gallery piped, "Raw work!"

Danny cursed Rivera openly, and forced him, while Rivera danced away. Also, Rivera made up his mind to strike no more blows at the body. In this he threw away half his chance of winning, but he knew if he was to win at all it was with the outfighting that remained to him. Given the least opportunity, they would lie a foul on him. Danny threw all caution to the winds. For two rounds he tore after and into the boy who dared not meet him at close quarters. Rivera was struck again and again; he took blows by the dozens to avoid the perilous clinch. During this supreme final rally of Danny's the audience rose to its feet and went mad. It did not understand. All it could see was that its favorite was winning after all.

"Why don't you fight?" it demanded wrathfully of Rivera. "You're yellow! You're yellow!" "Open up, you cur! Open up!" "Kill 'm, Danny! Kill 'm!" "You sure got 'm! Kill 'm!"

In all the house, bar none, Rivera was the only cold man. By temperament and blood he was the hottest-passioned there; but he had gone through such vastly greater heats that this collective passion of ten thousand throats, rising surge on surge, was to his brain no more than the velvet cool of a summer twilight.

Into the seventeenth round Danny carried his rally. Rivera, under a heavy blow, drooped and sagged. His hands dropped helplessly as he reeled backward. Danny thought it was his chance. The boy was at his mercy. Thus Rivera, feigning, caught him off his guard, lashing out a clean drive to the mouth. Danny went down. When he arose, Rivera felled him with a down-chop of the right on neck and jaw. Three times he repeated this. It was impossible for any referee to call these blows foul.

"Oh, Bill! Bill!" Kelly pleaded to the referee.

"I can't," that official lamented back. "He won't give me a chance."

Danny, battered and heroic, still kept coming up. Kelly and others near to the ring began to cry out to the police to stop it, though Danny's corner refused to throw in the towel. Rivera saw the fat police captain starting awkwardly to climb through the ropes, and was not sure what it meant. There were so many ways of cheating in this game of the Gringos. Danny, on his feet, tottered groggily and helplessly before him. The referee and the captain were both reaching for Rivera when he struck the last blow. There was no need to stop the fight, for Danny did not rise.

"Count!" Rivera cried hoarsely to the referee.

And when the count was finished, Danny's seconds gathered him up and carried him to his corner.

"Who wins?" Rivera demanded.

Reluctantly, the referee caught his gloved hand and held it aloft.

There were no congratulations for Rivera. He walked to his corner unattended, where his seconds had not yet placed his stool. He leaned backward on the ropes and looked his hatred at them, swept it on and about him till the whole ten thousand Gringos were included. His knees trembled under him, and he was sobbing from exhaustion. Before his eyes the hated faces swayed back and forth in the giddiness of nausea. Then he remembered they were the guns. The guns were his. The Revolution could go on.

THE PEARLS OF PARLAY

The Kanaka helmsman put the wheel down, and the *Malahini* slipped into the eye of the wind and righted to an even keel. Her headsails emptied, there was a rat-tat of reef-points and quick shifting of boom-tackles, and she was heeled over and filled away on the other tack. Though it was early morning and the wind brisk, the five white men who lounged on the poop-deck were scantily clad. David Grief, and his guest, Gregory Mulhall, an Englishman, were still in pajamas, their naked feet thrust into Chinese slippers. The captain and mate were in thin undershirts and unstarched duck pants, while the supercago still held in his hands the undershirt he was reluctant to put on. The sweat stood out on his forehead, and he seemed to thrust his bare chest thirstily into the wind that did not cool.

"Pretty muggy, for a breeze like this," he complained.

"And what's it doing around in the west? That's what I want to know," was Grief's contribution to the general plaint.

"It won't last, and it ain't been there long," said Hermann, the Holland mate. "She is been chop around all night—five minutes here, ten minutes there, one hour somewhere other quarter."

"Something makin', something makin'," Captain Warfield croaked, spreading his bushy beard with the fingers of both hands and shoving the thatch of his chin into the breeze in a vain search for coolness. "Weather's been crazy for a fortnight. Haven't had the proper trades in three weeks. Everything's mixed up. Barometer was pumping at sunset last night, and it's pumping now, though the weather sharps say it don't mean anything. All the same, I've got a prejudice against seeing it pump. Gets on my nerves, sort of, you know. She was pumping that way the time we lost the *Lancaster*. I was only an apprentice, but I can remember that well enough. Brand new, four-masted steel ship; first voyage; broke the old man's heart. He'd been forty years in the company. Just faded way and died the next year."

Despite the wind and the early hour, the heat was suffocating. The wind whispered coolness, but did not deliver coolness. It might have blown off the Sahara, save for the extreme humidity with which it was laden. There was no fog nor mist, nor hint of fog or mist, yet the dimness of distance produced the impression. There were no defined clouds, yet so thickly were the heavens covered by a messy cloud-pall that the sun failed to shine through.

"Ready about!" Captain Warfield ordered with slow sharpness.

The brown, breech-clouted Kanaka sailors moved languidly but quickly to head-sheets and boom-tackles.

"Hard a-lee!"

The helmsman ran the spokes over with no hint of gentling, and the *Malahini* darted prettily into the wind and about.

"Jove! she's a witch!" was Mulhall's appreciation. "I didn't know you South Sea traders sailed yachts."

"She was a Gloucester fisherman originally," Grief explained, "and the Gloucester boats are all yachts when it comes to build, rig, and sailing."

"But you're heading right in—why don't you make it?" came the Englishman's criticism.

"Try it, Captain Warfield," Grief suggested. "Show him what a lagoon entrance is on a strong ebb."

"Close-and-by!" the captain ordered.

"Close-and-by," the Kanaka repeated, easing half a spoke.

The *Malahini* laid squarely into the narrow passage which was the lagoon entrance of a large, long, and narrow oval of an atoll. The atoll was shaped as if three atolls, in the course of building, had collided and coalesced and failed to rear the partition walls. Cocoanut palms grew in spots on the circle of sand, and there were many gaps where the sand was too low to the sea for cocoanuts, and through which could be seen the protected lagoon where the water lay flat like the ruffled surface of a mirror. Many square miles of water were in the irregular lagoon, all of which surged out on the ebb through the one narrow channel. So narrow was the channel, so large the outflow of water, that the passage was more like the rapids of a river than the mere tidal entrance to an atoll. The water boiled and whirled and swirled and drove outward in a white foam of stiff, serrated waves. Each heave and blow on her bows of the upstanding waves of the current swung the *Malahini* off the straight lead and wedged her as with wedges of steel toward the side of the passage. Part way in she was, when her closeness to the coral edge compelled her to go about. On the opposite tack, broadside to the current, she swept seaward with the current's speed.

"Now's the time for that new and expensive engine of yours," Grief jeered good-naturedly.

That the engine was a sore point with Captain Warfield was patent. He had begged and badgered for it, until in the end Grief had given his consent.

"It will pay for itself yet," the captain retorted. "You wait and see. It beats insurance and you know the underwriters won't stand for insurance in the Paumotus."

Grief pointed to a small cutter beating up astern of them on the same course.

"I'll wager a five-franc piece the little *Nuhiva* beats us in."

"Sure," Captain Warfield agreed. "She's overpowered. We're like a liner alongside of her, and we've only got forty horsepower. She's got ten horse, and she's a little skimming dish. She could skate across the froth of hell, but just the same she can't buck this current. It's running ten knots right now."

And at the rate of ten knots, buffeted and jerkily rolled, the *Malahini* went out to sea with the tide.

"She'll slacken in half an hour—then we'll make headway," Captain Warfield said, with an irritation explained by his next words. "He has no right to call it Parlay. It's down on the admiralty charts, and the French charts, too, as Hikihoho. Bougainville discovered it and named it from the natives."

"What's the name matter?" the supercargo demanded, taking advantage of speech to pause with arms shoved into the sleeves of the undershirt. "There it is, right under our nose, and old Parlay is there with the pearls."

"Who see them pearl?" Hermann queried, looking from one to another.

"It's well known," was the supercargo's reply. He turned to the steersman: "Tai-Hotauri, what about old Parlay's pearls?"

The Kanaka, pleased and self-conscious, took and gave a spoke.

"My brother dive for Parlay three, four month, and he make much talk about pearl. Hikihoho very good place for pearl."

"And the pearl-buyers have never got him to part with a pearl," the captain broke in.

"And they say he had a hatful for Armande when he sailed for Tahiti," the supercargo carried on the tale. "That's fifteen years ago, and he's been adding to it ever since—stored the shell as well. Everybody's seen that—hundreds of tons of it. They say the lagoon's fished clean now. Maybe that's why he's announced the auction."

"If he really sells, this will be the biggest year's output of pearls in the Paumotus," Grief said.

"I say, now, look here!" Mulhall burst forth, harried by the humid heat as much as the rest of them. "What's it all about? Who's the old beachcomber anyway? What are all these pearls? Why so secretious about it?"

"Hikihoho belongs to old Parlay," the supercargo answered. "He's got a fortune in pearls, saved up for years and years, and he sent the word out weeks ago that he'd auction them off to the buyers to-morrow. See those schooners' masts sticking up inside the lagoon?"

"Eight, so I see," said Hermann.

"What are they doing in a dinky atoll like this?" the supercargo went on. "There isn't a schooner-load of copra a year in the place. They've come for the auction. That's why we're here. That's why the little *Nuhiva's* bumping along astern there, though what she can buy is beyond me. Narii Herring—he's an English Jew half-caste—owns and runs her, and his only assets are his nerve, his debts, and his whiskey bills. He's a genius in such things. He owes so much that there isn't a merchant in Papeete who isn't interested in his welfare. They go out of their way to throw work in his way. They've got to, and a dandy stunt it is for Narii. Now I owe nobody. What's the result? If I fell down in a fit on the beach they'd let me lie there and die. They wouldn't lose anything. But Narii Herring?—what wouldn't they do if he fell in a fit? Their best wouldn't be too good for him. They've got too much money tied up in him to let him lie. They'd take him into their homes and hand-nurse him like a brother. Let me tell you, honesty in paying bills ain't what it's cracked up to be."

"What's this Narii chap got to do with it?" was the Englishman's short-tempered demand. And, turning to Grief, he said, "What's all this pearl nonsense? Begin at the beginning."

"You'll have to help me out," Grief warned the others, as he began. "Old Parlay is a character. From what I've seen of him I believe he's partly and mildly insane. Anyway, here's the story: Parlay's a full-blooded Frenchman. He told me once that he came from Paris. His accent is the true Parisian. He arrived down here in the old days. Went to trading and all the rest. That's how he got in on Hikihoho. Came in trading when trading was the real thing. About a hundred miserable Paumotans lived on the island. He married the queen—native fashion. When she died, everything was his. Measles came through, and there weren't more than a dozen survivors. He fed them, and worked them, and was king. Now before the queen died she gave birth to a girl. That's Armande. When she was three he sent her to the convent at Papeete. When she was seven or eight he sent her to France. You begin to glimpse the situation. The best and most aristocratic convent in France was none too good for the only daughter of a Paumotan island king and capitalist, and you know the old country French draw no colour line. She was educated like a princess, and she accepted herself in much the same way. Also, she thought she was all-white, and never dreamed of a bar sinister.

"Now comes the tragedy. The old man had always been cranky and erratic, and he'd played the despot on Hikihoho so long that he'd got the idea in his head that there was nothing wrong with the king—or the princess either. When Armande was eighteen he sent for her. He had slews and slathers of money, as Yankee Bill would say. He'd built the big house on Hikihoho, and a whacking fine bungalow in Papeete. She was to arrive on the mail boat from New Zealand, and he sailed in his schooner to meet her at Papeete. And he might have carried the situation off, despite the hens and bull-beasts of Papeete, if it hadn't been for the hurricane. That was the year, wasn't it, when Manu-Huhi was swept and eleven hundred drowned?"

The others nodded, and Captain Warfield said: "I was in the *Magpie* that blow, and we went ashore, all hands and the cook, *Magpie* and all, a quarter of a mile into the cocoanuts at the head of Taiohae Bay—and it a supposedly hurricane-proof harbour."

"Well," Grief continued, "old Parlay got caught in the same blow, and arrived in Papeete with his hatful of pearls three weeks too late. He'd had to jack up his schooner and build half a mile of ways before he could get her back into the sea.

"And in the meantime there was Armande at Papeete. Nobody called on her. She did, French fashion, make the initial calls on the Governor and the port doctor. They saw her, but neither of their hen-wives was at home to her nor returned the call. She was out of caste, without caste, though she had never dreamed it, and that was the gentle way they broke the information to her. There was a gay young lieutenant on the French cruiser. He lost his heart to her, but not his head. You can imagine the shock to this young woman, refined, beautiful, raised like an aristocrat, pampered with the best of old France that money could buy. And you can guess the end." He shrugged his shoulders. "There was a Japanese servant in the bungalow. He saw it. Said she did it with the proper spirit of the Samurai. Took a stiletto—no thrust, no drive, no wild rush for annihilation—took the stiletto, placed the point carefully against her heart, and with both hands, slowly and steadily, pressed home.

"Old Parlay arrived after that with his pearls. There was one single one of them, they say, worth sixty thousand francs. Peter Gee saw it, and has told me he offered that much for it. The old man went clean off for a while. They had him strait-jacketed in the Colonial Club two days—"

"His wife's uncle, an old Paumotan, cut him out of the jacket and turned him loose," the supercargo corroborated.

"And then old Parlay proceeded to eat things up," Grief went on. "Pumped three bullets into the scalawag of a lieutenant—"

"Who lay in sick bay for three months," Captain Warfield contributed.

"Flung a glass of wine in the Governor's face; fought a duel with the port doctor; beat up his native servants; wrecked the hospital; broke two ribs and the collarbone of a man nurse, and escaped; and went down to his schooner, a gun in each hand, daring the chief of police and all the gendarmes to arrest him, and sailed for Hikihoho. And they say he's never left the island since."

The supercargo nodded. "That was fifteen years ago, and he's never budged."

"And added to his pearls," said the captain. "He's a blithering old lunatic. Makes my flesh creep. He's a regular Finn."

"What's that?" Mulhall inquired.

"Bosses the weather—that's what the natives believe, at any rate. Ask Tai-Hotauri there. Hey, Tai-Hotauri! what you think old Parlay do along weather?"

"Just the same one big weather devil," came the Kanaka's answer. "I know. He want big blow, he make big blow. He want no wind, no wind come."

"A regular old Warlock," said Mulhall.

"No good luck them pearl," Tai-Hotauri blurted out, rolling his head ominously. "He say he sell. Plenty schooner come. Then he make big hurricane, everybody finish, you see. All native men say so."

"It's hurricane season now," Captain Warfield laughed morosely. "They're not far wrong. It's making for something right now, and I'd feel better if the *Malahini* was a thousand miles away from here."

"He is a bit mad," Grief concluded. "I've tried to get his point of view. It's—well, it's mixed. For eighteen years he'd centred everything on Armande. Half the time he believes she's still alive, not yet come back from France. That's one of the reasons he held on to the pearls.

And all the time he hates white men. He never forgets they killed her, though a great deal of the time he forgets she's dead. Hello! Where's your wind?"

The sails bellied emptily overhead, and Captain Warfield grunted his disgust. Intolerable as the heat had been, in the absence of wind it was almost overpowering. The sweat oozed out on all their faces, and now one, and again another, drew deep breaths, involuntarily questing for more air.

"Here she comes again—an eight point haul! Boom-tackles across! Jump!"

The Kanakas sprang to the captain's orders, and for five minutes the schooner laid directly into the passage and even gained on the current. Again the breeze fell flat, then puffed from the old quarter, compelling a shift back of sheets and tackles.

"Here comes the *Nuhiva*," Grief said. "She's got her engine on. Look at her skim."

"All ready?" the captain asked the engineer, a Portuguese half-caste, whose head and shoulders protruded from the small hatch just for'ard of the cabin, and who wiped the sweat from his face with a bunch of greasy waste.

"Sure," he replied.

"Then let her go."

The engineer disappeared into his den, and a moment later the exhaust muffler coughed and spluttered overside. But the schooner could not hold her lead. The little cutter made three feet to her two and was quickly alongside and forging ahead. Only natives were on her deck, and the man steering waved his hand in derisive greeting and farewell.

"That's Narii Herring," Grief told Mulhall. "The big fellow at the wheel —the nerviest and most conscienceless scoundrel in the Paumotus."

Five minutes later a cry of joy from their own Kanakas centred all eyes on the *Nuhiva*. Her engine had broken down and they were overtaking her. The *Malahini's* sailors sprang into the rigging and jeered as they went by; the little cutter heeled over by the wind with a bone in her teeth, going backward on the tide.

"Some engine that of ours," Grief approved, as the lagoon opened before them and the course was changed across it to the anchorage.

Captain Warfield was visibly cheered, though he merely grunted, "It'll pay for itself, never fear."

The *Malahini* ran well into the centre of the little fleet ere she found swinging room to anchor.

"There's Isaacs on the *Dolly*," Grief observed, with a hand wave of greeting. "And Peter Gee's on the *Roberta*. Couldn't keep him away from a pearl sale like this. And there's Francini on the *Cactus*. They're all here, all the buyers. Old Parlay will surely get a price."

"They haven't repaired the engine yet," Captain Warfield grumbled gleefully.

He was looking across the lagoon to where the *Nuhiva's* sails showed through the sparse cocoanuts.

· II ·

The house of Parlay was a big two-story frame affair, built of California lumber, with a galvanized iron roof. So disproportionate was it to the slender ring of the atoll that it showed out upon the sand-strip and above it like some monstrous excrescence. They of the *Malahini* paid the courtesy visit ashore immediately after anchoring. Other captains and buyers were in the big room examining the pearls that were to be auctioned next day. Paumotan servants, natives of Hikihoho, and relatives of the owner, moved about dispensing whiskey and absinthe. And through the curious company moved Parlay himself, cackling and sneering, the withered wreck of what had once been a tall and powerful man. His eyes were deep sunken and feverish, his cheeks fallen in and cavernous. The hair of his head seemed to have come out in patches, and his mustache and imperial had shed in the same lopsided way.

"Jove!" Mulhall muttered under his breath. "A long-legged Napoleon the Third, but burnt out, baked, and fire-crackled. And mangy! No wonder he crooks his head to one side. He's got to keep the balance."

"Goin' to have a blow," was the old man's greeting to Grief. "You must think a lot of pearls to come a day like this."

"They're worth going to inferno for," Grief laughed genially back, running his eyes over the surface of the table covered by the display.

"Other men have already made that journey for them," old Parlay cackled. "See this one!" He pointed to a large, perfect pearl the size of a small walnut that lay apart on a piece of chamois. "They offered me sixty thousand francs for it in Tahiti. They'll bid as much and more for it to-morrow, if they aren't blown away. Well, that pearl, it was found by my cousin, my cousin by marriage. He was a native, you see. Also, he was a thief. He hid it. It was mine. His cousin, who was also my cousin—we're all related here—killed him for it and fled away in a cutter to Noo-Nau. I pursued, but the chief of Noo-Nau had killed him for it before I got there. Oh, yes, there are many dead men represented on the table there. Have a drink, Captain. Your face is not familiar. You are new in the islands?"

"It's Captain Robinson of the *Roberta*," Grief said, introducing them. In the meantime Mulhall had shaken hands with Peter Gee.

"I never fancied there were so many pearls in the world," Mulhall said.

"Nor have I ever seen so many together at one time," Peter Gee admitted.

"What ought they to be worth?"

"Fifty or sixty thousand pounds—and that's to us buyers. In Paris—" He shrugged his shoulders and lifted his eyebrows at the incommunicableness of the sum.

Mulhall wiped the sweat from his eyes. All were sweating profusely and breathing hard. There was no ice in the drink that was served, and whiskey and absinthe went down lukewarm.

"Yes, yes," Parlay was cackling. "Many dead men lie on the table there. I know those pearls, all of them. You see those three! Perfectly matched, aren't they? A diver from Easter Island got them for me inside a week. Next week a shark got him; took his arm off and blood poison did the business. And that big baroque there—nothing much —if I'm offered twenty francs for it to-morrow I'll be in luck; it came out of twenty-two fathoms of water. The man was from Raratonga. He broke all diving records. He got it out of twenty-two fathoms. I saw him. And he burst his lungs at the same time, or got the 'bends,' for he died in two hours. He died screaming. They could hear him for miles. He was the most powerful native I ever saw. Half a dozen of my divers have died of the bends. And more men will die, more men will die."

"Oh, hush your croaking, Parlay," chided one of the captains. "It ain't going to blow."

"If I was a strong man, I couldn't get up hook and get out fast enough," the old man retorted in the falsetto of age. "Not if I was a strong man with the taste for wine yet in my mouth. But not you. You'll all stay. I wouldn't advise you if I thought you'd go. You can't drive buzzards away from the carrion. Have another drink, my brave sailormen. Well, well, what men will dare for a few little oyster drops! There they are, the beauties! Auction to-morrow, at ten sharp. Old Parlay's selling out, and the buzzards are gathering—old Parlay who was a stronger man in his day than any of them and who will see most of them dead yet."

"If he isn't a vile old beast!" the supercargo of the *Malahini* whispered to Peter Gee.

"What if she does blow?" said the captain of the *Dolly*. "Hikihoho's never been swept."

"The more reason she will be, then," Captain Warfield answered back. "I wouldn't trust her."

"Who's croaking now?" Grief reproved.

"I'd hate to lose that new engine before it paid for itself," Captain Warfield replied gloomily.

Parlay skipped with astonishing nimbleness across the crowded room to the barometer on the wall.

"Take a look, my brave sailormen!" he cried exultantly.

The man nearest read the glass. The sobering effect showed plainly on his face.

"It's dropped ten," was all he said, yet every face went anxious, and there was a look as if every man desired immediately to start for the door.

"Listen!" Parlay commanded.

In the silence the outer surf seemed to have become unusually loud. There was a great rumbling roar.

"A big sea is beginning to set," some one said; and there was a movement to the windows, where all gathered.

Through the sparse cocoanuts they gazed seaward. An orderly succession of huge smooth seas was rolling down upon the coral shore. For some minutes they gazed on the strange sight and talked in low voices, and in those few minutes it was manifest to all that the waves were increasing in size. It was uncanny, this rising sea in a dead calm, and their voices unconsciously sank lower. Old Parlay shocked them with his abrupt cackle.

"There is yet time to get away to sea, brave gentlemen. You can tow across the lagoon with your whaleboats."

"It's all right, old man," said Darling, the mate of the *Cactus,* a stalwart youngster of twenty-five. "The blow's to the south'ard and passing on. We'll not get a whiff of it."

An air of relief went through the room. Conversations were started, and the voices became louder. Several of the buyers even went back to the table to continue the examination of the pearls.

Parlay's shrill cackle rose higher.

"That's right," he encouraged. "If the world was coming to an end you'd go on buying."

"We'll buy these to-morrow just the same," Isaacs assured him.

"Then you'll be doing your buying in hell."

The chorus of incredulous laughter incensed the old man. He turned fiercely on Darling.

"Since when have children like you come to the knowledge of storms? And who is the man who has plotted the hurricane-courses of the Paumotus? What books will you find it in? I sailed the Paumotus before the oldest of you drew breath. I know. To the eastward the paths of the hurricanes are on so wide a circle they make a straight line. To the westward here they make a sharp curve. Remember your chart. How did it happen the hurricane of '91 swept Auri and Hiolau? The curve, my brave boy, the curve! In an hour, or two or three at most, will come the wind. Listen to that!"

A vast rumbling crash shook the coral foundations of the atoll. The house quivered to it. The native servants, with bottles of whiskey and absinthe in their hands, shrank together as if for protection and stared with fear through the windows at the mighty wash of the wave lapping far up the beach to the corner of a copra-shed.

Parlay looked at the barometer, giggled, and leered around at his guests. Captain Warfield strode across to see.

"29:75," he read. "She's gone down five more. By God! the old devil's right. She's a-coming, and it's me, for one, for aboard."

"It's growing dark," Isaacs half whispered.

"Jove! it's like a stage," Mulhall said to Grief, looking at his watch. "Ten o'clock in the morning, and it's like twilight. Down go the lights for the tragedy. Where's the slow music!"

In answer, another rumbling crash shook the atoll and the house. Almost in a panic the company started for the door. In the dim light their sweaty faces appeared ghastly. Isaacs panted asthmatically in the suffocating heat.

"What's your haste?" Parlay chuckled and girded at his departing guests. "A last drink, brave gentlemen." No one noticed him. As they took the shell-bordered path to the beach he stuck his head out the door and called, "Don't forget, gentlemen, at ten to-morrow old Parlay sells his pearls."

· III ·

On the beach a curious scene took place. Whaleboat after whaleboat was being hurriedly manned and shoved off. It had grown still darker. The stagnant calm continued, and the sand shook under their feet with each buffet of the sea on the outer shore. Narii Herring walked leisurely along the sand. He grinned at the very evident haste of the captains and buyers. With him were three of his Kanakas, and also Tai-Hotauri.

"Get into the boat and take an oar," Captain Warfield ordered the latter.

Tai-Hotauri came over jauntily, while Narii Herring and his three Kanakas paused and looked on from forty feet away.

"I work no more for you, skipper," Tai-Hotauri said insolently and loudly. But his face belied his words, for he was guilty of a prodigious wink. "Fire me, skipper," he huskily whispered, with a second significant wink.

Captain Warfield took the cue and proceeded to do some acting himself. He raised his fist and his voice.

"Get into that boat," he thundered, "or I'll knock seven bells out of you!"

The Kanaka drew back truculently, and Grief stepped between to placate his captain.

"I go to work on the *Nuhiva*," Tai-Hotauri said, rejoining the other group.

"Come back here!" the captain threatened.

"He's a free man, skipper," Narii Herring spoke up. "He's sailed with me in the past, and he's sailing again, that's all."

"Come on, we must get on board," Grief urged. "Look how dark it's getting."

Captain Warfield gave in, but as the boat shoved off he stood up in the sternsheets and shook his fist ashore.

"I'll settle with you yet, Narii," he cried. "You're the only skipper in the group that steals other men's sailors." He sat down, and in lowered voice queried: "Now what's Tai-Hotauri up to? He's on to something, but what is it?"

·IV·

As the boat came alongside the *Malahini*, Hermann's anxious face greeted them over the rail.

"Bottom out fall from barometer," he announced. "She's goin' to blow. I got starboard anchor overhaul."

"Overhaul the big one, too," Captain Warfield ordered, taking charge. "And here, some of you, hoist in this boat. Lower her down to the deck and lash her bottom up."

Men were busy at work on the decks of all the schooners. There was a great clanking of chains being overhauled, and now one craft, and now another, hove in, veered, and dropped a second anchor. Like the *Malahini*, those that had third anchors were preparing to drop them when the wind showed what quarter it was to blow from.

The roar of the big surf continually grew, though the lagoon lay in the mirror-like calm. There was no sign of life where Parlay's big house perched on the sand. Boat and copra-sheds and the sheds where the shell was stored were deserted.

"For two cents I'd up anchors and get out," Grief said. "I'd do it anyway if it were open sea. But those chains of atolls to the north and east have us pocketed. We've a better chance right here. What do you think, Captain Warfield?"

"I agree with you, though a lagoon is no mill-pond for riding it out. I wonder where she's going to start from? Hello! There goes one of Parlay's copra-sheds."

They could see the grass-thatched shed lift and collapse, while a froth of foam cleared the crest of the sand and ran down to the lagoon.

"Breached across!" Mulhall exclaimed. "That's something for a starter. There she comes again!"

The wreck of the shed was now flung up and left on the sand-crest. A third wave buffeted it into fragments which washed down the slope toward the lagoon.

"If she blow I would as be cooler yet," Hermann grunted. "No longer can I breathe. It is damn hot. I am dry like a stove."

He chopped open a drinking cocoanut with his heavy sheath-knife and drained the contents. The rest of them followed his example, pausing once to watch one of Parlay's shell sheds go down in ruin. The barometer now registered 29:50.

"Must be pretty close to the centre of the area of low pressure," Grief remarked cheerfully. "I was never through the eye of a hurricane before. It will be an experience for you, too, Mulhall. From the speed the barometer's dropped, it's going to be a big one."

Captain Warfield groaned, and all eyes drew to him. He was looking through the glasses down the length of the lagoon to the southeast.

"There she comes," he said quietly.

They did not need glasses to see. A flying film, strangely marked, seemed drawing over the surface of the lagoon. Abreast of it, along the atoll, travelling with equal speed, was a stiff bending of the cocoanut palms and a blur of flying leaves. The front of the wind on the water was a solid, sharply defined strip of dark-coloured, wind-vexed water. In advance of this strip, like skirmishers, were flashes of wind-flaws. Behind this strip, a quarter of a mile in width, was a strip of what seemed glassy calm. Next came another dark strip of wind, and behind that the lagoon was all crisping, boiling whiteness.

"What is that calm streak?" Mulhall asked.

"Calm," Warfield answered.

"But it travels as fast as the wind," was the other's objection.

"It has to, or it would be overtaken and it wouldn't be any calm. It's a double-header. I saw a big squall like that off Savaii once. A regular double-header. Smash! it hit us, then it lulled to nothing, and smashed us a second time. Stand by and hold on! Here she is on top of us. Look at the *Roberta!*"

The *Roberta,* lying nearest to the wind at slack chains, was swept off broadside like a straw. Then her chains brought her up, bow on to the wind, with an astonishing jerk. Schooner after schooner, the *Malahini* with them, was now sweeping away with the first gust and fetching up on taut chains. Mulhall and several of the Kanakas were taken off their feet when the *Malahini* jerked to her anchors.

And then there was no wind. The flying calm streak had reached them. Grief lighted a match, and the unshielded flame burned without flickering in the still air. A very dim twilight prevailed. The cloud-sky, lowering as it had been for hours, seemed now to have descended quite down upon the sea.

The *Roberta* tightened to her chains when the second head of the hurricane hit, as did schooner after schooner in swift succession. The sea, white with fury, boiled in tiny, spitting wavelets. The deck of the *Malahini* vibrated under the men's feet. The taut-stretched halyards beat a tattoo against the masts, and all the rigging, as if smote by some mighty hand, set up a wild thrumming. It was impossible to face the wind and breathe. Mulhall, crouching with the others behind the shelter of the cabin, discovered this, and his lungs were filled in an instant with so great a volume of driven air which he could not expel that he nearly strangled ere he could turn his head away.

"It's incredible," he gasped, but no one heard him.

Hermann and several Kanakas were crawling for'ard on hands and knees to let go the third anchor. Grief touched Captain Warfield and pointed to the *Roberta.* She was dragging down upon them. Warfield put his mouth to Grief's ear and shouted:

"We're dragging, too!"

Grief sprang to the wheel and put it hard over, veering the *Malahini* to port. The third anchor took hold, and the *Roberta* went by, stern-first, a dozen yards away. They waved their hands to Peter Gee and Captain Robinson, who, with a number of sailors, were at work on the bow.

"He's knocking out the shackles!" Grief shouted. "Going to chance the passage! Got to! Anchors skating!"

"We're holding now!" came the answering shout. "There goes the *Cactus* down on the *Misi.* That settles them!"

The *Misi* had been holding, but the added windage of the *Cactus* was too much, and the entangled schooners slid away across the boiling white. Their men could be seen chopping and fighting to get them apart. The *Roberta,* cleared of her anchors, with a patch of tarpaulin set for'ard, was heading for the passage at the northwestern end of the lagoon.

They saw her make it and drive out to sea. But the *Misi* and *Cactus,* unable to get clear of each other, went ashore on the atoll half a mile from the passage.

The wind merely increased on itself and continued to increase. To face the full blast of it required all one's strength, and several minutes of crawling on deck against it tired a man to exhaustion. Hermann, with his Kanakas, plodded steadily, lashing and making secure, putting ever more gaskets on the sails. The wind ripped and tore their thin undershirts from their backs. They moved slowly, as if their bodies weighed tons, never releasing a hand-hold until another had been secured. Loose ends of rope stood out stiffly horizontal, and, when a whipping gave, the loose end frazzled and blew away.

Mulhall touched one and then another and pointed to the shore. The grass-sheds had disappeared, and Parlay's house rocked drunkenly. Because the wind blew lengthwise along the atoll, the house had been sheltered by the miles of cocoanut trees. But the big seas, breaking across from outside, were undermining it and hammering it to pieces. Already tilted down the slope of sand, its end was imminent. Here and there in the cocoanut trees people had lashed themselves. The trees did not sway or thresh about. Bent over rigidly from the wind, they remained in that position and vibrated monstrously. Underneath, across the sand, surged the white spume of the breakers.

A big sea was likewise making down the length of the lagoon. It had plenty of room to kick up in the ten-mile stretch from the windward rim of the atoll, and all the schooners were bucking and plunging into it. The *Malahini* had begun shoving her bow and fo'c'sle head under the bigger ones, and at times her waist was filled rail-high with water.

"Now's the time for your engine!" Grief bellowed; and Captain Warfield, crawling over to where the engineer lay, shouted emphatic commands.

Under the engine, going full speed ahead, the *Malahini* behaved better. While she continued to ship seas over her bow, she was not jerked down so fiercely by her anchors. On the other hand, she was unable to get any slack in the chains. The best her forty horsepower could do was to ease the strain.

Still the wind increased. The little *Nuhiva,* lying abreast of the *Malahini* and closer in to the beach, her engine still unrepaired and her captain ashore, was having a bad time of it. She buried herself so frequently and so deeply that they wondered each time if she could clear herself of the water. At three in the afternoon, buried by a second sea before she could free herself of the preceding one, she did not come up.

Mulhall looked at Grief.

"Burst in her hatches," was the bellowed answer.

Captain Warfield pointed to the *Winifred,* a little schooner plunging and burying outside of them, and shouted in Grief's ear. His voice came in patches of dim words, with intervals of silence when whisked away by the roaring wind.

"Rotten little tub . . . Anchors hold . . . But how she holds together . . . Old as the ark—"

An hour later Hermann pointed to her. Her for'ard bitts, foremast, and most of her bow were gone, having been jerked out of her by her anchors. She swung broadside, rolling in the trough and settling by the head, and in this plight was swept away to leeward.

Five vessels now remained, and of them the *Malahini* was the only one with an engine. Fearing either the *Nuhiva's* or the *Winifred's* fate, two of them followed the *Roberta's* example, knocking out the chain-shackles and running for the passage. The *Dolly* was the first, but her tarpaulin was carried away, and she went to destruction on the lee-rim of the atoll near the *Misi* and the *Cactus.* Undeterred by this, the *Moana* let go and followed with the same result.

"Pretty good engine that, eh?" Captain Warfield yelled to his owner.

Grief put out his hand and shook. "She's paying for herself!" he yelled back. "The wind's shifting around to the south'ard, and we ought to lie easier!"

Slowly and steadily, but with ever-increasing velocity, the wind veered around to the south and the southwest, till the three schooners that were left pointed directly in toward the beach. The wreck of Parlay's house was picked up, hurled into the lagoon, and blown out upon them. Passing the *Malahini,* it crashed into the *Papara,* lying a quarter of a mile astern. There was wild work for'ard on her, and in a quarter of an hour the house went clear, but it had taken the *Papara's* foremast and bowsprit with it.

Inshore, on their port bow, lay the *Tahaa,* slim and yacht-like, but excessively oversparred. Her anchors still held, but her captain, finding no abatement in the wind, proceeded to reduce windage by chopping down his masts.

"Pretty good engine that," Grief congratulated his skipper. "It will save our sticks for us yet."

Captain Warfield shook his head dubiously.

The sea on the lagoon went swiftly down with the change of wind, but they were beginning to feel the heave and lift of the outer sea breaking across the atoll. There were not so many trees remaining.

Some had been broken short off, others uprooted. One tree they saw snap off halfway up, three persons clinging to it, and whirl away by the wind into the lagoon. Two detached themselves from it and swam to the *Tahaa*. Not long after, just before darkness, they saw one jump overboard from that schooner's stern and strike out strongly for the *Malahini* through the white, spitting wavelets.

"It's Tai-Hotauri," was Grief's judgment. "Now we'll have the news."

The Kanaka caught the bobstay, climbed over the bow, and crawled aft. Time was given him to breathe, and then, behind the part shelter of the cabin, in broken snatches and largely by signs, he told his story.

"Narii ... damn robber ... He want steal ... pearls ... Kill Parlay ... One man kill Parlay ... No man know what man ... Three Kanakas, Narii, me ... Five beans ... hat ... Narii say one bean black ... Nobody know ... Kill Parlay ... Narii damn liar ... All beans black ... Five black ... Copra-shed dark ... Every man get black bean ... Big wind come ... No chance ... Everybody get up tree ... No good luck them pearls, I tell you before ... No good luck."

"Where's Parlay?" Grief shouted.

"Up tree ... Three of his Kanakas same tree. Narii and one Kanaka 'nother tree ... My tree blow to hell, then I come on board."

"Where's the pearls?"

"Up tree along Parlay. Mebbe Narii get them pearl yet."

In the ear of one after another Grief passed on Tai-Hotauri's story. Captain Warfield was particularly incensed, and they could see him grinding his teeth.

Hermann went below and returned with a riding light, but the moment it was lifted above the level of the cabin wall the wind blew it out. He had better success with the binnacle lamp, which was lighted only after many collective attempts.

"A fine night of wind!" Grief yelled in Mulhall's ear. "And blowing harder all the time."

"How hard?"

"A hundred miles an hour ... two hundred ... I don't know ... Harder than I've ever seen it."

The lagoon grew more and more troubled by the sea that swept across the atoll. Hundreds of leagues of ocean was being backed up by the hurricane, which more than overcame the lowering effect of the ebb tide. Immediately the tide began to rise the increase in the size of the seas was noticeable. Moon and wind were heaping the South Pacific on Hikihoho atoll.

Captain Warfield returned from one of his periodical trips to the engine room with the word that the engineer lay in a faint.

"Can't let that engine stop!" he concluded helplessly.

"All right!" Grief said. "Bring him on deck. I'll spell him."

The hatch to the engine room was battened down, access being gained through a narrow passage from the cabin. The heat and gas fumes were stifling. Grief took one hasty, comprehensive examination of the engine and the fittings of the tiny room, then blew out the oil-lamp. After that he worked in darkness, save for the glow from endless cigars which he went into the cabin to light. Even-tempered as he was, he soon began to give evidences of the strain of being pent in with a mechanical monster that toiled, and sobbed, and slubbered in the shouting dark. Naked to the waist, covered with grease and oil, bruised and skinned from being knocked about by the plunging, jumping vessel, his head swimming from the mixture of gas and air he was compelled to breathe, he laboured on hour after hour, in turns petting, blessing, nursing, and cursing the engine and all its parts. The ignition began to go bad. The feed grew worse. And worst of all, the cylinders began to heat. In a consultation held in the cabin the half-caste engineer begged and pleaded to stop the engine for half an hour in order to cool it and to attend to the water circulation. Captain Warfield was against any stopping. The half-caste swore that the engine would ruin itself and stop anyway and for good. Grief, with glaring eyes, greasy and battered, yelled and cursed them both down and issued commands. Mulhall, the supercargo, and Hermann were set to work in the cabin at double-straining and triple-straining the gasoline. A hole was chopped through the engine room floor, and a Kanaka heaved bilge-water over the cylinders, while Grief continued to souse running parts in oil.

"Didn't know you were a gasoline expert," Captain Warfield admired when Grief came into the cabin to catch a breath of little less impure air.

"I bathe in gasoline," he grated savagely through his teeth. "I eat it."

What other uses he might have found for it were never given, for at that moment all the men in the cabin, as well as the gasoline being strained, were smashed for'ard against the bulk-head as the *Malahini* took an abrupt, deep dive. For the space of several minutes, unable to gain their feet, they rolled back and forth and pounded and hammered from wall to wall. The schooner, swept by three big seas, creaked and groaned and quivered, and from the weight of water on her decks behaved logily. Grief crept to the engine, while Captain Warfield waited his chance to get through the companionway and out on deck.

It was half an hour before he came back.

"Whaleboat's gone!" he reported. "Galley's gone! Everything gone except the deck and hatches! And if that engine hadn't been going we'd be gone! Keep up the good work!"

By midnight the engineer's lungs and head had been sufficiently cleared of gas fumes to let him relieve Grief, who went on deck to get his own head and lungs clear. He joined the others, who crouched behind the cabin, holding on with their hands and made doubly secure by rope-lashings. It was a complicated huddle, for it was the only place of refuge for the Kanakas. Some of them had accepted the skipper's invitation into the cabin but had been driven out by the fumes. The *Malahini* was being plunged down and swept frequently, and what they breathed was air and spray and water commingled.

"Making heavy weather of it, Mulhall!" Grief shouted to his guest between immersions.

Mulhall, strangling and choking, could only nod. The scuppers could not carry off the burden of water on the schooner's deck. She rolled it out and took it in over one rail and the other; and at times, nose thrown skyward, sitting down on her heel, she avalanched it aft. It surged along the poop gangways, poured over the top of the cabin, submerging and bruising those that clung on, and went out over the stern-rail.

Mulhall saw him first, and drew Grief's attention. It was Narii Herring, crouching and holding on where the dim binnacle light shone upon him. He was quite naked, save for a belt and a bare-bladed knife thrust between it and the skin.

Captain Warfield untied his lashings and made his way over the bodies of the others. When his face became visible in the light from the binnacle it was working with anger. They could see him speak, but the wind tore the sound away. He would not put his lips to Narii's ear. Instead, he pointed over the side. Narii Herring understood. His white teeth showed in an amused and sneering smile, and he stood up, a magnificent figure of a man.

"It's murder!" Mulhall yelled to Grief.

"He'd have murdered Old Parlay!" Grief yelled back.

For the moment the poop was clear of water and the *Malahini* on an even keel. Narii made a bravado attempt to walk to the rail, but was flung down by the wind. Thereafter he crawled, disappearing in the darkness, though there was certitude in all of them that he had gone over the side. The *Malahini* dived deep, and when they emerged from the flood that swept aft, Grief got Mulhall's ear.

"Can't lose him! He's the Fish Man of Tahiti! He'll cross the lagoon and land on the other rim of the atoll if there's any atoll left!"

Five minutes afterward, in another submergence, a mess of bodies poured down on them over the top of the cabin. These they seized and held till the water cleared, when they carried them below and learned their identity. Old Parlay lay on his back on the floor, with closed eyes and without movement. The other two were his Kanaka cousins. All three were naked and bloody. The arm of one Kanaka hung helpless and broken at his side. The other man bled freely from a hideous scalp wound.

"Narii did that?" Mulhall demanded.

Grief shook his head. "No; it's from being smashed along the deck and over the house!"

Something suddenly ceased, leaving them in dizzying uncertainty. For the moment it was hard to realize there was no wind. With the absolute abruptness of a sword slash, the wind had been chopped off. The schooner rolled and plunged, fetching up on her anchors with a crash which for the first time they could hear. Also, for the first time they could hear the water washing about on deck. The engineer threw off the propeller and eased the engine down.

"We're in the dead centre," Grief said. "Now for the shift. It will come as hard as ever." He looked at the barometer. "29:32," he read.

Not in a moment could he tone down the voice which for hours had battled against the wind, and so loudly did he speak that in the quiet it hurt the others' ears.

"All his ribs are smashed," the supercargo said, feeling along Parlay's side. "He's still breathing, but he's a goner."

Old Parlay groaned, moved one arm impotently, and opened his eyes. In them was the light of recognition.

"My brave gentlemen," he whispered haltingly. "Don't forget ... the auction ... at ten o'clock ... in hell."

His eyes dropped shut and the lower jaw threatened to drop, but he mastered the qualms of dissolution long enough to omit one final, loud, derisive cackle.

Above and below pandemonium broke out. The old familiar roar of the wind was with them. The *Malahini,* caught broadside, was pressed down almost on her beam ends as she swung the arc compelled by her anchors. They rounded her into the wind, where she jerked to an even keel. The propeller was thrown on, and the engine took up its work again.

"Northwest!" Captain Warfield shouted to Grief when he came on deck. "Hauled eight points like a shot!"

"Narii'll never get across the lagoon now!" Grief observed.

"Then he'll blow back to our side, worse luck!"

· V ·

After the passing of the centre the barometer began to rise. Equally rapid was the fall of the wind. When it was no more than a howling gale, the engine lifted up in the air, parted its bed-plates with a last convulsive effort of its forty horsepower, and lay down on its side. A wash of water from the bilge sizzled over it and the steam arose in clouds. The engineer wailed his dismay, but Grief glanced over the wreck affectionately and went into the cabin to swab the grease off his chest and arms with bunches of cotton waste.

The sun was up and the gentlest of summer breezes blowing when he came on deck, after sewing up the scalp of one Kanaka and setting the other's arm. The *Malahini* lay close in to the beach. For'ard, Hermann and the crew were heaving in and straightening out the tangle of anchors. The *Papara* and the *Tahaa* were gone, and Captain Warfield, through the glasses, was searching the opposite rim of the atoll.

"Not a stick left of them," he said. "That's what comes of not having engines. They must have dragged across before the big shift came."

Ashore, where Parlay's house had been, was no vestige of any house. For the space of three hundred yards, where the sea had breached, no tree or even stump was left. Here and there, farther along, stood an occasional palm, and there were numbers which had been snapped off above the ground. In the crown of one surviving palm Tai-Hotauri asserted he saw something move. There were no boats left to the *Malahini,* and they watched him swim ashore and climb the tree.

When he came back, they helped over the rail a young native girl of Parlay's household. But first she passed up to them a battered basket. In it was a litter of blind kittens—all dead save one, that feebly mewed and staggered on awkward legs.

"Hello!" said Mulhall. "Who's that?"

Along the beach they saw a man walking. He moved casually, as if out for a morning stroll. Captain Warfield gritted his teeth. It was Narii Herring.

"Hello, skipper!" Narii called, when he was abreast of them. "Can I come aboard and get some breakfast?"

Captain Warfield's face and neck began to swell and turn purple. He tried to speak, but choked.

"For two cents—for two cents—" was all he could manage to articulate.

WONDER OF WOMAN

"Just the same, I notice you ain't tumbled over yourself to get married," Shorty remarked, continuing a conversation that had lapsed some few minutes before.

Smoke, sitting on the edge of the sleeping-robe and examining the feet of a dog he had rolled snarling on its back in the snow, did not answer. And Shorty, turning a steaming moccasin propped on a stick before the fire, studied his partner's face keenly.

"Cock your eye up at that there aurora borealis," Shorty went on. "Some frivolous, eh? Just like any shilly-shallyin', shirt-dancing woman. The best of them is frivolous, when they ain't foolish. And they's cats, all of 'em, the littlest an' the biggest, the nicest and the otherwise. They're sure devourin' lions an' roarin' hyenas when they get on the trail of a man they've cottoned to."

Again the monologue languished. Smoke cuffed the dog when it attempted to snap his hand, and went on examining its bruised and bleeding pads.

"Huh!" pursued Shorty. "Mebbe I couldn't 'a' married if I'd a mind to! An' mebbe I wouldn't 'a' been married without a mind to, if I hadn't hiked for tall timber. Smoke, d' you want to know what saved me? I'll tell you. My wind. I just kept a-runnin'. I'd like to see any skirt run me outa breath."

Smoke released the animal and turned his own steaming, stick-propped moccasins. "We've got to rest over to-morrow and make moccasins," he vouchsafed. "That little crust is playing the devil with their feet."

"We oughta keep goin' somehow," Shorty objected. "We ain't got grub enough to turn back with, and we gotta strike that run of caribou or them white Indians almighty soon or we'll be eatin' the dogs, sore feet an' all. Now who ever seen them white Indians anyway? Nothin' but hearsay. An' how can a Indian be white? A black white man'd be as natural. Smoke, we just oughta travel to-morrow. The country's plumb dead of game. We ain't seen even a rabbit-track in a week, you know that. An' we gotta get out of this dead streak into somewhere that meat's runnin'."

"They'll travel all the better with a day's rest for their feet and moccasins all around," Smoke counseled. "If you get a chance at any low divide, take a peep over at the country beyond. We're likely to strike open rolling country any time now. That's what La Perle told us to look for."

"Huh! By his own story, it was ten years ago that La Perle come through this section, an' he was that loco from hunger he couldn't know what he did see. Remember what he said of whoppin' big flags floatin' from the tops of the mountains? That shows how loco *he* was. An' he said himself he never seen any white Indians—that was Anton's yarn. An', besides, Anton kicked the bucket two years before you an' me come to Alaska. But I'll take a look to-morrow. An' mebbe I might pick up a moose. What d' you say we turn in?"

Smoke spent the morning in camp, sewing dog-moccasins and repairing harnesses. At noon he cooked a meal for two, ate his share, and began to look for Shorty's return. An hour later he strapped on his snow-shoes and went out on his partner's trail. The way led up the bed of the stream, through a narrow gorge that widened suddenly into a moose-pasture. But no moose had been there since the first snow of the preceding fall. The tracks of Shorty's snow-shoes crossed the pasture and went up the easy slope of a low divide. At the crest Smoke halted. The tracks continued down the other slope. The first spruce-trees, in the creek bed, were a mile away, and it was evident that Shorty had passed through them and gone on. Smoke looked at his watch, remembered the oncoming darkness, the dogs, and the camp, and reluctantly decided against going farther. But before he retraced his steps he paused for a long look. All the eastern sky-line was saw-toothed by the snowy backbone of the Rockies. The whole mountain system, range upon range, seemed to trend to the northwest, cutting athwart the course to the open country reported by La Perle. The effect was as if the mountains conspired to thrust back the traveler toward the west and the Yukon. Smoke wondered how many men in the past, approaching as he had approached, had been turned aside by that forbidding aspect. La Perle had not been turned aside, but, then, La Perle had crossed over from the eastern slope of the Rockies.

Until midnight Smoke maintained a huge fire for the guidance of Shorty. And in the morning, waiting with camp broken and dogs harnessed for the first break of light, Smoke took up the pursuit. In the narrow pass of the canyon, his lead-dog pricked up its ears and whined. Then Smoke came upon the Indians, six of them, coming toward him. They were traveling light, without dogs, and on each man's back was the smallest of pack outfits. Surrounding Smoke, they immediately gave him several matters for surprise. That they were looking for him was clear. That they talked no Indian tongue of which he knew a word was also quickly made clear. They were not white Indians, though they were taller and heavier than the Indians of the Yukon basin. Five of them carried the old-fashioned, long-barreled Hudson Bay Company musket, and in the hands of the sixth was a Winchester rifle which Smoke knew to be Shorty's.

Nor did they waste time in making him a prisoner. Unarmed himself, Smoke could only submit. The contents of the sled were distributed among their own packs, and he was given a pack composed of his and Shorty's sleeping-furs. The dogs were unharnessed, and when Smoke protested, one of the Indians, by signs, indicated a trail too rough for sled-travel. Smoke bowed to the inevitable, cached the sled end-on in the snow on the bank above the stream, and trudged on with his captors. Over the divide to the north they went, down to the spruce-trees which Smoke had glimpsed the preceding afternoon. They followed the stream for a dozen miles, abandoning it when it trended to the west and heading directly eastward up a narrow tributary.

The first night was spent in a camp which had been occupied for several days. Here was cached a quantity of dried salmon and a sort of pemmican, which the Indians added to their packs. From this camp a trail of many snow-shoes led off—Shorty's captors, was Smoke's conclusion; and before darkness fell he succeeded in making out the tracks Shorty's narrower snow-shoes had left. On questioning the Indians by signs, they nodded affirmation and pointed to the north.

Always, in the days that followed, they pointed north; and always the trail, turning and twisting through a jumble of upstanding peaks, trended north. Everywhere, in this bleak snow-solitude, the way seemed barred, yet ever the trail curved and coiled, finding low divides and avoiding the higher and untraversable chains. The snow-fall was deeper than in the lower valleys, and every step of the way was snow-shoe work. Furthermore, Smoke's captors, all young men, traveled light and fast; and he could not forbear the prick of pride in the knowledge that he easily kept up with them. They were travel-hardened and trained to snow-shoes from infancy; yet such was his condition that the traverse bore no more of ordinary hardship to him than to them.

In six days they gained and crossed the central pass, low in comparison with the mountains it threaded, yet formidable in itself and not possible for loaded sleds. Five days more of tortuous winding, from lower altitude to lower altitude, brought them to the open, rolling, and merely hilly country La Perle had found ten years before. Smoke knew it with the first glimpse, on a sharp cold day, the thermometer forty below zero, the atmosphere so clear that he could see a hundred miles. Far as he could see rolled the open country. High in the east the Rockies still thrust their snowy ramparts heavenward. To the south and west extended the broken ranges of the projecting spur-system they had crossed. And in this vast pocket lay the country La Perle had traversed —snow-blanketed, but assuredly fat with game at some time in the year, and in the summer a smiling, forested, and flowered land.

Before midday, traveling down a broad stream, past snow-buried willows and naked aspens, and across heavily timbered flats of spruce, they came upon the site of a large camp, recently abandoned. Glancing as he went by, Smoke estimated four or five hundred fires, and guessed the population to be in the thousands. So fresh was the trail, and so well packed by the multitude, that Smoke and his captors took off their snow-shoes and in their moccasins struck a swifter pace. Signs of game appeared and grew plentiful—tracks of wolves and lynxes that without meat could not be. Once, one of the Indians cried out with satisfaction and pointed to a large area of open snow, littered with fang-polished skulls of caribou, trampled and disrupted as if an army had fought upon it. And Smoke knew that a big killing had been made by the hunters since the last snow-flurry.

In the long twilight no sign was manifested of making camp. They held steadily on through a deepening gloom that vanished under a sky of light—great, glittering stars half veiled by a greenish vapor of pulsing aurora borealis. His dogs first caught the noises of the camp, pricking their ears and whining in low eagerness. Then it came to the ears of the humans, a murmur, dim with distance, but not invested with the soothing grace that is common to distant murmurs. Instead, it was in a high, wild key, a beat of shrill sound broken by shriller sounds—the long wolf-howling of many wolf-dogs, a screaming of unrest and pain, mournful with hopelessness and rebellion. Smoke swung back the crystal of his watch and by the feel of finger-tips on the naked hands made out eleven o'clock. The men about him quickened. The legs that had lifted through a dozen strenuous hours lifted in a still swifter pace that was half a run and mostly a running jog. Through a dark spruce-flat they burst upon an abrupt glare of light from many fires and upon an abrupt increase of sound. The great camp lay before them.

And as they entered and threaded the irregular runways of the hunting-camp, a vast tumult, as in a wave, rose to meet them and rolled on with them—cries, greetings, questions and answers, jests and jests thrust back again, the snapping snarl of wolf-dogs rushing in furry projectiles of wrath upon Smoke's stranger dogs, the scolding of squaws, laughter, the whimpering of children and wailing of infants, the moans of the sick aroused afresh to pain, all the pandemonium of a camp of nerveless, primitive wilderness folk.

Striking with clubs and the butts of guns, Smoke's party drove back the attacking dogs, while his own dogs, snapping and snarling, awed by so many enemies, shrank in among the legs of their human protectors, and bristled along stiff-legged in menacing prance.

They halted in the trampled snow by an open fire, where Shorty and two young Indians, squatted on their hams, were broiling strips of caribou meat. Three other young Indians, lying in furs on a mat of spruce-boughs, sat up. Shorty looked across the fire at his partner, but with a sternly impassive face, like those of his companions, made no sign and went on broiling the meat.

"What's the matter?" Smoke demanded, half in irritation. "Lost your speech?"

The old familiar grin twisted on Shorty's face. "Nope," he answered. "I'm a Indian. I'm learnin' not to show surprise. When did they catch you?"

"Next day after you left."

"Hum," Shorty said, the light of whimsy dancing in his eyes. "Well, I'm doin' fine, thank you most to death. This is the bachelor's camp." He waved his hand to embrace its magnificence, which consisted of a fire, beds of spruce-boughs laid on top of the snow, flies of caribou skin, and wind-shields of twisted spruce and willow withes. "An' these are the bachelors." This time his hand indicated the young men, and he spat a few spoken gutturals in their own language that brought the white flash of acknowledgment from eyes and teeth. "They're glad to meet you, Smoke. Set down an' dry your moccasins, an' I'll cook up some grub. I'm gettin' the hang of the lingo pretty well, ain't I? You'll have to come to it, for it looks as if we'll be with these folks a long time. They's another white man here. Got caught six years ago. He's a Irishman they picked up over Great Slave Lake way. Danny McCan is what he goes by. He's settled down with a squaw. Got two kids already, but he'll skin out if ever the chance opens up. See that low fire over there to the right? That's his camp."

Apparently this was Smoke's appointed domicile, for his captors left him and his dogs, and went on deeper into the big camp. While he attended to his foot-gear and devoured strips of hot meat, Shorty cooked and talked.

"This is a sure peach of a pickle, Smoke—you listen to me. An' we got to go some to get out. These is the real, blowed-in-the-glass, wild Indians. They ain't white, but their chief is. He talks like a mouthful of hot mush, an' if he ain't full-blood Scotch they ain't no such thing as Scotch in the world. He's the hi-yu, skookum top-chief of the whole caboodle. What he says goes. You want to get that from the start-off. Danny McCan's been tryin' to get away from him for six years. Danny's all right, but he ain't got go in him. He knows a way out—learned it on huntin' trips—to the west of the way you an' me came. He ain't had the nerve to tackle it by his lonely. But we can pull it off, the three of us. Whiskers is the real goods, but he's mostly loco just the same."

"Who's Whiskers?" Smoke queried, pausing in the wolfing-down of a hot strip of meat.

"Why, he's the top geezer. He's the Scotcher. He's gettin' old, an' he's sure asleep now, but he'll see you to-morrow an' show you clear as print what a measly shrimp you are on his stompin'-grounds. These grounds belong to him. You got to get that into your noodle. They ain't never been explored, nor nothin', an' they're hisn. An' he won't let you forget it. He's got about twenty thousand square miles of huntin' country here all his own. He's the white Indian, him an' the skirt. Huh! Don't look at me that way. Wait till you see her. Some looker, an' all white, like her dad—he's Whiskers. An' say, caribou! I've saw 'em. A hundred thousan' of good running meat in the herd, an' ten thousan' wolves an' cats a-followin' an' livin' off the stragglers an' the leavin's. We leave the leavin's. The herd's movin' to the east, an' we'll be followin' 'em any day now. We eat our dogs, an' what we don't eat we smoke 'n cure for the spring before the salmon-run gets its sting in. Say, what Whiskers don't know about salmon an' caribou nobody knows, take it from me.

"Here comes Whiskers lookin' like he's goin' somewheres," Shorty whispered, reaching over and wiping greasy hands on the coat of one of the sled-dogs.

It was morning, and the bachelors were squatting over a breakfast of caribou-meat, which they ate as they broiled. Smoke glanced up and saw a small and slender man, skin-clad like any savage, but unmistakably white, striding in advance of a sled team and a following of a dozen Indians. Smoke cracked a hot bone, and while he sucked out the steaming marrow gazed at his approaching host. Bushy whiskers and yellowish gray hair, stained by camp smoke, concealed most of the face, but failed wholly to hide the gaunt, almost cadaverous, cheeks. It was a healthy leanness, Smoke decided, as he noted the wide flare of the nostrils and the breadth and depth of chest that gave spaciousness to the guaranty of oxygen and life.

"How do you do," the man said, slipping a mitten and holding out his bare hand. "My name is Snass," he added, as they shook hands.

"Mine's Bellew," Smoke returned, feeling peculiarly disconcerted as he gazed into the keen-searching black eyes.

"Getting plenty to eat, I see."

Smoke nodded and resumed his marrow-bone, the purr of Scottish speech strangely pleasant in his ears.

"Rough rations. But we don't starve often. And it's more natural than the hand-reared meat of the cities."

"I see you don't like cities," Smoke laughed, in order to be saying something; and was immediately startled by the transformation Snass underwent.

Quite like a sensitive plant, the man's entire form seemed to wilt and quiver. Then the recoil, tense and savage, concentered in the eyes, in which appeared a hatred that screamed of immeasurable pain. He turned abruptly away, and, recollecting himself, remarked casually over his shoulder:

"I'll see you later, Mr. Bellew. The caribou are moving east, and I'm going ahead to pick out a location. You'll all come on to-morrow."

"Some Whiskers, that, eh?" Shorty muttered, as Snass pulled on at the head of his outfit.

Again Shorty wiped his hands on the wolf-dog, which seemed to like it as it licked off the delectable grease.

Later on in the morning Smoke went for a stroll through the camp, busy with its primitive pursuits. A big body of hunters had just returned, and the men were scattering to their various fires. Women and children were departing with dogs harnessed to empty toboggan-sleds, and women and children and dogs were hauling sleds heavy with meat fresh from the killing and already frozen. An early spring cold-snap was on, and the wildness of the scene was painted in a temperature of thirty below zero. Woven cloth was not in evidence. Furs and soft-tanned leather clad all alike. Boys passed with bows in their hands, and quivers of bone-barbed arrows; and many a skinning-knife of bone or stone Smoke saw in belts or neck-hung sheaths. Women toiled over the fires, smoke-curing the meat, on their backs infants that stared round-eyed and sucked at lumps of tallow. Dogs, full-kin to wolves, bristled up to Smoke to endure the menace of the short club he carried and to whiff the odor of this newcomer whom they must accept by virtue of the club.

Segregated in the heart of the camp, Smoke came upon what was evidently Snass's fire. Though temporary in every detail, it was solidly constructed and was on a large scale. A great heap of bales of skins and outfit was piled on a scaffold out of reach of the dogs. A large canvas fly, almost half-tent, sheltered the sleeping- and living-quarters. To one side was a silk tent—the sort favored by explorers and wealthy big-game hunters. Smoke had never seen such a tent, and stepped closer. As he stood looking, the flaps parted and a young woman came out. So quickly did she move, so abruptly did she appear, that the effect on Smoke was as that of an apparition. He seemed to have the same effect on her, and for a long moment they gazed at each other.

She was dressed entirely in skins, but such skins and such magnificently beautiful fur-work Smoke had never dreamed of. Her parka, the hood thrown back, was of some strange fur of palest silver. The mukluks, with walrus-hide soles, were composed of the silver-padded feet of many lynxes. The long-gauntleted mittens, the tassels at the knees, all the varied furs of the costume, were pale silver that shimmered in the frosty light; and out of this shimmering silver, poised on slender, delicate neck, lifted her head, the rosy face blonde as the eyes were blue, the ears like two pink shells, the light chestnut hair touched with frost-dust and coruscating frost-glints.

All this and more, as in a dream, Smoke saw; then, recollecting himself, his hand fumbled for his cap. At the same moment the wonder-stare in the girl's eyes passed into a smile, and, with movements quick and vital, she slipped a mitten and extended her hand.

"How do you do," she murmured gravely, with a queer, delightful accent, her voice, silvery as the furs she wore, coming with a shock to Smoke's ears, attuned as they were to the harsh voices of the camp squaws.

Smoke could only mumble phrases that were awkwardly reminiscent of his best society manner.

"I am glad to see you," she went on slowly and gropingly, her face a ripple of smiles. "My English you will please excuse. It is not good. I am English like you," she gravely assured him. "My father he is Scotch. My mother she is dead. She is French, and English, and a little Indian, too. Her father was a great man in the Hudson Bay Company. Brrr! It is cold." She slipped on her mitten and rubbed her ears, the pink of which had already turned to white. "Let us go to the fire and talk. My name is Labiskwee. What is your name?"

And so Smoke came to know Labiskwee, the daughter of Snass, whom Snass called Margaret.

"Snass is not my father's name," she informed Smoke. "Snass is only an Indian name."

Much Smoke learned that day, and in the days that followed, as the hunting-camp moved on in the trail of the caribou. These were real wild Indians—the ones Anton had encountered and escaped from long years before. This was nearly the western limit of their territory, and in the summer they ranged north to the tundra shores of the Arctic, and eastward as far as the Luskwa. What river the Luskwa was Smoke could not make out, nor could Labiskwee tell him, nor could McCan. On occasion Snass, with parties of strong hunters, pushed east across the Rockies, on past the lakes and the Mackenzie and into the Barrens. It was on the last traverse in that direction that the silk tent occupied by Labiskwee had been found.

"It belonged to the Millicent-Adbury expedition," Snass told Smoke.

"Oh! I remember. They went after musk-oxen. The rescue expedition never found a trace of them."

"I found them," Snass said. "But both were dead."

"The world still doesn't know. The word never got out."

"The word never gets out," Snass assured him pleasantly.

"You mean if they had been alive when you found them—?"

Snass nodded. "They would have lived on with me and my people."

"Anton got out," Smoke challenged.

"I do not remember the name. How long ago?"

"Fourteen or fifteen years," Smoke answered.

"So he pulled through, after all. Do you know, I've wondered about him. We called him Long Tooth. He was a strong man, a strong man."

"La Perle came through here ten years ago."

Snass shook his head.

"He found traces of your camps. It was summer time."

"That explains it," Snass answered. "We are hundreds of miles to the north in the summer."

But, strive as he would, Smoke could get no clew to Snass's history in the days before he came to live in the northern wilds. Educated he was, yet in all the intervening years he had read no books, no newspapers. What had happened in the world he knew not, nor did he show desire to know. He had heard of the miners on the Yukon, and of the Klondike strike. Gold-miners had never invaded his territory, for which he was glad. But the outside world to him did not exist. He tolerated no mention of it.

Nor could Labiskwee help Smoke with earlier information. She had been born on the hunting-grounds. Her mother had lived for six years after. Her mother had been very beautiful—the only white woman Labiskwee had ever seen. She said this wistfully, and wistfully, in a thousand ways, she showed that she knew of the great outside world on which her father had closed the door. But this knowledge was secret. She had early learned that mention of it threw her father into a rage.

Anton had told a squaw of her mother, and that her mother had been a daughter of a high official in the Hudson Bay Company. Later, the squaw had told Labiskwee. But her mother's name she had never learned.

As a source of information, Danny McCan was impossible. He did not like adventure. Wild life was a horror, and he had had nine years of it. Shanghaied in San Francisco, he had deserted the whaleship at Point Barrow with three companions. Two had died, and the third had abandoned him on the terrible traverse south. Two years he had lived with the Eskimos before raising the courage to attempt the south traverse, and then, within several days of a Hudson Bay Company post, he had been gathered in by a party of Snass's young men. He was a small, stupid man, afflicted with sore eyes, and all he dreamed or could talk about was getting back to his beloved San Francisco and his blissful trade of bricklaying.

"You're the first intelligent man we've had." Snass complimented Smoke one night by the fire. "Except old Four Eyes. The Indians named him so. He wore glasses and was short-sighted. He was a professor of zoology." (Smoke noted the correctness of the pronunciation of the word.) "He died a year ago. My young men picked him up strayed from an expedition on the upper Porcupine. He was intelligent, yes; but he was also a fool. That was his weakness—straying. He knew geology, though, and working in metals. Over on the Luskwa, where there's coal, we have several creditable hand-forges he made. He repaired our guns and taught the young men how. He died last year, and we really missed him. Strayed—that's how it happened—froze to death within a mile of camp."

It was on the same night that Snass said to Smoke:

"You'd better pick out a wife and have a fire of your own. You will be more comfortable than with those young bucks. The maidens' fires —a sort of feast of the virgins, you know—are not lighted until full summer and the salmon, but I can give orders earlier if you say the word."

Smoke laughed and shook his head.

"Remember," Snass concluded quietly, "Anton is the only one that ever got away. He was lucky, unusually lucky."

Her father had a will of iron, Labiskwee told Smoke.

"Four Eyes used to call him the Frozen Pirate—whatever that means—the Tyrant of the Frost, the Cave Bear, the Beast Primitive, the King of the Caribou, the Bearded Pard, and lots of such things. Four

Eyes loved words like these. He taught me most of my English. He was always making fun. You could never tell. He called me his cheetah-chum after times when I was angry. What is cheetah? He always teased me with it."

She chattered on with all the eager naiveté of a child, which Smoke found hard to reconcile with the full womanhood of her form and face.

Yes, her father was very firm. Everybody feared him. He was terrible when angry. There were the Porcupines. It was through them, and through the Luskwas, that Snass traded his skins at the posts and got his supplies of ammunition and tobacco. He was always fair, but the chief of the Porcupines began to cheat. And after Snass had warned him twice, he burned his log village, and over a dozen of the Porcupines were killed in the fight. But there was no more cheating. Once, when she was a little girl, there was one white man killed while trying to escape. No, her father did not do it, but he gave the order to the young men. No Indian ever disobeyed her father.

And the more Smoke learned from her, the more the mystery of Snass deepened.

"And tell me if it is true," the girl was saying, "that there was a man and a woman whose names were Paolo and Francesca and who greatly loved each other?"

Smoke nodded.

"Four Eyes told me all about it," she beamed happily. "And so he didn't make it up, after all. You see, I wasn't sure. I asked father, but, oh, he was angry. The Indians told me he gave poor Four Eyes an awful talking to. Then there were Tristan and Iseult—two Iseults. It was very sad. But I should like to love that way. Do all the young men and women in the world do that? They don't here. They just get married. They don't seem to have time. I am English, and I will never marry an Indian—would you? That is why I have not lighted my maiden's fire. Some of the young men are bothering father to make me do it. Libash is one of them. He is a great hunter. And Mahkook comes around singing songs. He is funny. Tonight, if you come by my tent after dark, you will hear him singing out in the cold. But father says I can do as I please, and so I shall not light my fire. You see, when a girl makes up her mind to get married, that is the way she lets young men know. Four Eyes always said it was a fine custom. But I noticed he never took a wife. Maybe he was too old. He didn't have much hair, but I don't think he was really very old. And how do you know when you are in love?—like Paolo and Francesca, I mean."

Smoke was disconcerted by the clear gaze of her blue eyes. "Why, they say," he stammered, "those who are in love say it, that love is dearer than life. When one finds out that he or she likes somebody better than everybody else in the world—why, then, they know they are in love. That's the way it goes, but it's awfully hard to explain. You just know it, that's all."

She looked off across the camp-smoke, sighed, and resumed work on the fur mitten she was sewing. "Well," she announced with finality, "I shall never get married anyway."

"Once we hit out we'll sure have some tall runnin'," Shorty said dismally.

"The place is a big trap," Smoke agreed.

From the crest of a bald knob they gazed out over Snass's snowy domain. East, west, and south they were hemmed in by the high peaks and jumbled ranges. Northward, the rolling country seemed interminable; yet they knew, even in that direction, that half a dozen transverse chains blocked the way.

"At this time of the year I could give you three days' start," Snass told Smoke that evening. "You can't hide your trail, you see. Anton got away when the snow was gone. My young men can travel as fast as the best white man; and, besides, you would be breaking trail for them. And when the snow is off the ground, I'll see to it that you don't get the chance Anton had. It's a good life. And soon the world fades. I have never quite got over the surprise of finding how easy it is to get along without the world."

"What's eatin' me is Danny McCan," Shorty confided to Smoke. "He's a weak brother on any trail. But he swears he knows the way out to the westward, an' so we got to put up with him, Smoke, or you sure get yours."

"We're all in the same boat," Smoke answered.

"Not on your life. It's a-comin' to you straight down the pike."

"What is?"

"You ain't heard the news?"

Smoke shook his head.

"The bachelors told me. They just got the word. To-night it comes off, though it's months ahead of the calendar."

Smoke shrugged his shoulders.

"Ain't interested in hearin'?" Shorty teased.

"I'm waiting to hear."

"Well, Danny's wife just told the bachelors," Shorty paused impressively. "An' the bachelors told me, of course, that the maidens' fires is due to be lighted to-night. That's all. Now how do you like it?"

"I don't get your drift, Shorty."

"Don't, eh? Why, it's plain open and shut. They's a skirt after you, an' that skirt is goin' to light a fire, an' that skirt's name is Labiskwee. Oh, I've been watchin' her watch you when you ain't lookin'. She ain't never lighted her fire. Said she wouldn't marry a Indian. An' now, when she lights her fire, it's a cinch it's my poor old friend Smoke."

"It sounds like a syllogism," Smoke said, with a sinking heart reviewing Labiskwee's actions of the past several days.

"Cinch is shorter to pronounce," Shorty returned. "An' that's always the way—just as we're workin' up our get-away, along comes a skirt to complicate everything. We ain't got no luck. Hey! Listen to that, Smoke!"

Three ancient squaws had halted midway between the bachelors' camp and the camp of McCan, and the oldest was declaiming in shrill falsetto.

Smoke recognized the names, but not all the words, and Shorty translated with melancholy glee.

"Labiskwee, the daughter of Snass, the Rainmaker, the Great Chief, lights her first maiden's fire to-night. Maka, the daughter of Owits, the Wolf-Runner—"

The recital ran through the names of a dozen maidens, and then the three heralds tottered on their way to make announcement at the next fires.

The bachelors, who had sworn youthful oaths to speak to no maidens, were uninterested in the approaching ceremony, and to show their disdain they made preparations for immediate departure on a mission set them by Snass and upon which they had planned to start the following morning. Not satisfied with the old hunters' estimates of the caribou, Snass had decided that the run was split. The task set the bachelors was to scout to the north and west in quest of the second division of the great herd.

Smoke, troubled by Labiskwee's fire-lighting, announced that he would accompany the bachelors. But first he talked with Shorty and with McCan.

"You be there on the third day, Smoke," Shorty said. "We'll have the outfit an' the dogs."

"But remember," Smoke cautioned, "if there is any slip-up in meeting me, you keep on going and get out to the Yukon. That's flat. If you make it, you can come back for me in the summer. If I get the chance, I'll make it, and come back for you."

McCan, standing by his fire, indicated with his eyes a rugged mountain where the high western range out-jutted on the open country.

"That's the one," he said. "A small stream on the south side. We go up it. On the third day you meet us. We'll pass by on the third day. Anywhere you tap that stream you'll meet us or our trail."

But the chance did not come to Smoke on the third day. The bachelors had changed the direction of their scout, and while Shorty and McCan plodded up the stream with their dogs, Smoke and the bachelors were sixty miles to the northeast picking up the trail of the second caribou herd. Several days later, through a dim twilight of falling snow, they came back to the big camp. A squaw ceased from wailing by a fire and darted up to Smoke. Harsh tongued, with bitter, venomous eyes, she cursed him, waving her arms toward a silent, fur-wrapped form that still lay on the sled which had hauled it in.

What had happened, Smoke could only guess, and as he came to McCan's fire he was prepared for a second cursing. Instead, he saw McCan himself industriously chewing a strip of caribou meat.

"I'm not a fightin' man," he whiningly explained. "But Shorty got away, though they're still after him. He put up a hell of a fight. They'll get him, too. He ain't got a chance. He plugged two bucks that'll get around all right. An' he croaked one square through the chest."

"Yes, I know," Smoke answered. "I just met the widow."

"Old Snass'll be wantin' to see you," McCan added. "Them's his orders. Soon as you come in you was to go to his fire. I ain't squealed. You don't know nothing. Keep that in mind. Shorty went off on his own along with me."

At Snass's fire Smoke found Labiskwee. She met him with eyes that shone with such softness and tenderness as to frighten him.

"I'm glad you didn't try to run away," she said. "You see, I—" She hesitated, but her eyes didn't drop. They swam with a light unmistakable. "I lighted my fire, and of course it was for you. It has happened. I like you better than everybody else in the world. Better than my father. Better than a thousand Libashes and Mahkooks. I love. It is very strange. I love as Francesca loved, as Iseult loved. Old Four Eyes spoke true. Indians do not love this way. But my eyes are blue, and I am white. We are white, you and I."

Smoke had never been proposed to in his life, and he was unable to meet the situation. Worse, it was not even a proposal. His acceptance was taken for granted. So thoroughly was it all arranged in Labiskwee's mind, so warm was the light in her eyes, that he was amazed that she did not throw her arms around him and rest her head on his shoulder. Then he realized, despite her candor of love, that she did not know the pretty ways of love. Among the primitive savages such ways did not obtain. She had had no chance to learn.

She prattled on, chanting the happy burden of her love, while he strove to grip himself in the effort, somehow, to wound her with the truth. This, at the very first, was the golden opportunity.

"But, Labiskwee, listen," he began. "Are you sure you learned from Four Eyes all the story of the love of Paolo and Francesca?"

She clasped her hands and laughed with an immense certitude of gladness. "Oh! There is more! I knew there must be more and more of love! I have thought much since I lighted my fire. I have—"

And then Snass strode in to the fire through the falling snowflakes, and Smoke's opportunity was lost.

"Good evening," Snass burred gruffly. "Your partner has made a mess of it. I am glad you had better sense."

"You might tell me what's happened," Smoke urged.

The flash of white teeth through the stained beard was not pleasant. "Certainly, I'll tell you. Your partner has killed one of my people. That sniveling shrimp, McCan, deserted at the first shot. He'll never run away again. But my hunters have got your partner in the mountains, and they'll get him. He'll never make the Yukon basin. As for you, from now on you sleep at my fire. And there'll be no more scouting with the young men. I shall have my eye on you."

Smoke's new situation at Snass's fire was embarrassing. He saw more of Labiskwee than ever. In its sweetness and innocence, the frankness of her love was terrible. Her glances were love glances; every look was a caress. A score of times he nerved himself to tell her of Joy Gastell, and a score of times he discovered that he was a coward. The damnable part of it was that Labiskwee was so delightful. She was good to look upon. Despite the hurt to his self-esteem of every moment spent with her, he pleasured in every such moment. For the first time in his life he was really learning woman, and so clear was Labiskwee's soul, so appalling in its innocence and ignorance, that he could not misread a line of it. All the pristine goodness of her sex was in her, uncultured by the conventionality of knowledge or the deceit of self-protection. In memory he reread his Schopenhauer and knew beyond all cavil that the sad philosopher was wrong. To know woman, as Smoke came to know Labiskwee, was to know that all woman-haters were sick men.

Labiskwee was wonderful, and yet, beside her face in the flesh burned the vision of the face of Joy Gastell. Joy had control, restraint, all the feminine inhibitions of civilization, yet, by the trick of his fancy and the living preachment of the woman before him, Joy Gastell was stripped to a goodness at par with Labiskwee's. The one but appreciated the other, and all women of all the world appreciated by what Smoke saw in the soul of Labiskwee at Snass's fire in the snow-land.

And Smoke learned about himself. He remembered back to all he knew of Joy Gastell, and he knew that he loved her. Yet he delighted in Labiskwee. And what was this feeling of delight but love? He could demean it by no less a name. Love it was. Love it must be. And he was shocked to the roots of his soul by the discovery of this polygamous strain in his nature. He had heard it argued, in the San Francisco studios, that it was possible for a man to love two women, or even three women, at a time. But he had not believed it. How could he believe it when he had not had the experience? Now it was different. He did truly love two women, and though most of the time he was quite convinced that he loved Joy Gastell more, there were other moments when he felt with equal certainty that he loved Labiskwee more.

"There must be many women in the world," she said one day. "And women like men. Many women must have liked you. Tell me."

He did not reply.

"Tell me," she insisted.

"I have never married," he evaded.

"And there is no one else? No other Iseult out there beyond the mountains?"

Then it was that Smoke knew himself a coward. He lied. Reluctantly he did it, but he lied. He shook his head with a slow indulgent smile, and in his face was more of fondness than he dreamed as he noted Labiskwee's swift joy-transfiguration.

He excused himself to himself. His reasoning was jesuitical beyond dispute, and yet he was not Spartan enough to strike this child-woman a quivering heart-stroke.

Snass, too, was a perturbing factor in the problem. Little escaped his keen black eyes, and he spoke significantly.

"No man cares to see his daughter married," he said to Smoke. "At least, no man of imagination. It hurts. The thought of it hurts, I tell you. Just the same, in the natural order of life, Margaret must marry some time."

A pause fell, and Smoke caught himself wondering for the thousandth time what Snass's history must be.

"I am a harsh, cruel man," Snass went on. "Yet the law is the law, and I am just. Nay, here with this primitive people, I am the law and the justice. Beyond my will no man goes. Also, I am a father, and all my days I have been cursed with imagination."

Whither his monologue tended, Smoke did not learn, for it was interrupted by a burst of chiding and silvery laughter from Labiskwee's tent, where she played with a new-caught wolf-cub. A spasm of pain twitched Snass's face.

"I can stand it," he muttered grimly. "Margaret must be married, and it is my fortune, and hers, that you are here. I had little hopes of Four Eyes. McCan was so hopeless I turned him over to a squaw who had lighted her fire twenty seasons. If it hadn't been you, it would have been an Indian. Libash might have become the father of my grandchildren."

And then Labiskwee came from her tent to the fire, the wolf-cub in her arms, drawn as by a magnet, to gaze upon the man, in her eyes the love that art had never taught to hide.

"Listen to me," said McCan. "The spring thaw is here, an' the crust is comin' on the snow. It's the time to travel, exceptin' for the spring blizzards in the mountains. I know them. I would run with no less a man than you."

"But you can't run," Smoke contradicted. "You can keep up with no man. Your backbone is limber as thawed marrow. If I run, I run alone. The world fades, and perhaps I shall never run. Caribou meat is very good, and soon will come summer and the salmon."

Said Snass: "Your partner is dead. My hunters did not kill him. They found the body, frozen in the first of the spring storms in the mountains. No man can escape. When shall we celebrate your marriage?"

And Labiskwee: "I watch you. There is trouble in your eyes, in your face. Oh, I do know all your face. There is a little scar on your neck, just under the ear. When you are happy, the corners of your mouth turn up. When you think sad thoughts they turn down. When you smile there are three and four wrinkles at the corners of your eyes. When you laugh there are six. Sometimes I have almost counted seven. But I cannot count them now. I have never read books. I do not know how to read. But Four Eyes taught me much. My grammar is good. He taught me. And in his own eyes I have seen the trouble of the hunger for the world. He was often hungry for the world. Yet here was good meat, and fish in plenty, and the berries and the roots, and often flour came back for the furs through the Porcupines and the Luskwas. Yet was he hungry for the world. Is the world so good that you, too, are hungry for it? Four Eyes had nothing. But you have me." She sighed and shook her head. "Four Eyes died still hungry for the world. And if you lived here always would you, too, die hungry for the world? I am afraid I do not know the world. Do you want to run away to the world?"

Smoke could not speak, but by his mouth-corner lines was she convinced.

Minutes of silence passed, in which she visibly struggled, while Smoke cursed himself for the unguessed weakness that enabled him to speak the truth about his hunger for the world while it kept his lips tight on the truth of the existence of the other woman.

Again Labiskwee sighed.

"Very well. I love you more than I fear my father's anger, and he is more terrible in anger than a mountain storm. You told me what love is. This is the test of love. I shall help you to run away back to the world."

Smoke awakened softly and without movement. Warm small fingers touched his cheek and slid gently to a pressure on his lips. Fur, with the chill of frost clinging in it, next tingled his skin, and the one word, "Come," was breathed in his ear. He sat up carefully and listened. The hundreds of wolf-dogs in the camp had lifted their nocturnal song, but under the volume of it, close at hand, he could distinguish the light, regular breathing of Snass.

Labiskwee tugged gently at Smoke's sleeve, and he knew she wished him to follow. He took his moccasins and German socks in his hand and crept out into the snow in his sleeping moccasins. Beyond the glow from the dying embers of the fire, she indicated to him to put on his outer foot-gear, and while he obeyed, she went back under the fly where Snass slept.

Feeling the hands of his watch Smoke found it was one in the morning. Quite warm it was, he decided, not more than ten below zero. Labiskwee rejoined him and led him on through the dark runways of the sleeping camp. Walk lightly as they could, the frost crunched crisply under their moccasins, but the sound was drowned by the clamor of the dogs, too deep in their howling to snarl at the man and woman who passed.

"Now we can talk," she said, when the last fire had been left half a mile behind.

And now, in the starlight, facing him, Smoke noted for the first time that her arms were burdened, and, on feeling, discovered she carried his snowshoes, a rifle, two belts of ammunition, and his sleeping-robes.

"I have everything fixed," she said, with a happy little laugh. "I have been two days making the cache. There is meat, even flour, matches, and skees, which go best on the hard crust and, when they break through, the webs will hold up longer. Oh, I do know snow-travel, and we shall go fast, my lover."

Smoke checked his speech. That she had been arranging his escape was surprise enough, but that she had planned to go with him was more than he was prepared for. Unable to think immediate action, he gently, one by one, took her burdens from her. He put his arm around her and pressed her close, and still he could not think what to do.

"God is good," she whispered. "He sent me a lover."

Yet Smoke was brave enough not to suggest his going alone. And before he spoke again he saw all his memory of the bright world and the sun-lands reel and fade.

"We will go back, Labiskwee," he said. "You will be my wife, and we shall live always with the Caribou People."

"No! no!" She shook her head; and her body, in the circle of his arm, resented his proposal. "I know. I have thought much. The hunger for the world would come upon you, and in the long nights it would devour your heart. Four Eyes died of hunger for the world. So would you die. All men from the world hunger for it. And I will not have you die. We will go on across the snow mountains on the south traverse."

"Dear, listen," he urged. "We must go back."

She pressed her mitten against his lips to prevent further speech. "You love me. Say that you love me."

"I do love you, Labiskwee. You are my wonderful sweetheart."

Again the mitten was a caressing obstacle to utterance.

"We shall go on to the cache," she said with decision. "It is three miles from here. Come."

He held back, and her pull on his arm could not move him. Almost was he tempted to tell her of the other woman beyond the south traverse.

"It would be a great wrong to you to go back," she said. "I—I am only a wild girl, and I am afraid of the world; but I am more afraid for you. You see, it is as you told me. I love you more than anybody else in the world. I love you more than myself. The Indian language is not a good language. The English language is not a good language. The thoughts in my heart for you, as bright and as many as the stars—there is no language for them. How can I tell you them? They are there— see?"

As she spoke she slipped the mitten from his hand and thrust the hand inside the warmth of her parka until it rested against her heart. Tightly and steadily she pressed his hand in its position. And in the long silence he felt the beat, beat of her heart, and knew that every beat of it was love. And then, slowly, almost imperceptibly, still holding his hand, her body began to incline away from his and toward the direction of the cache. Nor could he resist. It was as if he were drawn by her heart itself that so nearly lay in the hollow of his hand.

So firm was the crust, frozen during the night after the previous day's surface-thaw, that they slid along rapidly on their skees.

"Just here, in the trees, is the cache," Labiskwee told Smoke.

The next moment she caught his arm with a startle of surprise. The flames of a small fire were dancing merrily, and crouched by the fire was McCan. Labiskwee muttered something in Indian, and so lashlike was the sound that Smoke remembered she had been called "cheetah" by Four Eyes.

"I was minded you'd run without me," McCan explained when they came up, his small peering eyes glimmering with cunning. "So I kept an eye on the girl, an' when I seen her caching skees an' grub, I was on. I've brought my own skees an' webs an' grub. The fire? Sure, an' it was no danger. The camp's asleep an' snorin', an' the waitin' was cold. Will we be startin' now?"

Labiskwee looked swift consternation at Smoke, as swiftly achieved a judgment on the matter, and spoke. And in the speaking she showed, child-woman though she was in love, the quick decisiveness of one who in other affairs of life would be no clinging vine.

"McCan, you are a dog," she hissed, and her eyes were savage with anger. "I know it is in your heart to raise the camp if we don't take you. Very well. We must take you. But you know my father. I am like my father. You will do your share of the work. You will obey. And if you play one dirty trick, it would be better for you if you had never run."

McCan looked up at her, his small pig-eyes hating and cringing, while in her eyes, turned to Smoke, the anger melted into luminous softness.

"Is it right, what I have said?" she queried.

Daylight found them in the belt of foothills that lay between the rolling country and the mountains. McCan suggested breakfast, but they held on. Not until the afternoon thaw softened the crust and prevented travel would they eat.

The foothills quickly grew rugged, and the stream, up whose frozen bed they journeyed, began to thread deeper and deeper canyons. The signs of spring were less frequent, though in one canyon they found foaming bits of open water, and twice they came upon clumps of dwarf willow upon which were the first hints of swelling buds.

Labiskwee explained to Smoke her knowledge of the country and the way she planned to baffle pursuit. There were but two ways out, one west, the other south. Snass would immediately despatch parties of young men to guard the two trails. But there was another way south. True, it did no more than penetrate half-way into the high mountains, then, twisting to the west and crossing three divides, it joined the regular trail. When the young men found no traces on the regular trail they would turn back in the belief that the escape had been made by the west traverse, never dreaming that the runaways had ventured the harder and longer way around.

Glancing back at McCan, in the rear, Labiskwee spoke in an undertone to Smoke. "He is eating," she said. "It is not good."

Smoke looked. The Irishman was secretly munching caribou suet from the pocketful he carried.

"No eating between meals, McCan," he commanded. "There's no game in the country ahead, and the grub will have to be whacked in equal rations from the start. The only way you can travel with us is by playing fair."

By one o'clock the crust had thawed so that the skees broke through, and before two o'clock the web-shoes were breaking through. Camp was made and the first meal eaten. Smoke took stock of the food. McCan's supply was a disappointment. So many silver foxskins had he stuffed in the bottom of the meat bag that there was little space left for meat.

"Sure an' I didn't know there was so many," he explained. "I done it in the dark. But they're worth good money. An' with all this ammunition we'll be gettin' game a-plenty."

"The wolves will eat you a-plenty," was Smoke's hopeless comment, while Labiskwee's eyes flashed their anger.

Enough food for a month, with careful husbanding and appetites that never blunted their edge, was Smoke's and Labiskwee's judgment. Smoke apportioned the weight and bulk of the packs, yielding in the end to Labiskwee's insistence that she, too, should carry a pack.

Next day the stream shallowed out in a wide mountain valley, and they were already breaking through the crust on the flats when they gained the harder surface of the slope of the divide.

"Ten minutes later and we wouldn't have got across the flats," Smoke said, when they paused for breath on the bald crest of the summit. "We must be a thousand feet higher here."

But Labiskwee, without speaking, pointed down to an open flat among the trees. In the midst of it, scattered abreast, were five dark specks that scarcely moved.

"The young men," said Labiskwee.

"They are wallowing to their hips," Smoke said. "They will never gain the hard footing this day. We have hours the start of them. Come on, McCan. Buck up. We don't eat till we can't travel."

McCan groaned, but there was no caribou suet in his pocket, and he doggedly brought up the rear.

In the higher valley in which they now found themselves, the crust did not break till three in the afternoon, at which time they managed to gain the shadow of mountain where the crust was already freezing again. Once only they paused to get out McCan's confiscated suet, which they ate as they walked. The meat was frozen solid, and could be eaten only after thawing over a fire. But the suet crumbled in their mouths and eased the palpitating faintness in their stomachs.

Black darkness, with an overcast sky, came on after a long twilight at nine o'clock, when they made camp in a clump of dwarf spruce. McCan was whining and helpless. The day's march had been exhausting, but in addition, despite his nine years' experience in the arctic, he had been eating snow and was in agony with his parched and burning mouth. He crouched by the fire and groaned, while they made the camp.

Labiskwee was tireless, and Smoke could not but marvel at the life in her body, at the endurance of mind and muscle. Nor was her cheerfulness forced. She had ever a laugh or a smile for him, and her hand lingered in caress whenever it chanced to touch his. Yet, always, when she looked at McCan, her face went hard and pitiless and her eyes flashed frostily.

In the night came wind and snow, and through a day of blizzard they fought their way blindly, missing the turn of the way that led up a small stream and crossed a divide to the west. For two more days they wandered, crossing other and wrong divides, and in those two days they dropped spring behind and climbed up into the abode of winter.

"The young men have lost our trail, an' what's to stop us restin' a day?" McCan begged.

But no rest was accorded. Smoke and Labiskwee knew their danger. They were lost in the high mountains, and they had seen no game nor signs of game. Day after day they struggled on through an iron configuration of landscape that compelled them to labyrinthine canyons and valleys that led rarely to the west. Once in such a canyon, they could only follow it, no matter where it led, for the cold peaks and higher ranges on either side were unscalable and unendurable. The terrible toil and the cold ate up energy, yet they cut down the size of the ration they permitted themselves.

One night Smoke was awakened by a sound of struggling. Distinctly he heard a gasping and strangling from where McCan slept. Kicking the fire into flame, by its light he saw Labiskwee, her hands at the Irishman's throat and forcing from his mouth a chunk of partly chewed meat. Even as Smoke saw this, her hand went to her hip and flashed with the sheath-knife in it.

"Labiskwee!" Smoke cried, and his voice was peremptory.

The hand hesitated.

"Don't," he said, coming to her side.

She was shaking with anger, but the hand, after hesitating a moment longer, descended reluctantly to the sheath. As if fearing she could not restrain herself, she crossed to the fire and threw on more wood. McCan sat up, whimpering and snarling, between fright and rage spluttering an inarticulate explanation.

"Where did you get it?" Smoke demanded.

"Feel around his body," Labiskwee said.

It was the first word she had spoken, and her voice quivered with the anger she could not suppress.

McCan strove to struggle, but Smoke gripped him cruelly and searched him, drawing forth from under his armpit, where it had been thawed by the heat of his body, a strip of caribou meat. A quick exclamation from Labiskwee drew Smoke's attention. She had sprung to McCan's pack and was opening it. Instead of meat, out poured moss, spruce-needles, chips—all the light refuse that had taken the place of the meat and given the pack its due proportion minus its weight.

Again Labiskwee's hand went to her hip, and she flew at the culprit only to be caught in Smoke's arms, where she surrendered herself, sobbing with the futility of her rage.

"Oh, lover, it is not the food," she panted. "It is you, your life. The dog! He is eating you, he is eating you!"

"We will yet live," Smoke comforted her. "Hereafter he shall carry the flour. He can't eat that raw, and if he does I'll kill him myself, for he will be eating your life as well as mine." He held her closer. "Sweetheart, killing is men's work. Women do not kill."

"You would not love me if I killed the dog?" she questioned in surprise.

"Not so much," Smoke temporized.

She sighed with resignation. "Very well," she said. "I shall not kill him."

The pursuit by the young men was relentless. By miracles of luck, as well as by deduction from the topography of the way the runaways must take, the young men picked up the blizzard-blinded trail and clung to it. When the snow flew, Smoke and Labiskwee took the most improbable courses, turning east when the better way opened south or west, rejecting a low divide to climb a higher. Being lost, it did not matter. Yet they could not throw the young men off. Sometimes they gained days, but always the young men appeared again. After a storm, when all trace was lost, they would cast out like a pack of hounds, and he who caught the later trace made smoke signals to call his comrades on.

Smoke lost count of time, of days and nights and storms and camps. Through a vast mad phantasmagoria of suffering and toil he and Labiskwee struggled on, with McCan somehow stumbling along in the rear, babbling of San Francisco, his everlasting dream. Great peaks, pitiless and serene in the chill blue, towered about them. They fled down black canyons with walls so precipitous that the rock frowned naked, or wallowed across glacial valleys where frozen lakes lay far beneath their feet. And one night, between two storms, a distant volcano glared the sky. They never saw it again, and wondered whether it had been a dream.

Crusts were covered with yards of new snow, that crusted and were snow-covered again. There were places, in canyon- and pocket-drifts, where they crossed snow hundreds of feet deep, and they crossed tiny glaciers, in drafty rifts, wind-scurried and bare of any snow. They crept like silent wraiths across the faces of impending avalanches, or roused from exhausted sleep to the thunder of them. They made fireless camps above timber-line, thawing their meat-rations with the heat of their bodies ere they could eat. And through it all Labiskwee remained Labiskwee. Her cheer never vanished, save when she looked at McCan, and the greatest stupor of fatigue and cold never stilled the eloquence of her love for Smoke.

Like a cat she watched the apportionment of the meager ration, and Smoke could see that she grudged McCan every munch of his jaws. Once, she distributed the ration. The first Smoke knew was a wild harangue of protest from McCan. Not to him alone, but to herself, had she given a smaller portion than to Smoke. After that, Smoke divided the meat himself. Caught in a small avalanche one morning after a night of snow, and swept a hundred yards down the mountain, they emerged half-stifled and unhurt, but McCan emerged without his pack in which was all the flour. A second and larger snow-slide buried it beyond hope of recovery. After that, though the disaster had been through no fault of his, Labiskwee never looked at McCan, and Smoke knew it was because she dared not.

It was a morning, stark still, clear blue above, with white sun-dazzle on the snow. The way led up a long, wide slope of crust. They moved like weary ghosts in a dead world. No wind stirred in the stagnant, frigid calm. Far peaks, a hundred miles away, studding the backbone of the Rockies up and down, were as distinct as if no more than five miles away.

"Something is going to happen," Labiskwee whispered. "Don't you feel it?—here, there, everywhere? Everything is strange."

"I feel a chill that is not of cold," Smoke answered. "Nor is it of hunger."

"It is in your head, your heart," she agreed excitedly. "That is the way I feel it."

"It is not of my senses," Smoke diagnosed. "I sense something, from without, that is tingling me with ice; it is a chill of my nerves."

A quarter of an hour later they paused for breath.

"I can no longer see the far peaks," Smoke said.

"The air is getting thick and heavy," said Labiskwee. "It is hard to breathe."

"There be three suns," McCan muttered hoarsely, reeling as he clung to his staff for support.

There was a mock sun on either side the real sun.

"There are five," said Labiskwee; and as they looked, new suns formed and flashed before their eyes.

"By Heaven, the sky is filled with suns beyant all countin'," McCan cried in fear.

Which was true, for look where they would, half the circle of the sky dazzled and blazed with new suns forming.

McCan yelped sharply with surprise and pain. "I'm stung!" he cried out, then yelped again.

Then Labiskwee cried out, and Smoke felt a prickling stab on his cheek so cold that it burned like acid. It reminded him of swimming in the salt sea and being stung by the poisonous filaments of Portuguese men-of-war. The sensations were so similar that he automatically brushed his cheek to rid it of the stinging substance that was not there.

And then a shot rang out, strangely muffled. Down the slope were the young men, standing on their skees, and one after another opened fire.

"Spread out!" Smoke commanded. "And climb for it! We're almost to the top. They're a quarter of a mile below, and that means a couple of miles the start of them on the down-going of the other side."

With faces prickling and stinging from invisible atmospheric stabs, the three scattered widely on the snow surface and toiled upward. The muffled reports of the rifles were weird to their ears.

"Thank the Lord," Smoke panted to Labiskwee, "that four of them are muskets, and only one a Winchester. Besides, all these suns spoil their aim. They are fooled. They haven't come within a hundred feet of us."

"It shows my father's temper," she said. "They have orders to kill."

"How strange you talk," Smoke said. "Your voice sounds far away."

"Cover your mouth," Labiskwee cried suddenly. "And don't talk. I know what it is. Cover your mouth with your sleeve, thus, and do not talk."

McCan fell first, and struggled wearily to his feet. And after that all fell repeatedly ere they reached the summit. Their wills exceeded their muscles, they knew not why, save that their bodies were oppressed by a numbness and heaviness of movement. From the crest, looking back, they saw the young men stumbling and falling on the upward climb.

"They will never get here," Labiskwee said. "It is the white death. I know it, though I have never seen it. I have heard the old men talk. Soon will come a mist—unlike any mist or fog or frost-smoke you ever saw. Few have seen it and lived."

McCan gasped and strangled.

"Keep your mouth covered," Smoke commanded.

A pervasive flashing of light from all about them drew Smoke's eyes upward to the many suns. They were shimmering and veiling. The air was filled with microscopic fire-glints. The near peaks were being blotted out by the weird mist; the young men, resolutely struggling nearer, were being engulfed in it. McCan had sunk down, squatting, on his skees, his mouth and eyes covered by his arms.

"Come on, make a start," Smoke ordered.

"I can't move," McCan moaned.

His doubled body set up a swaying motion. Smoke went toward him slowly, scarcely able to will movement through the lethargy that weighed his flesh. He noted that his brain was clear. It was only the body that was afflicted.

"Let him be," Labiskwee muttered harshly.

But Smoke persisted, dragging the Irishman to his feet and facing him down the long slope they must go. Then he started him with a shove, and McCan, braking and steering with his staff, shot into the sheen of diamond-dust and disappeared.

Smoke looked at Labiskwee, who smiled, though it was all she could do to keep from sinking down. He nodded for her to push off, but she came near to him, and side by side, a dozen feet apart, they flew down through the stinging thickness of cold fire.

Brake as he would, Smoke's heavier body carried him past her, and he dashed on alone, a long way, at tremendous speed that did not slacken till he came out on a level, crusted plateau. Here he braked till Labiskwee overtook him, and they went on, again side by side, with diminishing speed which finally ceased. The lethargy had grown more pronounced. The wildest effort of will could move them no more than at a snail's pace. They passed McCan, again crouched down on his skees, and Smoke roused him with his staff in passing.

"Now we must stop," Labiskwee whispered painfully, "or we will die. We must cover up—so the old men said."

She did not delay to untie knots, but began cutting her pack-lashings. Smoke cut his, and, with a last look at the fiery death-mist and the mockery of suns, they covered themselves over with the sleeping-furs and crouched in each other's arms. They felt a body stumble over them and fall, then heard feeble whimpering and blaspheming drowned in a violent coughing fit, and knew it was McCan who huddled against them as he wrapped his robe about him.

Their own lung-strangling began, and they were racked and torn by a dry cough, spasmodic and uncontrollable. Smoke noted his temperature rising in a fever, and Labiskwee suffered similarly. Hour after hour the coughing spells increased in frequency and violence, and not till late afternoon was the worst reached. After that the mend came slowly, and between spells they dozed in exhaustion.

McCan, however, steadily coughed worse, and from his groans and howls they knew he was in delirium. Once, Smoke made as if to throw the robes back, but Labiskwee clung to him tightly.

"No," she begged. "It is death to uncover now. Bury your face here, against my parka, and breathe gently and do no talking—see, the way I am doing."

They dozed on through the darkness, though the decreasing fits of coughing of one invariably aroused the other. It was after midnight, Smoke judged, when McCan coughed his last. After that he emitted low and bestial moanings that never ceased.

Smoke awoke with lips touching his lips. He lay partly in Labiskwee's arms, his head pillowed on her breast. Her voice was cheerful and usual. The muffled sound of it had vanished.

"It is day," she said, lifting the edge of the robes a trifle. "See, O my lover. It is day; we have lived through; and we no longer cough. Let us look at the world, though I could stay here thus forever and always. This last hour has been sweet. I have been awake, and I have been loving you."

"I do not hear McCan," Smoke said. "And what has become of the young men that they have not found us?"

He threw back the robes and saw a normal and solitary sun in the sky. A gentle breeze was blowing, crisp with frost and hinting of warmer days to come. All the world was natural again. McCan lay on his back, his unwashed face, swarthy from camp-smoke, frozen hard as marble. The sight did not affect Labiskwee.

"Look!" she cried. "A snow bird! It is a good sign."

There was no evidence of the young men. Either they had died on the other side of the divide or they had turned back.

There was so little food that they dared not eat a tithe of what they needed, nor a hundredth part of what they desired, and in the days that followed, wandering through the lone mountain-land, the sharp sting of life grew blunted and the wandering merged half into a dream. Smoke would become abruptly conscious, to find himself staring at the never-ending hated snow-peaks, his senseless babble still ringing in his ears. And the next he would know, after seeming centuries, was that again he was roused to the sound of his own maunderings. Labiskwee, too, was light-headed most of the time. In the main their efforts were unreasoned, automatic. And ever they worked toward the west, and ever they were baffled and thrust north or south by snow-peaks and impassable ranges.

"There is no way south," Labiskwee said. "The old men know. West, only west, is the way."

The young men no longer pursued, but famine crowded on the trail.

Came a day when it turned cold, and a thick snow, that was not snow but frost crystals of the size of grains of sand, began to fall. All day and night it fell, and for three days and nights it continued to fall. It was impossible to travel until it crusted under the spring sun, so they lay in their furs and rested, and ate less because they rested. So small was the ration they permitted that it gave no appeasement to the hunger pang that was much of the stomach, but more of the brain. And Labiskwee, delirious, maddened by the taste of her tiny portion, sobbing and mumbling, yelping sharp little animal cries of joy, fell upon the next day's portion and crammed it into her mouth.

Then it was given to Smoke to see a wonderful thing. The food between her teeth roused her to consciousness. She spat it out, and with a great anger struck herself with her clenched fist on the offending mouth.

It was given to Smoke to see many wonderful things in the days yet to come. After the long snow-fall came on a great wind that drove the dry and tiny frost-particles as sand is driven in a sand-storm. All through the night the sand-frost drove by, and in the full light of a clear and wind-blown day, Smoke looked with swimming eyes and reeling brain upon what he took to be the vision of a dream. All about towered great peaks and small, lone sentinels and groups and councils of mighty Titans. And from the tip of every peak, swaying, undulating, flaring out broadly against the azure sky, streamed gigantic snow-banners, miles in length, milky and nebulous, ever waving lights and shadows and flashing silver from the sun.

"Mine eyes have seen the glory of the coming of the Lord," Smoke chanted, as he gazed upon these dusts of snow wind-driven into sky-scarfs of shimmering silken light.

And still he gazed, and still the bannered peaks did not vanish, and still he considered that he dreamed, until Labiskwee sat up among the furs.

"I dream, Labiskwee," he said. "Look. Do you, too, dream within my dream?"

"It is no dream," she replied. "This have the old men told me. And after this will blow the warm winds, and we shall live and win west."

Smoke shot a snow-bird, and they divided it. Once, in a valley where willows budded standing in the snow, he shot a snowshoe rabbit. Another time he got a lean, white weasel. This much of meat they encountered, and no more, though, once, half-mile high and veering toward the west and the Yukon, they saw a wild-duck wedge drive by.

"It is summer in the lower valleys," said Labiskwee. "Soon it will be summer here."

Labiskwee's face had grown thin, but the bright, large eyes were brighter and larger, and when she looked at him she was transfigured by a wild, unearthly beauty.

The days lengthened, and the snow began to sink. Each day the crust thawed, each night it froze again; and they were afoot early and late, being compelled to camp and rest during the midday hours of thaw when the crust could not bear their weight. When Smoke grew snow-blind, Labiskwee towed him on a thong tied to his waist. And when she was so blinded, she towed behind a thong to her waist. And starving, in a deeper dream, they struggled on through an awakening land bare of any life save their own.

Exhausted as he was, Smoke grew almost to fear sleep, so fearful and bitter were the visions of that mad, twilight land. Always were they of food, and always was the food, at his lips, snatched away by the malign deviser of dreams. He gave dinners to his comrades of the old San Francisco days, himself, with whetting appetite and jealous eye, directing the arrangements, decorating the table with crimson-leafed runners of the autumn grape. The guests were dilatory, and while he greeted them and all sparkled with their latest cleverness, he was frantic with desire for the table. He stole to it, unobserved, and clutched a handful of black ripe olives, and turned to meet still another guest. And others surrounded him, and the laugh and play of wit went on, while all the time, hidden in his closed hand, was this madness of ripe olives.

He gave many such dinners, all with the same empty ending. He attended Gargantuan feasts, where multitudes fed on innumerable bullocks roasted whole, prying them out of smoldering pits and with sharp knives slicing great strips of meat from the steaming carcasses. He stood, with mouth agape, beneath long rows of turkeys which white-aproned shopmen sold. And everybody bought save Smoke, mouth still agape, chained by a leadenness of movement to the pavement. A boy again, he sat with spoon poised high above great bowls of bread and milk. He pursued shy heifers through upland pastures and centuries of torment in vain effort to steal from them their milk, and in noisome dungeons he fought with rats for scraps and refuse. There was no food that was not a madness to him, and he wandered through vast stables, where fat horses stood in mile-long rows of stalls, and sought but never found the bran-bins from which they fed.

Once, only, he dreamed to advantage. Famishing, shipwrecked or marooned, he fought with the big Pacific surf for rock-clinging mussels, and carried them up the sands to the dry flotsam of the spring tides. Of this he built a fire, and among the coals he laid his precious trove. He watched the steam jet forth and the locked shells pop apart, exposing the salmon-colored meat. Cooked to a turn—he knew it; and this time there was no intruding presence to whisk the meal away. At last—so he dreamed within the dream—the dream would come true. This time he would eat. Yet in his certitude he doubted, and he was steeled for the inevitable shift of vision until the salmon-colored meat, hot and savory, was in his mouth. His teeth closed upon it. He ate! The miracle had happened! The shock aroused him. He awoke in the dark, lying on his back, and heard himself mumbling little piggish squeals and grunts of joy. His jaws were moving, and between his teeth meat was crunching. He did not move, and soon small fingers felt about his lips, and between them was inserted a tiny sliver of meat. And in that he would eat no more, rather than that he was angry, Labiskwee cried and in his arms sobbed herself to sleep. But he lay on awake, marveling at the love and the wonder of woman.

The time came when the last food was gone. The high peaks receded, the divides became lower, and the way opened promisingly to the west. But their reserves of strength were gone, and, without food, the time quickly followed when they lay down at night and in the morning did not arise. Smoke weakly gained his feet, collapsed, and on hands and knees crawled about the building of a fire. But try as she would Labiskwee sank back each time in an extremity of weakness. And Smoke sank down beside her, a wan sneer on his face for the automatism that had made him struggle for an unneeded fire. There was nothing to cook, and the day was warm. A gentle breeze sighed in the spruce-trees, and from everywhere, under the disappearing snow, came the trickling music of unseen streamlets.

Labiskwee lay in a stupor, her breathing so imperceptible that often

Smoke thought her dead. In the afternoon the chattering of a squirrel aroused him. Dragging the heavy rifle, he wallowed through the crust that had become slush. He crept on hands and knees, or stood upright and fell forward in the direction of the squirrel that chattered its wrath and fled slowly and tantalizingly before him. He had not the strength for a quick shot, and the squirrel was never still. At times Smoke sprawled in the wet snow-melt and cried out of weakness. Other times the flame of his life flickered, and blackness smote him. How long he lay in the last faint he did not know, but he came to, shivering in the chill of evening, his wet clothing frozen to the re-forming crust. The squirrel was gone, and after a weary struggle he won back to the side of Labiskwee. So profound was his weakness that he lay like a dead man through the night, nor did dreams disturb him.

The sun was in the sky, the same squirrel chattering through the trees, when Labiskwee's hand on Smoke's cheek awakened him.

"Put your hand on my heart, lover," she said, her voice clear but faint and very far away. "My heart is my love, and you hold it in your hand."

A long time seemed to go by, ere she spoke again.

"Remember always, there is no way south. That is well known to the Caribou People. West—that is the way—and you are almost there —and you will make it."

And Smoke drowsed in the numbness that is near to death, until once more she aroused him.

"Put your lips on mine," she said. "I will die so."

"We will die together, sweetheart," was his answer.

"No." A feeble flutter of her hand checked him, and so thin was her voice that scarcely did he hear it, yet did he hear all of it. Her hand fumbled and groped in the hood of her parka, and she drew forth a pouch that she placed in his hand. "And now your lips, my lover. Your lips on my lips, and your hand on my heart."

And in that long kiss darkness came upon him again, and when again he was conscious he knew that he was alone and he knew that he was to die. He was wearily glad that he was to die.

He found his hand resting on the pouch. With an inward smile at the curiosity that made him pull the draw-string, he opened it. Out poured a tiny flood of food. There was no particle of it that he did not recognize, all stolen by Labiskwee from Labiskwee—bread-fragments saved far back in the days ere McCan lost the flour; strips and strings of caribou-meat, partly gnawed; crumbles of suet; the hind-leg of the snow-shoe rabbit, untouched; the hind-leg and part of the fore-leg of the white weasel; the wing dented still by her reluctant teeth, and the leg of the snow-bird—pitiful remnants, tragic renunciations, crucifixions of life, morsels stolen from her terrible hunger by her incredible love.

With maniacal laughter Smoke flung it all out on the hardening snow-crust and went back into the blackness.

He dreamed. The Yukon ran dry. In its bed, among muddy pools of water and ice-scoured rocks, he wandered, picking up fat nugget-gold. The weight of it grew to be a burden to him, till he discovered that it was good to eat. And greedily he ate. After all, of what worth was gold that men should prize it so, save that it was good to eat?

He awoke to another sun. His brain was strangely clear. No longer did his eyesight blur. The familiar palpitation that had vexed him through all his frame was gone. The juices of his body seemed to sing, as if the spring had entered in. Blessed well-being had come to him. He turned to awaken Labiskwee, and saw, and remembered. He looked for the food flung out on the snow. It was gone. And he knew that in delirium and dream it had been the Yukon nugget-gold. In delirium and dream he had taken heart of life from the life sacrifice of Labiskwee, who had put her heart in his hand and opened his eyes to woman and wonder.

He was surprised at the ease of his movements, astounded that he was able to drag her fur-wrapped body to the exposed thawed gravel-bank, which he undermined with the ax and caved upon her.

Three days, with no further food, he fought west. In the mid third day he fell beneath a lone spruce beside a wide stream that ran open and which he knew must be the Klondike. Ere blackness conquered him, he unlashed his pack, said good-by to the bright world, and rolled himself in the robes.

Chirping, sleepy noises awoke him. The long twilight was on. Above him, among the spruce boughs, were ptarmigan. Hunger bit him into instant action, though the action was infinitely slow. Five minutes passed before he was able to get his rifle to his shoulder, and a second five minutes passed ere he dared, lying on his back and aiming straight upward, to pull the trigger. It was a clean miss. No bird fell, but no bird flew. They ruffled and rustled stupidly and drowsily. His shoulder pained him. A second shot was spoiled by the involuntary wince he made as he pulled trigger. Somewhere, in the last three days, though he had no recollection how, he must have fallen and injured it.

The ptarmigan had not flown. He doubled and redoubled the robe that had covered him, and humped it in the hollow between his right arm and his side. Resting the butt of the rifle on the fur, he fired again, and a bird fell. He clutched it greedily and found that he had shot most of the meat out of it. The large-caliber bullet had left little else than a mess of mangled feathers. Still the ptarmigan did not fly, and he decided that it was heads or nothing. He fired only at heads. He reloaded and reloaded the magazine. He missed; he hit; and the stupid ptarmigan, that were loth to fly, fell upon him in a rain of food—lives disrupted that his life might feed and live. There had been nine of them, and in the end he clipped the head of the ninth, and lay and laughed and wept he knew not why.

The first he ate raw. Then he rested and slept, while his life assimilated the life of it. In the darkness he awoke, hungry, with strength to build a fire. And until early dawn he cooked and ate, crunching the bones to powder between his long-idle teeth. He slept, awoke in the darkness of another night, and slept again to another sun.

He noted with surprise that the fire crackled with fresh fuel and that a blackened coffee-pot steamed on the edge of the coals. Beside the fire, within arm's length, sat Shorty, smoking a brown-paper cigarette and intently watching him. Smoke's lips moved, but a throat paralysis seemed to come upon him, while his chest was suffused with the menace of tears. He reached out his hand for the cigarette and drew the smoke deep into his lungs again and again.

"I have not smoked for a long time," he said at last, in a low calm voice. "For a very long time."

"Nor eaten, from your looks," Shorty added gruffly.

Smoke nodded and waved his hand at the ptarmigan feathers that lay all about.

"Not until recently," he returned. "Do you know, I'd like a cup of coffee. It will taste strange. Also flapjacks and a strip of bacon."

"And beans?" Shorty tempted.

"They would taste heavenly. I find I am quite hungry again."

While the one cooked and the other ate, they told briefly what had happened to them in the days since their separation.

"The Klondike was breakin' up," Shorty concluded his recital, "an' we just had to wait for open water. Two polin' boats, six other men—you know 'em all, an' crackerjacks—an' all kinds of outfit. An' we've sure been a-comin'—polin', linin' up, and portagin'. But the falls'll stick 'em a solid week. That's where I left 'em a-cuttin' a trail over the tops of the bluffs for the boats. I just had a sure natural hunch to keep a-comin'. So I fills a pack with grub an' starts. I knew I'd find you a-driftin' an' all in."

Smoke nodded, and put forth his hand in a silent grip. "Well, let's get started," he said.

"Started hell!" Shorty exploded. "We stay right here an' rest you up an' feed you up for a couple of days."

Smoke shook his head.

"If you could just see yourself," Shorty protested.

And what he saw was not nice. Smoke's face, wherever the skin showed, was black and purple and scabbed from repeated frost-bite. The cheeks were fallen in, so that, despite the covering of beard, the upper rows of teeth ridged the shrunken flesh. Across the forehead and about the deep-sunk eyes, the skin was stretched drum-tight, while the scraggly beard, that should have been golden, was singed by fire and filthy with camp-smoke.

"Better pack up," Smoke said. "I'm going on."

"But you're feeble as a kid baby. You can't hike. What's the rush?"

"Shorty, I am going after the biggest thing in the Klondike, and I can't wait. That's all. Start packing. It's the biggest thing in the world. It's bigger than lakes of gold and mountains of gold, bigger than adventure, and meat-eating, and bear-killing."

Shorty sat with bulging eyes. "In the name of the Lord, what is it?" he queried huskily. "Or are you just simple loco?"

"No, I'm all right. Perhaps a fellow has to stop eating in order to see things. At any rate, I have seen things I never dreamed were in the world. I know what a woman is,—now."

Shorty's mouth opened, and about the lips and in the light of the eyes was the whimsical advertisement of the sneer forthcoming.

"Don't, please," Smoke said gently. "You don't know. I do."

Shorty gulped and changed his thought. "Huh! I don't need no hunch to guess *her* name. The rest of 'em has gone up to the drainin' of Surprise Lake, but Joy Gastell allowed she wouldn't go. She's stickin' around Dawson, waitin' to see if I come back with you. An' she sure swears, if I don't, she'll sell her holdin's an' hire a army of gun-fighters, an' go into the Caribou Country an' knock the everlastin' stuffin' outa old Snass an' his whole gang. An' if you'll hold your horses a couple of shakes, I reckon I'll get packed up an' ready to hike along with you."

THE RED ONE

There it was! The abrupt liberation of sound, as he timed it with his watch, Bassett likened to the trump of an archangel. Walls of cities, he meditated, might well fall down before so vast and compelling a summons. For the thousandth time vainly he tried to analyze the tone-quality of that enormous peal that dominated the land far into the strongholds of the surrounding tribes. The mountain gorge which was its source rang to the rising tide of it until it brimmed over and flooded earth and sky and air. With the wantonness of a sick man's fancy, he likened it to the mighty cry of some Titan of the Elder World vexed with misery or wrath. Higher and higher it arose, challenging and demanding in such profounds of volume that it seemed intended for ears beyond the narrow confines of the solar system. There was in it, too, the clamor of protest in that there were no ears to hear and comprehend its utterance.

—Such the sick man's fancy. Still he strove to analyze the sound. Sonorous as thunder was it, mellow as a golden bell, thin and sweet as a thrummed taut cord of silver—no; it was none of these, nor a blend of these. There were no words nor semblances in his vocabulary and experience with which to describe the totality of that sound.

Time passed. Minutes merged into quarters of hours, and quarters of hours into half hours, and still the sound persisted, ever changing from its initial vocal impulse yet never receiving fresh impulse—fading, dimming, dying as enormously as it had sprung into being. It became a confusion of troubled mutterings and babblings and colossal whisperings. Slowly it withdrew, sob by sob, into whatever great bosom had birthed it, until it whimpered deadly whispers of wrath and as equally seductive whispers of delight, striving still to be heard, to convey some cosmic secret, some understanding of infinite import and value. It dwindled to a ghost of sound that had lost its menace and promise, and became a thing that pulsed on in the sick man's consciousness for minutes after it had ceased. When he could hear it no longer, Bassett glanced at his watch. An hour had elapsed ere that archangel's trump had subsided into tonal nothingness.

Was this, then, *his* dark tower?—Bassett pondered, remembering his Browning and gazing at his skeleton-like and fever-wasted hands. And the fancy made him smile—of Childe Roland bearing a slug-horn to his lips with an arm as feeble as his was. Was it months, or years, he asked himself, since he first heard that mysterious call on the beach at Ringmanu? To save himself he could not tell. The long sickness had been most long. In conscious count of time he knew of months, many of them; but he had no way of estimating the long intervals of delirium and stupor. And how fared Captain Bateman of the blackbirder *Nari?* he wondered; and had Captain Bateman's drunken mate died of delirium tremens yet?

From which vain speculations, Bassett turned idly to review all that had occurred since that day on the beach of Ringmanu when he first heard the sound and plunged into the jungle after it. Sagawa had protested. He could see him yet, his queer little monkeyish face eloquent with fear, his back burdened with specimen cases, in his hands Bassett's butterfly net and naturalist's shotgun, as he quavered in Beche de mer English: "Me fella too much fright along bush. Bad fella boy too much stop'm along bush."

Bassett smiled sadly at the recollection. The little New Hanover boy had been frightened, but had proved faithful, following him without hesitancy into the bush in the quest after the source of the wonderful sound. No fire-hollowed tree-trunk, that, throbbing war through the jungle depths, had been Bassett's conclusion. Erroneous had been his next conclusion, namely, that the source or cause could not be more distant than an hour's walk and that he would easily be back by mid-afternoon to be picked up by the *Nari's* whaleboat.

"That big fella noise no good, all the same devil-devil," Sagawa had adjudged. And Sagawa had been right. Had he not had his head hacked off within the day? Bassett shuddered. Without doubt Sagawa had been eaten as well by the bad fella boys too much that stopped along the bush. He could see him, as he had last seen him, stripped of the shotgun and all the naturalist's gear of his master, lying on the narrow trail where he had been decapitated barely the moment before. Yes, within a minute the thing had happened. Within a minute, looking back, Bassett had seen him trudging patiently along under his burdens. Then Bassett's own trouble had come upon him. He looked at the cruelly healed stumps of the first and second fingers of his left hand, then rubbed them softly into the indentation in the back of his skull. Quick as had been the flash of the long-handled tomahawk, he had been quick enough to duck away his head and partially to deflect the stroke with his up-flung hand. Two fingers and a nasty scalp-wound had been the price he paid for his life. With one barrel of his ten-gauge shotgun he had blown the life out of the bushman who had so nearly got him; with the other barrel he had peppered the bushmen bending over Sagawa, and had the pleasure of knowing that the major portion of the charge had gone into the one who leaped away with Sagawa's head. Everything had occurred in a flash. Only himself, the slain bushman, and what remained of Sagawa, were in the narrow, wild-pig run of a path. From the dark jungle on either side came no rustle of movement or sound of life. And he had suffered distinct and dreadful shock. For the first time in his life he had killed a human being, and he knew nausea as he contemplated the mess of his handiwork.

Then had begun the chase. He retreated up the pig-run before his hunters, who were between him and the beach. How many there were, he could not guess. There might have been one, or a hundred, for aught he saw of them. That some of them took to the trees and traveled along through the jungle roof he was certain; but at the most he never glimpsed more than an occasional flitting of shadows. No bow-strings twanged that he could hear; but every little while, whence discharged he knew not, tiny arrows whispered past him or struck tree-boles and fluttered to the ground beside him. They were bone-tipped and feather-shafted, and the feathers, torn from the breasts of humming-birds, iridesced like jewels.

Once—and now, after the long lapse of time, he chuckled gleefully at the recollection—he had detected a shadow above him that came to instant rest as he turned his gaze upward. He could make out nothing, but, deciding to chance it, had fired at it a heavy charge of number five shot. Squalling like an infuriated cat, the shadow crashed down through tree-ferns and orchids and thudded upon the earth at his feet, and, still squalling its rage and pain, had sunk its human teeth into the ankle of his stout tramping boot. He, on the other hand, was not idle, and with his free foot had done what reduced the squalling to silence. So inured to savagery had Bassett since become, that he chuckled again with the glee of the recollection.

What a night had followed! Small wonder that he had accumulated such a virulence and variety of fevers, he thought, as he recalled that sleepless night of torment, when the throb of his wounds was as nothing compared with the myriad stings of the mosquitoes. There had been no escaping them, and he had not dared to light a fire. They had literally pumped his body full of poison, so that, with the coming of day, eyes swollen almost shut, he had stumbled blindly on, not caring much when his head should be hacked off and his carcass started on the way of Sagawa's to the cooking fire. Twenty-four hours had made a wreck of him—of mind as well as body. He had scarcely retained his wits at all, so maddened was he by the tremendous inoculation of poison he had received. Several times he fired his shotgun with effect into the shadows that dogged him. Stinging day insects and gnats added to his torment, while his bloody wounds attracted hosts of loathsome flies that clung sluggishly to his flesh and had to be brushed off and crushed off.

Once, in that day, he heard again the wonderful sound, seemingly more distant, but rising imperiously above the nearer war-drums in the bush. Right there was where he had made his mistake. Thinking that he had passed beyond it and that, therefore, it was between him and the beach of Ringmanu, he had worked back toward it when in reality he was penetrating deeper and deeper into the mysterious heart of the unexplored island. That night, crawling in among the twisted roots of a banyan tree, he had slept from exhaustion while the mosquitoes had had their will of him.

Followed days and nights that were vague as nightmares in his memory. One clear vision he remembered was of suddenly finding himself in the midst of a bush village and watching the old men and children fleeing into the jungle. All had fled but one. From close at hand and above him, a whimpering as of some animal in pain and terror had startled him. And looking up he had seen her—a girl, or young woman, rather, suspended by one arm in the cooking sun. Perhaps for days she had so hung. Her swollen, protruding tongue spoke as much. Still alive, she gazed at him with eyes of terror. Past help, he decided, as he noted the swellings of her legs which advertised that the joints had been crushed and the great bones broken. He resolved to shoot her, and there the vision terminated. He could not remember whether he had or not, any more than could he remember how he chanced to be in that village or how he succeeded in getting away from it.

Many pictures, unrelated, came and went in Bassett's mind as he reviewed that period of his terrible wanderings. He remembered invading another village of a dozen houses and driving all before him with his shotgun save for one old man, too feeble to flee, who spat at him and whined and snarled as he dug open a ground-oven and from amid the hot stones dragged forth a roasted pig that steamed its essence deliciously through its green-leaf wrappings. It was at this place that a wantonness of savagery had seized upon him. Having feasted, ready to depart with a hind quarter of the pig in his hand, he deliberately fired the grass thatch of a house with his burning glass.

But seared deepest of all in Bassett's brain, was the dank and noisome jungle. It actually stank with evil, and it was always twilight. Rarely did a shaft of sunlight penetrate its matted roof a hundred feet overhead. And beneath that roof was an aërial ooze of vegetation, a monstrous, parasitic dripping of decadent life-forms that rooted in death and lived on death. And through all this he drifted, ever pursued by the flitting shadows of the anthropophagi, themselves ghosts of evil that dared not face him in battle but that knew, soon or late, that they would feed on him. Bassett remembered that at the time, in lucid moments, he had likened himself to a wounded bull pursued by plains' coyotes too cowardly to battle with him for the meat of him, yet certain of the inevitable end of him when they would be full gorged. As the bull's horns and stamping hoofs kept off the coyotes, so his shotgun kept off these Solomon Islanders, these twilight shades of bushmen of the island of Guadalcanal.

Came the day of the grass lands. Abruptly, as if cloven by the sword of God in the hand of God, the jungle terminated. The edge of it, perpendicular and as black as the infamy of it, was a hundred feet up and down. And, beginning at the edge of it, grew the grass—sweet, soft, tender, pasture grass that would have delighted the eyes and beasts of any husbandman and that extended, on and on, for leagues and leagues of velvet verdure, to the backbone of the great island, the towering mountain range flung up by some ancient earth-cataclysm, serrated and gullied but not yet erased by the erosive tropic rains. But the grass! He had crawled into it a dozen yards, buried his face in it, smelled it, and broken down in a fit of involuntary weeping.

And, while he wept, the wonderful sound had pealed forth—if by *peal*, he had often thought since, an adequate description could be given of the enunciation of so vast a sound so melting sweet. Sweet it was as no sound ever heard. Vast it was, of so mighty a resonance that it might have proceeded from some brazen-throated monster. And yet it called to him across that leagues-wide savannah, and was like a benediction to his long-suffering, pain-wracked spirit.

He remembered how he lay there in the grass, wet-cheeked but no longer sobbing, listening to the sound and wondering that he had been able to hear it on the beach of Ringmanu. Some freak of air pressures and air currents, he reflected, had made it possible for the sound to carry so far. Such conditions might not happen again in a thousand days or ten thousand days; but the one day it had happened had been the day he landed from the *Nari* for several hours' collecting. Especially had he been in quest of the famed jungle butterfly, a foot across from wing-tip to wing-tip, as velvet-dusky of lack of color as was the gloom of the roof, of such lofty arboreal habits that it resorted only to the jungle roof and could be brought down only by a dose of shot. It was for this purpose that Sagawa had carried the twenty-gauge shotgun.

Two days and nights he had spent crawling across that belt of grass land. He had suffered much, but pursuit had ceased at the jungle-edge. And he would have died of thirst had not a heavy thunderstorm revived him on the second day.

And then had come Balatta. In the first shade, where the savannah yielded to the dense mountain jungle, he had collapsed to die. At first she had squealed with delight at sight of his helplessness, and was for beating his brain out with a stout forest branch. Perhaps it was his very utter helplessness that had appealed to her, and perhaps it was her human curiosity that made her refrain. At any rate, she had refrained, for he opened his eyes again under the impending blow, and saw her studying him intently. What especially struck her about him were his blue eyes and white skin. Coolly she had squatted on her hams, spat on his arm, and with her finger-tips scrubbed away the dirt of days and nights of muck and jungle that sullied the pristine whiteness of his skin.

And everything about her had struck him especially, although there was nothing conventional about her at all. He laughed weakly at the recollection, for she had been as innocent of garb as Eve before the fig-leaf adventure. Squat and lean at the same time, asymmetrically limbed, string-muscled as if with lengths of cordage, dirt-caked from infancy save for casual showers, she was as unbeautiful a prototype of woman as he, with a scientist's eye, had ever gazed upon. Her breasts advertised at the one time her maturity and youth; and, if by nothing else, her sex was advertised by the one article of finery with which she was adorned, namely a pig's tail, thrust through a hole in her left ear-lobe. So lately had the tail been severed, that its raw end still oozed blood that dried upon her shoulder like so much candle-droppings. And her face! A twisted and wizened complex of apish features, perforated by upturned, sky-open, Mongolian nostrils, by a mouth that sagged from a huge upper-lip and faded precipitately into a retreating chin, and by peering querulous eyes that blinked as blink the eyes of denizens of monkey-cages.

Not even the water she brought him in a forest-leaf, and the ancient and half-putrid chunk of roast pig, could redeem in the slightest the grotesque hideousness of her. When he had eaten weakly for a space, he closed his eyes in order not to see her, although again and again she poked them open to peer at the blue of them. Then had come the sound. Nearer, much nearer, he knew it to be; and he knew equally well, despite the weary way he had come, that it was still many hours distant. The effect of it on her had been startling. She cringed under it, with averted face, moaning and chattering with fear. But after it had lived its full life of an hour, he closed his eyes and fell asleep with Balatta brushing the flies from him.

When he awoke it was night, and she was gone. But he was aware of renewed strength, and, by then too thoroughly inoculated by the mosquito poison to suffer further inflammation, he closed his eyes and slept an unbroken stretch till sun-up. A little later Balatta had returned, bringing with her a half dozen women who, unbeautiful as they were, were patently not so unbeautiful as she. She evidenced by her conduct that she considered him her find, her property, and the pride she took in showing him off would have been ludicrous had his situation not been so desperate.

Later, after what had been to him a terrible journey of miles, when he collapsed in front of the devil-devil house in the shadow of the breadfruit tree, she had shown very lively ideas on the matter of retaining possession of him. Ngurn, whom Bassett was to know afterward as the devil-devil doctor, priest, or medicine man of the village, had wanted his head. Others of the grinning and chattering monkey-men, all as stark of clothes and bestial of appearance as Balatta, had wanted his body for the roasting oven. At that time he had not understood their language, if by *language* might be dignified the uncouth sounds they made to represent ideas. But Bassett had thoroughly understood the matter of debate, especially when the men pressed and prodded and felt of the flesh of him as if he were so much commodity in a butcher's stall.

Balatta had been losing the debate rapidly, when the accident happened. One of the men, curiously examining Bassett's shotgun, managed to cock and pull a trigger. The recoil of the butt into the pit of the man's stomach had not been the most sanguinary result, for the charge of shot, at a distance of a yard, had blown the head of one of the debaters into nothingness.

Even Balatta joined the others in flight, and, ere they returned, his senses already reeling from the oncoming fever-attack, Bassett had regained possession of the gun. Whereupon, although his teeth chattered with the ague and his swimming eyes could scarcely see, he held onto his fading consciousness until he could intimidate the bushmen with the simple magics of compass, watch, burning glass, and matches. At the last, with due emphasis of solemnity and awfulness, he had killed a young pig with his shotgun and promptly fainted.

Bassett flexed his arm-muscles in quest of what possible strength might reside in such weakness, and dragged himself slowly and totteringly to his feet. He was shockingly emaciated; yet, during the various convalescences of the many months of his long sickness, he had never regained quite the same degree of strength as this time. What he feared was another relapse such as he had already frequently experienced. Without drugs, without even quinine, he had managed so far to live through a combination of the most pernicious and most malignant of malarial and black-water fevers. But could he continue to endure? Such was his everlasting query. For, like the genuine scientist he was, he would not be content to die until he had solved the secret of the sound.

Supported by a staff, he staggered the few steps to the devil-devil house where death and Ngurn reigned in gloom. Almost as infamously dark and evil-stinking as the jungle was the devil-devil house—in Bassett's opinion. Yet therein was usually to be found his favorite crony and gossip, Ngurn, always willing for a yarn or a discussion, the while he sat in the ashes of death and in a slow smoke shrewdly revolved curing human heads suspended from the rafters. For, through the months' interval of consciousness of his long sickness, Bassett had mastered the psychological simplicities and lingual difficulties of the language of the tribe of Ngurn and Balatta, and Gngngn—the latter the addle-headed young chief who was ruled by Ngurn, and who, whispered intrigue had it, was the son of Ngurn.

"Will the Red One speak to-day?" Bassett asked, by this time so accustomed to the old man's gruesome occupation as to take even an interest in the progress of the smoke-curing.

With the eye of an expert Ngurn examined the particular head he was at work upon.

"It will be ten days before I can say 'finish,'" he said. "Never has any man fixed heads like these."

Bassett smiled inwardly at the old fellow's reluctance to talk with him of the Red One. It had always been so. Never, by any chance, had Ngurn or any other member of the weird tribe divulged the slightest hint of any physical characteristic of the Red One. Physical the Red One must be, to emit the wonderful sound, and though it was called the Red One, Bassett could not be sure that red represented the color of it. Red enough were the deeds and powers of it, from what abstract clews he had gleaned. Not alone, had Ngurn informed him, was the Red One more bestial powerful than the neighbor tribal gods, ever a-thirst for the red blood of living human sacrifices, but the neighbor gods themselves were sacrificed and tormented before him. He was the god of a dozen allied villages similar to this one, which was the central and commanding village of the federation. By virtue of the Red One many alien villages had been devastated and even wiped out, the prisoners sacrificed to the Red One. This was true to-day, and it extended back into old history carried down by word of mouth through the generations. When he, Ngurn, had been a young man, the tribes beyond the grass lands had made a war raid. In the counter raid, Ngurn and his fighting folk had made many prisoners. Of children alone over five score living had been bled white before the Red One, and many, many more men and women.

The Thunderer, was another of Ngurn's names for the mysterious deity. Also at times was he called The Loud Shouter, The God-Voiced, The Bird-Throated, The One with the Throat Sweet as the Throat of the Honey-Bird, The Sun Singer, and The Star-Born.

Why The Star-Born? In vain Bassett interrogated Ngurn. According to that old devil-devil doctor, the Red One had always been, just where he was at present, forever singing and thundering his will over men. But Ngurn's father, wrapped in decaying grass-matting and hanging even then over their heads among the smoky rafters of the devil-devil house, had held otherwise. That departed wise one had believed that the Red One came from out of the starry night, else why—so his argument had run—had the old and forgotten ones passed his name down as the Star-Born? Bassett could not but recognize something cogent in such argument. But Ngurn affirmed the long years of his long life, wherein he had gazed upon many starry nights, yet never had he found a star on grass land or in jungle depth—and he had looked for them. True, he had beheld shooting stars (this in reply to Bassett's contention); but likewise had he beheld the phosphorescence of fungoid growths and rotten meat and fireflies on dark nights, and the flames of wood-fires and of blazing candle-nuts; yet what were flame and blaze and glow when they had flamed, and blazed and glowed? Answer: memories, memories only, of things which had ceased to be, like memories of matings accomplished, of feasts forgotten, of desires that were the ghosts of desires, flaring, flaming, burning, yet unrealized in achievement of easement and satisfaction. Where was the appetite of yesterday? the roasted flesh of the wild pig the hunter's arrow failed to slay? the maid, unwed and dead, ere the young man knew her?

A memory was not a star, was Ngurn's contention. How could a memory be a star? Further, after all his long life he still observed the starry night-sky unaltered. Never had he noted the absence of a single star from its accustomed place. Besides, stars were fire, and the Red One was not fire—which last involuntary betrayal told Bassett nothing.

"Will the Red One speak to-morrow?" he queried.

Ngurn shrugged his shoulders as who should say.

"And the day after?—and the day after that?" Bassett persisted.

"I would like to have the curing of your head," Ngurn changed the subject. "It is different from any other head. No devil-devil has a head like it. Besides, I would cure it well. I would take months and months. The moons would come and the moons would go, and the smoke would be very slow, and I should myself gather the materials for the curing smoke. The skin would not wrinkle. It would be as smooth as your skin now."

He stood up, and from the dim rafters grimed with the smoking of countless heads, where day was no more than a gloom, took down a matting-wrapped parcel and began to open it.

"It is a head like yours," he said, "but it is poorly cured."

Bassett had pricked up his ears at the suggestion that it was a white man's head; for he had long since come to accept that these jungle-dwellers, in the midmost center of the great island, had never had intercourse with white men. Certainly he had found them without the almost universal Beche de mer English of the west South Pacific. Nor had they knowledge of tobacco, nor of gunpowder. Their few precious knives, made from lengths of hoop-iron, and their few and more precious tomahawks, made from cheap trade hatches, he had surmised they had captured in war from the bushmen of the jungle beyond the grass lands, and that they, in turn, had similarly gained them from the salt water men who fringed the coral beaches of the shore and had contact with the occasional white men.

"The folk in the out beyond do not know how to cure heads," old Ngurn explained, as he drew forth from the filthy matting and placed in Bassett's hands an indubitable white man's head.

Ancient it was beyond question; white it was as the blond hair attested. He could have sworn it once belonged to an Englishman, and to an Englishman of long before by token of the heavy gold circlets still threaded in the withered earlobes.

"Now your head ..." the devil-devil doctor began on his favorite topic.

"I'll tell you what," Bassett interrupted, struck by a new idea. "When I die I'll let you have my head to cure, if, first, you take me to look upon the Red One."

"I will have your head anyway when you are dead," Ngurn rejected the proposition. He added, with the brutal frankness of the savage: "Besides, you have not long to live. You are almost a dead man now. You will grow less strong. In not many months I shall have you here turning and turning in the smoke. It is pleasant, through the long afternoons, to turn the head of one you have known as well as I know you. And I shall talk to you and tell you the many secrets you want to know. Which will not matter, for you will be dead."

"Ngurn," Bassett threatened in sudden anger. "You know the Baby Thunder in the Iron that is mine." (This was in reference to his all-potent and all-awful shotgun.) "I can kill you any time, and then you will not get my head."

"Just the same, will Gngngn, or some one else of my folk get it," Ngurn complacently assured him. "And just the same will it turn and turn here in the devil-devil house in the smoke. The quicker you slay me with your Baby Thunder, the quicker will your head turn in the smoke."

And Bassett knew he was beaten in the discussion.

What was the Red One?—Bassett asked himself a thousand times in the succeeding week, while he seemed to grow stronger. What was the source of the wonderful sound? What was this Sun Singer, this Star-Born One, this mysterious deity, as bestial-conducted as the black and kinky-headed and monkey-like human beasts who worshiped it, and whose silver-sweet, bull-mouthed singing and commanding he had heard at the taboo distance for so long?

Ngurn had he failed to bribe with the inevitable curing of his head when he was dead. Gngngn, imbecile and chief that he was, was too imbecilic, too much under the sway of Ngurn, to be considered. Remained Balatta, who, from the time she found him and poked his blue eyes open to recrudescence of her grotesque, female hideousness, had continued his adorer. Woman she was, and he had long known that the only way to win from her treason to her tribe was through the woman's heart of her.

Bassett was a fastidious man. He had never recovered from the initial horror caused by Balatta's female awfulness. Back in England, even at best, the charm of woman, to him, had never been robust. Yet now, resolutely, as only a man can do who is capable of martyring himself for the cause of science, he proceeded to violate all the fineness and delicacy of his nature by making love to the unthinkably disgusting bushwoman.

He shuddered, but with averted face hid his grimaces and swallowed his gorge as he put his arm around her dirt-crusted shoulders and felt the contact of her rancid-oily and kinky hair with his neck and chin. But he nearly screamed when she succumbed to that caress so at the very first of the courtship and mowed and gibbered and squealed little, queer, pig-like gurgly noises of delight. It was too much. And the next he did in the singular courtship was to take her down to the stream and give her a vigorous scrubbing.

From then on he devoted himself to her like a true swain as frequently and for as long at a time as his will could override his repugnance. But marriage, which she ardently suggested, with due observance of tribal custom, he balked at. Fortunately, taboo rule was strong in the tribe. Thus, Ngurn could never touch bone, or flesh, or hide of crocodile. This had been ordained at his birth. Gngngn was denied ever the touch of woman. Such pollution, did it chance to occur, could be purged only by the death of the offending female. It had happened once, since Bassett's arrival, when a girl of nine, running in play, stumbled and fell against the sacred chief. And the girl-child was seen no more. In whispers, Balatta told Bassett that she had been three days and nights in dying before the Red One. As for Balatta, the breadfruit was taboo to her. For which Bassett was thankful. The taboo might have been water.

For himself, he fabricated a special taboo. Only could he marry, he explained, when the Southern Cross rode highest in the sky. Knowing his astronomy, he thus gained a reprieve of nearly nine months; and he was confident that within that time he would either be dead or escaped to the coast with full knowledge of the Red One and of the source of the Red One's wonderful voice. At first he had fancied the Red One to be some colossal statue, like Memnon, rendered vocal under certain temperature conditions of sunlight. But when, after a war raid, a batch of prisoners was brought in and the sacrifice made at night, in the midst of rain, when the sun could play no part, the Red One had been more vocal than usual, Bassett discarded that hypothesis.

In company with Balatta, sometimes with men and parties of women, the freedom of the jungle was his for three quadrants of the compass. But the fourth quadrant, which contained the Red One's abiding place, was taboo. He made more thorough love to Balatta—also saw to it that she scrubbed herself more frequently. Eternal female she was, capable of any treason for the sake of love. And, though the sight of her was provocative of nausea and the contact of her provocative of despair, although he could not escape her awfulness in his dream-haunted nightmares of her, he nevertheless was aware of the cosmic verity of sex that animated her and that made her own life of less value than the happiness of her lover with whom she hoped to mate. Juliet or Balatta? Where was the intrinsic difference? The soft and tender product of ultra-civilization, or her bestial prototype of a hundred thousand years before her?—there was no difference.

Bassett was a scientist first, a humanist afterward. In the jungle-heart of Guadalcanal he put the affair to the test, as in the laboratory he would have put to the test any chemical reaction. He increased his feigned ardor for the bushwoman, at the same time increasing the imperiousness of his will of desire over her to be led to look upon the Red One face to face. It was the old story, he recognized, that the woman must pay, and it occurred when the two of them, one day, were catching the un-classified and unnamed little black fish, an inch long, half-eel and half-scaled, rotund with salmon-golden roe, that frequented the fresh water and that were esteemed, raw and whole, fresh or putrid, a perfect delicacy. Prone in the muck of the decaying jungle-floor, Balatta threw herself, clutching his ankles with her hands, kissing his feet and making slubbery noises that chilled his backbone up and down again. She begged him to kill her rather than exact this ultimate love-payment. She told him of the penalty of breaking the taboo of the Red One—a week of torture, living, the details of which she yammered out from her face in the mire until he realized that he was yet a tyro in knowledge of the frightfulness the human was capable of wreaking on the human.

Yet did Bassett insist on having his man's will satisfied, at the woman's risk, that he might solve the mystery of the Red One's singing, though she should die long and horribly and screaming. And Balatta, being mere woman, yielded. She led him into the forbidden quadrant. An abrupt mountain, shouldering in from the north to meet a similar intrusion from the south, tormented the stream in which they had fished into a deep and gloomy gorge. After a mile along the gorge, the way plunged sharply upward until they crossed a saddle of raw limestone which attracted his geologist's eye. Still climbing, although he paused often from sheer physical weakness, they scaled forest-clad heights until they emerged on a naked mesa or tableland. Bassett recognized the stuff of its composition as black volcanic sand, and knew that a pocket magnet could have captured a full load of the sharply angular grains he trod upon.

And then, holding Balatta by the hand and leading her onward, he came to it—a tremendous pit, obviously artificial, in the heart of the plateau. Old history, the South Seas Sailing Directions, scores of re-membered data and connotations swift and furious, surged through his brain. It was Mendana who had discovered the islands and named them Solomon's, believing that he had found that monarch's fabled mines. They had laughed at the old navigator's child-like credulity; and yet here stood himself, Bassett, on the rim of an excavation for all the world like the diamond pits of South Africa.

But no diamond this that he gazed down upon. Rather was it a pearl, with the depth of iridescence of a pearl; but of a size all pearls of earth

and time welded into one, could not have totaled; and of a color undreamed of any pearl, or of anything else, for that matter, for it was the
color of the Red One. And the Red One himself Bassett knew it to be
on the instant. A perfect sphere, fully two hundred feet in diameter, the
top of it was a hundred feet below the level of the rim. He likened the
color quality of it to lacquer. Indeed, he took it to be some sort of
lacquer, applied by man, but a lacquer too marvelously clever to have
been manufactured by the bush-folk. Brighter than bright cherry-red, its
richness of color was as if it were red builded upon red. It glowed and
iridesced in the sunlight as if gleaming up from underlay under underlay
of red.

In vain Balatta strove to dissuade him from descending. She threw
herself in the dirt; but, when he continued down the trail that spiraled
the pit-wall, she followed, cringing and whimpering her terror. That the
red sphere had been dug out as a precious thing, was patent. Considering the paucity of members of the federated twelve villages and their
primitive tools and methods, Bassett knew that the toil of a myriad
generations could scarcely have made that enormous excavation.

He found the pit bottom carpeted with human bones, among which,
battered and defaced, lay village gods of wood and stone. Some, covered
with obscene totemic figures and designs, were carved from solid tree
trunks forty or fifty feet in length. He noted the absence of the shark
and turtle gods, so common among the shore villages, and was amazed
at the constant recurrence of the helmet motive. What did these jungle
savages of the dark heart of Guadalcanal know of helmets? Had Mendana's men-at-arms worn helmets and penetrated here centuries before?
And if not, then whence had the bush-folk caught the motive?

Advancing over the litter of gods and bones, Balatta whimpering at
his heels, Bassett entered the shadow of the Red One and passed on
under its gigantic overhang until he touched it with his finger-tips. No
lacquer that. Nor was the surface smooth as it should have been in the
case of lacquer. On the contrary, it was corrugated and pitted, with here
and there patches that showed signs of heat and fusing. Also, the substance of it was metal, though unlike any metal or combination of metals
he had ever known. As for the color itself, he decided it to be no application. It was the intrinsic color of the metal itself.

He moved his finger-tips, which up to that had merely rested, along
the surface, and felt the whole gigantic sphere quicken and live and
respond. It was incredible! So light a touch on so vast a mass! Yet did
it quiver under the finger-tip caress in rhythmic vibrations that became
whisperings and rustlings and mutterings of sound—but of sound so
different; so elusive thin that it was shimmeringly sibillant; so mellow

that it was maddening sweet, piping like an elfin horn, which last was just what Bassett decided would be like a peal from some bell of the gods reaching earthward from across space.

He looked to Balatta with swift questioning; but the voice of the Red One he had evoked had flung her face-downward and moaning among the bones. He returned to contemplation of the prodigy. Hollow it was, and of no metal known on earth, was his conclusion. It was right-named by the ones of old-time as the Star-Born. Only from the stars could it have come, and no thing of chance was it. It was a creation of artifice and mind. Such perfection of form, such hollowness that it certainly possessed, could not be the result of mere fortuitousness. A child of intelligences, remote and unguessable, working corporally in metals, it indubitably was. He stared at it in amaze, his brain a racing wild-fire of hypotheses to account for this far-journeyer who had adventured the night of space, threaded the stars, and now rose before him and above him, exhumed by patient anthropophagi, pitted and lacquered by its fiery bath in two atmospheres.

But was the color a lacquer of heat upon some familiar metal? Or was it an intrinsic quality of the metal itself? He thrust in the blade-point of his pocket-knife to test the constitution of the stuff. Instantly the entire sphere burst into a mighty whispering, sharp with protest, almost twanging goldenly if a whisper could possibly be considered to twang, rising higher, sinking deeper, the two extremes of the registry of sound threatening to complete the circle and coalesce into the bull-mouthed thundering he had so often heard beyond the taboo distance.

Forgetful of safety, of his own life itself, entranced by the wonder of the unthinkable and unguessable thing, he raised his knife to strike heavily from a long stroke, but was prevented by Balatta. She upreared on her own knees in an agony of terror, clasping his knees and suppli-cating him to desist. In the intensity of her desire to impress him, she put her forearm between her teeth and sank them to the bone.

He scarcely observed her act, although he yielded atomically to his gentler instincts and withheld the knife-hack. To him, human life had dwarfed to microscopic proportions before this colossal portent of higher life from within the distances of the sidereal universe. As had she been a dog, he kicked the ugly little bushwoman to her feet and com-pelled her to start with him on an encirclement of the base. Part way around, he encountered horrors. Even, among the others, did he rec-ognize the sun-shriveled remnant of the nine-years girl who had acci-dentally broken Chief Gngngn's personality taboo. And, among what was left of these that had passed, he encountered what was left of one who had not yet passed. Truly had the bush-folk named themselves into the name of the Red One, seeing in him their own image which they strove to placate and please with such red offerings.

Farther around, always treading the bones and images of humans and gods that constituted the floor of this ancient charnel house of sacrifice, he came upon the device by which the Red One was made to send his call singing thunderingly across the jungle-belts and grass-lands to the far beach of Ringmanu. Simple and primitive was it as was the Red One's consummate artifice. A great king-post, half a hundred feet in length, seasoned by centuries of superstitious care, carven into dynasties of gods, each superimposed, each helmeted, each seated in the open mouth of a crocodile, was slung by ropes, twisted of climbing vegetable parasites, from the apex of a tripod of three great forest trunks, themselves carved into grinning and grotesque adumbrations of man's modern concepts of art and god. From the striker king-post, were suspended ropes of climbers to which men could apply their strength and direction. Like a battering ram, this king-post could be driven end-onward against the mighty, red-iridescent sphere.

Here was where Ngurn officiated and functioned religiously for himself and the twelve tribes under him. Bassett laughed aloud, almost with madness, at the thought of this wonderful messenger, winged with intelligence across space, to fall into a bushman stronghold and be worshiped by ape-like, man-eating and head-hunting savages. It was as if God's Word had fallen into the muck mire of the abyss underlying the bottom of hell; as if Jehovah's Commandments had been presented on carved stone to the monkeys of the monkey cage at the Zoo; as if the Sermon on the Mount had been preached in a roaring bedlam of lunatics.

The slow weeks passed. The nights, by election, Bassett spent on the ashen floor of the devil-devil house, beneath the ever-swinging, slow-curing heads. His reason for this was that it was taboo to the lesser sex of woman, and, therefore, a refuge for him from Balatta, who grew more persecutingly and perilously loverly as the Southern Cross rode higher in the sky and marked the imminence of her nuptials. His days Bassett spent in a hammock swung under the shade of the great breadfruit tree before the devil-devil house. There were breaks in this program, when, in the comas of his devastating fever-attacks, he lay for days and nights in the house of heads. Ever he struggled to combat the fever, to live, to continue to live, to grow strong and stronger against the day when he would be strong enough to dare the grass-lands and the belted jungle beyond, and win to the beach, and to some labor-recruiting, black-birding ketch or schooner, and on to civilization and the men of civilization, to whom he could give news of the message from other worlds that lay, darkly worshiped by beast-men, in the black heart of Guadalcanal's midmost center.

On other nights, lying late under the breadfruit tree, Bassett spent long hours watching the slow setting of the western stars beyond the black wall of jungle where it had been thrust back by the clearing for the village. Possessed of more than a cursory knowledge of astronomy, he took a sick man's pleasure in speculating as to the dwellers on the unseen worlds of those incredibly remote suns, to haunt whose houses of light, life came forth, a shy visitant, from the rayless crypts of matter. He could no more apprehend limits to time than bounds to space. No subversive radium speculations had shaken his steady scientific faith in the conservation of energy and the indestructibility of matter. Always and forever must there have been stars. And surely, in that cosmic ferment, all must be comparatively alike, comparatively of the same substance, or substances, save for the freaks of the ferment. All must obey, or compose, the same laws that ran without infraction through the entire experience of man. Therefore, he argued and agreed, must worlds and life be appanages to all the suns as they were appanages to the particular sun of his own solar system.

Even as he lay here, under the breadfruit tree, an intelligence that stared across the starry gulfs, so must all the universe be exposed to the ceaseless scrutiny of innumerable eyes, like his, though grantedly different, with behind them, by the same token, intelligences that questioned and sought the meaning and the construction of the whole. So reasoning, he felt his soul go forth in kinship with that august company, that multitude whose gaze was forever upon the arras of infinity.

Who were they, what were they, those far distant and superior ones who had bridged the sky with their gigantic, red-iridescent, heaven-singing message? Surely, and long since, had they, too, trod the path on which man had so recently, by the calendar of the cosmos, set his feet. And to be able to send such a message across the pit of space, surely they had reached those heights to which man, in tears and travail and bloody sweat, in darkness and confusion of many counsels, was so slowly struggling. And what were they on their heights? Had they won Brotherhood? Or had they learned that the law of love imposed the penalty of weakness and decay? Was strife, life? Was the rule of all the universe the pitiless rule of natural selection? And, and most immediately and poignantly, were their far conclusions, their long-won wisdoms, shut even then in the huge, metallic heart of the Red One, waiting for the first earth-man to read? Of one thing he was certain: No drop of red dew shaken from the lion-mane of some sun in torment, was the sounding sphere. It was of design, not chance, and it contained the speech and wisdom of the stars.

What engines and elements and mastered forces, what lore and mysteries and destiny-controls, might be there! Undoubtedly, since so much could be inclosed in so little a thing as the foundation stone of public building, this enormous sphere should contain vast histories, profounds of research achieved beyond man's wildest guesses, laws and formulæ that, easily mastered, would make man's life on earth, individual and collective, spring up from its present mire to inconceivable heights of purity and power. It was Time's greatest gift to blindfold, insatiable, and sky-aspiring man. And to him, Bassett, had been vouchsafed the lordly fortune to be the first to receive this message from man's interstellar kin!

No white man, much less no outland man of the other bush-tribes, had gazed upon the Red One and lived. Such the law expounded by Ngurn to Bassett. There was such a thing as blood brotherhood, Bassett, in return, had often argued in the past. But Ngurn had stated solemnly no. Even the blood brotherhood was outside the favor of the Red One. Only a man born within the tribe could look upon the Red One and live. But now, his guilty secret known only to Balatta, whose fear of immolation before the Red One fast-sealed her lips, the situation was different. What he had to do was to recover from the abominable fevers that weakened him and gain to civilization. Then would he lead an expedition back, and, although the entire population of Guadalcanal be destroyed, extract from the heart of the Red One the message of the world from other worlds.

But Bassett's relapses grew more frequent, his brief convalescences less and less vigorous, his periods of coma longer, until he came to know, beyond the last promptings of the optimism inherent in so tremendous a constitution as his own, that he would never live to cross the grass lands, perforate the perilous coast jungle, and reach the sea. He faded as the Southern Cross rose higher in the sky, till even Balatta knew that he would be dead ere the nuptial date determined by his taboo. Ngurn made pilgrimage personally and gathered the smoke materials for the curing of Bassett's head, and to him made proud announcement and exhibition of the artistic perfectness of his intention when Bassett should be dead. As for himself, Bassett was not shocked. Too long and too deeply had life ebbed down in him to bite him with fear of its impending extinction. He continued to persist, alternating periods of unconsciousness with periods of semi-consciousness, dreamy and unreal, in which he idly wondered whether he had ever truly beheld the Red One or whether it was a nightmare fancy of delirium.

Came the day when all mists and cobwebs dissolved, when he found his brain clear as a bell, and took just appraisement of his body's weakness. Neither hand nor foot could he lift. So little control of his body did he have, that he was scarcely aware of possessing one. Lightly indeed his flesh sat upon his soul, and his soul, in its briefness of clarity, knew by its very clarity, that the black of cessation was near. He knew the end was close; knew that in all truth he had with his eyes beheld the Red One, the messenger between the worlds; knew that he would never live to carry that message to the world—that message, for aught to the contrary, which might already have waited man's hearing in the heart of Guadalcanal for ten thousand years. And Bassett stirred with resolve, calling Ngurn to him, out under the shade of the breadfruit tree, and with the old devil-devil doctor discussing the terms and arrangements of his last life effort, his final adventure in the quick of the flesh.

"I know the law, O Ngurn," he concluded the matter. "Whoso is not of the folk may not look upon the Red One and live. I shall not live anyway. Your young men shall carry me before the face of the Red One, and I shall look upon him, and hear his voice, and thereupon die, under your hand, O Ngurn. Thus will the three things be satisfied: the law, my desire, and your quicker possession of my head for which all your preparations wait."

To which Ngurn consented, adding:

"It is better so. A sick man who cannot get well is foolish to live on for so little a while. Also, is it better for the living that he should go. You have been much in the way of late. Not but what it was good for me to talk to such a wise one. But for moons of days we have held little talk. Instead, you have taken up room in the house of heads, making noises like a dying pig, or talking much and loudly in your own language which I do not understand. This has been a confusion to me, for I like to think on the great things of the light and dark as I turn the heads in the smoke. Your much noise has thus been a disturbance to the long-learning and hatching of the final wisdom that will be mine before I die. As for you, upon whom the dark has already brooded, it is well that you die now. And I promise you, in the long days to come when I turn your head in the smoke, no man of the tribe shall come in to disturb us. And I will tell you many secrets, for I am an old man and very wise, and I shall be adding wisdom to wisdom as I turn your head in the smoke."

So a litter was made, and, borne on the shoulders of half a dozen of the men, Bassett departed on the last little adventure that was to cap the total adventure, for him, of living. With a body of which he was scarcely aware, for even the pain had been exhausted out of it, and with a bright clear brain that accommodated him to a quiet ecstasy of sheer lucidness of thought, he lay back on the lurching litter and watched the fading of the passing world, beholding for the last time the breadfruit tree before the devil-devil house, the dim day beneath the matted jungle roof, the gloomy gorge between the shouldering mountains, the saddle of raw limestone, and the mesa of black, volcanic sand.

Down the spiral path of the pit they bore him, encircling the sheening, glowing Red One that seemed ever imminent to iridesce from color and light into sweet singing and thunder. And over bones and logs of immolated men and gods they bore him, past the horrors of other immolated ones that yet lived, to the three-king-post tripod and the huge king-post striker.

Here Bassett, helped by Ngurn and Balatta, weakly sat up, swaying weakly from the hips, and with clear, unfaltering, all-seeing eyes gazed upon the Red One.

"Once, O Ngurn," he said, not taking his eyes from the sheening, vibrating surface whereon and wherein all the shades of cherry-red played unceasingly, ever a-quiver to change into sound, to become silken rustlings, silvery whisperings, golden thrummings of cords, velvet pipings of elfland, mellow-distances of thunderings.

"I wait," Ngurn prompted after a long pause, the long-handled tomahawk unassumingly ready in his hand.

"Once, O Ngurn," Bassett repeated, "let the Red One speak so that I may see it speak as well as hear it. Then strike, thus, when I raise my hand; for, when I raise my hand, I shall drop my head forward and make place for the stroke at the base of my neck. But, O Ngurn, I, who am about to pass out of the light of day forever, would like to pass with the wonder-voice of the Red One singing greatly in my ears."

"And I promise you that never will a head be so well cured as yours," Ngurn assured him, at the same time signaling the tribesmen to man the propelling ropes suspended from the king-post striker. "Your head shall be my greatest piece of work in the curing of heads."

Bassett smiled quietly to the old one's conceit, as the great carved log, drawn back through two-score feet of space, was released. The next moment he was lost in ecstasy at the abrupt and thunderous liberation of sound. But such thunder! Mellow it was with preciousness of all sounding metals. Archangels spoke in it; it was magnificently beautiful before all other sounds; it was invested with the intelligence of supermen of planets of other suns; it was the voice of God, seducing and commanding to be heard. And—the everlasting miracle of that interstellar metal! Bassett, with his own eyes, saw color and colors transform into sound till the whole visible surface of the vast sphere was a-crawl and titillant and vaporous with what he could not tell was color or was sound. In that moment the interstices of matter were his, and the inter-fusings and intermating transfusings of matter and force.

Time passed. At the last Bassett was brought back from his ecstasy by an impatient movement of Ngurn. He had quite forgotten the old devil-devil one. A quick flash of fancy brought a husky chuckle into Bassett's throat. His shotgun lay beside him in the litter. All he had to do, muzzle to head, was press the trigger and blow his head into noth-ingness.

But why cheat him? was Bassett's next thought. Head-hunting, can-nibal beast of a human that was as much ape as human, nevertheless Old Ngurn had, according to his lights, played squarer than square. Ngurn was in himself a fore-runner of ethics and contract, of consider-ation, and gentleness in man. No, Bassett decided; it would be a ghastly pity and an act of dishonor to cheat the old fellow at the last. His head was Ngurn's, and Ngurn's head to cure it would be.

And Bassett, raising his hand in signal, bending forward his head as agreed so as to expose cleanly the articulation to his taut spinal cord, forgot Balatta, who was merely a woman, a woman merely and only and undesired. He knew, without seeing, when the razor-edged hatchet rose in the air behind him. And for that instant, ere the end, there fell upon Bassett the shadow of the Unknown, a sense of impending marvel of the rending of walls before the imaginable. Almost, when he knew the blow had started and just ere the edge of steel bit the flesh and nerves, it seemed that he gazed upon the serene face of the Medusa, Truth— And, simultaneous with the bite of the steel on the onrush of the dark, in a flashing instant of fancy, he saw the vision of his head turning slowly, always turning, in the devil-devil house beside the breadfruit tree.

ON THE MAKALOA MAT

Unlike the women of most warm races, those of Hawaii age well and nobly. With no pretense of make-up or cunning concealment of time's inroads, the woman who sat under the hau tree might have been permitted as much as fifty years by a judge competent anywhere over the world save in Hawaii. Yet her children and her grandchildren, and Roscoe Scandwell, who had been her husband for forty years, know that she was sixty-four and would be sixty-five come the next twenty-second day of June. But she did not look it, despite the fact that she thrust reading glasses on her nose as she read her magazine and took them off when her gaze desired to wander in the direction of the half-dozen children playing on the lawn.

It was a noble situation—noble as the ancient hau tree, the size of a house, where she sat as if in a house, so spaciously and comfortably houselike was its shade furnished; noble as the lawn that stretched away landward, its plush of green at an appraisement of two hundred dollars a front foot, to a bungalow equally dignified, noble, and costly. Seaward, glimpsed through a fringe of hundred-foot cocoanut palms, was the ocean, beyond the reef a dark blue that grew indigo blue to the horizon, within the reef all the silken gamut of jade and emerald and tourmaline.

And this was but one of the half-dozen houses belonging to Martha Scandwell. Her town house, a few miles away in Honolulu, on Nuuanu Drive, between the first and second showers, was a palace. Hosts of guests had known the comfort and joy of her mountain house on Tantalus, and of her volcano house, her *mauka* (mountainward) house, and her *makai* (seaward) house on the big island of Hawaii. Yet this Waikiki house stressed no less than the rest in beauty, in dignity and in expensiveness of upkeep. Two Japanese yard boys were trimming hibiscus, a third was engaged expertly with the long hedge of night-blooming cereus that was shortly expectant of unfolding in its mysterious night-bloom. In immaculate ducks, a house Japanese brought out the tea things, followed by a Japanese maid, pretty as a butterfly in the distinctive garb of her race and fluttery as a butterfly to attend on her mistress. Another Japanese maid, an array of Turkish towels on her arm, crossed the lawn well to the right in the direction of the bath-houses, from which the children, in swimming suits, were beginning to emerge. Beyond, under the palms at the edge of the sea, two Chinese nurse maids, in their pretty native costume of white *yee-shon* and straight-lined trousers, their black braids of hair down their backs, attended each on a baby in a perambulator.

And all these—servants, and nurses, and grandchildren—were Martha Scandwell's. So likewise was the color of the skin of the grandchildren—the unmistakable Hawaiian color, tinted beyond shadow of mistake by exposure to the Hawaiian sun. One eighth and one sixteenth Hawaiian were they, which meant that seven eighths of fifteen sixteenths white blood informed that skin, yet failed to obliterate the modicum of golden tawny brown of Polynesia. But in this again, only a trained observer would have known that the frolicking children were aught but pure-blooded white. Roscoe Scandwell, grandfather, was pure white; Martha, three quarters white; the many sons and daughters of them seven eighths white; the grandchildren graded up to fifteen sixteenths white, or, in the cases when their seven eighths fathers and mothers had married seven eighths, themselves fourteen sixteenths or seven eighths white. On both sides the stock was good, Roscoe straight descended from the New England Puritans, Martha no less straight descended from the royal chief stocks of Hawaii whose genealogies were chanted in *meles* a thousand years before written speech was acquired.

In the distance a machine stopped and deposited a woman whose utmost years might have been guessed as sixty, who walked across the lawn as lightly as a well-cared-for woman of forty, and whose actual calendar age was sixty-eight. Martha rose to greet her in the hearty Hawaiian way, arms about, lips on lips, faces eloquent and bodies no less eloquent with sincereness and frank excessiveness of emotion. And it was "Sister Bella," and "Sister Martha," back and forth, intermingled with almost incoherent inquiries about each other, and about Uncle This and Brother That and Aunt Some One Else, until, the first tremulousness of meeting over, eyes moist with tenderness of love, they sat gazing at each other across their teacups. Apparently, they had not seen nor embraced for years. In truth, two months marked the interval of their separation. And one was sixty-four, the other sixty-eight. But the thorough comprehension resided in the fact that in each of them one fourth of them was the sun-warm, love-warm heart of Hawaii.

The children flooded about Aunt Bella like a rising tide and were capaciously hugged and kissed ere they departed with their nurses to the swimming beach.

"I thought I'd run out to the beach for several days—the trades had stopped blowing," Martha explained.

"You've been here two weeks already," Bella smiled fondly at her younger sister. "Brother Edward told me. He met me at the steamer and insisted on running me out first of all to see Louise and Dorothy and that first grandchild of his. He's as mad as a silly hatter about it."

"Mercy!" Martha exclaimed. "Two weeks! I had not thought it that long."

"Where's Annie?—and Margaret?" Bella asked.

Martha shrugged her voluminous shoulders with voluminous and forgiving affection for her wayward, matronly daughters who left their children in her care for the afternoon.

"Margaret's at a meeting of the Outdoor Circle—they're planning the planting of trees and hibiscus all along both sides of Kalakaua Avenue," she said. "And Annie's wearing out eighty dollars' worth of tires to collect seventy-five dollars for the British Red Cross—this is their tag day, you know."

"Roscoe must be very proud," Bella said, and observed the bright glow of pride that appeared in her sister's eyes. "I got the news in San Francisco of Ho-o-la-a's first dividend. Remember when I put a thousand in it at seventy-five cents for poor Abbie's children, and said I'd sell when it went to ten dollars?"

"And everybody laughed at you, and at anybody who bought a share," Martha nodded. "But Roscoe knew. It's selling to-day at twenty-four."

"I sold mine from the steamer by wireless—at twenty even," Bella continued. "And now Abbie's wildly dressmaking. She's going with May and Tootsie to Paris."

"And Carl?" Martha queried.

"Oh, he'll finish Yale all right—"

"Which he would have done anyway, and you *know* it," Martha charged, lapsing charmingly into twentieth-century slang.

Bella affirmed her guilt of intention of paying the way of her school friend's son through college, and added complacently:

"Just the same it was nicer to have Ho-o-la-a pay for it. In a way, you see, Roscoe is doing it, because it was his judgment I trusted to when I made the investment." She gazed slowly about her, her eyes taking in, not merely the beauty and comfort and repose of all they rested on, but the immensity of beauty and comfort and repose represented by them, scattered in similar oases all over the islands. She sighed pleasantly and observed: "All our husbands have done well by us with what we brought them."

"And happily . . ." Martha agreed, then suspended her utterance with suspicious abruptness.

"And happily, all of us, except Sister Bella," Bella forgivingly completed the thought for her.

"It was too bad, that marriage," Martha murmured, all softness of sympathy. "You were so young. Uncle Robert should never have made you."

"I was only nineteen," Bella nodded. "But it was not George Castner's fault. And look what he, out of the grave, had done for me. Uncle Robert was wise. He knew George had the far-away vision of far ahead, the energy, and the steadiness. He saw, even then, and that's fifty years ago, the value of the Nahala water rights which nobody else valued then. They thought he was struggling to buy cattle range. He struggled to buy the future of the water—and how well he succeeded, you know. I'm almost ashamed to think of my income sometimes. No; whatever else, the unhappiness of our marriage was not due to George. I could have lived happily with him, I know, even to this day, had he lived." She shook her head slowly. "No; it was not his fault. Nor anybody's. Nor even mine. If it was anybody's fault—" The wistful fondness of her smile took the sting out of what she was about to say. "If it was anybody's fault, it was Uncle John's."

"Uncle John's!" Martha cried with sharp surprise. "If it had to be one or the other, I should have said Uncle Robert. But Uncle John!"

Bella smiled with slow positiveness.

"But it was Uncle Robert who made you marry George Castner," her sister urged.

"That is true," Bella nodded corroboration. "But it was not the matter of a husband, but of a horse. I wanted to borrow a horse from Uncle John, and Uncle John said yes. That is how it all happened."

A silence fell, pregnant and cryptic, and, while the voices of the children and the soft mandatory protests of the Asiatic maids drew nearer from the beach, Martha Scandwell felt herself vibrant and tremulous with sudden resolve of daring. She waved the children away.

"Run along, dears, run along. Grandma and Aunt Bella want to talk."

And as the shrill, sweet treble of child voices ebbed away across the lawn Martha, with scrutiny of the heart, observed the sadness of the lines graven by secret woe for half a century in her sister's face. For nearly fifty years had she watched those lines. She steeled all the melting softness of the Hawaiian of her to break the half century of silence.

"Bella," she said. "We never knew. You never spoke. But we wondered, oh, often and often—"

"And never asked," Bella murmured gratefully.

"But I am asking now, at the last. This is our twilight. Listen to them! Sometimes it almost frightens me to think that they are grandchildren, *my* grandchildren—*I*, who only the other day, it would seem, was as heart-free, leg-free, care-free a girl as ever bestrode a horse, or swam in the big surf, or gathered *opihis* at low tide, or laughed at a dozen lovers. And here in our twilight let us forget everything save that I am your dear sister as you are mine."

The eyes of both were dewy moist. Bella palpably trembled to utterance.

"We thought it was George Castner," Martha went on; "and we could guess the details. He was a cold man. You were warm Hawaiian. He must have been cruel. Brother Walcott always insisted he must have beaten you—"

"No! No!" Bella broke in. "George Castner was never a brute, a beast. Almost have I wished, often, that he had been. He never laid hand on me. He never raised hand to me. He never raised his voice to me. Never—oh, can you believe it?—do, please, sister, believe it—did we have a high word nor a cross word. But that house of his, of ours, at Nahala, was gray. All the color of it was gray and cool and chill while I was bright with all colors of sun and earth and blood and birth. It was very cold, gray cold, with that cold gray husband of mine at Nahala— You know he was gray, Martha. Gray like those portraits of Emerson we used to see at school. His skin was gray. Sun and weather and all hours in the saddle could never tan it. And he was as gray inside as out.

"And I was only nineteen, when Uncle Robert decided on the marriage. How was I to know? Uncle Robert talked to me. He pointed out how the wealth and property of Hawaii was already beginning to pass into the hands of the *haoles*" (whites). "The Hawaiian chiefs let their possessions slip away from them. The Hawaiian chiefesses who married haoles had their possessions, under the management of their haole husbands, increase prodigiously. He pointed back to the original Grandfather Roger Wilton, who had taken Grandmother Wilton's poor *mauka* lands and added to them and built up about them the Kilohana Ranch—"

"Even then it was second only to the Parker Ranch," Martha interrupted proudly.

"—And he told me that had our father, before he died, been as far-seeing as grandfather, half the then Parker holdings would have been added to Kilohana, making Kilohana first. And he said that never, forever and ever, would beef be cheaper. And he said that the big future of Hawaii would be in sugar. That was fifty years ago, and he has been more than proved right. And he said that the young haole, George Castner, saw far and would go far, and that there were many girls of us, and that the Kilohana lands ought by rights to go to the boys, and that if I married George my future was assured in the biggest way.

"I was only nineteen. Just back from the Royal Chief School—that was before our girls went to the States for their educations. You were among the first, Sister Martha, who got their education on the mainland. And what did I know of love and lovers, much less of marriage? All women married. It was their business in life. Mother and grandmother, all the way back they had married. It was my business in life to marry George Castner. Uncle Robert said so in his wisdom, and I knew he was very wise. And I went to live with my husband in the gray house at Nahala.

"You remember it. No trees, only the rolling grass lands, the high mountains behind, the sea beneath, and the wind!—the Waimea and Nahala winds, we got them both, and the kona wind as well. Yet little would I have minded them, any more than we minded them at Kilohana, or than they minded them at Mana, had not Nahala itself been so gray, and husband George so gray. We were alone. He was managing Nahala for the Glenns, who had gone back to Scotland. Eighteen hundred a year, plus beef, horses, cowboy service, and the ranch house, was what he received—"

"It was a high salary in those days," Martha said.

"And for George Castner, and the service he gave, it was very cheap," Bella defended. "I lived with him for three years. There was never a morning that he was out of his bed later than half-past four. He was the soul of devotion to his employers. Honest to a penny in his accounts, he gave them full measure and more of his time and energy. Perhaps that was what helped make our life so gray. But listen, Martha. Out of his eighteen hundred, he laid aside sixteen hundred each year. Think of it! The two of us lived on two hundred a year. Luckily he did not drink or smoke. Also, we dressed out of it as well. I made my own dresses. You can imagine them. Outside of the cowboys who chored the firewood, I did the work. I cooked and baked and scrubbed—"

"You who had never known anything but servants from the time you were born!" Martha pitied. "Never less than a regiment of them at Kilohana."

"Oh, but it was the bare, naked, pinching meagerness of it!" Bella cried out. "How far I was compelled to make a pound of coffee go! A broom worn down to nothing before a new one was bought! And beef!

French beef and jerky, morning, noon, and night! And porridge! Never since have I eaten porridge or any breakfast food."

She arose suddenly and walked a dozen steps away to gaze a moment with unseeing eyes at the color-lavish reef while she composed herself. And she returned to her seat with the splendid, sure, gracious, high-breasted, noble-headed port of which no outbreeding can ever rob the Hawaiian woman. Very haole was Bella Castner, fair-skinned, fine-textured. Yet, as she returned, the high pose of head, the level-lidded gaze of her long brown eyes under royal arches of eyebrows, the softly set lines of her small mouth that fairly sang sweetness of kisses after sixty-eight years—all made her the very picture of a chiefess of old Hawaii full-bursting through her ampleness of haole blood. Taller she was than her sister Martha, if anything more queenly.

"You know we were notorious as poor feeders," Bella laughed lightly enough. "It was many a mile on either side from Nahala to the next roof. Belated travelers, or storm-bound ones, would, on occasion, stop with us overnight. And you know the lavishness of the big ranches, then and now. How we were the laughing-stock! 'What do we care?' George would say. 'They live to-day and now. Twenty years from now will be our turn, Bella. They will be where they are now, and they will eat out of our hand. We will be compelled to feed them, they will need to be fed, and we will feed them well; for we will be rich, Bella, so rich that I am afraid to tell you. But I know what I know, and you must have faith in me.'

"George was right. Twenty years afterward, though he did not live to see it, my income was a thousand a month. Goodness! I do not know what it is to-day. But I was only nineteen, and I would say to George: 'Now! now! We live now. We may not be alive twenty years from now. I do want a new broom. And there is a third-rate coffee that is only two cents a pound more than the awful stuff we are using. Why couldn't I fry eggs in butter—now? I should dearly love at least one new table-cloth. Our linen! I'm ashamed to put a guest between the sheets, though Heaven knows they dare come seldom enough.'

" 'Be patient, Bella,' he would reply. 'In a little while, in only a few years, those that scorn to sit at our table now or sleep between our sheets will be proud of an invitation—those of them who will not be dead. You remember how Stevens passed out last year—free living and easy, everybody's friend but his own. The Kohala crowd had to bury him, for he left nothing but debts. Watch the others going the same pace. There's your brother Hal. He can't keep it up and live five years, and he's breaking his uncles' hearts. And there's Prince Lilolilo. Dashes by me with half a hundred mounted, able-bodied, roystering Kanakas in his train who would be better at hard work and looking after their futures, for he will never be King of Hawaii. He will not live to be King of Hawaii.'

"George was right. Brother Hal died. So did Prince Lilolilo. But George was not *all* right. He, who neither drank nor smoked, who never wasted the weight of his arms in an embrace, nor the touch of his lips a second longer than the most perfunctory of kisses, who was invariably up before cock-crow and asleep ere the kerosene lamp had a tenth emptied itself, and who never thought to die, was dead even more quickly than Brother Hal and Prince Lilolilo.

" 'Be patient, Bella,' Uncle Robert would say to me. 'George Castner is a coming man. I have chosen well for you. Your hardships now are the hardships on the way to the promised land. Not always will the Hawaiians rule in Hawaii. Just as they let their wealth slip out of their hands, so will their rule slip out of their hands. Political power and the land always go together. There will be great changes, revolutions no one knows how many nor of what sort, save that in the end the haole will possess the land and the rule. And in that day you may well be first lady of Hawaii, just as surely as George Castner will be ruler of Hawaii. It is written in the books. It is ever so where the haole conflicts with the easier races. I, your Uncle Robert, who am half Hawaiian and half haole, know whereof I speak. Be patient, Bella, be patient.'

" 'Dear Bella,' Uncle John would say; and I knew his heart was tender for me. Thank God, he never told me to be patient. He knew. He was very wise. He was warm human, and, therefore, wiser than Uncle Robert and George Castner, who sought the thing, not the spirit, who kept records in ledgers rather than numbered heartbeats breast to breast, who added columns of figures rather than remembered embraces and endearments of look and speech and touch. 'Dear Bella,' Uncle John would say. He knew. You have heard always how he was the lover of the Princess Naomi. He was a true lover. He loved but the once. After her death they said he was eccentric. He was. He was the one lover, once and always. Remember that taboo inner room of his at Kilohana that we entered only after his death and found it his shrine to her. 'Dear Bella,' it was all he ever said to me, but I knew he knew.

"And I was nineteen, and sun-warm Hawaiian in spite of my three quarters haole blood, and I knew nothing save my girlhood splendors at Kilohana and my Honolulu education at the Royal Chief School, and my gray husband at Nahala with his gray preachments and practices of sobriety and thrift, and those two childless uncles of mine, the one with far cold vision, the other the broken-hearted, forever-dreaming lover of a dead princess.

"Think of that gray house! I, who had known the ease and the delights and the ever-laughing joys of Kilohana, and of the Parkers at old Mana, and of Puuwaawaa! You remember. We did live in feudal spaciousness in those days. Would you, can you, believe it, Martha?—at Nahala the only sewing machine I had was one of those the early missionaries brought, a tiny, crazy thing that one cranked around by hand!

"Robert and John had each given Husband George five thousand dollars at my marriage. But he had asked for it to be kept secret. Only the four of us knew. And while I sewed my cheap *holokus* on that crazy machine, he bought land with the money—the upper Nahala lands, you know—a bit at a time, each purchase a hard-driven bargain, his face the very face of poverty. To-day the Nahala Ditch alone pays me forty thousand a year.

"But was it worth it? I starved. If only once, madly, he had crushed me in his arms! If only once, he could have lingered with me five minutes from his own business or from his fidelity to his employers! Sometimes I could have screamed, or showered the eternal bowl of hot porridge into his face, or smashed the sewing machine upon the floor and danced a hula on it, just to make him burst out and lose his temper and be human, be a brute, be a man of some sort instead of a gray, frozen demigod."

Bella's tragic expression vanished, and she laughed outright in sheer genuineness of mirthful recollection.

"And when I was in such moods he would gravely look me over, gravely feel my pulse, examine my tongue, gravely dose me with castor oil, and gravely put me to bed early with hot stove lids and assure me that I'd feel better in the morning. Early to bed! Our wildest sitting up was nine o'clock. Eight o'clock was our regular bedtime. It saved kerosene. We did not eat dinner at Nahala—remember the great table at Kilohana where we did have dinner? But Husband George and I had supper. And then he would sit close to the lamp on one side the table and read old borrowed magazines for an hour, while I sat on the other side and darned his socks and underclothing. He always wore such cheap, shoddy stuff. And when he went to bed, I went to bed. No wastage of kerosene with only one to benefit by it. And he went to bed always the same way, winding up his watch, entering the day's weather in his diary, and taking off his shoes, right foot first invariably, left foot second, and placing them just so, side by side, on the floor, at the foot of the bed, on his side.

"He was the cleanest man I ever knew. He never wore the same undergarment a second time. I did the washing. He was so clean it hurt. He shaved twice a day. He used more water on his body than any Kanaka. He did more work than any two haoles. And he saw the future of the Nahala water."

"And he made you wealthy, but did not make you happy," Martha observed.

Bella sighed and nodded.

"What is wealth, after all, Sister Martha? My new Pierce-Arrow came down on the steamer with me. My third in two years. But oh, all the Pierce-Arrows and all the incomes in the world compared with a lover!—the one lover, the one mate, to be married to, to toil beside and suffer and joy beside, the one male man lover husband—"

Her voice trailed off, and the sisters sat in soft silence while an ancient crone, staff in hand, twisted, doubled, and shrunken under an hundred years of living, hobbled across the lawn to them. Her eyes, withered to scarcely more than peepholes, were sharp as a mongoose's, and at Bella's feet she first sank down, in pure Hawaiian mumbling and chanting a toothless *mele* of Bella and Bella's ancestry and adding to it an extemporized welcome back to Hawaii after her absence across the great sea to California. And while she chanted her mele, the old crone's shrewd fingers *lomied* or massaged Bella's silk-stockinged legs from ankle and calf to knee and thigh.

Both Bella's and Martha's eyes were luminous-moist, as the old retainer repeated the lomi and the mele to Martha, and as they talked with her in the ancient tongue and asked the immemorial questions about her health and age and great-great-grandchildren—she, who had lomied them as babies in the great house at Kilohana, as her ancestresses had lomied their ancestresses back through the unnumbered generations. The brief duty visit over, Martha arose and accompanied her back to the bungalow, putting money into her hand, commanding proud and beautiful Japanese housemaids to wait upon the dilapidated aborigine with *poi,* which is compounded of the roots of the water lily, with *iamaka,* which is raw fish, and with pounded *kukui* nut and *limu,* which latter is seaweed tender to the toothless, digestible and savory. It was the old feudal tie, the faithfulness of the commoner to the chief, the responsibility of the chief to the commoner; and Martha, three quarters haole with the Anglo-Saxon blood of New England, was four quarters Hawaiian in her remembrance and observance of the well-nigh vanished customs of old days.

As she came back across the lawn to the hau tree, Bella's eyes dwelt upon the moving authenticity of her and of the blood of her, and embraced her and loved her. Shorter than Bella was Martha a trifle, but the merest trifle, less queenly of port; but beautifully and generously proportioned, mellowed rather than dismantled by years, her Polynesian chiefess figure eloquent and glorious under the satisfying lines of a half-fitting, grandly sweeping, black silk *holoku* trimmed with black lace more costly than a Paris gown.

And as both sisters resumed their talk, an observer would have noted the striking resemblance of their pure, straight profiles, of their broad cheek bones, of their wide and loftly foreheads, of their iron-gray abundance of hair, of their sweet-lipped mouths set with the carriage of decades of assured and accomplished pride, and of their lovely, slender eyebrows arched over equally lovely long brown eyes. The hands of both of them, little altered or defaced by age, were wonderful in their slender, tapering fingertips, love-lomi'd and love-formed while they were babies by old Hawaiian women like to the one even then eating *poi* and iamaka and limu in the house.

"I had a year of it," Bella resumed, "and, do you know, things were beginning to come right. I was beginning to draw to Husband George. Women are so made. I was such a woman at any rate. For he *was* good. He *was* just. All the old sterling Puritan virtues were his. I was coming to draw to him, to like him, almost, might I say, to love him. And had not Uncle John loaned me that horse, I know that I would have truly loved him and have lived ever happily with him—in a quiet sort of way, of course.

"You see, I knew nothing else, nothing different, nothing better in the way of man. I came gladly to look across the table at him while he read in the brief interval between supper and bed, gladly to listen for and to catch the beat of his horse's hoofs coming home at night from his endless riding over the ranch. And his scant praise was praise indeed, that made me tingle with happiness—yes, Sister Martha, I knew what it was to blush under his precise, just praise for the things I had done right or correctly.

"And all would have been well for the rest of our lives together, except that he had to take steamer to Honolulu. It was business. He was to be gone two weeks or longer, first, for the Glenns in ranch affairs, and, next, for himself, to arrange the purchase of still more of the upper Nahala lands. Do you know, he bought lots of the wilder and up-and-down lands, worthless for aught save water, and the very heart of the watershed, for as low as five and ten cents an acre. And he suggested I needed a change. I wanted to go with him to Honolulu. But, with an eye to expense, he decided Kilohana for me. Not only would it cost him nothing for me to visit at the old home, but he saved the price of the poor food I should have eaten had I remained alone at Nahala, which meant the purchase price of more Nahala acreage. And at Kilohana Uncle John said yes, and loaned me the horse.

"Oh, it was like heaven, getting back those first several days. It was difficult to believe at first that there was so much food in all the world. The enormous wastage of the kitchen appalled me. I saw waste everywhere, so well trained had I been by Husband George. Why, out in the servants' quarters the aged relatives and most distant hangers-on of the servants fed better than George and I ever fed. You remember our Kilohana way, same as the Parker way, a bullock killed for every meal, fresh fish by runners from the ponds of Waipio and Kiholo, and the best and rarest at all times of everything. . . .

"And love, our family way of loving! You know what Uncle John was. And Brother Walcott was there, and Brother Edward, and all the younger sisters save you and Sally away at school. And Aunt Elizabeth, and Aunt Janet with her husband and all her children on a visit. It was arms around, and perpetual endearings, and all that I had missed for a weary twelve-month. I was thirsty for it. I was like a survivor from the open boat falling down on the sand and lapping the fresh, bubbling springs at the roots of the palms.

"And *they* came, riding up from Kawaihae, where they had landed from the royal yacht, the whole glorious cavalcade of them, two by two, flower-garlanded, young and happy, gay, on Parker Ranch horses, thirty of them in the party, a hundred Parker Ranch cowboys and as many more of their own retainers—a royal progress. It was Princess Lihue's progress, of course, she flaming and passing as we all knew with the dreadful tuberculosis; but with her were her nephews, Prince Lilolilo, hailed everywhere as the next king, and his brothers, Prince Kahekili and Prince Kamalau. And with the Princess was Ella Higginsworth, who rightly claimed higher chief blood lines through the Kauai descent than belonged to the reigning family, and Dora Niles, and Emily Lowcroft, and—oh, why enumerate them all! Ella Higginsworth and I had been roommates at the Royal Chief School. And there was a great resting time for an hour—no *luau*, for the luau waited them at the Parkers'— but beer and stronger drinks for the men, and lemonade, and oranges, and refreshing watermelon for the women.

"And it was arms around with Ella Higginsworth and me, and the Princess, who remembered me, and all the other girls and women, and Ella spoke to the Princess, and the Princess herself invited me to the progress, joining them at Mana whence they would depart two days later. And I was mad, mad with it all—I, from a twelvemonth of imprisonment at gray Nahala. And I was nineteen yet, just turning twenty within the week.

"Oh, I had no thought of what was to happen. So occupied was I with the women that I did not see Lilolilo, except at a distance, bulking large and tall above the other men. But I had never been on a progress. I had seen them entertained at Kilohana and Mana, but I had been too young to be invited along, and after that it had been school and marriage. I knew what it would be like—two weeks of paradise, and little enough for another twelvemonths at Nahala.

"And I asked Uncle John to lend me a horse, which meant three horses, of course—one mounted cowboy and a pack horse to accompany me. No roads then. No automobiles. And the horse for myself! It was Hilo. You don't remember him. You were away at school, then, and before you came home, the following year, he'd broken his back and his rider's neck wild-cattle-roping up Mauna Kea. You heard about it—that young American naval officer."

"Lieutenant Bowsfield," Martha nodded.

"But Hilo! I was the first woman on his back. He was a three-year-old, almost a four-year, and just broken. So black and in such vigor of coat that the high lights on him clad him in shimmering silver. He was the biggest riding animal on the ranch, descended from the King's Sparklingdew with a range mare for dam, and roped wild only weeks before. I never have seen so beautiful a horse. He had the round, deep-chested, big-hearted, well-coupled body of the ideal mountain pony, and his head and neck were true thoroughbred, slender, yet full, with lovely alert ears not too small to be vicious nor too large to be stubborn mulish. And his legs and feet were lovely, too, unblemished, sure and firm, with long springy pasterns that made him a wonder of ease under the saddle."

"I remember hearing Prince Lilolilo tell Uncle John that you were the best woman rider in all Hawaii," Martha interrupted to say. "That was two years afterward when I was back from school and while you were still living at Nahala."

"Lilolilo said that!" Bella cried. Almost as with a blush, her long brown eyes were illumined, as she bridged the years to her lover near half a century dead and dust. With the gentleness of modesty so innate in the women of Hawaii, she covered her spontaneous exposure of her heart with added panegyric of Hilo.

"Oh, when he ran with me up the long-grass slopes, and down the long-grass slopes, it was like hurdling in a dream, for he cleared the grass at every bound, leaping like a deer, a rabbit, or a fox terrier—you know how they do. And cut up, and prance, and high life! He was a mount for a general, for a Napoleon or a Kitchener. And he had, not a wicked eye, but, oh, such a roguish eye, intelligent and looking as if it cherished a joke behind and wanted to laugh or to perpetrate it. And I asked Uncle John for Hilo. And Uncle John looked at me, and I looked at him; and, though he did not say it, I knew he was *feeling* 'Dear Bella,' and I knew, somewhere in his seeing of me, was all his vision of the Princess Naomi. And Uncle John said yes. That is how it happened.

"But he insisted that I should try Hilo out—myself, rather—at private rehearsal. He was a *handful,* a glorious handful. But not vicious, not malicious. He got away from me over and over again, but I never let him know. I was not afraid, and that helped me keep always a *feel* of him that prevented him from thinking that he was even a jump ahead of me.

"I have often wondered if Uncle John dreamed of what possibly might happen. I know I had no thought of it myself, that day I rode across and joined the Princess at Mana. Never was there such festal time. You know the grand way the old Parkers had of entertaining. The pigsticking and wild-cattle shooting, the horse-breaking and the branding. The servants' quarters overflowing. Parker cowboys in from everywhere. And all the girls from Waimea up, and the girls from Waipio, and Honokaa, and Paauilo—I can see them yet, sitting in long rows on top the stone walls of the breaking pen and making *leis* (flower garlands) for their cowboy lovers. And the nights, the perfumed nights, the chanting of the meles and the dancing of the hulas, and the big Mana grounds with lovers everywhere strolling two by two under the trees.

"And the Prince . . ." Bella paused, and for a long minute her small fine teeth, still perfect, showed deep in her under lip as she sought and won control and sent her gaze vacantly out across the far blue horizon. As she relaxed, her eyes came back to her sister.

"He was a prince, Martha. You saw him at Kilohana before . . . after you came home from seminary. He filled the eyes of any woman, yes, and of any man. Twenty-five he was, in all glorious ripeness of man, great and princely in body as he was great and princely in spirit. No matter how wild the fun, how reckless mad the sport, he never seemed to forget that he was royal and that all his forbears had been high chiefs even to that one first one they sang in the genealogies, who had navigated his double canoes to Tahiti and Raiatea and back again. He was gracious, sweet, kindly, comradely, all friendliness—and severe, and stern, and harsh, if he were crossed too grievously. It is hard to express what I mean. He was all man, man, man, and he was all prince, with a strain of the merry boy in him, and the iron in him that would have made him a good and strong King of Hawaii had he come to the throne.

"I can see him yet, as I saw him that first day and touched his hand and talked with him ... few words and bashful, and anything but a year-long married woman to a gray haole at gray Nahala. Half a century ago it was, that meeting—you remember how our young men then dressed in white shoes and trousers, white silk shirts, with, slashed around the middle, the gorgeously colorful Spanish sashes—and for half a century that picture of him has not faded in my heart. He was the center of a group on the lawn, and I was being brought by Ella Higginsworth to be presented. The Princess Lihue had just called some teasing chaff to her which had made her halt to respond and left me halted a pace in front of her.

"His glance chanced to light on me, along there, perturbed, embarrassed. Oh, how I see him!—his head thrown back a little, with that high, bright, imperious, and utterly carefree poise that was so usual of him. Our eyes met. His head bent forward, or straightened to me. I don't know what happened. Did he command? Did I obey? I do not know. I know only that I was good to look upon, crowned with fragrant *maile,* clad in Princess Naomi's wonderful holoku loaned me by Uncle John from his taboo room; and I know that I advanced alone to him across the Mana lawn, and that he stepped forth from those about him to meet me halfway. We came to each other across the grass, unattended, as if we were coming to each other across our lives.

"Was I very beautiful, Sister Martha, when I was young? I do not know. I don't know. But in that moment, with all his beauty and truly royal-manness crossing to me and penetrating to the heart of me, I felt a sudden sense of beauty in myself—how shall I say?—as if in him and from him perfection were engendered and conjured within myself.

"No word was spoken. But, oh, I know I raised my face in frank answer to the thunder and trumpets of the message unspoken, and that, had it been death for that one look and that one moment I could not have refrained from the gift of myself that must have been in my face and eyes, in the very body of me that breathed so high.

"Was I beautiful, very beautiful, Martha, when I was nineteen, just turning into twenty?"

And Martha, threescore and four, looked upon Bella, threescore and eight, and nodded genuine affirmation, and to herself added the appreciation of the instant in what she beheld—Bella's neck, still full and shapely, longer than the ordinary Hawaiian woman's neck, a pillar that carried regally her high-cheeked, high-browed, high-chiefess face and head; Bella's hair, high-piled, intact, sparkling the silver of the years, ringleted still and contrasting definitely and sharply with her clean, slim, black brows and deep brown eyes. And Martha's glance, in modest over-whelming of modesty by what she saw, dropped down the splendid breast of her and generously true lines of body to the feet, silken clad, high-heeled-slippered, small, plump, with an almost Spanish arch and faultlessness of instep.

"When one is young, the one young time!" Bella laughed. "Lilolilo was a prince. I came to know his every feature and their every phase ... afterward, in our wonder days and nights by the singing waters, by the slumber-drowsy surfs, and on the mountain ways. I knew his fine, brave eyes, with their straight black brows, the nose of him that was assuredly a Kamehameha nose, and the last, least, lovable curve of his mouth. There is no mouth more beautiful than the Hawaiian, Martha.

"And his body. He was a king of athletes, from his wicked, wayward hair to his ankles of bronzed steel. Just the other day I heard one of the Wilder grandsons referred to as 'The Prince of Harvard.' Mercy! What would they, what could they, have called my Lilolilo could they have matched him against this Wilder lad and all his team at Harvard!"

Bella ceased and breathed deeply, the while she clasped her fine, small hands in her ample silken lap. But her pink fairness blushed faintly through her skin and warmed her eyes as she relived her prince days.

"Well—you have guessed?" Bella said, with defiant shrug of shoul-ders and a straight gaze into her sister's eyes. "We rode out from gay Mana and continued the gay progress—down the lava trails to Kiholo to the swimming and the fishing and the feasting and the sleeping in the warm sand under the palms; and up to Puuwaawaa, and more pig-sticking, and roping and driving, and wild mutton from the upper pas-ture lands; and on through Kona, now *mauka* (mountainward), now down to the King's palace at Kailua, and to the swimming at Keauhou, and to Kealakekua Bay, and Napoopoo and Honaunau. And everywhere the people turning out, in their hands gifts of flowers, and fruit, and fish, and pig, in their hearts love and song, their heads bowed in obei-sance to the royal ones while their lips ejaculated exclamations of amazement or chanted meles of old and unforgotten days.

"What would you, Sister Martha? You know what we Hawaiians are. You know what we were half a hundred years ago. Lilolilo was won-derful. I was reckless. Lilolilo of himself could make any woman reck-less. I was twice reckless, for I had cold, gray Nahala to spur me on. I knew. I had never a doubt. Never a hope. Divorces in those days were undreamed. The wife of George Castner could never be Queen of Ha-waii, even if Uncle Robert's prophesied revolutions were delayed, and if Lilolilo himself became king. But I never thought of the throne. What I wanted would have been the queendom of being Lilolilo's wife and mate. But I made no mistake. What was impossible was impossible, and I dreamed no false dreams.

"It was the very atmosphere of love. And Lilolilo was a lover. I was forever crowned with *leis* (wreaths) by him, and he had his runners bring me leis all the way from the rose gardens of Mana—you remember them; fifty miles across the lava and the ranges, dewy fresh as the moment they were plucked, in their jewel cases of banana bark; yard long they were, the tiny pink buds like threaded beads of Neapolitan coral. And at the *luaus* (feasts) the forever never-ending luaus, I must be seated on Lilolilo's Makaloa mat, the Prince's mat, his alone and taboo to any lesser mortal save by his own condescension and desire. And I must dip my fingers into his own *pa wai holoi* (finger bowl) where scented flower petals floated in the warm water. Yes, and careless that all should see his extended favor, I must dip into his *pa paakai* for my pinches of red salt, and limu, and kukui nut and chili pepper; and into his *ipu kai* (fish sauce dish) of *kou* wood that the great Kamehameha himself had eaten from on many a similar progress. And it was the same for special delicacies that were for Lilolilo and the Princess alone—for his *nelu*, and the *ake*, and the *palu*, and the *alaala*. And his *kahilis* were waved over me, and his attendants were mine, and he was mine; and from my flower-crowned hair to my happy feet I was a woman loved."

Once again Bella's small teeth pressed into her under lip, as she gazed vacantly seaward and won control of herself and her memories.

"It was on, and on, through all Kona, and all Kau, from Hoopuloa and Kapua to Honuapo and Punaluu, a lifetime of living compressed into two short weeks. A flower blooms but once. That was my time of bloom—Lilolilo beside me, myself on my wonderful Hilo, a queen, not of Hawaii but of Lilolilo and Love. He said I was a bubble of color and beauty on the black back of Leviathan; that I was a fragile dewdrop on the smoking crest of a lava flow; that I was rainbow riding the thunder cloud. . . ."

Bella paused for a moment.

"I shall tell you no more of what he said to me," she declared gravely; "save that the things he said were fire of love and essence of beauty, and that he composed hulas to me, and sang them to me, before all, of nights under the stars as we lay on our mats at the feasting, and I on the Makaloa mat of Lilolilo.

"And it was on to Kilauea—the dream so near its ending; and of course we tossed into the pit of sea-surging lava our offerings to *Pele*

(Fire Goddess) of maile leis and of fish and hard poi wrapped moist in the *ti* leaves. And we continued down through old Puna, and feasted and danced and sang at Kohoualea and Kamaili and Opihikao, and swam in the clear, sweet-water pools of Kalapana. And in the end came to Hilo by the sea.

"It was the end. We had never spoken. It was the end recognized and unmentioned. The yacht waited. We were days late. Honolulu called, and the news was that the King had gone particularly *pupule* (insane), that there were Catholic and Protestant missionary plottings, and that trouble with France was brewing. As they had landed at Kawaihae two weeks before with laughter and flowers and song, so they departed from Hilo. It was a merry parting, full of fun and frolic and a thousand last messages and reminders and jokes. The anchor was broken out to a song of farewell from Lilolilo's singing boys on the quarter-deck, while we, in the big canoes and whaleboats, saw the first breeze fill the vessel's sails and the distance begin to widen.

"Through all the confusion and excitement Lilolilo, at the rail, who must say last farewells and quip last jokes to many, looked squarely down at me. On his head he wore my *ilima* lei, which I had made for him and placed there. And into the canoes, to the favored ones, they on the yacht began tossing their many leis. I had no expectancy of hope ... And yet I hoped, in a small, wistful way that I know did not show in my face, which was as proud and merry as any there. But Lilolilo did what I knew he would do, what I had known from the first he would do. Still looking me squarely and honestly in the eyes, he took my beautiful ilima lei from his head and tore it across. I saw his lips shape, but not utter aloud, the single word *pau* (finish). Still looking at me, he broke both parts of the lei in two again and tossed the deliberate fragments, not to me, but down overside into the widening water. Pau. It was finished. . . ."

For a long space Bella's vacant gaze rested on the sea horizon. Martha ventured no mere voice expression of the sympathy that moistened her own eyes.

"And I rode on that day, up the old bad trail along the Hamakua coast," Bella resumed, with a voice at first singularly dry and harsh. "That first day was not so hard. I was numb. I was too full with the wonder of all I had to forget to know that I had to forget it. I spent the night at Laupahoe. Do you know, I had expected a sleepless night. Instead, weary from the saddle, still numb, I slept the night through as if I had been dead.

"But the next day, in driving wind and drenching rain! How it blew and poured! The trail was really impassable. Again and again our horses went down. At first the cowboy Uncle John had loaned me with the horses protested, then he followed stolidly in the rear, shaking his head, and, I know, muttering over and over that I was pupule. The pack horse was abandoned at Kukuihaele. We almost swam up Mud Lane in a river of mud. At Waimea the cowboy had to exchange for a fresh mount. But Hilo lasted through. From daybreak till midnight I was in the saddle, till Uncle John, at Kilohana, took me off my horse, in his arms, and carried me in, and routed the women from their beds to undress me and lomi me, while he plied me with hot toddies and drugged me to sleep and forgetfulness. I know I must have babbled and raved. Uncle John must have guessed. But never to another, nor even to me, did he breathe a whisper. Whatever he guessed he locked away in the taboo room of Naomi.

"I do have fleeting memories of some of that day, all a broken-hearted, mad rage against fate—of my hair down and whipped wet and stinging about me in the driving rain; of endless tears of weeping contributed to the general deluge, of passionate outbursts and resentments against a world all twisted and wrong, of beatings of my hands upon my saddle pommel, of asperities to my Kilohana cowboy, of spurs into the ribs of poor magnificent Hilo, with a prayer on my lips, bursting out from my heart, that the spurs would so madden him as to make him rear and fall on me and crush my body forever out of all beauty for man, or topple me off the trail and finish me at the foot of the *palis* (precipices), writing pau at the end of my name as final as the unuttered pau on Lilolilo's lips when he tore across my ilima lei and dropped it in the sea. . . .

"Husband George was delayed in Honolulu. When he came back to Nahala I was there waiting for him. And solemnly he embraced me, perfunctorily kissed my lips, gravely examined my tongue, decried my looks and state of health, and sent me to bed with hot stove lids and a dosage of castor oil. Like entering into the machinery of a clock and becoming one of the cogs or wheels, inevitably and remorselessly turning around and around, so I entered back into the gray life of Nahala. Out of bed was Husband George at half after four every morning, and out of the house and astride his horse at five. There was the eternal porridge, and the horrible cheap coffee, and the fresh beef and jerky. I cooked, and baked, and scrubbed. I ground around the crazy hand sewing machine and made my cheap holokus. Night after night, through the endless centuries of two years more, I sat across the table from him until eight o'clock, mending his cheap socks and shoddy underwear while he read the years'-old borrowed magazines he was too thrifty to subscribe to. And then it was bedtime—kerosene must be economized —and he wound his watch, entered the weather in his diary, and took off his shoes, the right shoe first, and placed them, just so, side by side, at the foot of the bed on his side.

"But there was no more of my drawing to Husband George, as had been the promise ere the Princess Lihue invited me on the progress and Uncle John loaned me the horse. You see, Sister Martha, nothing would have happened had Uncle John refused me the horse. But I had known love, and I had known Lilolilo; and what chance, after that, had Husband George to win from me heart of esteem or affection? And for two years, at Nahala, I was a dead woman, who somehow walked and talked, and baked and scrubbed, and mended socks and saved kerosene. . . . The doctors said it was the shoddy underwear that did for him, pursuing as always the high-mountain Nahala waters in the drenching storms of midwinter.

"When he died, I was not sad. I had been sad too long already. Nor was I glad. Gladness had died at Hilo when Lilolilo dropped my ilima lei into the sea, and my feet were never happy again. Lilolilo passed within a month after Husband George. I had never seen him since the parting at Hilo. La, la, suitors a-many have I had since; but I was like Uncle John. Mating for me was but once. Uncle John had his Naomi room at Kilohana. I have had my Lilolilo room for fifty years in my heart. You are the first, Sister Martha, whom I have permitted to enter that room. . . ."

A machine swung the circle of the drive, and from it, across the lawn, approached the husband of Martha. Erect, slender, gray-haired, of graceful military bearing, Roscoe Scandwell was a member of the "Big Five," which, by the interlocking of interests, determined the destinies of all Hawaii. Himself pure haole, New England born, he kissed Bella first, arms around, full-hearty, in the Hawaiian way. His alert eye told him that there had been a woman talk, and, despite the signs of all generousness of emotion, that all was well and placid in the twilight wisdom that was theirs.

"Elsie and the younglings are coming—just got a wireless from their steamer," he announced, after he had kissed his wife. "And they'll be spending several days with us before they go on to Maui."

"I was going to put you in the Rose Room, Sister Bella," Martha Scandwell planned aloud. "But it will be better for her and the children and the nurses and everything there, so you shall have Queen Emma's Room."

"I had it last time, and I prefer it," Bella said.

Roscoe Scandwell, himself well taught of Hawaiian love and love ways, erect, slender, dignified, between the two nobly proportioned women, an arm around each of their sumptuous wants, proceeded with them toward the house.

THE TEARS OF AH KIM

There was a great noise and racket, but no scandal, in Honolulu's Chinatown. Those within hearing distance merely shrugged their shoulders and smiled tolerantly at the disturbance as an affair of accustomed usualness. "What is it?" asked Chin Mo, down with a sharp pleurisy, of his wife, who had paused for a second at the open window to listen. "Only Ah Kim," was her reply. "His mother is beating him again."

The fracas was taking place in the garden, in back of the living rooms that were in back of the store that fronted on the street with the proud sign above: Ah Kim Company, General Merchandise. The garden was a miniature domain, twenty feet square, that somehow cunningly seduced the eye into a sense and seeming of illimitable vastness. There were forests of dwarf pines and oaks, centuries old yet two or three feet in height, and imported at enormous care and expense. A tiny bridge, a pace across, arched over a miniature river that flowed with rapids and cataracts from a miniature lake stocked with myriad-finned, orange-miracled goldfish that in proportion to the lake and landscape were whales. On every side the many windows of the several-storied shack buildings looked down. In the center of the garden, on the narrow graveled walk close beside the lake, Ah Kim was noisily receiving his beating.

No Chinese lad of tender and beatable years was Ah Kim. His was the store of Ah Kim Company, and his was the achievement of building it up through the long years from the shoestring of savings of a contract coolie laborer to a bank account in four figures and a credit that was gilt edge. An even half century of summers and winters had passed over his head, and, in the passing, fattened him comfortably and smugly. Short of stature, his full front was as rotund as a watermelon seed. His face was moon-faced. His garb was dignified and silken, and his black silk skullcap with the red button atop, now, alas, fallen on the ground, was the skullcap worn by the successful and dignified merchants of his race.

But his appearance, in this moment of the present, was anything but dignified. Dodging and ducking under a rain of blows from a bamboo cane, he was crouched over in a half-doubled posture. When he was rapped on the knuckles and elbows, with which he shielded his face and head, his winces were genuine and involuntary. From the many surrounding windows the neighborhood looked down with placid enjoyment.

And she who wielded the stick so shrewdly from long practice! Seventy-four years old, she looked every minute of her time. Her thin legs were encased in straight-lined pants of linen stiff-textured and shiny black. Her scraggly gray hair was drawn unrelentingly and flatly back from a narrow, unrelenting forehead. Eyebrows she had none, having long since shed them. Her eyes, of pinhole tinyness, were blackest black. She was shockingly cadaverous. Her shriveled forearm, exposed by the loose sleeve, possessed no more of muscle than several taut bowstrings stretched across meager bone under yellow, parchment-like skin. Along this mummy arm jade bracelets shot up and down and clashed with every blow.

"Ah!" she cried out, rhythmically accenting her blows in series of three to each shrill observation. "I forbade you to talk to Li Faa. Today you stopped on the street with her. Not an hour ago. Half an hour by the clock you talked. What is that?"

"It was the thrice accursed telephone," Ah Kim muttered, while she suspended the stick to catch what he said. "Mrs. Chang Lucy told you. I know she did. I saw her see me. I shall have the telephone taken out. It is of the devil."

"It is a device of all the devils," Mrs. Tai Fu agreed, taking a fresh grip on the stick. "Yet shall the telephone remain. I like to talk with Mrs. Chang Lucy over the telephone."

"She has the eyes of ten thousand cats," quoth Ah Kim, ducking and receiving the stick stingingly on his knuckles. "And the tongues of ten thousand toads," he supplemented ere his next duck.

"She is an impudent-faced and evil-mannered hussy," Mrs. Tai Fu accented.

"Mrs. Chang Lucy was ever that," Ah Kim murmured like the dutiful son he was.

"I speak of Li Faa," his mother corrected with stick emphasis. "She is only half Chinese, as you know. Her mother was a shameless kanaka. She wore skirts like the degraded haole women—also corsets, as I have seen for myself. Where are her children? Yet has she buried two husbands."

"The one was drowned, the other kicked by a horse," Ah Kim qualified.

"A year of her, unworthy son of a noble father, and you would gladly be going out to get drowned or be kicked by a horse."

Subdued chucklings and laughter from the window audience applauded her point.

"You buried two husbands yourself, revered mother," Ah Kim was stung to retort.

"I had the good taste not to marry a third. Besides, my two husbands died honorably in their beds. They were not kicked by horses nor drowned at sea. What business is it of our neighbors that you should inform them I have had two husbands, or ten, or none? You have made a scandal of me before all our neighbors, and for that I shall now give you a real beating."

Ah Kim endured the staccato rain of blows, and said when his mother paused, breathless and weary:

"Always have I insisted and pleaded, honorable mother, that you beat me in the house, with the windows and doors closed tight, and not in the open street or the garden open behind the house."

"You have called this unthinkable Li Faa the Silvery Moon Blossom," Mrs. Tai Fu rejoined, quite illogically and femininely, but with utmost success in so far as she deflected her son from continuance of the thrust he had so swiftly driven home.

"Mrs. Chang Lucy told you," he charged.

"I was told over the telephone," his mother evaded. "I do not know all voices that speak to me over that contrivance of all the devils."

Strangely, Ah Kim made no effort to run away from his mother, which he could easily have done. She, on the other hand, found fresh cause for more stick blows.

"Ah! Stubborn one! Why do you not cry? Mule that shameth its ancestors! Never have I made you cry. From the time you were a little boy I have never made you cry. Answer me! Why do you not cry?"

Weak and breathless from her exertions, she dropped the stick and panted and shook as if with a nervous palsy.

"I do not know, except that it is my way," Ah Kim replied, gazing solicitously at his mother. "I shall bring you a chair now, and you will sit down and rest and feel better."

But she flung away from him with a snort and tottered agedly across the garden into the house. Meanwhile recovering his skullcap and smoothing his disordered attire, Ah Kim rubbed his hurts and gazed after her with eyes of devotion. He even smiled, and almost might it appear that he had enjoyed the beating.

*   *   *

Ah Kim had been so beaten ever since he was a boy, when he lived on the high banks of the eleventh cataract of the Yangtze River. Here his father had been born and toiled all his days from young manhood as a towing coolie. When he died, Ah Kim, in his own young manhood, took up the same honorable profession. Farther back than all remembered annals of the family, had the males of it been towing coolies. At the time of Christ his direct ancestors had been doing the same thing, meeting the precisely similarly modeled junks below the white water at the foot of the cañon, bending the half mile of rope to each junk, and, according to size, tailing on from a hundred to two hundred coolies of them and by sheer, two-legged man power, bowed forward and down till their hands touched the ground and their faces were sometimes within a foot of it, dragging the junk up through the white water to the head of the cañon.

Apparently, down all the intervening centuries, the payment of the trade had not picked up. His father, his father's father, and himself, Ah Kim, had received the same invariable remuneration—per junk one-fourteenth of a cent, at the rate he had since learned money was valued in Hawaii. On long, lucky, summer days when the waters were easy, the junks many, the hours of daylight sixteen, sixteen hours of such heroic toil would earn over a cent. But in a whole year a towing coolie did not earn more than a dollar and a half. People could and did live on such an income. There were women servants who received a yearly wage of a dollar. The net makers of Ti Wi earned between a dollar and two dollars a year. They lived on such wages, or, at least, they did not die on them. But for the towing coolies there were pickings, which were what made the profession honorable and the guild a close and hereditary corporation or labor union. One junk in five that was dragged up through the rapids or lowered down was wrecked. One junk in every ten was a total loss. The coolies of the towing guild knew the freaks and whims of the currents, and grappled and raked and netted a wet harvest from the river. They of the guild were looked up to by lesser coolies, for they could afford to drink brick tea and eat No. 4 rice every day.

And Ah Kim had been contented and proud until, one bitter spring day of driving sleet and hail, he dragged ashore a drowning Cantonese sailor. It was this wanderer, thawing out by his fire, who first named the magic name Hawaii to him. He himself had never been to that laborer's paradise, said the sailor; but many Chinese had gone there from Canton, and he had heard the talk of their letters written back. In

Hawaii was never frost nor famine. The very pigs, never fed, were ever fat of the generous offal disdained by man. A Cantonese or Yangtze family could live on the waste of an Hawaiian coolie. And wages! In gold dollars, ten a month, or, in trade dollars, twenty a month, was what the contract Chinese coolie received from the white-devil sugar kings. In a year the coolie received the prodigious sum of two hundred and forty trade dollars—more than a hundred times what a coolie, toiling ten times as hard, received on the eleventh cataract of the Yangtze. In short, all things considered, an Hawaiian coolie was one hundred times better off, and, when the amount of labor was estimated, a thousand times better off. In addition was the wonderful climate.

When Ah Kim was twenty-four, despite his mother's pleadings and beatings, he resigned from the ancient and honorable guild of the eleventh cataract towing coolies, left his mother to go into a boss coolie's household as a servant for a dollar a year and an annual dress to cost not less than thirty cents, and himself departed down the Yangtze to the great sea. Many were his adventures and severe his toils and hardships ere, as a salt-sea junk sailor, he won to Canton. When he was twenty-six he signed five years of his life and labor away to the Hawaiian sugar kings and departed, one of eight hundred contract coolies, for that far island land, on a festering steamer run by a crazy captain and drunken officers and rejected of Lloyds.

Honorable, among laborers, had Ah Kim's rating been as a towing coolie. In Hawaii, receiving a hundred times more pay, he found himself looked down upon as the lowest of the low—a plantation coolie, than which could be nothing lower. But a coolie whose ancestors had towed junks up the eleventh cataract of the Yangtze since before the birth of Christ inevitably inherits one character in large degree; namely, the character of patience. This patience was Ah Kim's. At the end of five years, his compulsory servitude over, thin as ever in body, in bank account he lacked just ten trade dollars of possessing a thousand trade dollars.

On this sum he could have gone back to the Yangtze and retired for life a really wealthy man. He would have possessed a larger sum, had he not, on occasion, conservatively played che fa and fan-tan, and had he not, for a twelvemonth, toiled among the centipedes and scorpions of the stifling cane fields in the semi-dream of a continuous opium debauch. Why he had not toiled the whole five years under the spell of opium was the expensiveness of the habit. He had had no moral scruples. The drug had cost too much.

But Ah Kim did not return to China. He had observed the business life of Hawaii and developed a vaulting ambition. For six months, in order to learn business and English at the bottom, he clerked in the plantation store. At the end of this time he knew more about that particular store than did ever plantation manager know about any plantation store. When he resigned his position he was receiving forty gold a month, or eighty trade, and he was beginning to put on flesh. Also, his attitude toward mere contract coolies had become distinctively aristocratic. The manager offered to raise him to sixty gold, which, by the year, would constitute a fabulous fourteen hundred and forty trade, or seven hundred times his annual earning on the Yangtze as a two-legged horse at one-fourteenth of a gold cent per junk.

Instead of accepting, Ah Kim departed to Honolulu and in the big general merchandise store of Fong & Chow Fong began at the bottom for fifteen gold per month. He worked a year and a half, and resigned when he was thirty-three, despite the seventy-five gold per month his Chinese employers were paying him. Then it was that he put up his own sign: Ah Kim Company, General Merchandise. Also, better fed, there was about his less meager figure a foreshadowing of the melon-seed rotundity that was to attach to him in future years.

With the years he prospered increasingly, so that, when he was thirty-six, the promise of his figure was fulfilling rapidly, and, himself a member of the exclusive and powerful Hai Gum Tong and of the Chinese Merchants' Association, he was accustomed to sitting as host at dinners that cost him as much as thirty years of towing on the eleventh cataract would have earned him. Two things he missed: a wife, and his mother to lay the stick on him as of yore.

When he was thirty-seven he consulted his bank balance. It stood him three thousand gold. For twenty-five hundred down and an easy mortgage he could buy the three-story shack building and the ground in fee simple on which it stood. But to do this left only five hundred for a wife. Fu Yee Po had a marriageable, properly small-footed daughter whom he was willing to import from China and sell to him for eight hundred gold plus the costs of importation. Further, Fu Yee Po was even willing to take five hundred down and the remainder on note at six per cent.

Ah Kim, thirty-seven years of age, fat and a bachelor, really did want a wife, especially a small-footed wife; for, Chinese born and reared, the immemorial small-footed female had been deeply impressed into his fantasy of woman. But more, even more and far more than a small-footed wife, did he want his mother and his mother's delectable beatings. So he declined Fu Yee Po's easy terms, and at much less cost imported his own mother from servant in a boss coolie's house at a yearly wage of a dollar and a thirty-cent dress to be mistress of his

Honolulu three-story shack building with two household servants, three clerks, and a porter of all work under her, to say nothing of ten thousand dollars' worth of dress goods on the shelves that ranged from the cheapest cotton crêpes to the most expensive hand-embroidered silks. For be it known that even in that early day Ah Kim's emporium was beginning to cater to the tourist trade from the States.

For thirteen years Ah Kim had lived tolerably happily with his mother and by her been methodically beaten for causes just or unjust, real or fancied; and at the end of it all he knew as strongly as ever the ache of his heart and head for a wife and of his loins for sons to live after him and carry on the dynasty of Ah Kim Company. Such the dream that has ever vexed men from those early ones who first usurped a hunting right, monopolized a sand bar for a fish trap, or stormed a village and put the males thereof to the sword. Kings, millionaires, and Chinese merchants of Honolulu have this in common, despite that they may praise God for having made them differently and in self-likable images.

And the ideal of woman that Ah Kim at fifty ached for had changed from his ideal at thirty-seven. No small-footed wife did he want now, but a free, natural, out-stepping, normal-footed woman who, somehow, appeared to him in his daydreams and haunted his night visions in the form of Li Faa, the Silvery Moon Blossom. What if she were twice widowed, the daughter of a Kanaka mother, the wearer of white-devil skirts and corsets and high-heeled slippers? He wanted her. It seemed it was written that she should be joint ancestor with him of the line that would continue the ownership and management through the generations of Ah Kim Company, General Merchandise.

"I will have no half *paké* daughter-in-law," his mother often reiterated to Ah Kim, paké being the Hawaiian word for Chinese. "All paké must my daughter-in-law be, even as you, my son, and as I, your mother. And she must wear trousers, my son, as all the women of our family before her. No woman, in the she-devil skirts and corsets, can pay due reverence to our ancestors. Corsets and reverence do not go together. Such a one is this shameless Li Faa. She is impudent and independent, and will be neither obedient to her husband nor her husband's mother. This brazen-faced Li Faa would believe herself the source of life and the first ancestor, recognizing no ancestors before her. She laughs at our joss sticks and paper prayers and family gods, as I have been well told—"

"Mrs. Chang Lucy," Ah Kim groaned.

"Not alone Mrs. Chang Lucy, O son. I have inquired. At least a dozen have heard her say of our joss house that it is all monkey foolishness. The words are hers—she, who eats raw fish, raw squid, and baked dog. Ours is the foolishness of monkeys. Yet would she marry you, a monkey, because of your store that is a palace and of the wealth that makes you a great man. And she would put shame on me, and on your father before you long honorably dead."

And there was no discussing the matter. As things were, Ah Kim knew his mother was right. Not for nothing had Li Faa been born forty years before of a Chinese father, renegade to all tradition, and of a Kanaka mother whose immediate forebears had broken the taboos, cast down their own Polynesian gods, and weak-heartedly listened to the preaching about the remote and unimageable god of the Christian missionaries. Li Faa, educated, who could read and write English and Hawaiian and a fair measure of Chinese, claimed to believe in nothing, although in her secret heart she feared the kahunas (Hawaiian witch doctors), who she was certain could charm away ill luck or pray one to death. Li Faa would never come into Ah Kim's house, as he thoroughly knew, and kowtow to his mother and be slave to her in the immemorial Chinese way. Li Faa, from the Chinese angle, was a new woman, a feminist, who rode horseback astride, disported immodestly garbed at Waikiki on the surf boards, and at more than one luau had been known to dance the hula with the worst and in excess of the worst to the scandalous delight of all.

Ah Kim himself, a generation younger than his mother, had been bitten by the acid of modernity. The old order held, in so far as he still felt in his subtlest crypts of being the dusty hand of the past resting on him, residing in him; yet he subscribed to heavy policies of fire and life insurance, acted as treasurer for the local Chinese revolutionists that were for turning the Celestial empire into a republic, contributed to the funds of the Hawaii-born Chinese baseball nine that excelled the Yankee nines at their own game, talked theosophy with Katso Suguri, the Japanese Buddhist and silk importer, fell for police graft, played and paid his insidious share in the democratic politics of annexed Hawaii, and was thinking of buying an automobile. Ah Kim never dared bare himself to himself and thresh out and winnow out how much of the old he had ceased to believe in. His mother was of the old, yet he revered her and was happy under her bamboo stick. Li Faa, the Silvery Moon Blossom, was of the new, yet he could never be quite completely happy without her.

For he loved Li Faa. Moon-faced, rotund as a watermelon seed, a canny business man, wise with half a century of living—nevertheless Ah Kim became an artist when he thought of her. He thought of her in poems of names, as woman transmuted into flower terms of beauty and philosophic abstractions of achievement and easement. She was, to him, and alone to him of all men in the world, his Plum Blossom, his Tranquillity of Woman, his Flower of Serenity, his Moon Lily, and his Perfect Rest. And as he murmured these love endearments of namings, it seemed to him that in them were the ripplings of running waters, the tinklings of silver wind bells, and the scents of the oleander and the jasmine. She was his poem of woman, a lyric delight, a three dimensions of flesh and spirit delicious, a fate and a good fortune written, ere the first man and woman were, by the gods whose whim had been to make all men and women for sorrow and for joy.

But his mother put into his hand the ink brush and placed under it, on the table, the writing tablet.

"Paint," said she, "the ideograph of *to marry*."

He obeyed, scarcely wondering, with the deft artistry of his race and training painting the symbolic hieroglyphic.

"Resolve it," commanded his mother.

Ah Kim looked at her, curious, willing to please, unaware of the drift of her intent.

"Of what is it composed?" she persisted. "What are the three originals, the sum of which is it: to marry, marriage, the coming together and wedding of a man and a woman? Paint them, paint them apart, the three originals, unrelated, so that we may know how the wise men of old wisely built up the ideograph of *to marry*."

And Ah Kim, obeying and painting, saw that what he had painted was three picture signs—the picture signs of a hand, an ear, and a woman.

"Name them," said his mother; and he named them.

"It is true," said she. "It is a great tale. It is the stuff of the painted pictures of marriage. Such marriage was in the beginning; such shall it always be in my house. The hand of the man takes the woman's ear and by it leads her away to his house, where she is to be obedient to him and to his mother. I was taken by the ear, so, by your long honorably dead father. I have looked at your hand. It is not like his hand. Also have I looked at the ear of Li Faa. Never will you lead her by the ear. She has not that kind of an ear. I shall live a long time yet, and I will be mistress in my son's house, after our ancient way, until I die."

"But she is my revered ancestress," Ah Kim explained to Li Faa.

He was timidly unhappy; for Li Faa, having ascertained that Mrs. Tai Fu was at the temple of the Chinese Æsculapius making a food offering of dried duck and prayers for her declining health, had taken advantage of the opportunity to call upon him in his store.

Li Faa pursed her insolent, unpainted lips into the form of a half-opened rosebud, and replied:

"That will do for China. I do not know China. This is Hawaii, and in Hawaii the customs of all foreigners change."

"She is nevertheless my ancestress," Ah Kim protested, "the mother who gave me birth, whether I am in China or Hawaii, O Silvery Moon Blossom that I want for wife."

"I have had two husbands," Li Faa stated placidly. "One was a paké, one was a Portuguese. I learned much from both. Also am I educated. I have been to high school, and I have played the piano in public. And I learned from my two husbands much. The paké makes the best husband. Never again will I marry anything but a paké. But he must not take me by the ear—"

"How do you know of that?" he broke in suspiciously.

"Mrs. Chang Lucy," was the reply. "Mrs. Chang Lucy tells me everything that your mother tells her, and your mother tells her much. So let me tell you that mine is not that kind of an ear."

"Which is what my honored mother has told me," Ah Kim groaned.

"Which is what your honored mother told Mrs. Chang Lucy, which is what Mrs. Chang Lucy told me," Li Faa completed equably. "And I now tell you, O Third Husband To Be, that the man is not born who will lead me by the ear. It is not the way in Hawaii. I will go only hand in hand with my man, side by side, fifty-fifty, as is the haole slang just now. My Portuguese husband thought different. He tried to beat me. I landed him three times in the police court, and each time he worked out his sentence on the reef. After that he got drowned."

"My mother has been my mother for fifty years," Ah Kim declared stoutly.

"And for fifty years has she beaten you," Li Faa giggled. "How my father used to laugh at Yap Ten Shin! Like you, Yap Ten Shin had been born in China, and had brought the Chinese customs with him. His old father was forever beating him with a stick. He loved his father. But his father beat him harder than ever when he became a missionary paké. Every time he went to the missionary services, his father beat him. And every time the missionary heard of it he was harsh in his language to Yap Ten Shin for allowing his father to beat him. And my father laughed and laughed, for my father was a very liberal paké who had changed his customs quicker than most foreigners. And all the trouble was because Yap Ten Shin had a loving heart. He loved his honorable father. He loved the God of Love of the Christian missionary. But in the end, in me, he found the greatest love of all, which is the love of woman. In me he forgot his love for his father and his love for the loving Christ.

"And he offered my father six hundred gold for me—the price was small because my feet were not small. But I was half Kanaka. I said that I was not a slave woman, and that I would be sold to no man. My high-school teacher was a haole old maid who said love of woman was so beyond price that it must never be sold. Perhaps that is why she was an old maid. She was not beautiful. She could not give herself away. My Kanaka mother said it was not the Kanaka way to sell their daughters for a money price. They gave their daughters for love, and she would listen to reason if Yap Ten Shin provided luaus in quantity and quality. My paké father, as I have told you, was liberal. He asked me if I wanted Yap Ten Shin for my husband. And I said yes; and freely, of myself, I went to him. He it was who was kicked by a horse; but he was a very good husband before he was kicked by the horse.

"As for you, Ah Kim, you shall always be honorable and lovable for me, and some day, when it is not necessary for you to take me by the ear, I shall marry you and come here and be with you always, and you will be the happiest paké in all Hawaii; for I have had two husbands, and gone to high school, and am most wise in making a husband happy. But that will be when your mother has ceased to beat you. Mrs. Chang Lucy tells me that she beats you very hard."

"She does," Ah Kim affirmed. "Behold!" He thrust back his loose sleeves, exposing to the elbow his smooth and cherubic forearms. They were mantled with black and blue marks that advertised the weight and number of blows so shielded from his head and face.

"But she has never made me cry," Ah Kim disclaimed hastily. "Never, from the time I was a little boy, has she made me cry."

"So Mrs. Chang Lucy says," Li Faa observed. "She says that your honorable mother often complains to her that she has never made you cry."

A sibilant warning from one of his clerks was too late. Having regained the house by way of the back alley, Mrs. Tai Fu emerged right upon them from out of the living apartments. Never had Ah Kim seen his mother's eyes so blazing furious. She ignored Li Faa, as she screamed at him:

"Now will I make you cry. As never before shall I beat you until you do cry."

"Then let us go into the back rooms, honorable mother," Ah Kim suggested. "We will close the windows and the doors, and there may you beat me."

"No. Here shall you be beaten before all the world and this shameless woman who would with her own hand take you by the ear and call such sacrilege marriage! Stay, shameless woman."

"I am going to stay anyway," said Li Faa. She favored the clerks with a truculent stare. "And I'd like to see anything less than the police put me out of here."

"You will never be my daughter-in-law," Mrs. Tai Fu snapped.

Li Faa nodded her head in agreement.

"But just the same," she added, "shall your son be my third husband."

"You mean when I am dead?" the old mother screamed.

"The sun rises each morning," Li Faa said enigmatically. "All my life have I seen it rise—"

"You are forty, and you wear corsets."

"But I do not dye my hair—that will come later," Li Faa calmly retorted. "As to my age, you are right. I shall be forty-one next Kamehameha Day. For forty years I have seen the sun rise. My father was an old man. Before he died he told me that he had observed no difference in the rising of the sun since when he was a little boy. The world is round. Confucius did not know that, but you will find it in all the geography books. The world is round. Ever it turns over on itself, over and over and around and around. And the times and seasons of weather and life turn with it. What is, has been before. What has been will be again. The time of the breadfruit and the mango ever recurs, and man and woman repeat themselves. The robins nest, and in the springtime the plovers come from the north. Every spring is followed by another spring. The cocoanut palm rises into the air, ripens its fruit, and departs. But always are there more cocoanut palms. This is not all my own smart talk. Much of it my father told me. Proceed, honorable Mrs. Tai Fu, and beat your son who is my Third Husband To Be. But I shall laugh. I warn you I shall laugh."

Ah Kim dropped down on his knees so as to give his mother every advantage. And while she rained blows upon him with the bamboo stick, Li Faa smiled and giggled, and finally burst into laughter.

"Harder! O honorable Mrs. Tai Fu!" Li Faa urged between paroxysms of mirth.

Mrs. Tai Fu did her best, which was notably weak, until she observed what made her drop the stick by her side in amazement. Ah Kim was crying. Down both cheeks great round tears were coursing. Li Faa was amazed. So were the gaping clerks. Most amazed of all was Ah Kim, yet he could not help himself; and, although no further blows fell, he cried steadily on.

*   *   *

"But why did you cry?" Li Faa demanded often of Ah Kim. "It was so perfectly foolish a thing to do. She was not even hurting you."

"Wait until we are married," was Ah Kim's invariable reply, "and then, O Moon Lily, will I tell you."

Two years later, one afternoon, more like a watermelon seed in configuration than ever, Ah Kim returned home from a meeting of the Chinese Protective Association to find his mother dead on her couch. Narrower and more unrelenting than ever were the forehead and the brushed-back hair. But on her face was a withered smile. The gods had been kind. She had passed without pain.

He telephoned first of all to Li Faa's number, but did not find her until he called up Mrs. Chang Lucy. The news given, the marriage was dated ahead with ten times the brevity of the old-line Chinese custom. And if there be anything analogous to a bridesmaid in a Chinese wedding, Mrs. Chang Lucy was just that.

"Why," Li Faa asked Ah Kim when alone with him on their wedding night, "why did you cry when your mother beat you that day in the store? You were so foolish. She was not even hurting you."

"That is why I cried," answered Ah Kim.

Li Faa looked at him without understanding.

"I cried," he explained, "because I suddenly knew that my mother was nearing her end. There was no weight, no hurt, in her blows. I cried because I knew *she no longer had strength enough to hurt me.* That is why I cried, my Flower of Serenity, my Perfect Rest. That is the only reason why I cried."

SHIN BONES

They have gone down to the pit with their weapons
of war, and they have laid their swords under their
heads.

"It was a sad thing to see the old lady revert." Prince Akuli shot an apprehensive glance sideward to where, under the shade of a kukui tree, an old wahine was just settling herself to begin on some work in hand.

"Yes," he nodded, half sadly to me, "in her last years Hiwilani went back to the old ways and to the old beliefs—in secret, of course. And, *believe* me, she was some collector herself. You should have seen her bones. She had them all about her bedroom, in big jars, and they constituted most all her relatives, except a half dozen or so that Kanau beat her out of by getting to them first. The way the pair of them used to quarrel about those bones was awe-inspiring. And it gave me the creeps, when I was a boy, to go into that big, forever-twilight room of hers, and know that in this jar was all that remained of my maternal grand-aunt, and that in that jar was my great-grandfather, and that in all the jars were the preserved bone remnants of the shadowy dust of the ancestors whose seed had come down and been incorporated in the living, breathing me. Hiwilani had gone quite native at the last, sleeping on mats on the hard floor—she'd fired out of the room the great, royal, canopied four-poster that had been presented to her grandmother by Lord Byron, who was the cousin of the Don Juan Byron and came here in the frigate *Blonde* in 1825.

"She went back to all native at the last, and I can see her yet, biting a bite out of the raw fish ere she tossed them to her women to eat. And she made them finish her poi, or whatever else she did not finish herself. She—"

But he broke off abruptly, and by the sensitive dilation of his nostrils and by the expression of his mobile features I saw that he had read in the air and identified the odor that offended him.

"Deuce take it!" he cried to me. "It stinks to heaven. And I shall be doomed to wear it until we're rescued."

There was no mistaking the object of his abhorrence. The ancient crone was making a dearest-loved *lei* (wreath) of the fruit of the *hala,* which is the screw pine or pandanus of the South Pacific. She was cutting the many sections or nut envelopes of the fruit into fluted bell shapes preparatory to stringing them on the twisted and tough inner bark of the hau tree. It certainly smelled to heaven, but, to me, a *malachini,* the smell was more wine woody and fruit juicy and not unpleasant.

Prince Akuli's limousine had broken an axle a quarter of a mile away, and he and I had sought shelter from the sun in this veritable bowery of a mountain home. Humble and grass-thatched was the house, but it stood in a treasure garden of begonias that sprayed their delicate blooms a score of feet above our heads, that were like trees, with willowy trunks of trees as thick as a man's arm. Here we refreshed ourselves with drinking cocoanuts, while a cowboy rode a dozen miles to the nearest telephone and summoned a machine from town. The town itself we could see, the Lakanaii metropolis of Olokona, a smudge of smoke on the shore line, as we looked down across the miles of cane fields, the billow-wreathed reef lines, and the blue haze of ocean to where the island of Oahu shimmered like a dim opal on the horizon.

Maui is the Valley of Hawaii, and Kauai the Garden Isle; but Lakanaii, lying abreast of Oahu, is recognized in the present, and was known of old and always as the Jewel Isle of the group. Not the largest, nor nearly the smallest, Lakanaii is conceded by all to be the wildest, the most wildly beautiful, and, in its size, the richest of all the islands. Its sugar tonnage per acre is the highest, its mountain beef cattle the fattest, its rainfall the most generous without ever being disastrous. It resembles Kauai in that it is the first formed and therefore the oldest island, so that it has had time sufficient to break down its lava rock into the richest of soil, and to erode the cañons between the ancient craters until they are like Grand Cañons of the Colorado, with numberless waterfalls plunging thousands of feet in the sheer or dissipating into veils of vapor and evanescing in mid-air to descend softly and invisibly through a mirage of rainbows, like so much dew or gentle shower, upon the abyss floors.

Yet Lakanaii is easy to describe. But how can one describe Prince Akuli? To know him is to know all Lakanaii most thoroughly. In addition, one must know thoroughly a great deal of the rest of the world. In the first place, Prince Akuli has no recognized nor legal right to be

called "Prince." Furthermore, "Akuli" means the "squid." So that Prince
Squid could scarcely be the dignified title of the straight descendant of
the oldest and highest aliis of Hawaii—an old and exclusive stock,
wherein, in the ancient way of the Egyptian Pharaohs, brothers and
sisters had even wed on the throne for the reason that they could not
marry beneath rank, that in all their known world there was none of
higher rank, and that, at every hazard, the dynasty must be perpetuated.

I have heard Prince Akuli's singing historians (inherited from his father) chanting their interminable genealogies, by which they demonstrated that he was the highest alii in all Hawaii. Beginning with Wakea,
who is their Adam, and with Papa, their Eve, through as many generations as there are letters in our alphabet they trace down to Nanakaoko,
the first ancestor born in Hawaii and whose wife was Kahihiokalani.
Later, but always highest, their generations split from the generations
of Ua, who was the founder of the two distinct lines of the Kauai and
Oahu kings.

In the eleventh century A.D., by the Lakanaii historians, at the time
brothers and sisters mated because none existed to exceed them, their
rank received a boost of new blood of rank that was next to heaven's
door. One Hoikemaha, steering by the stars and the ancient traditions,
arrived in a great double canoe from Samoa. He married a lesser alii of
Lakanaii, and, when his three sons were grown, returned with them to
Samoa to bring back his own youngest brother. But with him he
brought back Kumi, the son of Tui Manua, which latter's rank was
highest in all Polynesia and barely second to that of the demigods and
gods. So the estimable seed of Kumi, eight centuries before, had entered
into the aliis of Lakanaii and been passed down by them in the undevi-
ating line to reposit in Prince Akuli.

Him I first met, talking with an Oxford accent, in the officers' mess
of the Black Watch in South Africa. This was just before that famous
regiment was cut to pieces at Magersfontein. He had as much right to
be in that mess as he had to his accent, for he was Oxford-educated and
held the Queen's Commission. With him, as his guest, taking a look at
the war, was Prince Cupid, so nicknamed, but true prince of all Hawaii,
including Lakanaii, whose real and legal title was Prince Jonah Kuhio
Kalanianaole and who might have been the living King of Hawaii Nei
had it not been for the haole revolution and annexation—this, despite
the fact that Prince Cupid's alii genealogy was lesser to the heaven-
boosted genealogy of Prince Akuli. For Prince Akuli might have been
King of Lakanaii, and of all Hawaii, perhaps, had not his grandfather
been soundly thrashed by the first and greatest of the Kamehamehas.

This had occurred in the year 1810, in the booming days of the sandalwood trade and in the same year that the King of Kauai came in and was good and ate out of Kamehameha's hand. Prince Akuli's grandfather, in that year, had received his trouncing and subjugating because he was "old school." He had not imagined island empire in terms of gunpowder and haole gunners. Kamehameha, farther-visioned, had annexed the service of haoles, including such men as Isaac Davis, mate and sole survivor of the massacred crew of the schooner *Fair American,* and John Young, captured boatswain of the scow *Eleanor.* And Isaac Davis and John Young and others of their waywardly adventurous ilk, with six-pounder brass carronades from the captured *Iphigenia* and *Fair American,* had destroyed the war canoes and shattered the morale of the King of Lakanaii's land fighters, receiving duly in return from Kamehameha, according to agreement: Isaac Davis, six hundred mature and fat hogs; John Young, five hundred of the same described pork on the hoof that was split.

And so, out of all incests and lusts of the primitive cultures and beast man's groping toward the stature of manhood, out of all red murders and brute battlings and matings with the younger brothers of the demigods, world-polished, Oxford-accented, twentieth century to the tick of the second, comes Prince Akuli, Prince Squid, pure-veined Polynesian, a living bridge across the thousand centuries, comrade, friend and fellow traveler, out of his wrecked seven-thousand-dollar limousine, marooned with me in a begonia paradise fourteen hundred feet above the sea and his island metropolis of Olokona, to tell me of his mother who reverted in her old age to ancientness of religious concept and ancestor worship and collected and surrounded herself with the charnel bones of those who had been her forerunners back in the darkness of time.

"King Kalakaua started this collecting fad, over on Oahu," Prince Akuli continued. "And his queen, Kapiolani, caught the fad from him. They collected everything—old makaloa mats, old *tapas,* old calabashes, old double canoes, and idols which the priests had saved from the general destruction in 1819. I haven't seen a pearl-shell fishhook in years, but I swear that Kalakaua accumulated ten thousand of them, to say nothing of human jawbone fish hooks, and feather cloaks, and capes and helmets, and stone adzes, and poi pounders of phallic design. When he and Kapiolani made their royal progresses around the islands, their hosts had to hide away their personal relics. For to the king, in theory, belongs all property of his people, and with Kalakaua, when it came to the old things, theory and practice were one.

"From him my father, Kanau, got the collecting bee in his bonnet, and Hiwilani was likewise infected. But father was modern to his finger tips. He believed neither in the gods of the *kahunas* (priests) nor of the missionaries. He didn't believe in anything except sugar stocks, horse breeding, and that his grandfather had been a fool in not collecting a few Isaac Davises and John Youngs and brass carronades before he went to war with Kamehameha. So he collected curios in the pure collector's spirit; but my mother took it seriously. That was why she went in for bones. I remember, too, she had an ugly old stone idol she used to yammer to and crawl around on the floor before. It's in the Deacon Museum now. I sent it there after her death, and her collection of bones to the Royal Mausoleum in Olokona.

"I don't know whether you remember her father was Kaaukuu. Well, he was, and he was a giant. When they built the Mausoleum, his bones, nicely cleaned and preserved, were dug out of their hiding place and placed in the Mausoleum. Hiwilani had an old retainer, Ahuna. She stole the key from Kamau one night, and made Ahuna go and steal her father's bones out of the Mausoleum. I know. And he must have been a giant. She kept him in one of her big jars. One day, when I was a tidy size of a lad and curious to know if Kaaukuu was as big as tradition had him, I fished his intact lower jaw out of the jar and the wrappings and tried it on. I stuck my head right through it, and it rested around my neck and on my shoulders like a horse collar. And every tooth was in the jaw, whiter than porcelain, without a cavity, the enamel unstained and unchipped. I got the walloping of my life for that offense, although she had to call old Ahuna in to help give it to me. But the incident served me well. It won her confidence in me that I was not afraid of the bones of the dead ones, and it won for me my Oxford education. As you shall see, if that car doesn't arrive first.

"Old Ahuna was one of the real old ones with the hall mark on him and branded into him of faithful born-slave service. He knew more about my mother's family, and my father's, than did both of them put together. And he knew, what no living other knew, the burial place of centuries where were hid the bones of most of her ancestors and of Kanau's. Kanau couldn't worm it out of the old fellow, who looked upon Kanau as an apostate.

"Hiwilani struggled with the old codger for years. How she ever succeeded is beyond me. Of course, on the face of it, she was faithful to the old religion. This might have persuaded Ahuna to loosen up a little. Or she may have jolted fear into him; for she knew a lot of the line of chatter of the old Huni sorcerers, and she could make a noise like being on terms of utmost intimacy with Uli, who is the chiefest god of sorcery of all the sorcerers. She could skin the ordinary *kahuna lanaau* (medicine man) when it came to praying to Lonopuha and Koleamoku; read dreams and visions and signs and omens and indigestions to beat the band; make the practitioners under the medicine god, Maiola, look like thirty cents; pull off a *pule hoe* incantation that would make them dizzy; and she claimed to a practice of *kahuna hoenoho,* which is modern spiritism, second to none. I have myself seen her drink the wind, throw a fit, and prophesy. The *aumakuas* were brothers to her when she slipped offerings to them across the altars of the ruined *heiaus* with a line of prayer that was as unintelligible to me as it was hair-raising. And as for old Ahuna, she could make him get down on the floor and yammer and bite himself when she pulled the real mystery dope on him.

"Nevertheless, my private opinion is that it was the *anaana* stuff that got him. She snipped off a lock of his hair one day with a pair of manicure scissors. This lock of hair was what we call the *maunu,* meaning the bait. And she took jolly good care to let him know she had that bit of his hair. Then she tipped it off to him that she had buried it, and was deeply engaged each night in her offerings and incantations to Uli."

"That was the regular praying-to-death?" I queried in the pause of Prince Akuli's lighting his cigarette.

"Sure thing," he nodded. "And Ahuna fell for it. First he tried to locate the hiding place of the bait of his hair. Failing that, he hired a *pahiuhiu* sorcerer to find it for him. But Hiwilani queered that game by threatening to the sorcerer to practice *apo leo* on him, which is the art of permanently depriving a person of the power of speech without otherwise injuring him.

"Then it was that Ahuna began to pine away and get more like a corpse every day. In desperation he appealed to Kanau. I happened to be present. You have heard what sort of a man my father was.

" 'Pig!' he called Ahuna, 'Swine brains! Stinking fish! Die and be done with it. You are a fool. It is all nonsense. There is nothing in anything. The drunken haole, Howard, can prove the missionaries wrong. Square-face gin proves Howard wrong. The doctors say he won't last six months. Even square-face gin lies. Life is a liar, too. And here are hard times upon us and a slump in sugar. Glanders has got into my brood mares. I wish I could lie down and sleep for a hundred years and wake up to find sugar up a hundred points.'

"Father was something of a philosopher himself, with a bitter wit and a trick of spitting out staccato epigrams. He clapped his hands. 'Bring me a high ball,' he commanded; 'no, bring me two high balls.' Then he turned on Ahuna. 'Go and let yourself die, old heathen, survival of darkness, blight of the pit that you are. But don't die on these premises. I desire merriment and laughter, and the sweet tickling of music and the beauty of youthful motion, not the croaking of sick toads and googly-eyed corpses about me still afoot on their shaky legs. I'll be that way soon enough if I live long enough. And it will be my everlasting regret if I don't live long enough. Why in hell did I sink that last twenty thousand into Curtis's plantation? Howard warned me the slump was coming, but I thought it was the square-face making him lie. And Curtis has blown his brains out, and his head luna has run away with his daughter, and the sugar chemist has got typhoid, and everything's going to smash.'

"He clapped his hands for his servants, and commanded: 'Bring me my singing boys. And the hula dancers—plenty of them. And send for old Howard. Somebody's got to pay, and I'll shorten his six months of life by a month. But above all, music. Let there be music. It is stronger than drink, and quicker than opium.'

"He with his music druggery! It was his father, the old savage, who was entertained on board a French frigate and for the first time heard an orchestra. When the little concert was over, the captain, to find which piece he liked best, asked which piece he'd like repeated. Well, when grandfather got done describing, what piece do you think it was?"

I gave up, while the prince lighted a fresh cigarette.

"Why, it was the first one, of course. Not the real first one, but the tuning up that preceded it."

I nodded, with eyes and face mirthful of appreciation, and Prince Akuli, with another apprehensive glance at the old wahine and her half-made hala lei, returned to his tale of the bones of his ancestors.

"It was somewhere around this stage of the game that old Ahuna gave in to Hiwilani. He didn't exactly give in. He compromised. That's where I come in. If he would bring her the bones of her mother, and of her grandfather (who was the father of Kaaukuu, and who, by tradition, was rumored to have been even bigger than his giant son), she would return to Ahuna the bait of his hair she was praying him to death with. He, on the other hand, stipulated that he was not to reveal to her the secret burial place of all the alii of Lakanaii all the way back. Nevertheless, he was too old to dare the adventure alone, must be helped by some one who of necessity would come to know the secret, and I was that one. I was the highest alii, besides my father and mother, and they were no higher than I.

"So I came upon the scene, being summoned into the twilight room to confront those two dubious old ones who dealt with the dead. They were a pair!—mother fat to despair of helplessness, Ahuna thin as a skeleton and as fragile. Of her one had the impression that if she lay down on her back she could not roll over without the aid of block and tackle; of Ahuna one's impression was that the tooth-pickedness of him would shatter to splinters if one bumped into him.

"And when they had broached the matter, there was more *pilikia* (trouble). My father's attitude stiffened my resolution. I refused to go on the bone-snatching expedition. I said I didn't care a whoop for the bones of all the aliis of my family and race.—You see, I had just discovered Jules Verne, loaned me by old Howard, and was reading my head off. Bones? When there were North Poles, and Centers of earths, and hairy comets to ride across space among the stars! Of course I didn't want to go on any bone-snatching expedition. I said my father was able-bodied, and he could go, splitting equally with her whatever bones he brought back. But she said he was only a blamed collector, or words to that effect only stronger.

"'I know him,' she assured me. 'He'd bet his mother's bones on a horse race or an ace-full.'

"I stood with father when it came to modern skepticism, and I told her the whole thing was rubbish. 'Bones?' I said. 'What are bones? Even field mice, and mangy rats, and cockroaches have bones, though the roaches wear their bones outside their meat instead of inside. The difference between man and other animals,' I told her, 'is not bones but brains. Why, a bullock has bigger bones than a man, and more than one fish I've eaten has more bones, while a whale beats creation when it comes to bone.'

"It was frank talk, which is our Hawaiian way, as you have long since learned. In return, equally frank, she regretted she hadn't given me away as a feeding child when I was born. Next she bewailed that she had ever borne me. From that it was only a step to anaana me. She threatened me with it, and I did the bravest thing I have ever done. Old Howard had given me a knife of many blades and corkscrews and screwdrivers and all sorts of contrivances, including a tiny pair of scissors. I proceeded to pare my finger nails.

"'There,' I said, as I put the parings into her hand. 'Just to show you what I think of it. There's bait and to spare. Go on and anaana me if you can.'

"I have said it was brave. It was. I was only fifteen, and I had lived all my days in the thick of the mystery stuff, while my skepticism, very recently acquired, was only skin deep. I could be a skeptic out in the open in the sunshine. But I was afraid of the dark. And in that twilight room, the bones of the dead all about me in the big jars, why, the old lady had me scared stiff. As we say to-day, she had my goat. Only I was brave and didn't let on. And I put my bluff across, for my mother flung the parings into my face and burst into tears. Tears in an elderly woman weighing three hundred and twenty pounds are scarcely impressive, and I hardened the brassiness of my bluff.

"She shifted her attack, and proceeded to talk with the dead. Nay, more, she summoned them there, and, though I was all ripe to see but couldn't, Ahuna saw the father of Kaaukuu in the corner and lay down on the floor and yammered. Just the same, although I almost saw the old giant, I didn't quite see him.

" 'Let him talk for himself,' I said. But Hiwilani persisted in doing the talking for him and in laying upon me his solemn injunction that I must go with Ahuna to the burial place and bring back the bones desired by my mother. But I argued that if the dead ones could be invoked to kill living men by wasting sicknesses, and that if the dead ones could transport themselves from their burial crypts into the corner of her room, I couldn't see why they shouldn't leave their bones behind them, there in her room and ready to be jarred, when they said good-by and departed for the middle world, the over world, or the under world, or wherever they abided when they weren't paying social calls.

"Whereupon mother let loose on poor old Ahuna, or let loose upon him the ghost of Kaaukuu's father supposed to be crouching there in the corner, who commanded Ahuna to divulge to her the burial place. I tried to stiffen him up, telling him to let the old ghost divulge the secret himself, than whom nobody else knew it better seeing that he had resided there upwards of a century. But Ahuna was old school. He possessed no iota of skepticism. The more Hiwalani frightened him, the more he rolled on the floor and the louder he yammered.

"But when he began to bite himself, I gave in. I felt sorry for him; but, over and beyond that, I began to admire him. He was sterling stuff, even if he was a survival of darkness. Here, with the fear of mystery cruelly upon him, believing Hiwilani's dope implicitly, he was caught between two fidelities. She was his living alii, his *alii kapo* (sacred chiefess). He must be faithful to her, yet more faithful must he be to all the dead-and-gone aliis of her line who depended solely on him that their bones should not be disturbed.

"I gave in. But I, too, imposed stipulations. Steadfastly had my father, new school, refused to let me go to England for my education. That sugar was slumping was reason sufficient for him. Steadfastly had my mother, old school, refused, her heathen mind too dark to place any value on education while it was shrewd enough to discern that education led to unbelief in all that was old. I wanted to study, to study science, the arts, philosophy, to study everything old Howard knew, which enabled him, on the edge of the grave, undauntedly to sneer at superstition and to give me Jules Verne to read. He was an Oxford man before he went wild and wrong, and it was he who had set the Oxford bee buzzing in my noddle.

"In the end Ahuna and I, old school and new school leagued together, won out. Mother promised that she'd make father send me to England, even if she had to pester him into a prolonged drinking that would make his digestion go back on him. Also, Howard was to accompany me, so that I could decently bury him in England. He was a queer one, old Howard, an individual if there ever was one. Let me tell you a little story about him. It was when Kalakaua was starting on his trip around the world. You remember, when Armstrong and Judd and the drunken valet of a German baron accompanied him. Kalakaua made the proposition to Howard—"

But here the long-apprehended calamity fell upon Prince Akuli. The old wahine had finished her lei hala. Barefooted, with no adornment of femininity, clad in a shapeless shift of much-washed cotton, with age-withered face and labor-gnarled hands, she cringed before him and crooned a mele in his honor, and, still cringing, put the lei around his neck. It is true, the hala smelled most freshly strong, yet was the act beautiful to me, and the old woman herself beautiful to me. My mind leaped into the prince's narrative so that to Ahuna I could not help likening her.

Oh, truly, to be an alii in Hawaii, even in this second decade of the twentieth century, is no light thing. The alii, utterly of the new, must be kindly and kingly to those old ones absolutely of the old. Nor did the prince without a kingdom, his loved island long since annexed by the United States and incorporated into a territory along with the rest of the Hawaiian Islands—nor did the prince betray his repugnance for the odor of the hala. He bowed his head graciously; and his royal condescending words of pure Hawaiian I knew would make the old woman's heart, until she died, warm with remembrance of the wonderful occasion. The very grimace he stole to me would not have been made had he felt any uncertainty of its escaping her.

"And so," Prince Akuli resumed, after the wahine had tottered away in an ecstasy, "Ahuna and I departed on our grave-robbing adventure. You know the Iron-bound Coast."

I nodded, knowing full well the spectacle of those lava leagues of weather coast, truly iron-bound so far as landing places or anchorages were concerned, great forbidding cliff walls thousands of feet in height, their summits wreathed in cloud and rain squall, their knees hammered by the trade-wind billows into spouting, spuming white, the air, from sea to rain cloud, spanned by a myriad leaping waterfalls, provocative, in day or night, of countless sun and lunar rainbows. Valleys, so called, but fissures, rather, slit the cyclopean walls here and there, and led away into a lofty and madly vertical back country, most of it inaccessible to the foot of man and trod only by the wild goat.

"Precious little you know of it," Prince Akuli retorted, in reply to my nod. "You've seen it only from the decks of steamers. There are valleys there, inhabited valleys, out of which there is no exit by land, and perilously accessible by canoe only on the selected days of two months in the year. When I was twenty-eight I was over there in one of them on a hunting trip. Bad weather, in the auspicious period, marooned us for three weeks. Then five of my party and myself swam for it out through the surf. Three of us made the canoes waiting for us. The other two were flung back on the sand, each with a broken arm. Save for us, the entire party remained there until the next year ten months afterward. And one of them was Wilson, of Wilson & Wall, the Honolulu sugar factors. And he was engaged to be married.

"I've seen a goat, shot down by a hunter above, land at my feet a thousand yards underneath. *Believe* me, that landscape seemed to rain goats and rocks for ten minutes. One of my canoemen fell off the trail between the two little valleys of Aipio and Luno. He hit first fifteen hundred feet beneath us, and fetched up in a ledge three hundred feet farther down. We didn't bury him. We couldn't get to him, and flying machines had not yet been invented. His bones are there now, and, barring earthquake and volcano, will be there when the Trumps of Judgment sound.

"Goodness me! Only the other day, when our promotion Committee, trying to compete with Honolulu for the tourist trade, called in the engineers to estimate what it would cost to build a scenic drive around the Iron-bound Coast, the lowest figures were a quarter of a million dollars a mile!

"And Ahuna and I, an old man and a young boy, started for that stern coast in a canoe paddled by old men! The youngest of them, the steersman, was over sixty, while the rest of them averaged seventy at the very least. There were eight of them, and we started in the nighttime so that none should see us go. Even these old ones, trusted all their lives, knew no more than the fringe of the secret. To the fringe, only, could they take us.

"And the fringe was—I don't mind telling that much—the fringe was Ponuloo Valley. We got there the third afternoon following. The old chaps weren't strong on the paddles. It was a funny expedition into such wild waters, with now one and now another of our ancient-mariner crew collapsing and even fainting. One of them actually died on the second morning out. We buried him overside. It was positively uncanny, the heathen ceremonies those gray ones pulled off in burying their gray brother. And I was only fifteen, *alii kapo* over them by blood of heathenness and right of hereditary heathen rule, with a penchant for Jules Verne and shortly to sail for England for my education! So one learns. Small wonder my father was a philosopher, in his own lifetime spanning the history of man from human sacrifice and idol worship, through the religions of man's upward striving, to the Medusa of rank atheism at the end of it all. Small wonder that, like old Ecclesiastes, he found vanity in all things and surcease in sugar stocks, singing boys, and hula dancers."

Prince Akuli debated with his soul for an interval.

"Oh, well," he sighed, "I have done some spanning of time myself." He sniffed disgustedly of the odor of the hala lei that stifled him. "It stinks of the ancient," he vouchsafed. "I stink of the modern. My father was right. The sweetest of all is sugar up a hundred points, or four aces in a poker game. If the Big War lasts another year, I shall clean up three quarters of a million over a million. If peace breaks to-morrow, with the consequent slump, I could enumerate a hundred who will lose my direct bounty and go into the old natives' homes my father and I long since endowed for them."

He clapped his hands, and the old wahine tottered toward him in an excitement of haste to serve. She cringed before him, as he drew pad and pencil from his breast pocket.

"Each month, old woman of our old race," he addressed her, "will you receive, by rural free delivery, a piece of written paper that you can exchange with any storekeeper anywhere for ten dollars gold. This shall be so for as long as you live. Behold! I write the record and the remembrance of it, here and now, with this pencil on this paper. And this is because you are of my race and service, and because you have honored me this day with your mats to sit upon and your thrice-blessed and thrice-delicious lei hala."

He turned to me a weary and skeptical eye, saying:

"And if I die to-morrow, not alone will the lawyers contest my disposition of my property, but they will contest my benefactions and my pensions accorded and the clarity of my mind.

"It was the right weather of the year; but even then, with our old weak ones at the paddles, we did not attempt the landing until we had assembled half the population of Ponuloo Valley down on the steep little beach. Then we counted our waves, selected the best one, and ran in on it. Of course, the canoe was swamped and the outrigger smashed, but the ones on shore dragged us up unharmed beyond the wash.

"Ahuna gave his orders. In the nighttime all must remain within their houses, and the dogs be tied up and have their jaws bound so that there should be no barking. And in the nighttime Ahuna and I stole out on our journey, no one knowing whether we went to the right or left or up the valley toward its head. We carried jerky, and hard poi and dried *aku,* and from the quantity of the food I knew we were to be gone several days. Such a trail! A Jacob's ladder to the sky, truly, for that first *pali,* almost straight up, was three thousand feet above the sea. And we did it in the dark!

"At the top, beyond the sight of the valley we had left, we slept until daylight on the hard rock in a hollow nook Ahuna knew and that was so small that we were squeezed. And the old fellow, for fear that I might move in the heavy restlessness of lad's sleep, lay on the outside with one arm resting across me. At daybreak, I saw why. Between us and the lip of the cliff scarcely a yard intervened. I crawled to the lip and looked, watching the abyss take on immensity in the growing light and trembling from the fear of height that was upon me. At last I made out the sea, over half a mile straight beneath. And we had done this thing in the dark!

"Down in the next valley, which was a very tiny one, we found evidences of the ancient population, but there were no people. The only way was the crazy footpaths up and down the dizzy valley walls from valley to valley. But lean and aged as Ahuna was, he seemed untirable. In the second valley dwelt an old leper in hiding. He did not know me, and when Ahuna told him who I was, he groveled at my feet, almost clasping them, and mumbled a mele of all my line out of a lipless mouth.

"The next valley proved to be the valley. It was long and so narrow that its floor had caught not sufficient space of soil to grow taro for a single person. Also, it had no beach, the stream that threaded it leaping a *pali* of several hundred feet down to the sea. It was a God-forsaken place of naked, eroded lava, to which only rarely could the scant vegetation find roothold. For miles we followed up that winding fissure through the towering walls, far into the chaos of back country that lies behind the Iron-bound Coast. How far that valley penetrated, I do not know, but, from the quantity of water in the stream, I judged it far. We did not go to the valley's head. I could see Ahuna casting glances to all the peaks, and I knew he was taking bearings, known to him alone, from natural objects. When he halted at the last, it was with abrupt certainty. His bearings had crossed. He threw down the portion of food and outfit he had carried. It was the place. I looked on either hand at the hard, implacable walls, naked of vegetation, and could dream of no burial place possible in such bare adamant.

"We ate, then stripped for work. Only did Ahuna permit me to retain my shoes. He stood beside me at the edge of a deep pool, likewise appareled and prodigiously skinny.

" 'You will dive down into the pool at this spot,' he said. 'Search the ruck with your hands as you descend, and, about a fathom and a half down, you will find a hole. Enter it, headfirst but going slowly, for the lava rock is sharp and may cut your head and body.'

" 'And then?' I queried. 'You will find the hole growing larger,' was his answer. 'When you have gone all of eight fathoms along the passage, come up slowly, and you will find your head in the air, above water, in the dark. Wait there then for me. The water is very cold.'

"It didn't sound good to me. I was thinking, not of the cold water and the dark, but of the bones. 'You go first,' I said. But he claimed he could not. 'You are my alii, my prince,' he said. 'It is impossible that I should go before you into the sacred burial place of your kingly ancestors.'

"But the prospect did not please. 'Just cut out this prince stuff,' I told him. 'It isn't what it's cracked up to be. You go first, and I'll never tell on you.' 'Not alone the living must we please,' he admonished, 'but, more so, the dead must we please. Nor can we lie to the dead.'

"We argued it out, and for half an hour it was stalemate. I wouldn't, and he simply couldn't. He tried to buck me up by appealing to my pride. He chanted the heroic deeds of my ancestors; and, I remember especially, he sang to me of Mokomoku, my great-grandfather and the gigantic father of the gigantic Kaaukuu, telling how thrice in battle Mokomoku leaped among his foes, seizing by the neck a warrior in either hand and knocking their heads together until they were dead. But this was not what decided me. I really felt sorry for old Ahuna, he was so beside himself for fear the expedition would come to naught. And I was coming to a great admiration for the old fellow, not least among the reasons being the fact of his lying down to sleep between me and the cliff lip.

"So, with true alii authority of command, saying, 'You will immediately follow after me,' I dived in. Everything he had said was correct. I found the entrance to the subterranean passage, swam carefully through it, cutting my shoulder once on the lava-sharp roof, and emerged in the darkness and air. But before I could count thirty, he broke water beside me, rested his hand on my arm to make sure of me, and directed me to swim ahead of him for the matter of a hundred feet or so. Then we touched bottom and climbed out on the rocks. And still no light, and I remember I was glad that our altitude was too high for centipedes.

"He had brought with him a cocoanut calabash, tightly stoppered, of whale oil that must have been landed on Lahaina beach thirty years before. From his mouth he took a water-tight arrangement of a match box composed of two empty rifle cartridges fitted snugly together. He lighted the wicking that floated on the oil, and I looked about and knew disappointment. No burial chamber was it, but merely a lava tube such as occurs on all the islands.

"He put the calabash of light into my hands and started me ahead of him on the way, which he assured me was long but not too long. It was long, at least a mile, in my sober judgment, though at the time it seemed five miles; and it ascended sharply. When Ahuna, at the last, stopped me, I knew we were close to our goal. He knelt on his lean old knees on the sharp lava rock, and clasped my knees with his skinny arms. My hand that was free of the calabash lamp he placed on his head. He chanted to me, with his old cracked, quavering voice, the line of my descent and my essential high aliiness. And then he said:

" 'Tell neither Kanau nor Hiwilani aught of what you are about to behold. There is no sacredness in Kanau. His mind is filled with sugar and the breeding of horses. I do know that he sold a feather cloak his grandfather had worn to that English collector for eight thousand dollars, and the money he lost the next day betting on the polo game between Maui and Oahu. Hiwilani, your mother, is filled with sacredness. She is too much filled with sacredness. She grows old and weak-headed, and she traffics overmuch with sorceries.'

" 'No,' I made answer. 'I shall tell no one. If I did, then would I have to return to this place again. And I do not want ever to return to this place. I'll try anything once. This I shall never try twice.'

" 'It is well,' he said, and arose, falling behind so that I should enter first. Also, he said: 'Your mother is old. I shall bring her, as promised, the bones of her mother and of her grandfather. These should content her until she dies; and then, if I die before her, it is you who must see to it that all the bones in her family collection are placed in the Royal Mausoleum.'

"I have given all the Islands' museums the once-over," Prince Akuli lapsed back into slang, "and I must say that the totality of the collections cannot touch what I saw in our Lakanaii burial cave. Remember, and with reason and history, we trace back the highest and oldest genealogy in the Islands. Everything that I had ever dreamed or heard of, and much more that I had not, was there. The place was wonderful. Ahuna, sepulchrally muttering prayers and meles, moved about, lighting various whale-oil lamp calabashes. They were all there, the Hawaiian race from the beginning of Hawaiian time. Bundles of bones and bundles of bones, all wrapped decently in tapa, until for all the world it was like the parcels-post department at a post office.

"And everything! Kahilis, which you may know developed out of the fly flapper into symbols of royalty until they became larger than hearse plumes with handles a fathom and a half and over two fathoms in length. And such handles! Of the wood of the *kauila,* inlaid with shell and ivory and bone with a cleverness that had died out among our artificers a century before. It was a centuries' old family attic. For the first time I saw things I had only heard of, such as the *pahoas,* fashioned of whale teeth and suspended by braided human hair, and worn on the breast only by the highest of rank.

"There were tapas and mats of the rarest and oldest; capes and leis and helmets and cloaks, priceless all, except the too ancient ones, of the feathers of the *mamo,* and of the *iwi* and the *akakano* and the *o-o.* I saw one of the mamo cloaks that was superior to that finest one in the Bishop Museum in Honolulu and that they value at between half a million and a million dollars. Goodness me, I thought at the time, it was lucky Kanau didn't know about it.

"Such a mess of things! Carved gourds and calabashes, shell scrapers, nets of *olona* fiber, a junk of *ié-ié* baskets, and fishhooks of every bone and spoon of shell. Musical instruments of the forgotten days—*ukukes* and nose flutes, and *kiokios* which are likewise played with one unstoppered nostril. Taboo poi bowls and finger bowls, left-handed adzes of the canoe gods, lava-cup lamps, stone mortars and pestles, and poi pounders. And adzes again, a myriad of them, beautiful ones, from an ounce in weight for the finer carvings of idols to fifteen pounds for the felling of trees, and all with the sweetest handles I have ever beheld.

"There were the *kaekeekes*—you know, our ancient drums, hollowed sections of the cocoanut tree, covered one end with sharkskin. The first kaekeeke of all Hawaii Ahuna pointed out to me and told me the tale. It was manifestly most ancient. He was afraid to touch it for fear the age-rotted wood of it would crumble to dust, the ragged tatters of the sharkskin head of it still attached. 'This is the very oldest and father of all our kaekeekes,' Ahuna told me. 'Kila, the son of Moikeha, brought it back from far Raiatea in the South Pacific. And it was Kila's own son, Kahai, who made that same journey, and was gone ten years, and brought back with him from Tahiti the first breadfruit trees that sprouted and grew on Hawaiian soil.'

"And the bones and bones! The parcel-delivery array of them! Besides the small bundles of the long bones, there were full skeletons, tapa-wrapped, lying in one-man, and two- and three-man canoes of precious *koa* wood, with curved outriggers of *wili-wili* wood, and proper paddles to hand with the *io* projection at the point simulating the continuance of the handle, as if, like a skewer, thrust through the flat length of the blade. And their war weapons were laid away by the sides of the lifeless bones that had wielded them—rusty old horse pistols, derringers, pepper boxes, five-barreled fantastiques, Kentucky long rifles, muskets handled in trade by John Company and Hudson's Bay, shark-tooth swords, wooden stabbing knives, arrows and spears bone-headed of the fish and the pig and of man, and spears and arrows wooden-headed and fire-hardened.

"Ahuna put a spear in my hand, headed and pointed finely with the long shin bone of a man, and told me the tale of it. But first he unwrapped the long bones, arms, and legs of two parcels, the bones, under the wrappings, neatly tied like so many fagots. 'This,' said Ahuna, exhibiting the pitiful white contents of one parcel, 'is Laulani. She was the wife of Akaiko, whose bones now placed in your hands, much larger and malelike as you observe, held up the flesh of a large man, a three-hundred pounder, seven-footer, three centuries agone. And this spear-head is made of the shin bone of Keola, a mighty wrestler and runner of their own time and place. And he loved Laulani, and she fled with him. But in a forgotten battle on the sands of Kalini, Akaiko rushed the lines of the enemy, leading the charge that was successful, and seized upon Keola, his wife's lover, and threw him to the ground, and sawed through his neck to the death with a shark-tooth knife. Thus, in the old days as always, did man combat with man for woman. And Laulani was beautiful, that Keola should be made into a spear-head for her! She was formed like a queen, and her body was a long bowl of sweetness, and her fingers lomi'd to slimness and smallness at her mother's breast. For ten generations have we remembered her beauty. Your father's singing boys to-day sing of her beauty in the hula that is named of her. This is Laulani, whom you hold in your hands.'

"And, Ahuna done, I could but gaze, with imagination at the one time sobered and fired. Old drunken Howard had lent me his Tennyson, and I had mooned long and often over the 'Idyls of the King.' Here were the three, I thought—Arthur and Launcelot and Guinevere. This, then, I pondered, was the end of it all, of life and strife and striving and love, the weary spirits of these long-gone ones to be invoked by fat old women and mangy sorcerers, the bones of them to be esteemed of collectors and betted on horse races and ace-fulls or to be sold for cash and invested in sugar stocks.

"For me it was illumination. I learned there in the burial cave the great lesson. And to Ahuna, I said: 'The spear headed with the long bone of Keola I shall take for my own. Never shall I sell it. I shall keep it always.'

" 'And for what purpose?' he demanded. And I replied: 'That the contemplation of it may keep my head sober and my feet on earth with the knowledge that few men are fortunate enough to have as much of a remnant of themselves as will compose a spearhead when they are three centuries dead.'

"And Ahuna bowed his head, and praised my wisdom of judgment. But at that moment the long-rotted olona cord broke and the pitiful woman's bones of Laulani shed from my clasp and clattered on the rocky floor. One shin bone, in some way deflected, fell under the dark shadow of a canoe bow, and I made up my mind that it should be mine. So I hastened to help him in the picking up of the bones and the tying, so that he did not notice its absence.

" 'This,' said Ahuna, introducing me to another of my ancestors, 'is your great-grandfather, Mokomoku, the father of Kaaukuu. Behold the size of his bones. He was a giant. I shall carry him, because of the long spear of Keola that will be difficult for you to carry away. And this is Lelemahoa, your grandmother, the mother of your mother that you shall carry. And day grows short, and we must still swim up through the waters to the sun ere darkness hides the sun from the world.'

"But Ahuna, putting out the various calabashes of light by drowning the wicks in the whale oil, did not observe me include the shin bone of Laulani with the bones of my grandmother."

The honk of the automobile, sent up from Olokona to rescue us, broke off the prince's narrative. We said good-by to the ancient and fresh-pensioned wahine, and departed. A half mile on our way, Prince Akuli resumed:

"So Ahuna and I returned to Hiwilani, and to her happiness, lasting to her death the year following, two more of her ancestors abided about her in the jars of her twilight room. Also, she kept her compact and worried my father into sending me to England. I took old Howard along, and he perked up and confuted the doctors so that it was three years before I buried him restored to the bosom of his family. Sometimes I think he was the most brilliant man I have ever known. Not until my return from England did Ahuna die, the last custodian of our alii secrets. And at his deathbed he pledged me again never to reveal the location in that nameless valley and never to go back myself.

"Much else I have forgotten to mention did I see there in the cave that one time. There were the bones of Kumi, the near demigod, son of Tui Manua of Samoa, who in the long before married into my line and heaven-boosted my genealogy. And the bones of my great-grandmother who had slept in the four-poster presented her by Lord Byron. And Ahuna hinted tradition that there was reason for that presentation, as well as for the historically known lingering of the *Blonde* in Olokona for so long. And I held her poor bones in my hands—bones once fleshed with sensate beauty, informed with sparkle and spirit, instinct with love and love warmness of arms around and eyes and lips together, that had begat me in the end of the generations unborn. It was a good experience. I am modern, 'tis true. I believe in no mystery stuff of old time nor the Kahunas. And yet I saw in that cave things which I dare not name to you, and which I, since old Ahuna died, alone of the living know. I have no children. With me my long line ceases. This is the twentieth century, and we stink of gasoline. Nevertheless these other and nameless things shall die with me. I shall never revisit the burial place. Nor in all time to come will any man gaze upon it through living eyes unless the quakes of earth rend the mountains asunder and spew forth the secrets contained in the hearts of the mountains."

Prince Akuli ceased from speech. With welcome relief of his face, he removed the lei hala from his neck, and, with a sniff and a sigh, tossed it into concealment in the thick lantana by the side of the road.

"But the shin bone of Laulani?" I queried softly.

He remained silent while a mile of pasture land fled by us and yielded to cane land.

"I have it now," he at last said. "And beside it is Keola, slain ere his time and made into a spearhead for love of the woman whose shin bone abides near to him. To them, those poor pathetic bones, I owe more than to aught else. I became possessed of them in the period of my culminating adolescence. I know they changed the entire course of my life and trend of my mind. They gave to me a modesty and a humility in the world from which my father's fortune has ever failed to seduce me.

"And often, when woman was nigh to winning to the empery of my mind over me, I sought Laulani's shin bone. And often, when lusty manhood stung me into feeling overproud and lusty, I consulted the spearhead remnant of Keaho, one time swift runner, and mighty wrestler and lover, and thief of the wife of a king. The contemplation of them has ever been of profound aid to me, and you might well say that I have founded my religion or practice of living upon them."

WHEN ALICE
TOLD HER SOUL

This, of Alice Akana, is an affair of Hawaii, not of this day, but of days recent enough, when Abel Ah Yo preached his famous revival in Honolulu and persuaded Alice Akana to tell her soul. But what Alice told concerned itself with the earlier history of the then surviving generation.

For Alice Akana was fifty years old, had begun life early, and, early and late, lived it spaciously. What she knew went back into the roots and foundations of families, businesses, and plantations. She was the one living repository of accurate information that lawyers sought out, whether the information they required related to land boundaries and land gifts, or to marriages, births, bequests, or scandals. Rarely, because of the tight tongue she kept behind her teeth, did she give them what they asked; and, when she did, it was when equity alone was served and no one could be hurt.

For Alice had lived, from early in her girlhood, a life of flowers and song and wine and dance; and, in her later years, had herself been mistress of these revels by office of mistress of the hula house. In such atmosphere, where mandates of God and man and caution are inhibited, and where woozled tongues will wag, she acquired her historical knowledge of things never otherwise whispered and rarely guessed. Her tight tongue had served her well, so that, while the old-timers knew she must know, none ever heard her gossip of the times of Kalakaua's boat-house, nor the high times of officers of visiting warships, nor of the diplomats and ministers and counsels of the countries of the world.

So, at fifty, loaded with historical dynamite sufficient, if it were ever exploded, to shake the social and commercial life of the Islands, still tight of tongue, Alice Akana was mistress of the hula house, manageress of the dancing girls who hula'd for royalty, for luaus, house parties, poi suppers, and curious tourists. Moreover, at fifty, she was not merely buxom, but short and fat in the Polynesian peasant way, with a constitution and lack of organic weakness that promised incalculable years. But it was, at fifty, that she strayed, quite by chance of time and curiosity, into Abel Ah Yo's revival meeting.

Now Abel Ah Yo, in his theology and word wizardry, was as much mixed a personage as Billy Sunday. In his genealogy he was much more mixed, for he was compounded of one fourth Portuguese, one fourth Scotch, one fourth Hawaiian, and one fourth Chinese. The Pentecostal fire he flamed forth was hotter and more variegated than could any one of the four races of him alone have flamed forth. For in him were gathered together the canniness and the cunning, the wit and the wisdom, the subtlety and the rawness, the passion and the philosophy, the agonizing spirit groping and the legs up to the knees in the dung of reality, of the four radically different breeds that contributed to the sum of him. His, also, was the clever self-deceivement of the entire clever compound.

When it came to word wizardry, he had Billy Sunday, master of slang and argot of one language, skinned by miles. For in Abel Ah Yo were the live verbs and nouns and adjectives and metaphors of four living languages. Intermixed and living promiscuously and vitally together, he possessed in these languages a reservoir of expression in which a myriad Billy Sundays could drown. Of no race, a mongrel par excellence, a heterogeneous scrabble, the genius of the admixture was superlatively Abel Ah Yo's. Like a chameleon, he titubated and scintillated grandly between the diverse parts of him, stunning by frontal attack and surprising and confounding by flanking sweeps the mental homogeneity of the more simply constituted souls who came in to his revival to sit under him and flame to his flaming.

Abel Ah Yo believed in himself and his mixedness, as he believed in the mixedness of his weird concept that God looked as much like him as like any man, being no mere tribal god but a world god that must look equally like all races of all the world even if it led to piebaldness. And the concept worked. Chinese, Korean, Japanese, Hawaiian, Porto Rican, Russian, English, French—members of all races—knelt without friction, side by side, to his revision of deity.

Himself, in his tender youth an apostate to the Church of England, Abel Ah Yo had for years suffered the lively sense of being a Judas sinner. Essentially religious, he had forsworn the Lord. Like Judas therefore he was. Judas was damned. Wherefore he, Abel Ah Yo, was damned; and he did not want to be damned. So, quite after the manner of humans, he squirmed and twisted to escape damnation. The day came when he solved his escape. The doctrine that Judas was damned, he concluded, was a misinterpretation of God, who, above all things, stood for justice. Judas had been God's servant, specially selected to perform a particularly nasty job. Therefore Judas, ever faithful, a betrayer only by divine command, was a saint. Ergo, he, Abel Ah Yo, was a saint by very virtue of his apostasy to a particular sect, and he could have access with clear grace any time to God.

This theory became one of the major tenets of his preaching, and was especially efficacious in cleansing the consciences of the backsliders from all other faiths who else, in the secrecy of their subconscious selves, were being crushed by the weight of the Judas sin. To Abel Ah Yo, God's plan was as clear as if he, Abel Ah Yo, had planned it himself. All would be saved in the end, although some took longer than others and would win only to back seats. Man's place in the ever-fluxing chaos of the world was definite and preordained—if, by no other token, by denial that there was any ever-fluxing chaos. This was a mere bugbear of mankind's addled fancy; and, by stinging audacities of thought and speech, vivid slang that bit home by sheerest intimacy into his listeners' mental processes, he drove the bugbear from their brains, showed them the loving clarity of God's design, and, thereby, induced in them spiritual serenity and calm.

What chance had Alice Akana, herself pure and homogeneous Hawaiian, against his subtle, democratic-tinged, four-race-engendered, slang-munitioned attack? He knew, by contact, almost as much as she about the waywardness of living and sinning—having been singing boy on the passenger ships between Hawaii and California, and, after that, bar boy, afloat and ashore, from San Francisco's Barbary Coast to Heinie's Tavern at Waikiki. In point of fact, he had left his job of Number One Bar Boy at Honolulu's University Club to embark on his great preachment revival.

So, when Alice Akana strayed in to scoff, she remained to pray to Abel Ah Yo's god, who struck her hard-headed mind as the most sensible god of which she had ever heard. She gave money into Abel Ah Yo's collection plate, closed up the hula house and dismissed the hula dancers to more devious ways of earning a livelihood, shed her gala colors and raiments and flower garlands, and bought a bible.

It was a time of religious excitement in the purlieus of Honolulu. The thing was a democratic movement of the people toward God. Place and caste were invited, but never came. The stupid lowly, and the humble lowly, only, went down on its knees at the penitent form, admitted its pathological weight and hurt of sin, eliminated and purged all its bafflements, and walked forth again upright under the sun, childlike and pure, upborne by Abel Ah Yo's god's arm around it. In short, Abel Ah Yo's revival was a clearing house for sin and sickness of spirit, wherein sinners were relieved of their burdens and made light and bright and spiritually healthy again.

But Alice was not happy. She had not been cleared. She bought and dispersed bibles, contributed more money to the plate, contralto'd gloriously in all the hymns, but would not tell her soul. In vain Abel Ah Yo wrestled with her. She would not go down on her knees at the penitent form and voice the things of tarnish within her—the ill things of good friends of the old days. "You cannot serve two masters," Abel Ah Yo told her. "Hell is full of those who have tried. Single of heart and pure of heart must you make your peace with God. Not until you tell your soul to God right out in meeting will you be ready for redemption. In the meantime you will suffer the canker of the sin you carry about within you."

Scientifically, though he did not know it and though he continually jeered at science, Abel Ah Yo was right. Not could she be again as a child and become radiantly clad in God's grace, until she had eliminated from her soul, by telling all the sophistications that had been hers, including those she shared with others. In the Protestant way, she must bare her soul in public, as in the Catholic way it was done in the privacy of the confessional. The result of such baring would be unity, tranquillity, happiness, cleansing, redemption, and immortal life.

"Choose!" thundered Abel Ah Yo. "Loyalty to God or loyalty to man." And Alice could not choose. Too long had she kept her tongue locked with the honor of man. "I will tell all my soul about myself," she contended. "God knows I am tired of my soul and should like to have it clean and shining once again as when I was a little girl at Kaneohe." "But all the corruption of your soul has been with other souls," was Abel Ah Yo's invariable reply; "when you have a burden, lay it down. You cannot bear a burden and be quit of it at the same time."

"I will pray to God each day, and many times each day," she urged. "I will approach God with humility, with sighs and with tears. I will contribute often to the plate, and I will buy bibles, bibles, bibles without end."

"And God will not smile upon you," God's mouthpiece retorted. "And you will remain weary and heavy laden. For you will not have told all your sin, and not until you have told all will you be rid of any."

"This rebirth is difficult," Alice sighed.

"Rebirth is even more difficult than birth," Abel Ah Yo did anything but comfort her. " 'Not until you become as a little child. . . .' "

"If ever I tell my soul, it will be a big telling," she confided.

"The bigger the reason to tell it then."

And so the situation remained at deadlock, Abel Ah Yo demanding absolute allegiance to God, and Alice Akana flirting on the fringes of paradise.

"You bet it will be a big telling, if Alice ever begins," the beach-combing and disreputable *kamaainas* (old-timers) gleefully told one another over their Palm Tree gin.

In the clubs the possibility of her telling was of more moment. The younger generation of men announced that they had applied for front seats at the telling, while many of the older generation of men joked hollowly about the conversion of Alice. Further, Alice found herself abruptly popular with friends who had forgotten her existence for twenty years.

One afternoon, as Alice, bible in hand, was taking the electric street car at Hotel and Fort, Cyrus Hodge, sugar factor and magnate, ordered his chauffeur to stop beside her. Willy-nilly, in excess of friendliness, he had her into his limousine beside him and went three quarters of an hour out of his way and time personally to conduct her to her destination.

"Good for sore eyes to see you," he burbled. "How the years fly! You're looking fine. The secret of youth is yours."

Alice smiled and complimented in return in the royal Polynesian way of friendliness.

"My, my," Cyrus Hodge reminisced. "I was such a boy in those days!"

"*Some* boy," she laughed acquiescence.

"But knowing no more than the foolishness of a boy in those long-ago days."

"Remember the night your hack-driver got drunk and left you—"

"S-s-sh!" he cautioned. "That Jap driver is a high-school graduate and knows more English than either of us. Also, I think he is a spy for his government. So why should we tell him anything? Besides, I was so very young. You remember ..."

"Your cheeks were like the peaches we used to grow before the Mediterranean fruit fly got into them," Alice agreed. "I don't think you shaved more than once a week then. You were a pretty boy. Don't you remember the hula we composed in your honor, the—"

"S-s-sh!" he hushed her. "All that's buried and forgotten. May it remain forgotten."

And she was aware that in his eyes was no longer any of the ingenuousness of youth she remembered. Instead, his eyes were keen and speculative, searching into her for some assurance that she would not resurrect his particular portion of that buried past.

"Religion is a good thing for us as we get along into middle age," another old friend told her. He was building a magnificent house on Pacific Heights, had but recently married a second time, and was even then on his way to the steamer to welcome home his two daughters just graduated from Vassar. "We need religion in our old age, Alice. It softens, makes us more tolerant and forgiving of the weaknesses of others; especially the weaknesses of youth of—of others, when they played high and low and didn't know what they were doing."

He waited anxiously.

"Yes," she said. "We are all born to sin, and it is hard to grow out of sin. But I grow. I grow."

"Don't forget, Alice, in those other days I always played square. You and I never had a falling out."

"Not even the night you gave that luau when you were twenty-one and insisted on breaking the glassware after every toast. But of course you paid for it."

"Handsomely," he asserted almost pleadingly.

"Handsomely," she agreed. "I replaced more than double the quantity with what you paid me, so that at the next luau I catered one hundred and twenty plates without having to rent or borrow a dish or glass. Lord Mainweather gave that luau—you remember him."

"I was pigsticking with him at Mana," the other nodded. "We were at a two weeks' house party there. But say, Alice, as you know, I think this religion stuff is all right and better than all right. But don't let it carry you off your feet. And don't get to telling your soul on me. What would my daughters think of that broken glassware!"

"I always did have an *aloha* (warm regard) for you, Alice," a member of the Senate, fat and bald-headed, assured her.

And another, a lawyer and a grandfather: "We were always friends, Alice. And remember, any legal advice or handling of business you may require I'll do for you gladly, and without fees, for the sake of our old-time friendship."

Came a banker to her late Christmas Eve, with formidable, legal-looking envelopes in his hand which he presented to her.

"Quite by chance," he explained, "when my people were looking up land records in Iapio Valley, I found a mortgage of two thousand on your holdings there—that rice land leased to Ah Chin. And my mind drifted back to the past when we were all young together, and wild, a bit wild, to be sure. And my heart warmed with the memory of you, and, so, just as an aloha, here's the whole thing cleared off for you."

Nor was Alice forgotten by her own people. Her house became a

Mecca for native men and women, usually performing pilgrimage privily after darkness fell, with presents always in their hands—squid fresh from the reef, opihis and limu, baskets of alligator pears, roasting corn of the earliest from windward Oahu, mangos and star apples, taro pink and royal of the finest selection, sucking pigs, banana poi, breadfruit, and crabs caught the very day from Pearl Harbor. Mary Mendaña, wife of the Portuguese consul, remembered her with a five-dollar box of candy and a mandarin coat that would have fetched three quarters of a hundred dollars at a fire sale. And Elvira Miyahara Makaena Yin Gap, the wife of Yin Gap, the wealthy Chinese importer, brought personally to Alice two entire bolts of piña cloth from the Philippines and a dozen pairs of silk stockings.

The time passed, and Abel Ah Yo struggled with Alice for a properly penitent heart, and Alice struggled with herself for her soul, while half of Honolulu wickedly or apprehensively hung on the outcome. Carnival Week was over, polo and the races had come and gone, and the celebration of Fourth of July was ripening, ere Abel Ah Yo beat down by brutal psychology the citadel of her reluctance. It was then that he gave his famous exhortation which might be summed up as Abel Ah Yo's definition of eternity. Of course, like Billy Sunday on certain occasions, Abel Ah Yo had cribbed the definition. But no one in the Islands knew it, and his rating as a revivalist uprose a hundred per cent.

So successful was his preaching that night, that he reconverted many of his converts, who fell and moaned about the penitent form and crowded for room amongst scores of new converts burned by the pentecostal fire, including half a company of negro soldiers from the garrisoned Twenty-fifth Infantry, a dozen troopers from the Fourth Cavalry on its way to the Philippines, as many drunken man-of-war's men, divers ladies from Iwilei, and half the riffraff of the beach.

Abel Ah Yo, subtly sympathetic himself by virtue of his racial admixture, knowing human nature like a book and Alice Akana even more so, knew just what he was doing when he arose that memorable night and exposited God, hell, and eternity in terms of Alice Akana's comprehension. For, quite by chance, he had discovered her cardinal weakness. First of all, like all Polynesians, an ardent lover of nature, he found that earthquake and volcanic eruption were the things of which Alice lived in terror. She had been, in the past, on the Big Island, through cataclysms that had shaken grass houses down upon her while she slept, and she had beheld Madame Pele fling red-fluxing lava down the long slopes of Mauna Loa, destroying fish ponds on the sea brim and licking up droves of beef cattle, villages, and humans on her fiery way.

The night before, a slight earthquake had shaken Honolulu and given

Alice Akana insomnia. And the morning papers had stated that Mauna Kea had broken into eruption, while the lava was rising rapidly in the great pit of Kilauea. So, at the meeting, her mind vexed between the terrors of this world and the delights of the eternal world to come, Alice sat down in a front seat in a very definite state of the "jumps."

And Abel Ah Yo arose and put his finger on the sorest part of her soul. Sketching the nature of God in the stereotyped way, but making the stereotyped alive again with his gift of tongues in pidgin English and pidgin Hawaiian, Abel Ah Yo described the day when the Lord, even His infinite patience at an end, would tell Peter to close his day book and ledgers, command Gabriel to summon all souls to judgment, and cry out with a voice of thunder: "Welakahao!"

This anthropomorphic deity of Abel Ah Yo thundering the modern Hawaiian-English slang of *welakahao* at the end of the world is a fair sample of the revivalists' speech tools of discourse. *Welakahao* means literally, "hot iron." It was coined in the Honolulu Iron Works by the hundreds of Hawaiian men there employed, who meant by it "to hustle," "to get a move on," the iron being hot meaning that the time had come to strike.

"And the Lord cried 'Welakahao,' and the Day of Judgment began and was over *wikiwiki* (quickly), just like that; for Peter was a better bookkeeper than any on the Waterhouse Trust Company, Limited, and, further, Peter's books were true."

Swiftly Abel Ah Yo divided the sheep from the goats and hastened the latter down into hell.

"And now," he demanded, perforce his language on these pages being properly Englished, "what is hell like? Oh, my friends, let me describe to you, in a little way, what I have beheld with my own eyes on earth of the possibilities of hell. I was a young man, a boy, and I was at Hilo. Morning began with earthquake. Throughout the day the mighty land continued to shake and tremble, till strong men became seasick, and women clung to the trees to escape falling, and cattle were thrown down off their feet. Myself I beheld a young calf so thrown. A night of terror indescribable followed. The land was in motion like a canoe in a Kona gale. There was an infant crushed to death by its fond mother stepping upon it whilst fleeing her falling house.

"The heavens were on fire above us. We read our bibles by the light of the heavens, and the print was fine even for young eyes. Those missionary bibles were always too small of print. Forty miles away from us, the heart of hell burst from the lofty mountains and gushed red blood of fire-melted rock toward the sea. The heavens in vast conflagration and the earth hulaing beneath our feet, was a scene too awful and too majestic to be enjoyed. We could think only of the thin bubble skin of earth between us and the everlasting lake of fire and brimstone, and of God to whom we prayed to save us. There were earnest and devout souls who there and then promised their pastors to give not their shaved tithes, but five tenths of their all to the church if only the Lord would let them live to contribute.

"Oh, my friends, God saved us. But first he showed us a foretaste of that hell that will yawn for us on the last day when he cries 'Welaka-hao!' in a voice of thunder. When the iron is hot! Think of it! When the iron is hot for sinners!

"By the third day, things being much quieter, my friend the preacher and I, being calm in the hand of God, journeyed up Mauna Loa and gazed into the awful pit of Kilauea. We gazed down into the fathomless abyss to the lake of fire far below, roaring and dashing its fiery spray into billows and fountaining hundreds of feet into the air like Fourth of July fireworks you have all seen, and all the while we were suffocating and made dizzy by the immense volumes of smoke and brimstone ascending.

"And I say unto you, no pious person could gaze down upon that scene without recognizing fully the bible picture of the Pit of Hell. Believe me, the writers of the New Testament had nothing on us. As for me, my eyes were fixed upon the exhibition before me, and I stood mute and trembling under a sense never before so fully realized of the power, the majesty, and terror of Almighty God—the resources of his wrath, and the untold horrors of the finally impenitent who do not tell their souls and make their peace with the Creator.*

"But oh, my friends, think you our guides, our native attendants, deep-sunk in heathenism, were affected by such a scene? No. The devil's hand was upon them. Utterly regardless and unimpressed, they were only careful about their supper, chatted about their raw fish, and stretched themselves upon their mats to sleep. Children of the devil they were, insensible to the beauties, the sublimities, and the awful terror of God's works. But you are not heathen I now address. What is a heathen? He is one who betrays a stupid insensibility to every elevated idea and to every elevated emotion. If you wish to awaken his attention, do not bid him to look down into the Pit of Hell. But present him with a calabash of poi, a raw fish, or invite him to some low, groveling, and sensuous sport. Oh, my friends, how lost are they to all that elevates the immortal soul! But the preacher and I, sad and sick of heart for

* See Dibble's "A History of the Sandwich Islands."

them, gazed down into hell. Oh, my friends, it *was* hell, the hell of the Scriptures, the hell of eternal torment for the undeserving . . ."

Alice Akana was in an ecstasy or hysteria of terror. She was mumbling incoherently: "O Lord, I will give nine-tenths of my all. I will give all. I will give even the two bolts of piña cloth, the mandarin coat, and the entire dozen silk stockings . . ."

By the time she could lend ear again, Abel Ah Yo was launching out on his famous definition of eternity.

"Eternity is a long time, my friends. God lives, and, therefore, God lives inside eternity. And God is very old. The fires of hell are as old and as everlasting as God. How else could there be everlasting torment for those sinners cast down by God into the Pit on the Last Day to burn forever and forever through all eternity? Oh, my friends, your minds are small—too small to grasp eternity. Yet is it given to me, by God's grace, to convey to you an understanding of a tiny bit of eternity.

"The grains of sand on the beach of Waikiki are as many as the stars, and more. No man may count them. Did he have a million lives in which to count them, he would have to ask for more time. Now let us consider a little, dinky, old minah bird with one broken wing that cannot fly. At Waikiki the minah bird that cannot fly takes one grain of sand in its beak and hops, hops, all day long and for many days, all the way to Pearl Harbor and drops that one grain of sand into the harbor. Then it hops, hops, all day and for many days, all the way back to Waikiki for another grain of sand. And again it hops, hops all the way back to Pearl Harbor. And it continues to do this through the years and centuries and the thousands and thousands of centuries, until, at last, there remains not one grain of sand at Waikiki, and Pearl Harbor is filled up with land and growing cocoanuts and pineapples. And then, oh my friends, even then, *it would not yet be sunrise in hell!*"

Here, at the smashing impact of so abrupt a climax, unable to withstand the sheer simplicity and objectivity of such artful measurement of a trifle of eternity, Alice Akana's mind broke down and blew up. She uprose, reeled blindly, and stumbled to her knees at the penitent form. Abel Ah Yo had not finished his preaching, but it was his gift to know crowd psychology, and to feel the heat of the pentecostal conflagration that scorched his audience. He called for a rousing revival hymn from his singers, and stepped down to wade among the hallelujah-shouting negro soldiers to Alice Akana. And, ere the excitement began to ebb, nine tenths of his congregation and all his converts were down on knees and praying and shouting aloud an immensity of contriteness and sin.

*   *   *

Word came, via telephone, almost simultaneously to the Pacific and University clubs, that at last Alice was telling her soul in meeting; and, by private machine and taxicab, for the first time Abel Ah Yo's revival was invaded by those of caste and place. The first comers beheld the curious sight of Hawaiian, Chinese, and all variegated racial mixtures of the smelting pot of Hawaii, men and women, fading out and slinking away through the exits of Abel Ah Yo's tabernacle. But those who were sneaking out were mostly men, while those who remained were avid-faced as they hung on Alice's utterance.

Never was a more fearful and damning community narrative enunci-ated in the entire Pacific, north and south, than that enunciated by Alice Akana, the penitent Phryne of Honolulu.

"Huh!" the first comers heard her saying, having already disposed of most of the venial sins of the lesser ones of her memory. "You think this man, Stephen Makekau, is the son of Moses Makekau and Minnie Ah Ling and has a legal right to the two hundred and eight dollars he draws down each month from Parke Richards Limited for the lease of the fish pond to Bill Kong at Amana. Not so. Stephen Makekau is not the son of Moses. He is the son of Aaron Kama and Tillie Naone. He was given as a present, as a feeding child, to Moses and Minnie by Aaron and Tillie. I know. Moses and Minnie and Aaron and Tillie are dead. Yet I know and can prove it. Old Mrs. Poepoe is still alive. I was present when Stephen was born, and in the nighttime, when he was two months old, I myself carried him as a present to Moses and Minnie, and old Mrs. Poepoe carried the lantern. This secret has been one of my sins. It has kept me from God. Now I am free of it. Young Archie Makekau, who collects bills for the Gas Company and plays baseball in the afternoons, and drinks too much gin, should get that two hundred and eight dollars the first of each month from Parke Richards Limited. He will blow it in on gin and a Ford automobile. Stephen is a good man. Archie is no good. Also he is a liar, and he has served two sen-tences on the reef, and was in reform school before that. Yet God de-mands the truth, and Archie will get the money and make a bad use of it."

And in such fashion Alice rambled on through the experiences of her long and full-packed life. And women forgot they were in the taber-nacle, and men, too, and faces darkened with passion as they learned for the first time the long-buried secrets of their other halves.

"The lawyers' offices will be crowded to-morrow morning," Mac-

Ilwaine, chief of detectives, paused long enough from storing away useful information to lean and mutter in Colonel Stilton's ear.

Colonel Stilton grinned affirmation, although the chief of detectives could not fail to note the ghastliness of the grin.

"There is a banker in Honolulu. You all know his name. He is 'way up, swell society because of his wife. He owns much stock in General Plantations and Interisland."

MacIlwaine recognized the growing portrait and forbore to chuckle.

"His name is Colonel Stilton. Last Christmas Eve he came to my house with big aloha and gave me mortgages on my land in Iapio Valley, all canceled, for two thousand dollars' worth. Now why did he have such big cash aloha for me? I will tell you . . ."

And tell she did, throwing the searchlight on ancient business transactions and political deals which from their inception had lurked in the dark.

"This," Alice concluded the episode, "has long been a sin upon my conscience and kept my heart from God.

"And Harold Miles was that time President of the Senate, and next week he bought three town lots at Pearl Harbor, and painted his Honolulu house, and paid up his back dues in his clubs. Also the Ramsay home at Honokiki was left by will to the people if the government would keep it up. But if the government, after two years, did not begin to keep it up, then would it go to the Ramsay heirs, who old Ramsay hated like poison. Well, it went to the heirs all right. Their lawyer was Charley Middleton, and he had me help fix it with the government men. And their names were:" Six names, from both branches of the legislature, Alice recited, and added: "Maybe they all painted their houses after that. For the first time have I spoken. My heart is mighty lighter and softer. It has been coated with an armor of house paint against the Lord. And there is Harry Werther. He was in the Senate that time. Everybody said bad things about him and he was never reëlected. Yet his house was not painted. He was honest. To this day his house is not painted, as everybody knows.

"There is Jim Lokendamper. He has a bad heart. I heard him, only last week, right here before you all, tell his soul. He did not tell all his soul, and he lied to God. I am not lying to God. It is a big telling, but I am telling everything. Now Azalea Akau, sitting right over there, is his wife. But Lizzie Lokendamper is his married wife. A long time ago he had the great aloha for Azalea. You think her uncle who went to California and died left her by will that two thousand five hundred dollars she got. Her uncle did not. I know. Her uncle died broke in

California, and Jim Lokendamper sent eighty dollars to California to bury him. Jim Lokendamper had a piece of land in Kohala he got from his mother's aunt. Lizzie, his married wife, did not know this. So he sold it to the Kohala Ditch Company and gave the twenty-five hundred to Azalea Akau—"

Here, Lizzie, the married wife, upstood like a fury long thwarted, and, in lieu of her husband, already fled, flung herself tooth and nail on Azalea.

"Wait, Lizzie Lokendamper!" Alice cried out. "I have much weight of you on my heart, and some house paint, too . . ."

And when she had finished her disclosure of how Lizzie had painted her house, Azalea was up and raging.

"Wait, Azalea Akau. I shall now lighten my heart about you. And it is not house paint. Jim always paid that. It is your new bathtub and modern plumbing that is heavy on me . . ."

Worse, much worse, about many and sundry, did Alice Akana have to say, cutting high in business, financial and social life, as well as low. None was too high nor too low to escape; and not until two in the morning, before an entranced audience that packed the tabernacle to the doors, did she complete her recital of the personal and detailed iniquities she knew of the community in which she had lived intimately all her days. Just as she was finishing, she remembered more.

"Huh!" she sniffed. "I gave last week one lot worth eight hundred dollars cash market price to Abel Ah Yo to pay running expenses and add up in Peter's account books in heaven. Where did I get that lot? You all think Mr. Fleming Jason is a good man. He is more crooked than the entrance was to Pearl Lochs before the United States Government straightened the channel. He has liver disease now; but his sickness is a judgment of God, and he will die crooked. Mr. Fleming Jason gave me that lot twenty-two years ago when its cash market price was thirty-five dollars. Because his aloha for me was big? No. He never had aloha inside of him except for dollars.

"You listen. Mr. Fleming Jason put a great sin upon me. When Frank Lomiloli was at my house, full of gin, for which gin Mr. Fleming Jason paid me in advance five times over, I got Frank Lomiloli to sign his name to the sale paper of his town land for one hundred dollars. It was worth six hundred then. It is worth twenty thousand now. Maybe you want to know where that town land is. I will tell you and remove it off my heart. It is on King Street, where is now the Come Again Saloon, the Japanese Taxicab Company Garage, the Smith & Wilson plumbing shop, and the Ambrosia Ice Cream Parlors, with the two more stories big Addison Lodging House overhead. And it is all wood, and always has been well painted. Yesterday they started painting it again. But that paint will not stand between me and God. There are no more paint pots between me and my path to heaven."

The morning and evening papers of the day following held an unholy hush on the greatest news story of years; but Honolulu was half a-giggle and half aghast at the whispered reports, not always basely exaggerated, that circulated wherever two Honoluluans chanced to meet.

"Our mistake," said Colonel Chilton, at the club, "was that we did not, at the very first, appoint a committee of safety to keep track of Alice's soul."

Bob Cristy, one of the younger islanders, burst into laughter so pointed and so loud that the meaning of it was demanded.

"Oh, nothing much," was his reply. "But I heard, on my way here, that old John Ward had just been run in for drunken and disorderly conduct and for resisting an officer. Now Abel Ah Yo finetooth combs the police court. He loves nothing better than soul-snatching a chronic drunkard."

Colonel Chilton looked at Lask Finneston, and both looked at Gary Wilkinson. He returned to them a similar look.

"The old beach comber!" Lask Finneston cried. "The drunken old reprobate! I'd forgotten he was alive. Wonderful constitution. Never drew a sober breath except when he was shipwrecked, and, when I remember him, into every deviltry afloat. He must be going on eighty."

"He isn't far away from it," Bob Cristy nodded. "Still beach-combs, drinks when he gets the price, and keeps all his senses, though he's not spry and has to use glasses when he reads. And his memory is perfect. Now if Abel Ah Yo catches him ...."

Gary Wilkinson cleared his throat preliminary to speech.

"Now there's a grand old man," he said. "A left-over from a forgotten age. Few of his type remain. A pioneer. A true kamaaina. Helpless and in the hands of the police in his old age! We should do something for him in recognition of his yeoman work in Hawaii. His old home, I happen to know, is Sag Harbor. He hasn't seen it for over half a century. Now why shouldn't he be surprised to-morrow morning by having his fine paid and by being presented with return tickets to Sag Harbor, and, say, expenses for a year's trip? I move a committee. I appoint Colonel Chilton, Lask Finneston, and, and myself. . . . As for chairman, who more appropriate than Lask Finneston, who knew the old gentleman so well in the early days? Since there is no objection, I hereby appoint Lask Finneston Chairman of the Committee for the Purpose of Raising and Donating money to Pay the Police-court Fine and the Expenses of a Year's Travel for that Noble Pioneer, John Ward, in Recognition of a Lifetime of Devotion of Energy to the Upbuilding of Hawaii."

There was no dissent.

"The Committee will now go into secret session," said Lask Finneston, arising and indicating the way to the library.

LIKE ARGUS OF THE
ANCIENT TIMES

It was the summer of 1897, and there was trouble in the Tarwater family. Grandfather Tarwater, after remaining properly subdued and crushed for a quiet decade, had broken out again. This time it was the Klondike fever. His first and one unvarying symptom of such attacks was song. One Chant only he raised, though he remembered no more than the first stanza and but three lines of that. And the family knew his feet were itching and his brain was tingling with the old madness, when he lifted his hoarse-cracked voice, now falsetto-cracked, in:

"Like Argus of the ancient times,
We leave this modern Greece,
Tum-tum, tum-tum, tum, tum, tum-tum,
To shear the Golden Fleece."

Ten years earlier he had lifted the chant, sung to the air of the "Doxology," when afflicted with the fever to go gold-mining in Patagonia. The multitudinous family had sat upon him, but had had a hard time doing it. When all else had failed to shake his resolution, they had applied lawyers to him, with the threat of getting out guardianship papers and of confining him in the state asylum for the insane—which was reasonable for a man who had, a quarter of a century before, speculated away all but ten meager acres of a California principality, and who had displayed no better business acumen ever since.

The application of lawyers to John Tarwater was like the application of a mustard plaster. For, in his judgment, they were the gentry, more than any other, who had skinned him out of the broad Tarwater acres. So, at the time of his Patagonian fever, the very thought of so drastic a remedy was sufficient to cure him. He quickly demonstrated he was not crazy by shaking the fever from him and agreeing not to go to Patagonia.

Next, he demonstrated how crazy he really was, by deeding over to his family, unsolicited, the ten acres on Tarwater Flat, the house, barn, outbuildings, and water-rights. Also did he turn over the eight hundred dollars in bank that was the long-saved salvage of his wrecked fortune. But for this the family found no cause for committal to the asylum, since such committal would necessarily invalidate what he had done.

"Grandfather is sure peeved," said Mary, his oldest daughter, herself a grandmother, when her father quit smoking.

All he had retained for himself was a span of old horses, a mountain buckboard, and his one room in the crowded house. Further, having affirmed that he would be beholden to none of them, he got the contract to carry the United States mail, twice a week, from Kelterville up over Tarwater Mountain to Old Almaden—which was a sporadically worked quicksilver mine in the upland cattle country. With his old horses it took all his time to make the two weekly round trips. And for ten years, rain or shine, he had never missed a trip. Nor had he failed once to pay his week's board into Mary's hand. This board he had insisted on, in the convalescence from his Patagonian fever, and he had paid it strictly though he had given up tobacco in order to be able to do it.

"Huh!" he confided to the ruined water wheel of the old Tarwater Mill, which he had built from the standing timber and which had ground wheat for the first settlers. "Huh! They'll never put me in the poor farm so long as I support myself. And without a penny to my name it ain't likely any lawyer fellows'll come snoopin' around after me."

And yet, precisely because of these highly rational acts, it was held that John Tarwater was mildly crazy!

The first time he had lifted the chant of "Like Argus of the Ancient Times," had been in 1849, when, twenty-two years of age, violently attacked by the California fever, he had sold two hundred and forty Michigan acres, forty of it cleared, for the price of four yoke of oxen and a wagon, and had started across the Plains.

"And we turned off at Fort Hall, where the Oregon emigration went north'ard, and swung south for Californy," was his way of concluding the narrative of that arduous journey. "And Bill Ping and me used to rope grizzlies out of the underbrush of Cache Slough in the Sacramento Valley."

Years of freighting and mining had followed, and, with a stake gleaned from the Merced placers, he satisfied the land-hunger of his race and time by settling in Sonoma County.

During the ten years of carrying the mail across Tarwater Township, up Tarwater Valley, and over Tarwater Mountain, most all of which land had once been his, he had spent his time dreaming of winning back that land before he died. And now, his huge gaunt form more erect than it had been for years, with a glinting of blue fires in his small and close-set eyes, he was lifting his ancient chant again.

"There he goes now—listen to him," said William Tarwater.

"Nobody at home," laughed Harris Topping, day laborer, husband of Annie Tarwater, and father of her nine children.

The kitchen door opened to admit the old man, returning from feeding his horses. The song had ceased from his lips; but Mary was irritable from a burnt hand and a grandchild whose stomach refused to digest properly diluted cow's milk.

"Now there ain't no use you carryin' on that way, father," she tackled him. "The time's past for you to cut and run for a place like the Klondike, and singing won't buy you nothing."

"Just the same," he answered quietly. "I bet I could go to that Klondike place and pick up enough gold to buy back the Tarwater lands."

"Old fool!" Annie contributed.

"You couldn't buy them back for less 'n three hundred thousand and then some," was William's effort at squelching him.

"Then I could pick up three hundred thousand, and then some, if I was only there," the old man retorted placidly.

"Thank God, you can't walk there, or you'd be startin', I know," Mary cried. "Ocean travel costs money."

"I used to have money," her father said humbly.

"Well, you ain't got any now—so forget it," William advised. "Them times is past, like roping bear with Bill Ping. There ain't no more bear."

"Just the same—"

But Mary cut him off. Seizing the day's paper from the kitchen table, she flourished it savagely under her aged progenitor's nose.

"What do those Klondikers say? There it is in cold print. Only the young and robust can stand the Klondike. It's worse than the north pole. And they've left their dead a-plenty there themselves. Look at their pictures. You're forty years older'n the oldest of them."

John Tarwater did look, but his eyes strayed to other photographs on the highly sensational front page.

"And look at the photys of them nuggets they brought down," he said. "I know gold. Didn't I gopher twenty thousand outa the Merced? And wouldn't it a-ben a hundred thousand if that cloud-burst hadn't busted my wing-dam? Now if I was only in the Klondike—"

"Crazy as a loon," William sneered in open aside to the rest.

"A nice way to talk to your father," Old Man Tarwater censured mildly. "My father'd have walloped the tar out of me with a single-tree if I'd spoke to him that way."

"But you *are* crazy, father—" William began.

"Reckon you're right, son. And that's where my father wasn't crazy. He'd a-done it."

"The old man's been reading some of them magazine articles about men who succeeded after forty," Annie gibed.

"And why not, daughter?" he asked. "And why can't a man succeed after he's seventy? I was only seventy this year. And mebbe I could succeed if only I could get to the Klondike—"

"Which you ain't going to get to," Mary shut him off.

"Oh, well, then," he sighed, "seein's I ain't, I might just as well go to bed."

He stood up, tall, gaunt, great-boned and gnarled, a splendid ruin of a man. His ragged hair and whiskers were not gray but snowy white, as were the tufts of hair that stood out on the backs of his huge bony fingers. He moved toward the door, opened it, sighed, and paused with a backward look.

"Just the same," he murmured plaintively, "the bottoms of my feet is itching something terrible."

Long before the family stirred next morning, his horses fed and harnessed by lantern light, breakfast cooked and eaten by lamplight, Old Man Tarwater was off and away down Tarwater Valley on the road to Kelterville. Two things were unusual about this usual trip which he had made a thousand and forty times since taking the mail contract. He did not drive to Kelterville, but turned off on the main road south to Santa Rosa. Even more remarkable than this was the paper-wrapped parcel between his feet. It contained his one decent black suit, which Mary had been long reluctant to see him wear any more, not because it was shabby, but because, as he guessed what was at the back of her mind, it was decent enough to bury him in.

And at Santa Rosa, in a second-hand clothes shop, he sold the suit outright for two dollars and a half. From the same obliging shopman he received four dollars for the wedding ring of his long-dead wife. The span of horses and the wagon he disposed of for seventy-five dollars, although twenty-five was all he received down in cash. Chancing to meet Alton Granger on the street, to whom never before had he mentioned the ten dollars loaned him in '74, he reminded Alton Granger of the little affair, and was promptly paid. Also, of all unbelievable men to be in funds, he so found the town drunkard for whom he had bought many a drink in the old and palmy days. And from him John Tarwater borrowed a dollar. Finally, he took the afternoon train to San Francisco.

A dozen days later, carrying a half-empty canvas sack of blankets and old clothes, he landed on the beach of Dyea in the thick of the great Klondike Rush. The beach was screaming bedlam. Ten thousand tons of outfit lay heaped and scattered, and twice ten thousand men struggled with it and clamored about it. Freight, by Indian-back, over Chilcoot to Lake Linderman, had jumped from sixteen to thirty cents a pound, which latter was a rate of six hundred dollars a ton. And the sub-arctic winter gloomed near at hand. All knew it, and all knew that of the twenty thousand of them very few would get across the passes, leaving the rest to winter and wait for the late spring thaw.

Such the beach old John Tarwater stepped upon; and straight across the beach and up the trail toward Chilcoot he headed, cackling his ancient chant, a very Grandfather Argus himself, with no outfit worry in the world, for he did not possess any outfit. That night he slept on the flats, five miles above Dyea, at the head of canoe navigation. Here the Dyea River became a rushing mountain torrent, plunging out of a dark canyon from the glaciers that fed it far above.

And here, early next morning, he beheld a little man weighing no more than a hundred, staggering along a foot-log under all of a hundred pounds of flour strapped on his back. Also, he beheld the little man stumble off the log and fall face-downward in a quiet eddy where the water was two feet deep and proceed quietly to drown. It was no desire of his to take death so easily, but the flour on his back weighed as much as he and would not let him up.

"Thank you, old man," he said to Tarwater, when the latter had dragged him up into the air and ashore.

While he unlaced his shoes and ran the water out, they had further talk. Next, he fished out a ten-dollar gold-piece and offered it to his rescuer.

Old Tarwater shook his head and shivered, for the ice-water had wet him to his knees.

"But I reckon I wouldn't object to settin' down to a friendly meal with you."

"Ain't had breakfast?" the little man, who was past forty and who had said his name was Anson, queried with a glance frankly curious.

"Nary bite," John Tarwater answered.

"Where's your outfit? Ahead?"

"Nary outfit."

"Expect to buy your grub on the Inside?"

"Nary a dollar to buy it with, friend. Which ain't so important as a warm bite of breakfast right now."

In Anson's camp, a quarter of a mile on, Tarwater found a slender, red-whiskered young man of thirty cursing over a fire of wet willow wood. Introduced as Charles, he transferred his scowl and wrath to Tarwater, who, genially oblivious, devoted himself to the fire, took advantage of the chill morning breeze to create a draught which the other had left stupidly blocked by stones, and soon developed less smoke and more flame. The third member of the party, Bill Wilson, or Big Bill as they called him, came in with a hundred-and-forty-pound pack; and what Tarwater esteemed to be a very rotten breakfast was dished out by Charles. The mush was half cooked and mostly burnt, the bacon was charred carbon, and the coffee was unspeakable.

Immediately the meal was wolfed down, the three partners took their empty packstraps and headed down trail to where the remainder of their outfit lay at the last camp a mile away. And old Tarwater became busy. He washed the dishes, foraged dry wood, mended a broken packstrap, put an edge on the butcher-knife and camp-ax, and repacked the picks and shovels into a more carryable parcel.

What had impressed him during the brief breakfast was the sort of awe in which Anson and Big Bill stood of Charles. Once, during the morning, while Anson took a breathing spell after bringing in another hundred-pound pack, Tarwater delicately hinted his impression.

"You see, it's this way," Anson said. "We've divided our leadership. We've all got specialties. Now I'm a carpenter. When we get to Lake Linderman, and the trees are chopped and whipsawed into planks, I'll boss the building of the boat. Big Jim is a logger and miner. So he'll boss getting out the logs and all mining operations. Most of our outfit's ahead. We went broke paying the Indians to pack that much of it to the top of Chilcoot. Our last partner is up there with it, moving it along by himself down the other side. His name's Liverpool, and he's a sailor. So, when the boat's built, he's the boss of the outfit to navigate the lakes and rapids to Klondike."

"And Charles—this Mr. Clayton—what might his specialty be?" Tarwater asked.

"He's the business man. When it comes to business and organization he's boss."

"Hum," Tarwater pondered. "Very lucky to get such a bunch of specialties into one outfit."

"More than lucky," Anson agreed. "It was all accident, too. Each of us started alone. We met on the steamer coming up from San Francisco, and formed the party.—Well, I got to be goin'. Charles is liable to get kicking because I ain't packing my share. Just the same, you can't expect a hundred-pound man to pack as much as a hundred-and-sixty-pounder."

"Stick around and cook us something for dinner," Charles, on his next load in and noting the effects of the old man's handiness, told Tarwater.

And Tarwater cooked a dinner that was a dinner, washed the dishes, had real pork and beans for supper, and bread baked in a frying-pan that was so delectable that the three partners nearly foundered themselves on it. Supper dishes washed, he cut shavings and kindling for a quick and certain breakfast fire, showed Anson a trick with foot-gear that was invaluable to any hiker, sang his "Like Argus of the Ancient Times," and told them of the great emigration across the Plains in Forty-nine.

"My goodness, the first cheerful and hearty-like camp since we hit the beach," Big Jim remarked as he knocked out his pipe and began pulling off his shoes for bed.

"Kind of made things easy, boys, eh?" Tarwater queried genially.

All nodded. "Well, then, I got a proposition, boys. You can take it or leave it, but just listen kindly to it. You're in a hurry to get in before the freeze-up. Half the time is wasted over the cooking by one of you that he might be puttin' in packin' outfit. If I do the cookin' for you, you all'll get on that much faster. Also, the cookin' 'll be better, and that'll make you pack better. And I can pack quite a bit myself in between times, quite a bit, yes, sir, quite a bit."

Big Bill and Anson were just beginning to nod their heads in agreement, when Charles stopped them.

"What do you expect of us in return?" he demanded of the old man.

"Oh, I leave it up to the boys."

"That ain't business," Charles reprimanded sharply. "You made the proposition. Now finish it."

"Well, it's this way—"

"You expect us to feed you all winter, eh?" Charles interrupted.

"No, siree, I don't. All I reckon is a passage to Klondike in your boat would be mighty square of you."

"You haven't an ounce of grub, old man. You'll starve to death when you get there."

"I've been feedin' some long time pretty successful," Old Tarwater replied, a whimsical light in his eyes. "I'm seventy, and ain't starved to death never yet."

"Will you sign a paper to the effect that you shift for yourself as soon as you get to Dawson?" the business one demanded.

"Oh, sure," was the response.

Again Charles checked his two partners' expressions of satisfaction with the arrangement.

"One other thing, old man. We're a party of four, and we all have a vote on questions like this. Young Liverpool is ahead with the main outfit. He's got a say so, and he isn't here to say it."

"What kind of a party might he be?" Tarwater inquired.

"He's a rough-neck sailor, and he's got a quick, bad temper."

"Some turbulent," Anson contributed.

"And the way he can cuss is simply God-awful," Big Jim testified.

"But he's square," Big Jim added.

Anson nodded heartily to this appraisal.

"Well, boys," Tarwater summed up, "I set out for Californy and I got there. And I'm going to get to Klondike. Ain't a thing can stop me, ain't a thing. I'm going to get three hundred thousand outa the ground, too. Ain't a thing can stop me, ain't a thing, because I just naturally need the money. I don't mind a bad temper so long's the boy is square. I'll take my chance, an' I'll work along with you till we catch up with him. Then, if he says no to the proposition, I reckon I'll lose. But somehow I just can't see 'm sayin' no, because that'd mean too close up to freeze-up and too late for me to find another chance like this. And, as I'm sure going to get to Klondike, it's just plumb impossible for him to say no."

Old John Tarwater became a striking figure on a trail unusually replete with striking figures. With thousands of men, each back-tripping half a ton of outfit, retracing every mile of the trail twenty times, all came to know him and to hail him as "Father Christmas." And as he worked ever he raised his chant with his age-falsetto voice. None of the three men he had joined could complain about his work. True, his joints were stiff—he admitted to a trifle of rheumatism. He moved slowly, and seemed to creak and crackle when he moved; but he kept on moving. Last into the blankets at night, he was first out in the morning, so that the other three had hot coffee before their one before-breakfast pack. And, between breakfast and dinner and between dinner and supper, he always managed to back-trip for several packs himself. Sixty pounds was the limit of his burden, however. He could manage seventy-five, but he could not keep it up. Once, he tried ninety, but collapsed on the trail and was seriously shaky for a couple of days afterward.

Work! On a trail where hard-working men learned for the first time what work was, no man worked harder in proportion to his strength than Old Tarwater. Driven desperately on by the near-thrust of winter, and lured madly on by the dream of gold, they worked to their last ounce of strength and fell by the way. Others, when failure made certain, blew out their brains. Some went mad, and still others, under the irk of the man-destroying strain, broke partnerships and dissolved lifetime friendships with fellows just as good as themselves and just as strained and mad.

Work! Old Tarwater could shame them all, despite his creaking and crackling and the nasty hacking cough he had developed. Early and late, on trail or in camp beside the trail, he was ever in evidence, ever busy at something, ever responsive to the hail of "Father Christmas." Weary back-trippers would rest their packs on a log or rock alongside of where he rested his, and would say: "Sing us that song of yourn, dad, about Forty-Nine." And, when he had wheezingly complied, they would arise under their loads, remark that it was real heartening, and hit the forward trail again.

"If ever a man worked his passage and earned it," Big Jim confided to his two partners, "that man's our old Skeezicks."

"You bet," Anson confirmed. "He's a valuable addition to the party, and I, for one, ain't at all disagreeable to the notion of making him a regular partner—"

"None of that!" Charles Crayton cut in. "When we get to Dawson we're quit of him—that's the agreement. We'd only have to bury him if we let him stay on with us. Besides, there's going to be a famine, and every ounce of grub'll count. Remember, we're feeding him out of our own supply all the way in. And if we run short in the pinch next year, you'll know the reason. Steamboats can't get up grub to Dawson till the middle of June, and that's nine months away."

"Well, you put as much money and outfit in as the rest of us," Big Bill conceded, "and you've a say according."

"And I'm going to have my say," Charles asserted with increasing irritability. "And it's lucky for you with your fool sentiments that you've got somebody to think ahead for you, else you'd all starve to death. I tell you that famine's coming. I've been studying the situation. Flour will be two dollars a pound, or ten, and no sellers. You mark my words."

Across the rubble-covered flats, up the dark canyon to Sheep Camp, past the overhanging and ever-threatening glaciers to the Scales, and from the Scales up the steep pitches of ice-scoured rock where packers climbed with hands and feet, Old Tarwater camp-cooked and packed and sang. He blew across Chilcoot Pass, above timber-line, in the first swirl of autumn snow. Those below, without firewood, on the bitter rim of Crater Lake, heard from the driving obscurity above them a weird voice chanting:

> *"Like Argus of the ancient times,*
> *We leave this modern Greece,*
> *Tum-tum, tum-tum, tum, tum, tum-tum,*
> *To shear the Golden Fleece."*

And out of the snow flurries they saw appear a tall, gaunt form, with whiskers of flying white that blended with the storm, bending under a sixty-pound pack of camp dunnage.

"Father Christmas!" was the hail. And then: "Three rousing cheers for Father Christmas!"

Two miles beyond Crater Lake lay Happy Camp—so named because here was found the uppermost fringe of the timber line, where men might warm themselves by fire again. Scarcely could it be called timber, for it was a dwarf rock-spruce that never raised its loftiest branches higher than a foot above the moss, and that twisted and groveled like a pig-vegetable under the moss. Here, on the trail leading into Happy Camp, in the first sunshine of half a dozen days, Old Tarwater rested his pack against a huge bowlder and caught his breath. Around this bowlder the trail passed, laden men toiling slowly forward and men with empty pack-straps limping rapidly back for fresh loads. Twice Old Tarwater essayed to rise and go on, and each time, warned by his shakiness, sank back to recover more strength. From around the bowlder he heard voices in greeting, recognized Charles Crayton's voice, and realized that at last they had met up with Young Liverpool. Quickly, Charles plunged into business, and Tarwater heard with great distinctness every word of Charles' unflattering description of him and of the proposition to give him passage to Dawson.

"A damn fool proposition," was Liverpool's judgment, when Charles had concluded. "An old granddad of seventy! If he's on his last legs, why in hell did you hook up with him? If there's going to be a famine, and it looks like it, we need every ounce of grub for ourselves. We only outfitted for four, not five."

"It's all right," Tarwater heard Charles assuring the other. "Don't get excited. The old codger agreed to leave the final decision to you when

we caught up with you. All you've got to do is put your foot down and
say no."

"You mean it's up to me to turn the old one down, after your encouraging him and taking advantage of his work clear from Dyea here?"

"It's a hard trail, Liverpool, and only the men that are hard will get
through," Charles strove to palliate.

"And I'm to do the dirty work?" Liverpool complained, while Tarwater's heart sank.

"That's just about the size of it," Charles said. "You've got the deciding."

Then Old Tarwater's heart uprose again as the air was rent by a
cyclone of profanity, from the midst of which crackled sentences like:
"Dirty skunks! . . . See you in hell first! . . . My mind's made up! . . .
Hell's fire and corruption! . . . The old codger goes down the Yukon
with us, stack on that, my hearty! . . . Hard? You don't know what hard
is unless I show you! . . . I'll bust the whole outfit to hell and gone if
any of you try to side-track him! . . . Just try to side-track him, that's
all, and you'll think the day of Judgment and all God's blastingness has
hit the camp in one chunk!"

Such was the invigoratingness of Liverpool's flow of speech that,
quite without consciousness of effort, the old man arose easily under
his load and strode on toward Happy Camp.

From Happy Camp to Long Lake, from Long Lake to Deep Lake,
and from Deep Lake up over the enormous hog-back and down to
Linderman, the man-killing race against winter kept on. Men broke their
hearts and backs and wept beside the trail in sheer exhaustion. But
winter never faltered. The fall gales blew, and amid bitter soaking rains
and ever increasing snow flurries, Tarwater and the party to which he
was attached piled the last of their outfit on the beach.

There was no rest. Across the lake, a mile above a roaring torrent,
they located a patch of spruce and built their saw-pit. Here, by hand,
with an inadequate whipsaw, they sawed the spruce-trunks into lumber.
They worked night and day. Thrice, on the night-shift, underneath in
the saw-pit, Old Tarwater fainted. By day he cooked as well, and, in
the betweenwhiles, helped Anson in the building of the boat beside the
torrent as the green planks came down.

The days grew shorter. The wind shifted into the north and blew
unending gales. In the mornings the weary men crawled from their
blankets and in their socks thawed out their frozen shoes by the fire
Tarwater always had burning for them. Ever arose the increasing tale
of famine on the Inside. The last grub steamboats up from Bering Sea
were stalled by low water at the beginning of the Yukon Flats hundred

of miles north of Dawson. In fact, they lay at the old Hudson Bay Company's post at Fort Yukon inside the Arctic Circle. Flour in Dawson was up to two dollars a pound but no one would sell. Bonanza and Eldorado Kings, with money to burn, were leaving for the Outside because they could buy no grub. Miners' Committees were confiscating all grub and putting the population on strict rations. A man who held out an ounce of grub was shot like a dog. A score had been so executed already.

And, under a strain which had broken so many younger men, Old Tarwater began to break. His cough had become terrible, and had not his exhausted comrades slept like the dead, he would have kept them awake nights. Also, he began to take chills, so that he dressed up to go to bed. When he had finished so dressing, not a rag of garment remained in his clothes bag. All he possessed was on his back and swathed around his gaunt old form.

"Gee!" said Big Bill. "If he puts all he's got on now, when it ain't lower than twenty above, what'll he do later on when it goes down to fifty and sixty below?"

They lined the rough-made boat down the mountain torrent, nearly losing it a dozen times, and rowed across the south end of Lake Linderman in the thick of a fall blizzard. Next morning they planned to load and start, squarely into the teeth of the north, on their perilous traverse of half a thousand miles of lakes and rapids and box canyons. But before he went to bed that night, Young Liverpool was out over the camp. He returned to find his whole party asleep. Rousing Tarwater, he talked with him in low tones.

"Listen, dad," he said. "You've got a passage in our boat, and if ever a man earned a passage you have. But you know yourself you're pretty well along in years, and your health right now ain't exciting. If you go on with us you'll croak surer'n hell.—Now wait till I finish, dad. The price for a passage has jumped to five hundred dollars. I've been throwing my feet and I've hustled a passenger. He's an official of the Alaska Commercial and just has to get in. He's bid up to six hundred to go with me in our boat. Now the passage is yours. You sell it to him, poke the six hundred into your jeans, and pull South for California while the goin's good. You can be in Dyea in two days, and in California in a week more. What d'ye say?"

Tarwater coughed and shivered for a space, ere he could get freedom of breath for speech.

"Son," he said, "I just want to tell you one thing. I drove my four yoke of oxen across the Plains in Forty-nine and lost nary a one. I drove them plumb to Californy, and I freighted with them afterward out of Sutter's Fort to American Bar. Now I'm going to Klondike. Ain't nothing can stop me, ain't nothing at all. I'm going to ride that boat, with you at the steering sweep, clean to Klondike, and I'm going to shake three hundred thousand out of the moss-roots. That being so, it's contrary to reason and common sense for me to sell out my passage. But I thank you kindly, son, I thank you kindly."

The young sailor shot out his hand impulsively and gripped the old man's.

"By God, dad!" he cried. "You're sure going to go then. You're the real stuff." He looked with undisguised contempt across the sleepers to where Charles Crayton snored in his red beard. "They don't seem to make your kind any more, dad."

Into the north they fought their way, although old-timers, coming out, shook their heads and prophesied they would be frozen in on the lakes. That the freeze-up might come any day was patent, and delays of safety were no longer considered. For this reason, Liverpool decided to shoot the rapid stream connecting Linderman to Lake Bennett with the fully loaded boat. It was the custom to line the empty boats down and to portage the cargoes across. Even then, many empty boats had been wrecked. But the time was past for such precaution.

"Climb out, dad," Liverpool commanded, as he prepared to swing from the bank and enter the rapids.

Old Tarwater shook his white head.

"I'm sticking to the outfit," he declared. "It's the only way to get through. You see, son, I'm going to Klondike. If I stick by the boat, then the boat just naturally goes to Klondike, too. If I get out, then most likely you'll lose the boat."

"Well, there's no use in overloading," Charles announced, springing abruptly out on the bank as the boat cast off.

"Next time you wait for my orders!" Liverpool shouted ashore as the current gripped the boat. "And there won't be any more walking around rapids and losing time waiting to pick you up!"

What took them ten minutes by river, took Charles half an hour by land, and while they waited for him at the head of Lake Bennett they passed the time of day with several dilapidated old-timers on their way out. The famine news was graver than ever. The Northwest Mounted Police, stationed at the foot of Lake Marsh where the gold-rushers entered Canadian Territory, were refusing to let a man past who did not carry with him seven hundred pounds of grub. In Dawson City a thousand men, with dog-teams, were waiting the freeze-up to come out over the ice. The trading companies could not fill their grub-contracts, and partners were cutting the cards to see which should go and which should stay and work the claims.

"That settles it," Charles announced, when he learned of the action of the mounted police on the boundary. "Old Man, you might as well start back now."

"Climb aboard!" Liverpool commanded. "We're going to Klondike, and old dad is going along."

A shift of gale to the south gave them a fair wind down Lake Bennett, before which they ran under a huge sail made by Liverpool. The heavy weight of outfit gave such ballast that he cracked on as a daring sailor should when moments counted. A shift of four points into the south-west, coming just at the right time as they entered upon Caribou Crossing, drove them down that connecting link to lakes Taggish and Marsh. In stormy sunset and twilight they made the dangerous crossing of Great Windy Arm, wherein they beheld two other boat-loads of gold-rushers capsize and drown.

Charles was for beaching for the night, but Liverpool held on, steering down Taggish by the sound of the surf on the shoals and by the occasional shore-fires that advertised wrecked or timid argonauts. At four in the morning, he aroused Charles. Old Tarwater, shiveringly awake, heard Liverpool order Crayton aft beside him at the steering-sweep, and also heard the one-sided conversation.

"Just listen, friend Charles, and keep your own mouth shut," Liverpool began. "I want you to get one thing into your head and keep it there: *old dad's going by the police. Understand? He's going by.* When they examine our outfit, old dad's got a fifth share in it, savvee? That'll put us all 'way under what we ought to have, but we can bluff it through. Now get this, and get it hard: *there ain't going to be any fall-down on this bluff—*"

"If you think I'd give away on the old codger—" Charles began indignantly.

"You thought that," Liverpool checked him, "because I never mentioned any such thing. Now—get me and get me hard: I don't care what you've been thinking. It's what you're going to think. We'll make the police post some time this afternoon, and we've got to get ready to pull the bluff without a hitch, and a word to the wise is plenty."

"If you think I've got it in my mind—" Charles began again.

"Look here," Liverpool shut him off. "I don't know what's in your mind. I don't want to know. I want you to know what's in my mind. If there's any slip-up, if old dad gets turned back by the police, I'm going to pick out the first quiet bit of landscape and take you ashore on it.

And then I'm going to beat you up to the Queen's taste. Get me, and get me hard. It ain't going to be any half-way beating, but a real, two-legged, two-fisted, he-man beating. I don't expect I'll kill you, but I'll come damn near to half-killing you."

"But what can I do?" Charles almost whimpered.

"Just one thing," was Liverpool's final word. "You just pray. You pray so hard that old dad gets by the police that he does get by. That's all. Go back to your blankets."

Before they gained Lake Le Barge, the land was sheeted with snow that would not melt for half a year. Nor could they lay their boat at will against the bank, for the rim-ice was already forming. Inside the mouth of the river, just ere it entered Lake Le Barge, they found a hundred storm-bound boats of the argonauts. Out of the north, across the full sweep of the great lake, blew an unending snow gale. Three mornings they put out and fought it and the cresting seas it drove that turned to ice as they fell in-board. While the others broke their hearts at the oars, Old Tarwater managed to keep up just sufficient circulation to survive by chopping ice and throwing it overboard.

Each day for three days, beaten to helplessness, they turned tail on the battle and ran back into the sheltering river. By the fourth day, the hundred boats had increased to three hundred, and the two thousand argonauts on board knew that the great gale heralded the freeze-up of Le Barge. Beyond, the rapid rivers would continue to run for days, but unless they got beyond, and immediately, they were doomed to be frozen in for six months to come.

"This day we go through," Liverpool announced. "We turn back for nothing. And those of us that dies at the oars will live again and go on pulling."

And they went through, winning half the length of the lake by nightfall and pulling on through all the night hours as the wind went down, falling asleep at the oars and being rapped awake by Liverpool, toiling on through an age-long nightmare while the stars came out and the surface of the lake turned to the unruffledness of a sheet of paper and froze skin-ice that tinkled like broken glass as their oar-blades shattered it.

As day broke clear and cold, they entered the river, with behind them a sea of ice. Liverpool examined his aged passenger and found him helpless and almost gone. When he rounded the boat to against the rim-ice to build a fire and warm up Tarwater inside and out, Charles protested against such loss of time.

"This ain't business, so don't you come horning in," Liverpool informed him. "I'm running the boat trip. So you just climb out and chop firewood, and plenty of it. I'll take care of dad. You, Anson, make a fire on the bank. And you, Bill, set up the Yukon stove in the boat. Old dad ain't as young as the rest of us, and for the rest of this voyage he's going to have a fire on board to sit by."

All of which came to pass; and the boat, in the grip of the current, like a river steamer with smoke rising from the two joints of stove-pipe, grounded on shoals, hung up on split currents, and charged rapids and canyons, as it drove deeper into the Northland winter. The Big and Little Salmon rivers were throwing mush-ice into the main river as they passed, and, below the riffles, anchor-ice arose from the river bottom and coated the surface with crystal scum. Night and day the rim-ice grew, till, in quiet places, it extended out a hundred yards from shore. And Old Tarwater, with all his clothes on, sat by the stove and kept the fire going. Night and day, not daring to stop for fear of the imminent freeze-up, they dared to run, an increasing mushiness of ice running with them.

"What ho, old hearty?" Liverpool would call out at times.

"Cheer O," Old Tarwater had learned to respond.

"What can I ever do for you, son, in payment?" Tarwater, stoking the fire, would sometimes ask Liverpool beating now one released hand and now the other as he fought for circulation where he steered in the freezing stern-sheets.

"Just break out that regular song of yours, old Forty-Niner," was the invariable reply.

And Tarwater would lift his voice in the cackling chant, as he lifted it at the end, when the boat swung in through driving cake-ice and moored to the Dawson City bank, and all waterfront Dawson pricked its ears to hear the triumphant pæan:

> *"Like Argus of the ancient times,*
> *We leave this modern Greece,*
> *Tum-tum, tum-tum, tum, tum, tum-tum,*
> *To shear the Golden Fleece."*

Charles did it, but he did it so discreetly that none of his party, least of all the sailor, ever learned of it. He saw two great open barges being filled up with men, and, on inquiry, learned that these were grubless ones being rounded up and sent down the Yukon by the Committee of Safety. The barges were to be towed by the last little steamboat in Dawson, and the hope was that Fort Yukon, where lay the stranded steamboats, would be gained before the river froze. At any rate, no matter what happened to them, Dawson would be relieved of their grub-consuming presence. So to the Committee of Safety Charles went, privily to drop a flea in its ear concerning Tarwater's grubless, money-less, and aged condition. Tarwater was one of the last gathered in, and when Young Liverpool returned to the boat, from the bank he saw the barges in a run of cake-ice, disappearing around the bend below Moose-hide Mountain.

Running in cake-ice all the way, and several times escaping jams in the Yukon Flats, the barges made their hundreds of miles of progress farther into the north and froze up cheek by jowl with the grub-fleet. Here, inside the Arctic Circle Old Tarwater settled down to pass the long winter. Several hours' work a day, chopping firewood for the steamboat companies, sufficed to keep him in food. For the rest of the time there was nothing to do but hibernate in his log cabin.

Warmth, rest, and plenty to eat, cured his hacking cough and put him in as good physical condition as was possible for his advanced years. But, even before Christmas, the lack of fresh vegetables caused scurvy to break out, and disappointed adventurer after disappointed adventurer took to his bunk in abject surrender to this culminating misfortune. Not so Tarwater. Even before the first symptoms appeared on him, he was putting into practice his one prescription, namely, exercise. From the junk of the old trading post he resurrected a number of rusty traps, and from one of the steamboat captains he borrowed a rifle.

Thus equipped, he ceased from wood-chopping, and began to make more than a mere living. Nor was he downhearted when the scurvy broke out on his own body. Ever he ran his trap-lines and sang his ancient chant. Nor could the pessimist shake his surety of the three hundred thousand of Alaskan gold he was going to shake out of the moss-roots.

"But this ain't gold-country," they told him.

"Gold is where you find it, son, as I should know who was mining before you was born, 'way back in Forty-Nine," was his reply. "What was Bonanza Creek but a moose-pasture? No miner'd look at it; yet they washed five-hundred-dollar pans and took out fifty million dollars. Eldorado was just as bad. For all you know, right under this here cabin, or right over the next hill, is millions just waiting for a lucky one like me to come and shake it out."

At the end of January came his disaster. Some powerful animal that he decided was a bob-cat, managing to get caught in one of his smaller traps, dragged it away. A heavy snow-fall put a stop midway to his pursuit, losing the trail for him and losing himself. There were but several hours of daylight each day between the twenty hours of intervening darkness, and his efforts in the gray light and continually falling snow succeeded only in losing him more thoroughly. Fortunately, when winter snow falls in the Northland the thermometer invariably rises; so, instead of the customary forty and fifty and even sixty degrees below zero, the temperature remained fifteen below. Also, he was warmly clad and had a full matchbox. Further to mitigate his predicament, on the fifth day he killed a wounded moose that weighed over half a ton. Making his camp beside it on a spruce-bottom, he was prepared to last out the winter, unless a searching party found him or his scurvy grew worse.

But at the end of two weeks there had been no sign of search, while his scurvy had undeniably grown worse. Against his fire, banked from outer cold by a shelter-wall of spruce-boughs, he crouched long hours in sleep and long hours in waking. But the waking hours grew less, becoming semi-waking or half-dreaming hours as the processes of hibernation worked their way with him. Slowly the sparkle point of consciousness and identity that was John Tarwater sank, deeper and deeper, into the profounds of his being that had been compounded ere man was man, and while he was becoming man, when he, first of all animals regarded himself with an introspective eye and laid the beginnings of morality in foundations of nightmare peopled by the monsters of his own ethic-thwarted desires.

Like a man in fever, waking to intervals of consciousness, so Old Tarwater awoke, cooked his moose-meat, and fed the fire; but more and more time he spent in his torpor, unaware of what was day-dream and what was sleep-dream in the content of his unconsciousness. And here, in the unforgetable crypts of man's unwritten history, unthinkable and unrealizable, like passages of nightmare or impossible adventures of lunacy, he encountered the monsters created of man's first morality that ever since have vexed him into the spinning of fantasies to elude them or do battle with them.

In short, weighted by his seventy years, in the vast and silent loneliness of the North, Old Tarwater, as in the delirium of drug or anæsthetic, recovered, within himself, the infantile mind of the child-man of the early world. It was in the dusk of Death's fluttery wings that Tarwater thus crouched, and, like his remote forebear, the child-man, went to myth-making, and sun-heroizing, himself hero-maker and the hero in quest of the immemorable treasure difficult of attainment.

Either must he attain the treasure—for so ran the inexorable logic of the shadow-land of the unconscious—or else sink into the all-devouring sea, the blackness eater of the light that swallowed to extinction the sun each night ... the sun that arose ever in rebirth next morning in the east, and that had become to man man's first symbol of immortality through rebirth. All this, in the deeps of his unconsciousness (the shadowy western land of descending light), was the near dusk of Death down into which he slowly ebbed.

But how to escape this monster of the dark that from within him slowly swallowed him? Too deep-sunk was he to dream of escape or feel the prod of desire to escape. For him reality had ceased. Nor from within the darkened chamber of himself could reality recrudesce. His years were too heavy upon him, the debility of disease and the lethargy and torpor of the silence and the cold were too profound. Only from without could reality impact upon him and reawake within him an awareness of reality. Otherwise he would ooze down through the shadow-realm of the unconscious into the all-darkness of extinction.

But it came, the smash of reality from without, crashing upon his ear drums in a loud, explosive snort. For twenty days, in a temperature that had never risen above fifty below, no breath of wind had blown movement, no slightest sound had broken the silence. Like the smoker on the opium couch refocusing his eyes from the spacious walls of dream to the narrow confines of the mean little room, so Old Tarwater stared vague-eyed before him, across his dying fire, at a huge moose that stared at him in startlement, dragging a wounded leg, manifesting all signs of extreme exhaustion, it, too, had been straying blindly in the shadow-land, and had wakened to reality only just ere it stepped into Tarwater's fire.

He feebly slipped the large fur mitten lined with thicknesses of wool from his right hand. Upon trial he found the trigger finger too numb for movement. Carefully, slowly, through long minutes, he worked the bare hand inside his blankets, up under his fur *parka,* through the chest openings of his shirts, and into the slightly warm hollow of his left armpit. Long minutes passed ere the finger could move, when, with equal slowness of caution, he gathered his rifle to his shoulder and drew bead upon the great animal across the fire.

At the shot, of the two shadow-wanderers, the one reeled downward to the dark and the other reeled upward to the light, swaying drunkenly on his scurvy-ravaged legs, shivering with nervousness and cold, rubbing swimming eyes with shaking fingers, and staring at the real world all about him that had returned to him with such sickening suddenness. He shook himself together, and realized that for long, how long he did not know, he had bedded in the arms of Death. He spat, with definite intention, heard the spittle crackle in the frost, and judged it must be below and far below sixty below. In truth, that day at Fort Yukon, the spirit thermometer registered seventy-five degrees below zero, which, since freezing-point is thirty-two above, was equivalent to one hundred and seven degrees of frost.

Slowly Tarwater's brain reasoned to action. Here, in the vast alone, dwelt Death. Here had come two wounded moose. With the clearing of the sky after the great cold came on, he had located his bearings, and he knew that both wounded moose had trailed to him from the east. Therefore, in the east, were men—whites or Indians he could not tell, but at any rate men who might stand by him in his need and help moor him to reality above the sea of dark.

He moved slowly, but he moved in reality, girding himself with rifle, ammunition, matches, and a pack of twenty pounds of moose-meat. Then, an Argus rejuvenated, albeit lame of both legs and tottery, he turned his back on the perilous west and limped into the sun-arising, re-birthing east. . . .

Days later—how many days later he was never to know—dreaming dreams and seeing visions, cackling his old gold-chant of Forty-Nine, like one drowning and swimming feebly to keep his consciousness above the engulfing dark, he came out upon the snow-slope to a canyon and saw below smoke rising and men who ceased from work to gaze at him. He tottered down the hill to them, still singing; and when he ceased from lack of breath they called him variously: Santa Claus, Old Christmas, Whiskers, the Last of the Mohicans, and Father Christmas. And when he stood among them he stood very still, without speech, while great tears welled out of his eyes. He cried silently, a long time, till, as if suddenly bethinking himself, he sat down in the snow with much creaking and crackling of his joints, and from this low vantage point toppled sidewise and fainted calmly and easily away.

In less than a week Old Tarwater was up and limping about the house-work of the cabin, cooking and dish-washing for the five men of the creek. Genuine sour-doughs (pioneers) they were, tough and hard-bitten, who had been buried so deeply inside the Circle that they did not know there was a Klondike Strike. The news he brought them was their first word of it. They lived on an almost straight-meat diet of moose, caribou, and smoked salmon, eked out with wild berries and somewhat succulent wild roots they had stocked up with in the summer. They had forgotten the taste of coffee, made fire with a burning glass, carried live fire-sticks with them wherever they traveled, and in their pipes smoked dry leaves that bit the tongue and were pungent to the nostrils.

Three years before, they had prospected from the head-reaches of the Koyokuk northward and clear across to the mouth of the Mackenzie on the Arctic Ocean. Here, on the whaleships, they had beheld their last white men and equipped themselves with the last whiteman's grub, consisting principally of salt and smoking tobacco. Striking south and west on the long traverse to the junction of the Yukon and Porcupine at Fort Yukon, they had found gold on this creek and remained over to work the ground.

They hailed the advent of Tarwater with joy, never tired of listening to his tales of Forty-Nine, and rechristened him Old Hero. Also, with tea made from spruce needles, with concoctions brewed from the inner willow bark, and with sour and bitter roots and bulbs from the ground, they dosed his scurvy out of him, so that he ceased limping and began to lay on flesh over his bony framework. Further, they saw no reason at all why he should not gather a rich treasure of gold from the ground.

"Don't know about all of three hundred thousand," they told him one morning, at breakfast, ere they departed to their work, "but how'd a hundred thousand do, Old Hero? That's what we figure a claim is worth, the ground being badly spotted, and we've already staked your location notices."

"Well, boys," Old Tarwater answered, "and thanking you kindly, all I can say is that a hundred thousand will do nicely, and very nicely, for a starter. Of course, I ain't goin' to stop till I get the full three hundred thousand. That's what I come into the country for."

They laughed and applauded his ambition and reckoned they'd have to hunt a richer creek for him. And Old Hero reckoned that as the spring came on and he grew spryer, he'd have to get out and do a little snooping around himself.

"For all anybody knows," he said, pointing to a hillside across the creek bottom, "the moss under the snow there may be plumb rooted in nugget gold."

He said no more, but as the sun rose higher and the days grew longer and warmer, he gazed often across the creek at the definite bench-formation half way up the hill. And, one day, when the thaw was in full swing, he crossed the stream and climbed to the bench. Exposed patches of ground had already thawed an inch deep. On one such patch he stooped, gathered a bunch of moss in his big gnarled hands, and ripped it out by the roots. The sun smoldered on dully glistening yellow. He shook the handful of moss, and coarse nuggets, like gravel, fell to the ground. It was the Golden Fleece ready for the shearing.

Not entirely unremembered in Alaskan annals is the summer stampede of 1898 from Fort Yukon to the bench diggings of Tarwater Hill. And when Tarwater sold his holdings to the Bowdie interests for a sheer half-million and faced for California, he rode a mule over a new-cut trail, with convenient road houses along the way, clear to the steam-boat landing at Fort Yukon.

At the first meal on the ocean-going steamship out of St. Michaels, a waiter, grayish-haired, pain-ravaged of face, scurvy-twisted of body, served him. Old Tarwater was compelled to look him over twice in order to make certain he was Charles Crayton.

"Got it bad, eh, son?" Tarwater queried.

"Just my luck," the other complained, after recognition and greeting. "Only one of the party that the scurvy attacked. I've been through hell. The other three are all at work and healthy, getting grub-stake to pros-pect up White River this winter. Anson's earning twenty-five a day at carpentering, Liverpool getting twenty logging for the saw-mill, and Big Bill's getting forty a day as chief sawyer. I tried my best, and if it hadn't been for scurvy . . ."

"Sure, son, you done your best, which ain't much, you being natu-rally irritable and hard from too much business. Now I'll tell you what. You ain't fit to work crippled up this way. I'll pay your passage with the captain in kind remembrance of the voyage you gave me, and you can lay up and take it easy the rest of the trip. And what are your circumstances when you land at San Francisco?"

Charles Crayton shrugged his shoulders.

"Tell you what," Tarwater continued. "There's work on the ranch for you till you can start business again."

"I could manage your business for you—" Charles began eagerly.

"No, siree," Tarwater declared emphatically. "But there's always post-holes to dig, and cord-wood to chop, and the climate's fine. . . ."

Tarwater arrived home a true prodigal grandfather for whom the fat-ted calf was killed and ready. But first, ere he sat down at table, he must stroll out and around. And sons and daughters of his flesh and of the law needs must go with him, fulsomely eating out of the gnarled old hand that had half a million to disburse. He led the way, and no opinion he slyly uttered was preposterous or impossible enough to draw dissent from his following. Pausing by the ruined water wheel which he had built from the standing timber, his face beamed as he gazed across the stretches of Tarwater Valley, and on and up the far heights to the sum-mit of Tarwater Mountain—now all his again.

A thought came to him that made him avert his face and blow his nose in order to hide the twinkle in his eyes. Still attended by the entire family, he strolled on to the dilapidated barn. He picked up an age-weathered single-tree from the ground.

"William," he said. "Remember that little conversation we had just before I started to Klondike? Sure, William, you remember. You told me I was crazy. And I said my father'd have walloped the tar out of me with a single-tree if I'd spoke to him that way."

"Aw, but that was only foolin'," William temporized.

William was a grizzled man of forty-five, and his wife and grown sons stood in the group, curiously watching Grandfather Tarwater take off his coat and hand it to Mary to hold.

"William—come here," he commanded imperatively.

No matter how reluctantly, William came.

"Just a taste, William, son, of what my father give me often enough," Old Tarwater crooned, as he laid on his son's back and shoulders with the single-tree. "Observe, I ain't hitting you on the head. My father had a gosh-wollickin' temper and never drew the line at heads when he went after tar.—Don't jerk your elbows back that way! You're likely to get a crack on one by accident. And just tell me one thing, William, son: is there any notion in your head that I'm crazy?"

"No!" William yelped out in pain, as he danced about. "You ain't crazy, father! Of course you ain't crazy!"

"You said it," Old Tarwater remarked sententiously, tossing the single-tree aside and starting to struggle into his coat. "Now let's all go in and eat."

THE PRINCESS

A fire burned cheerfully in the jungle camp, and beside the fire lolled a cheerful-seeming though horrible-appearing man. This was a hobo jungle, pitched in a thin strip of woods that lay between a railroad embankment and the bank of a river. But no hobo was the man. So deep-sunk was he in the social abyss that a proper hobo would not sit by the same fire with him. A gay-cat, who is an ignorant newcomer on the "Road," might sit with such as he, but only long enough to learn better. Even low down bindle-stiffs and stew-bums, after a once-over, would have passed this man by. A genuine hobo, a couple of punks, or a bunch of tender-yeared road-kids might have gone through his rags for any stray pennies or nickels and kicked him out into the darkness. Even an alki-stiff would have reckoned himself immeasurably superior.

For this man was that hybrid of tramp-land, an alki-stiff that has degenerated into a stew-bum, with so little self-respect that he will never "boil-up," and with so little pride that he will eat out of a garbage can. He was truly horrible-appearing. He might have been sixty years of age; he might have been ninety. His garments might have been discarded by a rag-picker. Beside him, an unrolled bundle showed itself as consisting of a ragged overcoat and containing an empty and smoke-blackened tomato can, an empty and battered condensed milk can, some dog-meat partly wrapped in brown paper and evidently begged from some butcher-shop, a carrot that had been run over in the street by a wagon-wheel, three greenish-cankered and decayed potatoes, and a sugar-bun with a mouthful bitten from it and rescued from the gutter as was made patent by the gutter-filth that still encrusted it.

A prodigious growth of whiskers, grayish-dirty and untrimmed for years, sprouted from his face. This hirsute growth should have been white, but the season was summer and it had not been exposed to a rain-shower for some time. What was visible of the face looked as if at some period it had stopped a hand-grenade. The nose was so variously malformed in its healed brokenness that there was no bridge, while one nostril, the size of a pea, opened downward, and the other, the size of a robin's egg, tilted upward to the sky. One eye, of normal size, dim-drown and misty, bulged to the verge of popping out, and as if from senility wept copiously and continuously. The other eye, scarcely larger than a squirrel's and as uncannily bright, twisted up obliquely into the hairy scar of a bone-crushed eyebrow. And he had but one arm.

Yet was he cheerful. On his face, in mild degree, was depicted sensuous pleasure as he lethargically scratched his ribs with his one hand. He pawed over his food-scraps, debated, then drew a twelve-ounce druggist's bottle from his inside coat-pocket. The bottle was full of a colorless liquid, the contemplation of which made his little eye burn brighter and quickened his movements. Picking up the tomato can, he arose, went down the short path to the river, and returned with the can filled with not-nice river water. In the condensed milk can he mixed one part of water with two parts of fluid from the bottle. This colorless fluid was druggist's alcohol, and as such is known in tramp-land as "alki."

Slow footsteps, coming down the side of the railroad embankment, alarmed him ere he could drink. Placing the can carefully upon the ground between his legs, he covered it with his hat and waited anxiously whatever impended.

Out of the darkness emerged a man as filthy ragged as he. The newcomer, who might have been fifty, and might have been sixty, was grotesquely fat. He bulged everywhere. He was composed of bulges. His bulbous nose was the size and shape of a turnip. His eyelids bulged and his blue eyes bulged in competition with them. In many places the seams of his garments had parted across the bulges of body. His calves grew into his feet, for the broken elastic sides of his Congress gaiters were swelled full with the fat of him. One arm only he sported, from the shoulder of which was suspended a small and tattered bindle with the mud caked dry on the outer covering from the last place he had pitched his doss. He advanced with tentative caution, made sure of the harmlessness of the man beside the fire, and joined him.

"Hello, grandpa," the newcomer greeted, then paused to stare at the other's flaring, sky-open nostril. "Say, Whiskers, how'd ye keep the night dew out of that nose o' yourn?"

Whiskers growled an incoherence deep in his throat and spat into the fire in token that he was not pleased by the question.

"For the love o' Mike," the fat man chuckled, "if you got caught out in a rainstorm without an umbrella you'd sure drown, wouldn't you?"

"Can it, Fatty, can it," Whiskers muttered wearily. "They ain't nothin' new in that line of chatter. Even the bulls hand it out to me."

"But you can still drink, I hope," Fatty at the same time mollified and invited, with his one hand deftly pulling the slip-knots that fastened his bindle.

From within the bindle he brought to light a twelve-ounce bottle of alki. Footsteps coming down the embankment alarmed him, and he hid the bottle under his hat on the ground between his legs.

But the next comer proved to be not merely one of their own ilk, but likewise to have only one arm. So forbidding of aspect was he that greetings consisted of no more than grunts. Huge-boned, tall, gaunt to cadaverousness, his face a dirty death's head, he was as repellant a nightmare of old age as ever Doré imagined. His toothless, thin-lipped mouth was a cruel and bitter slash under a great curved nose that almost met the chin and that was like a buzzard's beak. His one hand, lean and crooked, was a talon. The beady gray eyes, unblinking and unwavering, were bitter as death, as bleak as absolute zero and as merciless. His presence was a chill, and Whiskers and Fatty instinctively drew together for protection against the unguessed threat of him. Watching his chance, privily, Whiskers snuggled a chunk of rock several pounds in weight close to his hand if need for action should arise. Fatty duplicated the performance.

Then both sat licking their lips, guiltily embarrassed, while the unblinking eyes of the terrible one bored into them, now into one, now into another, and then down at the rock-chunks of their preparedness.

"Huh!" sneered the terrible one, with such dreadfulness of menace as to cause Whiskers and Fatty involuntarily to close their hands down on their cave-man's weapons.

"Huh!" the other repeated, reaching his one talon into his side coat pocket with swift definiteness. "A hell of a chance you two cheap bums 'd have with me."

The talon emerged, clutching ready for action a six-pound iron quoit.

"We ain't lookin' for trouble, Slim," Fatty quavered.

"Who in hell are you to call me 'Slim'?" came the snarling answer.

"Me? I'm just Fatty, an' seein' 's I never seen you before——"

"An' I suppose that's Whiskers, there, with the gay an' festive lamp tangoing into his eyebrow an' the God-forgive-us nose joy-riding all over his mug?"

"It'll do, it'll do," Whiskers muttered uncomfortably. "One monica's as good as another, I find, at my time of life. And everybody hands it out to me anyway. And I need an umbrella when it rains to keep from getting drowned, an' all the rest of it."

"I ain't used to company—don't like it," Slim growled. "So if you guys want to stick around, mind your step, that's all, mind your step."

He fished from his pocket a cigar stump, self-evidently shot from the gutter, and prepared to put it in his mouth to chew. Then he changed his mind, glared at his companions savagely, and unrolled his bindle. Appeared in his hand a druggist's bottle of alki.

"Well," he snarled, "I suppose I gotta give you cheap skates a drink when I ain't got more'n enough for a good petrification for myself."

Almost a softening flicker of light was imminent in his withered face as he beheld the others proudly lift their hats and exhibit their own supplies.

"Here's some water for the mixin's," Whiskers said, proffering his tomato-can of river slush. "Stockyards just above," he added apologetically. "But they say—"

"Huh!" Slim snapped short, mixing the drink. "I've drunk worse'n stockyards in my time."

Yet when all was ready, cans of alki in their solitary hands, the three things that had once been men hesitated, as if of old habit, and next betrayed shame as if at self-exposure.

Whiskers was the first to brazen it.

"I've sat in at many a finer drinking," he bragged.

"With the pewter," Slim sneered.

"With the silver," Whiskers corrected.

Slim turned a scorching eye-interrogation on Fatty.

Fatty nodded.

"Beneath the salt," said Slim.

"Above it," came Fatty's correction. "I was born above it, and I've never traveled second class. First or steerage, but no intermediate in mine."

"Yourself?" Whiskers queried of Slim.

"In broken glass to the Queen, God bless her," Slim answered, solemnly, without snarl or sneer.

"In the pantry?" Fatty insinuated.

Simultaneously Slim reached for his quoit, and Whiskers and Fatty for their rocks.

"Now don't let's get feverish," Fatty said, dropping his own weapon. "We aren't scum. We're gentlemen. Let's drink like gentlemen."

"Let it be a real drinking," Whiskers approved.

"Let's get petrified," Slim agreed. "Many a distillery's flowed under the bridge since we were gentlemen; but let's forget the long road we've traveled since, and hit our doss in the good old fashion in which every gentleman went to bed when we were young."

"My father done it—did it," Fatty concurred and corrected, as old recollections exploded long-sealed brain-cells of connotation and correct usage.

The other two nodded a descent from similar fathers and elevated their tin cans of alcohol.

By the time each had finished his own bottle and from his rags fished forth a second one, their brains were well-mellowed and a-glow, although they had not got around to telling their real names. But their English had improved. They spoke it correctly, while the argo of trampland ceased from their lips.

"It's my constitution," Whiskers was explaining. "Very few men could go through what I have and live to tell the tale. And I never took any care of myself. If what the moralists and the physiologists say were true, I'd have been dead long ago. And it's the same with you two. Look at us, at our advanced years, carousing as the young ones don't dare, sleeping out in the open on the ground, never sheltered from frost nor rain nor storm, never afraid of pneumonia or rheumatism that would put half the young ones on their backs in hospital."

He broke off to mix another drink, and Fatty took up the tale.

"And we've had our fun," he boasted. "And speaking of sweethearts and all," he cribbed from Kipling, " 'We've rogued and we've ranged—' "

" 'In our time,' " Slim completed the crib for him.

"I should say so, I should say so," Fatty confirmed. "And been loved by princesses—at least I have."

"Go on and tell us about it," Whiskers urged. "The night's young, and why shouldn't we remember back to the roofs of kings?"

Nothing loath, Fatty cleared his throat for the recital and cast about in his mind for the best way to begin.

"It must be known that I came of good family. Percival Delaney, let us say, yes, let us say Percival Delaney, was not unknown at Oxford once upon a time—not for scholarship, I am frank to admit; but the gay young dogs of that day, if any be yet alive, would remember him—"

"My people came over with the Conqueror," Whiskers interrupted, extending his hand to Fatty's in acknowledgment of the introduction.

"What name?" Fatty queried. "I did not seem quite to catch it."

"Delarouse, Chauncey Delarouse. The name will serve as well as any."

Both completed the handshake and glanced to Slim.

"Oh, well, while we're about it . . ." Fatty urged.

"Bruce Cadogan Cavendish," Slim growled morosely. "Go on, Percival, with your princesses and the roofs of kings."

"Oh, I was a rare young devil," Percival obliged, "after I played ducks and drakes at home and sported out over the world. And I was some figure of a man before I lost my shape—polo, steeple-chasing, boxing, wrestling, swimming. I won medals at buckjumping in Australia, and I held more than several swimming records from the quarter of a mile up. Women turned their heads to look when I went by. The women! God bless them!"

And Fatty, alias Percival Delaney, a grotesque of manhood, put his bulgy hand to his puffed lips and kissed audibly into the starry vault of the sky.

"And the Princess!" he resumed, with another kiss to the stars. "She was as fine a figure of a woman as I was a man, as high-spirited and courageous, as reckless and dare-devilish. Lord, Lord, in the water she was a mermaid, a sea-goddess. And when it came to blood, beside her I was parvenu. Her royal line traced back into the mists of antiquity.

"She was not a daughter of a fair-skinned folk. Tawny golden was she, with golden-brown eyes, and her hair that fell to her knees was blue-black and straight, with just the curly tendrilly tendency that gives to woman's hair its charm. Oh, there were no kinks in it, any more than were there kinks in the hair of her entire genealogy. For she was Polynesian, glowing, golden, lovely and lovable, royal Polynesian."

Again he paused to kiss his hand to the memory of her, and Slim, alias Bruce Cadogan Cavendish took advantage to interject:

"Huh! Maybe you didn't shine in scholarship, but at least you gleaned a vocabulary out of Oxford."

"And in the South Seas garnered a better vocabulary from the lexicon of Love," Percival was quick on the uptake.

"It was the island of Talofa," he went on, "meaning love, the Isle of Love, and it was her island. Her father, the king, an old man, sat on his mats with paralyzed knees and drank square-face gin all day and most of the night, out of grief, sheer grief. She, my princess, was the only issue, her brothers having been lost in their double canoe in a hurricane while coming up from a voyage to Samoa. And among the Polynesians the royal women have equal right with the men to rule. In fact, they trace their genealogies always by the female line."

To this both Chauncey Delarouse and Bruce Cadogan Cavendish nodded prompt affirmation.

"Ah," said Percival, "I perceive you both know the South Seas, wherefore, without undue expenditure of verbiage on my part, I am assured that you will appreciate the charm of my princess, the Princess Tui-nui of Talofa, the Princess of the Isle of Love."

He kissed his hand to her, sipped from his condensed milk can a man-size drink of druggist's alcohol, and to her again kissed his hand.

"But she was coy, and ever she fluttered near to me but never near enough. When my arm went out to her to girdle her, presto, she was not there. I knew, as never before, nor since, the thousand dear and delightful anguishes of love frustrate but ever resilient and beckoned on by the very goddess of love."

"Some vocabulary," Bruce Cadogan Cavendish muttered in aside to Chauncey Delarouse. But Percival Delaney was not to be deterred. He kissed his pudgy hand aloft into the night and held warmly on.

"No fond agonies of rapture deferred that were not lavished upon me by my dear Princess, herself ever a luring delight of promise flitting just beyond my reach. Every sweet lover's inferno unguessed of by Dante she led me through. Ah! Those tropic nights! Those swooning tropic nights, under our palm trees, the distant surf a languorous murmur as from some vast sea shell of mystery, when she, my Princess, all but melted to my yearning, and with her laughter, that was as silver strings by buds and blossoms smitten, all but made lunacy of my lover's ardency.

"It was by my wrestling with the champions of Talofa that I first interested her. It was by my prowess at swimming that I awoke her. And it was by a certain swimming deed that I won from her more than coquettish smiles and shy timidities of feigned retreat.

"We were squidding that day, out on the reef—you know how, un-doubtedly, diving down the face of the wall of the reef, five fathoms, ten fathoms, any depth within reason, and shoving our squid-sticks into the likely holes and crannies of the coral where squid might be lairing. With the squid-stick, bluntly sharp at both ends, perhaps a foot long, and held crosswise in the hand, the trick was to gouge any lazying squid until he closed his tentacles around fist, stick, and arm. Then you had him, and came to the surface with him, and bit him in the head which is in the center of him, and peeled him off into the waiting canoe. . . . And to think I used to do that!"

Percival Delaney paused a moment, a glimmer of awe on his rotund face, as he contemplated the mighty picture of his youth.

"Why, I've pulled out a squid, with tentacles eight feet long, and done it under fifty feet of water. I could stay down four minutes. I've gone down, with a coral-rock to sink me, in a hundred and ten feet to clear a fouled anchor. And I could back-dive with a once-over and go in feet-first from eighty feet above the surface—"

"Quit it, delete it, cease it," Chauncey Delarouse admonished testily. "Tell of the Princess. That's what makes old blood leap again. Almost can I see her. Was she very wonderful?"

Percival Delaney kissed unutterable affirmation.

"I have said she was a mermaid. She was. I know she swam thirty-six hours before being rescued, after her schooner was capsized in a double-squall. I have seen her do ninety feet and bring up pearl shell in each hand. She *was* wonderful. As a woman she was ravishing, sublime. I have said she was a sea-goddess. She was. Oh, for a Phidias or a Praxiteles to have made the wonder of her body immortal!

"And that day, out for squid on the reef, I was almost sick for her. Mad—I know I was mad for her. We would step over the side from the big canoe, and swim down, side by side, into the delicious depths of cool and color, and she would look at me, as we swam, and with her eyes tantalize me to further madness. And at last, down, far down, I lost myself and reached for her. She eluded me like the mermaid she was, and I saw the laughter on her face as she fled. She fled deeper, and I knew I had her for I was between her and the surface; but in the muck coral sand of the bottom she made a churning with her squid stick. It was the old trick to escape a shark. And she worked it on me, roiling the water so that I could not see her. And when I came up, she was there ahead of me, clinging to the side of the canoe and laughing.

"Almost I would not be denied. But not for nothing was she a princess. She rested her hand on my arm and compelled me to listen. We should play a game, she said, enter into a competition for which should get the more squid, the biggest squid, and the smallest squid. Since the wagers were kisses, you can well imagine I went down on the first next dive with soul aflame.

"I got no squid. Never again in all my life have I dived for squid. Perhaps we were five fathoms down and exploring the face of the reef-wall for lurking places of our prey, when it happened. I had found a likely lair and just proved it empty, when I felt or sensed the nearness of something inimical. I turned. There it was, alongside of me, and no mere fish-shark. Fully a dozen feet in length, with the unmistakable phosphorescent cat's eye gleaming like a drowning star, I knew it for what it was, a tiger shark.

"Not ten feet to the right, probing a coral fissure with her squid stick, was the Princess, and the tiger shark was heading directly for her. My totality of thought was precipitated to consciousness in a single all-embracing flash. The man-eater must be deflected from her, and what was I, except a mad lover who would gladly fight and die, or more gladly fight and live, for his beloved? Remember, she was the woman wonderful, and I was aflame for her.

"Knowing fully the peril of my act, I thrust the blunt-sharp end of my squid-stick into the side of the shark, much as one would attract a passing acquaintance with a thumb-nudge in the ribs. And the man-eater turned on me. You know the South Seas, and you know that the tiger shark, like the bald-face grizzly of Alaska, never gives trail. The combat, fathoms deep under the sea, was on—if by combat may be named such a one-sided struggle.

"The Princess, unaware, caught her squid and rose to the surface. The man-eater rushed me. I fended him off with both hands on his nose above his thousand-toothed open mouth, so that he backed me against the sharp coral. The scars are there to this day. Whenever I tried to rise, he rushed me, and I could not remain down there indefinitely without air. Whenever he rushed me, I fended off with my hands on his nose. And I would have escaped unharmed, except for the slip of my right hand. Into his mouth it went to the elbow. His jaws closed, just below the elbow. You know how a shark's teeth are. Once in they cannot be released. They must go through to complete the bite, but they cannot go through heavy bone. So, from just below the elbow he stripped the bone clean to the articulation of the wrist-joint, where his teeth met and my good right hand became his for an appetizer.

"But while he was doing this, I drove the thumb of my left hand, to the hilt, into his eye-orifice and popped out his eye. This did not stop him. The meat had maddened him. He pursued the gushing stump of my wrist. Half a dozen times I fended with my intact arm. Then he got the poor mangled arm again, closed down, and stripped the meat off the bone from the shoulder down to the elbow-joint, where his teeth met and he was free of his second mouthful of me. But, at the same time, with my good arm, I thumbed out his remaining eye."

Percival Delaney shrugged his shoulders, ere he resumed.

"From above, those in the canoe had beheld the entire happening and were loud in praise of my deed. To this day they still sing the song of me, and tell the tale of me. And the Princess." His pause was brief but significant. "The Princess married me. . . . Oh, well-a-day and lack-a-day, the whirligig of time and fortune, the topsy-turviness of luck, the wooden shoe going up and the polished heel descending, a French gunboat, a conquered island-kingdom of Oceania, to-day ruled over by a peasant-born, unlettered, colonial gendarme, and . . ."

He completed the sentence and the tale by burying his face in the down-tilted mouth of the condensed milk can and by gurgling the corrosive drink down his throat in thirsty gulps.

*   *   *

After an appropriate pause, Chauncey Delarouse, otherwise Whiskers, took up the tale.

"Far be it from me to boast of no matter what place of birth I have descended from to sit here by this fire with such as ... as chance along. I may say, however, that I, too, was once a considerable figure of a man. I may add that it was horses, plus parents too indulgent, that exiled me out over the world. I may still wonder to query: 'Are Dover's cliffs still white?'"

"Huh!" Bruce Cadogan Cavendish sneered. "Next you'll be asking 'how fares the old Lord Warden'?"

"And I took every liberty, and vainly, with a constitution that was iron," Whiskers hurried on. "Here I am with my three score and ten behind me, and back on that long road have I buried many a youngster that was as rare and devilish as I but who could not stand the pace. I knew the worst too young. And now I know the worst too old. But there was a time, alas all too short, when I knew the best.

"I, too, kiss my hand to the Princess of my heart. She was truly a princess, Polynesian, a thousand miles and more away to the eastward and the south from Delaney's Isle of Love. The natives of all around that part of the South Seas called it the Jolly Island. Their own name, the name of the people who dwelt thereon, translates delicately and justly into 'The Island of Tranquil Laughter.' On the chart you will find the erroneous name given to it by the old navigators to be Manatomana. The seafaring gentry the round ocean around called it the Adamless Eden. And the missionaries for a time called it God's Witness—so great had been their success at converting the inhabitants. As for me, it was, and ever shall be, Paradise.

"It was *my* Paradise, for it was there my Princess lived. John Asibeli Tungi was king. He was full-blooded native, descended out of the oldest and highest chief-stock that traced back to Manua which was the primeval sea home of the race. Also was he known as John the Apostate. He lived a long life and apostasized frequently. First converted by the Catholics, he threw down the idols, broke the tabus, cleaned out the native priests, executed a few of the recalcitrant ones, and sent all his subjects to church.

"Next he fell for the traders, who developed in him a champagne thirst, and he shipped off the Catholic priests to New Zealand. The great majority of his subjects always followed his lead, and, having no religion at all, ensued the time of the Great Licentiousness, when by all South Seas Missionaries his island, in sermons, was spoken of as Babylon.

"But the traders ruined his digestion with too much champagne, and after several years he fell for the Gospel according to the Methodists, sent his people to church, and cleaned up the beach and the trading crowd so spick and span that he would not permit them to smoke a pipe out of doors on Sunday, and fined one of the chief traders one hundred gold sovereigns for washing his schooner's decks on the Sabbath morn.

"That was the time of the Blue Laws, but perhaps it was too rigorous for King John. Off he packed the Methodists, one fine day, exiled several hundred of his people to Samoa for sticking to Methodism, and, of all things, invented a religion of his own, with himself the figurehead of worship. In this he was aided and abetted by a renegade Fijian. This lasted five years. Maybe he grew tired of being God, or maybe it was because the Fijian decamped with the six thousand pounds in the royal treasury; but at any rate the Second Reformed Wesleyans got him, and his entire kingdom went Wesleyan. The pioneer Wesleyan missionary he actually made prime minister, and what he did to the trading crowd was a caution. Why, in the end, King John's kingdom was blacklisted and boycotted by the traders till the revenues diminished to zero, the people went bankrupt, and King John couldn't borrow a shilling from his most powerful chief.

"By this time he was getting old, and philosophic, and tolerant, and spiritually atavistic. He fired out the Second Reformed Wesleyans, called back the exiles from Samoa, invited in the traders, held a general love-fest, took the lid off, proclaimed religious liberty and high tariff, and as for himself went back to the worship of his ancestors, dug up the idols, reinstated a few octogenarian priests, and observed the tabus. All of which was lovely for the traders, and prosperity reigned. Of course, most of his subjects followed him back into the heathen worship. Yet quite a sprinkling of Catholics, Methodists and Wesleyans remained true to their beliefs and managed to maintain a few squalid, one-horse churches. But King John didn't mind, any more than did he the high times of the traders along the beach. Everything went, so long as the taxes were paid. Even when his wife, Queen Mamare, elected to become a Baptist, and invited in a little, weazened, sweet-spirited, club-footed Baptist missionary, King John did not object. All he insisted on was that these wandering religions should be self-supporting and not feed a pennyworth's out of the royal coffers.

"And now the threads of my recital draw together in the paragon of female exquisiteness—my Princess."

Whiskers paused, placed carefully on the round his half-full condensed milk can with which he had been absently toying, and kissed the fingers of his one hand audibly aloft.

"She was the daughter of Queen Mamare. She was the woman wonderful. Unlike the Diana type of Polynesian, she was almost ethereal. She *was* ethereal, sublimated by purity, as shy and modest as a violet, as fragile-slender as a lily, and her eyes, luminous and shrinking tender, were as asphodels on the sward of heaven. She was all flower, and fire, and dew. Hers was the sweetness of the mountain rose, the gentleness of the dove. And she was all of good as well as all of beauty, devout in her belief in her mother's worship, which was the worship introduced by Ebenezer Naismith, the Baptist missionary. But make no mistake. She was no mere sweet spirit ripe for the bosom of Abraham. All of exquisite deliciousness of woman was she. She was woman, all woman, to the last sensitive, quivering atom of her—

"And I? I was a wastrel of the beach. The wildest was not so wild as I, the keenest not so keen, of all that wild, keen trading crowd. It was esteemed I played the stiffest hand of poker. I was the only living man, white, brown, or black, who dared run the Kuni-kuni Passage in the dark. And on a black night I have done it under reefs in a gale of wind. Well, anyway, I had a bad reputation on a beach where there were no good reputations. I was reckless, dangerous, stopped at nothing in fight or frolic; and the trading captains used to bring boiler-sheeted prodigies from the vilest holes of the South Pacific to try and drink me under the table. I remember one, a calcined Scotchman from the New Hebrides. It was a great drinking. He died of it, and we laded him aboard ship, pickled in a cask of trade rum, and sent him back to his own place. A sample, a fair sample, of the antic tricks we cut up on the beach of Manatomana.

"And of all unthinkable things, what did I up and do, one day, but look upon the Princess to find her good and to fall in love with her. It was the real thing. I was as mad as a March hare, and after that I got only madder. I reformed. Think of that! Think of what a slip of a woman can do to a lusty, roving man! By the Lord Harry, it's true. I reformed. I went to church. Hear me! I became converted. I cleared my soul before God and kept my hands—I had two then—off the ribald crew of the beach when it laughed at this, my latest antic, and wanted to know what was my game.

"I tell you I reformed, and gave myself in passion and sincerity to a religious experience that has made me tolerant of all religion ever since. I discharged my best captain for immorality. So did I my cook, and a better never boiled water in Manatomana. For the same reason I discharged my chief clerk. And for the first time in the history of trading my schooners to the westward carried bibles in their stock. I built a little anchorite bungalow up town on a mango-lined street squarely alongside the little house occupied by Ebenezer Naismith. And I made him my pal and comrade, and found him a veritable honey pot of sweetnesses and goodnesses. And he was a man, through and through a man. And he died long after like a man, which I would like to tell you about, were the tale of it not so deservedly long.

"It was the Princess, more than the missionary, who was responsible for my expressing my faith in works, and especially in that crowning work, the New Church, Our Church, the Queen-mother's church.

" 'Our poor church,' she said to me, one night after prayer-meeting. I had been converted only a fortnight. 'It is so small, its congregation can never grow. And the roof leaks. And King John, my hard-hearted father, will not contribute a penny. Yet he has a big balance in the treasury. And Manatomana is not poor. Much money is made and squandered. I know. I hear the gossip of the wild ways of the beach. Less than a month ago you lost more in one night, gambling at cards, than the cost of the upkeep of our poor church for a year.'

"And I told her it was true, but that it was before I had seen the light. (I'd had an infernal run of bad luck.) I told her I had not tasted liquor since, nor turned a card. I told her that the roof would be repaired at once, by Christian carpenters selected by her from the congregation. But she was filled with the thought of a great revival that Ebenezer Naismith could preach—she was a dear saint; and she spoke of a great church, saying:

" 'You are rich. You have many schooners, and traders in far islands, and I have heard of a great contract you have signed to recruit labor for the German plantations of Upolu. They say, next to Sweitzer, you are the richest trader here. I should love to see some use of all this money placed to the glory of God. It would be a noble thing to do, and I should be proud to know the man who would do it.'

"I told her that Ebenezer Naismith would preach the revival, and that I would build a church great enough in which to house it.

" 'As big as the Catholic church?' she asked.

"This was the ruined cathedral, built at the time when the entire population was converted, and it was a large order; but I was afire with love, and I told her that the church I would build would be even bigger.

" 'But it will take money,' I explained. 'And it takes time to make money.'

" 'You have much,' she said. 'Some say you have more money than my father, the King.'

" 'I have more credit,' I explained. 'But you do not understand money. It takes money to have credit. So, with the money I have, and the credit I have, I will work to make more money and credit, and the church shall be built.'

"Work! I was a surprise to myself. It is an amazement, the amount of time a man finds on his hands after he's given up carousing, and gambling, and all the time-eating diversions of the beach. And I didn't waste a second of all my new-found time. Instead I worked it over time. I did the work of half a dozen men. I became a driver. My captains made faster runs than ever and earned bigger bonuses, as did my supercargoes, who saw to it that my schooners did not loaf and dawdle along the way. And I saw to it that my supercargoes did see to it.

"And good! By the Lord Harry, I was so good it hurt. My conscience got so expansive and fine-strung it lamed me across the shoulders to carry it around with me. Why, I even went back over my accounts and paid Sweitzer fifty quid I'd jiggered him out of in a deal in Fiji three years before. And I compounded the interest as well.

"Work! I planted sugar cane—the first commercial planting on Manatomana. I ran in cargoes of kinky-heads from Malaita, which is in the Solomons, till I had twelve hundred of the blackbirds putting in cane. And I sent a schooner clear to Hawaii to bring back a dismantled sugar mill and a German who said he knew the field-end of cane. And he did, and he charged me three hundred dollars screw a month, and I took hold of the mill-end. I installed the mill myself, with the help of several mechanics I brought up from Queensland.

"Of course there was a rival. His name was Motomoe. He was the very highest chief blood next to King John's. He was full native, a strapping, handsome man, with a glowering way of showing his dislikes. He certainly glowered at me when I began hanging around the palace. He went back in my history and circulated the blackest tales about me. The worst of it was that most of them were true. He even made a voyage to Apia to find things out—as if he couldn't find a plenty right there on the beach of Manatomana! And he sneered at my falling for religion, and at my going to prayer-meeting, and, most of all, at my sugar-planting. He challenged me to fight, and I kept off of him. He threatened me, and I learned in the nick of time of his plan to have me knocked on the head. You see, he wanted the Princess just as much as I did, and I wanted her more.

"She used to play the piano. So did I, once. But I never let her know after I'd heard her play the first time. And she thought her playing was wonderful, the dear, fond girl! You know the sort, the mechanical one-two-three, tum-tum-tum school-girl stuff. And now I'll tell you something funnier. Her playing *was* wonderful, to me. The gates of heaven opened to me when she played. I can see myself now, worn out and dog-tired after the long day, lying on the mats of the palace veranda and gazing upon her at the piano, myself in a perfect idiocy of bliss. Why, this idea she had of her fine playing was the one flaw in her deliciousness of perfection, and I loved her for it. It kind of brought her within my human reach. Why, when she played her one-two-three, tum-tum-tum, I was in the seventh heaven of bliss. My weariness fell from me. I loved her, and my love for her was clean as flame, clean as my love for God. And do you know, into my fond lover's fancy continually intruded the thought that God in most ways must look like her.

"—That's right, Bruce Cadogan Cavendish, sneer as you like. But I tell you that's love that I've been describing. That's all. It's love. It's the realest, purest, finest thing that can happen to a man. And I know what I'm talking about. It happened to me."

Whiskers, his beady squirrel's eye glittering from out his ruined eyebrow like a live coal in a jungle ambush, broke off long enough to down a sedative draught from his condensed milk can and to mix another.

"The cane," he resumed, wiping his prodigious mat of face hair with the back of his hand. "It matured in sixteen months in that climate, and I was ready, just ready and no more, with the mill for the grinding. Naturally, it did not all mature at once, but I had planted in such succession that I could grind for nine months steadily, while more was being planted and the ratoons were springing up.

"I had my troubles the first several days. If it wasn't one thing the matter with the mill, it was another. On the fourth day, Ferguson, my engineer, had to shut down several hours in order to remedy his own troubles. I was bothered by the feeder. After having the niggers (who had been feeding the cane) pour cream of lime on the rollers to keep everything sweet, I sent them out to join the cane-cutting squads. So I was all alone at that end, just as Ferguson started up the mill, just as I discovered what was the matter with the feed-rollers, and just as Motomoe strolled up.

"He stood there, in Norfolk jacket, pigskin puttees, and all the rest of the fashionable get-up out of a bandbox, sneering at me covered with filth and grease to the eyebrows and looking like a navvy. And, the rollers now white from the lime, I'd just seen what was wrong. The rollers were not in plumb. One side crushed the cane well, but the other side was too open. I shoved my fingers in on that side. The big, toothed cogs on the rollers did not touch my fingers. And yet, suddenly, they did. With the grip of ten thousand devils, my finger-tips were caught, drawn in, and pulped to—well, just pulp. And, like a stick of cane, I had started on my way. There was no stopping me. Ten thousand horses could not have pulled me back. There was nothing to stop me. Hand, arm, shoulder, head, and chest, down to the toes of me, I was doomed to feed through.

"It did hurt. It hurt so much it did not hurt at all. Quite detached, almost may I say, I looked on my hand being ground up, knuckle by knuckle, joint by joint, the back of the hand, the wrist, the forearm, all in order slowly and inevitably feeding in. O engineer hoist by thine own petard! O sugar-maker crushed by thine own cane-crusher!

"Motomoe sprang forward involuntarily, and the sneer was chased from his face by an expression of solicitude. Then the beauty of the situation dawned on him, and he chuckled and grinned. No, I didn't expect anything of him. Hadn't he tried to knock me on the head? What could he do anyway? He didn't know anything about engines.

"I yelled at the top of my lungs to Ferguson to shut off the engine, but the roar of the machinery drowned my voice. And there I stood, up to the elbow and feeding right on in. Yes, it did hurt. There were some astonishing twinges when special nerves were shredded and dragged out by the roots. But I remember that I was surprised at the time that it did not hurt worse.

"Motomoe made a movement that attracted my attention. At the same time he growled out loud, as if he hated himself, 'I'm a fool.' What he had done was to pick up a cane-knife—you know the kind, as big as a machete and as heavy. And I was grateful to him in advance for putting me out of my misery. There wasn't any sense in slowly feeding in till my head was crushed, and already my arm was pulped half way from elbow to shoulder, and the pulping was going right on. So I was grateful, as I bent my head to the blow.

" 'Get your head out of the way, you idiot!' he barked at me.

"And then I understood and obeyed. I was a big man, and he took two hacks to do it; but he hacked my arm off just outside the shoulder and dragged me back and laid me down on the cane.

"Yes, the sugar paid—enormously; and I built for the Princess the church of her saintly dream, and ... she married me."

He partly assuaged his thirst, and uttered his final word.

"Alackaday! Shuttlecock and battledore. And this at the end of it all, lined with boiler-plate that even alcohol will not corrode and that only alcohol will tickle. Yet have I lived, and I kiss my hand to the dear dust of my Princess long asleep in the great mausoleum of King John that looks across the Vale of Manona to the alien flag that floats over the bungalow of the British Government House. . . ."

Fatty pledged him sympathetically, and sympathetically drank out of his own small can. Bruce Cadogan Cavendish glared into the fire with implacable bitterness. He was a man who preferred to drink by himself. Across the thin lips that composed the cruel slash of his mouth played twitches of mockery that caught Fatty's eye. And Fatty, making sure first that his rock-chunk was within reach, challenged.

"Well, how about yourself, Bruce Cadogan Cavendish? It's your turn."

The other lifted bleak eyes that bored into Fatty's until he physically betrayed uncomfortableness.

"I've lived a hard life," Slim grated harshly. "What do I know about love passages?"

"No man of your build and make-up could have escaped them," Fatty wheedled.

"And what of it?" Slim snarled. "It's no reason for a gentleman to boast of amorous triumphs."

"Oh, go on, be a good fellow," Fatty urged. "The night's still young. We've still some drink left. Delarouse and I have contributed our share. It isn't often that three real ones like us get together for a telling. Surely you've got at least one adventure in love you aren't ashamed to tell about—"

Bruce Cadogan Cavendish pulled forth his iron quoit and seemed to debate whether or not he should brain the other. He sighed, and put back the quoit.

"Very well, if you will have it," he surrendered with manifest reluctance. "Like you two, I have had a remarkable constitution. And right now, speaking of armor-plate lining, I could drink the both of you down when you were at your prime. Like you two, my beginnings were far distant and different. That I am marked with the hall-mark of gentlehood there is no discussion ... unless either of you cares to discuss the matter now ..."

His one hand slipped into his pocket and clutched the quoit. Neither of his auditors spoke nor betrayed any awareness of his menace.

"It occurred a thousand miles to the westward of Manatomana, on the island of Tagalag," he continued abruptly, with an air of saturnine disappointment in that there had been no discussion. "But first I must tell you of how I got to Tagalag. For reasons I shall not mention, by paths of descent I shall not describe, in the crown of my manhood and the prime of my devilishness in which Oxford renegades and racing younger sons had nothing on me, I found myself master and owner of a schooner so well known that she shall remain historically nameless. I was running blackbird labor from the West South Pacific and the Coral Sea to the plantations of Hawaii and the nitrate mines of Chili—"

"It was you who cleaned out the entire population of—" Fatty exploded, ere he could check his speech.

The one hand of Bruce Cadogan Cavendish flashed pocketward and flashed back with the quoit balanced ripe for business.

"Proceed," Fatty sighed. "I ... I have quite forgotten what I was going to say."

"Beastly funny country over that way," the narrator drawled with perfect casualness. "You've read this Sea Wolf stuff—"

"You weren't the Sea Wolf," Whiskers broke in with involuntary positiveness.

"No, sir," was the snarling answer. "The Sea Wolf's dead, isn't he? And I'm still alive, aren't I?"

"Of course, of course," Whiskers conceded. "He suffocated head-first in the mud off a wharf in Victoria a couple of years back."

"As I was saying—and I don't like interruptions," Bruce Cadogan Cavendish proceeded, "it's a beastly funny country over that way. I was at Taki-Tiki, a low island that politically belongs to the Solomons, but that geologically doesn't at all, for the Solomons are high islands. Ethnographically it belongs to Polynesia, Melanesia, and Micronesia, because all the breeds of the South Pacific have gravitated to it by canoe-drift and intricately, degeneratively, and amazingly interbred. The scum of the scrapings of the bottom of the human pit, biologically speaking, resides in Taki-Tiki. And I know the bottom and whereof I speak.

"It was a beastly funny time of it I had, diving out shell, fishing beche-de-mer, trading hoop-iron and hatchets for copra and ivory-nuts, running niggers and all the rest of it. Why, even in Fiji the Lotu was having a hard time of it and the chiefs still eating long-pig. To the westward it was fierce—funny little black kinky-heads, man-eaters the last Jack of them, and the jackpot fat and spilling over with wealth—"

"Jack-pots?" Fatty queried. At sight of an irritable movement, he added: "You see, I never got over to the West like Delarouse and you."

"They're all head-hunters. Heads are valuable, especially a whiteman's head. They decorate the canoe-houses and devil-devil houses with them. Each village runs a jack-pot, and everybody antes. Whoever brings in a whiteman's head takes the pot. If there aren't openers for a long time, the pot grows to tremendous proportions. Beastly funny, isn't it?

"I know. Didn't a Holland mate die on me of blackwater? And didn't I win a pot myself? It was this way. We were lying at Lango-lui at the time. I never let on, and arranged the affair with Johnny, my boat-steerer. He was a kinky-head himself from Port Moresby. He cut the dead mate's head off and sneaked ashore in the night, while I whanged away with my rifle as if I were trying to get him. He opened the pot with the mate's head, and got it, too. Of course, next day I sent in a landing boat, with two covering boats, and fetched him off with the loot."

"How big was the pot?" Whiskers asked. "I heard of a pot at Orla worth eighty quid."

"To commence with," Slim answered, "there were forty fat pigs, each worth a fathom of prime shell-money, and shell-money worth a quid a fathom. That was two hundred dollars right there. There were ninety-eight fathoms of shell-money, which is pretty close to five hundred in itself. And there were twenty-two gold sovereigns. I split it four ways: one-fourth to Johnny, one-fourth to the ship, one-fourth to me as owner, and one-fourth to me as skipper. Johnny never complained. He'd never had so much wealth all at one time in his life. Besides, I gave him a couple of the mate's old shirts. And I fancy the mate's head is still there decorating the canoe-house."

"Not exactly Christian burial of a Christian," Whiskers observed.

"But a lucrative burial," Slim retorted. "I had to feed the rest of the mate overside to the sharks for nothing. Think of feeding an eight-hundred-dollar head along with it. It would have been criminal waste and stark lunacy.

"Well, anyway, it was all beastly funny, over there to the westward. And, without telling you the scrape I got into at Taki-Tiki, except that I sailed away with two hundred kinky-heads for Queensland labor, and for my manner of collecting them had two British ships of war combing the Pacific for me, I changed my course and ran to the westward thinking to dispose of the lot to the Spanish plantations on Bangar.

"Typhoon season. We caught it. The *Merry Mist* was my schooner's name, and I had thought she was stoutly built until she hit that typhoon. I never saw such seas. They pounded that stout craft to pieces, literally so. The sticks were jerked out of her, deckhouses splintered to match-wood, rails ripped off, and, after the worst had passed, the covering boards began to go. We just managed to repair what was left of one boat and keep the schooner afloat only till the sea went down barely enough to get away. And we outfitted that boat in a hurry. The carpenter and I were the last, and we had to jump for it as she went down. There were only four of us—"

"Lost all the niggers?" Whiskers inquired.

"Some of them swam for some time," Slim replied. "But I don't fancy they made the land. We were ten days in doing it. And we had a spanking breeze most of the way. And what do you think we had in the boat with us? Cases of square-face gin and cases of dynamite. Funny, wasn't it? Well, it got funnier later on. Oh, there was a small breaker of water, a little salt horse, and some salt-water-soaked sea biscuit—enough to keep us alive to Tagalag.

"Now Tagalag is the disappointingest island I've ever beheld. It shows up out of the sea so as you can make its fall twenty miles off. It is a volcano cone thrust up out of deep sea, with a segment of the crater wall broken out. This gives sea entrance to the crater itself, and makes a fine sheltered harbor. And that's all. Nothing lives there. The outside and the inside of the crater are too steep. At one place, inside, is a patch of about a thousand coconut palms. And that's all, as I said, saving a few insects. No four-legged thing, even a rat, inhabits the place. And it's funny, most awful funny, with all those coconuts, not even a coconut crab. The only meat-food living was schools of mullet in the harbor—fattest, finest, biggest mullet I ever laid eyes on.

"And the four of us landed on the little beach and set up housekeeping among the coconuts with a larder full of dynamite and square-face. Why don't you laugh? It's funny, I tell you. Try it some time—Holland gin and straight coconut diet. I've never been able to look a confectioner's window in the face since. Now I'm not strong on religion like Chauncey Delarouse there, but I have some primitive ideas; and my concept of hell is an illimitable coconut plantation, stocked with cases of square-face and populated by ship-wrecked mariners. Funny? It must make the devil scream.

"You know, straight coconut is what the agriculturalists call an unbalanced ration. It certainly unbalanced our digestions. We got so that whenever hunger took an extra bite at us, we took another drink of gin. After a couple of weeks of it, Olaf, a squarehead sailor, got an idea. It came when he was full of gin, and we, being in the same fix, just watched him shove a cap and short fuse into a stick of dynamite and stroll down toward the boat.

"It dawned on me that he was going to shoot fish if there were any about; but the sun was beastly hot, and I just reclined there and hoped he'd have luck.

"About half an hour after he disappeared, we heard the explosion. But he didn't come back. We waited till the cool of sunset, and down on the beach found what had become of him. The boat was there all right, grounded by the prevailing breeze, but there was no Olaf. He would never have to eat coconut again. We went back, shakier than ever, and cracked another square-face.

The next day the cook announced that he would rather take his chance with dynamite than continue trying to exist on coconut, and that, though he didn't know anything about dynamite, he knew a sight too much about coconut. So we bit the detonator down for him, shoved in a fuse, and picked him a good fire-stick, while he jolted up with a couple more stiff ones of gin.

"It was the same program as the day before. After a while we heard the explosion and at twilight went down to the boat, from which we scraped enough of the cook for a funeral.

"The carpenter and I stuck it out two days more, then we drew straws for it and it was his turn. We parted with harsh words; for he wanted to take a square-face along to refresh himself by the way, while I was set against running any chance of wasting the gin. Besides, he had more than he could carry then, and he wobbled and staggered as he walked.

"Same thing, only there was a whole lot of him left for me to bury, because he'd prepared only half a stick. I managed to last it out till next day, when, after duly fortifying myself, I got sufficient courage to tackle the dynamite. I used only a third of a stick—you know, short fuse, with the end split so as to hold the head of a safety match. That's where I mended my predecessors' methods. Not using the match-head, they'd too-long fuses. Therefore, when they spotted a school of mullet and lighted the fuse, they had to hold the dynamite till the fuse burned short before they threw it. If they threw it too soon, it wouldn't go off the instant it hit the water, while the splash of it would frighten the mullet away. Funny stuff dynamite. At any rate, I still maintain mine was the safer method.

"I picked up a school of mullet before I'd been rowing five minutes. Fine big fat ones they were, and I could smell them over the fire. When I stood up, fire-stick in one hand, dynamite stick in the other, my knees were knocking together. Maybe it was the gin, or the anxiousness, or the weakness and the hunger, and maybe it was the result of all of them, but at any rate I was all of a shake. Twice I failed to touch the fire-stick to the dynamite. Then I did, heard the match-head splutter, and let her go.

"Now I don't know what happened to the others, but I know what I did. I got turned about. Did you ever stem a strawberry and throw the strawberry away and pop the stem into your mouth? That's what I did. I threw the fire-stick into the water after the mullet and held onto the dynamite. And my arm went off with the stick when it went off. . . ."

Slim investigated the tomato-can for water to mix himself a drink, but found it empty. He stood up.

"Heigh ho," he yawned, and started down the path to the river.

In several minutes he was back. He mixed the due quantity of river slush with the alcohol, took a long, solitary drink, and stared with bitter moodiness into the fire.

"Yes, but . . ." Fatty suggested. "What happened then?"

"Oh," said Slim. "Then the princess married me, of course."

"But you were the only person left, and there wasn't any princess ..." Whiskers cried out abruptly, and then let his voice trail away to embarrassed silence.

Slim stared unblinkingly into the fire.

Percival Delaney and Chauncey Delarouse looked at each other. Quietly, in solemn silence, each with his one arm aided the one arm of the other in rolling and tying his bindle. And in silence, bindles slung on shoulders, they went away out of the circle of fire-light. Not until they reached the top of the railroad embankment did they speak.

"No gentleman would have done it," said Whiskers.

"No gentleman would have done it," Fatty agreed.

THE WATER BABY

I lent a weary ear to old Kohokumu's interminable chanting of the deeds and adventures of Maui, the Promethean demigod of Polynesia who fished up dry land from ocean depths with hooks made fast to heaven, who lifted up the sky whereunder previously men had gone on all fours, not having space to stand erect, and who made the sun with its sixteen snared legs stand still and agree thereafter to traverse the sky more slowly—the sun being evidently a trade-unionist and believing in the six-hour day, while Maui stood for the open shop and the twelve-hour day.

"Now this," said Kohokumu, "is from Queen Liliuokalani's own family mele:

> *"'Maui became restless and fought the sun*
> *With a noose that he laid.*
> *And winter won the sun,*
> *And summer was won by Maui. . . .'"*

Born in the Islands myself, I know the Hawaiian myths better than this old fisherman, although I possessed not his memorization that enabled him to recite them endless hours.

"And you believe all this?" I demanded in the sweet Hawaiian tongue.

"It was a long time ago," he pondered. "I never saw Maui with my own eyes. But all our old men from all the way back tell us these things, as I, an old man, tell them to my sons and grandsons all the way ahead to come."

"You believe," I persisted, "that whopper of Maui roping the sun like a wild steer, and that other whopper of heaving up the sky from off the earth?"

"I am of little worth, and am not wise, O Lakana," my fisherman made answer. "Yet have I read the Hawaiian bible the missionaries translated to us, and there have I read that your Big Man of the Beginning made the earth and sky and sun and moon and stars, and all manner of animals from horses to cockroaches and from centipedes and mosquitoes to sea lice and jellyfish, and man and woman and everything, and all in six days. Why, Maui didn't do anything like that much. He didn't *make* anything. He just put things in order, that was all, and it took him a long, long time to make the improvements. And anyway, it is much easier and more reasonable to believe the little whopper than the big whopper."

And what could I reply? He had me on the matter of reasonableness. Besides, my head ached. And the funny thing, as I admitted to myself, was that evolution teaches in no uncertain voice that man did run on all fours ere he came to walk upright, that astronomy states flatly that the speed of the revolution of the earth on its axis has diminished steadily, thus increasing the length of day, and that the seismologists accept that all the islands of Hawaii were elevated from the ocean floor by volcanic action.

Fortunately, I saw a bamboo pole, floating on the surface several hundred feet away, suddenly up-end and start a very devil's dance. This was a diversion from the profitless discussion, and Kohokumu and I dipped our paddles and raced the little outrigger canoe to the dancing pole. Kohokumu caught the line that was fast to the butt of the pole and underhanded it in until a two-foot *ukikiki*, battling fiercely to the end, flashed its wet silver in the sun and began beating a tattoo on the inside bottom of the canoe. Kohokumu picked up a squirming, slimy squid, with his teeth bit a chunk of live bait out of it, attached the bait to the hook, and dropped line and sinker overside. The stick floated flat on the surface of the water, and the canoe drifted slowly away. With a survey of the crescent composed of a score of such sticks all lying flat, Kohokumu wiped his hands on his naked sides and lifted the wearisome and centuries-old chant of Kuali:

> " 'Oh, the great fishhook of Maui!
> Manai-i-ka-lani—"made fast to the heavens"!
> An earth-twisted cord ties the hook,
> Engulfed from lofty Kauiki!
> Its bait the red-billed Alae,
> The bird to Hina sacred!
> It sinks far down to Hawaii,
> Struggling and in pain dying!
> Caught is the land beneath the water,

Floated up, up to the surface,
But Hina hid a wing of the bird
And broke the land beneath the water!
Below was the bait snatched away
And eaten at once by the fishes,
The Ulua of the deep muddy places!' "

His aged voice was hoarse and scratchy from the drinking of too much swipes at a funeral the night before, nothing of which contributed to make me less irritable. My head ached. The sun glare on the water made my eyes ache, while I was suffering more than half a touch of mal de mer from the antic conduct of the outrigger on the blobby sea. The air was stagnant. In the lee of Waihee, between the white beach and the reef, no whisper of breeze eased the still sultriness. I really think I was too miserable to summon the resolution to give up the fishing and go in to shore.

Lying back with closed eyes, I lost count of time. I even forgot that Kohokumu was chanting till reminded of it by his ceasing. An exclamation made me bare my eyes to the stab of the sun. He was gazing down through the water glass.

"It's a big one," he said, passing me the device and slipping overside feetfirst into the water.

He went under without splash and ripple, turned over, and swam down. I followed his progress through the water glass, which is merely an oblong box a couple of feet long, open at the top, the bottom sealed water-tight with a sheet of ordinary glass.

Now Kohokumu was a bore, and I was squeamishly out of sorts with him for his volubleness, but I could not help admiring him as I watched him go down. Past seventy years of age, lean as a spear, and shriveled like a mummy, he was doing what few young athletes of my race would do or could do. It was forty feet to bottom. There, partly exposed but mostly hidden under the bulge of a coral lump, I could discern his objective. His keen eyes had caught the projecting tentacle of a squid. Even as he swam, the tentacle was lazily withdrawn, so that there was no sign of the creature. But the brief exposure of the portion of one tentacle had advertised its owner as a squid of size.

The pressure at a depth of forty feet is no joke for a young man, yet it did not seem to inconvenience this oldster. I am certain it never crossed his mind to be inconvenienced. Unarmed, bare of body save for a brief *malo* or loin cloth, he was undeterred by the formidable creature that constituted his prey. I saw him steady himself with his right hand on the coral lump, and thrust his left arm into the hole to the shoulder.

Half a minute elapsed, during which time he seemed to be groping and rooting around with his left hand. Then tentacle after tentacle, myriad-suckered and wildly waving, emerged. Laying hold of his arm, they writhed and coiled about his flesh like so many snakes. With a heave and a jerk appeared the entire squid, a proper devilfish or octopus.

But the old man was in no hurry for his natural element, the air above the water. There, forty feet beneath, wrapped about by an octopus that measured nine feet across from tentacle tip to tentacle tip and that could well drown the stoutest swimmer, he cooly and casually did the one thing that gave to him his empery over the monster. He shoved his lean, hawklike face into the very center of the slimy, squirming mass, and with his several ancient fangs bit into the heart and the life of the matter. This accomplished, he came upward slowly, as a swimmer should who is changing atmospheres from the depths. Alongside the canoe, still in the water and peeling off the grisly clinging thing, the incorrigible old sinner burst into the *pule* of triumph which had been chanted by countless squid-catching generations before him:

> " 'O Kanaloa of the taboo nights!
> Stand upright on the solid floor!
> Stand upon the floor where lies the squid!
> Stand up to take the squid of the deep sea!
> Rise up, O Kanaloa!
> Stir up! Stir up! Let the squid awake!
> Let the squid that lies flat awake! Let the squid that
> lies spread out. . . .' "

I closed my eyes and ears, not offering to lend him a hand, secure in the knowledge that he could climb back unaided into the unstable craft without the slightest risk of upsetting it.

"A very fine squid," he crooned. "It is a wahine squid. I shall now sing to you the song of the cowrie shell, the red cowrie shell that we used as a bait for the squid—"

"You were disgraceful last night at the funeral," I headed him off. "I heard all about it. You made much noise. You sang till everybody was deaf. You insulted the son of the widow. You drank swipes like a pig. Swipes are not good for your extreme age. Some day you will wake up dead. You ought to be a wreck to-day—"

"Ha!" he chuckled. "And you, who drank no swipes, who was a babe unborn when I was already an old man, who went to bed last night with the sun and the chickens—this day you are a wreck. Explain me that. My ears are as thirsty to listen as was my throat thirsty last night.

And here to-day, behold, I am, as that Englishman who came here in his yacht used to say, I am in fine form, in devilish fine form."

"I give you up," I retorted, shrugging my shoulders. "Only one thing is clear, and that is that the devil doesn't want you. Report of your singing has gone before you."

"No," he pondered the idea carefully. "It is not that. The devil will be glad for my coming, for I have some very fine songs for him, and scandals and old gossips of the high aliis that will make him scratch his sides. So let me explain to you the secret of my birth. The Sea is my mother. I was born in a double canoe, during a Kona gale, in the channel of Kahoolawe. From her, the Sea, my mother, I received my strength. Whenever I return to her arms, as for a breast clasp, as I have returned this day, I grow strong again and immediately. She, to me, is the milk giver, the life source—"

"Shades of Antæus!" thought I.

"Some day," old Kohokumu rambled on, "when I am really old, I shall be reported of men as drowned in the sea. This will be an idle thought of men. In truth, I shall have returned into the arms of my mother, there to rest under the heart of her breast until the second birth of me, when I shall emerge into the sun a flashing youth of splendor like Maui himself when he was golden young."

"A queer religion," I commented.

"When I was younger I muddled my poor head over queerer religions," old Kohokumu retorted. "But listen, O Young Wise One, to my elderly wisdom. This I know: as I grow old I seek less for the truth from without me, and find more of the truth from within me. Why have I thought this thought of my return to my mother and of my rebirth from my mother into the sun? You do not know. I do not know, save that, without whisper of man's voice or printed word, without prompting from otherwhere, this thought has arisen from within me, from the deeps of me that are as deep as the sea. I am not a god. I do not make things. Therefore I have not made this thought. I do not know its father or its mother. It is of old time before me, and therefore it is true. Man does not make truth. Man, if he be not blind, only recognizes truth when he sees it. Is this thought that I have thought a dream?"

"Perhaps it is you that are a dream," I laughed. "And that I and sky and sea and the iron-hard land are dreams, all dreams."

"I have often thought that," he assured me soberly. "It may well be so. Last night I dreamed I was a lark bird, a beautiful singing lark of the sky like the larks on the upland pastures of Haleakala. And I flew up, up toward the sun, singing, singing, as old Kohokumu never sang. I tell you now that I dreamed I was a lark bird singing in the sky. But may not I, the real I, be the lark bird? And may not the telling of it be the dream that I, the lark bird, am dreaming now? Who are you to tell me aye or no? Dare you tell me I am not a lark bird asleep and dreaming that I am old Kohokumu?"

I shrugged my shoulders, and he continued triumphantly.

"And how do you know but what you are old Maui himself asleep and dreaming that you are John Lakana talking with me in a canoe? And may you not awake, old Maui yourself, and scratch your sides and say that you had a funny dream in which you dreamed you were a haole?"

"I don't know," I admitted. "Besides, you wouldn't believe me."

"There is much more in dreams than we know," he assured me with great solemnity. "Dreams go deep, all the way down, maybe to before the beginning. May not old Maui have only dreamed he pulled Hawaii up from the bottom of the sea? Then would this Hawaii land be a dream, and you and I and the squid there only parts of Maui's dream? And the lark bird, too?"

He sighed and let his head sink on his breast.

"And I worry my old head about the secrets undiscoverable," he resumed, "until I grow tired and want to forget, and so I drink swipes, and go fishing, and sing old songs, and dream I am a lark bird singing in the sky. I like that best of all, and often I dream it when I have drunk much swipes—"

In great dejection of mood he peered down into the lagoon through the water glass.

"There will be no more bites for a while," he announced. "The fish sharks are prowling around, and we shall have to wait until they are gone. And so that the time shall not be heavy, I will sing you the canoe-hauling song to Lono. You remember:

" 'Give to me the trunk of the tree, O Lono!
Give me the tree's main root, O Lono!
Give me the ear of the tree, O Lono!—' "

"For the love of mercy, don't sing!" I cut him short. "I've got a headache, and your singing hurts. You may be in devilish fine form to-day, but your throat is rotten. I'd rather you talked about dreams, or told me whoppers."

"It is too bad that you are sick, and you so young," he conceded cheerily. "And I shall not sing any more. I shall tell you something you do not know and have never heard; something that is no dream and no whopper, but is what I know to have happened. Not very long ago there lived here, on the beach beside this very lagoon, a young boy whose name was Keikiwai, which, as you know, means Water Baby. He was truly a water baby. His gods were the sea and fish gods, and he was born with knowledge of the language of fishes, which the fishes did not know until the sharks found it out one day when they heard him talk it.

"It happened this way. The word had been brought, and the commands, by swift runners, that the king was making a progress around the island, and that on the next day a luau was to be served him by the dwellers here of Waihee. It was always a hardship, when the king made a progress, for the few dwellers in small places to fill his many stomachs with food. For he came always with his wife and her women, with his priests and sorcerers, his dancers and flute players and hula singers, and fighting men and servants, and his high chiefs with their wives, and sorcerers and fighting men and servants.

"Sometimes, in small places like Waihee, the path of his journey was marked afterward by leanness and famine. But a king must be fed, and it is not good to anger a king. So, like warning in advance of disaster, Waihee heard of his coming, and all food-getters of field and pond and mountain and sea were busied with getting food for the feast. And behold, everything was got, from the choicest of royal taro to sugar-cane joints for the roasting, from opihis to limu, from fowl to wild pig and poi-fed puppies—everything save one thing. The fishermen failed to get lobsters.

"Now be it known that the king's favorite food was lobster. He esteemed it above all *kao-kao* (food), and his runners had made special mention of it. And there were no lobsters, and it is not good to anger a king in the belly of him. Too many sharks had come inside the reef. That was the trouble. A young girl and an old man had been eaten by them. And of the young men who dared dive for lobsters, one was eaten, and one lost an arm, and another lost one hand and one foot.

"But there was Keikiwai, the Water Baby, only eleven years old, but half fish himself and talking the language of fishes. To his father the head men came, begging him to send the Water Baby to get lobsters to fill the king's belly and divert his anger.

"Now this, what happened, was known and observed. For the fishermen and their women, and the taro growers and the bird catchers, and the head men, and all Waihee, came down and stood back from the edge of the rock where the Water Baby stood and looked down at the lobsters far beneath on the bottom.

"And a shark, looking up with its cat's eyes, observed him, and sent out the shark call of 'fresh meat' to assemble all the sharks in the lagoon.

For the sharks work thus together, which is why they are strong. And the sharks answered the call till there were forty of them, long ones and short ones and lean ones and round ones, forty of them by count; and they talked to one another, saying: 'Look at that titbit of a child, that morsel delicious of human-flesh sweetness without the salt of the sea in it, of which salt we have too much, savory and good to eat, melting to delight under our hearts as our bellies embrace it and extract from it its sweet.'

"Much more they said, saying: 'He has come for the lobsters. When he dives in he is for one of us. Not like the old man we ate yesterday, tough to dryness with age, nor like the young men whose members were too hard-muscled, but tender, so tender that he will melt in our gullets ere our bellies receive him. When he dives in, we will all rush for him, and the lucky one of us will get him, and, gulp, he will be gone, one bite and one swallow, into the belly of the luckiest one of us.'

"And Keikiwai, the Water Baby, heard the conspiracy, knowing the shark language; and he addressed a prayer, in the shark language, to the shark god Moku-halii, and the sharks heard and waved their tails to one another and winked their cat's eyes in token that they understood his talk. And then he said: 'I shall now dive for a lobster for the king. And no hurt shall befall me, because the shark with the shortest tail is my friend and will protect me.'

"And, so saying, he picked up a chunk of lava rock and tossed it into the water, with a big splash, twenty feet to one side. The forty sharks rushed for the splash, while he dived, and by the time they discovered they had missed him, he had gone to the bottom and come back and climbed out, within his hand a fat lobster, a wahine lobster, full of eggs, for the king.

" 'Ha!' said the sharks, very angry. 'There is among us a traitor. The titbit of a child, the morsel of sweetness, has spoken, and has exposed the one among us who has saved him. Let us now measure the length of our tails!'

"Which they did, in a long row, side by side, the shorter-tailed ones cheating and stretching to gain length on themselves, the longer-tailed ones cheating and stretching in order not to be out-cheated and out-stretched. They were very angry with the one with the shortest tail, and him they rushed upon from every side and devoured till nothing was left of him.

"Again they listened while they waited for the Water Baby to dive in. And again the Water Baby made his prayer in the shark language to Moku-halii, and said: 'The shark with the shortest tail is my friend and will protect me.' And again the Water Baby tossed in a chunk of lava, this time twenty feet away off to the other side. The sharks rushed for the splash, and in their haste ran into one another, and splashed with their tails till the water was all foam and they could see nothing, each thinking some other was swallowing the titbit. And the Water Baby came up and climbed out with another fat lobster for the king.

"And the thirty-nine sharks measured tails, devouring the one with the shortest tail, so that there were only thirty-eight sharks. And the Water Baby continued to do what I have said, and the sharks to do what I have told you, while for each shark that was eaten by his brothers there was another fat lobster laid on the rock for the king. Of course, there was much quarreling and argument among the sharks when it came to measuring tails; but in the end it worked out in rightness and justice, for, when only two sharks were left, they were the two biggest of the original forty.

"And the Water Baby again claimed the shark with the shortest tail was his friend, fooled the two sharks with another lava chunk, and brought up another lobster. The two sharks each claimed the other had the shorter tail, and each fought to eat the other, and the one with the longer tail won—"

"Hold, O Kohokumu!" I interrupted. "Remember that that shark had already—"

"I know just what you are going to say," he snatched his recital back from me. "And you are right. It took him so long to eat the thirty-ninth shark, for inside the thirty-ninth shark were already the nineteen other sharks he had eaten, and inside the fortieth shark were already the nineteen other sharks he had eaten, and he did not have the appetite he had started with. But do not forget he was a very big shark to begin with.

"It took him so long to eat the other shark, and the nineteen sharks inside the other shark, that he was still eating when darkness fell and the people of Waihee went away home with all the lobsters for the king. And didn't they find the last shark on the beach next morning dead and burst wide open with all he had eaten?"

Kohokumu fetched a full stop and held my eyes with his own shrewd ones.

"Hold, O Lakana!" he checked the speech that rushed to my tongue. "I know what next you would say. You would say that with my own eyes I did not see this, and therefore that I do not know what I have been telling you. But I do know, and I can prove it. My father's father knew the grandson of the Water Baby's father's uncle. Also, there, on the rocky point to which I point my finger now, is where the Water Baby stood and dived. I have dived for lobsters there myself. It is a great place for lobsters. Also, and often, have I seen sharks there. And there, on the bottom, as I should know, for I have seen and counted them, are the thirty-nine lava rocks thrown in by the Water Baby as I have described."

"But—" I began.

"Ha!" he baffled me. "Look! While we have talked the fish have begun again to bite."

He pointed to three of the bamboo poles erect and devil-dancing in token that fish were hooked and struggling on the lines beneath. As he bent to his paddle, he muttered, for my benefit:

"Of course I know. The thirty-nine lava rocks are still there. You can count them any day for yourself. Of course I know, and I know for a fact."

NOTES

The stories in this edition are arranged chronologically by date of composition rather than date of publication. In the notes below, the first periodical publication and first book publication dates of each story are given along with relevant information about the composition and publication of each story. For this latter material the editors have relied on Jack London's meticulous magazine sales records, which provide a detailed account of his submissions and payments, and his correspondence which appears in *The Letters of Jack London*.

"Story of a Typhoon Off the Coast of Japan"

San Francisco *Morning Call*, November 12, 1893; *Dutch Courage and Other Stories* (New York: Macmillan, 1922). JL entered this story in the *Call's* writing contest for authors under twenty-two years old; it won first prize. London acknowledged his accomplishment in a letter to Houghton Mifflin, January 31, 1900: "Once ... I won a prize essay of twenty-five dollars from a San Francisco paper over the heads of Stanford and California Universities, both of which were represented by second and third place through their undergraduates. This gave me hope for achieving something ultimately."

"The White Silence" ✓

Overland Monthly 33 (February 1899): 138–42 (subtitled "Another Story of the 'Malemute Kid' "); *The Son of the Wolf: Tales of the Far North* (Boston: Houghton Mifflin, 1900). In a letter to Mabel Applegarth of February 28, 1899, London described a meeting he had with James Howard Bridge, editor of the *Overland*, the preceding week: "He ... was quite taken with my 'White Silence.' Said it was the most powerful thing which had appeared in the magazine for a year; but he was afraid it was a fluke and perhaps it would be impossible for me to repeat it.... If I sustained the promise I had given, he would give me a prominent place in the pages of his magazine, see that the newspapers, reviews, etc., puffed me, and inaugurate a boom to put my name before the public. You can readily see how valuable this would be—putting future employment into my hands from publications which could afford to pay well."

"To the Man on Trail" ✓

Overland Monthly 33 (January 1899): 36–40 (erroneously titled "To the Man on the Trail" and subtitled "A Klondike Christmas"); *The Son of the Wolf: Tales of the Far North* (Boston: Houghton Mifflin, 1900). In his letter to Mabel Applegarth of December 6, 1898, London expressed his dismay at the *Overland's* offer of five dollars for his story: "There are between three and four thousand words in it. Worth far more than five dollars, at the ordinary reportorial rate of so much per column." He tried to rationalize the situation: "Well, a newcomer must excel [established writers] in their own fields before he is accepted, or else he must create a new field. Perhaps it was the latter that impressed the editors in favor of my article; but be it what it may, if worthy of publication, it were worthy of proper pay."

"In a Far Country"

Overland Monthly 33 (June 1899): 540–49; *The Son of the Wolf: Tales of the Far North* (Boston: Houghton Mifflin, 1900). London, in a letter to Cloudesley Johns, May 18, 1899, asked his fellow writer for his opinion of "In a Far Country" and offered his own judgment of it: "... it is either bosh, or good; either the worst or the best of the series I have turned out." A month later, in another letter to Johns, London concurred with his friend's assessment: " 'In a Far Country' should have been the best of the series, but was not. As to the clumsiness of structure, you have certainly hit it. I doubt if I shall ever be able to polish. I permit too short a period—one to fifteen minutes—to elapse between the long-hand and the final MS. You see, I am groping, groping, groping for my own particular style, for the style which should be mine but which I have not yet found." For his story, London received $7.50.

"An Odyssey of the North" ✓

Atlantic Monthly 85 (January 1900): 85–100; *The Son of the Wolf: Tales of the Far North* (Boston: Houghton Mifflin, 1900). After having his story rejected by *McClure's*, London sent it to the *Atlantic*, which conditionally accepted it. He explained to Cloudesley Johns in a letter of July 29, 1899: "Did you ever write a yarn of, say, twelve thousand words, every word essential to atmosphere, and then get an order to cut out three thousand of those words, somewhere, somehow? That's what the Atlantic has just done to me. Hardly know whether I shall do it or not. It's like the pound of flesh." London did shorten the story, and for his tale he received $120 and a one-year subscription to the *Atlantic*.

"Semper Idem"

The Black Cat 6 (December 1900): 24–28; *When God Laughs and Other Stories* (New York: Macmillan, 1911). London originally entitled his story "Semper Idem; Semper Fidelis" and sent it to eight magazines and publishers before having it accepted. He wrote Cloudesley Johns on July 23, 1900: "I would have sold [the story] for a dollar. But the *Black Cat* gave me a sort of poor mouth . . . and that under the circumstances it could only offer me fifty dollars for it. Say! Most took my breath away."

"The Law of Life"

McClure's Magazine 16 (March 1901): 435–38; *Children of the Frost* (New York: Macmillan, 1902). Though London told a friend he thought this story was "good stuff," it was rejected by the *Atlantic Monthly* before it was accepted by *McClure's*. London explained the nature of his tale to Cloudesley Johns in a letter of December 22, 1900: "[The story] is short, applies the particular to the universal, deals with a lonely death, of an old man, in which beasts consummate the tragedy. My man is an old Indian, abandoned in the snow by his tribe because he cannot keep up. He has a little fire, a few sticks of wood. The frost and silence about him. He is blind. How do I approach the event? What point of view do I take? Why, the old Indian's, of course. It opens up with him sitting by his little fire, listening to his tribesmen breaking camp, harnessing dogs, and departing. The reader listens with him to every familiar sound; hears the last draw away; feels the silence settle down. The old man wanders back into his past; the reader wanders with him—thus is the whole theme exploited through the soul of the Indian. Down to the consummation, when the wolves draw in upon him in a circle. Don't you see, nothing, even the moralizing and generalizing, is done, save through him, in expressions of his experience." For this story London received fifty-five dollars.

"A Relic of the Pliocene"

Collier's Weekly 26 (January 12, 1901): 17, 20; *The Faith of Men and Other Stories* (New York: Macmillan, 1904). After having his story turned down by *McClure's* London sent it to *Collier's,* where it was accepted. When a fellow Klondike argonaut named Georges Dupuy claimed to have heard of this story in the winter of 1898 while he was in the northland, London corrected him in a letter of December 1, 1910: ". . . I absolutely invented this story. There were no hints of this tale in Klondike when I was there. I made it up altogether out of my own head. I finished it the first week of June, 1900. . . . This is one of the few stories I have not based on actual events."

"Nam-Bok the Unveracious"

Ainslee's Magazine 10 (August 1902): 29–37 (entitled "Nam-Bok, the Liar"); *Children of the Frost* (New York: Macmillan, 1902). London first sent this story to *McClure's* in August 1901, but it was rejected by *McClure's* and six other magazines before it was accepted by *Ainslee's* in February 1902. London received a hundred dollars for his story. Though "Nam-Bok" was eventually published, London confessed to Cloudesley Johns in a September 1902 letter that this story was not his best work: "The idea of it always appealed to me (including the satire), but I was not satisfied when I wrote it. I feel that I missed somewhere."

"The One Thousand Dozen"

National Magazine 17 (March 1903): 703–13; *The Faith of Men and Other Stories* (New York: Macmillan, 1904). Neither London nor Paul R. Reynolds, his literary agent, had much success in placing this "pretty long yarn" based upon an actual occurrence in the Klondike in 1898: Twenty-one magazines and publishing syndicates rejected it before it was accepted by the *National*. Deeply in debt and having to support a household of nine people, London balked at the paltry offer of twenty dollars for the story from Frank Putnam, managing editor of the *National*, and stated that he could receive $204 in transportation credit if he sold the story to a railroad magazine. Putnam agreed to get London this credit, in addition to the cash payment, but he did not fulfill his promise.

"To Build a Fire" ✓

The Youth's Companion 76 (May 29, 1902): 275. In a letter to Richard W. Gilder, editor of the *Century Magazine*, of December 22, 1908, London explained the difference between the first and second versions of this story: "A long, long time ago I wrote a story for boys which I sold to the *Youth's Companion* [for fifty dollars]. It was purely juvenile in treatment. Its motif was not only very strong, but was very true. Man after man in the Klondike has died alone after getting his feet wet, through failure to build a fire. As the years went by, I was worried by the inadequate treatment I had given that motif, and by the fact that I had treated it for boys merely. At last came the resolve to take the same motif and handle it for men. I had no access to the boys' version of it, and I wrote it just as though I had never used the motif before. I do not remember anything about the way I handled it for juveniles, but I do know, I am absolutely confident, that beyond the motif itself, there is no similarity of treatment whatever."

"Moon-Face"

The [San Francisco] *Argonaut* 51 (July 21, 1902): 36; *Moon-Face and Other Stories* (New York: Macmillan, 1906). In February 1902, London entered "Moon-

Face" in the *Black Cat* magazine fiction contest, but it lost. He submitted it to
three magazines for publication before *The Argonaut* agreed to buy it from him
for fifteen dollars. London's story turned out to be mildly controversial: It so
closely paralleled the plot of Frank Norris's "The Passing of Cock-Eye Black-
lock," which was published in the same month in the *Century,* that he was
suspected of plagiarism. London explained in a letter of April 10, 1906, to S. S.
McClure, publisher of *McClure's Magazine* and owner of the McClure newspaper
syndicate, "these two stories were quite different in manner of treatment, [but]
they were patently the same in foundation and motive. At once the newspapers
paralleled our stories. The explanation was simple: Norris and I had read the
same newspaper account, and proceeded to exploit it."

"BÂTARD"

Cosmopolitan 33 (June 1902): 218–26 (entitled "Diable—A Dog"); *The Faith of
Men and Other Stories* (New York: Macmillan, 1904). *Cosmopolitan* offered London a hundred dollars for his dog story in January 1902, but he declined and
made a counter offer of twenty-five dollars per thousand words; *Cosmopolitan*
agreed and paid London $141.25 for "Bâtard." In March 1903 London wrote
Anna Strunsky that *The Call of the Wild*—which he had recently completed—
was originally "a companion to my other dog story 'Bâtard.' . . ."

"THE STORY OF JEES UCK" ✓

The Smart Set 8 (September 1902): 57–70; *The Faith of Men and Other Stories*
(New York: Macmillan, 1904). London finished this story on March 28, 1902;
he sent it to *McClure's* and *Cosmopolitan,* but it was rejected by both magazines.
The Smart Set accepted it and agreed to pay him a hundred dollars. In a letter
to George P. Brett of February 16, 1903, London recalled an incident which
pointed up the fidelity of his story: "At the time [the story] was published
serially I was gratified to receive a letter from a man who had lived [a] wild
life, and who was so convinced by the story that I could not unconvince him
that I had never lived with a native wife, for only by so living, he contended,
could I have got the experience necessary to write the story."

"THE LEAGUE OF THE OLD MEN" ✓

Brandur Magazine 1 (October 4, 1902): 7–11; *Children of the Frost* (New York:
Macmillan, 1902). Originally entitled "The Perplexity of Imber," this story was
rejected by three magazines before it was accepted by *Brandur;* London received
$160 for it. In a letter published in the *Grand Magazine* 1 (August 1906), London
wrote: "Though 'The League of the Old Men' has no love motif, that is not
my reason for thinking it my best story. In ways, the motif of this story is
greater than any love-motif; in fact, its wide sweep includes the conditions and
situations for ten-thousand love-motifs. The voices of millions are in the voice

of Old Imber, the tears and sorrows of millions in his throat as he tells his story; and his story epitomises the whole vast tragedy of the contact of the Indian with the white man. In conclusion, I may say that nobody else agrees with me in the selection which I have made and which has been my selection for years."

✓ "Love of Life"

McClure's Magazine 26 (December 1905): 144–58 (simultaneously published serially in Edinburgh's *Blackwood's Magazine* 178 [December 1905]: 765–80); *Love of Life and Other Stories* (New York: Macmillan, 1907). Though London characterized "Love of Life" as his "song of success," this story proved to be rather problematical for him. A critic in the *Augusta Chronicle* challenged London's scientific accuracy in describing a scene in the story; another, in the *New York World,* suggested that the "similarity in thought and phraseology" between London's story and Augustus Bridle and J. K. MacDonald's "Lost in the Land of the Midnight Sun" (*McClure's,* December 1901) was more than coincidental. London dismissed the plagiarism implication by claiming that the earlier account was nonfiction and his was fiction. He wrote S. S. McClure: ". . . I, in the course of making my living by turning journalism into literature, used material from various sources which had been collected and narrated by men who made their living by turning the facts of life into journalism. Along comes the space-writer on the *World* who makes his living by turning the doings of other men into sensation. Well, all three of us made our living; and who's got any kick coming?"

"The Sun-Dog Trail"

Harper's Monthly 112 (December 1905): 83–91; *Love of Life and Other Stories* (New York: Macmillan, 1907). *Harper's* immediately accepted this story and paid London five hundred dollars for it.

"All Gold Canyon"

The Century Magazine 71 (November 1905): 117–26 ("Canyon" is spelled "Cañon" in the serial version); *Moon-Face and Other Stories* (New York: Macmillan, 1906). This story was another immediate success for London: *Century* accepted it for publication and paid London five hundred dollars.

"A Day's Lodging"

Collier's Weekly 39 (May 25, 1907): 18–21; *Love of Life and Other Stories* (New York: Macmillan, 1907). Two years after the publication of and payment ($750) for this story, Arthur Stringer, a Canadian novelist and poet, accused London and other writers of inaccurately portraying facts of Canadian life in order to meet their artistic needs. "A Day's Lodging," along with "Love of Life" and *White Fang*, were cited as examples of this "fakerism." Though London wanted Stringer to make amends for his inaccurate indictment publicly, he never did. London, along with Herbert Heron, adapted "A Day's Lodging" for the stage in their two plays, both entitled "Gold" (1910 and 1913).

"THE APOSTATE"

Woman's Home Companion 33 (September 1906): 5–7, 49 (subtitled "A Child Labor Parable" in the *Companion*); *When God Laughs and Other Stories* (New York: Macmillan, 1911). London's own experiences while working ten-hour days for ten cents an hour in a jute mill in 1893 were obviously used as the basis for this story of child labor. For his tale, the *Companion* paid London $767.30.

"THE WIT OF PORPORTUK" ✓

The Times Magazine (New York) 1 (January 1907): 39–44; *When God Laughs and Other Stories* (New York: Macmillan, 1911). London completed this story on July 17, 1906, and immediately sent it to S. S. McClure for publication in *McClure's*, with a note stating: "I prefer it to many of my Alaskan stories, in fact I think it's a pretty good one." Despite his boosting, the story was rejected. London then sent it, along with another letter promoting "The Wit of Porportuk" as "among my best half-dozen Alaskan short stories," to James Randolph Walker, editor of the short-lived *Times Magazine*. Walker offered London a thousand dollars for the story, but he never paid him.

"THE UNPARALLELED INVASION"

McClure's Magazine 35 (July 1910): 308–15; *The Strength of the Strong* (New York: Macmillan, 1914). London's story was turned down by a dozen magazines before being accepted by *McClure's*. This puzzled London. After having the story rejected by *Cosmopolitan*, London wrote Roland Phillips, the magazine's associate editor: "I thought, when writing 'The Unparalleled Invasion,' that I was making an interesting pseudo-scientific yarn. Can you tell me just what is wrong with it? Is it a good idea poorly handled, or is it an idea that in itself is of no value to magazine publications?" Phillips responded that the story was not accepted because *Cosmopolitan* had accepted two stories that were "similar in theme" to London's. It was not until February 1910 that *McClure's* agreed to publish "The Unparalleled Invasion" and to pay London four hundred dollars for it.

"TO BUILD A FIRE" ✓

The Century Magazine 76 (August 1908): 525–34; *Lost Face* (New York: Macmillan, 1910). For the most famous of all his short stories London was paid four hundred dollars by the *Century* in January 1908. See the note to the 1902 version of "To Build a Fire" above. The serial version of this story included an epigraph which was deleted when the story was collected in *Lost Face:* "He travels fastest who travels alone ... but not after the frost has dropped below fifty degrees or more.—Yukon Code."

"THE HOUSE OF PRIDE"

The Pacific Monthly 24 (December 1910): 598–607; *The House of Pride & Other Tales of Hawaii* (New York: Macmillan, 1912). London's manuscript of this story made the rounds to nineteen magazines before it was accepted; London received $267 for it. In a letter of November 19, 1910, to Lute Pease, editor of *The Pacific Monthly,* London whimsically commented, "Funny about 'The House of Pride.' I wonder if some of the disinclination for it is due to the fact that I didn't kill anybody in it. You know my reputed formula for a short story is to start with three characters and to kill four before the end. Possibly I erred in not killing anybody in 'The House of Pride.' The situation of the story itself was true. The story is real. What more could I say. Of course, I could have done more; I could have had them drown themselves in the surf, or murder each other; or fall on each other's necks in brotherly love. The only trouble is, life so rarely works out that way."

"THE HOUSE OF MAPUHI"

McClure's Magazine 32 (January 1909): 247–60; *South Sea Tales* (New York: Macmillan, 1911). Eleven magazines rejected this story before *McClure's* agreed to buy it for five hundred dollars.

"THE CHINAGO"

Harper's Monthly 119 (July 1909): 233–40; *When God Laughs and Other Stories* (New York: Macmillan, 1911). Eleven magazines also rejected this story before *Harper's Monthly* bought it for five hundred dollars.

"LOST FACE"

New York Herald (December 13, 1908): 7; *Lost Face* (New York: Macmillan, 1910). London explained the background of "Lost Face" to Newton A. Fuessle, a novelist and journalist, in a letter of May 5, 1910: "That 'Lost Face' story is based upon an actual occurrence that took place down in the Carolinas in the Indian Wars before the American Revolution. It was a British soldier who devised and put through this particular scheme to escape being tortured." London sent his story to thirteen magazines for publication before he submitted it in a short story contest in the *New York Herald.* It won the first prize of six hundred dollars.

"Koolau the Leper"

The Pacific Monthly 22 (December 1909): 752–60; *The House of Pride & Other Tales of Hawaii* (New York: Macmillan, 1912). London probably based this story on the actual murder of the father of Herbert Stolz, his fellow crewman aboard the *Snark*, by a native Hawaiian named Koolau. London tried for over a year to place his story with a magazine. It was finally accepted by *The Pacific Monthly* after eighteen other magazines rejected it. London received $299.55 in payment.

"Chun Ah Chun"

Woman's Magazine 21 (Spring 1910): 5–6, 38–40; *The House of Pride & Other Tales of Hawaii* (New York: Macmillan, 1912). This story was sent to eighteen magazines over the course of a year and a half before it was accepted for publication; London received $250 for it.

"The Heathen"✓

London Magazine 23 (September 1909): 33–42; *South Sea Tales* (New York: Macmillan, 1911). London's fictional depiction of the perfect Man-Comrade was published serially in England before it was published in *Everybody's Magazine* (August 1910) in America. For the English rights London was paid £16 16s; from *Everybody's* he received five hundred dollars.

"Mauki"

Hampton's Magazine 23 (December 1909): 752–60; *South Sea Tales* (New York: Macmillan, 1911). London, according to his second wife, Charmian, based "Mauki" on the story of a cook from the Solomon Islands whom he met during the *Snark* cruise. He circulated this story to a dozen magazines over a period of nine months before it was accepted by *Hampton's*, which paid London $250 for it.

"The Strength of the Strong"

Hampton's Magazine 26 (March 1911): 309–18; *The Strength of the Strong* (New York: Macmillan, 1914). In a letter to the editor of *Cosmopolitan* of August 30, 1909, London explained the reason why he wrote "The Strength of the Strong": "If you will remember, some time ago, Kipling made an attack on Socialism in the form of a parable or short story, entitled '[Adventures of] Melissa,' in which he exploited his Jingoism and showed that a co-operation of individuals strong enough to overcome war meant the degeneration of said individuals. I have written my 'Strength of the Strong' as a reply to his attack." Six years later he lamented to his fellow writer Mary Austin, "I have again and again written books that failed to get across.... [One] time I wrote an attack on ideas brought forth by Rudyard Kipling and entitled my attack 'The Strength of the Strong.' No one was in the slightest way aware of the point of my story." Perhaps because of this problem London had difficulty selling his story: He sent it to fifteen magazines over a period of twenty-two months before *Hampton's* bought it for two hundred dollars.

"SOUTH OF THE SLOT"

The Saturday Evening Post 181 (May 22, 1909): 3–4, 36–38; *The Strength of the Strong* (New York: Macmillan, 1914). London sold this story to the *Post* for $675. In 1910, he was approached by Walter H. Nichols to collaborate on a dramatic version of "South of the Slot." Originally entitled *The Light* and later *The Common Man,* the play was copyrighted by London and Nichols in 1913 as *The Damascus Road.*

"SAMUEL" ✓

The Bookman 37 (May 1913): 285–96; *The Strength of the Strong* (New York: Macmillan, 1914). Charmian London claimed that her husband was inspired to write this story by Robert McIlwaine, captain of the S. S. *Tymeric,* the ship on which the Londons sailed from Australia to Ecuador in May 1909. In a letter to John S. Phillips, editor and publisher of *The American Magazine,* London explained the circumstances under which the story was written and why he deserved to be paid more than Phillips offered: "... the material in that story 'Samuel' cost me at least $250 hard cash to acquire, and 43 days at sea between land and land, on a coal-laden tramp-steamer. Also, it took me two weeks to write. And my wife threw in 43 days of her time helping me in making a study of the vernacular, and in writing it down and classifying it. How the dickens I could sell that story for $250 and make both ends meet is beyond me." London accepted Phillips's offer in 1911, with the stipulation that "Samuel" be published serially in six months. When this did not occur, London, who had had the story rejected by nineteen other magazines, sold it to *The Bookman* in 1913 for a hundred dollars.

"A PIECE OF STEAK" ✓

The Saturday Evening Post 182 (November 20, 1909): 6–8, 42–43; *When God Laughs and Other Stories* (New York: Macmillan, 1911). In a letter of August 25, 1909, to Roland Phillips, associate editor of *Cosmopolitan,* London wrote: "I am glad that you like 'A Piece of Steak.' I have a sneaking liking for it myself. While it's just the story of a broken-down, second-rater Australian pug, nevertheless it has a motif that admits of the widest application." Two months later Phillips decided not to publish London's story because "there was a certain feeling among our staff that perhaps there was a little too much 'meat' in it for our half million lady readers." London then sent the story to the *Post,* which paid $787.70 for it.

"THE MADNESS OF JOHN HARNED"

Lady's Realm (London) 26 (May–October 1909): 570–81; *The Night-Born* (New York: Century, 1913). London wrote John O. Cosgrave, editor of *Everybody's Magazine,* in November 1909, that in "The Madness of John Harned" he "tried to boil down . . . the essential differences between the Spanish and Anglo-Saxon temperaments." He went on to admit to Lute Pease, editor of the *Pacific Monthly:* "I am afraid that personally I was guilty of some of the sensations my hero experienced at his bull fight. I know, among other things, that I jumped up, and in the tense silence cheered when the bull was getting the matador. And I didn't intend to, at all. I suddenly discovered myself doing it." London's story was rejected by three American magazines before it was published serially in the United States in *Everybody's* 23 (November 1910): 657–66.

"THE NIGHT-BORN"

Everybody's Magazine 25 (July 1911): 108–17; *The Night-Born* (New York: Century, 1913). Paul R. Reynolds, London's literary agent, sold this story to *Everybody's* for five hundred dollars in August 1910; from this sale London received $450.

"WAR"

The Coming Nation (London) 9 (July 29, 1911): 635–36; *The Night-Born* (New York: Century, 1913). After having his story rejected by ten American magazines, London "made a present" of it to England's *The Coming Nation,* which eventually compensated him at slightly less than three pounds. Charmian London noted that her husband considered "War" a "picture . . . which he deemed one of his gems."

"TOLD IN THE DROOLING WARD"

The Bookman 39 (June 1914): 432–37; *The Turtles of Tasman* (New York: Macmillan, 1916). When John O. Cosgrave, at this time managing editor of *Collier's,* rejected this story for publication in November 1911, London responded: ". . . I don't take it to heart, but I take it to head, your slam at my feebleminded yarn. It's real. It's true. I am on speaking terms with at least 500 of these imbeciles. Only last Sunday 30 of them paid me a call. The yarn was something new, something novel, something true—also, it was cheerful, optimistic, and eminently bourgeois." London's story was rejected by thirteen magazines before being bought by *The Bookman* for a hundred dollars.

"The Mexican" ✓

The Saturday Evening Post 184 (August 19, 1911): 6–8, 27–30; *The Night-Born* (New York: Century, 1913). London expressed his support for the Mexican Revolution against Porfirio Diaz's military dictatorship in this story. The *Post* paid him $750.

"The Pearls of Parlay" ✓

The Saturday Evening Post 184 (October 14, 1911): 9–11, 64–66; *A Son of the Sun* (New York: Doubleday, Page, 1912). London received $750 for this story from the *Post*.

"Wonder of Woman"

Cosmopolitan 52 (May 1912): 761–73; 52 (June 1912): 107–20; *Smoke Bellew* (New York: Century, 1912). London received $750 for this story, the twelfth and final one in his "Smoke Bellew" series. He wrote Roland Phillips, October 11, 1911, that in this story, "I bring in the tremendous love of a woman for Smoke. It ought to be a real good story. The tremendous love of this woman will drive him by its high impact, to marry Joy Castell—and finis Smoke."

"The Red One"

Cosmopolitan 65 (October 1918): 34–41, 132, 135–38; *The Red One* (New York: Macmillan, 1918). London originally entitled this story "The Message" and based the plot upon an idea which he got from his close friend George Sterling. London, in a letter to Sterling of March 7, 1916, inquired: "Do you remember another wonderful story you told me ... of the meteoric message from Mars or some other world in space, that fell amongst isolated savages, that was recognized for what it was by the lost explorer, who died or was killed before he could gain access to the treasure in the heart of the apparent meteor?"

"On the Makaloa Mat" ✓

Cosmopolitan 66 (March 1919): 16–23, 133–35; *On the Makaloa Mat* (New York: Macmillan, 1919). In June 1916, London sent the manuscript of this story to Edgar G. Sisson; in a cover letter he wrote: "This is true and genuine and correct and right of the old Hawaiian life, brought up to the present tick of the clock of Hawaiian life."

"The Tears of Ah Kim"

Cosmopolitan 65 (July 1918): 32–37, 136–38; *On the Makaloa Mat* (New York: Macmillan, 1919). London began writing his "light humorous Honolulu story" in mid-June 1916 and sent it to *Cosmopolitan,* where it was accepted for publication.

"Shin Bones"

Cosmopolitan 65 (November 1918): 74–81, 119–21 (entitled "In the Cave of the Dead"); *On the Makaloa Mat* (New York: Macmillan, 1919). Though London sent his story to Edgar G. Sisson, the editor of *Cosmopolitan,* on August 21, 1916, it was not published serially until over two years later.

"When Alice Told Her Soul"

Cosmopolitan 64 (March 1918): 28–33, 105–107; *On the Makaloa Mat* (New York: Macmillan, 1919). London submitted this story, along with "Like Argus of the Ancient Times," to *Cosmopolitan* in mid-September 1916, and commented to Edgar G. Sisson: "By glancing over these two you will note that the 'horror pedal' has not been pressed at all, and that neither of these two short stories is an 'article.'"

"Like Argus of the Ancient Times"

Hearst's Magazine 31 (March 1917): 176–78, 214–16; *The Red One* (New York: Macmillan, 1918). In *The Book of Jack London,* volume 2 (1921), Charmian London wrote that as the protagonist, Old Tarwater, "faces extinction in the Arctic forest, the influence of Jack's probings into the stuff of the psyche [is evident]. And to the lighter reader, I call attention to the fact that Jack himself walks across some of the pages as young Liverpool" (354–55).

"The Princess"

Cosmopolitan 65 (June 1918): 20–27, 145–49; *The Red One* (New York: Macmillan, 1918). In his letter to Edgar G. Sisson of September 19, 1916, London said: "Just now I am in the thick of a humorous tramp story, located in the United States, and to be entitled, I think, 'The Three One-Armed Pariahs.'" He changed the title to "The Princess" when he mailed the manuscript to Sisson a week later.

"The Water Baby"

Cosmopolitan 65 (September 1918): 80–85, 133; *On the Makaloa Mat* (New York: Macmillan, 1919). London sent this story, the last one he ever wrote, to Edgar G. Sisson on October 4, 1916.

BIBLIOGRAPHY

SELECTED SECONDARY READINGS

Baskett, Sam S. "Jack London's Heart of Darkness." *American Quarterly* 10 (September 1958): 66–77.

Beauchamp, Gorman. *Jack London.* Mercer Island, Washington: Starmont House, 1984.

Blackman, Gordon N., Jr. "Jack London: Visionary Realist." *Jack London Newsletter* 13 (September–December 1980): 82–94; Part II, *JLN* 14 (January–April 1981): 1–12.

Brown, Ellen. "A Perfect Sphere: Jack London's 'The Red One.'" *Jack London Newsletter* 11 (May–December 1978): 81–85.

Bykov, Vil. "Jack London in the Soviet Union." *The Book Club of California Quarterly Newsletter* 24 (Summer 1959): 52–58.

Campbell, Jeanne. "Falling Stars: Myth in 'The Red One.'" *Jack London Newsletter* 11 (May–December 1978): 87–101.

Chapman, Arnold. "Between Fire and Ice: A Theme in Jack London and Horacio Quiroga." *Symposium* 24 (Spring 1970): 17–26.

Clareson, Thomas D. "Notes" on "The Red One." In *A Spectrum of Worlds.* New York: Doubleday, 1973.

Courbin, Jacqueline M. "Jack London's Portrayal of the Natives in His First Four Collection of Arctic Tales." *Jack London Newsletter* 10 (September–December 1977): 127–37.

Day, A. Grove. "Introduction." *Stories of Hawaii by Jack London.* New York: Appleton-Century, 1965.

Dhondt, Steven T. "Jack London's Satire in *When God Laughs.*" Master's thesis. Logan: Utah State University, 1967.

———. "'There Is a Good Time Coming': Jack London's Spirit of Proletarian Revolt." *Jack London Newsletter* 3 (January–April, 1970): 25–34.

Foner, Philip S., ed. *Jack London, American Rebel: A Collection of his Social Writings together with an Extensive Study of the Man and His Times.* New York: Citadel, 1947.

Geismar, Maxwell. "Jack London: The Short Cut." In *Rebels and Ancestors: The American Novel, 1890–1915.* Boston: Houghton Mifflin, 1953.

Giles, James R. "Some Notes on the Red-Blooded Reading of Kipling by Jack London and Frank Norris." *Jack London Newsletter* 3 (May–August 1970): 56–62.

Hamilton, David Mike. *"The Tools of My Trade": Annotated Books in Jack London's Library.* Seattle: University of Washington Press, 1986.

Hendricks, King, ed. *Creator and Critic: A Controversy between Jack London and Philo M. Buck, Jr.* Logan: Utah State University Press, 1961.

———, ed. *Jack London: Master Craftsman of the Short Story.* Logan: Utah State University, 1966.

Johnston, Carolyn. *Jack London—An American Radical?* Westport, Conn.: Greenwood, 1984.

Kingman, Russ. *A Pictorial Life of Jack London.* New York: Crown, 1979.

Labor, Earle. *Jack London.* New York: Twayne, 1974.

———. "The Making of a Major Author: Jack London and the Politics of Literary Reputation." *Jack London Newsletter* 19 (September–December 1986): 100–104.

——— with King Hendricks. "Jack London's Twice-Told Tale." *Studies in Short Fiction* 4 (Summer 1967): 334–47.

Lachtman, Howard. "Criticism of Jack London: A Selected Checklist." *Modern Fiction Studies* 22 (Spring 1976): 107–25.

———. "Introduction." *Sporting Blood: Selections from Jack London's Greatest Sports Writing.* Novato, Calif.: Presidio Press, 1981.

Li, Shuyan. "Jack London in China." *Jack London Newsletter* 19 (January–April 1986): 42–46.

London, Charmian K. *The Book of Jack London.* 2 vols. New York: Century, 1921.

London, Joan. *Jack London and His Times: An Unconventional Biography.* New York: Doubleday, Doran, 1939. Reprinted by the University of Washington Press in 1968, with a new introduction by the author.

Lundquist, James. *Jack London: Adventures, Ideas, and Fiction.* New York: Ungar, 1987.

Lynn, Kenneth S. "Jack London: The Brain Merchant." In *The Dream of Success: A Study of Modern American Imagination.* Boston: Little, Brown, 1955.

McClintock, James I. *White Logic: Jack London's Short Stories.* Grand Rapids: Wolf House Books, 1975.

Mitchell, Lee Clark. "Keeping His Head: Repetition and Responsibility in London's 'To Build a Fire.'" *Journal of Modern Literature* 13 (March 1986): 76–96.

Moreland, David A. "Violence in the South Sea Fiction of Jack London." *Jack London Newsletter* 16 (January–April 1983): 1–35.

———. "The Quest That Failed: Jack London's Last Tales of the South Seas." *Pacific Studies* 8 (Fall 1984): 48–70.

Oriard, Michael. "Jack London: The Father of American Sports Fiction." *Jack London Newsletter* 11 (January–April 1978): 1–11.

Ownbey, Ray Wilson, ed. *Jack London: Essays in Criticism.* Santa Barbara, Calif.: Peregrine Smith, 1978.

Pattee, Fred Lewis. *The Development of the American Short Story.* New York: Harper Brothers, 1923.

Petersen, Per Serritslev. "Science-Fictionalizing the Paradox of Living: Jack London's 'The Red One' and the Ecstasy of Regression." *The Dolphin* (University of Aarhus, Denmark) 11 (April 1985): 35–58.

Peterson, Clell T. "Jack London's Alaskan Stories." *American Book Collector* 9 (April 1959): 15–22.

———. "The Theme of Jack London's 'To Build a Fire.'" *American Book Collector* 17 (November 1966): 15–18.

Pizer, Donald. "Jack London: The Problem of Form." *Studies in the Literary Imagination* 16 (Fall 1983): 107–15.

Reesman, Jeanne C. "The Problem of Knowledge in Jack London's 'The Water Baby.'" *Western American Literature* 23 (Fall 1988): 201–15.

Riber, Jørgen. "Archetypal Patterns in 'The Red One.'" *Jack London Newsletter* 8 (September–December 1975): 104–106.

Sherman, Joan R. *Jack London: A Reference Guide.* Boston: G. K. Hall, 1977.

Shivers, Alfred S. "The Romantic in Jack London." *Alaska Review* 1 (Winter 1963): 38–47.

———. "Jack London's Mate-Women." *American Book Collector* 15 (October 1964): 17–21.

Sinclair, Andrew. *Jack: A Biography of Jack London.* New York: Harper and Row, 1977.

Sisson, James E. "Introduction." *Jack London's Articles and Short Stories in "The Aegis."* Oakland, Calif.: Star Rover House, 1981.

Sisson, James E., III, and Robert W. Martens, comps. *Jack London First Editions —Illustrated—A Chronological Reference Guide.* Oakland, Calif.: Star Rover House, 1979.

Starr, Kevin. "The Sonoma Finale of Jack London, Rancher." In *Americans and the California Dream, 1850–1915.* New York: Oxford University Press, 1973.

Stasz, Clarice. "The Social Construction of Biography: The Case of Jack London." *Modern Fiction Studies* 22 (Spring 1976): 51–71.

Stone, Irving. *Sailor on Horseback: The Biography of Jack London.* Boston: Houghton Mifflin, 1938. Reprinted as *Jack London, Sailor on Horseback: A Biographical Novel* (New York: Doubleday, 1947); and as *Jack London: His Life, Sailor on Horseback (A Biography) and Twenty-Eight Selected Jack London Stories* (Garden City, N.Y.: Doubleday, 1977).

Tavernier-Courbin, Jacqueline. "The Many Facets of Jack London's Humor." *Thalia: Studies in Literary Humor* 2 (1979): 3–9. Reprinted in Tavernier-Courbin's *Critical Essays on Jack London.*

————, ed. *Critical Essays on Jack London.* Boston: G. K. Hall, 1983.

————. "Jack London's Science Fiction." *Jack London Newsletter* 17 (September–December 1984): 71–78.

Voss, Arthur. "Jack London." In *The American Short Story: A Critical Survey.* Norman: University of Oklahoma Press, 1973.

Walcutt, Charles Child. *Jack London.* University of Minnesota Pamphlets on American Writers. Minneapolis: University of Minnesota Press, 1966.

Walker, Dale L. *The Alien Worlds of Jack London.* Grand Rapids: Wolf House Books, 1973.

————, and James E. Sisson, III, eds. *The Fiction of Jack London: A Chronological Bibliography.* El Paso: Texas Western Press, 1972.

Walker, Franklin. "Ideas and Action in Jack London's Fiction." In *Essays on American Literature in Honor of Jay B. Hubell,* ed. Clarence Gohdes. Durham, N.C.: Duke University Press, 1967.

————. *Jack London and the Klondike.* San Marino, Calif.: Huntington Library, 1966.

————. *The Seacoast of Bohemia: An Account of Early Carmel.* San Francisco: The Book Club of California, 1966. Enlarged edition, Santa Barbara, Calif.: Peregrine Smith, 1973.

Ward, Susan. "Jack London's Women: Civilization vs. The Frontier." *Jack London Newsletter* 9 (May–August 1976): 81–85.

————. "Jack London and the Blue Pencil: London's Correspondence with Popular Editors." *American Literary Realism, 1870–1910* 14 (Spring 1981): 16–25.

Watson, Charles N., Jr. "Jack London's Yokohama Swim and His First Tall Tale." *Studies in American Humor* 3 (1976): 85–95.

————. "Jack London: Up from Spiritualism." In *The Haunted Dusk: American Supernatural Fiction, 1820–1920,* edited by Howard Kerr, John W. Crowley, and Charles L. Crow. Athens: University of Georgia Press, 1982.

Wilcox, Earl J. " 'The Kipling of the Klondike': Naturalism in London's Early Fiction," *Jack London Newsletter* 6 (January–April 1973): 1–12.

————. "Overtures of Literary Naturalism in *The Son of the Wolf* and *The God of His Fathers.*" In Tavernier-Courbin's *Critical Essays on Jack London.*

Woodbridge, Hensley C., John London, and George H. Tweney, comps. *Jack London: A Bibliography.* Georgetown, Calif.: Talisman, 1966. Enlarged edition, Millwood, N.Y.: Kraus, 1973.

Earle Labor, Wilson Professor of American Literature at Centenary College of Louisiana, has published more than forty essays and reviews as well as five books on Jack London, including the three-volume collection of *The Letters of Jack London* (1988), co-edited with Robert C. Leitz III, and I. Milo Shepard. In 1966, as a visiting professor at Utah State University, he taught the first course on Jack London ever offered in this country; in 1974, as a Fulbright lecturer at the University of Aarhus, Denmark, he presented the first Jack London course in Western Europe. In 1976 he served as guest editor for the Jack London Centennial Issue of *Modern Fiction Studies*. He lives in Shreveport, Louisiana.

Robert C. Leitz III, Professor of English at Louisiana State University in Shreveport, is co-editor of *The Letters of Jack London*. He edited volume three of *Selected Letters of W. D. Howells* (1980) and has published numerous articles and reviews on American Realistic and Naturalistic writers. Currently he is co-editor of *Frank Norris Studies* and co-editor of *Critical Essays on George Santayana*. He lives in Shreveport, Louisiana.

I. Milo Shepard, great-nephew of Jack London, manages the Jack London copyrights for the Trust of Irving Shepard and supervises the Jack London Vineyards. He has co-edited *The Letters of Jack London* with Professors Labor and Leitz. He lives in Glen Ellen, California.

To Build a Fire

He travels the fastest who travels alone.
frost has dropped below
fifty degrees or more. Yukon Co.

Day had just broken in
ed and gray — in
itely cold and gray—
hen the man turned a
ide from the main
Yukon trail and cli
e high earth-bank,
where a dim
and little-traveled tra
led eastward through
fat spruce timber-
timber-land. It was a
steep bank, and
paused for brea
at the top, exc
the act to himself
looking at his
It was nine o' clo